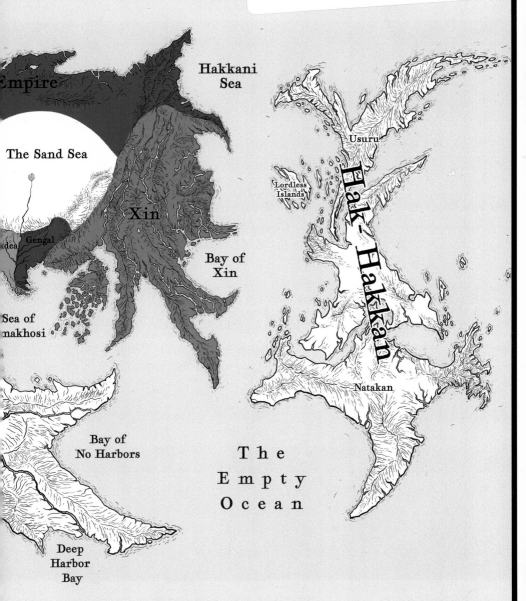

O c e a n

Hakkani
Sea

Empire

The Sand Sea

Usuru

Xin

Lordless
Islands

Hak-Hakkan

dea Gengal

Bay of
Xin

Sea of
nakhosi

Natakan

Bay of
No Harbors

The
Empty
Ocean

Deep
Harbor
Bay

O c e a n

THE SAND SEA

THE
SAND SEA

BOOK
1

THE RUBRIC OF CONQUEST

Michael McClellan

STORY GRID

A STORY GRID EDITION: 0002
STORY GRID PUBLISHING LLC

Story Grid Publishing LLC
223 Egremont Plain Road
PMB 191
Egremont, MA 01230

Copyright © 2019 by Michael Brandon McClellan
Cover Artwork by John Coulthart
Cover Design by Magnus Rex
Interior Design by Spring Hoteling
Maps and Additional Interior Artwork by Matthew Newman
Edited by Shawn Coyne

First Story Grid Publishing Hardback Edition June 2020

For Information About Special Discounts for Bulk Purchases,

Please Visit www.storygridpublishing.com

ISBN: 978-1-64501-021-0
Ebook: 978-1-64501-022-7

FIRST PRINTING

For Samantha, who has traveled this long journey with me, and without whom it would not be possible.

And for Catherine and Violet, who are long familiar with the phrase, "Daddy is doing his words."

May your own dreams and visions lead you to see farther than I ever could.

THE SAND SEA

PROLOGUE
Sixty-Nine Years Later

1948

She had left his desk exactly as it was. As had been true for weeks, she spent the afternoon seated in his easy chair, smelling him—the old books overflowing from their cases, the hint of cigar smoke that always hung about him in life, a smell that brought him back to her like a spirit upon the air.

She could not bear to move his things, as if rearranging his office or going through his papers would break the spell, as if then he would truly vanish from this place he loved more than any other.

Her daughter leaned against the windowsill, the morning sun on her back. Behind her, beyond the sloping lawn, beneath the branches of the willows, a mallard and her ducklings paddled in a line across the pond. Nearer to the house, the tulips and irises had returned, pushing up through the grass, adding patches of yellow and purple to the green. Her great-grandchildren chased each other around the flowers, their shouts faint but audible through the glass.

Her daughter repeated herself.

"Are you well enough to give the eulogy, Mother?"

She did not answer. As her daughter looked at her, she seemed, for the first time, to look her age of ninety-two years.

"I can help you write it."

Her mother continued staring out the window. "He loved this time of year, Elizabeth."

"I know."

"We planted those bulbs together. It took us hours. I did not think they would outlast him. He would be smiling at their color now. He stood where you are standing when he could not decide what to write, when the words refused to come."

"The funeral is in three days, Mother. If you are going to speak, we need to get to work."

"Is the Prime Minister coming?"

Elizabeth's eyes shifted, as if she did not want to answer. "He declined."

"He has always been a coward."

"He is a politician, Mother. They do what is popular."

"You are old enough to remember when Prime Ministers did their duty, Elizabeth. What did the Queen say?"

"The palace has not yet responded. Some say if she does come, there will be an uproar."

"Are they still trying to tear down his statues?"

"Some are."

"Have they succeeded?"

"Not yet."

The older woman nodded, closing her eyes.

"Should I just write it for you, Mother?"

"No. You are not ready."

"Not ready?"

"There are things you do not know."

"What things?"

"He would have told you," said the mother, still avoiding her daughter's eyes. "He wanted to. More than once he asked me if he could share parts of it with you, leaving out the parts I wished to keep secret. It was his love for me that stopped him."

"What are you talking about?" asked the daughter, growing impatient.

"I told him that we must share all of the story or none of it. But I was never ready to share all of it, even with you, and even in the end, when he asked me once more."

"What story?"

"He could always see, Elizabeth. The past, the present, that which was yet to come. He gained that vision in the desert, and it never fully left him. He saw all of this long ago. He knew they would try to diminish him, to erase his place in our history. To his credit, he did not let that change him."

"Mother, you are not making sense."

"Your father became as famous as a man can become, Elizabeth. Even those who do not care to know much of anything can still state the basic facts of his life. But those are not the things I am talking about. There are things we hid from the press, from his biographers, and from you and your sisters."

Elizabeth stared as if a stranger had suddenly replaced her mother. Her eyebrows furrowed, and the lines deepened across her forehead. Elizabeth was still beautiful in her late middle years, with the strong jawline of the woman in front of her, but the eyes and the auburn hair of her father.

"What are you trying to say? That I don't know my own father well enough to write his eulogy? I am a grandmother myself, Mother, not a child."

The older woman smiled. "Yes, but you are still my child, Elizabeth, and always will be. Open that drawer. The deep one on the bottom left-hand side of the desk."

Elizabeth walked to the desk, her cheeks flushed with frustration.

She pulled the drawer handle. It opened reluctantly, heavy with the contents inside. She lifted out an old dirty helmet made of pith and smelling of stale sweat and other things she could not identify.

She set it on the desk. "This?"

"No, underneath that. But when I am gone, you must protect that and treat it with reverence. That was his helmet."

Elizabeth reached lower into the drawer and found a leather folder stuffed with old paper.

"This?"

"Yes."

"What is this?"

"Put it on the desk," said her mother, slowly lifting herself out of her chair, gripping her cane.

Elizabeth ran her palm along the top of the leather, streaking a layer of dust. Her mother stood next to her, shorter and far frailer than she had been even a decade before.

With a wrinkled, bony hand, she lifted the edge of the leather. A handwritten note lay within, on top of a thick manuscript of yellowed paper. The writing was her husband's:

There are centuries in which nothing happens, and there are years in which centuries happen. Believe what you will about the events of 1879, but I will tell you—for I was there—the things their Prophecy predicted all came true, though not in the way that any of them had imagined.

She was the exception, and in the end, she was everything.

"That is Father's writing," said Elizabeth.

Her mother nodded, her eyes misting.

Elizabeth's mind moved quickly. "That was the year of the Stanwich Expedition."

"Yes."

"I know the story of the Stanwich Expedition, Mother. You have both told me, many times, across the years. It is in his biographies. Do you want me to include something about it in the eulogy?"

Her mother stood, staring down at her husband's pen strokes.

"I can put in a sentence or two," said Elizabeth.

Her mother let out a mocking laugh. "A sentence or two." A hint of the old beauty flashed across her face. "Sit down, Elizabeth. I am ready to tell you what your father wanted you to understand. It is time."

"We do not have time, Mother. The funeral—"

Her mother cut her off. "Who do you think he was referring to, when he wrote 'she was the exception, and in the end, she was everything'?"

Elizabeth sighed. "You, of course. That was when you first fell in love, in 1879."

"You are wrong. He is not referring to me."

Elizabeth's eyes shifted, the patronizing half-smile falling from her face.

"Sit," said her mother.

Elizabeth obeyed, taking her father's armchair, facing the desk.

"We should have taught you her name long ago, for without her, you would not exist, and there would be no statues of your father for them to tear down."

Elizabeth waited, her impatience gone, the eulogy forgotten.

"Her name was Selena," said the mother, "Selena Savanar."

As she said the name, her voice deepened with the strength of her younger self, a voice that reminded Elizabeth of the far more formidable woman she had once known.

"She was the daughter of Sah Seg Savanar, of the High Kezelboj of Alwaz Deem. Our true story begins and ends with her, Elizabeth, at the foot of the Great Mountain, in the Year of the Prophecy. I can see in your face that these names mean nothing to you, yet they are the root of all that followed. If you want to write the eulogy of the greatest man of this century and the last, then you should know how he actually came to be."

PART I
THE BESERIAN PROPHECY

By the God of the Mountain and
the Sands, perfect, holy, and wise:

In the seventh year of the
fortieth Qhaliffa, the Amahdi
of the west shall rise.

A stranger once and foreign born,
he will lead the Beserians home,

To the valley of the mountain,
where Mamet placed his throne.

From the east shall come another,
a child of Hom Hommuram,

To restore the Staff that was broken,
the Serpent, the Lion, and the Ram.

In worthy hands again,
the Three shall rule once more,

To return what was lost
and end the Usurper's war.

CHAPTER 1
The Unexpected Guests

Alwaz Deem
13th Day, Month of Norekah, 806
Anglian Calendar: November 22, 1878

"New girl."

Selena opened her eyes. For a moment, she looked around the dimly lit room, forgetting where she was. A woman stared down at her.

"You have a strange look about you. You know that?"

Selena swallowed, wishing she could return to the blankness and refuge of sleep. She placed a hand on her stomach, noting the absence of pain. She almost regretted it. She had yet to pay the price of her bread. That was to come, and soon.

The woman stood above her with hands on her hips. Heavy makeup covered the woman's face. Bright blush reddened her cheeks, round as pomegranates. Dark lines accentuated her eyebrows.

"How old are you?"

"Old enough," said Selena, trying to sound unafraid.

"Where did you work before?"

"The bazaar."

"Doing what?"

"It doesn't matter."

"You're right about that, new girl. No one cares."

"I made baskets and I sold them in the market," said Selena, still holding on to her vanished reality as a drowning man grasps for reeds at the river's edge.

The other woman poured herself a cup of wine. She lifted the cup to her lips and drank down a mouthful. "When did that stop?" she asked.

"My basketmaking?"

The woman nodded.

"A few weeks ago," said Selena. "I was robbed."

The woman smirked, knowingly. "So, is this your first?"

"First what?"

"What do you mean 'first what'? Don't talk back. Your first brothel."

Selena swallowed hard and nodded. She could still leave. She had not yet done the deed, not yet fulfilled her end of the bargain.

"Have you started working yet?"

Selena shook her head. "No."

"That's what I thought. So, this is your first night. Smile."

Selena looked at her.

"I said smile."

Selena opened her mouth, more grimacing than smiling.

"You have nice teeth. They will like that. You don't look like a brothel girl. By the God of the Mountain, you might even get a gold coin."

Selena closed her mouth, looking down at her body. A blanket covered her, but she wished she had two blankets. The look in the woman's eyes made her feel uncomfortable, as if she were naked.

The woman stepped closer and bent down over her, close enough that Selena could smell the wine on her breath. She looked at Selena the way her customers used to look at the baskets she made to sell in the bazaar, running their eyes along the details of the weaving. Except now Selena was the basket.

"Your face says you do not belong in the flatlands. There is something of the upper levels in you. Who was your mother?"

"I never knew her," said Selena, looking away, her voice barely a whisper.

"If I were a gambling woman," said the woman, "And I am—"

She paused and cupped Selena's chin in her hand, twisting Selena's face away from her, inspecting the profile of her nose, lips, and jawline, as if Selena were a sheep at auction. "I'd say your father was a Kezelboj lord. You're a child of sin."

"Take your hands off of me," said Selena. Despite her best efforts, tears welled in her eyes. Anger and shame reddened her face, heat rising on her cheeks.

"You best get used to having hands on you, new girl. Or you'll be back out on the street faster than you can blink. And if there's one thing I know, this is the last stop before the street. Once you go back out, there's no coming back. There'll be no more selling baskets in the bazaar if they know you've been here. Then you may as well just drown yourself in the Ring River."

Selena drew her knees up against her chest, looking at the wall.

"New girl," the voice was new.

Selena knew the voice. It was the voice of the one she owed, the voice of the madam—the one that gave her the food in her belly, the silk on her shoulders, and the blanket keeping her warm—the voice she had to answer. She turned her head toward the voice, her waking nightmare growing more real with each passing moment.

In an instant, the events of the past three weeks swirled through her mind.

The madam had approached her three weeks after the thieves broke open her cart and stole her baskets, smashing her locks with hammers in the middle of the night. By the night the madam came, offering Selena a way out, the hunger stabbed her like a serrated blade.

The Qhaliffa had laws against usury, outlawing the interest she was charged, but like with many things, the laws did little to protect those who lived in the twisted alleyways of the flatlands. In the flatlands, those who failed to repay the money-lenders disappeared, found later, usually at dawn, an example to others who might consider abandoning their debts. Selena knew this, and the madam knew it too.

The morning after the robbery, Selena rose with the sunrise and went to the nearest tower of the Grand Vizerian Guardsmen. She knew the foolishness of the idea as soon as it entered her mind. The guardsmen collected the taxes in the marketplace, and they always took more than the Qhaliffa required, skimming their own portion off the top. They were cruel and corrupt men, but she went to them anyway, for she had nowhere else to go. They laughed at her. Seeing their faces, she thought she recognized the same men who collected the taxes, but then again, all guardsmen tended to look a bit alike.

Selena had searched all that day on her own, looking for clues, seeing if she could find someone else selling her baskets. Some of the other merchants even took pity on her, shutting down their stalls in the bazaar early to search themselves, or sending their children to help Selena scour the flatlands, but they too found nothing, and Selena's debt mounted by the day. Three weeks later, she had still found nothing. She could work for another merchant's stall, but she could never make enough money without her own. She would owe more than she made, the gap growing ever greater. There was no way out, except death, or the madam, or escape, but where would she go? Sundar Dun? Meer Norekah? They would find her . . .

The madam's voice returned her to the present.

"New girl. A man is here for you. Get ready."

Selena felt the madam's eyes upon her as if they physically gripped her. The other woman, whose name she could not remember, still stared at her, drinking a new glass of wine. Her exaggerated eyebrows, her bright red cheeks, and her huge, heavy chest made her look to Selena particularly sinister, like a caricature of a fallen woman.

Selena's gut twisted despite the bread inside of her. She looked at the woman's face and felt, in a glance, that perhaps she peered into her own future.

Perhaps I should drown myself in the Ring River. There would be no more debt, and I would be free of this.

"I do not make my customers wait," said the madam. "In two minutes, be down the stairs. And replace that face with one that is smiling. Sadness does not sell. Do you hear me?"

"Yes."

At that, the madam left.

"Do you need help?" asked the other woman.

"No," said Selena. She lifted herself up off the cold wooden floor, still holding the blanket over her shoulders. Beneath, she wore a thin silk shift, which was insufficient to keep her warm against the night, even indoors.

"Remember," said the woman, "You are only acting out a role." Her voice softened further, as if conceding for the first time that she saw Selena as a woman—as a person worthy of compassion. "If it helps you, think about it that way."

The woman's eyes lingered on Selena's face, perhaps seeing, if only for a moment, a younger version of herself, a woman who had not yet made the choice from which it would be so hard to retreat.

Selena swallowed the lump of panic in her throat, feeling light-headed. Her heart pounded. She found a narrow mirror and looked at herself. She let the woolen blanket fall off of her shoulders and land on the wooden floor beneath her feet. Goosebumps covered her bare arms and the skin of her exposed upper chest. She looked thin, like a traveler nearing the end of a long journey across the sands. Her eyes were set deep behind her high cheekbones, almost sunken, given her thinness. Her eyes still pierced with their hazel-green, and her hair, newly washed, was still thick and auburn-brown. She imitated a smile for herself, though she could not, on her own, make her eyes sparkle. The eyes peering back at her—her own eyes—looked haunted, reminding her that though she stood on the river's edge, she had not yet crossed it. Selena the basket maker had not yet become Selena the—.

Selena shut the word off in her mind.

She turned and walked toward the stairs.

"Good luck," said the woman. "Remember, the first is the hardest."

Selena did not turn around, fearing that if she met anyone's eyes, even the other woman's, she would lose her resolve and run from this place. And if she did that . . .

She did not want to think of what would come next. She did not want to feel the gnaw of hunger again, the pain that mixed with the fear of knowing it would likely grow worse before it grew better, if it ever did. She did not want to dig through the rubbish piles outside of the great houses, fighting with other desperate men and women for old bread and little scraps of half-eaten meat hanging from bones. They lived more like dogs than humans. She had seen the beggars' way.

She reached the base of the stairs and passed through a door, turning right down a dark hall. Ahead, on the far side of a curtain, a sitting room awaited her.

Selena kept walking, dreamlike, as if observing some other woman walking down a hallway to do what she was told to do.

Part of her mind began to fight harder against the choice, even as her feet shuffled forward. *You do not have to do this. You can find someone to help you. What about the old fishmonger? Maybe he could loan you enough money to buy another supply of reeds. Perhaps he could even help fix the cart.*

Her practical mind, the one that tended to the needs of her hunger, fought back. *No, you fool. He has a family of his own. He has six little children, and what does he owe you? Nothing. You are out of options. You are alone. Here you will owe no one.*

But the rebel inside her mind grew fierce. *Owe no one! No, you will be a slave to the madam!*

Selena stood before the curtain. She felt the coldness on her skin and looked down at her bare feet. They were clean and washed, freed from the dirt of the street. Her chest held up the thin layer of silk, which hung loosely over the depression from her ribs to her hips, covering her legs past her knees. Her stomach twisted again. She looked at her wiry arms, reminding herself that her body was still strong. She stood on the threshold that would set the course of the rest of her life. She could feel it. She could still leave, even now . . .

She pulled back the curtain.

A young man waited, seated on a cushion. He looked at her with bright blue eyes set in a smooth, gentle face that did not fit what she expected. She expected to see the face of a guardsman or a man well like one—dark, bearded, and rough. Or perhaps she expected to see the frightening orange hair of an Erassian.

This was not such a man. She could see, even in her nervousness, that the young man looked nearly as frightened as she was.

His eyes fixed on her and widened. He lifted a fist to his mouth and cleared his throat.

She stood where she was, feeling exposed.

"Lady Savanar," he whispered.

Selena looked at him, twisting her head as if he had addressed someone else. She looked behind her, but there was no one. She took a hesitant step forward.

The man rose and stepped forward himself. He was not a short man, though Selena could see that she was nearly as tall as he was, standing almost eye to eye.

Her height had often drawn attention to her over the years, much of it unwanted. Even now, some pride inside of her prevented her from facing the world with the hunched shoulders of a broken woman. She met the man's eyes with a straight back and a level chin.

The man stood before her, wearing a simple traveler's cloak, his eyes racing over her form, then looking intently at the lines of her face.

"Lady Savanar," he said. "They have tasked me. I am to take you away from here."

Selena looked at the man as if he were a figment of her mind, speaking words that made no sense.

"Who has tasked you?" she asked.

"It is best if I do not say," said the young man, his blue eyes blazing with urgency.

Not knowing what else to say, she told him, "I am called Selena."

She smiled with her straight, bright teeth that were as unexpected in a flatlands whorehouse as the man who stood before her.

"Lady Savanar, for too long have we watched you from afar. We watched you sell your baskets in the bazaar. We saw when you borrowed from the moneylender. We nearly intervened when they robbed you, but perhaps it is best this way. The God of the Mountain and the Sands does not make mistakes."

Selena backed up, her eyes widening in confusion.

"What is this? What are you saying?"

Before the man could answer, Selena continued, "How do you know such things about me? I have never seen you before in my life."

The man glanced to his right and to his left, keeping his voice barely above a whisper. Selena felt a wave of cold air pass over her. A door had opened somewhere in an adjacent room.

The man sensed it too.

"I am called Trendan Rudar."

Selena's face remained blank. The name meant nothing.

"You must come with me now. You are no longer alone."

Selena looked at the man, wary of some cruel trick. Though he looked at her with kind eyes, she could not be certain this was not a trap or some new means to harm her. Perhaps this man secretly worked for the money-lender? Though as she looked at his face, she could not imagine this man ever talking to the money-lender. Perhaps that was why the money lender sent him.

"You are in danger," said the man. "Come with me now."

"Come with you? I do not know you. And we—we are not permitted to leave here with—with customers."

"Lady Savanar, I am not a customer, and you do not yet work here. You will never work here, for it is not your destiny. Come with me and you shall be free of this."

"Free of this?" said Selena. "And a slave to what other thing? Tell me quickly before I leave and tell the madam to have you thrown out."

"I cannot tell you here. It is not safe. Others listen and the walls are thin."

Footsteps approached. Selena saw a new tightness in Trendan Rudar's shoulders and watched his face tense.

A curtain flew open, ripped across its top bar. A tall, dark-featured man stood in the open space.

Selena jumped, stepping back.

"Rudar, it is time. We must go. Now."

The man's eyes locked on Selena, as intense as Trendan Rudar's. Selena considered running from the room, but her fear and surprise kept her standing in place.

There was an honesty and even a kindness in the tall man's face.

"Are you ready?" he asked, staring directly into Selena's eyes.

"Come, Lady Savanar," said the blue-eyed man, Trendan Rudar. "We are here to protect you."

"Protect me?"

"Others now know. They will come for you."

"Know what? Who will come for me?"

A voice rose from the direction of the alley.

"Open in the name of the Grand Vizer!"

A loud crash shattered the night air, the sound of iron breaking wood. Boots struck cobbles and then pounded across the wooden floor.

"Come!" barked the tall man. "They are here!"

Trendan Rudar pulled a hidden knife from within his robes, the curved blade flashing in the lamplight.

Selena stepped back against the wall, her heart slamming against her rib cage, her arms and legs tingling with fear.

Before she could move another step, dark shapes erupted into the room like projectiles. Trendan Rudar stepped forward, slashing wildly, and then the dark shapes were on top of him, striking him on the floor.

Selena turned and looked as a wide, bearded face beneath a steel helmet and a black turban rushed toward her. She froze.

Pressure surged against her head, and then sight and sound vanished . . .

CHAPTER 2
Stanwich's Invitation

Three Gods College, Crown University
South Anglia
December 7, 1878

Harold Milton Stanwich surveyed the sea of young Anglian faces from the podium. Most were Crown University men, and they filled the Three Gods College auditorium to its limit. Other students, from the other colleges of the university—though none quite as old or famous as Three Gods—had angled their way into obtaining tickets. Still others had snuck in after Stanwich began speaking, standing along the back wall. For the occasion, most wore white shirts beneath black waistcoats with black ties and black jackets bearing the shield of their college sewn onto the lapel. Most of the lapel shields showed three golden rings above a background of dark red, the sigil of Three Gods College.

The young men bent over wooden writing panels sliding up from slots in the small wooden chairs that bolted to the floor in long arcing rows. Those not taking notes stared at Stanwich with riveted attention that veered toward adoration the longer he spoke. Few more famous men than Harold Milton Stanwich inhabited either side of the Titanic Ocean, and, save for the Prime Minister himself, no more famous man had visited the university in the four years since the most senior classmen first walked the hallowed halls and campus greens.

Stanwich cleared his throat, flipped the page of his speech, and continued, "You will find, gentlemen, as you survey the world beyond these walls, that you are perhaps better positioned than any before you in history. You here at Three Gods are familiar with the history of these islands. There is no more historic college in this oldest of Anglian universities."

The Three Gods students beamed at the compliment.

"Perhaps, then," continued Stanwich, "you already have an inkling of what I shall now tell you. And if not, perhaps my words will at least find fertile ground in which to take root.

"First, you are Anglians, heirs to the greatest Imperium this world has yet known and perhaps ever shall know. Now, you might wonder, 'How could a New Anglian explorer say such a thing?' You would not be wrong to ask it. I am proud of my adopted country. It spans the width of a continent, newly connected by a great railway that links west with east and another tying north with south. New Anglia's industry grows at a rate that nearly ensures it will one day match and even surpass your own."

Several groaned in the audience.

"Come now!" said a heckling voice.

Stanwich heard and grinned in response, flashing his large, famous teeth. As he smiled, a twinkle illuminated his bright, blue-grey eyes.

"Fear not, Anglian friends. Our distinction this afternoon lies elsewhere, in something higher than industry. For all of my adopted nation's strengths, we have much to look up to in the spirit of this island nation, this epicenter of the vast Imperium. I speak of the difference between a country that looks outward toward empire and one that looks inward toward itself. For no nation can aspire to world leadership—and dare I say it, hegemony—by facing its gaze only inward. Certainly, one will find New Anglian men of trade on all of the continents and upon all of the oceans. But trade only takes a nation so far, and trade alone cannot mark a nation for enduring greatness.

"One might say that trade is necessary but not sufficient. Perhaps such is the difference between the outlook of a *republic* and that of an *empire*. While one looks inward, the other looks to the world, pushed by the drive to not only rule but to rule well, to bring light to the darkness, to bind with commerce but also with the rule of law, the faith of our forefathers, and that which can only follow the former—the glory of civilization."

Those taking notes now looked up as Stanwich's voice rose.

"Certainly, all must concede that the light of civilization follows wherever the Anglian flag flies—from the ancient harbors of Xin to the rugged shores of Omakhosi. But I have come not merely to affirm the goodness and bravery of those who have come before you. As Three Gods men, you already know your history and the debt of gratitude owed to your ancestors.

"Rather, I come to urge you, young men of Anglia, to answer history's call. I come to tell you that there are still empty places upon our maps, but also to remind you that *they are not empty* in the physical world. They are merely unexplored. I can assure you that the great Central Crater of Omakhosi and the Feathermen High-lands are not devoid of people!"

The audience burst into applause. Like the rest of the country, all had followed Stanwich's legendary journey to Omakhosi in their newspapers.

Stanwich waited for the applause to abate.

"The call of our age, gentlemen, is to find that which has been lost to Western man, but which is certainly known by the Three Gods. There comes a certain perspective, a higher credibility, when one can say that he is no mere armchair explorer, but rather, that he has confirmed the state of the world with his own eyes—eyes that have seen what others have not, eyes that have beheld the unknown wilderness and have thus made it known. I say that with the humility of knowing I could not have achieved what I did on my own. Generous men backed me, and *brave men went with me.*"

Stanwich paused, letting the implication of his last line set in. The young Anglians watched him in silent admiration, with the envy of believing that he had already achieved what the best of them could only hope for—a place in the history books, in the chapters to be written of their lifetimes.

"So now I ask you, men of Anglia. Where next?"

The faces looked back at him, bright winter sunlight pouring in through the windows in the high arch of the auditorium.

"You there," said Stanwich, pointing to a handsome student raising his hand in the front row. The young man rose with an aura of self-regard. Thick blond hair covered his head, swept into a severe, pomaded side-part and matched by a waxed, aristocratic mustache.

"Hak-Hakkan," said the young man, in a booming voice. "The great islands to the east of Xin. Their rulers have shut off the islands to outsiders for more than a century. While not blank, they are nonetheless unexplored."

Stanwich grinned, again revealing the trademark teeth he had shown so often to the illustrators of the world's newspapers, who had made his face among the most recognizable in Anglia, on a level with the greatest lords and ladies and the leaders of Parliament, though still not as known as the face of the Queen Empress, whose profile adorned every coin, gazing sideways from the Imperium's gold and silver sovereigns.

"Hak-Hakkan would be a bold choice," said Stanwich, "although one might think twice about landing upon those shores uninvited. Who here knows what happened to the Guildermen who landed thirty-five years ago?"

Several hands rose.

"You there in the back," said Stanwich, pointing toward the rear edge of the audience.

Several hundred faces turned, following Stanwich's extended hand.

"They were boiled alive," said a voice.

"Say that again," said Stanwich, cupping his ear. "And please stand so I can see you."

The voice rose, along with the young man. "They were boiled alive!"

"Indeed, they were," said Stanwich. "To which I must say to the first gentleman, the Lords of Hak-Hakkan chose to send a message, and the rest of the world heard it. For no Gerdic, nor LaFrentian, nor Spatanian, nor even Gressian has sought to test the Hakkani since. Perhaps that is due for a change, but those who wish to avoid a live boiling might wait for the sword of the Anglian Imperium to perhaps first open the way."

A spattering of laughter rose from the audience. The young man with the waxed mustache sat down, his cheeks red with embarrassment.

"Where else?" asked Stanwich. "To where should the lamp of progress next alight?"

Stanwich saw that the young man in the back of the room still stood, slouching with reddish-brown hair swept straight backward, lacking the fashionable side-part of the age.

"You there, in the back. What say you?"

The man lowered his raised hand and straightened himself, but not fully.

"Please first state your name," said Stanwich.

"Peter Harmon."

Hundreds of faces turned to look back at him again. His name was well-known, if not terribly popular, amongst the undergraduates at Three Gods College. He was the kind of Three Gods man who seemed more comfortable with his books than his fellow students, the type to someday pen a well-written tome that few would ever read.

"Tell me, Peter Harmon, where should an aspiring Anglian explorer go?"

Peter spoke, but Stanwich could not hear him, nor could the other students save for those seated nearest to him.

"Louder, please. Speak up so we can hear you!"

"I said the Sand Sea, perhaps!" Peter nearly shouted. His eyes darted around, awkwardly, as if wondering how many of his fellow students were judging his words.

"Perhaps the Sand Sea, says the young man. That is a most interesting selection, Peter Harmon," said Stanwich. "But pray tell us why. Of all of the choices, why would you choose there?"

"I did not say *I* would choose there," said Peter, crossing his arms.

"Speak up, please," said Stanwich, again, his voice carrying easily across the auditorium.

"The Year of the Prophecy," said Peter.

"Ahh, bravo," said Stanwich. He clapped his hands together. "And for those who do not know, what does the 'Year of the Prophecy' mean?"

"The Beserians—the people of the sands—have a prophecy. They claim a promised one will arrive from the west," said Peter, still standing with his long, lean arms folded in front of him and his shoulders hunched.

"And? What else?"

Peter looked around, seeming to grow more uncomfortable with all of the eyes upon him. "They say another will come from the east."

"Quite right," said Stanwich. He took his eyes off of Peter and surveyed the audience.

"The words say, 'In the seventh year of the fortieth Qhaliffa, the Amahdi of the west shall rise, and from the east shall come another.'"

A murmur moved through the auditorium. Peter began to sit down.

"One more question for the young Mr. Harmon. When does that year begin?"

Peter stood up again. "They use a different calendar, and it only has seven long months. However, like ours, it follows the solar year, so the answer is the first of January."

"And where did you learn that, Peter Harmon?"

"In a book."

"What book?"

Peter blushed. It was a short, strange book and most certainly not one that any of his professors would approve for a serious student to spend his time reading.

Stanwich waited.

"It is called *The Life of Hom Hommuram*."

Stanwich smiled. "And who says they do not teach practical information at this great university?"

Several students laughed tentatively, unsure whether Stanwich was mocking Peter or Three Gods College. A row of professors in academic gowns cast sideways glances at each other as if wondering whether bringing the famous explorer to Three Gods College had been a mistake. They had not approved this topic beforehand, nor had Stanwich included it in his advance lecture notes.

"The young man is correct," said Stanwich, looking at the professors, but speaking to their students. "As I hope your teachers could tell you, the seventh year of the reign of the fortieth Qhaliffa—the Year of the Prophecy—will begin in mere weeks."

Stanwich stopped abruptly. He reached for the cup of water resting on the podium and took a long sip. He looked out upon the crowd again, his face graver than it had been before. It was as if all he had said up to now was only a prelude to his real purpose.

"By a show of hands," he asked, "how many know the story of the Staff of the Prophet?"

Among the hundreds seated, only several hands rose. One of them belonged to Peter Harmon.

"Not very many, I see." Stanwich cleared his throat again. "Very well. Then I will tell you.

"Eight hundred years ago, a man climbed to the top of the Great Mountain at the center of the Sand Sea. When he came back down, he claimed there was only one God, not three, and that the one God spoke to him face to face. As proof of his encounter, he carried back down a wooden staff.

"It was a strange staff, the likes of which none had ever seen. The top, made from cedar, bore the head of a ram. The center, made from oak, held the face of a lion, and the bottom carried a coiled serpent, made of olive wood.

"The legend says the man soon wielded powers beyond explanation—miracles of the mind, body, and spirit. With this staff in his hands, he began seeing into the minds of men, knowing their secret thoughts. He saw deep into the past and far into the future, as if turning the pages of a book. So too could he see things that happened far away, as if he were there. In battle, the very earth and sky seemed to obey his commands. With these powers, none could stand against him. Within seven years of conquest, he united not only the river valleys of the Great Mountain but the entire Sand Sea from the edge of Hindea in the south to the borderlands of Gressia in the north, from the hills of Bulbania in the west to valleys of Xin in the East.

"When his conquest was complete, the man reigned for forty years of peace, ruling with justice and wisdom with the staff at his side. At the end of the fortieth year, however, he lay dying. He had fathered no children, and the question of his succession lay heavily upon the hearts of his subjects. On his death bed, he ordered the staff broken into its three parts."

Stanwich paused to drink a gulp of water. He wiped his lips with the back of his hand.

"He gave the Ram to his younger brother, Mamet. The Lion, he delivered to his greatest general, Hom Hommuram. And the Serpent, he entrusted to his chief priest, Beseri. The man, by now known to all as 'The Prophet,' explained to these men that they would each carry a portion of the powers the staff had granted to him, and that by dividing the powers amongst them, the God he met on the mountaintop would preserve justice across the kingdom.

"The Prophet then ordered each man to rule the kingdom for three years, one after the other. The Ram would rule first, then the Lion, and then the Serpent, meaning first Mamet, then Hom Hommuram, and last Beseri. He decreed that this cycle must continue in perpetuity, with each man choosing his replacement upon his death. Then the Prophet died.

"Mamet ruled first. But all did not go as the Prophet decreed. Mamet felt cheated that he did not receive the full staff and was angry that his brother had given equal powers to the others who did not share their blood.

"He devised a plan. He ordered Hom Hommuram, the Prophet's general, into the driest and most forbidding part of the Sand Sea. Who here knows the name of this part of the desert?"

No hands rose.

"No one?" asked Stanwich, frowning as he swept his eyes across the room. Peter Harmon slowly raised his hand.

"Yes?"

"The Hahst," said Peter.

"Correct," said Stanwich, lowering his voice. "The Hahst. The place of the white sands, direst and most desolate in all of the Sand Sea. Hom Hommuram followed Mamet's orders. He brought twelve men with him into the Hahst. There, as Mamet planned, Hom Hommuram disappeared with his companions and the Staff of the Lion. What happened to them no one knows, but they never returned, and they were never seen or heard from again."

Stanwich paused, again gripping the podium and scanning the crowd. Most of the students met his gaze, listening intently. Several professors yawned.

"With Hom Hommuram gone, Mamet made his move. He planned to kill Beseri, take the Staff of the Serpent, and rule the Seven Cities for the rest of his days. Beseri, however, using the power of his own staff, learned of Mamet's plan.

"Beseri and his people fled into the desert, never to return to the Great Mountain. They became nomads of the sands, living in tents with their herds. Today we know these same people as the Beserians, the wandering tribesmen of the Sand Sea.

"Mamet then gained his heart's desire and declared himself the first Qhaliffa. For forty generations, his descendants have ruled the Seven Cities of the Great Mountain. Indeed, as I speak to you today, the fortieth in Mamet's line, Sumetan, still sits upon the throne in the city of Saman Keer."

Stanwich finished his cup of water and raised his index finger into the air.

"But there is a twist in this story. It speaks to my previous question and our present moment. No one can say when the *Beserian Prophecy* first appeared. Some say Beseri himself uttered the words eight hundred years ago, using the power of the Staff of the Serpent to see into the future. I will quote you the most famous lines now."

Stanwich pulled a wrinkled piece of paper from his breast pocket, his voice resonant across the auditorium:

"By the God of the Mountain and the Sands, perfect, holy, and wise:
In the seventh year of the fortieth Qhaliffa, the Amahdi of the west shall rise.
A stranger once and foreign born, he will lead the Beserians home,
To the valley of the mountain, where Mamet placed his throne.
From the east shall come another, a child of Hom Hommuram,
To restore the Staff that was broken, the Serpent, the Lion, and the Ram.
In worthy hands again, the three shall rule once more,
To return what was lost and end the Usurper's war."

Stanwich set down the piece of paper.

"What does this mean? Are these merely the mystical words of an old legend? Some in this room would certainly say so."

As if on cue, a row of professors shook their heads, smirking at each other.

"Some will undoubtedly say I am a charlatan, filling your minds with nonsense. Those who think so can remain here in Anglia with their skepticism, cozy by their fireplaces. I will remind you, however, that most said the same things about my journey to the Feathermen Highlands. But then, I was there when they came riding out through the mists, mounted upon their birds the size of horses. No, I have never been deterred by the mocking of cynics.

"Gentlemen of Three Gods College, I will end this morning with an announcement. Like you, I endeavor to be a man of learning, but above all, I prefer to be a man of action, for men of action change the world.

"I see some newspapermen in the back of the room, which means you will all now learn tomorrow's news today. I hereby announce that I, Harold Milton Stanwich, intend to explore this legend. I will see for myself the merits of this Beserian Prophecy. I will lead my next expedition into the Sand Sea, and I will depart in less than a month's time."

Hundreds of young men crushed the space near the podium, hoping to shake the hand of Harold Milton Stanwich and angling to get a quick word. Swift as a fire in a dry field, the word spread that he might consider taking a young man or two on his journey with him, provided that such a young man could prove himself worthy.

Peter Harmon was not one of them. He went the opposite direction, making for the exit as soon as the speech ended.

A voice stopped him.

"Mr. Harmon," said the voice, LaFrentian and strongly accented.

"Yes?"

"A moment, please."

"Do I know you?" asked Peter.

"I am Hersen Expey."

Peter paused. The name sounded familiar. He searched his mind. He had read it somewhere, yes in the *Illustrated Telegraph*. Hersen Expey traveled with Stanwich, on his Omakhosian expedition to the Central Crater.

"Hersen Expey of the LaFrentian Legion?" asked Peter.

"Indeed," said the man, smiling beneath his trimmed mustache.

Peter's eyes widened. Even being a Harmon, he was not wholly immune to the allure of fame.

"Mr. Stanwich wishes to have a word with you," said Hersen Expey, his grey eyes twinkling as if something about Peter amused him.

"Stanwich wishes to speak with me? Why?"

"I will allow Mr. Stanwich to tell you his purposes."

Peter looked toward the crowd jostling around the podium.

"He appears rather occupied at the moment, no?"

"A moment's patience will serve you well, Mr. Harmon."

Peter hesitated, torn by his desire to see Sarah as soon as possible and his curiosity to hear what Stanwich had to say. Why would the world's most famous explorer have words for him? On the other hand, Sarah might already be there, waiting. He had counted down the hours to the lunch all week, to the rendezvous he had specially arranged with his aunt, who lived in a spacious townhouse several streets off-campus. Sarah was coming up from the City, and he had not seen her in a week . . .

"I'm afraid I have another pressing engagement, Mr. Expey. I really must go now."

"It will only be just a moment, Mr. Harmon. Come with me," said Hersen, placing a firm hand on Peter's back and turning him toward the podium. His tone was that of a command.

Peter obeyed, following the LaFrentian's quick pace.

They reached the edge of the undergraduate crowd, all seeking to grip the famous man's hand. Hersen slipped past them like the edge of a knife, moving through gaps Peter did not even see. Peter stepped behind him, slicing through the crowd in Hersen's wake.

Stanwich turned and saw Hersen, his eyes flashing recognition and some hidden sign. Peter followed the LaFrentian.

"Mr. Peter Harmon, meet Mr. Harold Milton Stanwich," said Hersen, introducing Peter and pushing him forward with a strong hand on his back.

Peter found himself suddenly face-to-face with the explorer, looking down. Stanwich, a short man, stood with ramrod posture and a chest as broad as his smile. Peter noticed the beads of sweat on his forehead.

"Yes, indeed!" said Stanwich. "Please follow me, Mr. Harmon."

"That will be all today, gentlemen. That will be all," said Hersen Expey, planting himself between the crowd and Stanwich while waving his arms with his back against Peter. "Thank you all. Your support means a great deal. Thank you very much."

"Mr. Stanwich!" bellowed a voice in the crowd. "One more question! Mr. Stanwich!"

"Thank you, thank you, gentlemen. Thank you very much," said Hersen, backing away.

Stanwich waved as he moved toward the door with Peter at his side.

A dark-skinned Omakhosian with a businesslike face stood guarding the exit. As he let him pass, Peter noted the man was as finely attired as Hersen, or for that matter, Stanwich himself. Peter, who had never taken his clothes very seriously, looked down at his shabby schoolboy suit and his slouched posture, and felt, for a fleeting moment, that he should perhaps try a bit harder in the way he presented himself to the world.

They stepped out into the cold, crisp early December air. The great sycamore trees on the quadrangle were naked and leafless overhead, and the grass was browned by the cold.

"This way," said Stanwich, the Omakhosian walking at his side. A crowd of well-wishers spotted them from a distance, waving and calling out.

"Mr. Stanwich! Mr. Stanwich!"

Stanwich smiled his best front-page smile and waved.

"Walk quickly," he said, under his breath.

Peter looked ahead at the stone building across the lawn, seeing another sharply dressed, dark-haired man standing beside a door. He looked to be a southerner from the continent.

Stanwich's smile tightened as the crowd of well-wishers advanced closer.

"Mr. Stanwich!"

"Mr. Stanwich, sir, one moment for the *Weekly Herald*!"

That voice caught his attention. He paused. Hersen, who was setting the pace, paused as well. The crowd advanced closer, led by a short round man awkwardly jogging forward with a pen and a notation pad.

The man huffed with exertion as he reached Stanwich and the others.

"Mr. Stanwich," he gasped, "Is it true that you said the Anglian Imperium is superior to the New Anglian Republic?"

Stanwich gazed across the crowd as he answered. "Both are great nations," he said.

"But is it true you said the Republic is insufficient because it does not have an eye toward empire?"

"I merely exhorted my listeners to follow the call of history, Mr.—?"

"Jones," said the reporter.

"Yes, good to see you, Mr. Jones. I would advise young New Anglians to do the same. Thank you, and good day to you all," he said, waving widely and flashing his smile in the bright cold air, the sunlight catching his grin.

At that, he turned and walked swiftly away.

Hersen Expey again led the way, Peter and the Omakhosian bringing up the rear. The dark-haired man stepped forward from the door of the great stone building that faced the quadrangle, positioning himself on the walkway and ushering the others in through the arched opening. He gave a suspicious look at Peter until the Omakhosian met his eyes, nodding that Peter was indeed part of the entourage.

Hersen did not stop in the stone hallway, his heels clicking on the floor as he marched through the corridor and passed through a second high-arched doorway into a sunlit room, where a table sat adorned with sandwiches and bottles of beer.

The door shut behind Peter. Stanwich dropped down onto a bench and exhaled, his entire body seeming to deflate as if he had just released a heavy load.

"Should have known that," he said, speaking to no one in particular. "That the papers would make hay out of those words, trying to set up Anglia against New Anglia, the land of my birth against my new adopted land." He reached for one of the beer bottles, popping the top.

"I told you," said Hersen, standing with his arms crossed. "When you asked about it before the speech."

"Perhaps someday I will listen to you," said Stanwich, looking up after swigging from the bottle.

"They were skeptical of my mission," said Stanwich.

"The students loved it," said Hersen.

"I mean the professors," said Stanwich.

"Naturally, they would be skeptical," said Hersen. "You were speaking of legends, little more than fairy tales to such men."

Stanwich smiled. He looked at Peter Harmon as if forgetting why he stood amongst his companions.

"Ah, yes, Peter Harmon. Please sit," he said.

"I really must be going," said Peter. "I have an engagemen—"

"Sit," said Stanwich, gesturing to an empty chair. "Have a sandwich."

Peter did as he was told, lowering himself into the wooden chair.

Stanwich looked at the sandwiches, each of which lay separately wrapped in a white paper band, stacked like ammunition in a wicker basket.

"Well, if you aren't going to eat one, pass one to me," said Stanwich.

"What kind would you like?" asked Peter, sounding hesitant to serve anyone their food.

"Beef."

Peter peered into the basket and selected a thick roasted beef sandwich stuck between two pieces of flaky, LaFrentian-style bread. He passed it across the table to Stanwich.

Stanwich gripped it with two hands, inserted a long section into his mouth, and chomped down. Peter watched him as he chewed.

"So," said Stanwich, still chewing. "Peter Harmon, eh? Sounded like you know a thing or two about the Sand Sea."

"I have done some reading, yes."

"You read *The Life of Hom Hommuram.*"

Peter nodded.

"Impressive," said Stanwich, his mouth still full of roast beef.

"It is only an obscure book I found in the library," said Peter.

"Is it?" Stanwich swallowed. "Are you certain you don't want a sandwich? This one is quite good." He took another large bite as if he had not eaten in a day.

"I am certain, yes. I have an engagement for which I am rapidly becoming tardy."

"Oh? With whom?"

"Pardon? I am scheduled to attend a luncheon with my aunt."

"I see," said Stanwich. "I do not want to detain you from your aunt, Mr. Harmon, but what I have to say should interest a young man such as you, I should think."

Peter waited.

"You may have heard that I am accepting volunteers for my next expedition into the Sand Sea."

"I heard," said Peter, tapping his foot. He could feel all of the eyes in the room staring at him.

"As you seem to know more than the others, how would you like to be one of those volunteers?" asked Stanwich.

"I am afraid that is impossible."

"Oh?"

"Yes. Quite impossible."

"If I am not mistaken, you have already graduated from Three Gods, have you not?"

Peter's face changed. "How did you know that?"

"I know a great deal about you, Peter Harmon. I know you are only here carrying out a self-directed study and that you plan to depart for Khyderbad next month to serve as the Personal Secretary to the Lord Governor."

"If you know that, Mr. Stanwich, you know why it is impossible for me to join your expedition."

Stanwich took another bite out of his sandwich, chewing vigorously with his large teeth.

Peter's brows furrowed in agitation. "Might I ask how you know these things about me? I would not think a person as esteemed as yourself would take an interest in a life as mundane as my own."

"All lives are mundane, young man, until they are not. I was raised in a West Anglian orphanage. Yet, here I am. What if I had taken the safe route, eh? I might be. . ." The smile fell from Stanwich's face as his voice drifted off.

"You might be what?" asked Peter.

"If one wishes to be something, one must take risks, Peter Harmon."

"I am sure that is true for some people," said Peter, standing up. "But I am nearly late for an important engagement, Mr. Stanwich, and I am afraid that joining your expedition is not a risk I am interested in taking. Good day."

Peter nodded politely to the others and began walking toward the door.

"Harmon," said Stanwich.

Peter stopped and turned around, arching an impatient eyebrow.

"One more thing you should know."

"And what is that?"

"Part of the funding for my expedition is coming from Calderon, in the New Anglian Republic. In particular, a man named Colonel Mason Caldwell."

"Oh?"

"He is your mother's brother. Is he not?"

"He is."

"Well, his son, your cousin, Jack Caldwell, will be joining us also."

Peter stared.

"I thought you should know," said Stanwich, looking as if he had just set down a winning hand at cards.

"If you knew me better, Mr. Stanwich, you would know that if Jack Caldwell is the sort you are looking for on your journey, I most certainly am not. Good day to you."

He walked out the door.

"Well?" asked Hersen Expey.

"He's a bit of a prig," said Stanwich. "We'll tell his father. I suppose he'll have to call Governor Freer and ask him to hire a new secretary in Khyderbad."

Hersen nodded.

"He'll come," said Stanwich. "Few can deny Lord Harmon what he wants, most of all his own son, I would imagine."

CHAPTER 3
Late for Lunch

Calderon State
New Anglian Republic
December 21, 1878

A hawk sailed high overhead, drifting in the breeze against the cloudless sky.

Kneeling, Hannah exhaled. Her open eye stared down the steel barrel of a new Mancaster repeater. The snake lay in her sights, coiled with its head raised and its tail rattling its signature warning.

She squeezed the trigger. The shot echoed off the mountain, sending half a dozen crows airborne from a tangle of red-barked manzanitas. The rattler's head vanished, and a splash of crimson struck the dirt on the trail.

Hannah lowered her rifle, a proud smile lifting across her sun-kissed face. Freckles adorned her high cheeks, and bright blue eyes flanked her well-shaped nose. She had her father's nose, the Huntington nose, which was slightly upturned and, in her feminine version, slightly provocative. A long, thick braid of yellow-blonde hair hung behind her head, dropping out of a wide-brimmed rancher's hat. Her mother had long disapproved of her wearing a man's hat, but on this subject, as in many, Hannah rested in the safe harbor of her father's indulgence.

Hannah stepped forward now, the mud of the trail sucking at her boots as she took the incline, leaving her horse tied to a protruding branch of a Calderon oak. She slung her rifle over her shoulder and crouched down over her prize. She had seen plenty of snakes on Mount Agabanzo thicker than her arm. This one, at its widest, looked to be as thick as her leg.

The body of the headless snake still moved in its coil. Undeterred, she picked up the heavy carcass and slid it into a leather sack. Windy whinnied loudly behind her, pulling against her reins and straining the oak branch.

"Easy, girl," said Hannah, looking over her shoulder.

She turned with the snake in the sack, hoisting it up with both arms. The horse's eyes strained with fear as she approached, showing white along the edges.

"It's dead, girl. Can't hurt you."

The horse did not agree. Windy whinnied again, long and shrill, the sound echoing off the mountain slope and down into the deep ravine below the trail. She pulled harder against her reins, threatening to break the branch.

"Come on, girl," said Hannah. "*Easy.*" She moved sideways, keeping herself between the snake and the horse and hiding the sack with her body. The horse tried to turn as Hannah walked past her, twisting her neck and stomping the mud with her hooves.

Hannah rested the sack on the edge of the trail. She approached the horse, slid her rifle into its holster, and pulled a thick carrot out of her saddlebag, holding it in front of the mare's nose.

The horse stared at the carrot with wide, suspicious eyes.

"Eat it."

Windy took a tentative bite, still eyeing Hannah with her ears perked, but the taste conquered the horse's willpower.

"Good girl," said Hannah, petting Windy's soft velvet nose as the carrot disappeared behind the square equine teeth. She turned and walked back to the leather sack, hoisting it again up over her shoulder.

"He'd better appreciate this," she said out loud, thinking of who the gift was for as she walked back toward her horse. "Easy, girl."

She smiled her prettiest smile while repeating the soothing words in her kindest voice. Holding the snake suspended in the sack behind her back, she slowly untied the reins and eased the horse's nose down the trail. She shoved a muddy boot into the near stirrup, grabbed the horn of her saddle with one hand, and vaulted herself up with the snake sack still hanging over her back.

Astride Windy, she looked westward, off the edge of the mountain toward the horizon and the sparkling blue expanse of the Great Western Ocean. Hannah Huntington had looked out upon the ocean countless times before and often from this very trail, three thousand feet above the water. From this elevation, the waters hinted at their vastness, and despite their familiarity, they had yet to lose their majesty in her eyes. She paused at the vista, knowing she gazed off the edge of the continent, off the end of the New Anglian Republic, standing on the western edge of Western civilization.

The Isle of Cadenza faced her from the sea like a mountain itself with its steep green canyons three dozen miles away on the far side of an oceanic trench, but seemingly close enough to touch in the bright morning light. She looked past Cadenza, knowing that beyond the island, a sailor would not strike land until the shores of Hak-Hakkan, ten thousand miles away, the shores of another world, the far-off lands of the east.

She lowered her gaze to the shoulder of Mount Agabanzo, to the rolling foothills beneath that, and to the coastal plain that ended in a thin line of beige-white sand that divided the green from the blue. The plain was bright green—almost lime—the color of new grass, coaxed from the ground by the winter rains. Patches of darker green dotted the plain, the green that remained even when the plain turned khaki and hard as rock in the high heat of summer. Those were the walnut and oak trees that kept their tough leaves year-round, whose roots stretched deep beneath the soil and into the aquifers that lay hidden from the eyesight of man.

"Come on, girl. We're late."

She touched her heels against Windy's sides. Between her legs, the horse glided forward, powerful and smooth, cantering down the soft trail. The ravine's edge lay mere feet away from her on her right, close enough to look straight down, the precipice cascading three hundred feet or more. However, she felt little fear, trusting the gait and footing of her mare. To her left, on the mountain side of the trail, the windswept slope ascended at a steep grade, held firmly by the roots of towering Calderon oaks with trunks as broad as wagon wheels. Beneath them, dense, tall thickets of manzanita covered the dirt and concealed the boulders.

As she rode, the offshore winds stretched Hannah's braid behind her, trailing her like a yellow banner. Even this high up the mountain, over the strong scent of the new grass, she could still smell the ocean air, salty and familiar, the smell of home.

She rounded a bend in the trail, the ravine still to her right, though growing less severe the further she descended. She looked south.

Miles beyond the foothills, a single mesa stood amid the plain like a volcano with the top shorn off, commanding the surrounding countryside. Atop the mesa, which at this distance looked flat as a table, amid a grove of avocado and citrus trees sat a large square house, laid out in the old Spatanian style with a great central courtyard. The groves surrounding the house covered the slopes of the peculiar hill in terraced rows, flanking a gravel road that led up from the plain, like a stream of grey through the greenery. The gravel beckoned to her now, and she increased her pace, clicking her tongue at Windy.

Her mind's eye turned to him, the one for whom she had shot the snake, Jack, the man she had known since he was a boy. Though he looked exactly as she thought a man should look, she knew he was very much still a boy, with the vanity and selfishness of youth. Did she love him? She could not say. He often occupied her thoughts, though not always pleasantly. She felt the burden of the snake in her sack. Jack said he wanted to shoot a snake for boots. Diego, the ranch hand, was able to make them—boots of rattler skin. She had set out in the early morning, well before the sunrise, to find a big enough snake.

Jack had grown up nearly like a brother to her, and to her older sister Carolyn as well. Carolyn was almost exactly Jack's age, but far less like him than Hannah. Carolyn was her mother's child, proper in all of the ways that mattered to society—the society Jack and Hannah had long mocked together, the society that wanted South Calderon to be like Port Calderon, or worse yet, like Laketown or Bay Port City, or one of the other great cities of the eastern Republic, with their balls and interminable dinners. They—she and Jack—lived the life of Westerners more than any of the others. Free. They were riders, hunters, ranchers, children of the outdoors. Jack had attended college in the east, but in her observation, he had returned even more committed to the Calderon way of life than before.

Together, their fathers owned the most important railroad in the Republic, the one that linked east and west, the one that cut across the spine of the continent. Since as long as Hannah could remember, adults—uncles, aunts, friends, and family—had joked about their future together, about a daughter of Mr. Samuel X. Huntington marrying the son of Colonel Mason Caldwell.

The gossip began even before the Transcontinental Railroad was completed. Since then, it had only intensified. Indeed, much of South Calderon society had discussed it. What could be more perfect than one of Sam Huntington's girls ending up with Colonel Caldwell's oldest, most-eligible bachelor?

The two families didn't own the railroad outright. No one could. But they were, respectively, the largest shareholders in the corporation that owned the railroad, and, fused by marriage, the families could maintain control far into the next generations. Such were the things society people liked to ponder.

Hannah made another swift turn on the trail. Her right arm burned from the weight of the rattlesnake, its body bouncing against her back at the curve, heavy and coiled in the leather sack. Windy kept cantering, seeming to have forgotten the snake. *The winds must be right*, thought Hannah. *She cannot smell it, thank the Three Gods.*

She looked over the edge of the last ravine, and her stomach tightened. The oak branches came together to form a corridor ahead. She centered her horse on the trail, floating above the earth. The grade flattened, and the air cooled as she entered the tunnel of trees, the oaks shading her from the bright overhead sun. She kicked her heels into Windy's flanks again, sending the mare into a gallop. If she was going to make lunch and avoid her mother's wrath, she needed to hurry.

Windy's hooves churned the soft earth beneath them, horse and rider emerging from the trees as if shot from a cannon. The wind rippled across Hannah's face as Windy charged forward, giving the floating sensation she loved more than perhaps any other, riding fast enough to make falling in the wrong way a matter of broken bones or worse.

They rode onward. Windy cut through the foothills, turning them into a leafy blur as they continued down onto the plain. Anyone at Caldwell House looking for her could certainly see her now, a lone figure galloping across the open green canvas.

Caldwell House grew more significant in her view, its red roof now clearly visible atop its broad, orchard-terraced hill. She gave a slight tug on Windy's reins, the horse now glistening with sweat, her sides heaving from the long run. The horse slowed to a walk, and Hannah's thoughts returned.

Jack. Perhaps he was looking down at her now. The thought made her self-conscious. She straightened her posture in her saddle.

He was pompous, and truth be told, he drank too much as well. The two were linked. The more he drank, the more arrogant he became. Hannah certainly did not love the man he became with too much wine or whiskey inside of him. But if not him, who? Who would she marry? A businessman from Laketown? A merchant from Port Calderon? Some other man her mother picked? She shuddered at the thought. Rich as her father was, and though she longed to see the world, her social circle in Calderon was not large, and she did not much trust those outside of it.

Jack seemed right, at least to the reasoning of her head, even if doubts rested heavily upon her heart. He would like the rattlesnake skin. She could bet on that. And after all, how many women could ride and shoot like her? He was a son of Calderon, of the wildness of the far west, and she was a daughter of the same place. Who else could be his partner and make him happy?

Hannah approached the fence line of the inner sanctum of the Caldwell Property, the fence that surrounded Caldwell Hill. It was no ordinary rancher's fence. The posts were tall and the beams long, straight, and painted white, a testament to the wealth of the family they served. The full property, which was merely one of the many land holdings of Colonel Caldwell, covered ten thousand acres, and no fence marked its outer boundaries. Seasoned ranch hands patrolled these, and the herdsmen of the other landowners knew where their masters' lands ended and those of Colonel Caldwell began.

As Hannah passed under the open gate, thousands of orange, lemon, lime, and avocado trees flanked her on either side. Gravel crunched under Windy's hooves. Familiar smells engulfed her like a blanket—citrus, and sea air, the same scents that had surrounded her South Calderon life for as long as she could remember. She felt as if she had spent as many memorable moments upon the Caldwell Property as on her own, if her parents' land could properly be called hers.

Her father satisfied himself with far less land than Colonel Caldwell, two thousand acres, to be precise, enough to justify his position in the world but less than he could afford. Hannah learned long ago, that unlike most other men, her father did not display the full extent of his wealth. She also now knew, because her father told her, that the Huntington fortune exceeded that of the Caldwells.

She had always assumed the opposite, and indeed, much of their social life had revolved around the Caldwell Property. But nor was she surprised, once she considered it. Colonel Caldwell was a large man, a man who expected others to call him "Colonel," a man that sat at the head of every table, rode the highest horse, stood tallest in the crowd.

Her father had helped her to see through such things. And as she began to see the colonel with new eyes, she began to see his son differently as well. It was no easy task being the oldest son of Colonel Mason Caldwell, the hero of the LaFrentian War, the most prominent landowner in South Calderon, and the most visible face to the national government behind the Transcontinental Railroad.

Hannah learned, with each passing year and with increased respect, that her father silently moved things for which the colonel often publicly took the credit. She had once assumed this made Colonel Caldwell a greater man than her father. She now understood the opposite.

"Remember, Hannah," said Samuel X. Huntington, only weeks before, "with credit comes fame, and with fame comes blame. Never court envy. It is dangerous enough to be rich."

Windy walked up the gravel slope, ascending the mesa. They had now passed the citrus trees, and the tallest, most mature avocados covered the path in pleasant shade. Hannah shifted the leather sack from one shoulder to the other to ease the ache in her back and arms, knowing she was almost there.

At the top of the wide path, the slope flattened, the orchard ended, and the great square of Caldwell House emerged. Flanked by a pair of mighty Calderon oaks that had stood for far longer than the house itself, Caldwell House looked as solid as the mesa beneath it. Though only a single story, its roof sloped in a bright mass of red tiles, both tall enough to accommodate the twelve-foot ceilings within and wide enough to cover the deep porches along the outer edges. It gave the Caldwells a commanding view of their domain in every direction.

The stables stood to the east, to Hannah's left, nearly as large as the house itself and built in the same style, but they were set lower on the hill so as not to obstruct the views.

In the center of the circular driveway, next to an imposing round fountain, atop which a trio of angels danced in stone, Diego stood with his hands on his hips.

Hannah smiled, stopping Windy with a small tug on the reins.

Diego, handsome and still not yet thirty, always took good care of her. In another life, perhaps, if she was not a Huntington, she would have married him—a man with the strong, lean body and tanned face of a life spent in the saddle. Unlike Jack, she had never seen him drunk or boastful, and he was nearly always kind.

"Miss Hannah," he said, smiling back. He had always called her that, even when she was a little girl.

"I'm late," she said.

"You are," said Diego, stepping forward.

"Are they already at the table?"

Diego nodded.

Hannah sighed, seeing a pair of large open carriages parked on the far side of the fountain in the turnabout. One of them belonged to her parents. The horses were unharnessed, meaning that Mr. and Mrs. Samuel X. Huntington had already been at Caldwell House for some time.

"Look," she said, pulling the sack around from her back.

Diego waited, cocking an eyebrow.

"Take it and look!" she said, grinning with a child's excitement.

Diego stepped forward, and Hannah exhaled as he took the weight from her arms.

"Open it."

Diego untied the thick leather string and peered in. His eyes widened in appreciation.

"You shot the head?"

Hannah nodded.

"One shot?"

"One shot."

"On Agabanzo?"

Hannah nodded again.

"How high?"

"Three thousand feet."

"No wonder you are late," said Diego, his eyes twinkling.

Hannah swung down out of her saddle, her boots crunching the gravel as she landed face-to-face with Diego. They stood nearly eye to eye.

"Do you think it's big enough for a pair of boots?" she asked.

"For certain."

"Could you make them?" Hannah asked.

"For you?"

"No, I want them to be a surprise . . . for Jack." She blushed as soon as she said it.

"Yes, I can make them," said Diego.

Hannah saw that his mouth still smiled, but the twinkle had left his eyes.

Diego stepped toward Windy, away from Hannah, taking his eyes off of her and looking at the horse. He rubbed the mare's shoulder, still glistening with sweat. He undid the saddle strap, smoothly taking the heavy load off of the horse's back and onto his own. Hannah's holstered Mancaster repeater hung down from the side, making it even heavier. Diego rested all of it upon his shoulder easily.

"I will take Windy," he said, reaching out for the reins.

"I'll give her some oats," said Hannah, still holding the reins and stepping toward the stables.

"I can give her oats," said Diego. "You will bring trouble on yourself if you don't go inside."

Hannah ignored him, leading Windy away.

If Mother grows angrier with each passing minute, let her, thought Hannah, smiling at her small defiance.

No doubt Carolyn, the obedient daughter, would be seated there already, looking as she was supposed to look and saying the things she was supposed to say. But Carolyn had never loved a horse like she loved Windy, Hannah reminded herself. Carolyn and her mother rode their horses like masters. They did not really know their animals, and their animals did not love them. Hannah reached the stable doors, smiling to herself at the contrast.

The doors were nearly closed, which was strange for the middle of a bright, sunny day when the horses would like the fresh air.

Hannah pushed, the hinges whining as the heavy wooden planks swung inward. She led Windy into the cool, dark building, the strong and familiar smells of hay and manure encircling her.

Hannah looked into the first stall. A Caldwell family horse stood there already, eyeing them warily as it chewed a mouthful of hay. Hannah saw one of the dappled geldings, a beautiful horse but also an irritable one.

"Come on. We'll find you another stall," she said to Windy, leading her by her bridle. Windy followed, the soft dirt floor muffling the clopping of her hooves.

A large black stallion occupied the next stall. He snorted.

"No, not in there either," said Hannah, shaking her head and leading Windy deeper into the stables.

The third stall lay empty but without any hay.

As she frowned at the empty stall, a strange noise came from the farthest side of the long row. Hannah froze, straining to hear more. There was a rustling. A deep sound. A high one.

She turned to Windy's bare back, reaching for her rifle that wasn't there. Diego had taken her saddle.

A shuffle, a grunt.

Adrenaline moved through her, raising the hair on her arms. Bandits had roamed the foothills and even the coastal plain in the past years but not recently, and none would dare come onto the Caldwell Property, much less up the mesa of Caldwell Hill, she thought, and certainly not in the middle of the day.

Another sound came from the farthest stall, softer. Her heart thundered. Windy could hear it too, and her ears perked.

Hannah let go of the horse's bridle. She looked around her. A pitchfork leaned against a wooden beam. She crept toward it across the dirt floor and grabbed its long wooden handle. She considered screaming for Diego. The noises continued, growing louder as she silently approached the source, the pitchfork raised in front of her. Moving forward, one soundless step after another, Hannah could hear her own rapid breathing as her chest tightened. She had nearly reached the final stall.

She heard a small shriek as she jumped around the corner, gripping the pitchfork like a trident. She landed as if sculpted in place, still as a statue as the image of them seared itself upon her mind.

The profile of Carolyn's face met her at eye level, unseeing with closed eyes, her palms flat against the wooden wall, her fingers extended wide, her long brown hair loose on her shoulders, swaying in motion. Jack stood close behind, leaning forward with his face hidden on the far side of Carolyn's, his hands gripping her chest, grunting as he slammed his hips against hers.

Hannah turned and ran, still carrying the pitchfork, rushing past Windy as if she were not there.

CHAPTER 4
The Ax or the Flames

Saman Keer
42nd Day, Month of Norekah, 806
Anglian Calendar: December 21, 1878

Torchlight flickered in the void, casting dancing shadows upon the wall. Selena had seen nothing but blackness for hours, and the flicker, faint as it was, glared in her eyes, waking her from her stupor. Perhaps it had been a day since the light last came, maybe longer. She had not eaten since then, though the moldy bread they brought her could hardly be called food. Her stomach now gurgled and gnawed as severely as it had on the night she agreed to the madam's proposal—a night that seemed as if it belonged to another life.

A bucket of water sat next to her, but it did not smell like anything she could drink. So, she sat, for countless hours, as her lips cracked from dehydration, her mind veering toward madness, silently arguing with herself about whether to drink or not drink. Every time she considered plunging her parched face into the bucket, she lowered her mouth to the surface, smelled its stench, and recoiled. Then, eventually, her thirst compelling her, she drank it down, nonetheless.

That was the clean bucket, the bucket for consumption. The other bucket was full of . . . Selena did not want to think about it, though the smell let her think of little else.

The cell's deep cold and the throbbing in her mouth kept her from sleeping for more than short spans. She shivered without a blanket. Her chains hung from iron rings embedded in the stone wall, their thick manacles rubbing the skin on her wrists and ankles to rawness. The abrasions hurt terribly, but compared to the pain in her mouth, they barely hurt at all.

At the precipice of her decision at the brothel, she did not think life could become worse. She now knew she had known nothing.

The men had come with their talk of rescuing her—Trendan Rudar with the blue eyes and the tall man—then the guardsmen came moments later. Selena had woken up after losing consciousness with bound hands and feet, facedown in a wagon with the guardsmen above her. They'd escorted her to this place beneath the earth, where she could not tell one day from the next.

The light came closer, and Selena shuddered. Down the stone corridor, the voices advanced like growls.

"Where?"

"This way, Your Excellency, in the dark hall."

The light grew brighter still. The voices grew louder as footsteps clacked and shadows retreated. Beyond the bars of her cell, the wall itself seemed to ooze in the light, as if the stones were sweating. The sweat looked vile, even poisonous. Perhaps that was why she coughed and why her breathing beneath the earth felt so strained. Or perhaps that was because of the putrid bucket in the corner, the bucket no one ever cleared and replaced. What happened when the bucket overflowed? Would she just sit in her own filth? How long could a person live like that? Weeks? Months? Years? Selena shuddered again as her heart picked up its pace, beating through her ragged ribs. How long since she had eaten? She could not say. Time did not travel at its accustomed pace in the darkness.

Selena crouched down toward the back of the small cell, a cave within the cave. She could not recall how many steps they had descended into the dungeon. She was hooded when it happened. Though she tried to count, her fear clouded her mind, and she could not remember. She was somewhere deep within a labyrinth, beneath the palace, in the underland where they kept the heretics.

The light continued to approach with the voices, the wall shifting from black to grey. A roach scrambled out through the bars of her cell, toward the darkness down the cavernous hall, fleeing the advancing torchlight that glistened upon its lacquered, shield-like back. Selena watched the insect as it disappeared in the shadows, envying its escape.

Her heart beat even faster, as if she were running. Not long ago, such an insect crawling upon her in the darkness would have frightened her. She now viewed the roach more as something to consider eating than something to fear. It was men that terrified her now, men advancing with torches.

When they chained her to the torture table, she had begged, she had pled, but they would not listen. They insisted she admit her treason. They said she was one of them, one of the heretics, one of the fanatics committed to the downfall of the Qhaliffa. Over and over, they had asked her, "How do you know Huralt Donadun? How do you know Trendan Rudar? Where is the lair of the Order? Who is the Serpent? Who is the Lion? Who is the Ram?" She whimpered that she did not know. She'd never heard of them. Then she screamed one last plea for mercy before they began. It made no difference.

The torturer seemed inhuman as he worked, calm and unyielding, pitiless as a hawk toward its prey, carrying out a task assigned to him. Selena had always assumed that for one human to torture another, they would be vicious, snarling like the guardsmen when they bullied vendors in the bazaar, but it was not that way. It was worse. The man merely carried out his mechanical operations, oblivious to her cries. The pain in her mouth flared as she remembered.

"The third cell, Your Excellency."

Selena crouched in the back corner, pinching her eyes closed against the flaming torches just beyond the iron bars. She felt naked and exposed in the light, covered in rough cloth that was little more than a long, dirty rag.

She could sense them standing over her now. In the absence of vision, one's other senses took on greater responsibility, greater power. She could hear things she had never heard before above ground, small sounds, the sounds of the walls, the sounds of rodents far away. She could hear the men breathing now.

She looked up at them, squinting like a mole. Several men stood above her. The light obscured their faces.

"This is her?" asked the voice.

"Yes, Your Excellency."

The men waited in silence except for the flickering of the torches and the heavy breathing of one of them.

Selena saw the outlines of the men take shape against the bright torchlight. In the center stood a man who was taller than the others, a large turban above a long, bearded face.

"Turn to the side, prisoner," he said.

In her fear and confusion, the man's words hung suspended in the air, deprived of any meaning.

A loud clang made her wince as a club struck her cell's bars.

"Obey the Grand Vizer!" shouted one of the others.

Selena obeyed, shaken from her daze, turning her head. The words stuck in her mind. *The Grand Vizer?*

"That is the Savanar jaw," said one of the men.

"Perhaps," said the tall man in the turban. Something seemed familiar in the man's voice, something that made Selena more afraid of him than of the others.

Selena crouched in silence, wishing, more than anything else, to say what was necessary to avoid another walk to the torture table.

"Do you know my voice?" asked the tall man.

Selena peered into the shadowed face, backlit by the dancing flames atop the torches.

Selena shook her head.

"Am I a stranger to you?"

Selena nodded her head in the affirmative.

"Do you still deny who *you* are?"

Selena stared, uncertain as to what she was expected to say.

"What is your name?"

"I am called Selena," she whispered, her voice hoarse from disuse.

The tall man smiled.

Selena's eyes looked up with confusion, with each passing moment seeing the contours of the man's face more clearly—its leanness, the high cheekbones, the sunken cheeks.

"Saliha Savanar," said the man. "That was the name of the little girl who escaped." He paused, his eyes closely examining Selena's face. "Tell me, who was your mother?"

Selena stayed silent, not wanting to say the wrong thing.

"Answer," said the man, his voice low and steady, almost bored.

"I—I never knew her."

"And your father?"

"I am an orphan, sir, a child of the street." Selena coughed, clearing her throat. "I did not know my father."

"And where did you grow up, Selena, the orphan girl?"

"The flatlands."

"Of Alwaz Deem?"

Selena nodded. "Yes."

"I would think," said the man, "that they would have given you a better alias. Saliha the Savanar becomes Selena the orphan girl. I suppose I suspected, all those years ago, that one day I would find you, perhaps far away upon the Sand Sea riding with the Beserians. Indeed, I have questioned many a caravan over the years. But what I never imagined was that they would hide you beneath my very nose, and in Alwaz Deem of all places—the one place where a face like yours was most likely to be recognized."

The man paused, staring down into Selena's face. Selena could now see the dark green of his eyes, the length of his nose, and the blackness of his small, sharp beard. She crouched in silence, unsure whether it was more dangerous to speak or not speak.

"I come here this evening to offer you a choice, Saliha, daughter of Sah Seg Savanar. You are the one that escaped my grasp. You are the one around whom others now place their hope. Do you know what year approaches?"

"807?"

"Yes. And do you know what year that is?"

Selena shook her head.

"It is the year that will mark the seventh year of the reign of our Qhaliffa, Sumetan the Magnificent. It is a malign year, for those of us whose duty it is to preserve the Qhaliffa's peace. Do you know why?"

Selena shook her head again.

"It is the year the heretics have awaited, the year of their prophecy. This, of course, makes the timing of your arrival in my hands particularly suspicious. Indeed, I doubted it. It is the kind of thing they would do—send me a false Savanar to distract from their treason and buy time for their rebellion. Except that as I place my eyes upon you now, though you are weak and thin with the filthy face of a prisoner, I can see that you are her."

"I am no one," whispered Selena, shaking her head again and fearing that any moment they would unlock her cell and take her back to the table.

"Yes, 'no one.' You may stop your protests. I can see into your eyes, and beyond that, into your heart. Your mind holds no secrets from me, even if it keeps them from you. You are no orphan from the flatlands. Nor are you a whore, though that is where I am told they found you, in a brothel."

Selena looked and saw that the man held a piece of wood in his hands, the length of the other men's torches. Against the man's chest, hidden from the others, it glowed as if it were aflame, though she saw no fire sprouting from it. The wood itself rippled and shimmered, as if the flame were buried within it, golden and bright.

"Please," said Selena, shaking her head in the golden light. "I know nothing of what you speak."

The man smiled, showing long, straight teeth, mildly discolored in the manner of those who drink too much strong tea.

"Most stop lying when the torture comes. Most seek leniency, admitting all they know, which leads me to consider the possibility that you may not even know your true identity. I suppose it was clever for them to keep you from yourself. It is something they would do. Although, was it not cruel to make a princess of the High Kezelboj believe she was a poor orphan? How long has it been now? Seventeen years? The time moves swiftly. How much did you suffer to protect their lie? I would think a great deal, if you were resorting to the brothel."

Selena struggled to breathe.

"I swear to you, s-sir." The tremor in her voice grew. "I . . . I am not who you think I am. I am a basket maker."

"Do you think you can convince me of what you do not know yourself? My guardsmen and my jailors have already told me your story, a story you kept, even when they took your teeth. Permit me, then, to tell you who I am."

Selena stared.

"I am Jemojeen Jongdar, Grand Vizer to the Qhaliffa of the Seven Cities of the Great Mountain, Sumetan the Magnificent, blessed be his name. Unlike you, Saliha of House Savanar, I was not born a princess of Alwaz Deem. I was born far to the west, in the Hill Country of Bulbania, like most Demissaries. Yes, I am the Demissary who rose to become Grand Vizer, the first to rise above the High Kezelboj in eight hundred years. Do you know who I am now?"

Selena nodded, her eyes widening, her fear growing. "Yes."

"Then you will also know I am the man who burned your father, Sah Seg Savanar and extinguished his family upon the orders of Selahim the Grim. Yes, Saliha, seventeen years ago, I burned your father. I stood next to the stake as the flames consumed him, and I oversaw the execution of your mother and your sisters."

Selena looked into his eyes between the flickering flames, nearly believing him.

"Your body was never found. Some say your family's servants smuggled you out of House Savanar that night. Some say the Order of the Ram, the Lion, and the Serpent then rode with you out of Alwaz Deem, out across the Approach of Alwaz and into the sands. Indeed, three veiled riders escaped Alwaz that very next morning. My Erassians chased them to the edge of the Hahst that day, where they disappeared amongst the white sands."

Selena watched him as he spoke.

"Do you remember? You were young—not yet five years old if my memory serves—but that is not so young that you could not remember."

Selena waited in silence, the chains weighing heavily upon her wrists and the manacles cutting into the raw flesh of her filthy ankles, slick with blood. Her gums throbbed.

"Answer the Grand Vizer!" barked one of the jailors to Jemojeen's side, again slamming his truncheon against the iron bars. The noise was as loud as a gunshot in the small cavern.

The Grand Vizer raised his hand as a look of sharp irritation flashed across his eyes.

"Do not. Do that. Again," he said.

Selena saw the fear in the jailor's face as he stepped back.

"I shall ask you once more, Saliha of House Savanar. What can you tell me about that night? Do you recall your escape? Do you remember the white sands?

A flicker of images moved across Selena's mind. She saw a face covered in cloth, with bright yellow-green eyes looking down into her own. She shuddered in surprise.

"What did you just see?"

"Nothing."

"Do not lie to me." Jemojeen lifted the piece of wood in his hands, his wide cloak still concealing it from the others.

Selena felt a tingle in her mind, like a soft blanket moving along the inside of her skull. Then it grew stronger and rougher, bordering on painful, making her spine, arms, and legs spasm and then stiffen. She nearly toppled over.

"I saw a face!" she cried out.

Her discomfort intensified as if hands squeezed her mind.

"What kind of face?" asked Jemojeen.

"It was covered," said Selena, speaking rapidly, shaking her head against the squeezing.

"With what?"

"Cloth!"

"What color?"

"It was . . . light."

"Light how? Like the color of sand?"

"Yes."

"Did you see eyes?"

"Yes!"

"Tell me about the eyes."

"They were green."

"And yellow?"

Selena nodded.

"My torturers should do better," said Jemojeen, turning his gaze toward the men next to him, his cloak closing over his arms and his piece of wood. The men all shrank in fear. "I find in moments what they cannot find in hours."

The feeling in Selena's mind relented, the grip releasing her. She exhaled in relief.

"I come here tonight to give you a choice, Saliha of House Savanar. Tomorrow you will be led out upon the platform with the heretics Trendan Rudar and Huralt Donadun. There you will be judged, found guilty of treason, chained to a stake, and burned alive. You will die as your father died."

Selena felt the breath fly out of her. She knew what a burning meant. There was no worse death, slow and terrible, the pain far beyond anything she had yet endured, even her torture.

"Your capture allowed me to convince the Qhaliffa that such must be done. Sumetan the Magnificent does not like burnings. He is gentler than his father. I, however, like his father, have always believed that burnings are useful things. I have seen a proud martyr face the ax that will take his head. I have seen others meet the rope that will hang them with their heads held high and their shoulders back. But the fire is different."

Selena looked at his face, too frightened to blink.

"You should be afraid now, for the flames await you. The oil soaks into the logs as we speak. But I come here in mercy. I bring you a choice to save the peace of this kingdom. If you admit your identity tomorrow—if you stand upon the platform and proclaim that you are indeed Saliha, the last Savanar, daughter of the heretic of the High Kezelboj, Sah Seg Savanar of Alwaz Deem, I will give you a clean death with the ax. You will avoid the flames. You must also renounce the prophecy."

Selena swallowed hard, closing her eyes.

"You will die tomorrow. The question is whether you wish to die slowly in unbearable pain, screaming in flames like your father, or in a swift instant. The choice is yours. Tell me now."

Selena willed herself to speak, finding only a faint whisper. "I will say whatever you want me to say."

"Then you have more wisdom than your father," said Jemojeen, turning to depart down the narrow stone corridor. The men with the torches followed him, rushing to keep his pace.

Selena again crouched alone, tears streaking her cheeks. In the darkness, the veiled face appeared again in her mind, looking into her face with the yellow-green eyes that, for the first time, she could remember.

And then, as if in a waking dream, the face spoke.

CHAPTER 5
I Will Not Have a Gelding

Offices of the *Illustrated Telegraph*, The City
South Anglia
December 21, 1878

His father gave no explanation when he summoned him, but Peter promptly obeyed, taking the express train down from Three Gods College. As he steamed into the City, the symbols of the Imperium passed by his window, imposing and familiar in the grey morning light. In the distance, through the mist, he saw the cathedral, then the palace, then Parliament, and then the ministries that handled domestic, colonial, and foreign affairs for Her Majesty's government. But for Peter, his destination loomed larger than them all.

Whether he liked it or not, as a Harmon of Hylebourne House, the center of the center, even more so than the great oval of Parliament, even more so than the Prime Minister's residence, even more so than the Queen's palace, was the office of the publisher of the *Illustrated Telegraph*, the most circulated paper in the home islands and across the colonies of the Anglian-speaking world—from the tip of Halex to the Xin Concession.

Lord George Harmon owned the *Illustrated Telegraph* outright, with no pesky shareholders to cater to and no board of directors to rein him in. It was the crown jewel of his newsprint empire, the paper that gave him the power his fellow conservatives in the Crown and Country Party envied and the opposition liberals in the Liberty and Commerce Party despised. Nearly all, however, regardless of party, feared public opinion, which meant they also feared Lord Harmon, for few could shape the public mind more swiftly and few could wield it more deftly.

Peter sat upon a green upholstered couch in the spacious waiting room, waiting like any other supplicant for his appointment. Theirs was not the kind of relationship that entitled the son to walk in to see his father without a prior, scheduled arrangement. Lord Harmon expected his son to wait like the others, all of whom were undoubtedly far more prominent than Peter. Peter was, as his father often reminded him, merely a college boy, who had much to achieve and much to learn about the world.

Peter looked up at the clock in the corner of the waiting room. 9:59 a.m.

He had one minute, one minute until Ulrich Ohms, his father's officious Gerdic secretary, would open the door that led to a carpeted walkway, past rows of clerks and to the stairs that rose to his father's office. Why had his father summoned him down from Three Gods College on short notice? He could not say, but it was a very odd thing for Lord Harmon to do, especially while Parliament was in session.

A door handle twisted. Peter looked up, seeing that it was the wrong door, the one that faced out into the alleyway from the outside.

Two men stepped in, wearing heavy raincoats and carrying umbrellas. A cold gust of wind accompanied them into the warmly heated room. They looked up, their eyes meeting Peter's. He recognized them in an instant.

"Good morning, Peter," said Harold Milton Stanwich, removing a top hat to reveal his sandy blond hair. "You remember Hersen Expey, yes?" He gestured with his head toward the tall, lean LaFrentian at his side.

Peter saw that Hersen Expey no longer dressed as a civilian. Beneath his overcoat, he wore an impeccable blue-and-red uniform with a high, stiff collar beneath a peaked cap, adorned with a gold braid where the brim met the peak, the uniform of an officer of the LaFrentian Legion. Peter's eyes moved to the insignia on the collar and identified the golden spade of a major.

"Mr. Harmon," said Hersen Expey, extending his hand to shake.

Baffled, Peter rose and took his hand. "Major Expey," he mumbled.

Stanwich looked at the clock. "Glad we made it on time. I forget how long it can take to go more than a few blocks at this hour, especially in the rain."

"Are you—"

"Joining you for your meeting with your father? Yes. Why did you think he summoned you?"

"I assumed—"

Stanwich smiled, looking at Hersen Expey.

Hersen smiled back beneath his trimmed mustache, declining to show his teeth.

Peter stood awkwardly, politeness demanding that he not sit down until the other gentlemen did first.

"Ahh," said Stanwich, not sitting. He looked up at the massive painting that covered the entire wall opposite the green couch.

"So, this is the great duke," said Stanwich, leaning forward on his long umbrella. He scanned the scene until his eyes rested upon the life-sized face of an Anglian General atop a chestnut horse.

The general in the painting wore a long, auburn wig beneath a plumed, bi-corn hat. Triple ranks of infantry stood in front of him with straight backs and steely eyes, awaiting the oncoming charge of LaFrentian cavalry. The front row knelt with their bayonets pointed upward like a steel hedge. From the right, a stampede of LaFrentian horsemen galloped with gleaming breastplates and plumed helmets, leveling their long, straight swords at the infantry. Above the infantry, an enormous Anglian flag—three golden rings over a red cross separating four white squares and bordered by an edge of dark blue—rippled above wafting musket smoke, eerily lifelike in the painted wind.

"How much do you know about this man?" asked Stanwich, still staring at the painted general.

"As much as I should, I suppose," said Peter, uneasy as to why Harold Milton Stanwich was there at all. After their last brief meeting, he did not expect to see him again.

Stanwich waited with his eyebrows arched. Outside the windows, cold rain spattered the awning, drenching the center of the alleyway. The silence grew awkward. Stanwich looked at Peter.

"Do you know much about him?" asked Peter, trying to make conversation, gesturing toward the battle scene.

"A bit," said Stanwich.

Hersen Expey stared at Peter, his grey LaFrentian eyes cool and evaluating.

Peter cleared his throat and nodded. "This depicts Mannhein Moor, the final battle against the LaFrentian Emperor."

Stanwich looked at Hersen and laughed. "Does a major of the LaFrentian Legion know a painting of Mannhein Moor when he sees it?"

He turned back to Peter. "Tell us something we might not know."

Peter felt his cheeks growing red.

"Very well, Mr. Stanwich."

Peter stepped closer to the painting, taking his eyes off of Stanwich and Hersen. As he had done countless times before, he looked up into the face of the general.

"Our forces had begun to turn the tide of the battle." Peter glanced at Hersen Expey's LaFrentian Legionnaire uniform, feeling a flicker of Anglian pride.

Hersen held his gaze steady.

"The Anglian forces advanced," said Peter, "opening a salient along the right flank. In his long record of victories, none had mastered decisive flanking maneuvers better than the Emperor. But now the Anglians used his own tricks against him. The Emperor saw the danger too late, they say."

Beneath his LaFrentian cap, Hersen Expey acknowledged this with a nod.

Peter's words flowed more freely as he looked into the face of his famous ancestor. "In response, the Emperor called up his reserve—his guards regiments, his personal Hussars, and the crown jewel of all his armies, the heavy cavalry brigade under the command of Marshall De Gonde, Constable of LaFrentia.

"Those plumed veterans, in their gleaming breastplates, nearly turned the day against our armies." Peter wagged his extended finger in front of the painting, now pacing like a lecturer. "This painting shows that moment. The Constable's horsemen came forward, cutting across two brigades of line infantry, slaughtering and trampling as they went. Then *he* saw them. At that point John Harmon, my great-great-grandfather, ordered his remaining line regiments into squares, despite the presence of the Emperor's artillery. He himself rode in front of the infantry, shouting that the Emperor's cannons would not shoot down the Emperor's own advancing cavalry, but that the cavalry would surely ride down any man not in the square.

"The squares formed. The squares prevailed. Against the triple volleys of musket fire and the triple-ranked hedges of bayonets, even De Gonde and the Guards could not break them. The cavalry charge failed, and so did the Emperor. My father says the true rise of the Anglian Imperium began that day. The grateful King elevated John Harmon, 7th Earl of Haden, to become John Harmon, the first Duke of Haden. That, of course, is the title my grandfather held in his lifetime and that which my father's older brother holds today."

Before Stanwich or Hersen Expey could respond, the inner door opened. A tall Gerdic functionary stood erect as a flagpole.

"Good morning. Lord Harmon will see you now. Please follow me."

Though he had met Peter many times, Ulrich Ohms showed him no more familiarity than that which he directed toward Harold Milton Stanwich or Hersen Expey, which is to say, none at all. Perhaps, had Peter been in a more reflective and generous frame of mind, he would have seen the remarkableness of this, for unlike the rest of Anglia, Ohms seemed unimpressed by Stanwich's fame. But Peter was not in such a frame of mind, and he remained, as always, offended by Ulrich Ohms' cold formality. If Ohms had any awareness that one day, he, Peter Harmon, stood to inherit the *Illustrated Telegraph*, which would make Ulrich Ohms his employee, Ohms concealed that realization extraordinarily well.

Ohms held the door open until Stanwich and Hersen Expey passed through it. Peter stood awkwardly in the hallway, his shoes sinking into the deep blue carpet. Desks flanked the corridor on either side. Peter did not recognize any of the occupying faces. The men leaned over stacks of papers, reading and annotating documents with intense, efficient strokes. They did not look up as Peter passed them. Ohms cleared his throat, walking quickly to regain the lead. Peter waited in irritable obedience.

Ohms passed by him. "Follow me, gentlemen."

Peter stood as tall as Ohms. He followed the narrow Gerdic shoulders down the narrow walkway and then to the left into a narrow hallway. They passed into a new room, larger than the first. Men hustled by, carrying folders with urgent, anxious looks upon their faces like men concerned with meeting deadlines.

Peter looked up at the far wall. A line of clocks hung just beneath the ceiling. Each timepiece bore the name of a place above it. CITY OF ANGLIA: 10:02 AM, BAY PORT CITY: 5:02 AM, LAKETOWN: 4:02 AM, VETENO: 2:02 PM, KHYDERBAD: 5:02 PM, XIN CONCESSION: 10:02 PM.

Peter returned his gaze to the back of Ulrich Ohms' perfectly coiffed head, reminded by the clock hands that his father's arms wrapped around the globe. They stretched as far as the limits of the Imperium and beyond, across the Continent, down to Omakhosi, and into the lands beyond the Titanic Ocean, Halex and the New Anglian Republic. The business of the *Illustrated Telegraph* never rested, nor did its employees, covering shifts around the clock.

Peter saw several men across the room pause and look up at them. He thought perhaps they had at last decided to take a look at the boss's son. Then he saw that their eyes moved past him without recognition, following Stanwich and his LaFrentian Legionnaire.

They turned to a flight of broad, carpeted stairs between a pair of imposing varnished railings. Ohms ascended in swift, silent steps. Peter and the others followed.

Atop the landing, they stopped at a set of massive double doors, oaken and solid. A small gold plaque lay above the door, which read, "Lord George Harmon, EMP, Publisher."

Ulrich Ohms knocked twice.

He waited three beats, twisted the knob, and pushed.

The door, despite its weight, slid silently open upon smooth hinges. Even amid the rainstorm outside, pleasant natural light flooded the room from tall windows to Peter's right, made all the brighter in contrast to the dimness of the stairwell. Peter followed Ohms, walking forward into the office that had never failed to make him feel small, like a child amongst men. Stanwich and Hersen followed behind him. Peter hunched his shoulders forward as if trying to make himself less visible.

He looked past Ohms. His father sat alone in a high-backed chair behind his huge desk. A bespectacled man sat across from him in one of the four chairs arrayed on the other side, closest to Peter, where supplicants approached Lord Harmon and the world received the decisions and judgments of the publisher of the *Illustrated Telegraph*.

Ohms stopped abruptly at the edge of an intricate Hindean rug. The vast rectangle covered the entire center of the room.

"My lord," said Ohms, standing stiffer than the towering palm trees in the corners of the office. "May I present Mr. Harold Milton Stanwich, the explorer, Major Hersen Expey, of the LaFrentian Legion, and your son, Mr. Peter Harmon."

"Good morning, Mr. Stanwich," said Lord Harmon, his voice booming.

His eyes had yet to acknowledge them, still focused upon the document in his hands. He rose, still holding the paper, showing his great height and his substantial girth. He was handsome in the manner of the middle-aged and prosperous, with full cheeks and lips, verging toward fleshy. A great walrus mustache adorned his upper lip. He looked forward, a monocle covering his left eye.

Stanwich and Hersen bowed.

"Lord Harmon," said Stanwich, slowly rising. "Your invitation honors us. Your paper has been most kind to our efforts across the years."

"We give credit where it is due," said Lord Harmon. "You know Jessup Jensen, of course. Our editor."

The much smaller man stood on the near side of the desk. He nodded respectfully, squinting through the pince-nez perched on the bridge of his long nose.

"Yes, most certainly," said Stanwich. "Good morning, Mr. Jensen."

Lightning flashed in the tall windows facing the street. In his nervous state, Peter winced. A heartbeat later, angry thunder roared. Peter looked to his right, toward the rivulets of rainwater moving down the glass panes.

"Please come and sit," said Lord Harmon, ignoring the storm and gesturing to the three open chairs to the left of Jessup Jensen. The desk was so large that it extended past the four chairs on either side.

Ohms sidestepped the central design upon the Hindean rug. A turbaned prince waved a saber above a rearing horse, brought forth magnificently by the tens of thousands of minute and precisely placed knots, each of them handwoven with immense effort. Peter did the same, looking down at the image as he walked by. He had always liked it, ever since he was a boy. He wished it rested somewhere other than in his father's office.

Stanwich stopped and looked down.

"Is this what I think it is?" he asked, Hersen Expey at his side.

"I suppose that depends upon what you think it is," said Lord Harmon.

"I once saw a very similar rug in the palace of the Crown Prince of Khyderbad. Almost identical."

Lord Harmon smiled. "Then you have seen two of a kind, Mr. Stanwich. The man to whom you refer gave me that which rests below you. Its sister rug adorns the throne room of the prince's palace."

Stanwich nodded, his face flushing with pride.

"I will also say," said Lord Harmon, "that you are the first person, of the very great many that have passed by it, to have made the connection between the two."

"Thank you, sir," said Stanwich.

"Please sit," said Lord Harmon.

Peter, Stanwich, and Hersen did as Lord Harmon asked. Ohms retreated to a small desk along the far side of the room, opposite from the windows and beneath the fronds of one of the palm trees.

Lord Harmon placed his elbows upon the desk, leaning forward. His coat sleeves retracted, revealing a pair of immense golden cuff links. Peter saw that they were in the shape of three interlocking rings, the same rings that adorned the Anglian flag—the rings of the Three Gods.

"Now, Peter, you may wonder why you are here," he said, acknowledging the presence of his son for the first time.

Peter sat, watching his father with anxious eyes.

"I understand, at my request, that Mr. Stanwich already spoke with you while he was at your school."

Peter's eyes widened. "At your request?" he asked, his voice higher than he would have preferred.

"Indeed. And I also understand that you rebuffed him in his request."

"Yes, I did," said Peter, Sarah's face coming into his mind's eye. "I told him the truth that I am slated to be the private secretary of the Lord Governor of Khyderbad."

"Ah, yes," said Lord Harmon. "Khyderbad raises its Hindean head again." He looked at Stanwich with a grin and a glint in his eye. "Much of my life seems to be drawn to that strange gem in our imperial crown."

Stanwich and Hersen mirrored Lord Harmon's smile, like those who are in on a joke.

"We already mentioned the prince of Khyderbad. Fine fellow, so far as those types go. We allow him his palace, his pleasures, and his deference. And, truth be told, the man is not unhelpful as a symbol. But, of course, the real ruling is done by my cousin, Bartimus Freer, the Lord Governor. Peter here has been dead set on becoming his secretary. I was nearly inclined to agree."

Peter shot an indignant look at his father.

"Nearly inclined, that is, until I realized my son does not need to serve as my cousin's secretary, not before he has seen a bit more of the world in the company of men such as yourselves."

He turned his gaze upon his son, the easy smile falling from his face, his left eye glaring at Peter from behind its gold-rimmed monocle.

"You have spent the last four years with books and pens and papers. It is time for you to see the world of action. When I was your age, I was en route to the Spatanian borderlands to fight the Gressians. If there were a war going now, I would expect you to do the same, but alas, there is not. So, I will settle for the next best thing. You are to accompany Mr. Stanwich here upon his expedition."

Peter opened his mouth to protest.

Lord Harmon lifted one of his substantial hands, his open palm facing Peter like a wall. "No, I did not give you leave to speak on the matter."

Peter felt the heat rising to his cheeks. Sarah would be leaving for Khyderbad with her mother and sisters, and would remain there for half a year at least. Her father, General Hesiger, had just taken a command with the Hindean Army.

"Your studies are concluded, and in my view, so is your boyhood. It is high time for you to gain a man's education in the presence of these men. Real men."

Peter felt dizzy as if the solid floor beneath his chair had suddenly begun to give way.

"I cannot," said Peter, looking down into his hands.

He felt the gazes of Lord Harmon, Jessup Jensen, Harold Milton Stanwich, and Hersen Expey upon his face.

"And why is that?" asked his father.

Peter's heart pounded in his chest. He felt ambushed, betrayed, powerless. Sarah's face again entered his mind. He saw her seated upon a park bench, Hindean palms rising above her. A young man sat next to her, wearing the uniform of a cavalry lieutenant. He spoke as she laughed, leaning toward him in her most flirtatious way. Peter's stomach twisted.

"Because we—we had an agreement," said Peter. "I am to be in Khyderbad. I already gave my word to Governor Freer."

"I spoke with Governor Freer," said Lord Harmon. "At my request, he has already found a replacement."

"But I—"

"You will depart with these men in two weeks. You will spend 1879 upon the Sand Sea. You will report on your journey for the *Illustrated Telegraph*, making a name for yourself, one that is worthy of the name you were given. I will not have a gelding for a son. There are enough of those in the Liberty and Commerce Party!"

Jessup Jensen smirked beneath his pince-nez, as Stanwich and Hersen Expey laughed aloud.

Peter's mind raced for another reason to object.

"What about—"

The men stopped laughing, and all eyes once again focused on Peter.

"What about the Gressians?" he asked.

The smile fell from his father's face. He glanced at Stanwich.

"What about them?"

"Well, historically," said Peter, "as you all surely know, the autocrats have resisted any incursion into the Sand Sea. It constitutes the vast majority of their southern border, and they like that it is closed off to the outside world. The tribesmen pose no real challenge to them, and the Qhaliffas have not launched a northern invasion for centuries. What makes you think they would tolerate an Anglian expedition prowling around their southern border any more than we would tolerate the Gressians exploring around the border of Hindea?"

Stanwich, Hersen, and Jessup Jensen all looked at Lord Harmon, waiting to follow his lead. Lord Harmon looked at his son, glaring through his monocle.

"The problem with a college boy," he said, "is that he always thinks he knows more than he does. If the Gressians did come south—which they won't—you'll have an even better story to tell for the *Illustrated Telegraph*. Maybe, if you're lucky, you'd even get a chance to fight a few of them as I did."

"But fear not, Peter," said Stanwich, forcing a laugh. "We are a peaceful, international expedition, exploring for the good of humanity, flying not only the Anglian flag but the New Anglian and the Spatanian flags as well. You're far more likely to get heatstroke than to meet a Gressian."

Hersen Expey said nothing, only smiling his sly, LaFrentian smile.

CHAPTER 6
Because You Are a Woman

Caldwell Ranch, Calderon State
New Anglian Republic
December 21, 1878

Little birds chirped from the bougainvillea branches that clung to the red tile roof, peering out from the pink flowers at the sunlit table below. In the courtyard, servants in aprons bustled to and from the house carrying trays of food and wine.

Hannah sat in silence, staring at her roasted chicken and potatoes, avoiding her mother's icy blue gaze across the table. Mrs. Sarah Gunderia Huntington was an imported Gerdic beauty, generally disapproving of her provincial life in Calderon despite the year-round good weather and the fact that her husband was likely the richest man in the state. She compensated for her deprivation with stern criticism of her youngest daughter, the one who did not live up to her expectations of what an ambitious young woman should be. Hannah was, among other things, unmarried at twenty-two.

"Carolyn and Jack went looking for you," she said.

"Did they?" asked Hannah, looking at one of the empty chairs.

"Yes, they did. And unlike you, they were not late for this luncheon." As Mrs. Huntington spoke, she looked out across the sparkling wine glasses, fine silver, and familiar faces, as if Hannah should place a much higher priority upon a meal with the assembled Caldwell, Huntington, and Johnson families.

Mrs. Nancy Caldwell leaned toward them. "Hannah, are you excited for the ball?"

"Yes, Mrs. Caldwell."

"Have you chosen your dress?"

"Not yet."

"No? You'd best do that soon if you are having it made."

"She is having her dress made in Bay Port City," said Mrs. Huntington. "She will be departing early on the Transcontinental."

"Did I hear that correctly?" asked Mrs. Johnson, leaning toward them as well. "Who is making it?"

"*Dardennes*," said Mrs. Huntington, answering for her daughter. "The fabric is already reserved, and measurements have been sent."

Mrs. Johnson's eyes widened at the name of the famous design house. "I suppose you must spend that kind of money on that kind of ball. There will be a matching ball in Anglia, yes?"

Mrs. Huntington nodded.

"At the Queen's palace, I heard," said Mrs. Caldwell.

"We are delighted to be attending," said Mrs. Huntington, with no shortage of pride. "The balls will, of course, be held on Three Gods Day. At midnight, Anglia time, they will send the first message across the Trans-Titanic cable, from Anglia to Bay Port City." She nodded importantly. "The Queen Empress herself will wish the New Anglian Republic a Happy Three Gods Day and a prosperous 1879. And then we in New Anglia, when it strikes midnight our time, shall send our reply."

"I must tell you, Sarah, I am envious," said Mrs. Caldwell.

"As am I," said Mrs. Johnson.

Mrs. Caldwell turned down the table toward her husband and the other men. "Colonel, why are we not going to the Three Gods Day Ball in Bay Port City?"

Colonel Mason Caldwell looked up from his conversation with Mr. Samuel X. Huntington and Mr. Jeremiah Johnson. He frowned, shook his head, and returned to whatever point he had been making to the men, gesturing with a butter knife.

"Because he has become cheap. That is why," whispered Mrs. Caldwell, turning back to the women.

"Jeremiah has as well," said Mrs. Johnson.

"By the Three Gods, we even travel on the Transcon for *free*," added Mrs. Caldwell.

"Well, for us, of course, it is very important," said Mrs. Huntington. "There will be many eligible bachelors attending." She looked at Hannah and raised her eyebrows, worry lines creasing her forehead. "We can, of course, expect all of the best unmarried sons from Bay Port City. However, I'm informed that many will also be coming in from both Laketown and Port Southern as well."

The other two mothers, both of whom had only sons, nodded at the seriousness of the matter. Nancy Caldwell and Judy Johnson had both long-consoled Mrs. Huntington regarding her difficult and disobedient youngest daughter. They had schemed together about finding her a suitable match when Hannah turned twenty, and again the following year when Carolyn Huntington married

Mr. Rex Shuler of Port Calderon. But now that Hannah was six months away from twenty-three, they considered it nearly a crisis. Neither woman, however, pushed hard for their sons to be the choice, partly out of fear of Mrs. Huntington's standards, and partly out of fear of Hannah's wildness, though both were aware that such a match would likely make the front page of the *Port Calderon Gazette* and perhaps even an appearance in the papers of Laketown and Bay Port City. Jack Caldwell was twenty-three, nearly twenty-four, the same age as Carolyn, and Jefferson Johnson was twenty-two, the same age as Hannah.

"Well, once the match is made, we all certainly look forward to a second Huntington wedding," said Mrs. Caldwell. "Carolyn's was no doubt the finest Port Calderon has ever seen."

"Oh, indeed," said Mrs. Johnson.

As if on cue, Jack and Carolyn stepped into the courtyard.

"There you are!" said Jack, loudly enough to stop all of the conversations at the table. A broad smile opened across his suntanned face as he locked his eyes upon Hannah. "Your sister and I went looking for you. We heard you might be lost up on the mountain."

Hannah did not smile back. "Oh, where did you look?"

Jack's mouth kept smiling, but his eyes flashed as if recognizing danger. Had she seen them?

Carolyn walked at a respectable distance behind him, the massive sapphire in her wedding ring glittering in the sunlight. Hannah saw that her hair was pinned up perfectly back in place, no doubt precisely as it had looked when she departed the luncheon to find her missing sister.

Jack and Carolyn took the remaining empty chairs, sitting at opposite ends of the table.

Colonel Caldwell cleared his throat, tapping his butter knife against his wine glass. All grew quiet. "Jack, since you are back, and since we are all here, why don't you go ahead and tell everyone."

Jack reached for a wine bottle and poured himself a tall glass, not waiting for a servant. With everyone's eyes upon him, he drank down a long sip of the golden wine and smiled again, white teeth flashing above his strong, prominent jaw.

"Very well," he said. "I will be leaving tomorrow. Up to Port Calderon in the morning and then to Bay Port City via the Transcon. I'll be keeping Hannah company on the train. Then I'll be boarding a steamer across the Titanic Ocean."

Hannah's eyes bulged.

The others all waited in silence. Jack swept his eyes along their faces, enjoying what he viewed as his rightful place at the center of their undivided attention.

"I trust you have all heard of Mr. Harold Milton Stanwich, the explorer?"
Jack saw at once in their faces that they had.

"He is launching a new expedition, and I am to be a part of it."

His mother, Mrs. Huntington, and Mrs. Johnson all looked at him as if he
were already a hero. Carolyn smiled possessively, her dark blue eyes the same
color as the sapphire on her hand.

"I have been dying to tell you," said Mrs. Caldwell, looking at her friends.

"Where will you be going, Jack?" asked Mrs. Johnson. She stole a glance at
her quiet son, Jefferson, doubting he would ever measure up to Jack.

"The Sand Sea," said Jack.

"The desert?" asked Mrs. Huntington. "Why?"

"Because young men must be formed," said Colonel Caldwell, interrupting.
He looked a great deal like his son, but his voice was deeper, and a thick brown
beard covered the lower half of his face. "And young men are not properly
formed," he continued, "by drinking wine with their families in the courtyards
of Calderon." He paused to look at Jack. "No, hardship, and only hardship,
forms boys into men."

Jeremiah Johnson nodded. He and the colonel were formed by the same
hardships, commanding a Howan State regiment together against the LaFrentians. Johnson served as his second in command in the war, and he continued as
his number two in the ensuing decades as they built the colonel's business empire. His son, Jefferson, was already diligently working under his direction,
learning the operations of Caldwell & Sons. Jefferson was not the kind that
needed to learn discipline on an expedition to the desert. But Jack most certainly was.

Jack blushed, seeming to grow smaller under his father's gaze. His father—
the founder of Caldwell & Sons, the famous regimental commander of the La-
Frentian War, and along with Sam Huntington, the largest shareholder of the
Transcontinental Railroad—was likely the only person who could cut his legs
out from under him with a word. He was also the only man who physically
frightened Jack.

Jack drained his wine glass, reaching for the bottle.

"Will it be dangerous?" asked Mrs. Huntington.

"It may," said Jack, pouring his wine, his voice softer than it had been only
a moment before.

"Well, dear, we shall eagerly read about you in the *Port Calderon Gazette*."

After two bottles of wine at lunch, Jack stood in his father's office, facing Samuel
X. Huntington, Jeremiah Johnson, and his father.

"If you ever want to run Caldwell & Sons, this is your first real test, son," said Colonel Caldwell.

Jack waited, swallowing heavily, feeling acutely that the three men before him held his fate in their hands.

"As you know, Sam here has agreed to fund a third of the expedition. I'm in for a third, and your Uncle Lord Harmon, across the ocean, is in for the final third. None of that comes for free. We want the minerals, plain and simple, and you're going to make sure we get them."

"Yes, the Beserite."

"Don't say that word."

Jack looked sheepishly at the closed door.

"I don't care if the door is closed," said the colonel. "Don't say the word until you get to the Sand Sea, and even there, you should say it with a whisper."

"Yes, sir," said Jack.

"And stop the drinking."

"Yes, sir."

"I mean it, stop the Three-Gods-damned drinking. This is real business. Our money is on the line, and we won't have you smashing it up because you can't control yourself."

"Yes, sir."

"As we have discussed, Barnes will be your protection and your guide. He is also going to keep an eye on you for us to make sure you're on track. He'll be disguised as your valet for the beginning of the trip until you get to the Sand Sea, but you better not think that makes him your damn servant. You understand?"

"Yes, sir."

"Jeremiah and I saw what he could do during the war. The man was the best soldier in our whole regiment." He paused, looking at Jeremiah Johnson.

Johnson nodded in agreement.

The colonel continued, "Barnes started as a private soldier and ended as a decorated sergeant. He fought in eight battles, including all five of the big ones. Wounded three times. He has remained very useful to all three of us since the war." The colonel glanced at Sam Huntington and Jeremiah Johnson.

Johnson nodded again.

"I've met him," said Jack. "I understand."

"Do you? Now, your cousin Peter is also supposed to go, but we're not counting on him for anything. I don't know him very well, and if you ask me, he's not really the sort for an expedition like this. He has always been a quiet, bookish young man. Frankly, knowing my sister and Lord Harmon, I'm not sure how a pair like them ends up with a boy like him. But that is neither here nor there. We're relying upon you. What are your questions while we are all standing here?"

Jack stood mute.

"Nothing? No questions?" asked the colonel. "I would have questions."

Jack waited, his head swirling and his mind too full of wine to formulate anything intelligent. His father and the other men stared at him.

"Fine," said the colonel, at last. "Sam, anything else?"

"No," said Samuel X. Huntington.

"Very well."

Sam Huntington shook hands with Colonel Caldwell, Jeremiah Johnson, and Jack.

"Good luck, Caldwell," he said, looking up into Jack's face with a stern gaze.

He pulled opened the door and walked out into the sunshine.

He made his way down the gravel path as the door clicked shut behind him. A whispered voice called out, "Father."

Sam Huntington spun around to see Hannah, her blonde hair popping up from behind a bush and her eyes darting to make sure she had not been discovered.

"Were you eavesdropping?" he asked.

"Yes," she said, standing up to her full height and walking quickly toward him. They stood nearly eye to eye with the same blue eyes. They had nearly the same color hair, though a touch of grey ran through Sam Huntington's. He smiled.

"You shouldn't do that."

"I want to go."

"Go where?"

"On the Stanwich Expedition."

"That's not going to happen, Hannah." He put a hand on her back, lightly leading her away from the colonel's office, along the side of the house toward the arbor overlooking the lemon groves and the ocean.

"Why not? I can ride and shoot as well as Jack."

"That is far from the point," said her father.

"If Colonel Caldwell has Jack as his representative, and Lord Harmon has his son going, who is your representative?"

"That is not how this works."

"Then how does it work?"

"Walk with me."

They walked in silence until they reached the archway of climbing roses. They stopped beneath it, looking out over the coast, their hair blowing in the offshore breeze. To the west, the Great Western Ocean softly rumbled as it met the shoreline several miles away.

"You have somewhere to be, Hannah—the Three Gods Day Ball in Bay Port City. It's important to your mother." He took a deep breath. "And to me."

Above the beach, a formation of pelicans flew southward in a long line.

"I don't want to go to the ball in Bay Port City."

"Hannah."

"I am serious, Father. I do not want Carolyn's life." Tears welled in her eyes.

Her father frowned. "Hannah, do not ask for things I cannot give you. You are going to Port Calderon, and from there Mrs. Smith will escort you to Bay Port City on the Transcontinental. That is the plan, and that is what you are going to do."

"Why? I don't even know Mrs. Smith."

"I know her, and she will keep you safe until I arrive."

Hannah shook her head. "Why do I need to be kept safe?"

"Because there are people that would hurt you because of who you are."

"What do you mean?"

"Because you are my daughter."

"What people? I have never seen them."

"That does not mean they are not there."

"Who is Mrs. Smith?"

"She is a woman I trust with your safety."

Hannah shook her head in frustration, looking away from her father and out toward the ocean, tracking the pelicans with her eyes.

"What is Beserite?"

"You should not have heard that word," said Sam Huntington, his eyes hardening.

"What is it?"

"Don't meddle there, Hannah."

"But Jack, the drunk, can know what it is?"

"I have concerns enough about that," said Sam Huntington.

Hannah could hear in her father's voice that she was treading upon dangerous terrain, but she pressed on nonetheless.

"Tell me why I can't go to the Sand Sea. Tell me why *I* have to go to some ridiculous ball instead."

"Because you are a woman, Hannah."

Hannah's face flushed. She opened her mouth, holding the words on the tip of her tongue that would expose Jack and Carolyn for what they were.

"What?" asked Sam Huntington, frowning.

"I will do as you ask, Father, only because *you* demand it, but don't ever expect me to be like them." She looked up toward the house.

"Like who, Hannah?"

"Any of them."

CHAPTER 7
No Place for a Silk Vest

Port Calderon
New Anglian Republic
December 22, 1878

Jack woke up, badly needing a drink.

The sun had set, and he had slept through the afternoon, nauseated after the choppy steamship ride, traveling with the Huntington women up the Calderonian coast. He never much liked the sea, despite having lived much of his life within sight of it. The fact that he still felt the effects of the previous night's whiskeys when they'd boarded did not help. He'd stayed up drinking with Diego and Jefferson Johnson, telling stories around the fire pit until well into the night.

On the steamship, Carolyn, faking seasickness, had slipped into his stateroom, ready to revisit their rendezvous in the stables while Hannah and her mother ate their lunch on the covered deck. Being actually seasick, Jack felt too physically awful to make use of the opportunity. Never one to sympathize with weakness, nor one with an inclination toward nursing the ill, Carolyn quickly departed. She called him "pathetic" as she closed the door, leaving him unfulfilled and vomiting into a wastebasket. Now that they were in Port Calderon, he knew he'd missed his chance. She would go back to her husband, Mr. Rex Shuler, for the night. Jack knew Carolyn's ways better than most.

The closest saloon to the Harris Hotel fronted a crowded alley, one streetblock up from the tangle of humanity on the wharf. In Port Calderon, the neighborhood could change dramatically in a single block, as Jack saw when he walked through the cold fog from the city's finest hotel toward the docks. The buildings grew dingier, and the people on the streets grew rougher. The alley smelled of fish and tar. The sign above the door said, "The Sail and Anchor." A life-sized wooden sailor stood outside, missing several of his fingers and the end of the gnarled pipe sticking out of his wooden mouth.

Jack stood looking at the mascot's missing fingers. Then he looked down at his own gentleman's clothes. They were the kind he wore in the city when he wished to make a good impression— silk vest, tailored pants, and shined shoes. He shrugged.

If they serve whiskey, I'll take my chances.

Jack pulled the door open and stepped inside. He waved his hand in front of him, swirling the dense fog of cigar and pipe smoke. It made no difference. The smoke was omnipresent. He coughed into the back of his hand.

He reached into the pocket of his vest and pulled out a gold watch, seeing that he still had an hour before he was to meet Barnes in the lobby of the Harris Hotel.

Someone sat on every stool at the bar, and other men stood behind those on the stools, barking their drink orders at the bartenders. Several sets of unfriendly eyes stared at Jack, peering over glasses of whiskey and mugs of beer. As his eyes adjusted to the darkness of the tavern, Jack looked for an open place at the bar, where he might order a drink without rubbing elbows with a sailor or a stevedore, but he saw only a solid wall of men's backs. Loud, indistinct voices assaulted his eardrums as hundreds of men spoke at once—some to each other and some to be heard over others. Several shouted lewd requests at a large-bosomed woman carrying a tray of beer. She carried a rough, hardened look on her face. A short, wide-shouldered man walked in behind Jack and shoved his way past him toward the bar.

Half way across the room, Jack saw a man point at him and whisper something to his companions. The companions laughed, but not kindly, looking at Jack with wolfish eyes. There looked to be a half-dozen of them. Jack resisted the urge to look down at the floor. If they saw his fear, he knew he would be worse off. Instead, he looked ahead of him, as if searching for someone he knew, feeling, with growing discomfort, the eyes of other men staring at him from the bar railings.

One of the men began walking toward him, moving through the dense crowd of working men spending their wages on whiskey they could ill afford. Jack saw that a second man followed the first, weaving his way directly toward him.

"Rich boy," said the first man, coming within earshot. Jack could barely hear the words over the din, but he could clearly read the words on the man's lips.

Jack pretended the man had addressed someone else.

"Hey, rich boy," repeated the man. "What are you doing here?"

Jack half turned, keeping his gaze upon a clock on the wall. It was a clock of one of the little free countries on the mountain border between LaFrentia and the Gerdic Empire. Little wooden men in an alpine scene moved in a never-ending circle, atop little wooden snow skis. It was a delicate instrument, and perhaps not surprisingly, it hung well above the reach of the tallest drunkard.

"Hey, rich boy!" repeated the voice, now shouting directly into Jack's face. Jack met the man's gaze, looking down at him. He saw with some satisfaction that he stood a half-head taller than the man. Jack looked down farther, at the man's arms and shoulders, and did not like what he saw. The man's muscles were thick around his neck, sloping downward into powerful trapezius muscles toward the shoulders and into the broad back of a stevedore—a man who lifted heavy loads for a living. Like most in the barroom, he looked to be one of the thousands that made their wages servicing the busiest port on the western coast of the Republic.

"You don't belong here," said the man, his voice slurred and menacing, as he looked Jack up and down.

Jack said nothing, staring into the man's face as adrenaline pumped through his long, strong limbs.

"Are you lookin' for someone?"

"No," said Jack.

"No? Then why do you keep lookin' like you're lookin'?"

"I'm not," said Jack.

"And I'm not blind," said the man. His light brown hair was cut short. Jack saw a sizeable scar moving down the man's cheek from the edge of his left eye as if a dagger had slashed him there some time ago.

"I'm not blind either," said Jack. "I'd ask you to back away."

"Yeah? What's the name of the man askin'?"

"My name? My name is none of your Three-Gods-damned business," said Jack.

"Oh, so you're a tough one? A tough one in a pretty vest, eh?"

The man's companion had slid to the side so he stood nearly parallel to the first man. The second man had not yet said a word. The silence of the second man worried Jack more than the words of the first. Jack lifted his head slightly into the air as if stretching his back while looking up at the ceiling. Then, in a flash, he swung his head forward and down, bringing the dead center of his forehead onto the shorter man's nose. As he struck, Jack could feel the crushing impact of his head into the cartilage.

The man's nose burst like a thrown tomato, spattering blood onto Jack's face, shirt, and vest.

Before the other man could strike, Jack's left fist hammered into his jaw. He hit him in the correct place, the place he had hit many others before. The man, however, did not fall. He staggered backward and then launched forward like a dog in a fighting pit. There was no growl, only physical movement. He surged toward Jack's throat—silent, swift, and deadly.

Jack threw another punch, this one from his right hand, the attack unconsciously surging across his body with all of the leverage of his height and with a boxer's shift of his hips. But the silent man ducked as Jack's hand pulled his weight forward—down and off-balance. The base of the man's palm slammed into Jack's sternum, striking him with the force of a brickbat. The air flew out of Jack's lungs, and his eyes widened in panic. He staggered backward, reflexively grabbing his chest like a man with a stopped heart.

"Enough."

The voice was low but audible through the shouts of the watching crowd.

The man who spoke did not rise from his stool. His hand remained on the bar, holding the handle of a pewter beer mug. The other men stepped away from his barstool, giving him a respectful distance in all directions.

The man who hit Jack stopped cold, like a trained dog hearing a command. The first man, the man Jack struck with his forehead, had taken his hands off of his nose and advanced toward Jack with clenched fists. Involuntary tears streamed down the man's cheeks, his smashed nose forcing them from his eyes. Blood continued to flow from his nostrils, covering his mouth and chin in scarlet. He now stopped as entirely as the other man.

Jack continued to gasp for air like a fish on a dock, grasping his chest. The man on the stool took a long, steady sip from his beer mug, slowly rising to his feet. Those nearby backed away another half-pace to give him more room, stepping back into those behind them.

The man walked toward Jack, a bowler hat resting low on his head, covering his forehead and half of his eyes.

"Breathe," he said.

Jack looked at him, unsure whether he was friend or foe. He could not breathe.

"Relax, and the air will return," said the man.

Jack felt like he was drowning on dry land. The man stepped closer. Jack looked into his face.

"Release your stomach," said the man. Jack looked into his face and saw eyes he knew.

His spasming diaphragm unclenched. The air rushed into his lungs as he took several deep, grateful breaths.

Sergeant Joshua Barnes turned toward the men who had just faced off against Jack. "Lads, meet Jack Caldwell, son of Colonel Mason Caldwell," he said.

Some of the men smiled. Others nodded respectfully. All looked at Jack with different eyes than those that had glared at him only seconds before.

"Come," said Joshua Barnes, putting his long, lean arm around Jack's shoulder. "Have an ale."

The bartender was already pumping the handle, filling a mug to the brim as Jack allowed Barnes to guide him to the bar.

"Drink," said Barnes.

Jack reached for the cold pewter mug, placed his lip into the thin layer of foam, and drank a deep gulp of the liquid beneath.

Barnes nodded to the bartender while Jack drank. A cloth filled with chunks of ice passed over the bar and landed in the hands of the man whose nose Jack had just smashed.

"Caldwell, this is Junger Dunderloff. He served as a private soldier in your father's regiment against the LaFrentians."

Jack put down his beer and looked into the face of the man who struck his sternum. Dunderloff nodded, offering a crooked smile.

"Pleased to meet you," said Jack, extending his hand to shake.

"Your father is an honorable man," said Dunderloff, taking Jack's hand, his voice deep and gruff.

"And this, Adam Adamson, is the man whose nose you struck," said Barnes.

Adamson looked at Jack, lowering the ice-filled cloth from his nose, but keeping his head tilted back.

"Mr. Adamson," said Jack, offering his hand.

Adamson shook it.

"Adamson fought with us as well," said Barnes.

Adamson smiled. Several teeth were missing, but the teeth that remained were in good shape, neither yellow nor cracked.

Barnes introduced Jack to half a dozen other men, all of whom had served in his father's regiment.

They turned back to the bar.

"Were you watching me the whole time?" asked Jack.

Barnes nodded.

"Did you want me to fight those men?"

"No."

"Why didn't you stop it?"

"I did stop it."

"Why didn't you stop it earlier?"

"A man best shows who he is when he does not know he is being watched. Finish your beer. You were unwise to come here. This is no place for a man in a silk vest. Even a Caldwell."

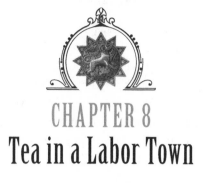

CHAPTER 8

Tea in a Labor Town

Harris Hotel, Port Calderon
New Anglian Republic
December 22, 1878

Matilda Smith raised a small porcelain teacup to her lips and took a dainty sip. She was, however, far from a dainty woman—thick in her shoulders and broad across her back with a wide neck and a round face. Her eyes were bright and kind, and she wore her sandy hair in a tight bun at the back of her head, showing several streaks of silver. Her dress was woolen, grey, and simple. She was not the kind of woman to artificially color her face, though the ruddiness of her cheeks made it look like she wore blush.

"And how did you meet my husband, Mrs. Smith?" asked Mrs. Sarah Huntington, peering down her nose. She could terrify most people with her cold blue stare, but Matilda Smith thus far seemed to be immune to her intimidation.

"Through Colonel Caldwell, ma'am."

"And how do you know Colonel Caldwell?" Mrs. Huntington's head seemed to tilt back farther with each passing question.

"I tended to him when he was wounded, ma'am. It was the spring of '58, after Franklinburg. Those were the worst weeks of the war, at least for us."

"I see," said Mrs. Huntington, not actually seeing much of anything in her mind's eye.

She was naturally incurious, knew little about the Battle of Franklinburg, and even less about the hellacious weeks that followed in the hospitals for nurses like Mrs. Smith. Colonel Caldwell was among those tasked with rooting the LaFrentians out from their trenches upon the heights. There was no bloodier day in the four-and-a-half-year war that had defined a New Anglian generation.

Mrs. Huntington sipped her tea slowly, examining Mrs. Smith with cold, judging eyes.

"One thing I would like to stress, Mrs. Smith, is the importance of this event in Hannah's life," said Mrs. Huntington. "Carolyn here is already married to the kind of man we can be proud to call our son-in-law. We wish the same for Hannah, that she might follow in her elder sister's footsteps."

Carolyn smiled with self-importance, her blue eyes sparkling beneath her dark, glossy hair. Unlike Hannah's, it was curled and looked freshly washed.

To emphasize her point, Mrs. Huntington reached out and took her eldest daughter's left hand in her right hand, feeling the bulge of the sapphire against her palm.

"As a Port Calderon woman, I trust you have heard of Mr. Rex Shuler?" said Mrs. Huntington, smiling proudly.

"I cannot say that I have, ma'am."

Carolyn looked at Mrs. Smith as if she were an idiot.

"You have not heard of the ship-owning Shulers?" asked her mother.

"No, ma'am. Should I know them?"

"If one reads a newspaper, I should think one should know them, yes," said Mrs. Huntington. "They are among the more prominent residents of your city. Thirty ships serve in the Shuler merchant fleet. It is thirty, yes?" She looked at Carolyn.

"Yes," said Carolyn, her eyes haughty.

"Last year," continued Mrs. Huntington, "our Carolyn here married the eldest Shuler son, Rex. *The Port Calderon Gazette* and the other papers covered it widely."

"You must be very proud, Mrs. Huntington."

"Yes, we are. But a mother cannot rest on her laurels, Mrs. Smith. I intend to place my second daughter into a successful marriage, as well. There will be few better opportunities than this Three Gods Day Ball, and opportunities do not exist to be squandered. Families from across the Republic are sending their sons to Bay Port City for this occasion, from Laketown to Port Southern. They are capping the ball at four hundred attendees, however, and it is a great honor for Hannah to be included."

Mrs. Smith sat in calm silence, a patient smile between her rosy cheeks.

"Hannah's dress is accordingly of the utmost importance," said Mrs. Huntington. "I will take no chances with this. We have hired Dardennes. You, of course, know *Dardennes?*"

"I can't say that I do, Mrs. Huntington."

Mrs. Huntington glanced at Carolyn, her eyes widening in disbelief and growing anger at her absent husband. What kind of lady's maid did not know Dardennes? And why would her husband hire an absurd person such as this? Because she was Colonel Caldwell's nurse during the war? Was this some sort of charity hiring, on her daughter's most important trip of her life?

"Well, Mrs. Smith," said Mrs. Huntington, a rush of air exiting her straight Gerdic nose, "Dardennes is generally considered to be the finest dressmaker in all of Bay Port City. Some would say the finest in the entire New Anglian Republic."

"I see," said Mrs. Smith.

Mrs. Huntington frowned as she reached for a tiny, fruit-speckled scone crusted with sugar crystals on the top. Her arms, like the rest of her body, were long and lean, kept attractive by both heredity and the active, leisured life available to a woman of her class. Her figure had done much to entice the rising Mr. Samuel X. Huntington in their early years, and she had retained it into her middle age. She looked at Mrs. Smith as she chewed the scone, her gaze flat and cold. Clearly, she determined, studying her face, Mrs. Smith was of sturdy peasant stock. It was evident in all of her features.

Mrs. Sarah Huntington was also built of sturdy stock, but sturdy in a manner that arose from generations of command, from ancestors who lived in castles of stone, from those who held the power of life and death over those who lived under thatched roofs. The lines in her face were sharp, striking, and angular—the result of powerfully built Gerdic warriors marrying Gerdic women of imposing beauty for generations upon generations. Gerdic warriors, it was said, preferred tall and strong women who could give them tall and strong sons. Such warriors would have liked Mrs. Huntington. She was of the class that on the old continent took twenty-five percent of the harvest while those like Mrs. Smith grew old early, working the land, breaking their backs so that the likes of Sarah Huntington— born Sarah Gunderia—could wear fine gowns in great halls and grand ballrooms.

"My father told me you once lived in the wilderness," said Hannah, speaking for the first time.

"Yes, when I was young," said Mrs. Smith.

"Here in Calderon?"

"In Calderon and other places along the border."

"The Halexan border?"

Mrs. Smith nodded.

"Was it wilder in those days?"

"It was," said Mrs. Smith.

"Why did you live there?"

"When I was a girl," said Mrs. Smith, "my father was a traveling deacon of the New Church of the Three Gods. We rode camels across the deserts. It was too dry for horses."

"Were there people in these deserts?" asked Mrs. Huntington. Her smile had tightened into a grimace. Like most in polite society, she did not approve of the New Church of the Three Gods.

"Not many people, Mrs. Huntington, but there were some. They lived hard lives. We wished to bring them the hope of our faith. We have a saying that a hard life here leads to greater riches in the next life."

"So, you are still a member of this church?"

"I am," said Mrs. Smith.

"That is similar to our faith," said Hannah. She reached for the tiered tray in front of her, taking one of the small crustless sandwiches. It held thinly sliced cucumbers between little bits of spongy white bread.

"Yes," said Mrs. Smith, looking at Hannah. "There are many similarities."

"And many differences," added Mrs. Huntington, with a mocker's smile.

"Were there still lions in the New Anglian desert in those days?" asked Hannah, ignoring her mother.

"There were."

"I am saddened that I never saw them, our desert lions."

"They were a thing to behold. But frightening," said Mrs. Smith. "As a girl, we would sleep with our camels hobbled and placed into a ring. The lions would circle us at night. More than once, we had to fend them off with our rifles."

"Did you ever shoot one?"

Mrs. Smith nodded. "Yes," she said softly.

"I am envious," said Hannah.

"Do not be. They were frightening evenings. I do not miss them."

"I should rather be frightened than bored," said Hannah, glancing at her mother and sister.

Mrs. Huntington looked into her teacup, pretending she had not heard her daughter.

Carolyn sat with perfect posture, staring out over the harbor. The sun sank in the sky, falling beneath the horizon of the Great Western Ocean. Its retreat painted the Calderonian sky in layers of purple, blue, and red above a forest of ships' masts in the harbor. Undoubtedly, Carolyn's husband owned several of the larger craft.

"Mrs. Huntington, get down," said Mrs. Smith.

"What did you say?"

"I said, get down!"

The glass behind her shattered. A rock sailed past Mrs. Huntington's face and landed on the table, toppling the tower of crustless sandwiches. Mrs. Smith leaped out of her chair, knocking Mrs. Huntington down onto the carpet and covering her with her body.

"Get down!" she shouted at Carolyn and Hannah.

The girls obeyed. Hannah could not believe how quickly Mrs. Smith had moved. Glass shattered as more rocks careened into the room. Other patrons rose from their tables and rushed toward the door. A running woman shrieked as a stone struck her back. Another ricocheted off of the ceiling, lodging in the carpet near Hannah. Then she saw that they were not rocks at all, but rather chunks of masonry and slate chipped off of buildings.

"In the name of the Three Gods!" exhaled Sarah Huntington at last.

"Stay down," said Mrs. Smith.

"Do not order me!" shouted Sarah Huntington. Mrs. Smith kept her girth upon Mrs. Huntington, pinning her onto the carpet. A new volley of thrown projectiles crashed through the window, shattering teacups and plates.

Hannah and Carolyn each crouched against the wall, their eyes wide with fear. They cowered on either side of the shattered bay window.

Threats and curses flooded into the room from outside. Hannah reassured herself that they were at least on the second floor, though her heart pounded violently in her chest.

"Come out, Huntington, you bastard!"

"Come out, you son of a whore!"

"You can't cheat the people forever!"

The words struck the room like gunshots. And then there were gunshots: one, two, three, staggeringly loud in the dusky air. One of the bullets hit the chandelier, exploding the glass of a gas lamp.

Carolyn let out a small shriek, covering her head with her hands.

Mrs. Smith looked into Mrs. Huntington's eyes beneath her, just as they widened in fear and understanding. The attack was not a random act of violence. The perpetrators used the name Huntington, and they had just fired a gun.

Whistles sounded in the distance, and angry voices rose up from outside the window. There were confused shouts and then shrieks of fear mixed with the sounds of galloping horses.

"Did you conceal your reservation?" asked Mrs. Smith. There was a tone of accusation in her voice as if Sarah Huntington were a fool.

Sarah Huntington shook her head.

"This is a labor town, Mrs. Huntington. You are not a person to those men out there. You are only a name, a force that keeps them down. Follow me."

Mrs. Smith led them from the room, taking Mrs. Huntington by the hand and crouching low as they made their way to the door. Dozens of police whistles pierced the air in the street below as Mrs. Huntington, at last, realized that perhaps her husband was not a fool to entrust their daughter to this woman.

CHAPTER 9
Trendan Rudar's Testimony

Saman Keer
43rd Day, Month of Norekah, 806
Anglian Calendar: December 22, 1878

Morning sun drenched the square in clean, bright light. The smaller of two boys shivered in the cold. Over his shoulders, he wore a ragged blanket, dirty and full of holes.

"Will the Qhaliffa come?" he asked.

"Who knows? Probably just the Grand Vizer," said the larger boy.

"Why wouldn't the Qhaliffa come?"

"You know what happened to the last boy who asked too many questions about the Qhaliffa?"

"What?

"He ended up there on one of those." The larger boy pointed to the elevated platform where three mounds of wood surrounded three wooden stakes. The smaller boy's eyes widened. He chomped down on the half-eaten apple in his little hand.

It seemed as if all of Saman Keer had turned out to watch. Though many said in private that they disapproved of the Grand Vizer's spectacle executions, most turned out to see them nonetheless, and few wished to miss the first burning since the reign of Selahim the Grim, the first burning in seven years.

A thump echoed out over the square, the sound of a large bass drum being struck. The crowd's chatter subsided as the drum struck again, again, and again.

The crowd grew quiet.

The drum continued its rhythmic beat. Three trumpeters emerged on the platform and blew their instruments. Three escalating short notes and one long one rang out over the crowd. Several thousand faces looked around anxiously, men and women craning their necks toward the platform. In front of each face, a little puff of breath was visible in the cold. In the crowd, all of the women wore head coverings of varying qualities of silk, cotton and wool. Scarves veiled most of their faces, protecting them against both the cold and accusations of immodesty. Most of the men wore turbans or other cloth coverings. Children alone watched with uncovered heads.

With visible effort, a herald mounted the stage and took his position next to the trumpeters. Bald, clean-shaven, and extremely fat, he had a voice like artillery that made his words heard over the rumble of thousands.

"People of the Great Mountain," he announced. "People of the Great Mountain!" he thundered again.

The murmurs of the crowd began to die down.

"People of the Great Mountain!" he proclaimed a third time. The crowd fell silent.

"People of Saman Keer, followers of the one true God, the God of the Mountain and his Qhaliffa, all hail Jemojeen Jongdar, the Grand Vizer!"

The crowd thundered back, "Hail the Grand Vizer!"

Jemojeen ascended a set of stairs to the platform where a throne-like chair awaited him, facing the three stakes at a diagonal. His ceremonial turban covered his head, large, bulbous, and dark green. In the center, a cherry-sized ruby anchored a long wing feather of a desert eagle, dyed crimson, and sticking up nearly three feet above him. His heavy winter cape lay across his shoulders fastened with a gold chain. Underneath the cape, he wore black robes, the color of a raven's feathers. Custom made for his disciplined body, they fit him impeccably. Before he took his seat, he raised his right palm into the air, acknowledging the crowd. The crowd repeated its cheer.

"Hail the Grand Vizer!"

Jemojeen nodded.

As Jemojeen took his seat, a line of three dozen Grand Vizerian Guardsmen streamed into the space between the platform and the crowd. They joined ranks with three dozen guardsmen already positioned there, facing the crowd behind armored tunics of grey chain mail. They stared out grimfaced beneath black turbans wrapped around conical helmets. Most were bearded. Some bore the visible scars of their flatlands upbringing. Jemojeen encouraged his Sipahis to recruit from the alley gangs in the roughest parts of the Seven Cities. In their right hands, they held the shafts of nine-foot spears topped with fourteen-inch triangular blades. At their hips, curved swords rested in dark scabbards.

At the far end of the line, closest to Jemojeen, a barrel-chested Sipahi barked out an order. Called Shaheni, and by reputation considered to be among the fiercest of Jemojeen's enforcers, he looked the part with a brawler's thick arms and a flattened nose. He wore the same uniform as his guardsmen, except that instead of a spear, he carried a mace, and the front of his chain mail held a bright brass badge indicating his Sipahi rank.

"Face!" he growled. The newly deployed guardsmen turned to face the crowd, adopting the same posture as those already there.

"Present!" said Shaheni.

The men lowered their spears in unison. The sharp points shimmered in the morning light. To any in the crowd thinking of interfering with the events to follow, it served as an unsubtle demonstration of deterrence. Those closest to the spears backed into those standing behind them, who groaned as heels stepped on toes.

"Return!"

As he barked his orders, Sipahi Shaheni swept his eyes over the crowd, scanning the faces for an anomaly. Most looked down, avoiding his gaze. The spears of his guardsmen returned to upright, their hands on their spear shafts and their feet planted a half-pace wider than their shoulders.

His men in place, Jemojeen nodded to the herald.

"Bring out the prisoners!" he cried.

The slow, deep beat of the drums resumed, filling the void. At the edge of the square, the sound of creaking wheels and clicking horseshoes advanced. The faces in the crowd turned, craning their necks and bobbing from side to side to see what approached.

Two black horses led a rattling cart along the cobbles. The cart was a cage with wheels, with three people seated inside: two men and a woman with filthy matted hair. Clothed in yellowed rags, the men had unkempt beards that made them look like beggars. A dozen guardsmen flanking the cart on each side marched in unison with two black-hooded executioners riding on the front, covered from head to toe with black robes. Under their hoods, black veils further hid their faces.

The cart rolled to the far side of a wooden barrier, which stood chest high and separated the public in the square from the prisoners' path toward the platform. At the bottom of the platform, the cart stopped. The cage faced the crowd, showing them the prisoners.

Jemojeen signaled to the herald.

The fat man opened his arms and shouted, "The upholders of the Faith!"

The crowd did not cheer. Many eyes darted nervously.

Opposite the prisoners' cage, ten priests in their middle and later years filed out from behind the platform. They ascended the platform's stairs, wearing rich, dark blue robes and walking in a single file line. Each man passed the three stakes and their mounds of wood. All were bearded, with short, cropped hair on their heads. They carried their Hats of Judgment in their hands in front of their chests as they walked. The hats were tall and rectangular, the same color as Jemojeen's dyed eagle feather, the color of fresh blood. From the peak of each hat, a long red veil hung down the back.

The priests continued in single file until they stopped before Jemojeen's chair. The first man in line approached Jemojeen and bowed. Jemojeen nodded. The man then rose, placed his Hat of Judgment upon his head, and took his place at the end of the long bench set slightly back from Jemojeen's chair. Each priest, in turn, bowed, rose, placed his Hat of Judgment on his head, and took a seat on the judges' bench. Like Jemojeen's chair, the bench was angled toward the stakes for unobstructed viewing. The last priest to sit would be the priest closest to the burning. This was considered the position of highest honor. When all of the priests were seated, Jemojeen rose.

The assembled thousands waited in silent anticipation.

Jemojeen extended his arms outward with his substantial open palms facing the crowd, his abnormally long fingers spread to the heavens.

"People of Saman Keer!" he shouted. His voice had neither the depth nor the carrying power of the herald's, but with the crowd's silence, all could hear him nonetheless.

"People of the Seven Cities! Like you, we on this platform have one duty above all others—to honor the God of the Mountain, the one true God, and his chosen Qhaliffa."

The crowd listened in silence, all eyes upon Jemojeen.

"Before you sit ten men tasked with upholding the law of God. Today, these men will decide the fate of those who dishonor the Qhaliffa, your Qhaliffa."

"They will burn!" shouted a voice in the crowd. Applause rippled. Other voices of support rose.

Jemojeen smiled and extended his arms out once again to silence the mob. The mob obeyed. When all was quiet, Jemojeen continued, "They may indeed burn, for that is the price of heresy. But before any man or woman burns, they shall first be judged. None shall writhe in flames before judgment."

"These men behind me wear the Hats of Judgment." Jemojeen gestured with his right hand toward the priests. "The fate of these prisoners lies in their hands."

Jemojeen slowly turned his head toward the three ragged bodies in the cage. The crowd followed his eyes, staring at the accused through the square iron bars.

"Bring them up!" said Jemojeen.

The veiled, hooded men in the black robes jumped off of the rider's mount on the cage. Each walked around the cage, one to the left, the other to the right. The man who went left inserted a key and twisted. He pulled the iron grate open and gave the crowd an unobstructed view of the prisoners. The crowd stirred with the energy of an awakening beehive.

The prisoners rose as one, each chained to the other. With as much dignity as their circumstances could allow, the two bearded, filth-covered men, and the equally grime-stained woman stood with their heads held high.

The first man exited the cage slowly on shaky, pale legs above bare feet. The dungeon grime made it look like he wore short black stockings up to his ankles. He was raggedly thin, like a skeleton covered in a soiled sheet. With his left hand chained to the woman's right hand, he descended from the wagon cage, followed by the woman and the other man behind her, chained to her left hand. Of the three, the last man to exit the pen was the tallest, standing a full head above the woman and the other man.

Jemojeen saw one of the executioners lean in toward the tall prisoner's head. The prisoner stared straight ahead as if he were looking at something well above the crowd. Even from this distance, Jemojeen could see the energy in the tall man's bright brown eyes. Jemojeen frowned and scratched a spot in his black beard.

As commanded, the three prisoners walked in a line toward the platform, with one of the executioners in front of them and the other trailing behind. The crowd could see that the hooded men in the black robes were both shorter than the prisoners, even the woman. The trailing executioner came up only to the tallest prisoner's shoulders.

"Heretics!" shouted a woman's voice, like a crack breaking across a dam.

A torrent of angry words rushed toward the prisoners. Jemojeen watched the faces in the front of the crowd. Women pulled down their veils to spit at the prisoners as they passed. Bearded men shook their fists and shouted curses. Bits of sentences hit Jemojeen's ears up on the platform.

"Burn them! Heretics! Beserian lovers! We'll hear you scream, traitors! In the fire! You'll know pain today! Your prophecy is a lie!"

Jemojeen allowed himself a small smile and did not gesture to silence them. *Let them pour out their frustration. It will increase the prisoners' fear. They will know that Saman Keer is against them. The people are against them and they are utterly alone.*

As the executioners led the prisoners up the steps to the platform, the rage of the crowd increased. Jemojeen could now no longer pick out individual words over the roar. He put his eyes on the prisoners' faces as they marched toward him. None made eye contact, staring straight ahead. Then they stood directly in front of him. The crowd's shouting swept over them like a wind. Jemojeen saw the executioners' eyes looking at his face, awaiting a command. He nodded.

"Kneel!" shouted the executioner on Jemojeen's right. Even as close as Jemojeen was, it was difficult to hear the executioner's words over the shouting of the crowd.

The prisoners did not immediately comply, as if paralyzed by the crowd's anger. The executioner kicked the first man's knee forward while pushing down on his shoulders. The man collapsed onto the hardwood platform and gasped as his kneecaps smashed into the wood. He tried to break his fall with his hands. Chained to his wrist, the woman went down with him, making a slightly more high-pitched gasp. The tall prisoner attached to her began to tip toward her. The executioner at his side grasped his other arm and yanked downward. From his position of greater height, the force that brought him to his knees was greater, and the crack was the loudest of all three as his knees struck the wood. The man closed his eyes against the pain and muttered words under his breath.

Jemojeen rose from his throne and stood above the three kneeling prisoners. He was a tall man, and he towered over them now. He again extended his hands with his palms facing the crowd.

"Silence!"

"Silence!" echoed the herald. Jemojeen Jongdar was not a man to disobey, even in the middle of a mob. The crowd quieted quickly.

"Are you in pain, Huralt?" Jemojeen stared into the tall man's face, which was clenched against the pain in his knees. "You have not begun to feel pain."

"Huralt Donadun. Selena Savanar. Trendan Rudar." Jemojeen said each name in an elevated tone, loudly enough for those on the platform and in the front of the crowd to hear him. Then the herald echoed his words, booming them out to everyone else watching in the square.

"You are accused of high treason against the Qhaliffa and heresy against the One True God, the God of the Mountain."

The herald echoed Jemojeen.

"The ten men assembled here will judge these accusations. As Grand Vizer, I do not make the Qhaliffa's laws. I only enforce them. Whatever the sentence of these judges, it will be carried out today." Jemojeen allowed himself a slow and deliberate glance toward the stakes, lest there be any doubt as to what the sentence might be.

At that, Jemojeen nodded to the priests seated on the bench and took his own chair before the kneeling prisoners. Each of the hooded executioners removed themselves to the edge of the platform, one to each side.

The bearded priest sitting farthest from Jemojeen rose. His crimson hat of judgment sat high atop his head, with its attached cloth draping down behind him, framing his face in a background of red. He was of average height and girth, with almost nothing to distinguish him at a distance. As one came closer, however, one could see that the priest had abnormally rounded cheeks and nearly black, circular eyes. The eyes were cold now, like a shark's.

"Trendan Rudar," said the man, "I am Chara, High Priest of Alwaz Deem, servant of the God of the Mountain."

The herald thundered Chara's words out over the crowd.

"You are accused of defiling the city of Alwaz Deem and heresy against the God of the Mountain. Do you deny it?"

Trendan Rudar did not speak quickly. His eyes were the opposite of Chara's—greenish-blue, expressive, and aflame with life. He looked into the High Priest's face, as if searching for something.

"I deny heresy," he barely whispered.

The herald looked to Chara, the High Priest, for instruction. Chara nodded.

"'I deny the heresy,' says the prisoner!"

The crowd grumbled.

Chara opened his mouth in an expression that on another face could be called a smile. In Chara's case, his mouth looked like a fish's preparing to eat. In the open chasm, Chara revealed his small brown teeth to the prisoners and the crowd. Quickly, the mouth snapped shut.

Chara spoke through nearly closed lips, "Prisoner, is the Qhaliffa God's emissary here on this earth?"

Trendan waited several moments before responding, knowing the ramifications of his answer. The herald proclaimed the question to the assembled thousands.

"The Qhaliffa is God's emissary, yes." said Trendan.

Chara looked both surprised and disappointed at once. Such were not the words of a heretic. If asked, all nine priests seated on the bench behind Chara would have agreed with Trendan Rudar.

The herald repeated the words. The crowd muttered in surprise. Some nodded in agreement and satisfaction that the heretic might have recanted.

Trendan looked at the platform beneath him.

Chara looked into Trendan's face. The prisoner continued to stare down.

"The Qhaliffa is God's emissary, you say?"

"Yes."

"How about me, am I God's emissary?"

"Yes."

"And how about you, are you God's emissary?"

Trendan hesitated. "Yes."

"Oh, you are?" Chara nodded to the herald, who repeated the exchange.

The crowd grumbled.

"Are you a High Priest, prisoner?"

"No."

"Are you a priest of any kind?"

"Yes."

"Oh, and what kind of priest is that?"

"A worshipper of God."

Chara paused for the herald to proclaim the questions and answers. Many in the crowd shook their heads in disagreement.

"How about her. Is she a priest, an emissary of God?" Chara gestured to Selena Savanar, who kept her eyes down. Trendan felt her squeeze his hand.

"Yes," he said.

The herald announced the words, and an uproar shook the crowd.

"I see," said Chara, raising his voice. "So the Qhaliffa is an emissary of God, but so is this woman?"

"You are correct."

"And how about a slave. Is a slave an emissary of God?"

"Yes."

"The same as the Qhaliffa?"

"In the eyes of God, yes."

Chara's voice continued to rise as he shook with outrage.

"And a prostitute. Is a prostitute an emissary of God?"

"Yes, in the same way."

"The same as the Qhaliffa?"

Trendan nodded.

"Speak your words!"

"Yes."

Chara, the High Priest, flushed a deeper red.

"And how about the Beserians of the sands? They who worship the God of the Sands, are they the same?"

"Yes, we are all equal before God," said Trendan.

Chara looked down at Trendan with rage in his round black eyes and scarlet in his round cheeks.

"Heresy!" he shouted. His voice cracked.

The herald repeated Trendan's words and Chara's response to the crowd. The crowd roared.

"Heresy! Heresy!"

Chara turned to his nine bearded colleagues on the bench and asked, "He defiles the faith. Should we take his tongue now?"

A majority of the priests nodded in the affirmative. One judge nodded with such force that he had to catch his hat of judgment as it fell from his head.

One priest near the middle of the bench did not nod.

The seated priest cleared his throat, raised his left hand, and said, "High Priest Chara, perhaps it is best to let the people decide?"

Others on the bench looked at him in disapproval. Chara was about to reject the suggestion when he noticed that the seated man had caught the eye of Jemojeen. Chara turned to Jemojeen. Ever so slightly, Jemojeen nodded in approval of the idea. Surprise replaced the rage on Chara's face. He did not know whether the suggestion was scripted in advance or not. Either way, the safe course was to follow the preference of the Grand Vizer.

"Very well," said Chara. He arranged his face into a mask of agreement that he did not feel. He wanted to see the heretic's tongue ripped out and lifted high into the air, dripping for all in the crowd to see as the man gagged in agony.

Chara looked to Jemojeen.

Jemojeen kept his eyes on Chara while speaking words for the herald to proclaim, "People of Saman Keer. The prisoner denies the holiness of the Qhaliffa. He says that a Beserian is his equal. Should we take his tongue?"

The herald's words washed over the crowd.

"Yes!" shouted back the crowd. "Take it! Take the tongue!"

Inspired by the shouts, Chara turned to look at the torture table. Many eyes in the crowd followed his own. The table rested near the stakes with their hanging chains and the piled wood around them. On top of the table, a variety of metal utensils and knives rested on top of a white cloth. Chara's eyes picked out the tongs and the long thin blade with the razor's edge.

From his chair, Jemojeen raised his right hand and kept it up until the crowd quieted.

"Or, should he keep his tongue so that he may be persuaded to renounce the heresy?"

The herald echoed Jemojeen.

"No! Take his tongue!" shouted voices from the crowd.

Other, deeper, and stronger voices began a different chant. They were the voices of men who Jemojeen's servants had paid handsomely in advance.

"Renounce! Renounce! Renounce!"

The chant grew louder and more widespread, with adults looking at each other for direction. Jemojeen looked out into the crowd and saw little children imitating the adults, shaking their small fists in the air, chanting, "Renounce!"

The voices shouting *renounce* slowly drowned out the voices that called for Trendan's tongue.

Jemojeen again lifted his hands with his palms facing the crowd. "Very well," he said. "It appears the people wish for further questioning."

Chara nodded, surprised by the crowd and still uncertain what to make of Jemojeen's intervention. Jemojeen again made eye contact with Chara. The edges of Jemojeen's mouth curled up inside of his beard. With his chin, he gestured toward the stakes. Had Chara blinked, he would have missed the gesture. But he did not blink, and he now understood. The Grand Vizer did not want the prisoner's tongue. He wanted the prisoner engulfed in flames, and believed the man would not renounce his heresy.

Trendan closed his eyes. To his left, Selena glanced sideways into his face. She knew that he prayed in his silence. Trendan ran his tongue along the roof of his mouth, still not sure if it would be ripped out with pincers and a knife. In his stomach, he felt a deep pit of fear. The tingling ran up his spine to the back of his head and out along his arms.

"Prisoner," said Chara, "you keep your tongue only so that you might admit the truth before God and these witnesses."

Chara made this proclamation far louder than anything he had said before. He looked out to confirm that the crowd had heard him. He lowered his voice, barely above a whisper, and leaned close to the herald's ear. "You need not repeat my words. They will hear me. Repeat only the words said by the prisoner."

"Yes, High Priest," said the herald, in a similar near-whisper.

Chara raised his voice and posed a question to Trendan.

"There are words in our Holy Book. They say if a part of your body causes you to sin against the God of the Mountain, something must be done. What does the Holy Book say should be done with the body part?"

"That is a metaphor," said Trendan, from his knees.

The herald repeated Trendan's answer. Faces in the crowd looked to each other for the meaning. Others shrugged. Some jeered.

"I did not ask your interpretation, prisoner!" said Chara. "What do the words say should be done?"

Chara's words struck like a whip.

Trendan obeyed. "Cut it off from the body," he said.

The herald repeated Trendan's words. The crowd roared.

"Cut it off! Cut it off!"

Chara looked out over the sea of faces with a squint. The crowd continued to shout.

Chara raised his voice to a level that almost matched the herald's.

"Correct, heretic, it is to be cut off. And why is that?"

Trendan kept silent, smart enough to see where the priest was leading him. "Answer me, prisoner!"

Trendan answered. "So that it does not lead the rest of the body astray."

"Astray toward evil, yes?"

"Yes."

Chara no longer looked into Trendan's face. He began to pace in front of the bench of his fellow priests with his eyes looking out toward the crowd as he spoke.

"The Holy Book says to cut off the offending part to save the rest of the body from evil and destruction."

"Yes," said voices in the crowd. "Truth!"

"The heretic has kept his tongue," said Chara. "But now his entire body is in jeopardy. Is it not?"

Men in the front row nodded. A woman behind them shouted out her agreement.

"So too," said Chara, "This is true for the body of the faithful. And we are that body. We are the faithful, and we must cut out those who would lead the rest of us to evil and destruction."

He paused in his pacing, standing above the three kneeling prisoners to let his meaning become obvious to the crowd.

He continued. "We are here in mercy to the larger body. We are here to cut out one part, or in this case, three parts, to keep the whole body from falling toward evil."

Chara paced in silence for several steps with his head jutted forward and his eyes on the platform. The red silk hanging off the back of his tall scarlet hat shone brilliantly in the bright morning sun. He stopped and snapped his head toward the crowd. The silk swung outward with the sudden movement.

"So tell me, people of Saman Keer, what is to be done with a part that is cut off from the body?"

"It is cast into the fire!" A man near the front shook his fist as he said the words.

"It is cast into the fire indeed," said Chara.

Chara walked back to Trendan and stood over him. He nearly shouted the words that he said.

"Trendan Rudar, I give you one final chance to renounce your heresy here before this assembled bench of holy priests and the people of Saman Keer. What say you now?"

Trendan stared at the ground, the knot of fear twisting violently in his stomach. He had seen men burn. There was no crueler death. There was no way to prepare for the pain. As he stared, he could see the tremor in his own shaking hands. An escape hatch opened in his mind. Selena had told him the Grand Vizer's offer from the dungeon. The ax or the flames.

They are only words. Is not any fate better than burning?

"Tell me, prisoner, do you renounce your heresy?"

Selena squeezed his hand, silently urging him to avoid the fire.

Then he heard Huralt, his mentor, the man who had trained him, praying under his breath. Trendan looked into his face. As their eyes met, another wave of thoughts rose in Trendan Rudar's mind.

Yes, but they are words that mean more than my life. A life is lived once, but memory endures. For such a time as this are men called. When we are victorious, when the Prophecy is fulfilled in all of its glory, what will men say of Trendan Rudar?

Trendan cleared his throat and spoke aloud. "A man may call the day the night and the night the day, but it does not make it so."

The herald repeated his words. The crowd rumbled like a swarm of locusts.

Chara stared at him. "What are you saying, prisoner? Speak clearly!"

Trendan raised his shaking voice, and with all of the strength he could muster, he shouted his words to the heavens, "In the name of the Prophet, by his priest Beseri, and upon the blood of the martyrs, I testify to truth alone! By the God of the Mountain and the Sands, perfect, holy, and wise! In the seventh year of the fortieth Qhaliffa, the Amahdi of the west shall rise! A stranger once and foreign born, he will lead the Beserians home, to *this* valley of the mountain, where Mamet placed his throne! From the east shall come another, a child of Hom Hommuram, to restore the Staff that was broken, the Serpent, the Lion, and the Ram! In worthy hands again, the three shall rule once more, to return what was lost and end the Usurper's war!"

The crowd stood in stunned silence.

"You serve the Usurper, High Priest, and you shall lose the coming war. Darkness cannot defeat the light, and from east and west, the light is coming!"

Chara's lip curled as he looked down at Trendan Rudar, his black eyes flashing first with rage and then triumph. He turned himself fully around, facing the bench of his peers, knowing that it was done. His fellow judges looked at him with admiration. Chara spoke his next words quietly with total confidence of victory.

"The prisoner's own words convict him. I need add nothing further. All in favor of death by burning, chained to the stake, indicate your judgment."

Nine bearded priests sat on the bench in their dark blue robes and tall crimson hats. Nine right arms rose, with the palms of the hands facing the crowd.

Chara slowly counted each raised hand. Then he turned toward the prisoners. "Trendan Rudar, in the name of the Qhaliffa and of this Holy Court, I sentence you to death by burning."

Tears streamed down Trendan's cheeks, and he looked like he struggled to breathe. Selena squeezed his hand again.

Chara continued, "Grand Vizer, in the name of the Qhaliffa, do you see any reason to relieve the prisoner of this sentence?"

"I do not," said Jemojeen.

Chara nodded once and turned to his right. The hooded executioner was already walking toward the prisoners. Chara looked to his left as the second black-robed man closed in from the other side. Trendan visibly shook, holding tightly to Selena's hand. The executioner's large gloved hands grabbed Trendan by his shoulders and pulled him up onto his feet. The other executioner reached for the chain that joined Selena's hand to Trendan's and twisted a key into the lock that bound them together. The chain fell down, but Trendan's hand remained clasped to Selena's.

"Look, he's holding the whore's hand!" shouted a voice from the crowd.

"Burn them together!" shouted another.

Cruel laughter rang out around the voices.

Trendan's legs looked like those of a puppet, hanging off of his body being held up by the executioner. The second executioner that had unlocked the chain grabbed Trendan's left side with the first executioner on his right. They walked him to the stake with his legs dragging along the platform. A small trail of urine stretched out behind them as they approached the stacked piles of wood.

Selena stared straight ahead, her fear overwhelming. She could not watch.

The executioners dragged Trendan up to the stake, stepping upon the wood they would soon light on fire. Around his waist, they affixed a chain. They then applied shackles to his ankles. The shackles opened on a hinge and snapped shut. Trendan's hands were bent behind the stake and shackled there. Trendan offered no resistance, his fear holding him to the stake as effectively as the shackles, preventing him from acting at all.

Jemojeen remained seated in his chair.

"Perhaps," he said, looking down at the two remaining prisoners, Selena and Huralt. "Perhaps, your friend's fate will affect the way you answer *your* questions. Look and see what flames do to flesh."

Selena looked at Jemojeen with hate in her eyes. Before he could make eye contact, she returned her gaze to the platform below her.

"Very well," said Jemojeen. "Listening can be just as effective."

He looked at Chara and nodded.

"Light him up," said Chara.

The executioners each took a lit torch and began to ignite the small kindling that had been stuffed under the larger logs, soaked in oil. Immediately they burst into flames, forming a low, crackling ring around Trendan, chained on his stake.

Smoke partially concealed him, but Trendan did not yet scream. The flames had not yet bitten into his bare feet. His eyes were as wide as saucers, wild with animal terror, darting back and forth as rising walls of flames approached him from all sides. The intense heat surrounded him, but he did not yet burn. Every eye in the crowd looked upon him. Every ear was attuned to hear, waiting for the screaming. Selena and Huralt closed their eyes, but they could not close their ears, waiting in horror for the gasps, the whimpers, and then the wailing that would come—the sounds of Trendan Rudar burning alive.

The flames rose to Trendan's body, but the sounds still did not come. Selena willed herself to look. Through the smoke, she saw that Trendan slumped forward like a dead man. A small puff of wind cleared the smoke, and Selena saw why Trendan did not scream. An arrow protruded from his throat, with white fletching on the shaft.

My God.

"Huralt," she said, her voice barely audible. She cleared her throat. "Huralt, look."

Huralt looked, his mouth still moving in silent prayer. He saw the white fletching and gasped aloud. Tears filled his eyes as a sob convulsed him.

"My God, my God," he cried, "they are here."

Chara did not yet see the arrow in Trendan's throat. He looked out at the crowd, waiting for the screams. The screams always came, no matter how strong the man. None could resist the fire.

"People of Saman Keer! People of the Seven Cities! See the price of heresy!" he shouted, turning toward the flaming pyre and throwing out his hand, like a barker introducing a troupe of dancers. And then Chara saw the arrow. A look of confusion swept across his face. He turned back to the crowd. It was the last living expression Chara the High Priest would ever give to the people of Saman Keer.

CHAPTER 10
They Came

Saman Keer
43rd Day, Month of Norekah, 806
Anglian Calendar: December 22, 1878

The next arrow punched through Chara's throat almost to the end of the shaft, the swan-white fletching sticking out of his windpipe. He fell to his knees, opening and closing his mouth like a fish. He drew both hands to his ruined airway as blood seeped through his fingers. His eyes widened with the panic of a drowning man, his lungs no longer able to draw air. From his knees, Chara fell forward onto his face. The arrow stuck out the back of his neck, propping his red veil up in the air with the edges hanging down around his head like a scarlet tent.

In the crowd, fingers pointed at the dead priest and at the limp man on the stake. He was not writhing or screaming in flames, but hanging from the chains, still as a corpse. Several quiet seconds of stunned recognition passed. Then a wave of panic crashed through the crowd, and a thousand voices spoke at once. In the densely packed square, men began to shove. Some sought freedom to the left, others to the right. Few tried to rush toward the platform. Most ran in the other direction, fleeing to the rear. Men, women, and children toppled and thrashed, fighting to regain their footing amongst the stampede.

Jemojeen reacted faster than the others. Seeing the arrow in Trendan Rudar's throat, he dove from his chair, rolling onto his side as he hit the wood of the platform. The arrow meant for his chest struck his empty chair, the shaft of the arrow quivering in the cedarwood.

From the ground, Jemojeen saw the arrow strike Chara's neck. He did not move to his aid. By the time the first priests rose from the bench, Jemojeen had scrambled behind his chair, using it as a shield, scanning the roofline for the attackers. As he looked, he slid his three-barreled Demissary pistol out from his robes.

The priests dithered as the arrow storm came. A silver-bearded priest cried out, grasping the wound in his chest. The priests on the ends of the bench scrambled outward, running laterally toward the edges of the platform. Two priests ran past Trendan's burning corpse, their red silk veils trailing behind them. They shielded their faces from the intense heat with their arms. Arrows knocked them both down, tumbling one priest to the fire's edge as the other fell into the flames. The man on the edge of the fire recoiled, frantically drawing in his robes and panting in terror.

The priest on the pyre let loose a high-pitched shriek of overwhelming pain, the scream he had waited to hear from Trendan Rudar only moments before. He thrashed wildly to remove his robes but succeeded only in further stoking the fire. He rolled onto the platform, his clothes burning from his ankles to his head. His screams caught the attention of some in the crowd, and a knot of children pointed. They would see a burning today after all. Others heard and increased their efforts to depart the square, striking down those in their way with thrashing arms.

On the stage, two more priests fell with arrows protruding from their legs and arms.

Peeking out from behind his chair-shield, Jemojeen gripped his pistol.

"Sipahi!" he shouted.

Sipahi Shaheni stood on the end of the line of guardsmen, stationed between the crowd and the execution platform. The fat herald hid under the torture table with wide, frightened eyes.

"Sipahi!" shouted Jemojeen again.

Shaheni turned and made eye contact. His men held their line with lowered spears, keeping the crowd at bay. Below the guardsmen, a dozen luckless men and women lay sprawled out on the ground. Some were unconscious. Others moaned in pain.

On Shaheni's command, the guardsmen had not yet killed anyone with their spearpoints, instead striking people with the hardwood of the shafts, knocking them down. The crowd flowed away from them, and a gap opened between the stampeding spectators and Shaheni's line of spears.

The screaming of the burning priest reached a fevered pitch as the flames consumed him. The priest closest to him backed away with an arrow lodged in his shoulder. His hat lay apart from him, on the edge of the flame. Its veil caught fire and burned as hotly as the shrieking priest. From the ground, still slinking away, the hatless priest raised his hand and made a blessing of mercy onto his colleague. It did not reduce the horrific sounds.

Jemojeen, unable to shout over the screams, signaled to Sipahi Shaheni. Shaheni grabbed the four closest guardsmen and ran toward the prisoners. Selena and

Huralt no longer knelt. Ahead of Shaheni, they ran away from the flaming pyre, their wrists still shackled together, Huralt's right arm bound to Selena's left.

Rushing forward, mace in hand, Shaheni roared his orders to his guardsmen.

"Stop them!"

On the platform, one of the executioners grabbed a long-handled beheading ax from the torture table. With his black hood and floor-length robe, he chased after the fleeing prisoners, gliding across the platform like the image of death itself. At the other end, the second executioner barred the escape route, a faceless black cloak holding a long knife. Selena and Huralt ran at him unarmed, their arms still chained together.

Propelled by her fear and adrenaline, Selena sprinted behind Huralt, trying to keep his pace, the tall man bending his right arm behind him to give her as much slack as possible. Huralt's long, pale legs raced across the platform, his tattered tunic barely covering his thighs.

With only his left hand free, Huralt made for the executioner barring their way. Standing before the ragged pair, the executioner raised a knife and bellowed through his veil, "Stop or die, heretic!"

Huralt and Selena increased their pace, running directly at him.

The executioner brought his knife down in a wide, slashing arc.

With agility he did not look capable of, Huralt lurched to the right, arching his back as the blade swept past him, missing his nose by a hair's breadth. In the same fluid movement, Huralt swung the bony point of his elbow into the executioner's temple. The man crumpled onto the platform.

"The knife," shouted Huralt, his emaciated chest heaving with exertion. He bent down and smashed the hooded figure's face with his fist.

Selena had already picked it up, and it was heavier than she expected, with the blade protruding beneath her grip.

"Huralt!" she shouted.

Huralt looked up to see the second executioner running at them with the raised beheading ax. Chained together, they could not outrun him.

"Stab him!" shouted Huralt, crouching down behind Selena, his right hand still chained to her left as the man fell upon them.

The executioner lifted the ax high over his head and swung down at Selena, throwing his body weight forward, with the power to chop a limb from her body. Without thinking, Selena dipped down and sideways, toward her chained left arm, almost falling off the platform as the ax-head missed her. From the edge, she stabbed wildly to her right, striking the executioner's exposed side. The knife pierced his robes, met flesh, slipped between ribs, and slid in to the hilt.

The executioner collapsed, gasping as the breath flew out of him.

Selena looked up to see a dark blur of guardsmen in front of her. She jerked out the knife, her heart thundering too violently for her to contemplate that she had just killed a man.

Sipahi Shaheni's guardsmen charged straight at her with their spears lowered.

"Run!" she screamed into Huralt's face.

Huralt had already launched forward, yanking her away from them and running along the edge of the platform. She followed, struggling to keep up with her chained arm extended in front of her. The balls of her filthy bare feet pounded the wood of the platform as she ran with the bloody knife still in her hand.

They'd neared the end of the platform when the pistol fired.

Huralt and Selena kept running, their heads ducked.

A second blast sounded, and then a third. The shackle on Selena's wrist ripped her downward.

She fell, her chest landing on Huralt's back.

He lay motionless beneath her, a bloody gash in the cloth behind his right shoulder, inches from her face. Another wound, the size of a medallion, marked the back of his head. Panting, Selena pushed herself up, rolling Huralt's body over as she rose. She screamed. In his remaining cheek, one brown eye stared up at her. The other half of his face was gone as if shorn off with a cleaver.

Selena looked behind her with frantic eyes. Crouched behind the wooden back of his chair, his red-eagle feather broken off of his turban, the Grand Vizier held a three-barreled Demissary pistol in his left hand. Smoke still wafted from the barrels as Jemojeen's eyes met her own.

He smiled as he shouted, "Catch her, Shaheni! Bring her alive!"

Another arrow slammed into the chair, inches from his head. He winced, crouching so that only a sliver of his face remained exposed to the square.

Jemojeen scanned the roofline with narrowed eyes. He could not see the archers, but he knew they were there, amongst the sloping green tiles, crouched behind the chimneys more than one hundred yards away on the far side of the square. His mind raced, considering possibilities, knowing that only a handful of men in the entire Seven Cities could wield a bow so well.

The guardsmen ran at full speed past him, toward Selena, thundering forward in their heavy boots and rattling chain mail, their spearpoints lowered to kill.

"Alive!" roared Jemojeen again.

Selena placed her knife at the joint in Huralt's dead wrist and cut as deeply as she could. The cut passed halfway through the joint, sticking on the bone. Selena yanked her hand up with as much force as she could muster. Her arms were sinewy, thin, and malnourished—weak from the dungeon and the weeks of near starvation before. The chain on Huralt's wrist still held her, attached to his corpse as heavy as an anvil. She thrust her hand back down onto the platform and cut again. She sawed the blade back and forth, pushing down with all of her body weight.

"Ayah!" she shouted with the effort.

The ligaments in the wrist gave way, and the blade met the wood beneath. Out of the corner of her eye, she saw the rushing guardsmen nearly upon her. She launched up into a crazed, scrambling run, a hare fleeing a pack of wolves. Huralt's severed hand still stuck in the shackle, somehow still caught in the iron, dangling from her left hand as she sprinted across the wood with her matted hair flying behind her. No one stood between her and the edge of the platform.

"Stop her!" shouted Jemojeen, still crouching behind his chair, pointing with his empty pistol.

Selena leaped from the edge, taking the ten wooden steps down to the ground in two bounds. Pain burst in her bare feet and knee joints as she landed, but she kept running. Her feet barely touched the cold stones below. She ran past the cage that carried her from the dungeon, past the harnessed black horses. She ran for the edge of the square, where the alleyways separating the tall buildings could give her a chance to escape. No guardsmen barred her way. She ran faster than she had ever run before, gasping for air.

Spectators in the crowd watched her as she fled. None tried to stop her. Some stood with mouths agape. Most fled before her with fear in their faces, seeing her wild, tangled hair, her missing front teeth as she panted for breath, the long, bloodied knife in one hand, and Huralt's severed hand dangling from the chain on the other.

She closed in on the shadow beneath the dark stone buildings.

Two figures appeared like apparitions, standing at the edge of the alley. Selena stumbled in fright, nearly falling. Tightly wrapped cloth covered their bodies from head to feet, the color of Hahst desert sand, almost white. Only their eyes showed. From sheaths slung across their backs, they pulled long scimitari swords, wide-bladed and curved like crescent moons.

The one on the left of the alley gestured to Selena, waving her toward himself.

Selena slowed her pace in indecision. If they were false help, they would capture her and bring her to Jemojeen. She would be better off dying at her own hand now, stabbing herself with the knife. She would not submit to torture again.

With her own eyes, she had never seen them before, but she knew what the cloth meant—if they were real and her eyes did not deceive her. Panicked thoughts flew through her mind, fast as arrows.

They are the Oath Holders of the Order, and you have seen them before. The face in the dungeon, the yellow-green eyes, the veils are the same. Run to them. They are your only hope.

One of the men yelled from behind his face covering, "Run!"

Something in the man's tone—the fierce urgency—convinced her.

Selena lurched forward, reaching out her free hand toward the man on the left side of the alley. The man reached out his hand and grabbed hers. He pulled her behind him. As he did so, Selena turned and saw the full extent of what pursued her. The man stepped forward, blocking her from the charging guardsmen, facing them down.

Their force had grown, joined by others deployed in the square. Fifty guardsmen closed in on the alley, running with lowered spears. Dozens more came from the distance, running to reinforce them.

"Stay behind me," said the man, his voice calm.

Again, something in his voice made her obey. Selena took ragged breaths, her chest heaving for air. She crouched behind the sand-colored cloth that covered the man's back, and the smell of his sweat filled her nostrils.

The man stood steadfast as the horde advanced. Selena glanced across the alley at the other man and watched him withdraw a hidden pistol. The man in front of Selena pulled a gun of his own, gripping its red handle. He aimed the wide barrel at an angle, higher than the guardsmen's heads as if he were firing at a man on camelback.

"Close your eyes!" he said roughly, into Selena's face.

She obeyed, but not entirely, squinting through her eyelids.

He pulled the trigger. With a hiss, a thin stream of red-orange powder launched out from the barrel toward the guardsmen—a running wall of chain mail and spearpoints. The dust hung in the air, suspended for a long moment without falling as if someone had emptied a pail filled with red chalk from a high window. Slowly, the cloud drifted toward the ground as the guardsmen charged directly into it. Then the cloud burst, flashing across the square.

Selena cried out, covering her slitted eyelids. It was the brightest flash she had ever seen, more brilliant than lightning, like powdered sunlight.

The guardsmen staggered. Some dropped their spears. Others stopped in place, only to be run over by the charging men behind them. Those in front grasped at their faces, blinded by the flash.

The second man held his pistol at the ready. He lowered the weapon to the same angle the other man had used and pulled the trigger. The barrel flashed and boomed. Above the guardsmen, the air exploded, knocking a dozen men to the ground like a volley from the sky.

The two men thrust their pistols back into their concealed holsters beneath the cloth on their chests. Wounded guardsmen cried out in pain, writhing on the stone pavers. Selena had never seen a flash pistol or a shrapnel pistol in action, but like most in the Qhaliffa's realm, she had heard what the Qhaliffa's Demissaries could do with them. How these men had such weapons, she did not know.

"Follow me!" said the man standing in front of her.

He turned and grabbed her arm, his grip powerful. Leading her, he ran down the narrow alley. The other man followed behind her, shielding her back from any pursuers. The alley led deep between two tall stone buildings that reached up at least forty feet above, blocking out the sunlight. At the end of the lane, another alley ran perpendicular to the first. They reached the intersecting path and turned to the right at a full run. Selena's feet nearly slid out from under her, but the man in front of her kept her steady. The men in the wrapped cloth ran with sure-footed steps, wearing soft leather shoes with rough grips on the bottom.

Behind them, furious shouts echoed down the passageway they had just fled. In front of them, twenty yards away, another masked face peered out from behind a doorway.

A man stepped out into the alley wearing the same sand-colored cloth as Selena's companions. He was larger than any man Selena had ever seen before. In his right hand, he held a two-handed scimitarus, its blade curved, wide, and enormous. It was an unusable weapon for all but the strongest men. With his left hand, he pointed to the doorway. Selena slowed, afraid of the figure in front of her. As they reached the giant man with the giant sword, the man holding her arm pulled her toward him, turning her left and into the doorway. The giant followed them inside and closed the door.

He slammed a thick iron bolt into place and gestured down a dark hallway. Aside from a candle burning at the end of the hall, the windowless room was black as night. Another masked man, barely visible in the hall, stood near the candle, holding up a trapdoor in the floor.

"Follow me," said the giant man, passing Selena and her two rescuers.

Even whispering, his voice held a deep rumbling power, like the sound of distant cannon fire. The giant walked past the man holding the trapdoor, ducked his head, and descended the steep stairs beneath. Selena and her two rescuers followed him. As she passed through the trapdoor, Selena saw that his eyes stared intently into her face. When they had all descended into the stairwell, the first man closed the trapdoor behind him.

The candle threw a dim, eerie light into the stairwell as he reached down. Using both hands and significant effort, he picked up an iron bar with the thickness of a man's wrist. He slid it into three iron hoops beneath the trapdoor, with the ends of the iron bar sticking out underneath the stone of the passageway where they fit into a pair of iron hoops drilled into the rock itself. For a moment, he paused, inspecting the iron bar, making sure it was secure.

"This way," said the large man, already moving down the stone passageway. Selena followed him with the others close behind.

CHAPTER 11
Oath Holders of the Order

Saman Keer
43rd Day, Month of Norekah, 806
Anglian Calendar: December 22, 1878

After forty stairs—Selena had counted each one—the passageway flattened, and they walked in a more or less straight line that seemed to curve slightly to the left. In the dark, it was hard to tell, and Selena was not sure whether she could even trust her senses. But if they were following the natural curve of the mountain, they were moving north, in a tunnel beneath the center of the city. Selena and the four veiled men walked in silence for minutes that seemed much longer.

"Wait," said the enormous man, at last, breaking the silence.

He paused to inspect the stones on the wall.

"Bring me the candle." His voice rumbled, echoing down the passageway.

The man in the back of the line did as the veiled giant asked. He drew the small, flickering flame close to the wall on his left, and the light revealed a symbol on the stone. It was an animal with a ram's head, a lion's body, and the tail of a serpent.

"Stand back."

Selena and the three other men did as instructed. The giant lowered to a knee, still nearly as tall as Selena standing at her full height. "Do you see these?"

In the dim candlelight, he pointed to five triangular stones dispersed at diagonals from each other in the next stretch of the passageway.

"If you step on one," he said, stopping mid-sentence. Then he slowly moved the candle up the stone wall of the tunnel, until he came to a small hole. "A spear comes out of here and into you."

Selena looked at the wall and saw the hole that held the spring-trapped spear. She brought her gaze down onto the ground. Beneath a layer of dust, she could discern the outlines of the triangular trap stones in the candlelight.

"Follow me," said the giant. "And watch my feet."

The man then stepped with his left foot along the left wall, deliberate and decisive. With his right foot, he reached out forward and at a diagonal. In between his two feet lay the first of the triangular stones. He then moved his left foot out, skipping the next one. He held the candle out to his side so his body did not block the light.

"Go after him," said one of Selena's masked rescuers.

Selena looked down to place her bare foot into the much larger footprint in the dust ahead of her. The man behind her followed closely, putting his shoes into her prints. After the large man had taken seven or eight exaggerated steps, he stopped and turned to face the others.

"After here, there are no more trap stones. Follow my steps to here."

Selena reached his place and exhaled with relief, still holding the knife she had used to kill the executioner. She noticed for the first time since they had entered the tunnel how fast her heart beat and how hard she was still breathing. She also saw that Huralt's severed hand had fallen from the shackle, no longer dangling from the chain at her wrist.

"Move forward to make way for the others," said the large man, moving forward as well but carefully holding the candle out to keep the light upon the trap stones. Selena obeyed. The other men followed Selena's steps through the traps.

The large man looked back down toward the blackness of the tunnel from which they had just come.

"If they follow us, they will pay the price," he said, sheathing his scimitarus sword over his shoulder by smoothly sliding it into the scabbard on his back.

"Sheath your knife," he said to Selena.

"I don't have a sheath," she said.

"Then give it to me."

She hesitated.

His massive gloved hand remained extended. She gave him the handle, and the knife disappeared beneath the cloth wrapped across his chest.

The giant then handed the lone candle back to the man who had operated the trapdoor at the beginning of the tunnel and continued forward. As he walked, the candlelight illuminated him from behind. His body seemed to fill up the entire passageway, the cloth covering his head grazing the stone ceiling. He came to a set of ascending stairs made of the same smooth stone as the floor and walls of the tunnel. He walked up without looking back at the others. As the candlelight followed, a closed, iron-studded door emerged in front of him.

The giant reached the door, grasped its metal handle, and shoved it forward. The door gave way, creaking on heavy hinges.

The group followed through, onto a landing, beneath more steps that led farther upward ahead. Light poured through an opening, coming down from whatever lay above the last staircase.

The large man ascended the steps with Selena and the others close behind. They stepped out into the light and onto a flat stone foyer, surrounded by raised levels on all sides. It looked like an arena for prize fighting, except they stood upon a smooth stone floor, not a pit of sand. Thousands of candles encircled them. Compared to the darkness of the tunnel they had just left, the candles shone brightly as day. Selena blinked and looked around her, squinting in disbelief.

Upon the stone steps, dozens of people all sat in the same way, with erect postures and their hands laid open upon their legs, as if they waited to receive a blessing. All wore the same cloth coverings as her rescuers, showing nothing but their eyes. No one spoke. Selena could hear herself breathing as her bare feet walked across the cold stone floor. The veiled faces scrutinized her and her companions emerging from the tunnel, their eyes following them to the center of the floor.

After a long moment of silence, a lone veiled figure stood up from the front stone bench. At the same moment, the seated figures clasped their hands together, as if in silent communal prayer.

"Three set out from the dungeon this morning, but only one arrives," said a woman's voice, speaking through her veil.

The four masked men with Selena bowed their heads as one. Selena's eyes darted around her, her mind racing and her breath shallow.

"The Savanar stands before us. Where are Huralt Donadun and Trendan Rudar?" asked the veiled woman.

Selena waited, unsure if she was expected to speak. She looked into the woman's face, seeing that it held the same veil as the face that appeared to her in the dungeon, but her eyes were grey, not yellow-green.

"They fell," said the giant.

Selena turned to see that all of the veiled Oath Holders had knelt when the woman stood. She now did the same, feeling self-conscious, ignorant of the unspoken ritual. The stone was hard and uncomfortable on her bony knee.

"What befell them?" asked the woman.

"Trendan Rudar fell to an arrow of mercy," said the giant, his voice like thunder. "He'd been chained to the stake, but he did not burn alive."

The masked woman's eyes glistened.

"He could not be saved?" she asked.

"Not without losing her," said the giant.

Selena realized that he referred to *her*. A feeling of unworthiness rose in her chest.

"Whose arrow struck Rudar?" asked the woman.

"The Ram you tasked with the deed," said the giant.

The woman nodded.

"And Huralt Donadun?" Her voice seemed to catch in her throat.

"The Grand Vizer killed him," said the giant, "while he escaped, chained to the Savanar."

The woman looked at the chain still hanging from Selena's wrist, the iron shackle still glistening with Huralt's blood.

"How?" she asked.

"A Demissary pistol," said the giant.

Selena saw the woman's chest rise as if she were catching her breath. The open eye of Huralt's half-face stared up at her in her mind.

"Did they keep the faith?" asked the woman.

"Yes," said the giant. "Unto the end. Rudar proclaimed the Prophecy from the platform before the assembled thousands. Donadun would have done the same."

Trendan Rudar's final words echoed in Selena's ears. *From east and west, the light is coming.*

The woman raised her voice, her words clear and loud. "Praise be to the God of the Mountain and the Sands. The people will remember their courage."

She turned around slowly, sweeping her eyes across all of the veiled faces.

"Their journey has ended. They are martyrs of the Prophecy, true servants to our God. They await us now on the other side, alive and free."

The crowd waited.

"Trendan Rudar and Huralt Donadun," she said.

"Trendan Rudar and Huralt Donadun," said the faces from behind their veils, loudly, nearly shouting. Their voices echoed off the ceiling of the cavern.

Selena watched, afraid the noise would carry up into Saman Keer and into the ears of her pursuers.

"May they look over us from paradise and glory," said the woman.

"May they look over us from paradise and glory," said the crowd.

"May we honor their faithfulness with our deeds," said the woman.

"May we honor their memory with faithfulness to the Prophecy!" said the others in unison.

Selena was the only one not speaking the words. A tingle of shame moved up her spine as the others spoke as one.

The woman returned her eyes to Selena.

"We have long watched you."

The words hung in the air of the silent cavern. Candles flickered.

"You do not know our faces, but we have long known yours. Trendan Rudar and Huralt Donadun gave their lives so that you might be saved. They were not of our Order, but they are heroes of the Prophecy. We here assembled are Oath Holders of the Order of the Ram, the Lion, and the Serpent."

Selena shifted uncomfortably. With all of the eyes upon her, her tongue self-consciously moved to the gap at the front of her mouth. Her matted hair hung raggedly below her shoulders. Dungeon grime streaked her face and her thin, exposed limbs. She felt filthy and hideous, unworthy of the attention surrounding her. She looked down at the stone beneath her.

The woman stepped closer to Selena. She stopped when her eyes were only inches from Selena's face.

"You have suffered," said the woman. "Though you did not know why."

Selena looked into the woman's eyes, seeing that they bore an even brighter intensity than those of Rudar and Donadun, as if they held majestic power.

"You still see the world as shadows upon the wall. With time, you will see beyond the shadows, and through you, so shall we. In time, you will remember your own story, the story that still hides itself from you. You will remember that you are not a stranger to us, nor we to you. When you do—when the truth of your past unveils itself—you will see not only what was, but what is, and what is yet to come."

Selena looked to the ground, tears flowing from her eyes as the brutal pain of the last months released itself. She resisted the urge to shout out that this was all a mistake, that she was merely Selena from the flatlands, Selena the basket maker, Selena the no one.

"Today, you wear the rags and filth of the dungeon," continued the woman.

Selena met her gaze.

"And you bear scars far more difficult to remedy than filth and rags—scars of sacrifice," said the woman, slowly placing her hands upon the wounds where the manacles had rubbed the skin from her wrists.

"Rise, daughter of Sah Seg Savanar."

Selena obeyed.

The woman knelt and placed her hands upon Selena's raw ankles. Then she rose. "Show me your mouth."

Selena let the woman reach up to touch her face. She opened her cracked lips to reveal where her two beautiful front teeth were ripped from her gums with iron tongs. She shuddered as the agony of the moment returned. The woman gently placed her fingertips upon Selena's chin.

"Do not be afraid," said the woman. "Banish fear from your heart. You now carry a wound of glory, not shame, a mark of your destiny. Know this, Lady Savanar, what has been taken from you shall be returned, and the God of the Mountain and the Sands shall restore all things. As you are restored, so too will be the Prophet's true kingdom."

Selena's eyes flashed through her tears. Whatever mysticisms these people might believe, and however fiercely they could fight, even a poor basket maker from the flatlands knew that teeth, once taken, did not grow back.

The woman stepped away from Selena, standing alongside the giant.

"Show your face to Lady Saliha of House Savanar," said the woman, looking at the giant.

The man reached up, removed his face veil, and pulled back the cloth covering his head.

Selena's eyes gaped.

With his veil removed, the man looked even larger. He was obviously an Omakhosian, from the southern continent across the sea. His skin was darker than even the darkest Beserians. His head was razor-shaved and big as a boulder, and his neck was as thick as a large man's thigh, with cord-like musculature going down into his upward sloping trapezii and bulging shoulders. He looked as if he could rip apart an enemy with his bare hands, as if the two-handed scimitarus sword slung across his back was an unnecessary weapon.

The giant Omakhosian remained upon one knee. The woman approached him. Though she stood straight, and he knelt, his eyes were still higher than hers.

The masked woman placed a hand on his shoulder. Then she looked at Selena with an intense and unblinking gaze.

"Rise, Oapah the Hohsa."

The giant rose, towering over Selena as if she were a child.

"We have long prepared for this day," continued the woman with the grey eyes, "The day your journey will begin, Lady Savanar."

Journey? Selena's eyes widened. *What journey?*

"Our enemies are liars, deceivers in most things, but they are correct to fear you. For you are who they say you are. You are Saliha Savanar. We would know, for it was we that took you from the evil one's hands on the night he planned to kill you, we that took you to the desert, we that named you Selena."

Selena closed her eyes, wishing she would wake up with her baskets in the bazaar, with her teeth still in her mouth, exhaling as she realized it had all been a dream.

The woman continued, "Why did we save you today and before? Because you are Sah Seg Savanar's heir, the last of his line. And one day, when all is done, you will return to Alwaz Deem, the city that by ancient rights belongs to you and your family. But now you must leave the Seven Cities. You must return to the sands once again."

"The desert?" asked Selena, finally speaking aloud. Though she had seen the desert countless times from the flatlands of Alwaz Deem, looking out across the

Ring River from the bazaar, she could not remember ever crossing over the Ring River and venturing into that stark, brutal land.

The woman nodded. "To the Sand Sea. Our enemy will pursue you, for he had you in his grasp, and we have taken you from him again. He will not rest, for he knows what is at stake."

She turned to the giant Omakhosian. "But you shall not journey alone, Lady Savanar. Oapah the Hohsa will not leave your side."

Oapah looked down into Selena's face.

Selena looked up, high into the mighty warrior's gaze. A strange gentleness rested upon his face, and a brightness shone in his eyes—the same light she had seen in the eyes of Trendan Rudar, Huralt Donadun, and the woman before her. As he looked down at her, she felt a sudden and unexpected warmth, as if near him, she might find safety. She had not felt such a feeling since her baskets were stolen, and likely long before that.

"So too will another guide and protect you on your journey," said the woman, "one who has traveled with you already."

Selena looked to her side, where the men from the alleyway now stood next to each other in a line.

"Gulana of Nor Gandus, show yourself."

One of the masked warriors from the alley stepped forward, the taller of the two, removing his veil.

Selena's eyes flashed again, her face as surprised as it had been to see the Omakhosian face of Oapah the Hohsa.

The veil removed, a long narrow face of a woman looked down into Selena's eyes. She looked barely older than Selena. She nodded gravely, her eyes fierce and brown, her hair straight, cut short above her shoulders, and as brown as her eyes.

She was one of the two that had faced fifty Grand Vizerian Guardsmen without fear. She had stood in the alley, firing the shrapnel pistol that flattened them.

"Oapah the Hohsa and Gulana of Nor Gandus, Lions of our Order, will guard your life with theirs until your journey is complete."

"But where are we going?"

"To the west, Lady Savanar . . . far to the west, to Abu Akhsa and the Staff of Beseri."

Selena looked around, into the unblinking eyes of the veiled faces surrounding her, eyes that seemed to understand her destination far more than she did. She stepped closer to the woman.

"Do I have a choice?" she asked, her voice barely more than a whisper.

"A choice?" the woman paused as if this were an extraordinary question. Then she shook her veiled head. "No, Lady Savanar. The blood of the line runs through your veins. You are chosen."

CHAPTER 12
Sherman Sterling

The Transcontinental Railroad
New Anglian Republic
December 23–30, 1878

Between the shores of Calderon and the metropolis of Laketown, the snow-capped peaks of the Spine divided the Republic. Looking out the window, Hannah could see the staggering height of the mountains rising in front of them. The peaks slowly rose on the horizon for the better part of the morning, growing with each quarter hour as the train steamed ever closer. They were now three days of nearly constant movement out from Port Calderon, headed east. In those three days, the express train stopped only three times. The flatness of the deserts gave way to the scrub brush and oak-lands of the foothills. The tall grasses stood dry and winter-browned as they gained elevation. A herd of antelope grazed on the slope of a hill in the distance. The toll of the hunters notwithstanding, the antelope were still plentiful on the western slope of the Spine, far more abundant than the relentlessly hunted herds of the eastern descent.

After the pistol attack at the Harris Hotel, Mrs. Smith ushered the Huntington women out a side door and into a covered carriage with dark curtains pulled across the glass. In her astonishment, Mrs. Sarah Huntington offered no resistance. Mrs. Smith had a clear plan, and she did not. The man above the cab into which Mrs. Smith guided them carried a loaded shotgun with two barrels. Inside the enclosure, with the three Huntington women, Mrs. Smith herself held a small revolver with a little snubbed nose. Carolyn whispered to her mother that the barrel matched Mrs. Smith's actual nose. Seeing her staring at the weapon, Mrs. Smith assured Mrs. Huntington that while the barrel was small, the bullets most certainly were not.

They stayed the night in a small, modest boardinghouse run by a deacon of Mrs. Smith's New Church of the Three Gods. Mrs. Smith told them the Huntington women were special guests from the south and did not give their names.

The rooms were sparse but clean, and the breakfast in the morning was simple but nourishing, with a chunk of hearty bread to dip into a simple broth. The deacon asked no further questions of his visitors from the south. Those of the New Church, so often in need of refuge themselves, gladly provided it when asked. Such was the fruit of their persecution.

After their breakfast, served at sunrise, the deacon organized a group of six armed men to accompany Hannah and Mrs. Smith to the train station. Hannah said goodbye to her mother at the boardinghouse. The New Churchmen sent word to Mr. Rex Shuler, who rushed to retrieve his wife and Mrs. Huntington, furious that he had not been informed as to Carolyn's whereabouts sooner.

Hannah and Carolyn nodded to each other but did not embrace. Their mother noticed but was too exhausted from the night before to pay more than desultory attention to her daughters. She would have a story for Nancy Caldwell, Judy Johnson, and the rest of her set in South Calderon regarding the horrid barbarism of Port Calderon and its awful labor movement. It would be their favorite kind of story—the kind that confirmed what they already believed.

As the engine pulled the train toward the Spine, Jack sat across from Hannah. Mrs. Smith and Sergeant Barnes sat across the aisle. All traveled in a first-class cabin, courtesy of Mr. Samuel X. Huntington and Colonel Mason Caldwell. Among the benefits they had extracted from the shareholders was a lifetime of first-class travel for all members of the Caldwell and Huntington families. That did not include Sergeant Barnes and Mrs. Smith.

At the Port Calderon station, with Hannah and Mrs. Smith still trailing a guard of six New Churchmen behind her, the Transcontinental Railroad had requested payment for the express tickets in the name of Joshua Barnes and Matilda Smith. Jack Caldwell, red-faced and with a rising voice, asked the clerk if he knew with whom he was speaking. The ticketing manager arrived shortly after that with prolific apologies and first-class tickets for Mrs. Smith and Sergeant Barnes.

Jack Caldwell's voice was now as low, quiet, and mundane as the first-class cabin.

"I could use a drink," he said, leaning against the green velvet back of the varnished wooden booth. The seat was wide enough to accommodate three adult travelers, but Jack reclined with his legs spread apart, having the row to himself. He held his hands steepled in front of him, his foot tapping the floor in boredom.

Hannah looked at him over the edge of her book. She, too, had a row to herself. As in many things, it was useful to be a Caldwell or a Huntington when riding on the Transcontinental. The rest of the first-class cabin was fully occupied.

"Care to join me?" asked Jack, standing up and arching his back to stretch his broad chest. It was only ten minutes past noon.

"For a drink?"

Jack nodded.

"No, thank you," said Hannah, returning her eyes to the passage in the book in front of her.

Matilda Smith looked up from her book, her eyes affirming the prudence of Hannah's decision. Sergeant Barnes appeared to be napping, and his eyes were almost closed.

Jack turned and walked down the center aisle, moving toward the dining car. Hannah's eyes followed him as he walked. From girlhood, she had known the curves of his body, the breadth of his shoulders, the narrowness of his hips, and the way he walked with his shoulders held back in a posture of utter confidence. He moved easily, and he slept easily as though unburdened by life or its choices. Unlike the others in the first-class car, he wore the rough pants and loose shirt of a rancher. Some of the other men sitting in the car, all of whom wore frock coats over silk vests and shirtsleeves, looked at Jack with disapproving eyes, as if he were a man who did not know his place.

Hannah could not see Jack's face as he walked past them, but she was almost certain he did not notice the critical looks. If they heard his name, they would have looked differently, with deference and hunger for his approval. By virtue of his birth, he was likely to be richer than any of them. He was younger, stronger, better looking, and blessed with a quick, practical mind. He was very much his father's son, with a strong touch of his mother's beauty. And beneath his easy, casual manner, Hannah knew Jack Caldwell was more arrogant than them all.

Hannah returned her eyes to her book. She scanned the page to find the sentence she was reading. She read the sentence. She reread it, the words failing to pass through her eyes and into her mind. She put the book down on the velvet seat next to her, the green cover of the book nearly matching the forest green of the bench. She stood up, smoothed the front of her dress, and followed Jack down the center aisle. Her hair was more put together than usual, with blonde ringlets framing her face on either side. Her skin was still sun-kissed from the long horseback ride up Mount Agabanzo.

Plush dark blue carpet cushioned her steps as she walked. She wore light green, underneath a small, dark blue jacket. It was a simple dress, hugging her rib cage, and then billowing out at her hips. The same men who had sneered at Jack's attire noted hers as she strode past them. Their gazes lingered. Several of the men looked awkwardly back down into their newspapers, pretending they had not just stared at her chest as she passed. Several smiled up at her with hungry eyes. Most were old enough to have fathered her. She increased her pace, reached the door of the car, and pulled it open. She stepped into the space between the cars. It was colder here, and the rumble of the train thundered in her ears.

She pulled the door of the next car and stepped inside. The rattling in her ears ceased, and the peaceful tranquility of the insulated first-class train returned. Jack stood at the bar, leaning on the lacquered wood with his elbows, talking to the barman. The barman looked at Hannah as Jack spoke, his eyes taking her in from her shoes to her hair. Several other men, all a bit older than Jack, and standing farther down the bar, momentarily stopped their conversations. Jack, self-centered as he was, noticed the distraction in the men around him. He turned and saw Hannah. She looked better than usual, beautiful even, thought Jack. For a brief moment, he saw her as if through the eyes of a stranger.

Jack raised a glass of whiskey and water to his lips.

"You changed your mind," he said, finishing his sip without looking at her.

Hannah nodded.

"Whiskey?"

"Fine," said Hannah.

The bartender pulled the bottle and started mixing Hannah's drink.

"I heard about the mix-up at the Harris," said Jack.

Hannah shook her head. "Terrible."

"You want to tell me about it?"

Hannah nodded.

"Odd that a crowd gathered that quickly," said Jack. "Who knew you were staying at the hotel?"

"I suppose anyone who checked. My mother made no effort to conceal our arrival."

Jack sipped his drink. A pleasant chill hit his palate before the familiar burn moved down his throat.

"Are we really that hated?" asked Hannah.

"It's Port Calderon, a town of agitators and crazies."

"They wanted to kill us."

"Maybe," said Jack, sipping his drink again, "maybe not. They just want what they don't have. Rioting's easier than working."

The bartender handed Hannah her whiskey in a cold glass. She could see the other men at the bar still looking at her with sideways glances as they carried on their conversations.

Hannah drank a healthy sip, building up her courage. Frightening as it had been, it was not the gunshots at the Harris Hotel that held her mind hostage. She could tell Jack now. Jack would be gone a long time before he was face-to-face with anyone back in Calderon.

"I saw something," said Hannah.

Jack raised his eyebrows.

"On the last day, we were at your property. At the Caldwell Ranch, I saw something."

"Oh?"

"In the stables, before lunch, before you met with your father and mine, I saw you." There was a slight tremor in Hannah's voice. "I saw you in the stables."

Jack's face changed. It was only for a moment, but in that moment, Hannah knew it was not the first time. He looked away toward the mirrored back of the bar and drank down the remainder of his whiskey. He gestured with his glass to the bartender that he would like more.

"What of it, Hannah?" A flash of belligerence passed across Jack's eyes.

"How could you?" said Hannah, her face tightening.

Jack looked down at his empty glass.

"Leave that all behind," he said. "I am going far away on the orders of my father. You are going to find yourself a husband in Bay Port City. You are going to the big Three Gods Ball. Be happy, like all of the other rich girls."

Hannah stared, gripping the bar as a wave of nausea careened through her.

"Do what is expected of you, as I do," said Jack.

More waves struck Hannah, one immediately after the other, like the breakers from the Great Western Ocean on the Calderon shore in a storm. She drank down the remainder of her whiskey. It burned her throat. She coughed, lifting a fist to her lips.

"I killed that rattlesnake up on Agabanzo," she said.

Jack listened, leaning on the bar, saying nothing.

"I shot it for *you* because I thought *you* would like the skin." She kept her voice low, eyeing the bartender, wearing a false mask of pleasantry as she spoke.

The bartender handed Jack his second whiskey and then walked to the other end of the bar, leaving Hannah and Jack to their privacy.

"And then what?" asked Jack. His voice grew suddenly hard.

Hannah looked at Jack with widened eyes and lifted eyebrows, as if she did not understand.

"I'd like the skin, and then what?" asked Jack.

"Then. Then maybe you could have some boots made," said Hannah.

"And then what?"

Hannah did not know what to say.

"And then nothing," said Jack. His blue-grey eyes were iron. "I am going to the desert in the middle of the Three-Gods-damned old continent, as my father demands. You should do what they demand of you. Stop being a girl. Become a woman."

"Like my sister?" said Hannah, her voice acid.

She drank more whiskey. This time she did not cough.

Jack smiled, cruelly. "You could learn things from your sister."

His words lashed Hannah like a whip.

"Jack Caldwell?" said a man's voice at the far end of the dining car. "By the Three Gods, it is you."

Jack turned.

"Sherman Sterling," said Jack. "On the honor of the Republic, that is a face I never thought I would see west of the Spine."

Hannah turned away and wiped the tears from the corners of her eyes with a tissue she kept in a small hidden pocket of her dress. She looked toward the window. She thought of walking away, but the only means of escape was to the wrong end of the dining car. She did not want to speak with this new friend of Jack's. The shades were pulled nearly all of the way down, sparing those in the dining car from the glare of the noonday sun. She felt grateful for the shade. The altitude made the whiskey hit her twice as fast.

A tall, thin young man with a massive smile and a severely pomaded side-part strode down the length of the lacquered bar with long, smooth steps. He grasped Jack Caldwell's hand and shook it vigorously.

"Been far too long, Sterling," said Jack, matching Sterling's grin with his own. All of the hardness fled Jack's voice, leaving only a natural, friendly charm.

"Even we of Bay Port City must leave our paradise to see the rest of the Republic now and then," said Sherman Sterling. He wore a finely tailored black frock coat over garishly striped pants. A thick gold chain dangled from his waistcoat. He looked like a cartoonist's rendering of a rich young man of enterprise.

Sherman looked down at Jack's rancher's clothing. "Still trying to prove you are richer than the rest of us, I see."

"You are the one with the gold chain," said Jack.

"You are the one with the Transcontinental Railroad," said Sherman, his brown eyes twinkling. "And with a lovely traveling companion." He faced Hannah Huntington and bowed. "I beg for the privilege of an introduction," said Sterling, keeping his eyes on Hannah's face and away from her chest.

Jack nodded. "Miss Hannah Huntington of Calderon, please allow me to introduce Mr. Sherman Sterling of Bay Port City. I am honored to know Sterling from our years together at the University of the Vine." At the word "Huntington," Sterling's eyes perceptibly widened.

"I am honored," said Sterling, smiling as wide as Hannah had ever seen a person smile before.

Her tears freshly wiped, Hannah deployed her own most charming smile, the one that caused her cheeks to dimple. "A pleasure to meet you, Mr. Sterling."

Sterling took Hannah's hand and held it for a moment or two longer than manners would have declared appropriate. Hannah allowed her hand to linger as their eyes remained locked. She did not find him particularly attractive. He was a strange-looking man, thin with an enormous mouth. Yet still, her eyes remained fixed upon his.

"So, Sterling, what brings you to our western wildlands?" said Jack, speaking in the way of one old college friend to another.

"Business, I am afraid," said Sterling, his eyes still on Hannah's face.

"Oh?"

"Indeed." Sterling pulled his eyes away from Hannah.

"What kind of business is that these days?" asked Jack. "Buying another bank? I'd think three were enough, even for the Sterlings of Bay Port City."

"No, no, no," said Sterling, shaking his head. "Shipping."

"What kind of shipping?"

"Down the Great Western. Long haul. Port Calderon to Halex, Halex to Omakhosi, Omakhosi to Xin. And we're on the front end of it, I daresay. Many nickels to be made, dimes to be earned. But enough of that. What object pulls both a Huntington and a Caldwell eastward? Inspecting the family business?"

"No," said Jack. "I'm traveling to meet Stanwich."

Sterling wrinkled his forehead in concentration and narrowed his eyes. Then his eyes opened, and his brow relaxed, an idea located in the filing cabinet of his mind.

"Stanwich, the explorer?"

"The same," said Jack.

"And you as well?" asked Sterling, looking at Hannah.

"No," she said. "Bay Port City."

"On behalf of my humble city, I bid you an early welcome," said Sterling, smiling again, his eyes transfixed on Hannah's.

She felt herself smiling back with both her mouth and her eyes.

"For what purpose do you visit us, might I ask?"

"You may," said Hannah, tilting her head in a flirtatious way that Jack had never before seen. "I will be attending a ball."

"Would that be the Anglia to New Anglia Three Gods Day Ball celebrating the Trans-Titanic cable?"

Hannah nodded.

"Then, Miss Huntington, I dare say we are headed to the same place."

Jack looked at Sterling, looking at Hannah. He saw her smiling back and knew it was a real smile. At that moment, Jack Caldwell felt something he had not ever felt before regarding a daughter of Samuel X. Huntington. Jealousy.

———————————•————————————•———————————

They did not tarry in Laketown. Both Jack and Hannah risked the ire of their respective aunts and uncles by not staying over for the evening. In particular, Mrs. Gertrude Sanderson, elder sister of Colonel Mason Caldwell, would no doubt be sending Jack a stern missive reminding him of what manners in a gentleman are supposed to look like and that if he could not take the time to visit his family perhaps his family would not take the time to visit him. He had, to this point in his life, always refrained from sending her a response note in kind. He had, however, written her a host of them in his mind. "Dear Aunt Gertrude, I am delighted by your future anticipated forbearance. Please do not visit. Your nephew, Jack."

At nine, twelve, and six o'clock each day, the express trains departed for Bay Port City via the Laketown and Bay Port Railroad, the L&B. One of those trains, every other day, came straight through via the Transcontinental, making the full journey across the continent from Port Calderon. After consulting with Sergeant Barnes and Mrs. Smith, Hannah and Jack stayed on the train they had taken from Port Calderon to Laketown, waited for the recoal, and steamed out two hours later on the eastbound L&B.

To Jack's newfound dismay, Sherman Sterling altered his previous plans to stay over in Laketown and remained onboard the train for the final leg to Bay Port City. He had also moved his cabin so he was now seated in the same first-class car as Jack and Hannah.

Out the car's window, the sun set over the rolling farmland of Howan State. Large barns flanked by naked oaks and maples towered above straight fences dividing barren and empty winter fields.

Seeing her proximity to Hannah, Sterling discovered a newfound fascination in Mrs. Smith, asking her questions and listening in rapt attention to her invariably long answers. Under ordinary circumstances, Jack knew Sterling would have little use for the thoughts of a matronly and earnest member of the New Church of the Three Gods, and a servant at that. Yet, there Sterling was, sitting in convincingly undivided attention. Jack had never seen Sterling as a competitor, at least not until three days prior at the bar, when he noticed the way he looked at Hannah Huntington and the way she looked back at him.

"It was several years ago," said Sterling, sitting next to Hannah with his long legs crossed, one over the other. Hannah and Mrs. Smith had been laughing at his stories for hours. Jack saw that Sterling had traded out his bright striped trousers for a pair of more sedate, plain grey pants. So too had his flashy silk waistcoat disappeared in favor of a black woolen variety. The gold chain that had adorned him on their first meeting did not appear again. Whatever in Sterling's mind told him to reduce his natural foppishness, he was correct in anticipating Hannah's discomfort with flash. Her father was an exceedingly wealthy, but simple man. Sam Huntington did not take seriously men who wore their wealth in their attire, and he had relentlessly exhorted his daughters to be wary of the same. *It is fine in a woman. They are the fairer of the two sexes, and they should show their beauty to the world. But a man was not made to be a peacock. A man should adorn his wife, not himself.* Hannah had heard those words hundreds of times in the long years of her girlhood, and Sam Huntington was not a man to hide his opinions under a bushel.

Sterling cleared his throat. The gaslight flickering on the walls accentuated Sterling's high cheekbones and made the skin on his face look healthy and young.

"Yes, it was several years ago that Mr. Harold Milton Stanwich dined with us," he said, gesturing with his hands. "He had just finished his Omakhosian explorations. I remember it well. His eyes still shone with excitement when he talked of first descending the slope of the great crater into the Feathermen Highlands. He told of the first day at dawn when the Feathermen first approached him, emerging through the morning mist, carrying bamboo lances and riding their great birds—birds larger than horses with great sharp beaks, longer than a man's arm. He is a great man, Stanwich."

Jack pretended to read an evening paper from Laketown. Sterling had been talking for an hour, and Mrs. Smith and Hannah kept asking him questions. Jack frowned. *He tells a fine story, but the man talks far, far too much.*

"I would be most delighted to host you at the very same dining table at which we hosted Stanwich," said Sterling. "Do you have the dinner hours free, on the night of the Three Gods Ball?"

"We do," said Hannah, looking at Mrs. Smith.

Mrs. Smith nodded in approval.

"Then I believe we would be honored to join you, Mr. Sterling," said Hannah smiling with her dimples beneath her straight freckled nose.

"Most excellent," said Sterling, smiling his broad, toothy grin. "My mother shall be most delighted. And what about you, Caldwell? Care to join us before you board the steamer across the Titanic?"

Several ways to say *no* twisted around Jack's mind.

"I promised Fish I would see him on the night of the ball," said Caldwell. It was not true, but it was the first thing that came to his mind.

"Aaron Fish? You telegraphed him from Port Calderon or Laketown?" asked Sterling. Aaron Fish was a shared acquaintance. Indeed, Jack Caldwell was likely acquainted with no one in Bay Port City who was not also acquainted with Mr. Sherman Sterling.

"Oh, uh," said Jack, looking, as liars do, up and to his right, "Port Calderon. I believe."

"As you know, Caldwell, I count Fish a good friend," said Sterling. "You are welcome to bring him with you. I thought he was away, though?"

Jack swallowed the liar's lump in his throat. "That would be most strange," said Jack, his voice slightly altered.

"Yes, we conversed not long ago," said Sterling. "I thought he was down in LaFrentian Halex for the entire month. It is, after all, December in Bay Port City, which no one likes, including me. It is, of course, presently summer down in South Halex and quite nice these days. The spas improve with each passing year. One might even think one was on the south Spatanian coast in June. The climates are so similar! But perhaps Fish has returned early? I also could have misheard, of course."

Hannah looked at Sterling and the landscape behind him. She had a far-off look in her eyes and seemed to like Sterling's words the way a kitten likes a patch of sunshine on the carpet beneath a window. In the window behind Sterling, the Howan farmland continued to stream past. A group of blotchy black-and-white cattle huddled near each other against the cold.

"I, I will ask Fish," said Jack.

"Very well," said Sterling. "You will call upon him when we arrive?"

Jack nodded. "Yes."

Barnes leaned back in his chair, as usual, appearing to sleep while the others conversed. He seemed to care little what Sherman Sterling had to say. *For that matter*, thought Jack, *he seems to care little what any of us have to say.* An unopened newspaper rested on Barnes' chest, slowly rising and falling with each breath.

When Jack finally left for his sleeping cabin, Sterling and Hannah were still speaking, Mrs. Smith looking bleary-eyed and exhausted in her corner. Sterling told yet another story, and Hannah still listened. Sterling had asked Hannah nearly every question there was to ask about Calderon, from the names of her horses to the kinds of fruit they grew on the Huntington estate. Hannah answered them all, never tiring of telling Sherman Sterling about her life. The only topic about which Hannah refused to talk was her sister Carolyn. Sterling saw a shift in her eyes when he asked, and he stayed well away from the subject for the remainder of the evening.

Crossing from the plateau of Howan into the rolling foothills of Bay State in the middle of the night, the train steamed into Bay Port City's Central Crescent Station at six o'clock in the morning. The immaculate, starched-and-pressed, uniformed attendants walked through the first-class cabin, knocking on varnished cherrywood doors with bright brass handles, telling the weary faces that opened them that it would shortly be time to exit the train.

Before Jack opened his eyes to the dawn light, Barnes had already packed both his own small canvas bags and Jack's trunk. Jack splashed water on his face from his brass shaving basin, lathered his neck and jaw, and eliminated any stubble that had appeared on the last day with short, clean strokes from the straight blade of his razor. He spread some cologne on his neck, and for the first time since departing Calderon, he exchanged his rancher's clothes for those of the city. He looked in the large rectangular mirror to see a man transformed. He was every bit a gentleman of the Republic, wearing a perfectly tailored frock coat, black trousers cut from the finest wool, thick for winter but still soft to the touch, and a brilliant black waistcoat with dark red paisley worked into it. So too, did he slip out of his clunky rancher's boots, well-worn and the color of Calderonian mud. He put his feet into a pair of stiff black city shoes, shiny as dining room silver, narrow and laced from the top.

Second and third class exited the train first, allowing the first-class passengers time to dress and permitting their servants time to finalize the logistics of transporting their employers' substantial luggage. Jack emerged from his cabin, looking clean and smelling fresh. Barnes stepped from his adjacent servant's quarters. He, too, was clean with a freshly shaved face beneath his hard, alert eyes. Jack was still uncomfortable asking Barnes to assist him. Barnes was twice his age and in his mid-forties. Barnes had commanded and killed men in battle. Yet, despite Jack's hesitation to ask, Barnes did not hesitate to assist. He was not overly deferential, merely professional. He gave the impression of a man with a job to do, and his job at the moment in Bay Port City was to be Jack Caldwell's personal valet. They could travel together in this manner while arousing the least suspicion.

Jack could see in Sterling's eyes that he was skeptical of the story that he was merely joining Harold Milton Stanwich for a journey of exploration, which is to say, for little more than a lark. Jack had few doubts Sterling would ask him more, should he get the chance. The Sterlings were as commercially minded as any family in the Republic. For the moment, however, at least Sterling knew no more than he was supposed to. Hannah might have loose lips with him if she knew, but she did not know about the Beserite.

Others might furrow their brows with cynicism, but the cover story was the story. *I wish to travel with Stanwich to learn from him. Like Stanwich, I believe in geographic exploration, in breaking into the unknown. I am, after all, the son of a railroad man. Our world requires being knit together from the steaming jungles to the driest deserts, from the valleys to the peaks.* So long as the word *Beserite* was never mentioned aloud, his head start over any other ambitious, enterprising New Anglians should be sufficient.

Jack stepped out onto the red bricks of the platform. A deep chill wrapped around him, piercing through his overcoat. Bay Port City was cold in the winter. The air did not carry a dry cold, as it did upon the high deserts east of Calderon or in the hill country approaching the snowy peaks of the Spine. Bay Port City was cold and wet, the moisture of Deep Bay and the Titanic Ocean mixing with the frozen December air that came down from the wildlands of the north, with the wetness making it feel far, far colder.

Jack pulled his overcoat tighter around him as Barnes hailed a group of railroad porters to move their luggage. Two men strained to lift Jack's trunk. It was a familiar scene alongside the first-class cars of the train—lowly paid railroad porters with foreign faces and unfamiliar accents heaving the massive chests of first-class passengers, who themselves carried nothing but the silk in their waistcoats and the wool on their backs.

Hannah walked ahead, her yellow-blonde braid dangling beneath a fur hat. Mrs. Smith trailed behind her, leading a small armada of trunks and porters.

"Caldwell!"

Jack turned to see Sterling, walking toward him through the cloud of his breath. A rim of fur lined his overcoat, far thicker than Jack's. Despite the terrible chill, Sterling still looked warm.

"May I ask you something?"

Jack cocked an eyebrow. It was cold enough alongside the track to make him shiver. The station, a mere one hundred yards away, would be heated and comfortable. Sterling placed one of his lean gloved hands on Jack's shoulder. It was a stronger grip than Jack would have liked. He resisted the urge to throw the arm off of him.

Sterling pressed Jack's back, leading him away from Sergeant Barnes, who was blowing into his ungloved hands.

"Just a quick question for you, old friend."

Jack's shoulders tightened as his eyes narrowed. Sterling's eyes were forward, following Hannah's braid as she walked toward the station.

"Is there anyone there I should know of?"

"Anyone where?" asked Jack. His voice was hard enough to reorient Sterling's gaze.

Sterling looked into Jack's eyes with some surprise. Jack looked back into his brown eyes, disliking his thick black mustache, his full mouth, and his thin lips. Jack had never known before the train ride just how much he disliked Sherman Sterling.

Sterling looked at him with some surprise. Sterling's face was close to Jack's.

They were nearly the same height, which, as tall men, was a rarity for them both.

"Is there anyone there, *with Hannah*? Back in Calderon?"

"Why do you ask?" said Jack. He could feel adrenaline in his shoulders. Sterling took his hand off of Jack's back, which had tightened into a rock.

"Is it you?" asked Sterling, his eyes widening, and his voice rising in disbelief.

"Of course not," said Jack, far too quickly.

"I didn't think so," said Sterling, his voice again lowering. After a pause, he said, "Do you disapprove?" His voice rose again as he asked.

"No," said Jack.

"I shouldn't think so," said Sterling, the confidence rushing back into his voice like a river after heavy rain.

An image of his fist in Sterling's teeth flashed across Jack's mind.

"Oh?" said Jack.

Sterling leaned back away from Jack. "I should rather think we would be a good fit."

Jack said nothing.

"Very well then," said Sterling. His mouth still smiled. His eyes did not. "I hope you can join us for supper before the ball. That is, of course, if you are not detained with Aaron Fish."

CHAPTER 13
Two Proposals

Bay Port City
New Anglian Republic
Three Gods Day, December 31, 1878

As it was, Jack's alibi became a real one. Aaron Fish had indeed just re-turned from LaFrentian Halex, concluding one of his many annual holi-days. Jack called upon the Fish Mansion from the Grand Mariner Hotel, fully expecting the errand boy to return with a note stating that Mr. Fish was not presently in the New Anglian Republic. Aaron Fish instead re-sponded that he would be most delighted to dine with Jack before the Three Gods Ball.

Fish suggested the Vine Club. Overlooking the ships' masts and smoke-stacks of Deep Bay Harbor, the club for graduates of their shared universi-ty was located three short city blocks away from the Grand Mariner Hotel in Bay Port City's Central Crescent.

"You have the evening off," said Jack, fixing his black cravat.

Barnes nodded. "Where are you going?" he asked.

"I will be at the Vine University Club, dining with an old friend. Then we will be off to the Three Gods Ball. Do not plan on waiting up."

"Our ship departs at seven in the morning," said Barnes. "I should think we will depart here at five o'clock in the morning. No later."

"I shall not be late," said Jack.

"They will not hold the ship for us," said Barnes, returning to his desk.

Ten minutes later, carrying his top hat in one hand and his walking stick in the other, Jack walked through the double doors of the Member's Room. The clock, which rested on the floor and stood taller than Jack, showed that it was six o'clock in the evening. A cloud of cigar smoke greet-ed him, thick enough to obscure his vision of the back of the room.

"May I help you, sir?" asked the uniformed reception man. Jack stood alone, scanning for familiar faces through the indoor fog. The look on his face showed that he found none.

"I am meeting Mr. Aaron Fish," said Jack as he coughed.

The occupants of each table appeared to be competing with the others to see who could speak more loudly. In the confined space, the sound was as overwhelming as the smoke.

"Mr. Fish?" said the waiter, summoned by the reception man.

"Yes," said Jack, raising his voice.

"Your name, please?"

"I am John J. Caldwell. I am a member."

"You're a member of the Vine Club, sir?"

"Yes," said Jack.

The man nodded. His eyes slipped down and then up again, assessing Jack from his shoes, which were shined, to his shaggy, longish hair, which was not. In early '78, the style of Bay Port City was to wear one's hair shorter, with what hair remained slicked back and parted with the assistance of a shiny pomade. By December of '78, few men in Bay Port City of a certain class remained with hair that was not as shiny as their shoes. The waiter's eyes evaluated Jack Caldwell's hair as decidedly unstylish. The eyes moved to the hat in Jack's right hand. It was shaped like the smokestack of a steamship, the edges of the brim curving up at the sides, black and hard to the touch beneath its silk covering. The waiter's eyes seemed to at least approve of the hat.

"This way, sir."

Jack followed him into the tobacco fog, his feet cushioned by the deep carpet, winding around tables into the very back of the room.

A small man at a small, crowded table locked eyes with Jack. Jack's face relaxed with the comfort of at last being recognized in a room of strangers.

"Caldwell of Calderon," said the man, rising.

His body was small, but his voice was not. Aaron Fish was handsome and lean with a face as brown as the expensive cigar in his small mouth. His smile was as compact as his body, showing straight little teeth in a face tanned by far warmer days than those offered by Bay Port City in December.

The others at the table stood and turned toward Jack as he made the final steps to the table. They were all there: Jurious Jackson, Austen Blake, Tom Beardsley, and even Lucas Alexander. As one, they let up a cheer, loud enough for those at other tables to stop their conversations in mid-sentence and look toward the back of the Member's Room.

"I may be a selfish man," said Fish, "but I could not deprive these fine gentle-men of the rare chance to see Jack Caldwell on this end of the Transcontinental."

"The Three Gods know we do not see any of you in Calderon," said Jack. His eyes sparkled with surprise and joy. His head shook in the manner of a man encountering an unexpected kindness.

"If you had given me more than a half-day notice, we could have had a doz-en of us, you know," said Fish, his eyes twinkling as brightly as Jack's. "As it is the evening of the Three Gods Ball, however, others could not be diverted from their present plans."

Jack said greetings around the rest of the table, embracing each man in turn: Fish, Jackson, Blake, and Beardsley. At Lucas Alexander, however, he extended his hand to shake, which Lucas took with a clammy palm. He was farthest away, but mostly Jack would have felt odd embracing Lucas Alexander.

"Sit," said Aaron Fish, playing the role of host.

Jack took the empty chair. A cut-glass decanter rested on the table. From the flushed cheeks of those who had preceded him to the table, Jack could see it was not the first decanter. Not waiting for their waiter, Fish reached out into the center of the table and poured the dark-purplish wine into Jack's crystal goblet. He topped off the wine in everyone else's crystal and raised his glass.

"If the Three Gods see fit to loan us Caldwell for only one evening, let us ensure that it is an evening worthy of remembrance!" Fish drained his glass.

As the delicious red wine went down Jack's throat, he thought of the hour at which he was to depart for his steamship that would take him across the Ti-tanic Ocean to the Veteno and Stanwich. But it was only six o'clock in the eve-ning, and the Three Gods Ball would not begin in earnest for another four hours.

The Sterling Mansion sat on a row of similar mansions, each of which took up nearly one-third of the space available on a full city block. There were perhaps thirty or forty like it in all of Bay Port City, but only a dozen such mansions stood upon Admiral's Hill, overlooking Deep Bay Harbor from the highest point in the city. Only the oldest families—those that had been around long enough to take the very best land—had mansions on Admiral's Hill, and those families were not in the habit of selling or making room for others.

The coachman helped Hannah Huntington down, grasping her gloved hand as she stepped onto the damp cobbles of the street. A flurry of snow dust-ed the city, making the metropolis seem soft and quiet beneath the gaslight in the high streetlamp above her. The old trees of Admiral's Hill towered forty or even fifty feet above her, far higher than the streetlamps, with thick gnarled trunks supporting broad, sturdy branches. She glanced up, imagining what the naked trees would look like when fully dressed in their summer leaves.

The coachman led Hannah across the stone sidewalk to the base of the great brick steps leading up to the high front doors of the mansion.

Hannah stood with the coachman, waiting for a handsome, clean-shaven Sterling family footman to lead her up the steps, taking care that she did not lose her footing as her delicate shoes left marks on the fresh coat of snow. Despite being nearly twenty years Hannah's senior, Mrs. Smith waived off assistance as she trailed behind her.

Between tall, black wrought-iron railings, they approached the brick landing beneath the mighty front doors. Nearly life-sized lion heads glared out at them in brass, set in oakwood painted with shiny black paint. On either side of the door, tongues of gaslight blazed in large lamps behind panes of glass set in brass. The door swung open, and Sherman Sterling stepped into the opening, looking down at Hannah. He smiled his broadest smile. Chandeliers in the entry hall behind him blazed with warm, welcoming light.

"Miss Huntington, welcome to our home," said Sterling. His face showed that he was aware his home was magnificent.

Hannah looked into his face, feeling, despite her own father's wealth, a touch of awe. She had heard of Bay Port City wealth, but she had never beheld it with her own eyes in all of its metropolitan splendor.

"Good evening, Mr. Sterling," she said with inviting eyes. Sterling bent down to kiss her gloved hand.

"Please allow me the privilege of introducing my mother."

Florenta Fredericks Sterling looked very much like her son, a testament to the Fredericks genes. She was tall and lanky, with dark hair and a broad mouth. The massive smile on the narrow face, which on her son was a compelling feature, dazzling if not entirely attractive, failed to impress on the mother's face. Her teeth were older, lacking the sparkle of the son's, and in the female face, the mouth looked very much like that of a horse. The thought crossed Hannah's mind that she saw the future of Sherman's smile. The glory of the entryway and the Sterling Mansion receded before this realization.

"You are as beautiful as Sherman proclaimed, and you honor us as our guest on Three Gods Day," said Mrs. Sterling, smiling her horse smile. Her eyes were set too close together, giving her the appearance of concentrating on some object just beyond her nose.

Hannah smiled, dipping into a deep curtsy.

"Mrs. Sterling, you are kind to welcome an empty-handed traveler." As Hannah spoke, a household maid led Mrs. Smith along the sidewall of the foyer, speaking in hushed tones.

Mrs. Florenta Fredericks Sterling looked at Mrs. Smith as she was ushered along, wondering why a servant had the impertinence to enter through her front door. She looked at Hannah again, her eyes hardening, as if to say, *they have no manners in Calderon.*

"And this is my father, Mr. George Sterling," said Sherman to Hannah, who now stood alone, her skin glowing radiantly in the chandelier light. A servant had taken her fur-lined coat at the door, leaving Hannah in her floor-length, cream-colored Dardennes gown. Her arms were bare, as was her upper chest. Like her mother and sister, Hannah was well-shaped in that region of her body, even without the aid of a corset, and she saw that the elder Mr. Sterling had taken the time to notice.

George Sterling looked nothing like his son. Hannah looked into his face. For a moment, her surprise showed before she consciously reapplied the mask of her courteous smile. George Sterling was short, fat, and bald. He was, it appeared, the opposite of Sterling in nearly every way.

"I know and admire your father," said George Sterling.

As Hannah heard the words, she realized Sherman Sterling did inherit one thing from his father—his voice. The son, like his mother, was tall, lean, and horsey. The father was short, fat, and porcine. But with her eyes closed, Hannah would have struggled to tell their voices apart.

"Thank you, sir," said Hannah.

"Pity that they did not arrive in time to join us."

"They will be most disappointed," said Hannah.

Swift and silent servants brought Hannah and each of the Sterlings a glass of sparkling wine, delivered on a silver tray. Sherman and his mother each took a glass, but Mr. George Sterling waived the wine away with a whisk of his hand. As he spoke with Hannah, he bent forward, with his hands clasped behind his back, making himself even shorter. Mrs. Smith disappeared down into the servants' quarters below, where she would dine with those of her own class, leaving Hannah to face the Sterlings alone.

George Sterling led Hannah into the dining room on his arm. Looking over, she could see the shining top of his balding head as they walked. Both Mrs. Sterling and Sherman Sterling seemed content to remain quiet in George Sterling's presence. He spoke incessantly but asked few questions.

"You see, young lady, there are many reasons to diversify from banking, not that banking is a poor place to begin. Indeed, I would say it is the ideal place to begin. Capital is the lifeblood of all industries, and banks control capital. Don't you agree?"

Hannah nodded half-heartedly.

Not looking at her nod, George Sterling said, "I would presume your father would agree as well. Try building a railroad without the capital of banks! Ha!

Nonsense! Never! There would be no railroads but for the banks—and certainly no Transcontinental—which is to say there is no Calderon without Bay Port City. But few ever care to thank those to whom they are indebted."

A footman pulled out Hannah's chair as they reached the table. George Sterling continued talking about his banks and their importance. Hannah looked across the table at Sherman, who was seated next to his mother. It appeared that only the four of them would be dining. Hannah would have appreciated other guests to reduce the attention upon her, or at the very least, to reduce George Sterling's attention upon her. She realized she had not asked Sherman Sterling who else would be dining with them other than his parents.

"Do you have other siblings?" asked Hannah when George Sterling had paused for a moment to drink a sip of water. She looked at Sterling as she spoke. Her eyes were nearly pleading.

"No," said George Sterling before his son could speak.

Hannah looked down at her plate of shelled shrimp, wishing she could be in the basement with Mrs. Smith.

Except to relieve themselves in the toilets, no one rose from Aaron Fish's table in the Vine Club Member's Room for three and a half hours. Food arrived. Decanters of wine came with it. It was dense food, rich and full of meat, flour, and cheese. Roasted potatoes, carrots, and onions adorned the main course of beef, cooked in a flaky browned crust of fine flour. A thick cream sauce was poured over it. The red wines became heavier as the meal progressed. The light LaFrentian reds of the early meal gave way to the bolder Gerdic varietals paired with the roasted meat courses. Jack lost count of the decanters long before he finished his cream-drenched beef pastry. He had already eaten a full pheasant and, before that, a course of freshwater stream fishes, caught from the highlands of Bay State and served in butter and lemon with their heads still affixed to their bodies.

Between each course, Aaron Fish insisted upon a round of cigars. Jack was now puffing the smoke from his fourth. A waiter placed several large wedges of cheese in front of him, along with a candied plum. The Gerdic wines were replaced by Spatanian brandy, strong and aromatic. Jack ate every course, drank every wine, and smoked every cigar Fish gave him.

Austen Blake swirled his brandy in a wide glass goblet. Blake's family was perhaps the least exalted of those at the table, his father being merely a prosperous lawyer in Howan State. Among his clients were the L&B Railroad, and all of its subsidiaries that linked the economic capillaries of Howan State and Bay State to the three great commercial arteries of the Republic: the Laketown and

Bay Port City Railroad, the Laketown and Port Southern Railroad, and the Laketown and Port Calderon Railroad. To anyone of the Republic, however, those railroads were known as the L&B, the L&S, and the Transcontinental. Blake came from a town of only several thousand. Rather than return, he had chosen to stay in Bay Port City. Blake was ambitious.

"Is it time?" he asked.

"For the ball?" asked Fish, pulling a gold watch from his waistcoat. "Nearly ten o'clock. I say let's have one more round, eh?"

"We'll be late," said Lucas Alexander, looking at his own watch.

"Why should you care?" asked Jurious Jackson. "You barely dance."

"I dance well enough," said Lucas Alexander.

"Well enough for what?" asked Tom Beardsley, exhaling a mouthful of smoke.

"What say you, Caldwell?" asked Fish. "To the ball or not?"

Jack Caldwell swirled his brandy, a broad smile on his face. "You know I am heading to the desert in the morning."

"Yes, yes, the Sand Sea, what of it?" asked Fish.

"Do you know what there are few of in the Sand Sea?"

"Rivers?" asked Fish. "Green hills?"

Jurious Jackson laughed.

"Women," said Jack.

"Is that your way of saying you want to go to the ball?" asked Fish.

"No," said Jack. He puffed on his cigar, letting the smoke slowly leave his mouth. "What was that place? The place in Gressia Town?"

Austen Blake shot a look at Tom Beardsley, raising his eyebrows and grinning. With the wine in his teeth, he looked like a pirate.

Fish lowered his voice and leaned forward. "Madame Nadia's?"

"Yes," said Jack, nodding.

"Caldwell, are you asking us to abandon the Three Gods Ball to go to Madame Nadia's?" Fish spoke in a conspiratorial whisper, his eyes nearly as wide as his smile.

"That would be devious," said Jurious Jackson.

"Our families would undoubtedly be very cross with us," said Tom Beardsley.

"And we would certainly miss the delivery of the Queen's message from the new telegraph line," said Austen Blake, suppressing a laugh.

"Which would be tragic," said Jurious Jackson.

"Let's let Lucas decide," said Fish.

"I think we should go to the Three Gods Ball," said Lucas Alexander. His cheeks were flushed above his red beard. Alexander's family was old, rich, and had called Bay Port City home for more than two hundred years.

"Then Madame Nadia's it is!" said Fish.

"That is a bad idea," said Lucas Alexander, exhaling his cigar smoke and looking up at the ceiling. It was among his numerous gestures that Jack Caldwell found annoying.

"I'm sure they've forgiven you, Lucas," said Jurious Jackson, smiling brightly, and patting Lucas on the shoulder. Jackson was darker than even Fish. His father was an old-time New Anglian, but his mother was a south Spatanian, from one of the countless finger peninsulas where the Continent faced southward toward Omakhosi, and where the sun was bright and hot from the early spring until the late fall. Jackson had none of his father's coloring and all of his mother's. His hair hung about his head in loose curls, neither blond nor brown, but something in between.

"You're the one with the steamer to catch, so what say you, Caldwell?" asked Tom Beardsley, bearded, green-eyed, and pale as a ghost. Beardsley was the son of a long line of North Anglian merchants, narrow-shouldered and tall as a Gressian grenadier.

Jack exhaled more smoke with narrowed eyes. His head had begun to swirl. "It was my idea, was it not?"

Beardsley nodded. "Alright, then. Are we doing this?"

Jack looked at Aaron Fish. Fish was smoking yet another cigar with his eyes closed.

"Yes, it's time," said Fish, blowing a smoke ring toward the ceiling. His eyes were still closed. "We owe it to Caldwell."

"Are you in, Lucas?" asked Jurious Jackson. "Or are you going to the ball alone?"

Austen Blake grinned his purple smile.

"I'll come with you," said Lucas Alexander with anxiety in his voice and fear on his face.

After dinner, Hannah tried several different ways to excuse herself, yet George Sterling refused to relent in his ceaseless monologues. Each time Hannah made a polite nod, he took it for validation that his self-aggrandizing story was indeed significant, interesting, or entertaining. Hannah had then stopped nodding altogether. Yet, George Sterling carried on, appearing to gain momentum as the night went on. Several times Sherman Sterling tried to change the subject.

"Hannah, remind me of the produce you grow on the Huntington Property," asked the son, who was not oblivious to Hannah's boredom and whose anxiety had begun to show upon his face. Sherman Sterling himself had started to count the minutes until he could escort Hannah to the ball and leave his parents.

Hannah began to answer, "We grow fruit, mostly—pears, peaches, nectarines, lemons—"

"You know, Hannah," interrupted George Sterling, "we have several farms ourselves. Few understand how much fine produce we grow here in Bay State, even on the very borders of Bay Port City."

"Yes, we saw many fine fields from the train—" attempted Hannah.

"Yes, yes," said George Sterling, raising his voice. "Some things can be seen from the train, but little that is worthwhile. The finest farmland is farther away. That is the farmland we own, the finest and most productive in the entire Republic, I'll tell you, by the Three Gods."

"I must be going," said Hannah, at last, "I am afraid this travel has left me feeling unwell." Her voice was definitive. "Would it be possible for word to be sent down to Mrs. Smith?"

"What about the ball?" asked Mrs. Sterling, incredulous.

"I don't know that I can attend," said Hannah, gathering her resolve as she inserted a quaver into her voice. "I am feeling ill. Quite ill." She frowned and placed a hand upon her stomach.

Hearing the words, Sherman Sterling himself looked ill.

"Should I have some medicine brought?" asked Mrs. Sterling.

Mr. Sterling looked annoyed to have the table's attention placed upon something other than himself and his stories.

"George, please see what can be done for Miss Huntington here. We cannot have her missing the Three Gods Ball after traveling all of this way."

"I— yes, yes, of course," said George Sterling, rising from the table.

"You too, Sherman," said Mrs. Sterling, her voice edged. "Help your father."

"Of course," said Sherman, bowing to Hannah.

Father and son departed out a side door from the dining room as a waiting, liveried servant silently opened and shut it. The rich of Bay Port City made sure to never fall below the trappings of wealth shown by the highest of the Anglian aristocracy across the Titanic Ocean. Indeed, wherever possible, they endeavored to exceed it. With a look, Mrs. Sterling told the servant he should disappear on the other side of the door as well. Most conversations in the Sterling Mansion were held in front of servants, but not all, and Mrs. Sterling's eyes made clear that this was to be one of those.

"I was hoping we might be able to speak for a few moments, dear, just us ladies," said Mrs. Sterling, looking intently across the table. "As you are feeling ill, it appears that time is now."

"Oh?" said Hannah, smiling weakly.

Mrs. Sterling pressed swiftly. "Yes, we should have a few quiet minutes while word is sent down to your Mrs. Smith. The servants may not have yet finished their meal. They eat a bit later than we do, once the bulk of the serving is done. You would prefer to allow your maid to finish her meal, I presume?"

Hannah nodded, seeing no way out of Mrs. Sterling's box.

Mrs. Sterling looked to the door, making sure they had the dining room to themselves. She smiled her horsey grin across the bottom of her long oval face, revealing her large, mildly discolored teeth. She reached her long arms across the table and took Hannah's hands into her own.

"You must forgive my husband his stories. Like many men who have seen too much success at too young an age, he assumes that all delight in the sound of his voice as much as he himself does."

I cannot imagine there is such a person in all of the Republic, thought Hannah, smiling at her own silent quip.

"There is nothing to forgive," said Hannah aloud. "Mr. Sterling is most accomplished."

"You are a polite, sweet girl. But I do not wish to waste our small amount of time here tonight talking about George. You have captured my son's eye. Sherman is most taken with you."

Hannah forced herself to smile as she felt the walls moving in upon her. Mrs. Sterling's grip upon her wrists felt like a jailer's restraints. She kept her hands in Mrs. Sterling's grip and fought to keep her feelings from her eyes.

"You have a most exceptional son," said Hannah.

Mrs. Sterling smiled again, broadly. Hannah again saw the vision of Sherman Sterling's future smile—massive, ugly, and unavoidable.

"I am so glad you agree," said Mrs. Sterling. "Sherman was insistent that you dine with us here tonight up on Admiral's Hill, especially as it is the night of the ball. So many women have tried to ensnare my son. As I am sure you can understand, all of *this* is not readily shared with any pretty girl who comes calling."

To emphasize her point, Mrs. Sterling waved her arm around the dining room, as if to encompass the glory of the Sterling Mansion, Admiral Hill, Bay Port City, and perhaps even all of the old wealth of the Republic. In doing so, Mrs. Sterling released Hannah's left hand, which she withdrew into her lap. With some awkwardness, Mrs. Sterling kept Hannah's remaining hand firmly in her grip.

"But you," said Mrs. Sterling, letting out a small laugh and gesturing with her free hand, "You are at last a young woman worthy of my son! Imagine the daughter of the Transcontinental paired with a Sterling of Admiral Hill. Oh, we would be the talk of the town, Hannah. You would be the talk of Bay Port City, the toast of the Republic!"

Hannah fought the urge to rip her hand from Mrs. Sterling's grip and run for the front doors of the mansion, bursting through the brass lions and out into the snowy street. Her smile remained tenuously on her face.

"You are most kind, Mrs. Sterling," Hannah managed to say.

Jammed into the back of a carriage, Jack sat next to Jurious Jackson and across from Tom Beardsley. They were all tall men, and their knees extended past each other's, dangerously close to the others' groins, as the carriage wheels rattled along the snow-swept streets of the Bay Port City Central Crescent, in the direction of Gressia Town, which was in the most disreputable southeastern part of the city.

"When were you last at Madame Nadia's?" asked Jurious with mischief in his eyes.

"Several years ago," said Jack, looking out the carriage window and feeling the wine in his stomach. His mind was elsewhere.

"A bit different from the Vine Club," said Beardsley, grinning at Jurious.

Jack said nothing and continued staring out the window. Long moments passed. Iron horseshoes tapped rhythmically on pavement—click, clock, click, clock. Under the falling snow, the streets were largely deserted. The door of a drinking hall opened, and foreign, drunken voices washed out over the snow-covered street. The carriage continued, and the voices receded. The horseshoes kept their rhythmic beat. Click, clock, click, clock.

"You ever see Sterling?" asked Jack, trying to sound casual. The wine had slurred his voice, but not enough that Beardsley or Jurious could tell. They had both drunk more than Jack.

"Old Sherman Sterling? The Mouth of Admiral's Hill? Certainly," said Beardsley.

Jack laughed. He would call Sterling that to Hannah. *The Mouth of Admiral's Hill. Three Gods bless you, Beardsley.*

"I see him now and then," said Jurious. "Arrogant bastard."

Beardsley nodded. "Why do you ask about Sterling, Caldwell? Are Caldwell & Sons looking for a loan?"

"No," said Jack, his shoulders bristling. *Never,* he thought. *I'd rather lose the railroad.*

"Why do you bring him up?" asked Jurious.

"No reason," said Jack, feeling drunk. "We saw him on the train."

"Who's we? You and your valet?"

"No," said Jack, without thinking. "Hannah."

"Hannah?" asked Jurious. "Hannah who?"

"Hannah? No one that warrants discussion. Just someone else from Calderon." Jack's cheeks flushed. He had not mentioned Hannah all evening, though she had never been far from his thoughts. The wine brought her from the back of his mind to the forefront.

Jurious and Beardsley both looked at him, sobered by the obvious lie.

"You are traveling with a woman?" asked Beardsley.

"Did you run off and get married?" asked Jurious. "I daresay I am offended."

"Did the postman misplace my invitation as well?" asked Beardsley.

"No, I am not married," said Jack, his voice now matching the embarrassment of his cheeks. He was not a man to be rattled by the mentioning of a young woman, especially when drinking, and the others knew it.

"Scandalous," said Jurious Jackson.

"Indeed," said Beardsley, who pulled a cigar from his waistcoat and struggled with a match. He struck the first match, lost his grip, and flung it at Jack's face. Jack twisted his head and swatted the tiny flame into the fogged glass of the carriage window.

"You Calderonians are bold," said Jurious Jackson. "Pray, tell us more."

"Indeed, in the name of the Three Gods," said Beardsley, trying to light another match and failing.

"It is not that way," said Jack. "She is the daughter of a business associate of my father's. She is like a sister to me."

"Like a sister and a sister are not the same thing," said Jurious.

"Indeed, not in any way the same thing," said Beardsley, the cigar between his teeth protruding from his beard.

"I trust she is attractive?" said Jurious.

"Yellow-haired? Busty?" asked Beardsley.

Both, thought Jack. "Enough," he said. He looked out the carriage. They were on yet another dark, snow-covered street in a part of the city he did not know at all.

"Are we close?" he asked.

"Close enough," said Jurious. "And far enough for you to answer our questions."

"Where is this mysterious almost-sister tonight?" asked Beardsley.

If I tell them, they will ask more. If I tell them, they may even talk to Sterling. I must not tell them.

"Attending the ball, I should think," said Jack.

"Then perhaps we should go there, after all. Eh, Beardsley?" said Jurious Jackson.

"Don't make me throw you out of a moving carriage, Jackson," said Jack Caldwell. Beardsley finally lit his cigar.

After a half-hour more of continuous movement, the carriage stopped beneath an awning covering a narrow alleyway. The canopy kept the alley's cobblestones free of snow, but it did not block the wind that seemed to kick up as soon as they crossed over into Gressia Town. On the southeastern edge of the city, well outside the Central Crescent, Gressia Town was exposed to all of the elements that blew down the length of Deep Harbor, driven by the frozen winds of the north Titanic Ocean. The carriage door swung open, and a cold wind whipped into Jack's face.

"Three Gods," he said, shielding his face with a gloved hand.

"Welcome to Gressia Town," said Jurious Jackson, stepping out of the carriage.

"Madame Nadia's," said the driver, holding open the door. His fur hat hid his face, and the thick woolen collar of his greatcoat muffled his voice. He grabbed Jack's arm to steady him as he stepped down from the carriage. Jack followed Tom Beardsley into the opened door in the stone wall along the side of the alley. There was no sign to denote the establishment, merely an opening in the dark wall of the dark building. There were no streetlights along the alleyway, and the awning blocked any moonlight that had managed to punch through the snow clouds overhead.

The second carriage bearing Aaron Fish, Austen Blake, and Lucas Alexander pulled into the alleyway just as Jack crossed the threshold into the heated room. The ceiling was low. There was no light but for that of the blazing fireplace to the right.

"Welcome," said a woman's voice.

"Good evening," said Jurious Jackson.

An attractive woman of middle age stepped forward out of the shadows at the back of the room. Another figure stepped forward from the corner, not nearly as far ahead as the woman, but forward enough for any entering the place to see him. He was a giant with the broad face of a Gressian forester and a massive black beard covering his jaw. It was not a beard like Tom Beardsley's, trimmed, and light brown. Instead, it was the beard of a peasant or a steppe warrior—long, black, and shaggy. Jack saw that the man's tangle of hair nearly touched the ceiling. Nor was it a gentle tangle, like Jurious Jackson's brown-blond locks. It was a rough, coarse mass, like the loops of the metal pads used to scrub rust from a barrel ring.

"Good evening," said a loud voice behind them.

Jack turned to see Aaron Fish. He walked swiftly with the gait of a man entering a familiar place and expecting a warm reception. The woman's face opened into an expansive smile.

"Ah, it is you. Mr. Fish, welcome." The woman opened her arms and flashed her beaming smile up at each of the men in the small waiting room. Only Aaron Fish stood at her eye level. Even in the dimness of the firelight, Jack could see that she had once been a woman of staggering beauty. Her face was almost perfectly symmetrical with bright brown eyes flanking the kind of nose that one might see in sculpture, neither large nor small, but perfect in its shape and straight as a nose can be. Beneath luxuriant black hair pulled back tightly about her head, she revealed all of her face between tiny, symmetrical ears, flat against the side of her head. The skin on her chest was milky against the black silk of her dress.

"I bring you a special guest this evening, Madame Nadia," said Aaron Fish.

"Oh?" said Madame Nadia, sweeping her eyes across the faces of Fish's companions. Her eyes stopped on the face of Lucas Alexander. Her smile disappeared.

"Mr. Fish, I believe we discussed this matter last month." Her eyes remained focused on the face of Lucas Alexander.

Jack turned. Lucas's face was red as a berry. His head shrugged down into his shoulders, retreating like a turtle's.

"Did we not discuss this, Mr. Alexander?" Her voice was a dagger. In response, like a guard dog sensing his master's displeasure, the Gressian in the corner moved forward, taking a large step into the firelight.

"Madame, Madame!" There was laughter in Aaron Fish's voice. "That is not your surprise. We nearly had to drag Lucas here. He shall be on his best behavior. Bohrus taught him a lesson last time that he is not likely to forget." As he finished speaking, Fish looked at the massive man lurking on the edge of the shadows. The man did not acknowledge Fish's words, staring at the group with cold, steely eyes.

Lucas's head retreated deeper into his shoulders.

There was breezy confidence in Aaron Fish's voice as if Bohrus the giant was no more than an ornamental gargoyle. "Your surprise, Madame Nadia, is a gentleman visiting us all the way from Calderon. This is Jack Caldwell. He is a Caldwell of *the* Caldwells—the Caldwells of the Transcontinental. You know the railroad on the other end of the L&B, the one that connects Laketown to Calderon? Well, Caldwell owns it."

Madame Nadia corrected her face, reapplying her smile as convincingly as an actor upon a stage.

"Then you must be Mr. Caldwell," said Madame Nadia, guessing correctly. She stepped forward, looking at Jack's face. She stepped close to him, close enough for her perfume to engulf and entice him. As he inhaled Madame Nadia's scent, Hannah Huntington's face receded from his mind like a spent wave upon the sand.

Madame Nadia extended her hand. As he had been quite drunk on his last visit several years before, Jack was unsure whether to shake it or bend down to kiss it. He decided upon the latter. Her skin was smooth on his lips and daubed with the same perfume. Jack felt Madame Nadia's hand tense in surprise.

Aaron Fish let out a laugh, followed by Jurious Jackson.

"You are a gentleman," said Madame Nadia.

Jack's cheeks flushed.

"Well done, Caldwell," said Tom Beardsley, slapping Jack on his shoulder.

"I am Madame Nadia, and I welcome you to my establishment." Jack had expected a strong foreign accent, but he could detect none. Indeed, she spoke with the flatness of the central Republic, like a woman from Howan State.

"Whatever you prefer, we shall endeavor to provide," she continued. She swept her eyes across the group, lingering for a moment on the face of Lucas Alexander and losing her smile. The smile returned as she moved her eyes back to Aaron Fish. "As Mr. Fish can attest, we offer only the finest. And we can satisfy all tastes."

On the word *all*, Jack thought he heard an edge in Madame Nadia's voice.

"Thank you," said Jack, nodding, and not knowing what else to say.

"Very well then," said Madame Nadia. "Follow me." She turned and walked toward a door that Bohrus, the bearded Gressian, had already pulled open. They entered a narrow, dark hallway that smelled of dusty carpets and stale smoke. Aaron Fish walked directly in front of Jack, his head only coming up to Jack's chin.

"Fish," whispered Jack.

Fish half turned his head.

"Why doesn't she have an accent?"

"Because she's not Gressian," said Fish.

In his wine-altered state, Jack turned that over in his mind, trying to make sense of it.

They exited the hallway and entered a large receiving room. A host of glass bottles rested on an unattended bar. Gas lamps around the periphery faintly illuminated the room with their flames burning low. A series of long couches were set up directly in front of them, facing a large open area. To the left, in the direction of the bar, several tables, surrounded by large upholstered chairs, sat empty.

"Please sit," said Madame Nadia. Aaron Fish led the way, taking the left most position of the most left couch.

"Join me, Caldwell," he said. Jack followed him and sat down on the couch to Fish's right. Jack took in the room with his eyes. Large mirrors hung on left of the walls. Between the mirrors, large paintings displayed naked women in the old imperial style, positioned in various poses. Some reclined, eating bunches of grapes with looks of unhurried contentment upon their painted faces. Others stood, looking out into the distance over rolling, green countryside, marked with rivers and mountains on the horizon.

When the last man, Lucas Alexander, found his place on the couch, the women entered. There were nine of them, all young, beautiful, and nearly naked. Jack noticed that they all walked strangely, standing on the balls of their feet with their heels raised above the ground, emphasizing the lines of their uncovered legs. The second thing Jack noticed was that one of them made all of the others recede into the background of his vision.

His eyes locked upon her, hungrily tracing every curve of her body.

She caught his glance and walked directly at him, her hips swaying. Jack stared at her feet, slowly moving up the lean muscles of her legs, and ending at her golden-brown eyes, which were now directly in front of his own.

She bent over him with her hands upon Jack's knees. Her chest pressed up against his own.

"I am Katya," she said, with her warm breath in Jack's ear.

"I am terribly embarrassed," said Hannah, standing upon the front doorstep of the Sterling Mansion. "It must be the traveling."

Are you sure I cannot escort you back to the Grand Mariner Hotel?" asked Sherman Sterling. "The Three Gods Ball will be far less bright without you."

"I am just so ill, Mr. Sterling . . . I wouldn't want you to fall ill too."

"I will gladly—"

"I will be in good hands with Mrs. Smith, Mr. Sterling."

"Please, you must call me Sherman, truly."

"I will send you a telegram," said Hannah. "I am envious that I will not be with you . . . Sherman. Please dance a waltz for me."

Sterling looked as if he might cry.

"Thank you for a lovely evening," said Hannah.

Sterling took her hand and kissed it.

Hannah withdrew it as quickly as she could without making it evident that she wished to run to the carriage.

"When will I see you again?" he asked.

"Soon, I hope," said Hannah, taking the arm of the waiting footman who helped her across the snow-covered sidewalk. She climbed into the carriage and gave a small polite wave to Sterling, who still stood between the brass lions on the stairs. The carriage door closed behind her.

"Are you ill?" asked Mrs. Smith.

"In a way," said Hannah, sighing deeply.

"Are you prepared to miss the ball?"

"How can I go now?"

"I suppose you could say you are suddenly feeling better."

Hannah shook her head. "No, Mrs. Smith. I cannot meet any more bachelors from Bay Port City or *Admiral's Hill*."

The horseshoes clicked softly upon the snow-covered pavement. The carriage wheels rolled smoothly, as there were no divots or bumps on the pristine, sloped streets of Admiral's Hill.

"Your mother and father will be there," said Mrs. Smith.

"I hope they enjoy it," said Hannah, looking out the window at the snow-dusted city below them.

"They are expecting you."

"They will have to endure their disappointment," said Hannah.

They rode in silence for several long moments.

"Have you wondered why your father selected me to escort you here?" asked Mrs. Smith.

Hannah looked at her. "Because of your expertise with ball gowns?"

Mrs. Smith smiled. She had indeed sat very awkwardly during Hannah's final fitting at Dardennes.

"Yes, I have wondered that," said Hannah, her face growing serious.

"And what have you wondered?"

"You do not seem like a lady's maid."

"Because I am not."

Hannah shifted uncomfortably in her seat.

"What does that mean?"

"It means you must go to the ball," said Mrs. Smith.

"Why?"

"Because you must see your father."

"What will I tell Sherman Sterling? Or his parents?"

"It doesn't matter," said Mrs. Smith, sharply rapping the wall of the carriage with her fist.

The carriage stopped.

"What are you doing?" asked Hannah, her eyes widening.

"Telling our coachman that we have a new destination."

"Why? Where?"

"To the Three Gods Ball, Miss Huntington, at the Hall of the Republic. Your father has ordered me to deliver you to him, and I will."

CHAPTER 14
A Lady's Love

The Royal Palace
City of Anglia
Three Gods Day, December 31, 1878

At last, the massive, black, four-horse towncoach stopped. The Harmon coat of arms was painted in gold on the side. A footman leaped down and opened the door, causing the Harmon crest to swing forward. Peter Harmon stepped out behind it, smoothing his waistcoat and looking askance at the long line of similar carriages stretched out behind him. They carried the leading personages and nobility of Anglia, clogging the stone drive back to the palace gates and beyond. A full squadron of mounted Royal Guardsmen flanked either side of the driveway as if to remind the guests that however much power Parliament might hold, and however much wealth the City's merchant princes might possess, Anglia was still a monarchy.

Like nearly every other gentleman emerging from the carriages, Peter wore a white bow tie and a black jacket. He stepped toward the imposing, four-story, stone façade of the palace, gripping his walking stick in his right hand and adjusting his black top hat with his left. The ceaseless rain of the past weeks had given way to a brilliant and clear winter night, moonlit, and cold against the freshly shaved skin on his face. Before he left Hylebourne House, he took care to daub some LaFrentian cologne on his wrists, the scent Sarah had once complimented.

His father stood next to him, as tall as Peter and substantially bulkier. As the footman stepped forward to assist his wife, Lord Harmon glared out at the crowd, looking every bit as fierce as his reputation.

Lady Glencora Caldwell Harmon emerged from the carriage last, placing a gloved hand into that of the footman before gingerly stepping down onto the carriage step. She stepped down once more onto the broad, smooth stone of the palace entrance. The hem of her violet gown drifted behind her. Brilliant hothouse orchids from the Hylebourne House conservatory festooned her strawberry-blonde hair, which her maids had expertly and painstakingly piled atop her head, her shapely neck rising above the white fox fur of her shawl. A triple strand of pearls stretched across her bare clavicles, resting upon the exposed, milky skin of her upper chest. Sapphire drop earrings dazzled beneath round diamonds in each of her ears.

Faces reflexively turned toward her as she stepped forward, taking her husband's arm.

"You are radiant, Cora," he said with possessive pride in his voice.

She smiled, looking past him toward the crowd. Twenty-four years before, her marriage to Lord George Harmon had captured the imaginations of both the press and the people, and in the intervening years, she had lost neither her beauty nor the crowd's eye. She was then the twenty-two-year-old daughter of Leon Caldwell, the Laketown millionaire, wedding the second son of the Duke of Haden, pairing the energy of New Anglian commerce with the dignity of one of Anglia's oldest and most glorified families. Readers on both sides of the Titanic had lived vicariously through their union. They lived vicariously through her still.

Her husband at her side, she strode toward the palace with utter confidence, secure in her beauty and bolstered by wealth and title. Peter walked like a ghost behind his famous parents, barely reflective of their social glory, little known and little noticed.

His eyes darted from familiar face to familiar face. Though many forgot his own face, he forgot none himself. Such was the curse of his memory, which he had rarely if ever seen surpassed amongst society for certain, and even amongst the professors and students of Three Gods College, which was, by reputation and design, supposed to collect the finest minds in Anglia. His eyes searched for Sarah.

Following his parents, he ascended the wide, shallow steps toward the entrance, the double doors held open, Queen's Guardsmen in long capes standing on either side. They stood with sabers drawn, resting against their shoulders, the brass badges on their plumed helmets gleaming in the moonlight. Tall gas lamps flickered behind them, flanking either side of the entryway.

A court herald waited inside, wearing an overcoat to weather the cold air wafting in through the open doors.

The crowd waited, each arriving couple standing in a line to be announced.

Peter stood behind his parents, frowning, waiting impatiently for the right to enter, to exit the cold, and to find Sarah.

"The Lord and Lady George Harmon of Hylebourne House!" cried the herald, at last.

The crowd inhaled a sharp breath, eyes shifting and heads bobbing to see them—the press lord and the society beauty.

"Mr. Peter Harmon of Hylebourne House!" said the herald.

Lord and Lady Harmon walked in through the palace doors, smiling broadly, drinking in the adulation. Peter walked with hunched shoulders behind them, drawing few looks as his name was announced.

Lord Harmon caught the eye of the Prime Minister.

The leader of Her Majesty's government nodded his head, his dark curls glistening in the gaslight of the chandeliers overhead, the little beard on his chin pointed and sharp.

Lord Harmon nodded back.

"Lord Harmon!" cried a voice, sounding of North Anglia. Peter looked up to see a physically enormous Crown and Country lord who led an obscure ministry, something to do with canals and tolls.

Lord Harmon stepped forward, bowing politely to the man.

The man bowed back, deeper and with more reverence.

A footman wearing the canary yellow of the royal livery approached, presenting a tray of sparkling wine. Lord Harmon took two glasses, handing one to his wife.

Peter cleared his throat, stepping awkwardly toward the retreating footman.

"Pardon me," he said, a tinge of irritation in his voice.

The footman stopped.

"I will have a glass," said Peter.

The man elevated his chin and retreated his shoulders, waiting stone-faced as Peter lifted a glass from his tray. Peter raised the flute to his lips and tasted the cold, extraordinary wine, bubbling and dry. He exhaled, having drunk sparkling LaFrentian wine for most of his life. It calmed him now.

His parents drifted ahead of him, talking with the Crown and Country EMs—Elected Members of Parliament—who flocked to them as if magnetized. The EMs quickly abandoned their previous conversations to shake the hand of the man most credited with putting both the Prime Minister and the party back on top.

Peter's eyes searched the edges of the crowd. Attractive faces flitted across his gaze. He looked past them, his eyes seeking her face and hers alone. He had not seen her in two long weeks, though he had written her every day. She had responded only three times, each letter shorter than the one preceding it. Peter had thought of little else since waking up, growing more nervous as the day darkened and the ball approached.

Peter had thought of one other thing since waking up, Khyderbad. How could he go if Uncle Bartimus refused to take him on as his private secretary?

Peter knew that no amount of pleading to Uncle Bartimus was likely to do any good. Even the Lord Governor of Khyderbad would not dare defy a direct request from Lord Harmon, especially for someone as insignificant as Peter. His father, in a simple declaration, had checkmated him.

Peter's eyes stopped. She stood across the hall, along the far wall, speaking to an older man. Her father stood next to her, his long, brown spade-shaped beard hanging down from his long oval face. Unlike Peter or Lord Harmon, or most of the gentlemen in the room, he did not wear the black jacket, white waistcoat and white tie of a civilian. He stood out, bright as blood, in his red tunic with the insignia of a senior officer of Her Majesty's army. A large contingent of medals covered the left side of his chest, and the brass of his buttons gleamed nearly as brightly as the medals.

Peter cleared his throat. General August Hesiger was consistent in his terse unfriendliness, at least toward him, and Peter never felt at ease in his presence. It would be better if Sarah would step away from him. Perhaps if he could catch her eye . . .

Peter waited in indecision. Sarah continued in her conversation, ignoring the young man standing by himself in the middle of the crowded foyer, staring at her. He drained the remainder of his sparkling wine, his heart beating faster.

He inhaled deeply through his nose and began walking toward her, cutting across the crowd. He bumped into a woman his mother's age. She glared at him with indignant eyes.

"Pardon me, *sir*," said the woman's husband, scowling above a set of silver mutton-chop whiskers.

"Pardon me, sir," said Peter, stopping and bowing.

Before the man could say another word, Peter continued, taking more care to not step into anyone else, coming closer to the wall, closer to Sarah.

General Hesiger saw Peter before his daughter did, stopping him in his tracks with a severe gaze, peering down his long nose.

"Good evening, General," said Peter.

"Good evening," said General Hesiger, inverting Peter's smile with a frown of his own.

"It is a lovely evening, now that the rain has gone," said Peter.

"Say that again," said the general, raising his bearded chin.

"I said it is a lovely evening," said Peter, speaking louder. He felt the moisture growing on his temples.

General Hesiger nodded. He glanced over Peter's shoulder as if looking for another person with whom to speak.

"My father says you will be taking command in Khyderbad, sir."

"Yes," said General Hesiger, still looking past Peter.

"Congratulations, sir, on the command."

"Thank you."

"My uncle—well, he is technically my father's cousin—Sir Bartimus Freer is Lord Governor in Khyderbad. I presume you might work together?"

"If he is your father's cousin, then he is your second cousin, not your uncle," said General Hesiger.

"Yes, sir, it is only that we call him uncle—"

"If you will excuse me," said General Hesiger, cutting him off and stepping past him.

Peter again stood alone, feet away from Sarah.

"Miss Hesiger," he said.

She turned, seeing him.

He stepped closer, his eyes wide and expectant.

"I presume you know Mr. Barrington of the City?" she said.

"How do you do, sir?" said Peter.

"Elbridge Barrington," said the man, shaking Peter's hand, "You are?"

"Peter Harmon, sir."

"Are you a relation of the Duke of Haden?"

"Yes, sir, he is my uncle."

The man nodded.

"Which would make you?"

"I am the son of Lord George Harmon."

"Ah, yes, I now recall that he has a son."

"Two sons, actually, sir. I have a brother—"

"I disagree with your father's politics, of course," said Mr. Barrington, "as I am a Liberty and Commerce man myself."

"Mr. Hammerstone and Mr. Browne are patriotic Anglians," said Peter, referring to the opposition party leaders, both of whom his father routinely lampooned in his papers.

"Does your father know you think that?"

"Let us hope not," said Peter, smiling.

Mr. Barrington did not smile.

Sarah's eyes searched the crowd as the two men spoke.

"Are you in business in the City?" asked Peter.

"I am."

"And what kind of business—"

A trumpet sounded. All in the cavernous marble room turned toward the staircase, the herald standing expectantly at the base of the stairs.

The doors opened at the top of the landing. The crowd waited in silence, all eyes looking up. With a broad, puffed-out chest, the herald boomed, "Her

Imperial Majesty, Queen of Anglia, Empress of Hindea and the Imperium, Her Royal Highness . . ."

All eyes watched as the royal titles rolled on, and the widowed Queen Empress descended the stairwell. An elderly duke in uniform escorted her, her gloved hand upon his arm.

Peter watched Sarah as she watched the Queen. He had yet to tell her the news.

When the Queen reached the base of the stairs, the doors to the ballroom opened.

"Shall we?" asked Peter, offering his arm.

Sarah took it.

They walked behind her parents, Sarah keeping an inch or two more than was socially necessary between her and Peter. They took their place on the dance floor.

The orchestra struck up a Spatanian waltz, and they began to follow the movements, dancing in time with the others. Peter, who had cared nothing for dancing before, had taken lessons at Sarah's request. He danced with high concentration now, his steps and timing correct, but with a hunched stiffness as he kept looking down at his feet. The sweat continued to accumulate on his temples.

Then the music changed, slowing. Couples around them stepped closer together. Sarah's face looked stunning and bright, her skin flawless in the warm light of the chandeliers.

"I have been meaning to tell you something," said Peter.

"Is it something that you have not already told me in your daily letters?"

Peter winced, the strangeness of the response registering in his eyes. "Yes, there is something else, something I have waited to tell you in person." He looked at her gloved hand in his own.

"And what is that?" she said, her hand stiffening. They stepped to the side of the dance floor.

"Khyderbad."

"What of it?"

"My father forbids me to go."

"Oh?"

"Yes."

"Then where will you go?"

"He tells me—" He paused. "He tells me I must go with Stanwich."

"Who is Stanwick?"

Peter looked at her with surprise, stopping dancing entirely.

"Stan*wich*. He is an explorer. I know I have mentioned him."

"An explorer of what?"

"Stanwich? You know I am referring to Harold Milton Stanwich, yes? He discovered the Central Crater of Omakhosi."

Sarah's face remained blank.

"The Feathermen Highlands?" tried Peter again.

"Is that where you are going?"

"No, that is what Stanwich discovered in the Central Crater several years ago."

Sarah's eyes flashed recognition. "Ah, he is the man who made you late for our luncheon at your aunt's."

"Yes," said Peter nodding.

"So, you will go with him to where?"

"To explore the Sand Sea."

"What is the Sand Sea?"

"A desert."

"Why would you go there?"

"According to my father, I will be reporting for the *Illustrated Telegraph*."

"I would like to have some punch," said Sarah.

Peter looked up toward the wall, seeing a silver bowl of punch large enough to hold a child's bath.

"Of course," he said.

They walked to it, and each accepted a crystal cup from the server.

"I have not accepted his proposal," Peter continued. "I am inclined to defy him."

"Oh?" said Sarah, raising an eyebrow as she sipped her punch. "Have you ever done that before?"

"Done what? Defied my father?"

Sarah nodded.

"Of course I have," said Peter, blushing with embarrassment.

"When was that?"

Peter looked at her lips and nose. They were very well shaped.

"There have been many times," he said.

Sarah smiled, but not kindly.

"And I think I shall defy him again," continued Peter. "To speak the truth, the idea of being away from you for six months is agony to me."

"Six months? Father says we will be in Khyderbad for a year."

"A year?" Peter felt his stomach twist.

Sarah nodded. "He says it will require at least that long to clean up the messes of his predecessor."

"And will you and your mother stay there for the entire year?"

"Would you have us abandon him?"

"No, of course not," said Peter drinking down his punch, tasting the alcohol, feeling unsteady.

"Sarah," said Peter, "If you ask it of me, I will defy him, and I will come to Khyderbad. We will be together."

"Pardon me," said a voice, the accent foreign.

Peter turned to see a line of bright white teeth set in olive skin. The man stood as tall as Peter, dark-haired and lean, his tunic green with the markings of the Spatanian cavalry.

"How do you do?" asked Peter.

The man did not look at him but rather at Sarah.

"May I have this dance?" he asked.

Peter's heart lurched.

"Yes," said Sarah, smiling far more brightly than she had smiled at Peter all night.

As they walked away from him, Peter saw two young women, both nearly his age. Both watched Sarah and the Spatanian officer with the white teeth.

"Pardon me," said Peter. "Who is that?"

They looked at him, disliking the scowl on his face.

"Miss Sarah Hesiger," said one.

"Not her," he said. "Who is the Spatanian?"

"Captain Ernesto Ruggiero," said one of the young women.

"He is with the embassy," said the other.

The name galloped across Peter's mind as his eyes narrowed. *Ruggiero. Ruggiero. Ruggiero.*

"Peter Harmon," said a voice behind him.

Peter turned.

Harold Milton Stanwich stood before him. The young women behind him said something else, but he was no longer listening.

"Mr. Stanwich," said Peter, fighting the urge to turn back around to see Sarah dancing with the Spatanian.

"Pardon me, sir," said the female voice, the one who had identified Ruggiero for Peter.

"Are you?"

Peter saw her blush.

"Are you Mr. Harold Milton Stanwich?"

"Yes," said Stanwich, smiling with his big teeth.

"We have read about you in the papers." They smiled back at Stanwich, their cheeks red beneath their wide eyes.

"I am honored," said Stanwich, bowing. "You must excuse us," he said, taking Peter by the elbow and leading him to a more sparsely occupied spot along the wall.

"How may I help you, Mr. Stanwich?" said Peter.

Stanwich tilted his head, hearing the edge in Peter's voice. "I come only to tell you that our expedition does not need any who do not wish to come. The Sand Sea is no place for the reluctant."

"Very well," said Peter, looking back out over his shoulder, out toward the dance floor. Sarah's head was tilted back, laughing, her hand in the Spatanian's. His stomach twisted harder. He met Stanwich's eyes again, channeling his envy into anger.

"Then I shall make it easy for you, Mr. Stanwich. I do not now, nor have I ever intended to go with you upon your expedition. If your game here is to bring a rich man's son, you should find another."

Stanwich took a step back, the hint of a smile hanging on his face.

Peter's voice rose as he leaned forward, his head towering over the explorer. "Do you not believe I can do other than what my father wishes? Then you are in for a surprise. As is he!"

"As is whom?" asked a voice.

Peter froze.

Lord Harmon stood erect with his shoulders held back, the light glinting off of the glass of his gold-rimmed monocle. His eyes stared into the face of his son, hard as steel.

Peter paused, speechless, looking like a boy who had just been caught stealing sweets from the pantry.

"To my eye," said Lord Harmon, "it looked as if you were speaking disrespectfully to our friend Mr. Stanwich."

"I told him," said Peter, breathing hard. "I told him that I am not going to the Sand Sea."

"Is that so? Where will you go, then?"

Peter turned without answering, walking swiftly away from them, his heart thundering.

"Ladies and gentlemen!" cried the herald, barring the door to the foyer and the front entrance. "The Prime Minister!"

The Prime Minister stepped forward, and the crowd quieted. "Good evening. It is my distinct privilege to announce that the awaited moment approaches." He looked down to his right as a pair of palace servants wheeled in a machine, trailing a wire. "In seven minutes, Her Majesty, the Queen, will send Anglia's transmission to Bay Port City. This will be the first message sent across the new Trans-Titanic cable, connecting our islands to the New Anglian Republic as never before . . ."

The crowd, now well lubricated with wine, sparkling and otherwise, applauded loudly. Those near the door closed in around the telegraph machine, blocking Peter's exit. He wheeled and walked across the dance floor, his head down to avoid eye contact with Sarah or her Spatanian.

He reached the far door that led to the next room, a cavernous portrait gallery where older guests, tiring of the noise and energy of the ballroom, sat on couches and upholstered chairs, discussing the unpleasant pace of the present age, of which the telegraph machine in the adjacent room was a glaring example.

Peter continued walking with his head down.

"They are *all* in a hurry these days," said a woman's voice. "Everyone is off to make their fortune. Even the girls are in a rush."

Peter glanced at her, recognizing her as a countess in possession of strong opinions. He walked faster, avoiding her gaze, no doubt affirming the countess's view of young Anglians in a hurry.

He reached the end of the long room and saw a closed door at the end of the gallery. To his surprise and relief, it stood unattended. The gallery grew less occupied the farther he walked, as the elderly guests realized they should not miss the Prime Minister's remarks.

Peter reached the door and turned the handle. It opened into a library, dimly lit. A fire crackled in an enormous fireplace, the mantle of which was nearly as tall as he was. Above it, in the empty room, he saw a familiar face.

He stopped and exhaled, his mind still spinning, and his heart still pounding.

He looked up into the face. Like the painting in the lobby of the *Illustrated Telegraph*, it showed General John Fitzroy Harmon, First Duke of Haden, at life-size. Though in this picture, his face was different, older than the man's on the battlefield, looking with mild deference at his monarch, the King of Anglia, seated upon a throne. The duke stood amongst a group of others, but he stood out amongst them, first of his peers, a half-smile upon his face. He looked like a man that had discovered life's higher secrets—one that had made it to the far side of the mountain, enduring not only the battles, but the triumphs and fame that followed.

Peter stood, a destabilizing, almost nauseated feeling moving across his gut. He turned away from the painting, wanting to get away from the duke, as if his eyes accused him of some unnamed crime.

Peter walked across the library. At the other end of the room was another closed door. He walked toward it, fleeing the eyes of John Harmon, fleeing his father and Stanwich, fleeing Sarah and her Spatanian. He pushed the door open. A man in a bright yellow tunic embraced a woman in a violet gown, his face nearly against hers. His arms were around her, and her arms were around him.

Before Peter could speak, both looked at him. His eyes widened, and his cheeks blushed cherry red. He knew the man's face, the face above the bright yellow tunic. The head was balding, and a shadow of a beard hung about his face. He was shorter than Peter and a great deal stockier, with a chest like a bulldog.

"Good evening," said the man, smiling like a buccaneer.

The woman only stared, looking at her son from above the white fur shawl, and her triple strand of pearls, her sapphire eyes first indignant, then amused, as if Peter had just said something terribly funny. Peter stood in stunned indecision. He had, of course, heard the rumors, but he had always ignored them. They were rumors no longer, for his mother stood before him, in the arms of Colonel Willem Spinner of the Gengali Lancers.

"Peter, darling, you know your father's and my dear friend, Colonel Spinner, yes?" said Lady Harmon, her eyes twinkling.

"Yes. How are you, sir?" said Peter.

"Well, quite well," said Colonel Spinner.

"Are you—on leave, sir?"

"From Hindea, yes."

"You see, Peter," said Lady Harmon, "the colonel was just telling me something quite troubling, something about his time in Hindea."

"I see," said Peter, not knowing what to do other than go along with the lie.

"As we have been friends for so many years—as we have seen so many of life's journeys together, I am consoling him."

Peter gaped, marveling at his mother's stark boldness.

"Now, if you don't mind," said Lady Harmon, "the colonel has not finished telling me his story, and I must hear it all out if I am to be able to help him work through the matter."

"Yes, certainly," said Peter, turning to leave.

"And Peter," said his mother. "As this is both an important and private matter, I trust you will use discretion?"

Peter nodded.

"It would be most unfortunate if someone were to have the wrong impression of our friendship. There are so many gossips and liars about, yes?"

"Yes," said Peter.

His heart beat violently as if he had just run the length of the palace. His face was still flushed red as he left the library for the gallery. *Have they no shame? Do they think I am still a little child, that I cannot see what is before my own face?* He shook his head, indignant that it was he who felt humiliated, not they—they that had just been caught embracing in the library. Peter had long known that his mother cared about her parties and country weekends with her friends more than her children, including during the years when her children were still young and very much wished to see and know their mother.

As if compelled, Peter looked up again at the face of General John Fitzroy Harmon. The eyes seemed to follow him, mockingly, as he walked onward, back into the gallery, which was now nearly empty. From the ballroom, he could hear the people, the ruling class of Anglia, shouting out the countdown to the sending of the telegraph message across the sea, allowing the east to speak directly with the west, marking the beginning of the new year, 1879.

"Five! Four! Three!"

Peter slowed his pace.

A wave of bitter resolve rose inside of him, a resolve to flee, growing with each step. He reached the end of the gallery. He stepped back through the open door into the ballroom after the cheering subsided.

Sarah stood before him, in the midst of the crowd, still arm in arm with Ernesto Ruggiero in his green tunic, her eyes locked upon his, their faces close together. He saw his father speaking with the Prime Minister, fixated upon whatever they were discussing, surely a matter of paramount public importance.

"Fool," said Peter under his breath, feeling that for perhaps the first time in his life, he knew something that could humiliate his father.

"Fool," he said again, shaking his head more violently, this time speaking to himself.

He saw Stanwich standing at the center of a crescent-shaped crowd. The explorer spoke as the others all listened. He gestured with an empty wine flute. The crowd laughed. Stanwich smiled his big, toothy smile. Peter walked directly at him, into the crescent. None in the group seemed to notice his arrival.

"Mr. Stanwich!" he said, stepping forward, breathing heavily, and interrupting with an awkward loudness. He stood face-to-face with the explorer, all in the crowd now looking at him with baffled frowns.

"Mr. Harmon," said Stanwich, stiffly.

"I'll go!" said Peter, nearly shouting.

"Go where, sir?"

"With you!"

"To the Sand Sea?"

Stanwich smiled, already knowing the answer to his question.

Peter stepped away, through the marble foyer, past the Queen's guardsmen and out into the cold dark night, into the first hours of 1879.

CHAPTER 15
Two Escapes

Bay Port City
New Anglian Republic
Three Gods Day, December 31, 1878

Mrs. Smith remained with the rented carriage on the avenue, watching Hannah through the falling snow. She would have walked her to the doors, but the outer barrier permitted none but the four hundred guests beyond it, and the name "Matilda Smith" did not appear on the list. Brass stanchion posts and velvet ropes separated the sidewalk from the steps to the Hall of the Republic, keeping the gawking crowd in control as the rich and famous of Bay Port City passed by them. Some of the guests smiled at the admirers, but most rushed from their carriages to the checkpoint without so much as a nod. A line of Bay Port City police officers manned the velvet ropes, wearing tall, blue helmets and heavy overcoats, watching with stern eyes for any citizens that did not belong.

None challenged Hannah Huntington, but half of a dozen blue helmets turned to watch her walk up the wide stone stairs. Under their gaze, she approached the towering white columns of the Hall. The sounds of an orchestra and a vast rectangle of light beckoned to her from the open doors.

Men in black top hats and evening attire ascended the steps at the same time, their bejeweled women glittering on their arms. Most looked at Hannah's face, flushed against the cold, at the high cheekbones and strong jaw, at the thick blonde hair, pulled tight and piled atop her head. Some traced the curves of her tall, athletic body as she took the stairs with long, steady strides. Others noted the quality of her ballgown beneath her fitted, fur-lined coat. But all saw that she was the only woman approaching the Hall of the Republic unescorted by a man.

Feeling the gazes around her, Hannah looked up at the old and famous marble columns, both excited and frightened by her plan, the plan she had told no one, not even Mrs. Smith, who would have detained her until she'd changed her mind.

An errant voice pierced the air behind her, in the direction of the broad avenue, on the far side of the lined-up carriages.

"Thieves!"

Hannah slowed her ascent and turned back to see.

"You are all thieves!"

A woman in a ratty shawl shouted through the snow, waving her fist in the air. "Shame on you! Shame on those who feast while others starve and on the day of the Three Gods no less!"

A knot twisted in Hannah's stomach, her mind's eye suddenly back to Port Calderon, hearing the crash as the bullets struck the chandelier and smelling the tearoom carpet just beneath her nose. She remembered the words she heard through the windows, "Come out, Huntington, you bastard! Come out, you son of a whore!"

A pair of policemen walked across the avenue, toward the shouting woman, aiming to silence her. Hannah glanced toward the carriages where Mrs. Smith still waited. No, Mrs. Smith would be fine. She was more like those on the far side of the police line than those within it. Hannah turned and walked faster toward the doors and the growing sound of the music.

She passed beneath the enormous New Anglian flag hanging between the columns. The flag's sun, rising from the green against the open blue sky, was meant to convey the hope of New Anglia, that the future belonged not to the empires of the old continent, but to the Republic of the new. Hannah glanced up at the flag, feeling a defiant hope of her own. She was about to spurn her mother, and there was nothing she could do to stop her. Mrs. Sarah Gunderia Huntington and the forces of convention for which she so stridently stood would be aghast.

So be it.

Hannah stopped abruptly at the doors, coming face-to-face with a tall, severe-looking man in a uniform dripping with golden braid. He looked at her with confused eyes, searching for her escort. He cleared his throat into his fist.

"Your name, Madam?"

Hannah's chin jutted forward as she looked him in the eyes.

"I am Hannah Huntington."

The man ran his finger along the list he held in his white-gloved hands.

"Of Calderon state?"

"Yes."

The man still stood before her, barring her way.

"I am here to meet my parents, Mr. and Mrs. Samuel X. Huntington."

The man's face relaxed.

"Should I summon them for you, Madam?"

"That will not be necessary," said Hannah, smiling widely enough to dimple her cheeks.

The man nodded, his own cheeks reddening as he stepped back.

"Enjoy the ball, madam."

Hannah walked through the doors.

The warmth of the Hall embraced her like a blanket. Another uniformed man stepped forward to take her coat. Hannah relinquished it, revealing the full beauty of her cream-colored gown. She looked up as she did so, toward the cavernous ceiling, feeling a moment of awe. Above her, ten thousand crystals sparkled, dangling from a dozen chandeliers, each as large as a four-horse city coach.

A line of couples waited ahead of her, chatting with each other in hushed tones, preparing for their brief moment on display before the pinnacle of New Anglian society. The men had all removed their top hats. Like Hannah, the women had all piled their hair—whether black, brown, blonde, or auburn—fashionably upon their heads, each secured by unseen clips and pins, the result of hours of assistance from their ladies' maids. Many wore little glittering tiaras, a testament to their towering wealth, looking more like duchesses of the old world than merchants' wives of the new, their jewels flashing in the soft gaslight.

Ahead, a silver-haired Master of Ceremonies announced each couple as they stood before him. As he said their names, each couple bowed, walked across the open marble floor, and then took their place with the growing crowd on the far side of the room. The man's mouth was as big as his voice, thundering out each pair of names from beneath a bushy mustache that connected to a pair of mutton-chop whiskers.

Hannah's heart raced as the line in front of her shortened. She could still leave the line before the moment arrived. She could walk back now to the man with the gold-braid uniform and ask him to summon her father.

Two by two, the Master of Ceremonies continued his work, speaking loudest when he called out a famous name. He waited several moments after each announcement, allowing each couple its moment of glory, as the leading citizens of the Republic acknowledged their arrival.

Then only one couple stood between Hannah and the mutton-chopped announcer. She looked over the last couple's shoulders, fighting the urge to hunch her own or even turn around. She saw the Master of Ceremonies holding a list that looked like a scroll, the list of the four hundred. Who had decided who appeared on the list? Hannah could not say.

Then she stepped forward, feeling nearly dizzy as dozens of strangers' eyes rested upon her. Her arms and upper chest lay bare above the cream-colored gown. Her curled hair shimmered like gold in the gaslight, a diamond pendant glittering at her throat. She felt heat on her cheeks and her chest, knowing that her skin was flushing under the undivided attention of so many eyes.

Hundreds of faces now stared at her, for a moment dazzled into silence by the Dardennes dress, the beauty of the woman wearing it, and the fact that she stood *alone*.

The Master of Ceremonies hesitated, his eyes darting. Was he to announce only Hannah's name and not also that of a gentleman escorting her? Was there a father? A brother? No one?

The crowd waited, staring at Hannah in silence.

Then the exigency of the situation overcame the man with the mutton-chops. He raised his chin and roared, "Miss Hannah Huntington of Calderon!"

Hannah smiled broadly as her name echoed off the marble, her teeth bright and radiant, the attention of the room upon her and her alone. She walked forward with slow, measured steps, her heels clicking on the floor.

She came closer to the broad line of black coats and bright ballgowns, making eye contact with the faces above them. Though she did not know them, they looked as if they perhaps knew her, or at least the name they had just heard.

Ever since the completion of the Transcontinental, few from Admiral's Hill or similar neighborhoods in Port Calderon, Port Southern, Laketown, or the lesser cities across the land would fail to know the name *Huntington*—one of the two names behind the longest railroad in the Republic. To them, the name invoked progress, Calderon, the far west, and, most importantly, a great deal of money.

Despite the familiarity in their glances, however, none extended Hannah a word of greeting now. She walked along the line, trailing whispers as she passed. She kept her smile frozen in place, seeking the refuge of even a single familiar face. She found none.

She walked deeper into the foyer toward the doors of the ballroom ahead, her anxiety growing. Perhaps she had been foolish to be so bold?

"Hannah."

She turned around.

"Father!" the word burst out of her. "Thank the Three Gods."

"You are radiant," said Samuel X. Huntington. His teeth flashed beneath a sharp mustache. He had parted and pomaded his golden hair for the occasion, in the current style of Bay Port City.

He did not stand alone.

Hannah nearly winced as her eyes met her mother's.

Sarah Gunderia Huntington stared at her daughter, unsmiling above a Dardennes gown of her own.

"Your mother was correct about the Dardennes dresses," said Sam Huntington, ignoring the face-off between his wife and youngest daughter. "On you and your mother, they are worth the price."

Hannah smiled.

"What in the Three Gods' name was that?" asked Mrs. Huntington, stepping closer.

"What?" asked Hannah, taking a half step back.

"Where is the Sterling boy?"

Hannah inhaled. "Not here."

"Where is Jack Caldwell?"

"I don't know."

"Were you not dining at the Sterling Mansion, on *Admiral's Hill?*"

"I was."

"Then how is it that you are here, and Sherman Sterling is not?"

"I left."

"You left where?" asked Mrs. Huntington.

"His home. On *Admiral's Hill.*" Hannah said the last words with contempt.

"Why?"

"Because I did not wish to be there."

Mrs. Huntington stared, her eyes demanding more.

Hannah kept silent, staring back.

"What does that mean?" asked Mrs. Huntington, stepping closer again.

"I did not care to stay any longer," said Hannah.

"Why?"

"Because they are horrid."

"Horrid?" asked Sarah Huntington, looking past Hannah at the crowd around them. She caught a pair of familiar eyes and smiled sweetly.

Then her gaze returned to Hannah, cold and blue, as her voice descended to a vicious whisper. "That is hardly a thing to say, daughter, especially here. You should take greater care with your words."

"His father is the vainest man I have ever met," said Hannah.

Knowing George Sterling, Samuel Huntington smirked.

Knowing only that the Sterlings owned three banks and a home on Admiral's Hill, Sarah Huntington scowled.

"He talks without end," said Hannah. "And then the mother told me she would welcome my marriage to her son."

Sarah Huntington winced. "And yet you left them? Because the father talks too much and because the mother suggested a perfectly sensible match?"

"Yes."

"You are a foolish girl."

It was Hannah's turn to wince.

"You have embarrassed your family," said her mother.

"That was not my intent, I—"

Mrs. Huntington cut her off, "No one sees your intent, only your actions."

Hannah swallowed.

Sarah Huntington continued, "You could have requested your father to escort you. You could have entered like all of the other young women your age. Instead, you have pulled this, this—" Sarah Huntington stuttered as her eyes narrowed.

"This stunt."

Hannah's cheeks flushed a deeper shade of red.

"You have now likely ruined your chances here," said her mother, her face now pale with cold, Gerdic fury. "And not only with the Sterlings. What do you think the others are whispering behind you? Oh yes, they're whispering about *you*."

Hannah glanced around her, wondering if it was true.

But her mother was not finished. "What did you tell the Sterlings when you left early?"

"I told them I was ill."

"You do not look ill to me," said Mrs. Huntington.

A murmur of excitement rose behind them.

The three Huntingtons glanced toward the entrance with the rest of the crowd.

A dozen policemen walked in through the door, standing at full attention with serious, self-important looks upon their faces.

"Ladies and gentlemen!" shouted the Master of Ceremonies, barking out the words between his mutton-chops. A hushed silence followed.

The policemen stiffened further.

"May I have your eyes and your ears! It is our privilege on this Three Gods Day to welcome the President and the First Lady of the Republic!"

Applause rippled across the Hall.

Mrs. Huntington stepped forward, angling for a better look. Unlike her husband, she had yet to meet the President. A woman next to her spoke excitedly into her ear. Sarah Huntington nodded.

"Hannah," said her father, seeing his wife's distraction. "Walk with me."

He put his hand on Hannah's elbow, leading her deeper into the crowd and away from the applause.

"What is it?" said Hannah, still reeling from her mother's tongue-lashing.

"This way."

"Where are we walking?"

Samuel X. Huntington acted as if he had not heard her, weaving Hannah through black coats and bright ball gowns, nodding to several older men that Hannah did not know. Several young men stared as they passed, seemingly more interested in Hannah than in the President of the Republic.

They walked onward, passing an enormous ice sculpture garnished with concentric circles of shelled shrimp. Hannah frowned, thinking of the shrimp she had eaten several hours earlier while George Sterling droned on about his banks. They continued in silence until they reached an open area of the ballroom beyond the earshot of the crowd.

"What did Mrs. Smith tell you?" asked Sam Huntington, still walking.

"That I must come here to see you," said Hannah.

Samuel Huntington nodded. "She is reliable."

"I did not want to come."

"It is important that you did."

"Mother seems to think it is all a waste."

Sam Huntington waved his hand in dismissal. "Your stunt is not important."

They stopped at the far wall, near a broad window, the segmented glass panes reaching up three times taller than either of them. They stood side by side, overlooking the gas lamps above the sidewalks, and the line of carriages on the snow-covered avenue below. Sam Huntington stepped to the edge of the massive blue drapes held back by a golden cord, blocking him from the eyes of the crowd.

"Step closer."

Hannah obeyed.

"Do you know why I hired her?"

"Mrs. Smith?"

Samuel X. Huntington nodded.

"To keep me safe."

"Has she?"

Hannah nodded. "I am here."

Samuel Huntington stepped closer to his daughter. "Mrs. Smith is a war nurse, raised in the wild deserts, tested under hardship."

"And she is not a lady's maid," said Hannah.

Samuel Huntington shook his head in agreement, his face suddenly serious. "No, she is not."

He glanced over Hannah's bare shoulder, toward the crowd, making sure that no one else could hear him. "Do you still want to go?"

Hannah's heart beat faster.

"Go where?"

"You know where."

"With Stanwich?"

Sam Huntington nodded.

"Yes," said Hannah.

"The Sand Sea is no place for a soft man," said Sam Huntington, "much less a woman."

Hannah's skin began to tingle with adrenaline. "You know I am not like the others. I am not like Carolyn and mother."

"No, you are like me."

Hannah nodded, her blue eyes bright and full.

"But you are not me. You are a young woman. You attract attention here. You will attract far more attention there."

He gestured with his chin toward the young men across the room, standing near the ice sculpture.

Hannah turned to look. Several of the young men looked back at her over their sparkling wine flutes.

"Men look at you, and I will not be there to protect you."

"I understand."

"Do you? There are dangers from which even Mrs. Smith cannot keep you safe."

"I will be careful."

"Being announced alone here was foolish—a childish rebellion."

"I do not want this life," said Hannah, her eyes sweeping across the ballroom.

"No, you do not," said Sam Huntington.

"If I wanted it, I would not rebel."

"Perhaps."

"What would you have me do?" asked Hannah.

"I would have you do whatever she tells you to do."

"Mrs. Smith?"

"Yes. Tell me you will obey her."

"I will," said Hannah, shuffling her feet. "Tell me why you are changing your mind."

"If I were changing my mind, Mrs. Smith would not have accompanied you across the Republic."

Hannah's head tilted. "Do you mean you planned this all along?"

"You are worthier than Jack, Hannah, and the stakes are high. He is reckless, and I do not mean in your way. He is a drunk. The colonel sends him because he is his son and because he must test him if he is ever to make him his successor. But I do not trust the boy."

"Trust him for what?"

"To do what needs to be done."

A fierce pride rose in Hannah's chest. "You mean I am to secure the Beserite?"

"Yes," whispered Sam Huntington. "But do not say that word again until you are far from here. Do not say it in the Veteno. Do not say it on the ship."

"What ship?" asked Hannah.

Sam Huntington pulled a sealed envelope from his breast pocket. "The rest of what I have to say to you is written here."

Hannah took the letter, looking at it uncertainly in her hands as doubt began to creep into her eyes.

"How am I to get there? To Stanwich and the Sand Sea?"

Sam Huntington peered for long silent moments into his daughter's young, beautiful face.

Hannah swallowed heavily, feeling a new nervousness that surprised her.

"You are afraid," said her father.

Hannah did not correct him.

For a long moment, she considered a retreat, nearly conceding that the desert would be too much for her, that she was only a rebellious daughter of a rich man, playacting with her desires. Images flashed across her mind, visions of the life her mother planned for her—a life with someone like Sherman Sterling or Rex Shuler, a life of elegant houses and carriages and boats and balls. *Admiral's Hill.*

"Your fear can stop you," said Sam Huntington. "Or it can set you free. You are right to fear the Sand Sea, and you are right to fear a wasted life. You must decide which of the two you fear more."

Hannah did not answer.

He continued, "I have secured you a stateroom on the Ship of the Republic *Agobasto*. It is the same ship that will carry Jack Caldwell and Sergeant Barnes across the Titanic Ocean to the Veteno, where they will meet Stanwich and the others. It departs in the morning."

"Does he know I am coming?"

"Stanwich? Yes."

"Does Jack?"

"No," said Sam Huntington.

"What will I tell them?"

"You will tell them that you represent Mr. Samuel X. Huntington, a one-third backer of the expedition, just as Jack Caldwell represents the colonel."

Hannah nodded.

"I am not telling you to go," said Sam Huntington. "Indeed, much of me will be relieved if you do not. A father does not readily send his daughter out into the world, much less into the Sand Sea."

Hannah's heart felt like a locomotive in her chest.

Her father continued, "But you must decide. You will either choose the life your mother has set before you, or you will choose this other way, but there is no longer any in-between."

"And if I say no? What will the other part feel, the part of you that is not relieved?"

Samuel X. Huntington looked into her eyes.

"It does not matter," he said. "You will always be my daughter and entitled to my love."

Hannah inhaled several short breaths.

"I choose Stanwich."

"Then follow me."

Jack Caldwell lay on his back in the candlelight with his hands clasped behind his head. The room was warm, and Jack made no effort to cover his nakedness. His long legs stretched out on the bed. He smiled, content from the physical exertion. Katya had untied the knots inside of him, including the ones he did not know were there, relieving pressures he had carried with him for weeks. She lay next to him tightly against his body, running her hands through his chest hair. Her exquisite skin touched his for her entire length, with one of her smooth, shaved legs hooked over his.

"I wish I could save you for myself," said Jack, utterly indifferent to the hour of the night, his ship's departure in the morning seemingly an event belonging to another man living another life.

"You can have me anytime you come to Bay Port City," said Katya. Her sparkling eyes looked more golden than brown in the candlelight, matching the gold of her hair. They were almond-shaped, flanking a tiny nose. Her ears stuck out slightly from her heart-shaped face, in a way that reminded Jack of the ancient fairy tales, the ones with elves and dwarves. Surely Katya was what the legend-makers thought of when they spoke of the elvish women. Her features were all sharp and small. Her body was compact, muscular, and proportional. In every movement, Katya had the grace of a cat—from the way she observed through her intelligent eyes to the way she walked on her little feet. Jack compared Katya to Hannah in his mind and smiled. *Hannah is a clumsy giant next to you, Katya. Let her have Sterling and the Three Gods Ball. I will be here.*

"More wine?" asked Katya, her accent heavy.

Jack nodded. Katya reached over to the carafe on the side of the table and poured Jack a small glass. She brought it up to his lips. It was a sweet dessert wine, stronger than the wines he had been drinking all night.

"Smoke?" asked Katya.

Jack turned and looked at the box of small cigars on the side table.

"Don't you mind?" he asked. "Here in the bed?"

"No. Do not mind." Katya rolled out of bed, stood, and opened the cigar box. Jack's eyes feasted on her naked body, moving from her feet and up her legs. He paused on the firm bubble of her buttocks, sweeping up the hollow of her back to the long, golden hair that hung down loosely past her shoulders. Expertly, Katya punched a hole in one end of the cigar with a small metal rod, blew into it, and lit the other end with a match, striking a flame in the first try. She started the cigar, puffing decisively to get the tobacco leaves fully burning. Jack watched her profile as she did so, seeing that her chest was perfectly proportioned to her body, above a lean stomach that swept down into her equally lean legs. Jack looked down at her bare feet. He liked the shape of her toes, symmetrical, and petite like the rest of her. Her nails were all clean and cut.

Katya looked at Jack, staring at her feet. She smiled, flashing small straight teeth, and climbed back up onto the bed, resting on her knees. She put the lit cigar between Jack's lips.

"I am traveling on the ocean tomorrow," said Jack between puffs of his cigar.

"Where are you going?" asked Katya, again running her fingertips along Jack's chest, down to his stomach and up to his chin.

"East."

"East is into the great ocean," said Katya.

"Across the Titanic, yes," said Jack.

"I am from across the great ocean," said Katya.

"I know. You are Gressian."

"No, not Gressian."

"Not Gressian? Are the rest of the women here Gressian?"

"Most."

"What are you?"

"I am from a small country."

"Which one?"

"It is called Bulbania."

Jack nodded. "On the border of the Sand Sea."

At the words "Sand Sea," Jack saw a flash of something he had not seen before in Katya's eyes, a flash of pain or fear.

"Yes," she said. Her voice had lowered. "That is where my country is."

"That is where I am going," said Jack. "To the Sand Sea."

Katya's eyes changed again, and Jack could feel her body tense against his. She pushed away from him slightly. The room seemed to grow darker, their cocoon of pleasure fracturing around them.

"Did I say something?" asked Jack, ashing his cigar into the empty glass next to the bed. He sat up, feeling suddenly self-conscious in his nakedness.

Katya shook her head.

"When I said 'the Sand Sea,' your face changed. I saw it," said Jack.

Katya leaned away from Jack and shook her head again. He could not see her eyes.

"I left all of that behind. I left a long time ago."

"What did you leave?" asked Jack. He felt the urge to protect Katya and her perfect little body. "Look at me."

She turned her cat's eyes onto his. She seemed smaller, vulnerable. There was a new intensity in her gaze.

"One does not come to this place to talk of the world left behind."

"What about the Sand Sea?"

Katya was silent for long moments. Jack pulled deeply on the cigar and released a mouthful of aromatic smoke.

"The Sand Sea is a bad place, a dangerous place." Katya's face had altered with her voice. The kitten was gone. The face of a weary woman with a furrowed brow looked down at him. She had looked younger than him a moment ago. She suddenly now looked ten years older.

"Why are you saying that? What do you know about the Sand Sea?"

"I am here now—in this place," she said.

Jack looked into her eyes. "Tell me."

"I am here, in this place, because it is better to be here, to be this, than to go to the East . . . to the Great Mountain."

"I do not understand," said Jack. He sat up and pulled the sheet up over himself, concealing his nakedness.

"You would not understand, Westerner."

"Let me try. I leave for the Sand Sea tomorrow morning, on a boat." *The boat, the boat departs early. I am far from my hotel.* "What time is it?" Reality rushed into the room like a torrent.

"I do not know the hour," she said. "Likely, it is half-past two in the morning."

The pleasant mask of the playful kitten returned to Katya's face. Whatever moment had just intruded into the room had departed as quickly as it arrived, like a thief in the night.

"What were you fleeing? What were you fleeing in the East?" asked Jack, trying again.

Katya smiled easily. She crawled onto Jack, straddling his naked body. "One more time before you must leave?" she asked. She brought her lips close to Jack's, her playful young face returning, and her cat's eyes again drawing him in. He wrapped his arms around her as she reached one of her hands down beneath her.

A scream ripped through the air. Katya flinched, jerking her head up and her hand as well, looking over her shoulder. It was a woman's scream.

"Oh no," she said.

"What is it?" asked Jack, lurching out of bed.

"Put on your clothes," said Katya. "Quickly!"

Another scream sounded down the hall. Jack grabbed his undergarments from the chair and stepped into them. In his haste, he nearly tripped, catching his heel in the fabric. The sounds of thunderous footsteps rolled down the hallway, followed by the crash of a door being thrown open against the wall. A man's voice pleaded—a growl. Something was smashed. Jack's eyes widened, and he fumbled with his pants. His heart pounded. Katya grabbed his shirt and helped him slide his arms into the sleeves. The door to their room flew open. Aaron Fish stood in the doorway; he was shoeless, coatless, and missing his vest, wearing a pair of pants and an unbuttoned shirt.

"Caldwell, come with me," his voice was urgent, his eyes wide.

More violent crashing sounds came from down the hall.

"Caldwell, now!"

Jack followed Fish out into the hall, leaving the rest of his things. Fish ran to an open door from which the crashing sounds were coming. Jack turned to look into the room. The chair lay smashed in jagged wooden pieces. The bulbous body of a lamp had been shattered like a thrown water jug with bits of ceramic and glass covering the ground in shards. A half-naked woman cowered in the corner. It was the small orange-haired one, the only other one Jack could remember well from the lineup.

Bohrus, the Gressian bear, held Lucas Alexander in the air, bleeding, naked, and still conscious. Lucas was soft in his middle section, and the side of his stomach hung down.

"No," said Lucas.

Gripping one leg and one shoulder, the Gressian hurled Lucas across the room into the plastered wall. Lucas flew through the air as easily as a doll hurled by a toddler. But Lucas was not a doll. His heavy body smashed into the plaster, cracking it. He fell to the ground with a sickening crunch. Bohrus took no notice of Aaron Fish and Jack Caldwell in the hallway. Nor was he done punishing Lucas. He lumbered over to Lucas, and Lucas weakly adjusted himself, covering his neck with one of his hands.

"No, please," he said. The Gressian stood over him.

"Enough," said Jack, his voice like thunder. The Gressian stopped and looked at him. He turned back to Lucas and kicked him in the side with his heavy black boots. Lucas shrieked in pain.

"Oh! Oh!"

Jack rushed forward. The Gressian turned to face him. Jack was a tall man, the tallest man in most rooms. Bohrus, the Gressian, was a full head taller and twice as wide. Jack slammed his fist into the Gressian's jaw, punching with his hips and letting the power come from his legs. His punch landed on the man's beard, and the Gressian staggered a step backward.

But it was only a step. The giant threw a fist forward from his right hand, which Jack blocked. The force of the Gressian's blow threw Jack backward, and the arm that had blocked the punch felt as if he had just taken a full swing from a wooden club. The Gressian swung from his left. Jack ducked, the pain in his arm calling out to him through his adrenaline.

The Gressian's massive arm whiffed the air above Jack's head. The Gressian stepped forward, swinging again. Jack dodged backward and to his left side. The years of boxing with Diego had created instincts in him that he drew upon without thinking. The Gressian launched another vicious blow. Jack evaded it again, moving down and to his right. Jack did not see the wall behind him. For years, he and Diego had boxed out in the driveway on the gravel, shirtless and under the sun. There was no such space here.

The Gressian charged. Jack tried to back away but instead hit the plaster of the wall behind him. He followed the only option available to him. He crouched beneath the Gressian's attack and tried to roll to the side. The Gressian landed on top of him with his enormous mass, heavy as a draft horse. Beneath the suffocating weight, Jack panicked. He hated small spaces and had a deep fear of not being able to breathe.

"Three Gods, help me, Fish!"

Aaron Fish attacked the Gressian like a terrier.

The Gressian covered Jack with all of his weight, bringing his arms down to try to strangle him by his throat. Jack had jammed his hands up in between the Gressian's arms and his neck, but even still, he could feel the air and the life being squeezed out of him. Jack could smell nothing but the foul sourness of the Gressian's breath and the sulfuric stink of his body odor, blasting into Jack's face from his huge hairy armpits.

Fish kicked the Gressian with his bare feet. It was as useless as a little girl kicking a stone. The Gressian did not flinch.

"Jackson! Beardsley!" shouted Fish. "By the Three Gods, get in here! Damn you, hurry!"

"Get off of him, Bohrus! He is a customer!" shouted Katya. "Help me, Anika!" she cried.

The girl with the red hair, the girl that Lucas Alexander had been with in the room, shook her head, still cowering in her corner. Katya looked at Lucas

Alexander. He was still lying on the floor, writhing in pain from Bohrus's hammer blows from his fists and the bone-breaking kicks from his heavy boots.

The half-open door exploded as it was thrown against the wall behind it. Jurious Jackson flew into the room. Pantless and shoeless, he wore only his shirt-sleeves. His legs were long and tan, having spent the last several months swimming in the ocean of warmer climates. Tom Beardsley appeared directly behind him with his fists in the air, wearing only his underwear, revealing long pale legs and a thin hairy chest.

Jurious surveyed the situation in a glance, rushed at Bohrus, and dove onto his back. "Off of him, you bastard!" he shouted. He aimed a fist at the Gressian's ear and punched it as hard as he could.

The Gressian growled in pain and loosened his grip on Jack Caldwell's throat. Jurious hit him again in the same ear. The Gressian released Jack with an arm and swung at Jurious. It was a backhanded swing. Jurious blocked it with his two free arms. Tom Beardsley threw a punch at the Gressian's head, hitting the back of the giant man's skull. His fist connected with the massive cranium with an audible crunch, but the crunch came from Beardsley's hand, not Bohrus's head. Beardsley bent over his wounded hand, crying out from the pain.

The Gressian released Jack beneath him and launched another wild blow in the direction of Jurious Jackson. This time Bohrus rose up and brought more leverage behind the sweeping movement of his arm. The arm caught Jurious and knocked him reeling into the middle of the room. On his way down to the floor, Jurious stumbled into Tom Beardsley, knocking them both over. The Gressian stood up. Jack gasped for air, still crumpled on the ground. Only three stood now: fully clothed Bohrus, still in his heavy boots, Aaron Fish, wearing only a pair of pants, and Katya, utterly naked.

"Cease." It was a woman's voice.

The Gressian stopped.

Madame Nadia stepped into the room, her eyes aflame. She stood in the doorway, looking down at the carnage strewn across the floor: the broken lamp, the shattered glass and ceramic, the beaten bodies of her customers, and one of her finest courtesans still cowering in the corner. In a glance, she could see all that had happened, recreating with near-perfect accuracy the history of the last several minutes in her mind. And as she suspected—as she had suspected the moment the man with the red beard walked into her establishment—it had all begun with Lucas Alexander.

She looked down at him. His soft body, in her view, far too soft and flabby for a young man to ever have, was bloodied and crumpled on the floor. He was naked, covering himself in the opposite corner of Anika, her customers' favorite redhead, week after week, and month after month. Madame Nadia paid her better than any of her other girls, better even than Katya.

"What happened here?" asked Madame Nadia. Bohrus stared down at Lucas Alexander with cold hard eyes.

"Anika?" she asked.

Anika merely shook her head, saying nothing.

"Was it Lucas Alexander?"

Anika stopped shaking her head from side to side and nodded up and down several times, making herself very clearly understood.

"He did it again?"

"Yes," Anika's voice was always soft and low. Now it was barely a whisper.

Madame Nadia shook her head in the disgust of self-reproach.

"Know this, Mr. Alexander," said Madame Nadia, her voice colder than the windswept alley outside, "but for your friends coming to your aid—aid which you in no way deserve—I would have let Bohrus beat you far worse than he did. Indeed, I may have let him make you into an accident. We are nearly on a canal on the backside of this building. People disappear in this city, you know. People fall into the canals. Some slip on the ice."

Jack looked up at Madame Nadia and her intense dark eyes. He could not tell whether she was exaggerating for effect or whether she might actually order one of them murdered. He looked up at Bohrus. He had a murderer's eyes, and Jack did not much like Gressians to begin with. He had inherited that prejudice. Indeed, one of Colonel Caldwell's favorite sayings was: "Never trust a banker of any race or a Gressian in any profession." Jack assumed that included whorehouse strongmen.

Jack lifted himself up, leaning back against the wall, pulling his feet up, readying himself to rise.

"You will all pay for this. You are fortunate that you have money. If you did not, you would pay in other ways." Madame Nadia looked at each of the young men, resting her dark, furious eyes on each of their faces long enough to force each of them to look away from her.

A new man appeared in the doorway. He was nearly as tall as Bohrus, but he was clean-shaven and much thinner. He had a long, ugly face with a bulbous nose and a protruding chin.

"Katya. Anika. Leave us," said Madame Nadia.

Anika lifted herself from the ground, covering her body with a blanket. She walked out of the room swiftly, making eye contact with no one. Katya moved more slowly. As she came within inches of Madame Nadia, she said something rapidly in a foreign language that Jack could not understand. He looked at Fish, but Fish shook his head enough for Jack to see that he also could not understand the words. Katya turned and looked at Jack with wide, fearful eyes before she disappeared through the door.

She leaned into him as she walked past. "Do as they say," she whispered.

The new tall man walked into the room. Malice advanced in front of the man like an odor. Jack looked at the man's face and felt a shiver of fear move through him.

"Buhrl will see that you find your way downstairs quickly. Collect your things. Do not delay. You are no longer welcome here." At that, Madame Nadia turned and walked out of the room. Bohrus followed her, barely fitting through the door laterally, and having to duck to make his way under the doorframe.

Her fur-lined coat retrieved, Hannah followed her father down an empty marble corridor and into a closed, dark wing of the Hall of the Republic. Samuel X. Huntington opened a door out onto an alleyway. The cold air rushed in, making Hannah cross her arms and pull her collar tighter around her neck. An enclosed carriage waited in the falling snow behind two harnessed dark horses.

One of the two coachmen saw them and leaped down from his perch. He depressed the latch and pulled open the coach door.

Matilda Smith looked out from within, a wool shawl wrapped around her neck.

She looked at Samuel Huntington and his daughter, her eyes flashing with understanding.

Hannah turned to her father, a strange feeling overcoming her. It was the same feeling she had when she was a little girl, poised upon a cliff overlooking the Great Western Ocean, deciding whether she dared to leap into the water below.

"What will you tell Mother?" she asked.

"I will tell her what I told you in my letter."

"What if she is furious—with you?"

"I will endure her wrath."

"I love you," said Hannah.

The coachman waited with an open umbrella.

Hannah turned and embraced her father, her arms wrapping around his strong, compact shoulders.

He raised his arms and placed them around her. His arms had protected her like a ship in harbor for as long as she could remember.

She remained there for long moments, her grip lingering.

"It is time," he said.

Hannah turned and walked across the alley, stepping up into the coach.

The door closed, and the coachman mounted his perch. Horseshoes clicked against the pavement.

Samuel X. Huntington waited in silence in the doorway, wearing only his evening attire, watching through the falling snow as the carriage turned down the avenue, out of sight.

Jack helped Lucas Alexander down the flight of wooden stairs as he staggered down them, limping and weak. His face tensed with pain after every step. Jack had helped him dress and saw that Bohrus had bruised him from his legs up to his neck. One of the giant's blows had struck Lucas on his face, shutting his left eye with a bright red swelling. Jack knew it would be black as a ripe Calderon avocado rind in the morning.

Buhrl, the tall thin man with the long, ugly face, herded them all into the small reception room they had first entered from the alley. He ordered them all to stand in a line. They obeyed, with Lucas still leaning heavily on Jack's shoulder for support and only seeing out of one eye.

Aaron Fish wandered forward a step.

"Back in line!" growled Buhrl. He spoke with a heavy foreign accent. Jack assumed it was Gressian. They were in Gressia Town. But Jack had little experience telling one inland continental accent from another.

"These bastards could learn some manners," whispered Fish to no one in particular.

"What did you say, boy?" asked Buhrl.

"Nothing," said Fish. Buhrl stared at him with an expression that suggested his capacity for violence was only just barely contained.

A gap opened in the wood paneling of the wall. The paneling showed no door handle. Indeed, there was nothing to mark it as a door until it creaked open. Madame Nadia walked through, trailed by Bohrus. Another man followed Bohrus. Next to anyone else, he would have seemed a giant. Next to Bohrus, he looked like a younger brother, a few inches shorter and a few inches narrower across the shoulders. He was still a half-head taller than Jack and easily seventy pounds heavier.

With Bohrus and the other man flanking her, Madame Nadia stopped to face the line of six young men: Jack Caldwell, Lucas Alexander, Aaron Fish, Austen Blake, Tom Beardsley, and Jurious Jackson. Four of the five men standing to Jack's left came from families that were among the wealthiest of Bay Port City, which meant they were among the wealthiest citizens of the twenty-eight million souls that called the New Anglian Republic their home.

"I believed I was very clear the last time Mr. Alexander chose to exercise his perversion."

No one spoke. They were all still drunk. Yet fear had sobered them all into silence.

"Was I not clear?" Madame Nadia's voice rose. "What did I say, Mr. Alexander? What did I say last time?"

Lucas Alexander said nothing. His face, however, was bright red, and his unbattered eye was wide open.

"I will remind you what I said," said Madame Nadia. "I said that if you do it again to one of my girls, I will have Bohrus do it to you."

Jack felt Lucas Alexander weaken on his arm, leaning on him more heavily, sinking toward the ground.

"Should I have him do that now, in front of your friends?"

"Enough games," said Aaron Fish, his own face reddening, not in fear but anger. Fish was the smallest of them all. He was also their leader in most things. All of them knew the fire inside of Aaron Fish was easily lit, and once lit, difficult to extinguish.

"Games? This is not a game, Mr. Fish," said Madame Nadia. She looked at Buhrl. He stepped forward and pulled back his overcoat, revealing the black handle of a long knife on his belt. It was half the length of a grown man's arm and nearly as wide.

Fish's eyes widened. He was an experienced game player, but only of a certain kind and with specific stakes. He had mastered the games of young men in the Vine University set, not the kind of games in which men carry knives.

"What do you want?" asked Jack. Lucas tapped his leg nervously next to him, like a child that needed to use the toilet.

"What do I want? That is the question, visiting friend. Isn't it? I am sure I want no more than what the group of you can readily provide." She slowly drew her eyes across each of their faces, menacing as an auctioneer looking at a line of slaves.

"Just tell us what you want," said Fish, his voice edged and angry.

"Hold your tongue, Fish," said Madame Nadia, "or I will have Buhrl hold it for you." Buhrl stared, gripping his knife handle. Bohrus and his smaller, still-giant companion followed Buhrl's lead, staring without speaking. Bohrus pulled back his overcoat to reveal an iron-studded truncheon, the kind of club the Gressian gangs used to break each other's skulls.

Jack raised his palms up in a gesture of peace and took half a step forward.

"Stay," said Bohrus, tapping his truncheon in his right hand onto the open palm of his left.

"Tell us what we can do to remedy our situation," said Jack.

"As Mr. Fish knows," said Madame Nadia. "Indeed, as most of you know, your fee would have been four hundred dollars each."

Jack's eyes widened. That was a fortune. That was what a senior Transcontinental engineer made in a month, what a regular laborer made in half a year if he was working very hard.

"But that was before Mr. Alexander decided to indulge in his disgusting appetites," continued Madame Nadia. "My women are here to serve all of my customers; they are not to be damaged. You will now each pay me four thousand dollars."

"Four thousand!" Tom Beardsley shouted first.

"Nonsense," said Jurious Jackson, laughing nervously.

Lucas Alexander was incapable of saying anything, paralyzed as he was by his fear and his shame. Austen Blake narrowed his eyes, his gaze darting between Madame Nadia and each of her three grim enforcers.

"One thousand," said Blake, son of the railroad lawyer.

"What? Do you think this is a negotiation?" Madame Nadia turned and looked at Bohrus.

"They think this is a negotiation." She smiled. Bohrus did not smile.

"Everything is a negotiation," said Austen Blake, crossing his arms.

"I think this is extortion," said Fish, shaking his fist in the air.

"Silence. boy," she said.

"Do you know what our families could do to you? And to your shit-stained little place?" Fish shook his fist again.

"The only shit stains will be from you, Fish, if I let Buhrl do what he is patiently waiting to do to you and your friends," said Madame Nadia. Buhrl, as if on cue, slid the knife from its leather sheath. An ugly black blade emerged from the leather, long and wide as a half-sword.

A knock struck the door in the alley like a rifle shot. Jack and the others jumped in surprise, all except for Lucas Alexander, who was barely conscious on his feet.

"We are closed," said Madame Nadia, signaling to the man at her left. He turned and walked to the door. Bohrus remained at her right, staring at the young men in their disheveled evening dress. Buhrl stood stone-faced, holding his black-bladed knife.

The knock on the door struck again, loud and demanding.

"We are closed," said the large Gressian.

The knock struck the door again, as insistent as a patrol of policemen. The Gressian looked out the peephole in the door. No one stood on the other side. He turned to Madame Nadia, his face confused.

There was another knock, sharp and urgent. The Gressian turned back around, slid open the bolt lock, and opened the heavy oaken door. The frozen air from the alley swirled into the room.

"Closed," barked the Gressian. He cracked open the door only wide enough for half of his face to peer into the alley. None in the room could hear the words being said from the other side of the door.

"I said closed!" shouted the Gressian, shifting his palm on the door to slam it shut. An iron bar caught between the doorjam and the door as the Gressian tried to push it closed. Enraged, the Gressian pulled the door open wider and pulled his truncheon out of his belt. Like Bohrus's club, it was thick and iron-studded.

"You learn slow!" he said to whoever stood outside the door. He lifted his weapon and swung it down. A dull crack sounded in the alleyway, the sound of metal on bone.

The Gressian froze. There was another crack and another. The Gressian dropped his truncheon, and then he dropped to his knees. A man kicked him over with a boot to his chest and stepped into the room, cold air and snowflakes swirling in behind him. The collar of his overcoat was pulled up high with his bowler hat shoved down low on his head. A scarf covered his mouth.

Bohrus turned and swung at the man with his iron-studded club, pushing Madame Nadia to the side as he did so. The man sidestepped the swing, stepping around Bohrus like a Spatanian dodging a bull.

The man in the overcoat slipped by Bohrus, moving under a second swing, which came dangerously close to the bun atop Madame Nadia's head. The man glided past Madame Nadia, paying her no attention. He stepped toward Jack Caldwell and then turned to face Bohrus and Buhrl. The man held out his thin iron bar, gripping it in a leather-gloved hand. Buhrl stabbed forward with his knife. Jack instinctively stepped backward, fear coursing through his body. The rest of the young men did the same, seeking refuge along the back wall.

The man in front of Jack did the opposite. He stepped toward Buhrl, un-flinching, gripping Buhrl's sleeve as the Gressian's long arm thrust the long blade forward. The man, a full foot shorter than Buhrl, stepped forward as if he were about to give Buhrl a kiss. His thin iron bar flew fast as a viper's strike, meeting Buhrl's face with the vicious kiss of iron against flesh. It was enough. Buhrl's arms tightened, extending out. The man kneed Buhrl in the groin, once, with the full momentum of a grown man firmly planted on the ground and throwing his full weight upward into the knee thrust. Buhrl's face contorted in astonishment and pain. The man struck Burhrl's exposed temple with the iron bar. Buhrl fell to the ground, unconscious.

Bohrus pushed Madame Nadia behind him. He advanced slowly, holding his truncheon out. Bohrus's head skimmed the ceiling above him. It was far from an ideal space in which to swing his massive weapon, which was easily three times longer than the small iron bar that had just knocked Buhrl unconscious.

"If you lower your weapon, Gressian, I shall lower mine," said the man with the small iron bar.

"Do as he says," said Madame Nadia. Slowly and beneath suspicious eyes, the Gressian half lowered his club.

The man in the bowler hat kept his scarf in front of his face, his collar high and his hat low. His eyes shone with intensity.

"These men owe me a great deal of money," said Madame Nadia, her voice still calm but less certain than it had been moments ago when she had three men at her command.

"How much money?" asked the man.

"Four thousand each," said Madame Nadia.

"Twenty-four thousand dollars?" asked the man. "Are they buying your whorehouse?"

"I do not negotiate with cowards," said Madame Nadia. "Show your face."

"Yet you negotiate with armed men against unarmed gentlemen in evening dress. Who is the coward?"

Bohrus glared, his face tensing.

"Mr. Fish," asked the man. "How much money do you owe this woman?"

"Nothing!" said Fish, feeling brave and belligerent with the man standing between him and Bohrus.

"Mr. Fish, I shall ask you again. What is the fee owed to this woman?"

"Four hundred each," said Fish.

"Pay her."

"I don't have four hundred," said Beardsley.

"Mr. Fish, pay her the full sum she is owed. You may collect from your friends."

The man's eyes flashed back at Aaron Fish before immediately returning to Bohrus. Fish pulled a Sterling Republic Bank cheque from his waistcoat and handed it over the man in the bowler hat's shoulder. The man took it in his free hand. Glancing down, he saw that it was in the amount of $2,500.

"There are an extra hundred dollars there for your trouble," said the man. He crouched down and set the cheque on the floor, keeping his eyes on Bohrus.

Bohrus and Madame Nadia stood looking at the cheque on the ground.

Madame Nadia slipped by Bohrus, reached down, and picked up the cheque.

She stood directly in front of the man who had just struck two of her massive enforcers unconscious.

"Be gone," she said, scanning each of the young men's faces slowly and deliberately. "And know this. None of you are ever welcome here again. If you come back, I will kill you."

Bohrus stepped to the side, and they began to file out into the snow-swept cold of the alleyway.

"Mr. Alexander," said Madame Nadia, just as he was about to pass through the door. "I am not finished with you. When the sunlight comes in the morning, you are not free."

Still leaning on Jack for support, Lucas glanced back at her with his right eye, the one through which he could still see. It was wide and frightened.

"Yes, you best look over your shoulders," she said. "One day soon, you will be repaid."

Lucas let go of Jack and scrambled out the door like a drunkard fleeing a burning building.

The man in the bowler hat stepped out last, never taking his eyes off of the giant, bearded Gressian.

"This way," said the man, his scarf still covering his face. Down the alleyway, facing northwest on the avenue, two carriages waited on the street in the heavily falling snow.

"Friend," said Aaron Fish, "who are you?" He was leaning off the side of the carriage, one foot already inside.

"A valet," said Sergeant Joshua Barnes, his face still hidden.

"I am in your debt, valet," said Fish.

Barnes closed the door to Aaron's Fish's carriage and signaled for the driver to leave.

CHAPTER 16
Dawn

SOTR *Agobasto*, Deep Bay Harbor
New Anglian Republic
January 1, 1879

Hannah Huntington had barely slept, boarding the Ship of the Republic *Agobasto* with Mrs. Smith in the dark. She leaned against the varnished wood railing of her private deck now, facing the eastern shoreline of the Republic. It would be her first time leaving the country without the company of her parents, and despite having Mrs. Smith at her side, she could feel the difference. A mug of steaming coffee warmed her hands as the grey light of dawn broke over the city.

She looked down, marveling at the scope of the ship beneath her, larger than any she had ever boarded before. The *Agobasto* was a floating steel behemoth, a mighty trans-Titanic liner made to withstand the fiercest storms of the North Titanic in winter and fast enough to make the long passage to the Eastern Spatanian Empire in less than two weeks. The great boilers below would soon awaken, and the three massive funnels, painted blue, green, and gold for the New Anglian Steam Ship Line, would belch their dark clouds of coal smoke, turning the screws that would speed Hannah across the Titanic Ocean. They would not stop until they reached the ancient harbor of the Veteno.

But for the moment, all lay quiet.

The snowstorm had departed Bay Port City before the SOTR *Agobasto*, leaving a cold clear morning and, from Hannah's deck, a remarkable view of the metropolis. In the distance, towering over the Central Crescent, the mansions of Admiral's Hill first caught the eastern light. Hannah stared at the sunstruck windows, looking as if they were paned with gold. She could not tell, at this distance, which mansion belonged to the Sterlings.

A pang of guilt struck her.

Sherman Sterling would now surely know that she had gone to the Three Gods Day Ball without him. *He is not a bad man. A man does not choose his parents, and I have poorly repaid his kindness*, she thought, her guilt deepening.

She looked away, pushing the thought from her mind as her eyes left Admiral's Hill and peered down into the city.

No looking backward, she told herself.

The buildings spread out in a vast, deep arc as the sun rose, the city clearer than she had ever seen it before, lining the waters of Deep Bay Harbor and stretching back as far as Hannah could see into the hinterlands. She looked now to the south, to the only place where a haze still seemed to linger. From more chimneys than Hannah could count, wood smoke slithered upward, rising like a thousand snakes into the cold morning sky.

"Where is that?" she asked.

Mrs. Smith looked up from her newspaper, a crisp copy of the *Bay Port Tribune*.

"Where?"

Hannah pointed to the southern edge of the city, the end of the unbroken arc of buildings.

"Gressia Town," said Mrs. Smith. "A bad place."

Hannah glanced down at the headline of Mrs. Smith's paper.

QUEEN EMPRESS CABLES FIRST TRANS-TITANIC MESSAGE: "A THREE GODS BLESSING TO THE NEW WORLD IN THE COMING YEAR."

"You missed the President reading the Queen's message at the ball," said Mrs. Smith, her eyes still on the paper.

"I am seeing it now," said Hannah.

"I never thought I would see the day," said Mrs. Smith, "When the old world could speak directly to the new, and the new world could reply across the width of the Titanic." She shook her head with amazement. "Even the ocean seems smaller."

Hannah kept looking out at the city. She had watched every arriving coach on the pier below. Jack Caldwell had yet to emerge from any of them.

"I remember when your father completed his railroad across the Spine, and a four-month journey across the Republic became a mere seven days. It was a similar feeling then. The world is coming together as never before."

Hannah looked at Mrs. Smith, her face anxious as if she had not heard a word. "What will we do for supplies?" she asked.

Mrs. Smith twisted her head, meeting Hannah's gaze. "What supplies? For the desert?"

Hannah nodded.

"You needn't worry about that. Much is already in your trunk, including your Mancaster repeater."

"My rifle? How? Did you pack it in Calderon?" asked Hannah, her eyebrows arching.

"No, your father did."

Hannah shook her head, the tension easing in her face. *No*, she thought, *of course, he would not send me off without first preparing the way.*

"The rest we will find in the Veteno when we meet Stanwich," said Mrs. Smith, returning her eyes to her paper. "It has all been arranged."

Hannah continued staring over the edge of the railing as she blew on her coffee, still scanning the wharf below.

"Where are they?" she asked.

Farther down the length of the ship, bundled passengers boarded slowly in the cold, walking up the ramps to the second- and third-class decks.

"They will come," said Mrs. Smith. "I never wager against Sergeant Barnes."

"I thought followers of the New Church didn't wager at all?"

"We don't," said Mrs. Smith, smiling between her rosy cheeks.

Hannah reached into her coat, feeling her father's letter. She pulled it out.

"My father gave me this," she said, staring at the fine paper of the envelope, at her father's blue wax seal, and her name written across the front.

"Read it," said Mrs. Smith, still reading the *Tribune*'s take on the Trans-Titanic cable.

Hannah broke the seal with her finger, pulling out the thick, folded paper within. Her father's pen strokes lay before her in dark blue ink.

My Dearest Hannah,

If you are reading these words, you have chosen what I expected. You will find few better companions than Mrs. Smith. Follow her example and obey her instructions. You may also trust and rely upon Sergeant Barnes. Be wary of all others.

You will learn what else you need to know from Stanwich. He is a bold and able man, motivated to achieve our mission. But remember that you are more precious to me than anything Stanwich may find upon the Sand Sea. Money can be remade. It is replaceable. You are not.

Go now with my blessing, and the blessing of the Three Gods. If I had done what was expected of me, I would still be a grocer in Howan State. The same fire that forged the rails of the Transcontinental burns in you. I will never be the one to snuff it out. When the going is hard—as it will be—remember that I too have disliked the things that made me stronger when they were actually happening. But I have found them to be nearly always worth the struggle.

I have long known that your path would carry you far away from me. Walk upon your path boldly now, for you are better prepared than you know. Remember always that your father's greatest pride is reserved for you. May Mrs. Smith keep you safe, and with luck, your mother's rage will have subsided by the time you return to us.

Your Loving Father,
Samuel X. Huntington

Hannah lowered the letter as the first "all aboard" horn sounded, deep, long, and low.

The engines rumbled beneath her, in the heart of the *Agobasto*. She looked back down onto the pier, her heartbeat quickening. Near the gangplanks leading up to the first-class cabins, uniformed men from the New Anglian Steam Ship Line paced, checking their passenger lists.

A lone carriage skidded to a halt in front of them, the coachman heaving on his reins.

Despite the freezing air, the horses panted for breath, as if the driver had galloped them halfway across the city.

A man quickly stepped out of the coach, as small as a toy soldier beneath the hull of the mighty *Agobasto*.

Even in the distance, Hannah could see his lean, straight-backed efficiency, and the bowler hat set low upon his head. He reached up to pay the coachman as a taller, broad-shouldered man stepped out of the coach behind him, his overcoat unbuttoned and his top hat askew. He rushed forward toward the ship, staggering on the dock as if still drunk.

The man reached the dock's edge, bent over, and violently vomited into the dark grey water of the bay.

"Mrs. Smith," said Hannah. "Perhaps you *should* wager."

Mrs. Smith looked up from her *Tribune*.

Hannah pointed down to the dock. "It appears Sergeant Barnes and Jack Caldwell will be joining us after all."

The man on the dock's edge retched again.

PART II
THE SEVENTH YEAR OF
THE FORTIETH QHALIFFA

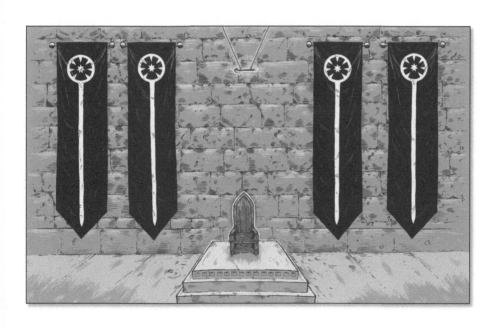

CHAPTER 17
Sumetan the Magnificent

Saman Keer
1st Day, Month of Gandus, 807
Anglian Calendar: January 1, 1879

Jemojeen Jongdar stood alone in a black cape and turban, his hands clasped behind his back, facing the broad mullioned windows of his chambers. On the table next to him, his breakfast remained untouched. The three boned fish, the little loaf of bread, the small bowl of olive oil, the soft-boiled egg, the peeled orange, the tea, and the vase of pale-blue winter flowers were all exactly as Baydar had placed them hours before. Despite his thinness, Jemojeen had always been a man with a voracious appetite, and it was rare for a piece of food to remain upon any of his plates for longer than a few minutes into a meal. But not today. Today, he stared in silence, the magnitude of his failure encircling him like a cloud.

Indeed, Jemojeen had hardly eaten or slept in the week since the debacle in the Square, since Selena Savanar had escaped, since the Oath Holders had humiliated him, killing the priests, his guardsmen, and his executioners, all while rescuing her. How many Oath Holders had even attacked? A dozen? Half that number? He had only seen two, near the alley, the men covered in cloth the color of Hahst sand from their heads to their feet.

His first meeting with the Qhaliffa had been a disaster. Sumetan, usually so pliable in Jemojeen's hands, threw his own words back into his face, making Jemojeen, for the first time in seven years, wonder if his enemies might actually be able to bring him down. This escape had emboldened the Qhaliffa in a way he had not seen in years, making him speak almost like his father, Selahim the Grim, a man that all rightly feared, including Jemojeen. Had Maja not given Sumetan enough tar? He would have to speak with the little Erassian if she was not doing as she was told.

The stakes had now grown too high and, if he was not careful—incredibly careful—any further mistakes could forever deprive him of his goal. His true goal, the goal he had never shared with anyone, had now come so close that he could feel it in his bones. He could not afford this distraction with the Savanar, not now, and with each passing day, it was becoming far more than a distraction.

How the meeting with the Qhaliffa today would be any better, Jemojeen could not say, but it had to be. He would will it to be so. He would do whatever necessary even if the facts were against him. Saliha, the daughter of Sah Seg Savanar, remained at large, and he had yet to catch a single Oath Holder. Heretics, yes, he had caught dozens in the past week, so many that the dungeon was growing full, but not a single Oath Holder. He needed to find one, or two, or ten—the more, the better. Whether a Ram, a Lion, or a Serpent did not matter, but he needed to show Sumetan and all of the others that *he* was in command, and he needed to show them soon. The Oath Holders would break under torture like any other man. Of that, he had few doubts. Even fanatics yield to the blade and the flame.

And he needed to catch the Savanar girl. Alive was better, but at this point, even dead would do. At all costs, she could not escape. Jemojeen had been too explicit, too clear in convincing the Qhaliffa to reinstate the burnings, too emphatic in saying that she was the linchpin of the rebellion, the critical part of the survival of the Beserian Heresy. It had never crossed his mind that he might fail to burn her. Never before in his seventeen years as Grand Vizer had a prisoner escaped his grasp.

As these thoughts swirled through his restless mind, Jemojeen scanned the capital spread out beneath him under his broad windows, wondering where they lay hidden, for certainly, beneath his view, he believed that Oath Holders hid. Bright morning sunlight struck the thousands of green tile rooftops in his view, rooftops that could conceal his enemies, rooftops that might hide the Savanar girl.

He looked north, to his left, toward the high, rocky mountain ridge, beyond which lay the city of Nor Wasura. Might they take her there? It was among the more tranquil of the Qhaliffa's cities, a place where little happened, a city that was neither poor nor rich, a place where quiet merchants, artisans, and terrace farmers went about their daily business. Perhaps an ideal place to hide her.

Then he looked south, toward the forested shoulder of the mountain that divided the capital from the next city to the south, Ganjar en Oxus. Perhaps they might take her there, to the river, for Ganjar en Oxus was a place through which many people moved. It was the city of the little Oxus, the stream that flowed most directly into the mighty river.

Yes, perhaps they might take the little Oxus to the greater Oxus, the real Oxus, the river that flowed south through the sands for a thousand miles to the Harafhan Mountains and the border of Hindea. Yes, he must post the River Galleys along the Oxus, and they must check all boats, all rafts, all barges, even pieces of debris that floated southward, for the Oxus was broad and busy, and the Savanar was only a girl, easily hidden.

Then he looked east again, his eyes squarely on the central part of the capital beneath him, following the bright blue ribbon of the River Keer, flowing along the valley floor, the river that divided the city in two. His eyes tracked the Keer until it emptied into the flank of the Ring River at the bottom of the valley—seven miles away from him, and a vertical mile beneath him—past where the shoulders of the valley ended, and the thousands of buildings and tangled alleyways of the flatlands filled the alluvial plain in a great arc along the Ring River's banks.

His eyes shifted a fraction of an inch, looking a half-mile north, up the Ring River to the great stone bridge that crossed it, the Approach of the East, the only way to cross the Ring River by land from Saman Keer into the eastern Sand Sea. Of course, he had already tripled the garrison of guardsmen on the bridge, and they were presently checking every single cart, caravan, and person that passed through the Bridge Gate on the near side of the bridge or the Sand Gate on the far side.

His eyes moved past the Sand Gate, out into the desert, to the eastern expanse of the Sand Sea itself, stretching to the horizon. Would they go east with her, toward Xin and the Barban Mountains? It would be contrary to their prophecy. Or would it? For the words said, "From the East shall come another." Surely, that must mean that they would take the Savanar to the west. Or would they take her east and from there return?

"Your Excellency?" said a small voice behind him.

Broken from his train of thought, Jemojeen spun around, his eyes murderous, and his hand moving to the curved dagger at his belt.

"What is it?"

Seeing who had interrupted him, his eyes narrowed. He sneered. Baydar. The little servant with the strange, heart-shaped face and the huge ears.

"Are you stupid, Bat?" He nearly spat the words.

Baydar winced at the name, his face flushing red, with an empty tray in his hands.

"How many times have I told you to never come up behind me like that?" said Jemojeen. "The next time, I may treat you like an assassin and cut your throat."

Baydar swallowed heavily.

"Perhaps if I had your bat ears, I would hear you coming, but as it stands, you sneak up on me like a little rodent. I should have you flogged in the Square."

Baydar stood, his heart thundering and his shaky legs barely keeping him standing. "You t-told me to c-come at this hour, Your Excellency."

"What time is it?" asked Jemojeen.

Baydar stared with his mouth open. No words came out.

"By the God of the Mountain, Bat, speak!"

"The n-ninth hour, Y-Your Excellency," Baydar stuttered, barely whispering. Jemojeen glared.

"The S-Sipahi Shaheni is h-here."

Jemojeen looked past Baydar.

The Sipahi was indeed there, wide-bodied and thick across the chest and shoulders, wearing a black tunic beneath dark chain mail and a black turban wrapped around a dark steel helmet. His eyes were set wide apart, flanking a flat, smashed nose from his years as a flatlands gang leader in the most lawless of the Seven Cities, the City of the Red Rooftops, Sundar Dun. Shaheni still did much of what he did in his gang years. Only now, he carried the mace of a Sipahi and the authority of the Grand Vizer of the Qhaliffa behind him.

"Your Excellency," said Shaheni, saluting with a gloved fist across his mailed chest.

"Is it time already?" said Jemojeen.

Shaheni nodded, stepping forward. "Yes, Your Excellency."

Jemojeen again glanced out the window and down toward the rooftops, as if trying to solve a puzzle in his mind.

"Take my breakfast away, Bat."

"Y-yes, Your Excellency," said Baydar, rushing forward with his tray.

Jemojeen turned his eyes toward Baydar.

"But before you do, I have one question, Bat."

Baydar froze over Jemojeen's breakfast, his arm extended toward the un-touched egg.

"What color are these flowers?"

"B-blue, Your Excellency," said Baydar, glancing up at Jemojeen and quick-ly returning his gaze down as he loaded Jemojeen's uneaten meal onto his tray.

"Yesterday, do you recall me requesting a specific color with my breakfast, Bat?"

"Yes, Your Excellency."

"And that color was purple, was it not?"

"Y-yes, Your Excellency."

"Are you able to distinguish one color from another, Bat?"

"Y-yes, Your Excellency," said Baydar.

"Ah, very good," said Jemojeen. He turned toward Shaheni. "I am of the impression that servants should do what they are told. Aren't you?"

"Yes, Your Excellency," said Shaheni, his voice deep and gravelly.

"Indeed, the farther along one proceeds in this endeavor of ruling, the hard-er it is to avoid the conclusion that there are certain men born to lead, others born to serve, and still yet others, so devoid of gifts they are barely fit even to serve."

Shaheni gave a half-hearted smile, unclear where exactly he fit into Jemojeen's categories.

Baydar continued loading the tray.

"Bat, since you have revealed your ability to discern one color from another, remind me of the color of the flowers you delivered with my breakfast."

"Blue, Your Excellency."

"Yes, they are blue. Tell me, Bat, is blue purple?"

"N-no, Your Excellency."

"N-no, it isn't," said Jemojeen, imitating Baydar's stutter. "Did you willfully do other than what I asked, or are you simply that careless?" Jemojeen's voice was low, but it carried an edge as sharp as the dagger at his waist.

Baydar visibly shook, spilling Jemojeen's soft-boiled egg off of its tiny bowl and onto the tray. The egg rolled off of the tray and landed on an open scroll, smudging it with a small grease mark.

"Did you just spill food onto my scroll, Bat?"

"I am s-sorry, Your Excellency," Baydar panted.

Jemojeen stepped closer to him, looming over him, seemingly twice the servant's height.

"I noticed something else, Bat. Do you know what I noticed?"

Baydar looked down at his feet, too frightened to speak and too afraid to even pick the egg up off of the scroll.

"I noticed that it is winter."

Baydar nodded, his chest rising and falling.

"Sipahi Shaheni," said Jemojeen, "Do you notice a chill in my chambers?"

"Perhaps, Your Excellency."

"'Perhaps,' he says. Bat, the Sipahi is too kind. It is cold in my chambers because you failed to bring in a new log. Would you prefer that I tend to my own fire?"

Baydar turned his head toward the vast marble fireplace, seeing that within the veined green slabs, the fire had indeed burned low, the final log crumbling into embers.

"No, Your Excellency." Baydar's voice was a whisper, like the voice of a ghost.

"That is three mistakes in a single morning, Bat. Perhaps I should ask Shaheni to punish you right now?"

Shaheni's face grew solemn. For all other than the Qhaliffa, the Demissaries, the Kezelboj, and those under their direct protection, Jemojeen's word bore the force of law. Shaheni was a man who did his duty, whether he liked it or not.

If the Grand Vizer asked him to carve up the servant on the table, he would do it. Such efficient obedience was among the reasons Jemojeen had continued to elevate him above his peers.

"Or perhaps," said Jemojeen, "you would learn to be more careful after a stay in the dungeon?"

"P-please forgive me, Your Excellency."

Jemojeen now stood only inches away from Baydar, staring down at the top of his bowed head. "Pick. That. Egg. Up. Off of my scroll, Bat," he whispered, "and get out of my sight . . . *now!*"

Jemojeen screamed the last word into Baydar's ear. Baydar physically jumped, his eyes widening like he'd been touched by a heated iron. He lurched forward, grasped the egg, placed it onto the tray, and scrambled toward the door, nearly running. As he reached the door, however, he skidded to a stop, almost spilling the tray. A man with flaming orange hair and a small pointed beard of the same color stood in his way.

Baydar bowed as the man stared at him.

Baydar stepped out of the way, the plates rattling on the tray in his shaking hands.

Turkelan the Erassian was a man rightly feared.

The man stepped into the room, watching contemptuously as the servant rushed out of the room behind him.

"We may have to make an example out of that one, Shaheni," said Jemojeen loudly enough to make sure Baydar could hear him as he raced down the hallway. He smiled but without mirth.

"Good morning, Your Excellency," said the orange-haired man.

Rather than saluting as the Sipahi had, Turkelan bowed with one arm extended out to the side, the other against his chest, in the manner of the Erassian cavalry.

"Captain," said Jemojeen.

Shaheni nodded to the Erassian.

"Close the door," said Jemojeen.

Turkelan did as the Grand Vizer commanded, the heavy wooden door shutting softly. He slid the bolt lock in place.

"Sit," said Jemojeen. "We have much to discuss. You will both accompany me to meet with the Qhaliffa," said Jemojeen.

A look of surprise came across both men's faces. The anxiousness showed more upon Shaheni's face than Turkelan's. For the fierce Erassian to show any emotion at all was unusual.

"First, what news do you bring me?"

Neither man rushed to speak, each looking at the other.

"Sipahi? What news?"

"There is no news."

"That is not a sufficient answer, Sipahi."

"My men are overextended, Your Excellency. They are not resting. I have used my reserve. There are too many places to patrol, too many checkpoints to man. The Great Mountain is large, and the Seven Cities hold many hiding places."

"Do not make excuses, Sipahi. And do not tell me things I already know. Tell me what you have found. Tell me what new efforts you have made since yesterday."

Sipahi Shaheni hesitated. "There is no new news since yesterday, Your Excellency."

Jemojeen stared into Shaheni's face, his eyes boring into him like drills.

To his credit, Shaheni held his gaze for several moments before staring down at the chain mail on his belly.

"And how about you, Turkelan? What have your Erassians found me?"

"It is the same as for Shaheni, Your Excellency. We have rounded up heretics."

"Oath Holders?"

"None yet."

"I trust," said Jemojeen, "that I need not remind either of you that you hold your positions because I have given them to you."

Both men stood looking down at the floor. Neither had any answer that could mollify the Grand Vizer, and they knew it. Best to let the rage wash over them. At the moment, he needed them.

"I have an idea," said Jemojeen.

Turkelan and Shaheni looked up. To their astonishment, the Grand Vizer was smiling.

Sumetan the Magnificent, Qhaliffa of the Seven Cities, reclined upon a cushion, his favorite concubine curled up at his side with her fingertips stroking his arm. Blazing fireplaces roared on either side of the receiving room, making the three standing men before him sweat despite the frigid winter air beyond the windows.

In his black cape and turban, Jemojeen stood in the center. Armored, beneath steel helmet and mailed shirt, Shaheni stood a step behind him on his right, with Captain Turkelan in the same position on his left, in a loose linen tunic and trousers beneath his Erassian cap and scarf. All stood unarmed, for none were permitted with weapons in the presence of the Qhaliffa. None, that is, except for the Qhaliffa's guards, who for generations had been Demissary

Lancers, the men of the orange capes and turbans, chosen for their height, their strength, and their ruthlessness. Compared to the lancers, Shaheni knew that even his hardest guardsmen were little better than amateurs.

The lancers alone stood armed, a pair of them flanking the door at the back of the room, still and stone-faced with their long, wide-bladed scimitari swords sheathed at their sides. They were the visible reminder that the Qhaliffa held the power of life and death over his subjects, even the men standing before him.

The Qhaliffa looked at Jemojeen beneath his jeweled turban with red, puffy eyes. He gazed lazily out from above dark half-moons, the lingering signs of his nighttime activities. Jemojeen noted that he looked worse than he had in months, as if he had smoked more tar than usual, as if he had not slept at all. Were he not the Qhaliffa, his bearded face would be common enough to be mistaken for a Nor Wasuran merchant.

Maja, his emerald-eyed, flame-haired Erassian concubine sat next to him like an exotic cat, her legs tucked underneath her and her little feet sticking out from the edge of her silk covering. The jewels on her anklets sparkled in the firelight as her fingertips lightly grazed the exposed skin on the Qhaliffa's forearm. All of the Qhaliffa's concubines were beautiful, but Maja stood out even amongst them. Most declared Maja the Erassian to be perfect in face and form, physically exquisite in every way, and she had held the Qhaliffa's attention, almost without interruption, across the seven years of his reign. Sumetan grew bored with most things quickly. However, Jemojeen had learned that there were two things of which he never tired: Xinish tar and Maja.

"What news today, Jemojeen?" asked the Qhaliffa, his voice low and far-away.

"Our hunt continues, Your Majesty," said Jemojeen, speaking with his head partially bowed and his long fingers steepled beneath his chin. "May I also congratulate you, Your Majesty, upon the seventh year of your reign."

The Qhaliffa gestured to Maja. She reached for the table next to them, retrieving a small pipe of Hindean leaf. Sumetan relied upon the Hindean leaf to keep him awake after a sleepless night with the tar. Unlike the Xinish tar, the leaf did not pulverize his mind. Maja put the pipe to her lips and took a series of small rapid puffs, preparing it for Sumetan.

"Does that mean that she is still on the run?" asked the Qhaliffa. "The Savanar?"

Maja handed Sumetan the pipe.

"Yes, Your Majesty," said Jemojeen, making another small bow with his head.

Sumetan inhaled deeply from the pipe. "Why," began Sumetan, exhaling a jet of the aromatic smoke up toward the vaulted ceiling, "is she not caught?"

The smoke seemed to lessen the irritation in the Qhaliffa's face.

"A Grand Vizer might be tempted to say, Your Majesty, that the Great Mountain is large and that there are many hiding places in your realm, but you will hear no such excuses from me, nor from the Sipahi Shaheni or Captain Turkelan this morning."

The Qhaliffa inhaled again, opening his mouth to let the smoke slowly drift up past his face.

"Then what will I hear, Jemojeen?" The Qhaliffa said the Grand Vizer's name slowly as if it were three names, Jemm-oh-jeeen. Before Jemojeen could answer, the Qhaliffa gestured to Maja the Erassian again. She retrieved a cup of wine from the table and lifted it to the Qhaliffa's lips. He kept the pipe in his hand, and his other hand upon Maja's shoulder, allowing her to hold the cup while he drank.

He licked his lips.

"I believe, Your Majesty," said Jemojeen, speaking slowly, his tone honeyed with respect and deference, "that there may be traitors amongst our forces, traitors that are feeding information to the Order to help the Savanar and the others stay a step ahead of us."

The Qhaliffa did not immediately react, as if Jemojeen's words took a long time to travel across the room and into his ears. He drew again from his pipe.

"Why do you think this?"

"In the Square, Your Majesty, during the attack, certain weapons were used, weapons that rebels should not be able to obtain."

The Qhaliffa exhaled again, shifting his position upon his cushion.

"What kind of weapons?"

"Most notably, Your Majesty, Demissary pistols. A shrapnel pistol and a flash pistol."

The Qhaliffa listened.

Jemojeen continued. "Those are not weapons easily replicated, Your Majesty. Many have tried, but only the Demissary armorers can make them."

"Do you think there are traitors in the armory, Jemojeen?"

"It is possible, but I find it doubtful, Your Majesty."

"Who used the pistols?"

"The Oath Holders."

"Are you saying you think there are Oath Holders that are—" the Qhaliffa paused to inhale more smoke. "That are Demissaries?"

"Perhaps, Your Majesty."

"Which Legion?" as he asked, Sumetan looked toward the pair of Demissaries guarding his door. They bore the symbol "II" upon the leather straps that crisscrossed their chest, the mark of the Second Legion, famous for its cruelty.

Jemojeen resisted the urge to look back at the Demissaries. He knew they would not react regardless, not in the presence of the Qhaliffa.

"I do not know, Your Majesty. We have only begun our inquiry into the matter."

"That is a dangerous thing to say, Jemojeen, what you are saying. Pistols can be stolen."

"There is more, Your Majesty."

The Qhaliffa waited. His eyes became slightly less hooded as he focused them on Jemojeen.

"The archer that killed the priests on the platform—the one that killed the heretic while he was on the stake and saved him from the flames—he loosed his arrows from the rooftops all the way across the Square."

The Qhaliffa exhaled more smoke as he considered this.

"In my observations, Your Majesty, only several men in the Seven Cities can wield a bow like that, and most of them are Demissaries that wear the green turban."

The Qhaliffa waited, still not speaking.

"I should say that the man hit Trendan Rudar's throat—not to mention Chara the High Priest's—from that distance. In the case of Rudar, it was with his first arrow, from more than a hundred yards away."

"What are you asking, Jemojeen?" the Qhaliffa's face grew more agitated as he asked his question. He attempted to inhale again from his pipe and nearly dropped it as his chest convulsed with a cough. He coughed again and again, bending over as he hacked from deep within his lungs, the lungs that had inhaled so much of the Xinish tar.

The coughing continued.

"Your Majesty," said Jemojeen, taking a step forward.

The Demissaries at the door took a step forward, their eyes and faces altering as they considered rushing to the Qhaliffa.

Maja, the Erassian, reached over to the table and picked up a cup of water.

The Qhaliffa continued coughing.

Jemojeen took another step forward, as did the Demissary lancers.

At last, the Qhaliffa stopped. He reached for the cup of water in Maja's hand and slowly sipped it, involuntary tears dripping down his cheeks.

"Your Majesty—" said Jemojeen. "Perhaps we should continue our discussion at a later time?"

"No," said Sumetan, his voice barely audible. "Continue."

"Are you certain, Your Majesty?"

The Qhaliffa nodded.

"As you wish, Your Majesty. I was saying that we must take seriously the possibility that there is a traitor amongst your Demissaries, possibly more than one."

"I suppose it is possible that amongst the Three Legions there is a traitor somewhere. But I would suspect them less than anyone else, Jemojeen. It is more likely that there are traitors amongst your men, I would think."

Turkelan and Sipahi Shaheni stood in silence as the Qhaliffa's suggestion washed over them.

"Or perhaps amongst the Kezelboj," said the Qhaliffa.

Jemojeen waited.

"Have you spoken with Ottovan?" asked the Qhaliffa.

Jemojeen inhaled through his nose, making sure his face was an indecipherable mask. Ottovan Fanfar, Commander of the Third legion of Demissaries, the most famous Demissary of his generation, was the last person with whom Jemojeen wished to discuss this matter or what he was about to propose. They had been harvested in the same spring reaping, he and Ottovan, so many years ago. They had risen together, he and Ottovan. Jemojeen was well aware of the Qhaliffa's love for the Third Legion Commander, and he was well aware that Commander Fanfar was the only Demissary who could match him in most things. He also knew, with certainty, that Ottovan Fanfar would not respond favorably to the suggestion that there were traitors in his Legion or any other Demissary Legion.

"Commander Fanfar is in Alwaz Deem. I can summon him if you insist, but he is preparing to deploy the Third Legion to the western desert, Your Majesty. The Third will meet the rising Beserian threat, if they try to move east against us."

"What threat? Abu Akhsa?" As he said the name, the Qhaliffa began coughing again, hacking violently on his cushion. He drank more of Maja's cup of water, and at last set down his pipe.

"Yes, Your Majesty," said Jemojeen. "Though it pains me to hear such a vile name upon your lips."

"I hear he gathers an army."

"He does, Your Majesty. In the Valley of Kordon, tribesmen gather in unprecedented numbers."

"How many?"

"The Erassian scouts say thousands, Your Majesty."

Turkelan, the Erassian, nodded in agreement.

The Qhaliffa flared his nostrils in contempt.

"Some say tens of thousands," added Jemojeen.

Turkelan did not nod again, but nor did he deny it.

The Qhaliffa shook his head. "How many of them even live upon the sands? Do they not fight each other?"

"Some say they have put aside their differences, Your Majesty, to gather in the name of the prophecy," said Jemojeen.

"In the name of the *heresy*," said Sumetan.

"Of course, Your Majesty, it is heresy. They are deluded and foolish, but they gather nonetheless."

"Is this linked to the Savanar?"

"We think so, Your Majesty."

The Qhaliffa's face looked suddenly even wearier than before. "What would you have me do, Jemojeen?"

Jemojeen lowered his head and his voice. "In light of the threats we face, Your Majesty, I would ask for temporary command of the Three Demissary Legions."

The Qhaliffa's eyes widened. "The Grand Vizer has never directly commanded the Demissaries. They answer only to the legion commanders . . . and to me."

"Of course, Your Majesty. My preference would be for you to take command yourself."

Sumetan's face seemed to relax at the suggestion.

"My concern is only for your health, Your Majesty."

The Qhaliffa inhaled slowly, placing a hand over his abdomen.

"I would only wish to relieve you of this burden for a short while, until your health improves," said Jemojeen.

"For how long?"

"Only for as long as it takes to root out the traitors and find the Savanar, Your Majesty."

The Qhaliffa considered this. He looked at Maja the Erassian. He leaned toward her and whispered something into her ear. She placed her lips against his ear and whispered back, speaking at some length.

Sumetan turned back to Jemojeen, nodding slowly. "I will do as you suggest, Jemojeen, until you find the Savanar. But you will tell me before you act upon any suspected traitors . . . especially in the Demissaries."

"Of course, Your Majesty."

Sumetan stood up. Maja quickly rose behind him, revealing the stunning allure of her body. Jemojeen and the others bowed, averting their eyes.

"I am retiring to my rooms above," said Sumetan, using his preferred phrase for his harem.

"One more thing, Your Majesty," said Jemojeen, slowly rising from his bow. "Given the extraordinary nature of this present requirement to defend the realm, and having been a Demissary Legion Commander myself, Your Majesty, I know they would wish to hear it from your own mouth, or at the very least from your own hand—"

The Qhaliffa waited impatiently, his foot tapping.

"I have prepared an edict—"

"Let me see it," said Sumetan, extending his hand.

Jemojeen removed a scroll from beneath his cape and handed it to the Qhaliffa, bowing again as he did so.

The Qhaliffa's eyes darted along the lines of neatly written words, prepared in Jemojeen's own hand, but with the precision of a scribe.

"Quill," said the Qhaliffa.

Maja turned to the table, dipped one of the long eagle feathers into an ink pot and placed it carefully into the Qhaliffa's outstretched hand. He carried the scroll to the table and bent over it.

Beneath the words that said, By Edict of His Majesty the Qhaliffa, Sovereign of the Seven Cities and the Sand Sea, True and Upright Heir to the Prophet, Protector of the Great Mountain of God, First Among All Beneath the Heavens, He Who is Called Magnificent, he signed,

SUMETAN

Sumetan looked up, dropping the quill. "Do not fail me again, Jemojeen."

"Your Majesty, we will destroy them all," said Jemojeen, bowing deeply. "And I am merely the sword wielded by your hand, Your Majesty."

But the Qhaliffa was already nearing the door. Maja the Erassian trailed behind him, her curves exquisite beneath her thin silk gown, her hips swaying as she walked, her jeweled anklets flashing as she departed in the firelight.

The Demissaries turned and followed them, towering over them, leaving Jemojeen standing in the middle of the room with Shaheni and Turkelan.

Jemojeen leaned toward the Erassian Captain.

"Did you tell her what to say?" he asked.

Turkelan nodded.

"She has done well, Turkelan."

Turkelan nodded again, his face a mask.

"Tell her she can expect one hundred gold pieces this month, not fifty. If she keeps him on the tar, the next month may be the same."

Turkelan nodded again. His sister Maja normally shared twenty-five percent of whatever Jemojeen secretly paid her through the eunuchs that were loyal to him. The edges of Turkelan's lips turned upward into a tiny smile above his pointed orange beard. He could think of many things upon which to spend twenty-five gold pieces. Indeed, even in the finest brothels, it was hard to spend twenty-five gold pieces, even in a month.

CHAPTER 18
The Mountain Path

Saman Keer
5th Day, Month of Gandus, 807
Anglian Calendar: January 5, 1879

Gulana of Nor Gandus, Oath Holder of the Order, lifted the heavy wooden door. Pushing it an inch over her head, she scanned above ground. The full moon shone brightly, bathing the Upper Ring Road in light. By the faith, it was an auspicious night to travel, but by the moon, a poor night for concealment. She peered to her left, looking down the Valley of Saman, at the main road leading up the Great Mountain, the way that paralleled the River Keer.

The Keer, this high up the mountain, even in winter, still moved swiftly down the steep upper slope of the valley, its water level low, foaming over the jagged rocks just below the surface. It was loud enough to muffle other sounds. The stone road next to it lay empty in the moonlight, but Gulana knew that at any moment, Jemojeen's forces could appear, leaving their eastern stronghold to search up the mountain.

As Gulana scanned, the stones of the road lay as silent as those in the tunnel beneath her. The River Keer gurgled. Over the two weeks they had hidden, Selena regained much of her strength. Gulana and Oapah insisted that they were safer traveling with only the three of them than with a party of twelve. But The Ram, the only one of the three supreme leaders of the Order presently in Saman Keer, had decided otherwise.

"No matter how hard you and Oapah fight, Gulana, if even a single patrol catches you, it will be unlikely she'll survive. Our enemies travel by the dozen, and more often by the score. Jemojeen will scatter his men throughout the Seven Cities. He will be indecisive because he knows not where our forces lie. He will accordingly dispatch his men by patrols. With a dozen Oath Holders, you will slaughter their finest patrols, so a dozen you shall have." The Ram's fierce grey eyes flashed as she said this, jamming her finger down on the table with finality, before wishing them well by the God of the Mountain and the Sands.

Gulana and Oapah argued that three might hide far more easily than a dozen. The Ram was nonetheless adamant, and they obeyed. The Ram spoke with the authority of the Order, and though they were a revolutionary order, they were also a deeply disciplined one. Commited to sowing chaos for the Qhaliffa and his Grand Vizer, they tolerated little within themselves. A Sworn Oath Holder did not defy the authority of The Ram, The Lion, or The Serpent when they issued a command.

Gulana continued scanning. She looked to her right, down the road toward Ganjar en Oxus, the place they were going, the next city south on the path to the open desert and freedom. They could not travel upon the Upper Ring Road itself. That was the main thoroughfare the Qhaliffa's forces would use to reach any one of the Seven Cities from another. Jemojeen would heavily guard and patrol it. If the reports were true, the Grand Vizer had even called up his reserve men, placing nearly his entire force of guardsmen on duty to find Selena Savanar.

Gulana glanced down at Selena, Oapah, and the others, all crouched in the narrow, dark tunnel. Gulana paused on Selena's anxious eyes, her face veiled like the others, knowing she would willingly give her own life to save her, and that Oapah and the others would do the same. She knew the risks when she accepted the mission. She'd volunteered nonetheless. She had already faced down four dozen guardsmen in the square for the daughter of Sah Seg Savanar. She would do it again.

Selena's hands clung to the ladder directly below her, in the vertical passageway up from the tunnel. Oapah held the ladder directly beneath Selena. Ten more Oath Holders of the Order waited behind Selena, some Rams, some Lions, like Gulana and Oapah, and even two Serpents. The Serpents were strange-looking people. Beneath their veils were clean, hairless faces and the same yellow-green eyes Selena remembered. Their rituals—the same practices that gave them their unique powers—also tended to make them all look alike, men and women, young and old. They were fearsome warriors in their own strange ways, but Gulana had always been grateful that she was not a Serpent.

"It is clear," she whispered at last.

She looked across the path, seeing that she would have to cross twelve feet before reaching the shrubs on the side of the Upper Ring Road. From the shrub line, they would proceed across sharp, broken ground up to the mountain paths, and then farther up still, to the goat paths the Rams of the Order had charted out and used across the centuries. Typically, the Rams would clear and scout the way before the Lions followed, but this was Gulana's mission, and she insisted upon going first, at least until they reached the high mountain paths. She was not, however, used to traveling in a party of twelve.

"You must hold the tunnel cover," said Oapah in his deep low voice. His words reverberated like a bass drum off of the narrow walls of the tunnel. "Wait for Gulana's sign to cross. I will follow you."

Selena nodded, swallowing heavily beneath her veil.

The Rams in the party, four of them, looked up at Oapah and Selena with inscrutable eyes. Oapah knew that Rams did not like allowing others to scout ahead of them.

Gulana slid herself out from under the wooden slab on her belly, the gravel and dirt of the edge of the Upper Ring Road still concealing the panel to the tunnel beneath. Beneath the gravel, the Upper Ring Road itself held wide, flat paving stones. They were solid and thick enough to support carts carrying the heaviest loads in all weather, including those towing the Great Guns of the Kezelboj, the enormous bronze cannons that faced out into the desert from each of the Seven Cities.

As Gulana moved into the open, Selena stepped up and placed her hands onto the wooden door above her. Gulana had held the door as if it were light, but Selena grunted in exertion.

Gulana scrambled on her hands and feet, galloping into the thicket on the side of the road. She reached the bushes and turned around in a crouch, her body tensed to pounce, scanning the area she had just vacated. From her position, she could see down the road for hundreds of yards in each direction, all the way until the curve of the road bent around the mountain to both the north and the south.

Gulana gestured to Selena with a closed fist, the signal to follow her. Selena slid out from beneath the heavy door. Oapah reached up to take the weight of the wooden plank as she did so. Her hands felt the rough gravel beneath her, and she inhaled the cold, clean night air through her nose. After the dark stuffiness of the tunnel, the air felt pure and liberating on her face. The moon shone as brightly as the morning.

Selena scrambled toward the thicket, following Gulana's example on her hands and feet, the gravel rough on her bare hands. Oapah moved swiftly after her. For all of his size, he did not lumber. Selena felt his presence behind her, massive and strong. As she tried to keep ahead of him, she felt a surge of confidence, trying to imagine fighting a man as large and as powerfully constructed as Oapah. Beneath the sand-colored cloth, his arms were like stone pillars, his shoulders like dark granite boulders, and he was there, above all other tasks, to protect her.

The remainder of the Oath Holders surfaced, rushed across the path, and concealed themselves in the bushes. Gulana and Oapah watched the road with zealous, expert eyes. If anyone approached, they would not approach unseen. Of that, Selena was certain.

The Rams came after Oapah, their faces concealed, their eyes alert and calm. All of them carried bows on their backs, the same horn bows the Demissary archers had used with great deadliness over the generations.

The Serpents came last, strange and languid in their movements, carrying their thin, reedlike windpipes, through which they blew poisoned darts at their enemies. Serpents rejected the scimitari swords of the Lions and the light but deadly fighting staffs of the Rams, preferring their short, curved, razor-sharp daggers instead. Others called them their "fangs."

"On the mountain paths," said Gulana, looking at the senior Ram, Rondus Rungar. "You lead us."

Rondus nodded. He signed several quick symbols to his fellow Rams. Like Rondus, beneath their veils, they were bearded and sturdily built men. Two of them crawled silently through the brush on their hands and feet, keeping low to the ground, beneath even the lowest branches. Selena looked and saw long thick thorns on the branches above them. The Rams moved purposefully, like men traveling a well-known path toward a clearly understood destination. Rondus signaled for Gulana and Oapah to follow him. He turned and passed through the thicket on his hands and feet, bent low to the ground.

"Follow me," said Gulana, looking at Selena. Oapah nodded behind her.

Gulana moved on her hands and feet, rushing after the Rams. Selena again struggled to keep their pace. The Rams moved fast in a manner that evoked the animals for which their class of Oath Holders was named. Selena considered herself a hardy person, restored by the food and rest the Oath Holders had given her, lean of body and swift of movement. Still, she could already feel the fatigue in her shoulders as she crawled after Gulana, and her breathing grew heavy. Gulana and Oapah, moving faster than she was, made not a sound. Selena placed her hand on something sharp and resisted the urge to cry out as the pain of a puncture shot upward from her palm. In the darkness of the bushes, she could not see the wound. Whether she was bleeding, she could not say, but the pain called to her like an alarm bell in a tower. Oapah nudged her to keep moving.

"We cannot stop, Lady Savanar," he said, his whisper like faint thunder.

"My hand," she whispered back.

"Thorns will not kill you," said Oapah, placing his hand upon her back, pushing her forward. "But guardsmen will. Do not stop."

They moved farther through the thornbushes, staying beneath the branches. And then, after a time, they crouched above the thorns, resting upon a sunken path, behind a granite ridge, invisible to the Upper Ring Road, which now lay hundreds of feet beneath them.

Then at long last, even higher up the mountain, Selena Savanar and a dozen Oath Holders of the Order stood upright. Cloth coverings concealed all of their faces, men and women alike, Rams, Lions, and Serpents. Alone among them, Selena panted for air with the exertion of the climb.

"Now we run," said Rondus, unable to hide his eagerness.

He'd already scanned the ridge above them, a nearly sheer rock face, and his sharp, discerning eyes saw no spies upon the mountain. He launched southward on the narrow trail cut into the rock, barely wide enough for two grown men to pass each other, yet he took it at a dead run.

"They should be there by now," said Oapah.

Gulana nodded.

"The eyes of our enemy are distracted," said Oapah. "I can sense it. Can you?"

Gulana nodded again.

"I believe the plan will succeed," said Oapah, gazing back over his shoulder toward Saman Keer.

Selena could not tell from his voice whether he was trying to reassure Gulana.

Gulana turned and said a prayer, her eyes clenched tight. "God of the Mountain and the Sands, protect them with Your power."

"Protect who?" asked Selena, still breathing heavily.

"No one, Lady Savanar," said Gulana. "Run."

And then she turned to the south and ran, following Rondus and his Rams.

CHAPTER 19
Aurelio Demassi

Merchant House Gremanian, Port of the Veteno
Eastern Spatanian Empire
January 16, 1879

Peter waited beside the window, looking out at a sky as cold and grey as the ocean beneath it. The fire behind him crackled, warming the room enough that Peter had removed his coat. Even in his shirtsleeves, he felt like he might start sweating. He watched as the great steamship approached, looking for the emblem of the New Anglian liner. The liner his eyes sought would fly the New Anglian flag, the flag of the earth, the sky, and the rising sun, the rising sun orange-gold against a bright blue sky, moving upward from green earth.

Peter would see the flag long before he saw the markings on the hull, whipping in the wind of the Bay of the Veteno, moving north from the choppy South Spatanian Sea. The steamship in front of him flew the orange banner of the Guildermen. He could see that even without his telescope. In the rising, wind-driven waves, the ship had only two of its four mainsails flying, drawing it toward the sandy lowlands of the coastline.

Five miles to the east or west in either direction, the coastline transformed into a jagged rocky affair with ridges that extended well out into the sea, each capable of shredding the underbelly of a ship as easily as if it were mortal flesh. But the receiving bay of the Veneto was a broad expanse of gentle, sloping sand resting along a deep ancient harbor, protected on either side by tall, fierce rocks. For generations upon generations, ships sought the bay of the Veteno's refuge, the great stopping point between Hindea to the east and the protrusion of Spatania to the west.

The winds had pushed strong and steady for days on end, blowing cold salty air upward from the Sea of Omakhosi. It began as warm air, far to the south, but it chilled by the time it reached the Bay of the Veteno. Peter hoped it did not mean Caldwell's ship had been blown off course. The Ship of the Republic

Agobasto was a powerful vessel, but not as powerful as the southerly winds in winter.

"A watched pot does not boil, Peter Harmon." The voice was LaFrentian, at once urbane and contemptuous.

"Well, Expey, *not* watching has not brought the ship any closer, either," said Peter, salting his own words with a tone of contempt. Most rich Anglians could, especially when speaking to a LaFrentian.

Hersen Expey was not a born LaFrentian. Peter had learned in the past weeks, however, that there was no more pride-filled LaFrentian than he who earned his citizenship through service in the Legion. Hersen Expey had risen to the rank of major in the New Anglian War, as the legionnaires called it. He had, like all legionnaires, begun as a private. There were no officers that had not first been noncommissioned officers, and there were no noncommissioned officers that had not first been private soldiers. As Hersen Expey was quick to say, in his tone of superiority, "Unlike any other army in the world, every general that serves in the LaFrentian Legion was once a private. We are fighting officers, all of us."

Peter had twice resisted reminding Hersen that such did not keep the Legion from losing the war against the New Anglians or, for that matter, the great decades-long war against Anglia that had brought down the LaFrentian Emperor in the age of his great-great-grandfather, General John Fitzroy Harmon. Peter learned that Hersen Expey had fought in many of the same battles as Colonel Mason Caldwell of Calderon, except that he was, of course, on the other side.

Stanwich had told Peter not to worry about such things, that the war was long ago and that its veterans—on both sides—had moved on. It had been nearly twenty years since the peace, and the peace had held.

"I myself am a New Anglian, Peter, and yet Hersen and I have led a half-dozen expeditions together. We are nearly like brothers."

Peter had his doubts.

Few New Anglians shared Stanwich's view. Indeed, in the early newspaper reports of Stanwich's expeditions, all references of Hersen Expey, former Major of the LaFrentian Legion, had been omitted from the New Anglian editions, including in all of the Harmon papers.

Jack Caldwell's bodyguard was rumored to be a New Anglian veteran, a sergeant named Barnes. Peter suspected such men did not easily forgive the things done to their countrymen or readily forget the things they had done themselves. He would wait to see how the man responded to meeting the LaFrentian Legionnaire.

Peter looked over his shoulder at Hersen.

"They are three days late."

"Have you ever traveled across the Titanic in winter?" asked Hersen. The man's accent made it seem as if he was always accusing Peter of something.

"No."

Hersen nodded his head and spoke slowly. "It is a different ocean in the winter."

Peter continued looking out the window.

The Brothers Leboveckian and Stanwich had gone into the other room, holding yet another meeting from which he'd been omitted. What they were discussing, Peter could not say. The brothers, Aaran and Yekov, both Macmenians, had married a pair of exceedingly wealthy sisters and ran Merchant House Gremanian for their father-in-law. In the Veteno, the center point of the east-west trading routes, the leading merchants had more money than most princes. In the past century, with the relaxation of laws requiring that all merchants carry a Royal Spatanian Charter—a charter requiring that the applicant be a member of the Church of the Three Gods—the Macmenian merchant houses had cut significantly into the export-import business once dominated by the old Vetenan families. As far as Peter could tell, few of the Macmenians had cut into the trade more effectively than Merchant House Gremanian and the Brothers Leboveckian.

Overlooking one of the Veteno's central squares on one side and the harbor on the other, Merchant House Gremanian was part residence, part place of business, as large as a hotel. Large as it was, however, Peter had spent the past six days cooped up inside of it, and he was beginning to grow stir-crazy. Indeed, every time he tried to open a window for fresh air, one of the Brothers Leboveckian or one of their minions would remind him that in the Veteno, there were many listening ears and the windows were to remain closed.

Lord Harmon, characteristically, had explained very little to his son before the expedition departed from Anglia, and neither Stanwich nor Hersen seemed inclined to answer Peter's straightforward questions as to what role the Brothers Leboveckian were playing.

In response to Peter's questions, Stanwich repeatedly answered with some version of, "They are friends of your father's, they are acquaintances of mine, and they are to be trusted," before departing into yet another closed-door meeting from which he would emerge with an anxious face.

The door opened.

"We have our guides," said a New Anglian voice—flat, loud, and nasal.

Peter half turned to see Stanwich's face. For the first time in several days, he was smiling.

"Oh?"

"Damn fine guides, too," said Stanwich, "Beserians. Macmenian caravan men."

"How many?" asked Peter.

As best he could piece together from Stanwich's vague answers, except for waiting for Jack and his sergeant to arrive, finalizing the terms with their desert guides was the last major unfilled caravan piece they still needed.

"You can turn around and see," said Stanwich, with his hands on his hips. He wore khaki pants, pulled up high on his hard, flat stomach, nearly to his belly button, with a dark-brown shirt tucked into them.

Peter turned around.

A half-dozen Beserians in long cotton headscarves, baggy shirts, and wide trousers streamed into the room before him. Presumably, to gird themselves against the cold, they wore patchy blankets wrapped around their shoulders. To a man, they were wire-thin with dark, sunbaked faces, all wearing various lengths of beards. At a glance, Peter found it difficult to tell their ages. They could all be very healthy men in their forties, very weathered men in their twenties, or something in between. *Stanwich thinks these men are fine guides?*

"How do you do," said Peter, nodding politely. "I am Peter Harmon." He stepped forward toward the line of men and extended his hand to shake.

The line of men stared at him with stone faces, neither smiling nor frowning, unexpressive as wax figures in an Anglian museum. Peter's hand remained held out awkwardly.

He frowned, feeling insulted. *If it is not the way of the Beserians to shake hands, they should at least have a sense of how to treat an Anglian with manners.*

"Peter Harmon, I am called Aurelio, of House Demassi," said a man to Peter's left, the man standing one in from the end. Peter saw that against the dark brown of his face, the man's teeth looked remarkably white. His beard was short but shaggy as if it had been trimmed with scissors without a mirror.

They clasped hands and shook in the Anglian manner. The man had long, strong hands with a firm grip. Peter stood several inches taller than Aurelio Demassi but saw that Demassi was the tallest of his companions.

"You are a Beserian?" asked Peter.

The stone-faced men in the line of guides smiled. One let out a small laugh.

"I am of the Veteno, of House Demassi," said Demassi. As he said the words, Peter could hear the hint of the Spatanian imperial accent.

"Demassi here comes from an old Vetenan trading family. They've been in the Sand Sea trade with the Macmenians for three generations," said Stanwich, reaching for the teakettle hanging above an open fire.

"You have traveled the Sand Sea often?" asked Peter.

"Since I was nine years old," said Aurelio Demassi.

"And how about the rest of you?" asked Peter in Anglian.

They looked back at him as he looked at them, but they said nothing.

"They do not speak your Anglian tongue," said Demassi.

"What do they speak?" asked Peter, still looking into the dark bearded faces beneath the headscarves. *If they don't speak Anglian, why did they laugh when I asked Demassi if he was a Beserian?*

Stanwich blew on the surface of his freshly poured cup of strong tea. The bitter-floral aroma wafted around the room. "They speak Beserian, Macmenian, even a touch of Spatanian, that is, if you can speak it with the Vetenan lisp."

"Yes," said Demassi.

"Harmon," said Hersen Expey. "It looks as if your New Anglians have arrived." Peter turned around. Since he had been away from the window, a massive trans-Titanic liner had steamed into the bay. He saw the blue and green banner on the bow, with its unmistakable golden-orange rising sun blown out to its full length by the wind. Peter reached for the brass telescope that he had left extended and sitting on the table. He adjusted the lens, fixing it upon the bow of the incoming vessel.

SOTR *Agobasto*.

"Thank the Three Gods," said Peter. "Three days late is better than four."

"And better than not at all," said Hersen Expey, revealing a small gap between his front two teeth as he smiled.

The ship steamed forward, its three smokestacks belching like factory chimneys. Nearly black against the grey sky, the ship's prow carved through the water of the bay, tall and formidable, built to withstand transoceanic storms. A foghorn sounded, deep and resounding. A trio of tugboats steamed out from the pier to meet the *Agobasto* and maneuver her against the dock. Peter looked out the window and saw, with satisfaction, that the *Agobasto's* dock would be directly in front of them.

"I am going to meet them," said Peter, reaching for his coat.

"Don't waste your time, Anglian," said Hersen. "They won't be off the ship for an hour, at least."

"I will accompany you," said Aurelio Demassi.

Peter looked at the Vetenan merchant's son dressed like a Beserian. "Alright, Demassi."

A dense chill hung in the air. Peter wore a black wool overcoat in the Anglian naval style with dual rows of large brass buttons. To not draw attention to himself, Peter had left his top hat in his quarters and instead wore the peaked cap of a naval officer or a merchant ship's mate. He would never pass as a worker, but he might be mistaken for a ship's owner. Heavy wool trousers covered his legs, and underneath them, his feet rested in thick woolen stockings stuck inside of leather voyaging boots with sturdy soles. In his bulky attire, he looked massive compared to Demassi in his light tribesman's garb.

Peter looked down at Demassi's Beserian raiment—at his pants that did not come down to his ankles, at the shirtsleeves that did not come down to his wrists, and at the ratty blanket slung across his bony shoulders. *Why would the son of an old Vetenan trading house dress himself as a poor tribesman?* Demassi's feet were nearly bare, sockless, and stuck inside of leather sandals.

"If I may ask," said Peter.

Demassi met Peter's gaze.

"Why do you dress as a Beserian?" Peter looked down at Demassi's feet as he spoke. They were slightly purplish in the cold.

"I wear the clothing of the sands."

"Would you not perhaps be warmer if you wore the clothing of the Veteno while you are here?"

Demassi shook his head. "I wear the clothing of my people."

"Your people?"

Demassi nodded.

"Those who share my faith."

"Your faith?"

"Faith in the God of the Sands," said Demassi.

The SOTR *Agobasto* now rested alongside the dock, its smokestacks and masts taller than the ancient stone battlements of the Veteno looming behind Peter and Demassi. The two young men stood idly on the stone approach to the wharf. Others scurried by: tattooed dockmen preparing to receive the cargo from the Agobasto, sharp-eyed merchant clerks with their pens and notebooks, preparing to confirm and reconfirm that all that was supposed to arrive did indeed arrive and in acceptable status.

"Do you mean to say that you are not a follower of the Three Gods?" asked Peter, looking up behind him at the vast Vetenan church towers. In the Veteno, there seemed to be a church on every square, which seemed strange for a town renowned for its loose morals and commercial greed.

"I was a follower of that faith once, long ago," said Demassi, watching the flurry of activity and the dockmen walking up and down the gangplanks like ants on twigs.

Peter waited for more. Demassi watched the unloading of the huge steamship in silence.

"And then what?" asked Peter.

"Then what?"

"You were a follower of the Three Gods, and then what?"

"The religion of my father and the religion of this place," Demassi paused and swept his arm across the air as if to encompass all of the Veteno. "That is no longer my faith. I sought truth and truth I found."

"You found truth in the religion of the tribesmen?"

Demassi shook his head. "I found *the* truth, Anglian."

"They are unloading the first-class cabins," said Peter, pointing toward the gangplank that extended to the highest elevation on the port side of the *Agobasto*. Women wearing fur coats over long dresses walked slowly down the ramp way, gripping the varnished wooden rails as they made their way. Men in tall top hats and black overcoats accompanied them, taking the arms of the ladies in black, gloved hands. Servants carried children, bundled up like balls of cloth, their little faces barely visible in the layers meant to keep them warm.

"What does that mean, you found *the* truth?" asked Peter. His eyes were skeptical, and lines of doubt creased his forehead.

"Answers suffice only for those who are ready to hear," said Demassi.

Peter looked into Demassi's face, his eyes curious.

"And? You judge me ready to hear or not ready to hear?"

"Not ready to hear."

"Oh?" Peter's face reddened slightly. A lesser Harmon he might be, but he was still a Harmon of Hylebourne House, and he did not appreciate being dismissed by a mere guide dressed like a beggar.

Demassi's face remained completely calm, even tranquil, amongst the bustling around them.

"Am I mistaken, or have I just been insulted?" Peter's voice rose.

"By no means, Anglian. A man who has not known the desert can hardly be expected to know the truth. Few are ready to hear desert truths while standing upon the stone wharf of the Veteno."

"What does that mean?"

"Truth becomes clear when one is in the presence of truth. This is a city of lies, as are most places."

"You speak in riddles, man," said Peter, shaking his head dismissively.

Aurelio Demassi turned to face him and dropped his voice an octave. His eyes took on a kind of grave seriousness, with any hint of mocking or playfulness gone. "I have seen things in the sands, Anglian, things that are not readily believed here amongst the stone warehouses, ships that belch steam, and the ocean's shore."

Peter looked at him, staring down into the Vetenan's eyes with his own.

"The God of the Sands is a living God," said Demassi. "I have seen the God bring storms and make them go away. I have seen sick men healed."

"I believe, Vetenan, that such is called weather and illness, or its absence. I, too, have seen storms and sick men healed."

"As I said," said Demassi, tilting his head, "some truths are not understood in this city or in any other, where men delude themselves to believe that they hold control, that they are the authors of the story. No, Beserian truths are not readily understood in Spatania."

"That does not sound a great deal like truth to me," said Peter Harmon. But he could see that the Vetenan was not listening. Aurelio Demassi's eyes were locked onto the gangplank, staring with the look of a jilted lover that has just seen the object of his desire walking with another suitor, staring in a way that makes all other objects become merely background.

Peter looked. Jack Caldwell was on the gangplank, tall and broad, flashing a winning smile beneath a black top hat, waving with his extended right arm. At his side walked a beautiful blonde, tall and substantial, with thick braided hair underneath a round fur hat in the Gressian style.

Peter waved back.

Behind Jack and the blonde, Peter saw a lean, severe-looking man walking alongside a round-looking matron in her forties or fifties.

Demassi looked at Peter waving. "That is the rest of our party?" asked Demassi.

"Yes," said Peter. "My cousin, Mr. Jack Caldwell of Calderon, of the New Anglian Republic."

"Who is the woman?"

"I don't know," said Peter, staring himself . . . not at Jack, but at *her*.

"They are married?" asked Demassi.

"No, most certainly not," said Peter. "I just said I don't know who she is."

Demassi continued staring at the group of four as they made the long descent down the polished wooden walkway to the floating wooden dock.

"He is your same age?" asked Demassi. He seemed to have no interest in the women.

"Jack?"

Demassi nodded.

"No, one year older."

"How old is that?"

"He is in his twenty-third year," said Peter.

Demassi's eyes shifted, and his color drained as if he had just seen a ghost.

CHAPTER 20
Ottovan's Plan

Alwaz Deem—Saman Keer
5th Day, Month of Gandus, 807
Anglian Calendar: January 5, 1879

Few would deny that Ottovan Fanfar was brilliant. Many claimed he won his battles before they even began. They said Ottovan knew his enemies' moves before they themselves did. Across the years, even when outnumbered, which he often was, he had ambushed the ambushers, outflanked the flank attacks, and arrived first upon the high ground, whenever there was high ground to be had. His achievements were too numerous to ascribe to luck.

In the fight itself, Ottovan famously led from the front. His scimitarus sword had killed dozens, and even more had fallen before the barrels of his pistols, his shotgun, and when he used to operate one, his long gun. His courage, charisma, and competence made him beloved amongst the men he led. His long string of victories drove even the skeptics to declare Ottovan the greatest Demissary of his generation, and the best young Demissaries all sought to serve in the legion he commanded, the Third.

The truest testament to Ottovan's brilliance, however, was a secret known only to his wife and a handful of Oath Holders in the Order.

He was, and had been for nearly seventeen years, a traitor.

He was a traitor of the most dangerous kind—a traitor above suspicion, of nearly unlimited patience and positioned close to the pinnacle of power. Like the handful of other rising Demissaries that secretly followed him into treason so many years before, Ottovan joined the Order of the Ram, the Lion, and the Serpent in the year that Selahim the Grim burned Sah Seg Savanar alive.

As a young man, Ottovan had watched Lord Savanar, coming to know him as well as any young Demissary could, seeing that he was a rare, natural leader, revered by his fellow subjects, respected in the palaces of the Kezelboj, and adored in the alleyways of the flatlands. In Alwaz Deem, Savanar's fellow lords witnessed his wisdom, the merchants felt his fairness, and the poor welcomed his generosity. In the days of his youth, Ottovan often heard others say it was a shame that Lord Savanar had not been born Qhaliffa, instead of Selahim, who the people had already begun calling "the Grim." In the secret recesses of his heart, even then, Ottovan knew they were right.

Selahim the Grim, who was cunning but not wise, with little interest in fairness, and known for his greed, watched Lord Savanar's popularity with growing rage. With each passing year, the contrast with Lord Savanar made his deficiencies all the more glaring. Enflamed with envy and refusing to change himself, Selahim brooded that his people would never love him like they loved the Lord of Alwaz Deem.

Selahim had already resolved to destroy Lord Savanar when a young and ambitious Demissary commander showed him how. With Selahim's support, Ottovan's fellow Demissary, Jemojeen Jongdar, planned the fatal charges of heresy and high treason—bribing the witnesses, inventing the evidence, and coercing the lords and priests who would serve as Savanar's judges. When Jemojeen succeeded, Selahim elevated him above all others, making him his Grand Vizer.

Ottovan observed all of this as it happened, seventeen years before.

Then he watched Sah Seg Savanar burn. With his own eyes, Ottovan saw the courage and honor of the man as he kept his screams at bay, only succumbing in the last minutes, as the flames climbed higher and the pain overwhelmed him.

But it was Jemojeen's slaughter of the Savanar family and his stealing of the Savanar property that pushed Ottovan across the line. In the days after the murders, when The Serpent, The Lion, and The Ram visited him together in the darkness, he reached for his dagger, but the knowledge of Jemojeen killing the Savanar children stayed his hand. That night, Ottovan knew he could no longer serve the line of the Qhaliffas, and his secret life began.

Ottovan had risen in the years since, both visibly as a Demissary and behind the veil of the Order because he did not think like ordinary men. He was the rare man whose fame, if anything, understated his abilities and failed to capture the supreme discipline that governed his every action.

In the Game of the Squares of War, a game that nearly all men in the Seven Cities learned to play as boys and continued playing when they became men, Ottovan was rarely if ever defeated. In his early years in the Demissary barracks—years in the Academy when the young, heartsick Bulbanian boys had few entertainments beyond the Game of the Squares of War—only one could match him with any consistency, and that was Jemojeen Jongdar.

Jemojeen had now risen as far as a man who was not born Qhaliffa could ascend. Second only to the Qhaliffa himself, he now stood above the Highest

Kezelboj, while Ottovan still commanded Demissaries. Yet, despite his power, Jemojeen still watched him as a rival. Only two other Demissaries shared Ottovan's rank of legion commander, elected on merit by their peers and confirmed by the Qhaliffa. Equally troubling to Jemojeen, the three Demissary Legions remained as a separate source of strength, outside the authority of either the Grand Vizer or the Kezelboj, and by design, accountable only to the Qhaliffa himself.

As Commander of the Third Legion, Ottovan still spoke directly with the Qhaliffa, though not as often as he once did. Sumetan liked him and always had, despite Jemojeen's efforts to poison the Qhaliffa's mind against him with each passing year. Sumetan viewed Ottovan as a mentor, and that view, formed in boyhood, was not easily altered.

On orders from Sumetan's father, Selahim the Grim, Ottovan trained Sumetan in the way of the scimitarus. He was a natural swordsman in all of the ways that the young Qhaliffa-in-waiting was not, but rare among such blade handlers, Ottovan was also a natural teacher. That the Qhaliffa could now defend himself with a blade, years later, he owed almost entirely to Ottovan.

Across countless hours, Ottovan had taught the young Sumetan how to slash, how to parry, how to create force with leverage, how to feel with one's body where the other man is going to swing his blade, how to avoid that place, and how to exploit the other man's decisions. Ottovan showed him how every swing creates its own vulnerability and how in the moment of attack, the attacker is most exposed. That was the way of the Demissary, the way of Hom Hommuram, the teaching of the Great Lion himself.

And so it was, that Ottovan, in his secret treason, planned the next great act of the rebellion—taking the Staff of the Ram from its perch in the Throne Room of the Qhaliffa. He had waited for a great distraction. Selena Savanar's escape from the stake had at last provided it. Across the long years, he had never seen Jemojeen more distracted. His failure to burn the last Savanar had rattled him. In his power, he had grown unaccustomed to failure. Ottovan could now see that power, like rot inside of wood, had weakened part of Jemojeen's mind. Power had given birth to pride, and pride clouded his judgment.

With the same vision he used to defeat Jemojeen in the Game of the Squares of War, Ottovan saw that Jemojeen's mind hunted obsessively for Selena. When Jemojeen scattered his men all over the Seven Cities, Ottovan saw his chance. Jemojeen had slashed forward, and now his flank lay exposed. The Throne Room, Ottovan predicted, would be barely guarded.

In a general mobilization, all forces were required to heed the call: the Erassian Scouts, the Grand Vizerian Guardsmen, the Levies of the Kezelboj, and of course, once the Qhaliffa agreed, the most elite part of the army, the Demissary Legions.

Ottovan had foreseen this too. And so, he requested, days before, that the Third Legion be granted the honor of leading the attack on the Beserians, should the reports coming back from the Erassian scouts pan out to be true. Through intermediaries, he had convinced Jemojeen that if the Beserian, Abu Akhsa, had truly massed a force in the western deserts, plans must be made to attack him.

As Ottovan devised, his legion waited in the western city of Alwaz Deem, the place of their barracks, relieved of making far-flung patrols or manning guard posts to catch the fugitive Selena Savanar.

Ottovan then ensured that Ulgur Uggatar, Captain of the Third Legion's lancers—who had secretly been reporting to Jemojeen for years—would leave Ottovan's stone house just as Captain Nemakar Hasdruba arrived to discuss his orders for the fire Demissaries. Ottovan would make a show of explaining to them both that he would meet with Ozgar to discuss the role of the archers last, deep into the night.

But Ozgar Ogatonia, Captain of the Third Legion's archers and Oath Holder of the Order, would not be in Alwaz Deem. Ozgar would already be hiding in the capital of Saman Keer, on the other side of the Great Mountain. When Selena Savanar escaped onto the alpine trails south to Ganjar en Oxus, and Jemojeen spread out his forces trying to find her, Ozgar and his Oath Holders would descend upon the palace.

And there, they would take the Staff of the Ram before the Qhaliffa or his Grand Vizer understood what lay within their grasp, before they realized that the Year of the Prophecy could give them a weapon not used in eight hundred years since the days of the Prophet and Mamet the First.

For they still believed the Prophecy was a lie . . .

Ozgar surveyed his fighters. Five were Rams, four were Lions, and three were Serpents. They had approached the palace from above, from the west, where the steep slope of the Great Mountain met the limestone and granite walls of the Qhaliffa's fortress home. They were now close enough to see the outlines of the few Grand Vizerian Guardsmen and Demissary Lancers guarding the palace. Approaching from above, the ramparts were shortest, and the forest of upper Saman Keer came to within fifty yards of the palace walls. The cedars, ancient and massive, had stood since the years of the Prophet.

Ozgar looked out from behind one of them now. He and his fighters had exchanged their usual cream-colored robes, the color of Hahst sand, for the dark robes of a night attack. To call them robes was perhaps misguided, as they were bands of cloth, tightly wrapped around each of the Oath Holder's bodies, covering them from their ankles to their wrists, to the hair on their heads. On their hands, they wore gloves. Soft leather shoes covered their feet, shoes that allowed them to move silently along stone passageways. The cloth wrappings covered their faces, leaving only a narrow strip for their eyes. There was no looseness anywhere on their bodies, as loose fabric could snag a branch, catch a stray nail, or pull down a piece of stone. Slack cloth made accidents more likely, and the wrong sound at the wrong time could condemn them all.

Ozgar looked out over the covered faces of his men and women, making eye contact with each of them. His Lions carried their pistols. His Rams had their bows. The Serpents held their dart tubes. He gripped a bow of his own. Like the other archers, Ozgar exchanged his white fletched arrows of the Order in favor of dark arrows that could have been used by anyone. At the stakes in the Square of the Qhaliffa, it was important for all of Saman Keer to know who had rescued Selena Savanar and who had defied the power of Jemojeen, the Qhaliffa, and the priests. But tonight, it was better for no one to know.

A cloud moved across the moon. The space between the trees and the palace walls darkened. It was time.

"Go," said Ozgar, looking to the Rams who would lead the approach.

They nodded in acknowledgment, emerged from the tree line, and silently ran toward the fortress. The upper approach—moving down the mountain from the west—was always sparsely guarded compared to the northern, southern, or eastern approaches, even on an ordinary night. The great curtain wall of the east, the wall from which Jemojeen hung his net of severed heads after executions, faced outward toward the desert and, being above the center of the city of Saman Keer, carried the largest contingent of guards.

The west was always less protected. This night, Ozgar could see no more than a half-dozen guards along the entire western wall.

Ozgar's Rams moved more like cats than Rams across the dark ground, silent and swift. The ground was grassy but firm, with no stones marring the field. Through centuries of care, the trimmed sloped lawn beyond the west wall had taken on the domesticated appearance of a pleasure garden. Ozgar watched as the Rams reached the wall's shadow. The guards on the top of the wall, the half-dozen tasked with surveying four hundred yards of stone perimeter, did not stir. Ozgar looked up. The cloud still masked the moon.

"Now," he said.

He stepped out from behind the tree and ran, crouching low as he did so. He kept his eyes upon the wall, looking up at the closest guardsman. The guardsman did not move, staring out toward the cedar forest, never looking down at the line of darkly clothed fighters running in darkness over dark grass.

As they reached the even darker shadow of the palace wall, the clouds moved. Moonlight flooded the field they had just crossed. Ozgar placed a hand on the cold stone of the wall, crouching with the others. All eleven of his fighters waited, poised to continue.

"The God of the Mountain and the Sands is with us this night," said one of Ozgar's Rams.

"With us indeed," said Ozgar. "Remain vigilant." He pointed to the north.

The Rams moved first, staying close against the wall. They reached the door. It was low and wooden, studded with iron, and barely wide enough for one person to enter, too short for a grown man to stand in. The Rams waited for Ozgar.

The first test had been crossing the field. The second requirement was for the door to be unlocked. If it was still barred—if they had been betrayed— they would have to scale the walls. They would have to kill the guardsmen, and in killing guardsmen, they would likely alert the others. Their mission was not to fight, but to get in and out undetected, while Jemojeen was distracted, seeking those fleeing from him, not those attacking his very center.

Ottovan had explained all of this to him, but Ozgar alone knew of Ottovan's involvement this night. Such was the way of the Order. The less a captured fighter could say under the knives, the straps, and the flames of Jemojeen's torturers, the better.

One of the Rams knocked upon the door while one of the Serpent men crouched beside Ozgar, his eyes bright, even in the shadows. Ozgar had long ago learned that under the ground, none were superior to Sworn Serpents of the Order.

Ozgar nodded to the Ram. He knocked again.

Only silence answered.

Ozgar looked up at the positioning of the moon, knowing that his timing was correct.

Hoofbeats sounded in the distance. The horses were walking, and they carried riders on their backs.

Ozgar identified the sound in an instant.

"Knock again."

The Ram knocked.

The hoofbeats came nearer.

A muffled sound arose behind the door—a cry, followed by a thud.

The door swung open.

A purple-robed eunuch stumbled backward out the door, gripping a dagger, a spear jammed deep into his chest. His eyes were open but unmoving above a mouth still frozen in a gasp.

"There are more!" said a man from the darkness. Whatever torches had illuminated the passageway were snuffed out. Through the door lay pitch blackness. The sounds of footsteps rushed toward them.

The Sworn Serpents—two of them—stepped forward into the darkness without hesitation. Their blowguns already raised to their lips, each made a small thump as they sent their darts forward into the tunnel.

The footsteps stopped.

"There are no more," said one of the Sworn Serpents looking ahead into the blackness with narrowed, yellow-green eyes.

The hoofbeats grew louder outside.

"Into the tunnel. Hurry," said Ozgar, pushing the last of the Sworn Lions in as she passed him.

He entered last.

Standing in the darkness of the doorway, he looked out across the field toward the edge of the cedars. A patrol of three riders approached in dark armor and dark clothing. Conical helmets covered their heads, with strands of colorful ribbons hanging down from the top.

Kezelboj cavalry. God of the Mountain, Jemojeen has called forth everyone, thought Ozgar.

He did not reach for his bowstring. He could drop them all before they saw him, sending them down to the turf with arrows in their chests, but then there would be dead horsemen, and dead horsemen have a way of being found, even in the middle of the night, especially when the moon is full and guardsmen man the ramparts. Ozgar slipped inside the studded oaken door, into the darkness.

One of the Sworn Lions found the edge of the door and began to push it shut, the dense wood creaking on its hinges as it moved toward the stone mouth of the tunnel. It closed with a thud. Ozgar heard one of his companions grasp the iron bolts and slide them into their grooves.

Unless the Kezelboj horsemen had brought a battering ram and team to swing it, they would not be entering through the door. There was only one way to go now, and that was forward, deeper into the tunnel, underneath the palace of the Qhaliffa.

The blackness was total. A man moaned, breathing in gasps.

"Give me light," said Ozgar with urgency in his whisper.

An Oath Holder lit a torch.

A dozen faces emerged in the cramped corridor. Sworn Lions, Rams, and Serpents looked back into Ozgar's eyes, their heads nearly grazing the low stone roof. They were all experienced fighters, each chosen carefully for the mission.

Ozgar fought the fear in his stomach, swallowing hard. The tunnel was no place for a man frightened of tight spaces. Ozgar was such a man. He feared nothing while on horseback, charging across the open desert, even when a hail of bullets or a rain of arrows fell upon him. But Ozgar hated tunnels, especially narrow tunnels with low ceilings. He looked down.

At his feet, several heaps of cloth did not move.

In the torchlight, he looked toward the moaning and the heavy breathing. The man wore the clothes of a palace servant. Ozgar did not recognize the face of the small man with abnormally large ears. The man had given his life to open the door, and he had speared a eunuch of the Qhaliffa to do it.

"We owe our lives to you, friend," he whispered, looking down at the little man.

The man looked up at him with pain in his eyes.

"Check the eunuchs," said Ozgar, crouching down over the dying servant.

The Serpents approached the eunuchs without hesitation. Ozgar saw their small thin knives in the torchlight, their fangs, the razor-sharp killing blades, slightly curved and shorter than a grown man's forearm.

The Serpents bent down and slashed the throats of the bodies beneath them. If the men in the eunuch robes still had life in them, they did no longer.

"What does it mean?" asked one of the Rams, looking warily into the darkness of the tunnel beyond the limits of the torchlight.

Ozgar shook his head. He looked down at the body of the servant. Shallow, ragged breaths still lifted his chest.

"Friend, you will soon be in Paradise, beside the Eternal Stream with the God of the Mountain and the Sands. Tell me your name."

The man spoke faintly, "Bayd—"

"You have done your duty to the Order and to the God we all serve. May blessings be upon you."

The man nodded his head, slight but definite. He opened his eyes, burning with fierce urgency. "He . . . knows."

"Who knows?"

"He . . . knows the power—"

"The power of what?"

"The power . . . of the sta . . . Jemoj—" The man's head collapsed.

"How did the eunuchs find you?"

The man gurgled, trying to speak.

Ozgar could not make out the words.

"Friend, tell me, how did the eunuchs know you were here?"

The man made another effort to speak, but his words were unclear.

"Were you followed?"

"No," said the man, shaking his head with effort. Then he opened his eyes wide, and drew in a last gasping breath. "They were . . ."

"They were already here? Did they know?"

The man's head fell back against the stone of the wall, tilting toward one of his shoulders.

"Did they know we were coming?" asked Ozgar.

One of the Serpents reached toward the servant, grabbing his wrist.

"He is gone," said the Serpent.

"Are you sure?"

The Serpent moved his hand up to the man's neck. "He is dead and gone."

"May he drink from the Eternal Stream," said Ozgar.

The others all echoed his words.

"Someone knows we are here," said one of the Rams.

"We should go back out the door, kill the Kezelboj riders and return to the forest," said one of the Lions.

"If they were waiting for us, we are entering a trap. They will capture and torture us all," said another Ram.

"If we are to flee, we must flee now," said a third Ram.

"No," said Ozgar, shaking his head and remembering Ottovan's words.

"If it is a trap? If the eunuchs knew to be here, would you have us continue into the palace? Those eunuchs guard the Qhaliffa's harem. They are men accustomed to guarding narrow spaces. Why would they be here in the tunnels except to trap someone coming in from that door?" It was the first Ram that spoke again. Nothing he said was false.

Ozgar looked into the eyes of the Serpent nearest him. She was very young, but among the best Sworn Serpents in all of the Order. Sendata. He had requested her for a reason. She had, beyond all of the skills required of her, the judgment to lead.

"What say you, Sendata?"

"Tonight, we take the Staff of the Ram," she said. "There will not be another opportunity such as this. Our enemy's eyes are elsewhere, seeking the Savanar. Tonight is the night."

Ozgar nodded. "We will not flee. Tonight, we take the Staff of the Ram in fulfillment of the Prophecy. Follow me."

He grabbed the torch from the hand of one of the Rams and walked deeper into the darkness, conquering his fear of the tunnel and whatever else might lie ahead.

CHAPTER 21
The Lure of Katya

Altadige
Eastern Spatanian Empire
January 18–19, 1879

Stanwich's agitation seemed to grow with each passing day. He was always a man that gave the impression of constant movement, but while waiting for the New Anglians, he had seemed to grow positively anxious. When the New Anglians finally arrived, he wasted no time.

On Stanwich's orders, the entire expedition, fifty-two strong, boarded a Spatanian Imperial train from the Veteno to the mountain border town of Altadige, where they would meet their camels and pick up their final supplies. Though no one told Peter that two women would now be joining them, neither Stanwich nor Hersen seemed surprised by Hannah Huntington and Mrs. Smith's arrival, reminding Peter that there was much about the expedition he still did not know.

A handful of others who would not be venturing into the Sand Sea joined the expedition for the train ride to Altadige, including the Brothers Leboveckian, their servants, and Jones, Peter's valet from Hylebourne House. Peter sat with Jones, periodically looking over his book to catch glimpses of Hannah on the far side of the first-class car. When she found him looking at her, she did not smile, so Peter raised his book over his face where she could not see him blushing.

Like many things in the Spatanian Empire, their train, said to be among the most modern in all of eastern Spatania, was ornate and sluggish. Its compartments were gilded, full of mirrors, and lined with big windows that gave them all a comprehensive view of the coastal plain as the lower Veteno slipped past them. The marshlands receded as they steamed past the tidy farms and woods of the upper Veteno. Then the snowcapped peaks came into view, and all became steep ridges, evergreen forests, and deep valleys as the train slowly chugged its way up into the border mountains and Altadige.

As the landscapes passed by and the train climbed the mountain, Peter tried more than once to strike up a conversation with his cousin, but Jack Caldwell sat with his arms crossed, napping. When he was awake, he seemed as disinterested in talking with Peter as the New Anglian sergeant at his side. When Peter asked him his thoughts on their mission and the articles he had in mind to write for the *Illustrated Telegraph*, Jack had merely smirked and nodded, as if he knew things Peter did not, as if he were an adult and Peter still a child, though they were only one year apart.

When they arrived, Altadige was cold, dark, and eerily still.

The winds, when they came from the east, blowing off of the Sand Sea through the Mountain Gate, were said to be ferocious, but there was no wind now, not even a faint breeze. The Imperial Spatanian Flag, with its silver lion against a red-brown background, hung like a limp, dark cloth from its three-story staff in the center of the square.

They stepped off the train into a silent city.

Minutes before midnight, the totality of the town appeared to be sleeping. The streets consisted of smooth stone pavers, newly refurbished by an ambitious imperial architect. The architect, a young Baron from the Bulbanian borderlands, had plans for the Imperial Spatanian Capital itself, nearly one thousand miles to the west. But he first sought to perfect the improvements in Altadige, treating the place as an experimental canvas, a proving ground for his vision.

Altadige was a difficult city to define—part imperial outpost, part trade route bazaar, part playground to the continental aristocracy. For generations, the Spatanian royal family, House Adomingo, and its extensive band of courtiers had taken their annual trips to Altadige, generally once in the high winter and once in the high summer. And where the court of the Monarch-Emperor traveled, so too did the aristocracy.

One generation prior, when Peter's parents were still young, the Anglian nobility had seemingly discovered Altadige all at once. Soon it became common to see the likes of Anglian Parliamentary leaders like Orlando Browne and, in younger days, even the Prime Minister, Binyam Aurelian, skating on the ice in the winter season and dining at the cafes in the summer after long hikes in the green, alpine valleys.

Jack Caldwell blew into his hands, remembering how few places were better than Calderon in the winter months.

"It is cold, but at least it is dry," said Peter Harmon with a pleasant smile.

Jack looked down at Peter's hands, enveloped by warm, fur-lined leather gloves. Jack shook his head. "I just feel the cold."

Peter's eyes moved to the stairs of the first-class carriage where Hannah Huntington descended in a full-length coat, lined in ermine with a matching round hat. In the gaslight overhead, Peter looked at the beautiful lines of her high cheekbones framing the deep blue of her eyes.

Aurelio Demassi exited the second-class cabin at nearly the same moment. Over his shoulders, he wore a thin blanket, and his feet were still bare in his leather sandals. Peter looked at him as if he were a madman.

"Look at him," said Peter, elbowing Jack and pointing at Aurelio. "Naked as a beggar."

Aurelio gazed at Peter from several train lengths away. His dark eyes, as usual, met Peter's with a piercing intensity.

"I am disinterested in your guide, Peter," said Jack.

"He is a strange one, Jack," whispered Peter. "There is something off about him. I spoke with him at the docks when you were arriving, he said —"

Jack turned away. "Hello, Hannah."

Hannah walked toward them with Mrs. Matilda Smith in tow. Joshua Barnes held one end of a heavy trunk as Mrs. Smith gripped the other handle.

Strange New Anglians, thought Peter. *They could just wait for the porters. Why carry your own trunk?*

Hannah walked unencumbered, seemingly floating along the pavement, the edge of her coat grazing just inches above the stones. Hannah smiled, and Peter felt his heart flutter. She was tall, strong, and utterly compelling to his eyes.

"Did you sleep on the train?" asked Jack with a relaxed familiarity.

"A bit," said Hannah, glancing around the empty square. Shops lined the edges with heavy wooden shutters covering their windows. The cafe tables and chairs that would line the square in summer were all stowed away. Small piles of old snow rested against the corners of the buildings.

Peter stared at Hannah's face, saying nothing.

"I spoke with Stanwich," said Hannah. "He says we will wait until dawn the day after tomorrow, and then we will begin the march to the Mountain Gate. We will pass through by midday and make the descent into the sands by sundown."

Peter watched this woman in an elegant, fur-lined coat discussing a march into the desert and found himself liking every part of her in a way that he had not desired a woman before. Sarah Hesiger crossed his mind—the subject that had been the equivalent of an open wound ever since his father had told him he was to go to the Sand Sea instead of Khyderbad. He thought of her, dancing with Ernesto Ruggiero, and for the first time, he did not care, as if Hannah's presence had rendered Sarah's magic impotent to command his desire.

Hannah glanced at Peter, her eyes meeting his intense, hungry stare. She quickly looked back at Jack. Peter's cheeks flushed.

"Very well," she said. "We are off to our sleeping quarters. Tomorrow will be full of tasks."

"Sleep well," said Jack, as easily as if he were speaking to his sister.

"Yes," said Peter, his voice sounding odd and forced to his own ears.

Mrs. Smith glanced at him, askance as they walked away.

"Not to gossip, but that one has an eye for you," she said, once they were out of earshot.

"Who?" asked Hannah.

"The young Anglian."

"Peter Harmon?"

Mrs. Smith nodded.

"I hadn't noticed," she lied.

Jack reached his sleeping quarters and sat on his bed. A pair of flickering gas lamps illuminated the walls, flanking oil paintings of imposing Altadige landscapes. *An excellent combination to make a fire*, thought Jack, idly.

His trunk rested at the foot of his bed, where Barnes had instructed the porters to place it. Jack's nightclothes waited on the bed. A chamber pot sat on the polished planks of the hardwood floor. A small fire burned, giving warmth as well as light to supplement the gas lamps. Barnes's room was adjacent to his own, smaller and sparsely appointed in the manner of a servant's quarters.

"Barnes, I'll be going to bed early tonight," said Jack. "So, goodnight."

The door handle clicked, and the adjoining door cracked open. Barnes appeared in the gap, already wearing his nightclothes.

"Seven thirty tomorrow?" he asked.

"We meet Stanwich at eight? Yes, I'd rather sleep than bathe. Seven thirty," said Jack.

Barnes nodded and closed the door. Jack considered locking it but then thought better of it. Barnes would undoubtedly hear the lock turn, even in the dead of sleep. He was that kind of man. If he ever really slept, he never slept with his guard fully down. But nor was Barnes the sort of man to open the door without reason.

Jack pulled his boots off of his feet and walked around his bed to his trunk. He dug down and found his evening clothes. Barnes always operated with an organized mind. The tie, the waistcoat, the shirt, the trousers, and the jacket were all there, packaged together. He found his black city shoes, well-shined, and covered with a slip of cloth to keep the polish away from the clothes.

Jack dressed in silence. Fully clothed, he tied his tie and looked in the mirror. *Not bad for no valet!*

He turned sideways and admired himself. He took a small glop of pomade from his jar and used it to slick back his hair. He found his comb and executed a precise, if somewhat severe, side-part. Standing on the rug to muffle the sound of his feet, he tied his shoes and took one last look in the mirror. He looked every bit the oligarch that he intended to be this evening. They would treat him well.

He stepped with extreme caution toward the hallway door. Barnes, if he was asleep, was barely so. He would have to make it down the hallways briskly. He had already located the servants' door at the end of the hall and the stairway no one else of their party would be using. Peter's room was at the other end. He and Jones went in at the same time as he and Barnes. Stanwich and Hersen were on a different floor. Hannah and Mrs. Smith went to bed earlier than he did. The hallway would be vacant.

He turned the door handle. It clicked far more loudly than he remembered it clicking when he went into the room. He froze.

He heard nothing. He waited long moments with the door handle held in his hand. Satisfied that he had not awakened anyone—Barnes in particular—he took a series of quick furtive steps out onto the rug in the center of the hallway. The carpet muffled his feet, but he walked on his toes nonetheless. After covering the length of the hallway, dreading each door he passed, he finally reached the end of the hall. He turned and looked down the softly lit corridor. It was as empty as when he had stepped into it. He passed into the stairwell beyond the door. The stairs were dark, with only the moonlight of the window and a few nearly spent candles showing him the steps beneath his feet. He descended the steps quickly, pulled the door handle in his finely gloved hands, and the frigid night air embraced him. It was still windless and calm. The alley on the side of the hotel was empty, except for the greying piles of old snow pushed up against stone walls.

He shrugged against the cold, pulling his dark overcoat tighter around his shoulders, and buttoned up one more button than was fashionable. He adjusted his scarf around his neck. He reached up and pushed the brim of his top hat down firmly on his head. Yes, it would make him conspicuous—a man walking alone in a fine overcoat and top hat—but Altadige was not a terribly dangerous place, and he was a large man with a considerable silver head on his walking stick.

He turned down the alley. At the boulevard, he made a left, in the direction of the Mountain Gate. The street was largely deserted. A pair of men in top hats eyed him from the other side of the street as he walked. They smoked cigars, talking quietly under a gas lamp.

Jack continued forward.

After a quarter of a mile, passing a series of closed shops with large, brightly colored signs above them, he turned down a narrower, less well-lit street and headed south. He walked for a hundred yards or so, and then made another turn.

There, in front of him, hung a row of red signs flanking a narrow alley. Jack walked faster. He did not turn to see the figure tracking his movements from several blocks behind him.

Jack walked past the first few signs.

"The sixth door on the right beneath the number seven." That was what the man in the hotel had told him. Jack had given him a fifty-ducat note and asked him to be quiet and tell no one about their conversation.

The man's eyes had widened, and he said, "Thank you, sir. I recall neither your face nor our conversation."

Jack had nodded and walked away, confident the sum was more than the man would likely earn in a week of work at the hotel desk.

Jack came to the sixth door on the right. Through the cloudy glass, Jack could see a warm light within. He heard voices and the sounds of a lewd Spatanian song. He pulled on the door, but it was locked.

He knocked.

A small, dark-haired woman with large, corseted breasts opened the door. "Sir?"

"May I come in?" asked Jack.

She quickly looked him up and down, smiled, and said, "Welcome."

Jack stepped through the entryway.

A dozen voices washed over him, and the warmth of the room embraced him. The scents of a half-dozen perfumes entered his nostrils at once. There was no foyer like at Madame Nadia's, just a handful of men scattered across the room.

None paid him much attention beyond a cursory glance. Most of the men had young women sitting on their laps in various states of undress. There were platters of food strewn about the room and carafes of wine everywhere he looked. Everyone seemed to be either drunk or well on their way to drunkenness. A tall woman with long red hair resumed her song in the middle of the room. She wore a light pink dress of thin, almost translucent silk so that Jack could see every contour of her lithe, well-proportioned figure.

"May I take your coat, sir?" asked the large-breasted woman in the corset.

"Yes," said Jack, handing her his walking stick and top hat before removing his coat and gloves.

As quickly as the corseted woman walked away with his hat, stick, and coat, another woman approached him.

She was a dark-haired beauty in the classic eastern Spatanian style. Perhaps she was a Venetan, maybe even a native Altadigean. Jack could not tell. Nor did he particularly care. She was magnificent to behold. She stood close to him, and her perfume embraced him. Her skin was olive-colored and without blemish. She wore silk slippers that stuck out from beneath the bottom hem of her silken dress.

"Wine?" she asked.

"Yes," said Jack, resigning himself to the energy of the place, the warmth moving across his skin like a liquid.

He took a glass of golden wine and raised it to his lips. It was neither sweet nor dry, neither warm nor cold, but it reminded him of flowers and honey and freshly dug soil all at once.

"What else may I bring you?"

Jack smiled, feeling bold.

"Do you have any blonde Bulbanians?" His Spatanian accent was just passable.

The woman looked at him with a flirtatious twinkle in her bright brown eyes.

"Of course we do."

And then he saw her.

She looked so much like Katya that he nearly jumped. She walked toward him with the same jaunty bobbing of her hips, back and forth. She had the same full lips and the same lean, muscular legs. And her hair was as golden as sunlight itself.

The flash of her brilliantly colored hair, and the twinkling of her golden-brown eyes . . . that was the last thing he remembered.

CHAPTER 22
Mist over the Red Rooftops

Sundar Dun
13th Day, Month of Gandus, 807
Anglian Calendar: January 13, 1879

In the darkness of the third hour past midnight, Sundar Dun looked as clean and peaceful as any of the other Seven Cities. Even its bloodred rooftops looked merely dark in the soft moonlight, little different from the roofs of Meer Norekah or Nor Gandus.

But Selena knew that darkness deceives. They had made their way along the side paths of the Upper Ring Road, from Saman Keer, moving south and west to Ganjar en Oxus and westward still across the Great Mountain to the upper valley of Sundar Dun.

They had avoided the Grand Vizer's Guardsmen, the Kezelboj patrols, and even a company of Demissary Lancers. Selena had marveled at her companions. They led her high up the mountain, up paths and down hidden trails along the steep slopes of the upper southern valleys, taking ways that she did not know existed, filling their waterskins in the rivers, and eating only the dried strips of meat and little meal cakes they carried with them.

Selena crouched now below a stunted, wind-tortured cedar, its thick trunk gnarled from years of struggle, growing out of a crack in a slab of granite. Oapah crouched beneath her on the slope, his oxlike shoulders rising and falling with his breath. Gulana squatted to her right, her eyes focused on the city below. They were all in need of a bath, a real bath with soap and a good scrubbing. Their smell took Selena's mind back to her days as a street girl in the flatlands, amongst the poor for whom meals were uncertain and bathing, at best, a semi-monthly event. Anyone downwind would smell their stench.

"This will be the most perilous part," said Gulana, frowning.

A deep crease of worry ran from her hairline down to her eyebrows, dividing her forehead in two. A vague sense of dread had grabbed hold of her since they had first set out on the southwestern path to Ganjar en Oxus. Her veil was pulled down, revealing her face.

Selena looked at Gulana's dark olive skin and large, intelligent eyes in the moonlight.

"They will be down there in force," said Gulana. "They will foresee an escape down the Oxus, or into the Semissari."

Oapah grunted in assent.

The other Oath Holders spread out along the ridgeline, crouching and squatting amongst the scrub brush. An enemy was more likely to smell them than see them, thought Selena. All knew how to conceal themselves. Close as she was, Selena could barely pick them out amongst the bushes.

"Will there be mist on the river?" asked Gulana.

Oapah stared forward. "Yes, see there."

Even whispering, as always, his voice was deep and powerful. Oapah pointed down into the River Oxus, extending southward to the horizon, a stripe of darkness against the pale grey of the southern desert in the faint moonlight. Gulana could see that the usual glassiness of the river was cloudy as if covered in haze.

"The mist rises," said Oapah. "Praise be to the God of the Mountain and the Sands."

"We must go now," said Rondus Rungar, the lead Ram.

He was a broad-shouldered man with a wide forehead, a large nose, and a recessed chin. He had lowered his veil, letting Selena see his face as his large hands gripped an iron-studded battle staff, the close combat weapon of choice amongst the Rams.

"We will be fortunate to reach the river line by the sunrise, and that is if we move swiftly."

Selena watched as the others debated her fate.

"And what if we do not reach the Ring River by sunrise?" she asked.

Rondus, the Ram, shook his head. He spoke with an accent of the east, like a man from the Xin borderlands. "Then we will find a safe house. But no house is safe in Sundar Dun. Not now."

"What if we waited the night and day here?" asked Selena.

"Then a Kezelboj patrol might find us. A shepherd might find us. And if we are discovered, we will fail. Do not underestimate how badly our enemies desire you, and the Grand Vizer has many eyes and ears on this mountain, Lady Savanar."

Selena nodded, considering.

Rondus continued. "If we are not waiting at the sunrise, our rowers will fear the worst. They may linger longer than they should. They will risk capture if the Grand Vizer's River Galleys are patrolling. They will then have to hide their rowboats again. That means two more trips in and out of hiding in which they can be seen. We will then have to hope they return on the morrow to wait in the same place, hoping that we will be there waiting."

"Is there any way to get them a message?" asked Selena.

"Yes, but it is the same way we would take to get you on the boat."

"Then lead the way," said Selena. She had begun asserting herself, and more so with each passing day on the mountain, the farther they had traveled together.

Oapah nodded.

Gulana stared down onto the rooftops of Sundar Dun, bloodred by day, but almost black in the night. The crease in her forehead deepened.

Selena walked down the steep mountain slope with her hand on Oapah's back. Scrub oaks and dwarf cedars blocked out the moonlight, darkening their way. Yet despite the darkness, none of Selena's twelve companions lost their footing down the ravines. Gulana, always walking just behind her, kept a hand on Selena Savanar more often than not, and Oapah's massive form remained in front of her. If she fell, she would fall into him, and Selena did not believe she was capable of altering the Sworn Lion's balance, even if she were to push him with all her strength when he was not expecting it.

They stopped seven times at the bidding of the Sworn Serpents.

As always, they heard things others did not hear and saw things others did not see.

The Rams, led by Rondus, staked out the best terrain—the less-traveled and the most secret. Always moving down the mountain, they slid laterally across rock faces and moved in and out of trees and shrubs. As the grade lessened, the number of buildings increased, and Selena could feel the worry emanating from Gulana like an added body odor.

When Selena turned back to look at her, Gulana shook her head.

"We are almost there," said Selena, not knowing whether her words were true or not.

"We should not have chosen Sundar Dun," whispered Gulana.

"We will move through quickly," said Selena.

"We should have gone through Ganjar en Oxus."

"Sundar Dun is closer to the Semissari," whispered Selena, parroting the argument of Rondus the Ram.

One of the Sworn Serpents looked back, silencing them with her eyes.

Gulana shook her head at Selena in disagreement.

The red-roofed buildings rose all around them. The darkness hid the grime that clung to the unwashed plaster and dirty stone. The better parts of Sundar

Dun would hold the most Grand Vizerian Guardsmen, so they had avoided the better parts, descending through the territory of the gangs.

The grade had almost diminished to nothing. That meant that they were close to the Ring River, approaching the flatlands. In the flatlands of Sundar Dun, the Qhaliffa's rule was nominal at best. Neither Demissaries, nor Kezelboj levies, nor even Jemojeen's Grand Vizerian Guardsmen often waded into the muck of the flatlands of Sundar Dun. The Demissaries had bigger things to worry about, the levies were afraid, and the guardsmen were bribed to stay away.

The gangs ran the flatlands, and the gangs did not care for the Order any more than they cared for the Qhaliffa. The difference, however, was that most of the gangs had paid Jemojeen's Sipahis to keep their guardsmen out of the flatlands.

In exchange for their freedom, the gangs promised to take care of trouble-makers, as the Grand Vizer understood the term, and there were no worse trou-blemakers in the eyes of Jemojeen Jongdar than the Oath Holders of the Order of the Ram, the Lion, and the Serpent. No, there would be no friendly faces in the flatlands of Sundar Dun.

As they crept along in the darkness, Selena could see that Oapah's right hand gripped the handle of his curved, two-handed scimitarus. It was an old and powerful weapon, used by few. To use a two-handed scimitarus, a man had to wield great strength. Walking behind him, Selena again felt reassured, knowing she could not envision a man wielding more physical strength than Oapah the Hohsa.

They moved down the alley swiftly, moving in groups of three, first the Serpents, then the Rams, then Oapah, Selena and Gulana, and then the three Lions in the rear. The tiles of the buildings on either side of them leaned over the alley, nearly touching the rooftops on the other side and blocking out the moonlight.

"Who goes there?" said a man's voice, deep and grumbling.

Selena felt Gulana's hand on her back, pushing her down.

Selena was already crouching. Her face almost touched Oapah's back, his smell at such range nearly overpowering. There was no wind in the alley, only darkness and the ringing of the man's voice.

A torch advanced into the alley, throwing its light up onto the overhanging buildings above and illuminating the dirty walls flanking the cobblestones below.

Selena could not hear the sound of the blow dart as it left the Serpent's hollow tube. The man fell onto his face, limp as an eel in a monger's stall. His torch landed on the cobbles with a clang.

The Sworn Serpents rushed forward along the alley walls, signaling that all should follow with haste.

Gulana's firm grip lifted Selena onto her feet. Selena's movements never seemed to be swift enough to avoid a push, a pull, or a nudge from Gulana.

"We must move. Where there is one, there are more," said Gulana.

Selena could hear her anxious tone, picturing the crease in her forehead deepening even farther behind her sand-colored veil. Selena looked down at the man's silent corpse as Gulana shoved her forward.

They ran.

Selena could hear her own footsteps on the cobbles. The others seemed to run in silence as if their feet never actually touched the ground. Selena had noticed that about the Oath Holders of the Order. They could all move with stunning speed and silence, even the giant Lions like Oapah the Hohsa.

Selena had no idea which direction they ran, slipping in and out of twisting alleyways. The darkness was almost total, and once one descended into the flatlands, the alleys and winding lanes became a tangle of ancient roads, some short, some incredibly long. Most were narrow and refused to follow a straight line. To those who did not know their way, the flatlands were nearly an impenetrable maze, a fact the gangs had used to their advantage for generations upon generations to maintain their violent semi-freedom from Qhaliffan rule.

The Sworn Serpents leading the way moved with decisive speed, never pausing to decide which alley to cut down or lane to run across. They moved at a dead run, and the others followed.

They ran for long minutes. Selena's lungs began to protest, and her legs began to weaken. The Oath Holders of the Order all ran as if they could continue at the same pace for hours. And then as suddenly as they had turned down yet another narrow alley, they stood at the wharf, on the edge of the Ring River, looking down on the Great Pool at the base of the Great Mountain. Large as a vast lake, it was the starting point of the Oxus, the mighty life-giving river that flowed south through the Sand Sea, cutting through the Harafhan Mountains, into the verdant plains of Hindea, dividing Hindea from Gengal, and finally ending in the Sea of Omakhosi one and a half thousand miles to the south.

Gulana's hand pulled down on Selena's back.

Each time Gulana pushed and pulled, it irritated Selena a little. But as she looked, all of the others in their party already crouched down at the edge of the open stone wharf, searching for danger. As usual, she was the last to duck, the last to be where she should.

Perhaps Gulana will stop pushing me when I move as well as the others. As she crouched, still trying to catch her breath and looking out over the Great Pool, Selena's cheeks reddened in frustration and embarrassment.

The sunrise was not far away.

To the west lay starlit blackness, but the sky had begun to turn pink in the east. Selena heard the sound of boots striking stone in the rhythmic beat of soldiers marching. The sound came from the west, from the direction of Alwaz Deem. Selena stared out from between two crates, her back against the stone wall of a Ring River warehouse. Trash lay strewn on the cobbles in front of her, old rotting rinds of melons, bits of rag, and reeking piles of manure.

"In Nor Gandus, any merchant who treated the road that way would be flogged," whispered Gulana into Selena's ear, speaking of her native city on the north side of the mountain. "But of course, no merchant of Nor Gandus would ever treat the road that way."

The thumping sound of the marching boots grew louder, mixing with the sounds of swinging weapons on leather belts and the rustling of chain mail.

"Guardsmen from the barracks beneath Alwaz Deem," said Gulana. "An entire company of them."

Selena saw them as they appeared, nearly one hundred strong. Their clothing, armor, helmets, and turbans were all dark and menacing in the early morning light. Where they marched was not clear, but their faces all looked forward. A Sipahi led them, carrying a mace in his hands.

They marched with the certainty that their numbers protected them. There were no advanced men, no scouts, no screening forces, just a column of marching men, four men across. Even the boldest Sundar Dun gang would not be so mad as to challenge an entire company of mailed guardsmen on the march.

Selena sat as still as the stone wall behind her as the guardsmen filed past. They were close enough that she could smell them—leather, oiled mail, and the pungent body odor of a large body of men that had not recently bathed. For a moment, a surge of fear moved through her as she thought that perhaps they could smell her too. It had been long days since she had scrubbed the grime off of her. But no man so much as glanced in her direction. The breath caught in her throat as they stomped past, as if they might hear the sound of air moving in and out of her lungs.

They marched onward, with the Great Pool at the base of the Ring River to their right and the stone warehouses of the flatlands of Sundar Dun to their left. The sky continued to brighten in the east.

"Where are they?" asked Selena, at last taking in a full breath while scanning the edge of the river beneath the stone wharf.

A stagnant armada of river ships lay at anchor. Others gently swayed on their moorings in the slow-moving water of the Great Pool. They bobbed in and out of Selena's line of sight through the swirling mists, but Selena could not yet see a single ship moving through the fog. Surely the fishermen would head out for their morning efforts soon? She heard no oars, and there was still little wind to push a sail.

"Shh," whispered Gulana, putting her finger to her lips.

"They will come," said Oapah. "They are Oath Holders of the Order."

"They will come," said Gulana, agreeing.

Selena stared out into the mist-covered river, the mists that would shield them from prying eyes. The tightness in her chest lessened.

The God of the Mountain and the Sands has granted us this mist. It will mask our escape upon the water. We will not die here in Sundar Dun.

The mists continued to thicken, moving over the stone cobbles upon which they crouched, washing over the warehouses, covering the flatlands of Sundar Dun like a moist, floating blanket, and rising up the valley of central Sundar Dun itself, as if a hungry cloud had moved in to swallow the city.

CHAPTER 23
The Staff of the Ram

Saman Keer
5th Day, Month of Gandus, 807
Anglian Calendar: January 5, 1879
Eight Days Earlier

The Order's map of the palace was accurate, down to the smallest details. Ozgar had studied that map for weeks, and he made sure the others knew it as well as he did. They had planned in total secrecy, with the individual Rams, Lions, and Serpents he selected not even knowing who else would be joining them. Each understood their role, and they knew only that Ozgar Ogatonia would lead the mission.

From the tunnels, they traveled deep into the central underbelly of the palace.

Over the centuries, the tunnels had proliferated. It was now possible to move from one end of the palace to another entirely underground. If someone was waiting to ambush them, it was a very patient ambush.

As they walked—and they had been moving for the better part of half an hour—Ozgar began to suspect that the eunuchs they'd confronted in the hallway had been waiting for something else. Who could say what motivated those odd and secretive gelded men to do anything, or where they ventured when they were not guarding the Qhaliffa's harem? Certainly not Ozgar Ogatonia.

Sendata, Sworn Serpent, walked first, swift and silent as a snake. At certain places where the tunnels turned, she stopped them abruptly, hearing some distant sound far before Ozgar or any of the Rams or Lions. There were parties of guards down in the tunnels, mostly Grand Vizerian Guardsmen, moving in groups of two and three. Even underground, they carried their spears, and they wore their heavy chain mail shirts and black-cone helmets beneath their black turbans. In Sendata's ears, their movements were as noisy and obvious as those of panting bulls.

One patrol came within ten feet of Sendata, but they did not turn down the tunnel in which a dozen Oath Holders hid in the shadow of the wall. Sendata had halted the others with a single soft sound.

In the tunnels, there lay total darkness but for the flickering light coming from the torches in sconces, mounted along the stone corridors. There were not many torches on the walls of the larger passageways, and in some of the smaller passages, there was no light at all.

At the place where the map indicated they would find the stairway to the ground level, the level beneath the Throne Hall, they found a closed door with an arched top, barely visible in the faint torchlight. The door matched the contours of the stone ceiling above it. Ozgar tensed, on high alert, his limbs already tingling with adrenaline. As he looked at the door, his heart beat faster.

Even in the middle of the night, the ground floor would be perilous. There were doors in every direction, and the enemy could come from any point on the compass. The ground floor was open, intended to be a grand place of gathering, a place to awe all supplicants with the might and majesty of the Qhaliffa.

Sendata crouched. Ozgar squatted down behind her. The sweat on her neck smelled sweet.

Ozgar spoke in a whisper, startlingly loud in the silence. "Remember, we must return to this door. When we have the staff, we come through here and move down through the tunnels, using the same path from which we just arrived."

In the flickering torchlight, Ozgar looked into the faces of his sworn fighters. They were all covered, with only their eyes showing. He did not see fear in their eyes.

"In the name of the God of the Mountain and the Sands," said Ozgar.

All of his fighters whispered the words back.

"In the name of the believers who have burned for the cause."

The fighters repeated the words.

Ozgar felt a wave of pride rush through him. These were the best of the Order, and he was their leader, the one Ottovan chose above all others for this task of tasks, a fulfillment of the Prophecy.

Ozgar rose, stepped past Sendata, and placed his hand on the door.

He grasped the heavy iron ring and pulled. The door creaked open, moving on old hinges. *The servants delivered as they promised. Praise be to the God of the Mountain and the Sands.* After the darkness of the tunnels, the light in front of them seemed to blaze with the brightness of daylight.

Ozgar slipped forward at a swift walk, nearly a run but more controlled, gliding up the stone stairs with silent steps. Sendata and the others followed, as soundless as Ozgar. No door barred the top of the steps, and the ceiling above them rose fifty feet high.

Ozgar reached the top of the stairs, crouching now in the Hall of the Qhaliffas, adjacent to the Throne Hall itself. He looked around him with an arrow nocked in his double-arched horn bow. The bow bore no markings, but with it, Ozgar had killed scores of enemies. It was a bow made of layers of wood and horn. Twisted and tortured to perfection, the bow was of rarely paralleled power or beauty. With the same bow, Ozgar shot the arrow of mercy into the throat of Trendan Rudar, sparing him from the flames. And another arrow loosed from the same bow—from a rooftop across the Square of the Qhaliffa—sent Chara, the torturing priest, into the fires of hell.

As his eyes searched the hall, Ozgar saw no one, not even a single guard.

They crept beneath the great vaulted ceiling of the Hall of the Qhaliffas, quickly approaching the Throne Hall. Soon, their eyes would behold the Prophet's Chair, which the Qhaliffas had made their throne so many centuries ago.

Above the chair, suspended from a pair of chains, they would see it—the Staff of the Ram, which was the Staff of Ruling, the broken top third of the Staff the God of the Mountain and the Sands gave to his Prophet atop the Great Mountain.

Oil lamps lined the walls. Hundreds of candles shone from their hanging fixtures, illuminating the flat stone floor and the tiled designs of palms, rivers, and animals of the mountain and the sands.

Praise be to the God of the Mountain and the Sands.

"To the Throne," said Ozgar. He broke into a controlled run, crouched forward and tense as a cat preparing to launch, an arrow still nocked on his bowstring.

The dozen Oath Holders ran forward behind him, spreading out into a wedge formation with Ozgar and Sendata at the fore. Sendata carried each of her razor-sharp "serpent fangs" in her hands, the small curved blades shimmering in the candlelight. The Lions carried bared scimitari swords, knowing that their pistols would cause far too much noise and would only be used as a last resort.

The twelve crossed the floor in short seconds, scanning in all directions, ready to knock down any who appeared with an arrow or a dart, silent and deadly. They saw no guards, no attendants, no servants.

They reached the Door of the Throne, the massive twin gilded doors studded with polished steel spikes embedded in dense steel disks, the spikes sticking out far enough to impale.

Ozgar turned around at the door, nestling up next to the steel spikes, again scanning behind him with an arrow at the ready.

He saw no one. He heard nothing. He nodded to the nearest two Lions. Their swords drawn, they placed their hands on the door handle and pushed forcefully. The hinges on the Throne Door were well greased, and despite its massive size, the gilded hardwood and steel moved easily.

Ozgar crept forward into the darkness, all the darker having come from the torchlit brightness of the Hall of the Qhaliffas. Dim moonlight penetrated from small windows near the roofline, windows designed to let in natural sunlight during the day. The Prophet's Chair—the Throne of the Qhaliffas—sat directly ahead of them.

It was too dark to see the throne. At his side, Ozgar could feel Sendata tense. She could see and hear things in the dark that he could not.

"Welcome," said a man's voice, the sound stopping Ozgar like a blade to his throat.

Ozgar's heart lurched as he aimed his arrow in the direction of the voice. Adrenaline set his skin ablaze as he prepared to fight or flee.

The flames of two torches burst into light, one on either side of the vast Hall.

The light was still faint, given the immensity of the hall, but the throne came into view, and Ozgar could see that a man sat upon it. In the same glance, Ozgar could see that the Staff of the Ram did not hang in its usual place above the throne. Even with only the single word, Ozgar knew the voice that spoke. He knew it to be evil, the sound of his enemy.

He loosed his arrow at the body on the throne, aimed straight for the man's throat. The arrow punched through the air with deadly speed.

There was a flash of light—blinding as a flash pistol, but darker and brighter at once—the light more golden than white.

Ozgar turned his face away. The flash spread out through the Throne Hall, illuminating the space like the noonday sun. All of Ozgar's fighters closed their eyes or turned their faces from the throne.

"Seize them," said the voice.

Ozgar opened his eyes.

Torches were lit on all of the walls. The darkness was gone. At least forty flames shone in the hands of guardsmen, illuminating their hard, dark faces.

In one of their hands, the men held torches; in the other, they held bared blades of dark, sharpened steel. For every guardsman holding a torch and a blade, there stood another guardsman holding a heavy spear, and yet another behind him. A line of guardsmen rushed in behind the dozen Oath Holders of the Order, cutting them off from the door they had entered.

The Oath Holders crept forward, tightening their formation and carrying their weapons at the ready. If they were to fight their way out, they would have to fight now.

The guardsmen advanced slowly inwards from the walls of the Throne Hall, stepping toward the center in short disciplined steps, moving in unison like a tightening net.

"Before you try to leave us," said the voice.

Ozgar looked up and saw the long face of the Grand Vizer.

"Observe what will happen to all of you before we are through."

From the rafters, high up near the roof, two bodies dropped on ropes.

One rope held their arms, and a second rope held their legs. The bodies fell nearly twenty feet from the ceiling's beams. The lines caught their legs and arms with a sickening force, sufficient to rip a man's arms from his sockets. The bodies now settled, hanging ten feet or so above the stone floor. Ozgar could see that their mouths were gagged.

"I am told," said the Grand Vizer, still sitting on the Qhaliffa's throne, "No, no—I am shown, that your type does not like seeing your friends burning. You will have to move quickly, then, archer."

Jemojeen stared into Ozgar's eyes, the only visible part of his covered face. *Does he know it is me?*

Ozgar looked ahead, to the left and the right, to the bodies hanging from the ceiling. Behind the gags around their mouths, Ozgar could see the faces contorted in agony. Both of the hanging men wore the clothes of palace servants. *By the God of the Mountain, he caught them.*

Dread crawled up Ozgar's back, swift as a spider.

Small piles of wood lay under where each of the bodies dangled. The bodies twisted like fish on a line, trying to free themselves, still very much alive. The guardsmen from the wall approached the piles of wood with their lit torches.

Jemojeen stood up from the ancient cedar, oak, and olive wood of the Prophet's Chair, the throne of the Qhaliffa upon which he had comfortably sat as if it were his own.

He stepped forward with the torchlight illuminating him in full view. With one arm, he tapped the piece of wood against the palm of his other hand. It was not quite three feet long with a bulbous top in the shape of the Ram's head, its horns curled on either side. The bottom of the staff was jagged as if it had been broken off from another piece.

Ozgar gaped.

The Staff of the Ram. You have no business holding that, Grand Vizer! Impostor! Ozgar's words nearly escaped him as they burned across his mind. If he shouted, Jemojeen would know his voice.

"And yet the Staff of the Ram is in my hands. Is it not?" said Jemojeen, speaking as if Ozgar had spoken aloud. "As is its power!"

The fear inside of Ozgar twisted. He could sense it in his bones: a far deeper force now loomed inside of the Grand Vizer, one that had not been present in the Square of the Qhaliffa when they rescued Selena Savanar.

Jemojeen pulled his arms apart, gripping the Staff of the Ram by its midsection with his right hand and brandishing the Ram's head like a giant wooden mace.

Jemojeen's guardsmen walked inward from the walls, coming ever closer toward the dozen Oath Holders of the Order, tightening the net, outnumbering them ten to one. The guardsmen closest to the woodpiles put their torches to the oil-soaked kindling. The logs erupted in flames, sending searing heat up into the two, dangling, live prisoners above them. Even through their cloth gags, Ozgar could hear their shrieking.

"Put them out of their misery, archer! Show them mercy!" taunted Jemojeen. His laugh rang out across the Throne Hall, haggard and vicious as it echoed off the stone.

Ozgar nocked a new arrow onto his bowstring.

Jemojeen walked toward him, slowly stepping down the limestone steps of the platform that held the Qhaliffa's throne. His chest was exposed. Ozgar could have easily hit the center of his chest from the back of a moving horse. Standing as he was, he could put the arrow in the dead center of Jemojeen's long neck ten times out of ten.

Ozgar ignored the burning bodies and focused both of his eyes on Jemojeen's throat. *He must die; I must kill him. If we all must be sacrificed so that the many might be free, so be it. We are Oath Holders of the Order.*

Ozgar's bowstring snapped; the horn and wood of his bow vibrated with its familiar shudder of released power. The arrow flew forward, straight and true.

As the arrow released, a blinding flash again erupted around Jemojeen.

On reflex, Ozgar turned his face away. He turned back, looking up at the Grand Vizer, unseeing, like a boy trying to stare into the sun.

"Serpents!" he said, breaking his silence, his voice panicky. "I cannot see! The Grand Vizer! Is he down?" In his heart, Ozgar already knew the answer.

"The Grand Vizer walks toward us still," said Sendata, her voice still quiet and calm in the manner of the Sworn Serpents, even in battle.

"My arrow was straight and true!" Ozgar closed his eyes, squeezing his eyelids tight and then opening them again. He could still see only flashes of light.

"The Staff of the Ram protects him. He has found its magic," said Sendata.

The tingle of fear gripped Ozgar's limbs. *God of the Mountain and the Sands protect us.* He blinked again. The objects of the room came into a loose focus.

"You should have chosen mercy, archer!" roared Jemojeen, still walking forward.

The shrieks of the slowly roasting men hanging above the fires tore at Ozgar's ears. He pulled another arrow from the quiver on his back. He blinked again and looked up at Jemojeen. He could not see well, perceiving only faint outlines. The aged cedarwood of the Staff of the Ram was transformed, glowing with a golden metallic light. Jemojeen's skin glowed with the same golden light as if he had swallowed sunlight, and it was seeping out of his pores.

From the head of the ram, the staff brightened further. Light flooded the Throne Room, bright as a thousand torches.

The dangling servants continued to shriek above their fires.

"Give them the mercy," said Ozgar.

Sendata signaled to a second Serpent.

They raised blowguns to their mouths and sent poisoned darts into the dangling bodies. One of the darts struck true, hitting the man's neck, even as he writhed above the fire. The other body twisted, taking the dart in the arm. The man with the dart in his throat stopped spinning immediately, the poison seizing him and extinguishing the pain, snuffing out his life, and any consciousness of the fire below him. The second man twisted for another span of seconds in conscious and terrible torment, pain engulfing him, removing all thoughts except those of the fire, and the pain and *God of the Mountain make it stop!* And then the poison worked its way through him, and he hung silently, the sickening smell of roasting human flesh filling the Throne Hall.

"You have failed, Oath Holders. And now, I will burn you all," said Jemojeen, walking toward them.

The guardsmen shouted their battle cry as they rushed inward.

Before Ozgar ordered them, the Lions fired their flashguns into the faces of the oncoming guardsmen, and then their other pistols too, pulling them from their holsters in rapid succession, the noise deafening.

The moment of last resort had come.

CHAPTER 24
Galleys in the Mist

Great Pool of the Oxus, South of Sundar Dun
13th Day, Month of Gandus, 807
Anglian Calendar: January 13, 1879

The rowboat had taken them well out into the Great Pool of the Oxus when they heard the rhythmic rowing of the galleys. Even through the heavy mists, the drumbeat and the sound of sixty oars striking the water at once was unmistakable.

"They know we are here," said Gulana, sitting up in the bow and staring into the impenetrable fog. The two rowers on the tiny boat were both Oath Holders, Rams of the Order, short and broad-shouldered. With each pull of the oars, they shifted their weight, getting the most out of each stroke in the way expert rowers can. Selena, seated next to her, could feel Gulana's growing worry. Gulana worried without ceasing since she had set her eyes upon the red roofs of Sundar Dun.

Selena looked down at the flat glassy surface of the Great Pool. They glided along with it, building up speed with each new stroke by the rowers.

"Have faith," said Selena. "You were worried about Sundar Dun, and we made it through."

Gulana continued peering into the mists, scowling with her face taut as a bowstring.

Oapah, heavy and huge, sat in the stern. The boat had sunk low in the water when he'd stepped in on the shoreline of Sundar Dun, in the shadows of the stone wharf.

The other Oath Holders—the ten who traveled with them from Saman Keer—scattered on the shoreline, each to make his or her way back north through the alleyways and hidden paths. They had fulfilled their task. Selena Savanar was in a boat, out of the Seven Cities, and on her way to the Semissari Swamp, when she would come under the care of Asatan, The Serpent of the Order, one of the governing three.

Boom. Splash.

The drum struck, the oars splashed, the sound now closer than before.

Boom, boom. Splash, splash.

A second boom moved through the fog, like an echo, followed by another series of splashes.

Oapah turned and looked behind them. There was nothing to see but a wall of slowly swirling fog.

Boom, boom, splash, splash.

"There is a second boat," said Oapah, "not far behind the first. How far are we from the reeds of the Semissari?" His voice sounded like one of the drums in the fog.

"A half of a mile," said the oarsman on the right.

"Perhaps a little more," said the other.

Oapah looked at the padding on the Rams' oar blades. The strokes of their rowers were nearly soundless.

"They cannot hear us," said one of the Rams.

"We are well muffled," whispered the other.

"They are rowing as if they can hear us," said Gulana.

Selena looked into the fog wall, beginning to agree with Gulana.

"How many men on a galley?" asked Selena.

"Forty, fifty, at least," said Gulana. "They are separate from the rowers. The men on top are Galley Guardsmen, riders of the Ring River. Nasty men, no better than the gangmen of Sundar Dun. Maybe worse."

Oapah drummed his fingers on the long handle of his two-handed scimitarus.

Boom! Splash!

The sounds were now frighteningly close.

"Should we shift course?" asked Gulana.

"We are on the shortest course to the reeds," said one of the Rams, speaking with his back to her as he heaved on his oar handle.

"Perhaps they are on the same course," said Gulana, her voice rising.

Boom! Splash!

"Row faster, you bastards! We're moving to catch the traitor! Faster!" The voice sounded as if it were in the rowboat next to Selena. Her heart jumped.

Yet, still, the mists hid the oncoming Galley.

"South," said Oapah, whispering. "South now. Turn!"

The Rams obeyed.

They had rowed to the southwest. The Ram to Oapah's right pulled his oar out of the water. The Ram to his left pulled mightily, sticking his oar deep into the dark grey-green waters of the Great Pool. As he heaved on the handle, sending the long wooden blade into the water, the little rowboat turned sharply, shifting course nearly ninety degrees.

In the next stroke, the other Ram returned his oar to the water, timing his stroke to exactly match that of his companion's. The boat launched south as surely as one of the surface-skating insects of the Semissari. The two Rams pulled in unison again, sending the vessel further south, not a moment too soon.

From the mists, the River Galley emerged tall, magnificent and deadly, and on nearly the exact line upon which the little rowboat had been moving to the southwest.

On the River Galley's prow, above the scythe-shaped battle ram, the loaded scorpion came into view first. Its bowstring was already pulled back, waiting on its sturdy hook and bending the thick arms of the horizontal bow. Resting in its slot lay the spear it would launch, heavy and longer than a man. The tip was an elongated pyramid of iron, heavy enough to punch a hole through the iron armor of a River Galley. Men stood by the scorpion on the prow. Behind them, stretching back along the decks, dozens of black-turbaned archers looked out into the mists. Beneath them, the oars lifted.

Boom, sounded the drum.

Splash. Thirty oars on the port side of the Galley plunged into the water at once.

The oars pulled the water, sending the Galley forward toward the Semissari Swamp, swift and elegant as the ship glided across the water.

"Row," said Oapah, "Row!"

It was the closest thing to fear Selena had yet heard in his voice. Selena looked at the River Galley in stunned silence. Gulana grabbed her by the shoulders, pulled her into the bottom of the bow, and lay down on top of her.

"What are you doing?"

"Silence," said Gulana, her mouth inches from Selena's ear, her heavy body pressing Selena against the wooden floorboards of the boat, her breath terrible. The Rams above them heaved. They lurched a boat-length farther to the south.

A clear voice sounded from the high, front deck of the River Galley. "Boat sighted! Boat sighted!"

Oapah looked up at the River Galley. It had moved almost out of view, nearly receding into the thick mist, but they were still close enough that Oapah could see the archers nocking their arrows on their bowstrings. There was nowhere to hide, and the rowboat offered no cover.

The first arrows struck the water just behind Oapah, sitting in the stern. They made tiny splashes as they hit the surface of the Great Pool.

"Row!" said Oapah. "Row for the Semissari!"

He could see that the River Galley had already begun to change course, shifting south to cut them off, as if knowing they could never outrun them with two oars against sixty.

"Row!"

The two Rams heaved with the supreme effort of men rowing for their lives. The little rowboat shot further south.

Another group of arrows skimmed over Oapah's head, striking the water just south of the rowboat's bow.

"They are bracketing us," said Oapah. "By the God of the Mountain and the Sands, row!"

Gulana continued covering Selena like a human shield.

The Rams pulled again in unison.

Oapah turned back and could see that the Galley was turning farther to chase them, its angle correcting. The rowers on the port side of the boat began rowing backward. Despite its forward momentum, the Galley turned quickly with its sharp, sickle-shaped iron prow aiming ever closer to being in line with their tiny boat.

Oapah looked just above the ramming-prow. As he watched, the artillerymen turned their scorpion toward them.

"Use evasion!" shouted Oapah.

One of the oarsmen pulled hard. The other stopped rowing. The little boat swerved. Gulana's full weight shifted onto Selena. Another cluster of arrows struck where Oapah's body had just been. One of the arrows hit the side of the rowboat, quivering with its sharp head buried in the wood.

"Again!"

The oarsmen shifted further to the east, moving away from the Semissari swamp.

The Galley's prow-scorpion fired.

The snap of the mighty bow made Oapah duck reflexively. The scorpion's bolt, longer than a guardsman's spear and three times as heavy, shot forward through the air, fast as an arrow. It struck the water no more than a boat length from the little rowboat, drenching Oapah and the Rams, sending a towering geyser of river water into the air. Gulana's body shielded Selena from most of the water, but she felt coldness all around her as it landed and pooled in the bottom of the boat.

Selena strained her neck to breathe, her face just above the water.

"Do not rise," said Gulana.

Selena moved her hands underneath her to prop up her chin. The water was now inches deep in the boat.

"South!" ordered Oapah.

The Rams heaved on their oars, turning the vessel almost due south. Oapah looked to the west, to the line of reeds on the banks of the Semissari. There was a channel-like clearing in the mists. They were closer to the shoreline than Oap-ah realized.

The galley archers loosed another volley of arrows. They had found their range.

"Row!" shouted Oapah

The Rams did not row. The arrows had found their targets.

Each man slumped forward with half a dozen shafts bristling out of his body. Both men still clung to the oars with open eyes. In an instant, Oapah could see in their faces that life had left them.

He lurched forward, pulling each of their bodies down into the stern, roughly throwing them like meat on top of Gulana and Selena. Oapah grabbed each of the oars, and pulled, doing the work of two men.

Selena stuck her head up above the beam and saw that the Rams were no longer on their bench. She felt their suffocating weight upon her.

"They struck the oarsmen!" she shouted.

"Stay down!" barked Gulana, adjusting her body with the dead men on top of her. She shifted herself to cover more of Selena and pushed Selena's face down toward the pool of cold river water beneath them.

"I can't breathe!" gasped Selena.

"We are close to the shore, Gulana! Keep her down!" growled Oapah, pant-ing with the strain of pulling both of the oars. It was a two-man rower, but he was strong enough and broad enough to do the work himself.

Another volley of arrows struck the water just behind them.

Above the deadly scythe-prow, the scorpion's horizontal bowstring snapped powerfully again, its thump carrying over the water, just a moment faster than its giant, iron-tipped bolt.

The thump was the last thing Selena Savanar heard before she hit the sur-face of the Great Pool, face-first. As the rowboat flipped up into the air, the cold struck her skin like ten thousand tiny needles, and then all fell silent under the water.

CHAPTER 25
New Reasons to Hurry

Altadige
Eastern Spatanian Empire
January 19–20, 1879

"What do you mean they found out?" asked Stanwich. His hands shook with rage and adrenaline.

"I mean just that." Yekov Leboveckian kept his voice calm. He was nearly as angry as Stanwich, but he had long ago learned to keep his rage quiet and still.

"Does Lord Harmon know?" asked Stanwich.

"He should," said Aaran Leboveckian, a leaner, taller, and slightly younger version of his brother Yekov.

"Have you told him?" asked Stanwich

"We told you first," said Yekov.

"Well, I appreciate that, I suppose," said Stanwich, pushing out his chair to vigorously pace alongside the table.

Hersen Expey sat in silence, wearing the blue officer's tunic of the LaFrentian Legionnaire he once was. A lit cheroot sat in his lips, filling the small room with its strong, aromatic smoke. The room was little more than a clerk's office attached to a warehouse. Much of Merchant House Gremanian's trade traffic flowed through the Mountain Gate and Altadige, but their buildings there were sparse and functional.

"I trust that you kept matters confidential in all of your words and communications, in letters, spoken conversations, and of course, in your telegraph messages?" said Aaran.

"Of course," said Stanwich with a wave of his hand.

"Perhaps the young Harmon?"

"No," said Stanwich, shaking his head. "He doesn't even know."

"No?" said Yekov, raising an eyebrow.

"His father has told him nothing, and neither have I." Stanwich looked at Hersen.

Hersen nodded in agreement.

"How about the New Anglians?" asked Aaran Leboveckian. "Huntington, Caldwell, and their children?"

"Yes, they know. At least the Caldwell boy does, but Three Gods! How am I to know what they have said? I did not travel with them."

"Have you asked them?"

"Asked them about this? You are just now telling me."

"Did you tell them of the importance of confidentiality?"

Stanwich looked at Yekov with a deep frown and reddening cheeks. "Do you think I am an idiot? Of course, everyone knew from the beginning that this is a secret. And if they failed to keep this secret, it is their own Three-Gods-damned money that they will be losing!"

"Perhaps," said Yekov, his arms folded across his chest.

"Hersen and I get our fee, whether the Gressians get there first or not!"

"Perhaps not," said Aaran, his arms folded in precisely the same manner as his older brother's.

"I signed a contract," said Stanwich.

Yekov could see the danger in Stanwich's eyes. A man did not conquer the wildlands of central Omakhosi by being tame. Yekov modified his tone, speaking softer, more gently.

"Of course, you have a contract, but it is best to get there first."

"No, it is necessary," said Stanwich. "And we will get there first. I am not going to be bested by a Three-Gods-damned Gressian."

Hersen smoked in silence, his eyes missing nothing.

"It is unlikely that even if the New Anglians had loose lips that the news would have time to make its way to the Court of the Autocrat. Perhaps it was the professors," said Aaran.

"Perhaps," agreed Yekov. "There are Gressians at the Anglian universities."

"Lord Harmon would crush them," said Stanwich.

"Perhaps," said Yekov.

"Where is he now? Where is this Nepopolous?"

"Our sources tell us," said Yekov, "that Count Usor Nepopolous departed into the Sand Sea from the Gressian borderlands two weeks ago with a sharp southerly bearing, along a route that would keep him near the Bulbanian hill country."

"How strong is his party?" asked Stanwich.

"I am told he left with at least one hundred riflemen, not counting his porters and others."

"So, they are probably two hundred and fifty men," said Stanwich.

"At least," said Hersen, exhaling a mouthful of smoke.

"That's five times the size of us," said Stanwich, shaking his head.

"It is also worth noting," said Aaran Leboveckian, "that they travel underneath the imperial flag of the Gressian Autocrat."

Yekov nodded.

Stanwich shook his head more vigorously in frustration. Hersen Expey continued to smoke.

"He has stolen our idea, our very same idea! He is going for the Beserite. He travels under diplomatic protection. He wagers that if he can secure a deal with the Beserians first, no Anglian Prime Minister would be mad enough to wage war over it."

"Especially not Binyam Aurelian," said Yekov with a twinkle of pride in his eyes. Aurelian had converted to the Faith of the Three Gods two decades ago before his first campaign to stand for Parliament, but Macmenians across the world did not doubt that he was by birth, and always would be, one of their own.

"Damn! Damn, damn, damn!" said Stanwich, shaking his fists in the air and then pounding them on the table beneath him.

The Brothers Leboveckian were correct. His window to achieve his mission was narrow and rapidly closing. If Usor Nepopolous beat him to the Valley of Kordon and struck a deal with the Beserians, he would fail, and Lord George Harmon, Colonel Mason Caldwell, and Samuel X. Huntington would have wasted their money betting on him. That is if they still decided to pay him for the rest of the contract at all.

Stanwich did not need to say the words aloud that all were thinking. *None of those three are forgiving men.* Nor did Stanwich wish to think of what Lord Harmon could do to his reputation with his papers . . . and Stanwich and Hersen very much needed the money.

"If we leave tomorrow, how many days are we from the Valley of Kordon, if we are willing to really push the camels?" asked Stanwich. He had done the calculations a half-dozen times, but he asked anyway.

"It is a day to the Mountain Gate because of the steep grade. It is nine days on camelback from the Mountain Gate, if the weather holds," said Yekov. "Perhaps, if you do not rest yourselves or your mounts, which is dangerous, you can make it in seven and a half days from the Mountain Gate."

Stanwich nodded. "How many days is the count from reaching the Valley of Kordon?"

"That depends how hard he is pushing his men and his mounts," said Aaran Leboveckian.

"He is a Gressian," said Hersen Expey. "We may safely assume he is pushing his men and their mounts to their limits. He will drive them like dogs."

Stanwich considered this. "How long? How long until he is in the valley?"

"Assuming that his weather holds and that he is pushing his column in the way that Major Expey believes, he could be there in eight days, maybe seven."

"We must leave tomorrow," said Stanwich.

"But the supplies—" began Aaran.

"Damn the supplies. We have enough. We will have to do without. I will not give Nepopolous that extra day. That day can make the difference between victory and disaster."

Aaran Leboveckian's eyes widened. "In my experience, unless one is a Beserian, one should never venture into the Sand Sea without necessary supplies." He glanced at Yekov.

The look in his brother's eyes told him to keep any further thoughts to himself. So he did.

Stanwich opened the door and stormed off into the night in the direction of the hotel. Hersen got up slowly, nodded at the Leboveckians, and followed him, still smoking his cheroot.

Peter rose with the sun and, despite the pillow beneath his head, felt tired and stiff. The list of tasks ahead of him made him wish to stay under the warm blanket that covered him. He glanced at the dying fire in the hearth, burned down to a small pile of glowing coals. He felt the chill seeping through the stone walls and the thickly paned windows as he rolled over and emptied his bladder into the chamber pot. Stanwich had ordered that all were to be present for a meeting at 8:00 a.m. to discuss the descent into the Sand Sea.

"Jones!" shouted Peter, loudly but not unkindly.

His valet had not once complained about the journey to the edge of the Sand Sea. He had not even asked for extra wages. *The man is a testament to the Anglian valet, that unique and outstanding species of man.* That was what Peter had said to Jack the night before.

Rex Jones, valet to Peter Harmon since his fourteenth birthday, was well aware that the young man would struggle to dress himself in the manner to which he was accustomed. So, with little inducement, he volunteered to travel to the edge of the desert with him, leaving the predictable schedule and comforts of Hylebourne House behind. *Hylebourne House will always be here, and a Harmon should not travel without his valet.* Peter remembered Jones's words and smiled.

"Good morning," said Jones, opening the door.

Jones was fully dressed and sharply groomed, as always.

"I will need a bath," said Peter.

"It is already drawn," said Jones.

Peter stepped out of his bed, stark naked, his pale skin covered in goose bumps.

Jones held open Peter's robe. Peter stepped into it and placed his feet into the slippers Jones had placed upon the cold wooden floor.

His mind still groggy, Peter walked down the hallway to the bath. As he sank his body into the steaming soapy water, Peter wondered when he would next enjoy such luxuries. The following day, they would leave well before the sun rose, and he would leave Jones behind in Altadige, on his father's orders.

Peter closed his eyes, and Hannah Huntington entered his mind.

He saw her face and imagined the various ways he had seen her since she had walked down the gangplank of the SOTR *Agobasto*. He pictured her wearing the light-yellow dress she had worn on the train, the one that was cut lower than the others so that he could see her chest. He thought about the light freckles on her chest. Peter then thought about Hannah sitting in her own bath, in the very same hotel as him.

Perhaps she was thinking about him at this very moment, sitting naked in her own warm bath? He felt himself stiffen in the hot water. He reached down with his hand.

"Harmon."

Peter jolted in the bath, splashing water over the edge. His cheeks flushed, ripening like a cherry. He turned to see Joshua Barnes standing in the doorway. Barnes frowned with a furrowed brow. The rest of his face looked tight with worry.

"My apologies, sir. I told him you were bathing," said Jones.

"Your cousin," said Barnes, "Have you seen him?"

"Jack? Not since last night," said Peter.

Peter wondered how much Barnes, or for that matter, Jones had seen. He glanced down at the water. The bubbles were thick enough to render anything beneath them invisible.

"He is not in his room," said Barnes.

"Perhaps he woke early?" said Peter, lowering himself deeper in the tub.

"His boots, his belt, and his hat are still in his room."

"Perhaps he wore other footwear. Have you checked with Stanwich? Perhaps he is with them." Peter's voice edged.

Without saying anything further, Barnes turned and left.

"Poor manners," said Jones. "I apologize."

"Never mind, Jones, not on you," said Peter. "Please close the door."

Peter tried to picture Hannah again in her bath, but another face entered his mind: Aurelio Demassi's. The moment was gone. There was something not right about the guide. Peter could not say what, but he felt an uneasiness about the man. Peter pulled himself up out of the tub.

He pulled his bathrobe off of the hook on the wall and trudged down the hallway with the heavy steps of a man in a foul mood.

Peter walked into the dining room at five minutes to eight. Stanwich and Hersen Expey were already seated at the far end of the table, poring over a map and a checklist of items.

"Please close the door behind you," said Stanwich. Hersen Expey continued staring down at the map.

Peter walked toward them. A basket of pastries and a pot of coffee waited on the table.

"Have you seen Jack?" said Peter.

"No," said Stanwich, not taking his eyes off of the map.

"Has he been here at all?"

Stanwich glanced up. "He has not."

"Has Barnes been here?"

"Yes, now that you mention it, asking for Jack Caldwell." Stanwich stood up. "Is he missing?"

"Apparently, yes," said Peter.

The door opened.

Hannah Huntington stepped in, wearing a simple dark overcoat and a woolen hat that covered her hair, which was piled up to fit entirely inside of the hat. Mrs. Smith trailed behind her, serious and unsmiling.

"No, I have not seen him," said Hannah before anyone could ask her a question. "Should we be alarmed?"

All eyes turned to Stanwich.

"Is anyone else missing?" he asked.

For a moment, all were silent.

"Where is the guide?" asked Peter. "The Vetenan who dresses like a tribesman, Aurelio Demassi?"

Stanwich glanced at Hersen Expey.

"He should be here," said Hersen.

"And yet he is not," said Stanwich.

Peter felt his anxiety rising inside of him, like gas in a hot spring.

"Major Expey, find Barnes," said Stanwich. "And with him, find Caldwell. And for that matter, find Demassi."

"Yes, Commander," said Hersen Expey, rising from his chair overlooking the map. He walked out of the room, leaving Peter, Hannah Huntington, Mrs. Smith, and Harold Milton Stanwich.

Stanwich stood with his hands on his hips, looking from Hannah to Peter and back again.

Hannah's forehead creased in a way it had not before that very minute.

"Major Expey will find them all, Miss Huntington. You may rest assured of that," said Stanwich.

"Thank you, Mr. Stanwich," said Hannah. "I am sure he is somewhere in Altadige. It would not be the first time he spent an evening out of his bed."

Mrs. Smith nodded knowingly.

Peter looked at Hannah, trying to sift her meaning from her words.

Stanwich was more direct. "What does that mean, Miss Huntington?"

Hannah's eyes narrowed, and she looked out toward the window. "Let us give it some time. If he is not accounted for in the next hour or so, I would begin searching the whorehouses."

Mrs. Smith nodded again.

Stanwich stared, and then he smiled. "Is that so?"

"But then again," said Hannah, her forehead crease deepening, "Barnes is well aware of that proclivity, so I am sure he will do so anyway. If not, I would make sure it is done. Tell me when I am needed," said Hannah, turning toward the door. Mrs. Smith grabbed a pastry and followed her out.

Stanwich said nothing to stop them.

Peter watched them leave. A torrent of conflicting thoughts swirled inside of him: first, astonishment at how Hannah had casually referred to Jack in a whorehouse, second, excitement in that casual manner. Third, he felt thoughts of condemnation that Jack was the kind of man that visited brothels. Fourth, he felt hurt that Jack had not invited him to come along.

Peter stood up to leave as well.

"A word if I may," said Stanwich. Only the two of them remained in the room.

"Yes?"

"There is something we need to discuss."

Peter waited with one of his eyebrows arched. Stanwich had discussed almost nothing of substance with him since their departure from Anglia.

Stanwich glanced toward the door, making sure it was closed.

"How much do you know, Peter, about minerals?"

"Minerals?"

Stanwich nodded.

"I suppose as much as the next Three Gods College graduate. I earned high marks in geology."

Stanwich frowned as if debating with himself whether to continue. "How much has your father spoken to you about minerals?"

"My father? I can't say that my father has ever spoken to me about minerals."

"That's what I thought," said Stanwich, beginning to pace. "Sit, please." He pointed at a chair.

Peter sat.

Stanwich inhaled a deep breath, looking uncomfortable. "This expedition . . . is different from the journey to the Central Crater of Omakhosi."

"Indeed," said Peter.

"Can I trust you to keep what I tell you in confidence?"

Peter nodded.

"The utmost confidence?"

"Yes."

Stanwich's cheeks began to redden. "You see, expeditions are costly. And in the past years, to maintain certain appearances, I incurred, or rather, Major Expey and I incurred certain debts. The City, as you know, is an expensive place . . . "

Peter waited.

"Your father approached me some months ago. Through several sources at your university, he became aware of certain minerals, well, one mineral in particular."

Peter sat in solemn silence with his hands folded together on the table in front of him.

"Have you heard of Beserite?"

Peter shook his head. "No."

"It is a remarkable thing, really," said Stanwich. "Some professors at your university came to realize that Beserite, if mixed with coal, even in minimal quantities, can have a—well, a very dramatic impact upon the performance of engines. In fact, it could make every railway, every steamship, and every factory that uses the steam engine far more efficient—far, far more efficient."

"Is it a catalyst?"

"Yes, a catalyst. Not many people know this. In fact, before what I learned today, you could count them on two hands. You are now one of them."

Peter waited, understanding that the real story was yet to come.

"Beserite has not been discovered in very many places in the world. There is only one known massive deposit presently located."

"The Sand Sea," said Peter.

"You are a bright young man," said Stanwich. "Yes, the Sand Sea, and in particular, the Valley of Kordon. It is there that we journey. That is the true purpose of our expedition, Peter Harmon."

Peter waited in silence, his hands still folded, allowing this to sink in.

"Do you mean to say that all of this, the speech at Three Gods College, the prophecy, all of that, is a front?"

Stanwich nodded.

"But the Year of the Prophecy is real. I read about it in—"

"Yes, in *The Life of Hom Hommuram*." Stanwich allowed himself a small, weary laugh. "Peter, you will come to learn that men do not fund expeditions as expensive as this one to pursue ancient legends, especially not men like your father and your uncle."

Peter felt a twisting sensation in his stomach. "Why are you telling me this? Why are you telling me now?"

"Because you now need to know."

"Why?"

Stanwich paced several times without speaking.

"Our true purpose, Peter, is to trade several crates of Anglian Army rifles to the Beserian tribesmen for the mineral rights to the Beserite in the Valley of Kordon. And for a right of way to build a railway from there to here, to Altadige."

Peter leaned back, his eyes even wider than before.

"That is why, Peter, the New Anglians are with us. Their fathers are helping pay for the expedition, and they will split the profits too, a third each to Huntington and Caldwell. That is why I had no choice but to allow those women to join us."

Peter shook his head, speechless.

"There is more," said Stanwich. "Last night, I spoke with Mr. Yekov and Mr. Aaran Leboveckian."

Peter waited, wondering what more there could possibly be.

Stanwich paced, peculiarly twisting his lips, as if deciding how to phrase what he was about to say.

"They told me another expedition has taken a head start on our own."

"Who?" asked Peter.

"Have you heard the Huntington girl or Caldwell or anyone else mention the Beserite?" Stanwich's tone was gentle, but his eyes were hard.

"No," said Peter. "You just told me now."

"I did not think so," said Stanwich. His steely blue eyes were still cold. "I nonetheless must ask."

"Who is the rival expedition?"

"They are Gressians."

Peter shook his head. "Do you know the name? The name of their leader?"

"Usor Nepopolous. He is a Count. Royal blood. Not terribly close to the throne but close enough to matter at court. He is traveling under the flag of the Autocrat. He will have as much diplomatic protection as we will."

"Did he also leave from Altadige? Before us?"

"No, he left from the Gressian borderlands, just north of Bulbania."

"That is hundreds of miles from here," said Peter, seeing a map in his mind. Geography was another subject in which he received high marks. "That is also hundreds of miles north and west of the Valley of Kordon."

"Yes, it is," said Stanwich. "Which is why Nepopolous embarked into the Sand Sea several weeks ago."

"How long until he reaches the Valley of Kordon?"

"The Leboveckians say seven days if they have moved without delay at a breakneck pace."

"And if not?"

"Another day. Three more. Five more. I do not know. They are somewhere on the sands now, moving south to steal our Beserite out from under us. And they do so under the flag of the Autocrat of all of the Gressias."

"Which means to wrest it from them would mean war," said Peter.

Stanwich nodded.

"And no Anglian government," Peter continued, "either Crown and Country or Liberty and Commerce, whether under Aurelian or Hammerstone, would risk such a thing."

Stanwich nodded again.

"Then we must leave now," said Peter Harmon.

"Yes," said Stanwich.

"What are we waiting for?"

"For final supplies, without which I am willing to depart at once, and now apparently your cousin Jack, without whom I am less willing to depart."

"Three Gods," said Peter.

"Three Gods, indeed."

"If he is truly in a whorehouse and that causes our delay . . ." Peter did not finish his sentence.

"Prepare your things, Peter. We must depart before the sun sets," said Harold Milton Stanwich, returning his eyes to the map.

"You know, Stanwich," said Peter. "If we fail, you may rest assured of one thing, my father's blame will fall on me, not you."

"I sincerely doubt that," said Stanwich, glancing up again.

"You shouldn't," said Peter.

He turned to leave, to gather his things at the hotel, walking more quickly and with more purpose in his step than he had since their departure from Anglia.

The brothels of Altadige concentrated in a series of alleys in the southern part of the city. The red sign district looked wrong in the daylight, like an exposed face, accustomed to hiding its blemishes behind dense layers of makeup.

Barnes walked with Hersen Expey at his side. Neither man was comfortable with the other. They had each expertly killed each other's countrymen in the LaFrentian War. Seventeen years had healed many wounds in both nations, and in both nations' warriors. But some wounds inside of some men were still open, and even if they were scabbed, the scab was still easily lifted.

"Fond of the whorehouses, is he?" said Hersen.

His accent grated on Barnes's ears. Try as he may, he still heard it as the voice of the enemy.

"No more than the ordinary boy of his age," said Barnes.

"Boy, eh? At three years past twenty, what were we? Veterans is what we were, made hard by battle. Hardly boys, we were at twenty-three."

Barnes looked askance at Hersen, hating the sound of his voice as much as the words he used.

"I wish our lives upon no generation," he said. "Our boyhoods were robbed from us."

They continued walking, the frost on the stones crackling underneath their boots. The morning was otherwise silent, windless, and cold.

"The whorehouse business is not a morning business," said Hersen, smirking beneath his mustache. In the bright morning light, the signs revealed cracked and chipped paint.

Barnes looked suspiciously at both sides of the alley.

Red signs flanked both stone walls, lined up like Anglian grenadiers standing guard above narrow closed doors.

I should never have let him out of my sight. I spent two hours talking with Matilda Smith, and in that time, he disappeared. Barnes frowned. His job was to keep his eyes on Jack Caldwell, and he had taken his eyes away. Joshua Barnes feared few men, but Colonel Mason Caldwell and Samuel X. Huntington were two of them.

With each breath, Hersen and Barnes made small visible clouds in front of their faces.

"Tell me, Barnes, what do you think of this Beserite mission? Did they make it worth your while?"

Barnes looked at Hersen Expey with an eyebrow raised in equal parts suspicion and dislike. He had always viewed LaFrentians as greedy mercenaries, and the legion men, in his eyes, were even worse than the others.

"Whatever my dealings are, they are my own, LaFrentian."

There were undoubtedly more disarming ways to answer.

Hersen Expey scowled, reflecting Barnes's dislike in his own eyes.

"The best way to do this," said Barnes, "is for us to divide each side of the street. Spend money at the door if you have to. The whores will talk if you flash enough money in front of them."

"Whose money am I to spend?" asked Hersen.

Barnes made a sound between a snort and a grunt. "We will make it *worth your while*, Major Expey."

Hersen Expey extended his hand. "I am happy to take the left side of the street," he said.

Barnes shook Hersen's hand. When he withdrew his own hand, Hersen's was still extended.

"The bills, Sergeant. Cash. Spatanian currency is preferable."

Barnes stared into Hersen's LaFrentian face, frowning with disdain. He considered striking him then and there. Barnes was hard as iron. He had killed men with a blade; he had killed with his bare hands. But he knew what kind of man Hersen was. *He is scum, but the kind of scum that knows how to kill, the kind that enjoys killing more than a man should.* Barnes had learned that one does not strike such a man lightly, not unless he is prepared to go further than the scum, and often that meant being willing to kill. Barnes was not willing to kill.

His hands remained at his sides. He reached into his pocket and pulled out a stack of Spatanian bills, enough to pay for a small arsenal of supplies or a series of memorable nights in the most expensive brothels in the most expensive cities.

Hersen took the money, walked toward the door under the first hanging red sign, and knocked. The sound of his knuckles against the wood struck the crisp morning air, making a sharp crack like a distant rifle shot. He hit again harder, again, and again.

Barnes shook his head. *If he knocks like that, they are going to come to the door with a pistol.* Hersen continued his knuckle barrage on the door.

The door flew open.

"What, man? Three Gods! We are closed!" The voice was a man's, shouting in accented Spatanian.

Hersen stood and stared at him.

The man slammed the door.

Hersen jammed his boot in the bottom.

"I said *closed*, you stupid bastard!" shouted the man, his voice indignant in the manner of the formerly drunk on the following morning.

Hersen stepped forward.

Barnes could not hear the words that he said, but he did see the man's face in the doorway. The man's face changed in the span of a heartbeat. He lowered his head and shook it. Hersen turned, walked to the next door beneath a red sign and knocked as ferociously as he had knocked at the first door.

A woman answered the second door. She spoke softly, and Hersen did as well. She nodded and then shook her head. Hersen moved on to the third door. Barnes knocked on his first. A woman answered almost immediately.

She had large attractive brown eyes. She eyed Barnes from his hat to his shoes.

"Yes?"

"Good morning. I am looking for someone."

"We are closed."

"Yes."

"Who are you looking for?"

"May I speak in Anglian?" asked Barnes.

"I do not speak that language."

"Very well," continued Barnes, in poorly accented but passable Spatanian. "I am looking for a young man. Taller than I am," Barnes gestured with his hand to show how tall Jack Caldwell was. "He would have been in evening dress. Top hat, silver-topped walking stick. He had a foreign accent."

The woman smiled. Her teeth were clean, white, and slightly crooked. It was not a beautiful smile, but not unattractive either.

"You describe half of our customers," she said.

"His accent was like mine."

"So many foreign accents sound the same to me, sir."

Barnes pulled a ten-ducat note from the internal coat pocket, the one against his chest. "For your time," he said, "And any memories you can locate."

"Now that you mention it," she said, leaning forward and looking up toward the opposite end of the alleyway, as if looking for someone to appear from one of the closed, shuttered windows. "There was a man with a voice like yours, tall, young, strong-looking."

"Oh?" asked Barnes.

The woman placed her hand on her chin as if trying to coax the memory from her mind. Barnes handed her another ten-ducat note. He was saving the fifties and hundreds unless absolutely necessary.

"Yes, tall and strong-looking, with a silver-tipped walking stick."

"Bearded or clean-shaven?" asked Barnes.

"Clean face, like yours," said the woman. She winked flirtatiously.

"He was here? Inside?"

"No, not here. He went to the last door. This side of the alley."

"Thank you," said Barnes, already walking toward the end of the cobblestone lane.

"Come back sometime," said the woman, leaning forward with her hands on either side of the doorframe, emphasizing her large and well-formed chest.

"Barnes!" the voice was Hersen Expey's. "Barnes, he went to the last door on the right, your side of the street."

"Yes," said Barnes, walking.

Hersen caught up to him. They were of similar heights, and both men were lean.

They reached the last door on the right. Its red sign was less cracked and better maintained than the others as if it had been painted far more recently. There was no name on the sign, merely the number seven.

Barnes looked at the number. "I will do the talking."

"As you wish," said Hersen.

Barnes and Hersen, a New Anglian Army master sergeant and a major of the LaFrentian Legion, as unlikely a couple as there ever was, stood facing the door, shoulder to shoulder.

Barnes knocked softly. A sudden cold breeze blew down the alley as he did so. A cluster of old newspapers rustled past Barnes and Hersen's feet, driven by the wind as the yellowed pages danced across the cobbles.

No one answered the door.

Barnes knocked again, harder than the first time. Tap, tap, tap.

Hersen stood next to him, not speaking, but holding a smug look on his mustachioed LaFrentian face.

"Not a word," said Barnes, staring forward at the closed door.

"I have not spoken," said Hersen, glancing at Barnes.

Barnes knocked harder and more rapidly. Still, the door remained unanswered. Barnes knocked harder. At last, they both heard the sound of a body moving toward the locked door.

"You see," said Hersen, smirking, "I move to the last step first."

"And that is your error," said Barnes.

The door opened. The woman stared at them, looking tired. She was pale in an unhealthy way, her eyes cloudy and bloodshot. Her hair was unkempt, and her eyes darted nervously from Barnes to Hersen.

"We need to know what happened to one of your customers," said Barnes.

"No customers here. We are closed," said the woman. She wore an old woolen sweater over a cotton dress, the kind few would choose to wear in winter. Barnes suspected she did not have a dress better suited to the season.

"Were you working here last night?" asked Barnes.

She shook her head and then paused and glanced behind her as if making sure no one inside was within earshot.

"I only work mornings. I do cleaning up."

Barnes, who did not have a particularly well-suited ear for such things, could hear in her accent that she was a foreigner.

"Where is home?" asked Hersen in nearly flawless Spatanian. He had even accented his words in the manner of the Altadigean mountain dwellers, lisping some of his consonants. Barnes did grant him that. The man had a knack for languages.

"Bulbania," said the woman. There was nervousness in her voice, and she kept glancing over her shoulder as if someone might come up upon her from behind.

"South Bulbania, yes?"

"Yes."

Hersen nodded. His ear for accents was as good as his ability to adopt them, and he rarely asked questions to which he did not already know the answer.

"How long have you been here in Altadige?"

"One year."

"Not much longer than us," said Hersen, smiling his most charming La-Frentian smile beneath his mustache. He had small teeth with a small gap in the front, but they were straighter than most.

"I must go. Much cleaning to do." She gripped the door as if to slam it closed. Barnes could see as plainly as Hersen that this was a woman being paid barely enough to buy a dinner of bread and water.

"Before you go back to your cleaning," said Barnes.

She turned her head at his accent, understanding him, but only with effort.

"We would like to thank you for your time." Barnes pulled a one-hundred-ducat note from his breast pocket.

She stared openly, and then her eyes focused on the note with intensity, as if willing it to come to her. It was, to her, a nearly unattainable fortune.

"Answer our questions," said Barnes, "and this shall be yours. Have you seen a man who looks like this?" Barnes pulled a small, grainy photograph from his opposite coat pocket and placed it in front of her.

The woman glanced at the hundred-ducat note. Then she looked Barnes directly in the eyes.

"Yes," she said. "He was here last night."

"Did you see him with your own eyes?" asked Barnes.

She nodded.

"Where is he now? Is he inside? You must tell us now. Is he inside?"

"No, he left sometime between the middle night and the sunrise, closer to the sunrise."

"Was he walking? Walking on his own?" Barnes heard the urgency in his own voice and did not like it.

She shook her head. The fear in her eyes seemed to grow. "He was not walking. He was lying down when they pulled him out."

"Who is they?"

"They? The Vetenan who looks like a Beserian. It was him and the others." Barnes turned and looked at Hersen.

"What others?" asked Hersen.

"Beserians," she said. "The sand people."

"Where did they go?" asked Hersen. There was a deadly calm in Hersen's voice. Barnes felt a wave of respect move through him before he reminded himself that Hersen was a LaFrentian.

"That way," said the woman, pointing east, in the direction of the Mountain Gate.

"To the Mountain Gate?" asked Barnes.

"No, to the Sand Sea," she said. Her face seemed to have grown even paler, and her eyes were wide with fear.

CHAPTER 26
Oapah's Sword

Great Pool of the Oxus
13th Day, Month of Gandus, 807
Anglian Calendar: January 13, 1879

Selena gasped for air as her head breached the surface. Her clothes clung to her as if glued to her skin. Whereas for a moment they were buoyant, they soon began taking on water, dragging her down into the frigid depths of the Great Pool as if they were trying to drown her. The waters that filled the Ring River water began as ice, flowing down from the frozen upper reaches of the Seven Streams of the Great Mountain. In winter, no blazing summer sun struck them as they descended the mountain, and now nothing warmed them before they reached the Great Pool of the Oxus.

Selena was not a great swimmer. She tore violently at her cloak. She freed a shoulder and then she saw them. The Galley was close enough for her to see the faces of the individual archers on the railing. They were not shooting their arrows, but their eyes stared directly at her. A pair of them held a net and were spreading it out to toss.

They aim to capture me.

She freed her other shoulder, thrashing wildly. The cloak released, sinking without her. She rose like a cork freed from beneath the surface.

The Galley oars struck the surface of the pool with a coordinated splash. The scythe-shaped iron on the prow lurched toward her. Selena put her head down and began swimming toward the shoreline with violent, thrashing strokes as mists still swirled around her. When she lifted her head to breathe, she heard the words.

"Loose!"

The word launched off of the Galley's deck just before arrows sailed far over her head. They were not for her.

She looked up and saw them: two canoes, long and narrow, only wide enough for one man and a paddle, but long enough for a dozen in a line. She could see that the rowers were all Sworn Serpents, Oath Holders of the Order. The arrows slammed into them, directly on target, but the Serpents were protected. They carried thin light shields, made of layered hardwood fronted by cork. The arrows stuck in the shields, but they did not pierce through.

The scorpion on the galley's bow launched a bolt. The bolt struck the water, splashing like some demonic pelican splitting the difference between the two canoes, drenching both, but hitting neither.

"Help me! Here!" she shouted.

"Lady Savanar!" shouted the lead rower in the canoe.

The canoe men paddled in unison, and then they were upon her. Selena grabbed the side railing of the canoe, barely inches above the surface of the Great Pool as more arrows flew.

The rower pulled the shield over both himself and Selena.

"Get the scales over her!" shouted one.

Powerful hands grabbed her from farther back in the canoe. She looked up to see Oapah's face as he lifted her as effortlessly as a grown man lifting a child and placed her facedown into the base of the canoe.

"Stay down. The arrows cannot pierce the Serpents' scales," he said. His massive body loomed above her, barely fitting inside the narrow width of the dugout.

The River Galley lurched closer.

The canoe cut a perpendicular line to the approaching larger ship, slipping directly in front of the Galley's scythe-shaped ram. In a smooth, long stroke, the rowers pulled their paddles again. Oapah had joined them, finding their rhythm, digging into the water with his paddle, his powerful shoulders flexing beneath his wet, sand-colored robes.

The canoe passed underneath the Galley's decks, close enough to the bow that the archers did not have an angle to shoot down at them. They continued northeast, toward the Great Mountain, sliding along the side of the longer ship, as the Galley moved southwest, toward the Semissari Swamp.

"Stay on the side! Close! Close!" roared Oapah.

He had dropped his paddle into the canoe. He held his two-handed scimitarus unsheathed in a high guard position, the immense blade over his head. Then he stood up, facing away from the galley. A line of thirty oars lay directly in front of him, sticking out as if to knock him into the water. Oapah did not duck.

"Faster!" he roared.

The canoe paddlers pulled, moving directly at the oars.

The Galley's oars moved up and then down into the water, splashing in their rhythmic dance.

The bow of the canoe slipped beneath the first oar of the galley, the wooden belly of the ship within an arm's length of Oapah, just to his right at the waterline.

Selena looked above her, clenching her teeth as Oapah's chest headed straight for the oars.

Oapah swung his two-handed scimitarus.

The long oar in front of him splintered.

He slashed again.

The oar snapped.

He swung again, breaking the next oar clean. The Galley's oar holes at the water's surface were tiny, barely larger than the oar itself.

The rowers inside were helpless to protect their oars unless they pulled them inside the ship itself, and even then, the oars' wooden blade would be exposed to Oapah's steel one.

Selena heard them shouting through the oar-holes.

"The oars! The oars! Shoot that man!"

Oapah hacked at the next oar, snapping it as cleanly as the second. He broke the fourth oar, roaring with effort, then the fifth, and the sixth.

An archer leaned far over the railing, exposing his entire torso.

One of the back rowers in the canoe—a Serpent—blew a dart before the archer could loose his arrow. The dart struck the man's neck, and he fell onto the railing, rebounding off of it, falling limp into the cold water below with a splash.

The second canoe reemerged, paddling out from the mist, its Serpents' scales raised. The archers on the deck took the bait, riddling the thin cork-and-hardwood shields with their arrows. In seconds, the shields bristled like pin-cushions, but the men behind them sat unharmed in their seats.

On the other side of the Galley, Oapah continued to chop relentlessly at the oars as the canoe slipped down the length of the long ship. The seventh and eighth oars snapped before his blade.

"Oapah, enough!" shouted Selena, sitting up behind him in the canoe.

But he was past the point of hearing, in full battle rage. He shouted as he swung, having perfected his rhythm. More oars snapped like sticks. Nine, ten, eleven, twelve.

"Turn!" screamed Selena, cupping her hands over her mouth toward the veiled Serpent rowers. Oapah chopped four more oars. Selena could see that the time to escape was now.

"Hold the shield," said the rower behind her.

He passed it forward, and she grasped its handle, bracing her forearm on the railing of the canoe as she saw the others had done. The shield stuck out at an angle.

"More angle!" shouted the rower. "I cannot row!"

Selena angled the base of the shield out further, her arms shaking with the effort, seeing that the Serpents' scales were far more demanding than the Serpents made them look. The rower behind her dipped his steering paddle into the water and turned the canoe away from the side of the Galley.

Oapah, still hacking, did not lose his footing. "Nineteen, twenty!" he roared.

"Oapah, get down!" shouted Selena, struggling with the shield.

Oapah was of no mind to take an order. As the canoe lurched away from the Galley, Oapah twisted backward and took one final swipe at an oar, separating its wooden blade from its shaft.

"Twenty-one!"

It was one swing too many.

An archer on the railing above found his angle. He loosed his shaft into Oapah as open water separated the canoe from the Galley.

"God of the Mountain!" Oapah cried out in pain.

He dropped to the base of the canoe like a stone, nearly dipping the sides beneath the surface of the Great Pool but still holding the giant blade of his scimitarus upright in his lap. The canoe rocked wildly with his weight, and Selena nearly dropped her shield into the water.

A trio of arrows slammed into the top of her shield. An arrow stuck out from Oapah's left shoulder.

"Is it poisoned?" asked Selena. If it was not lost in the pool, she carried the antidote in her belt, a gift from The Ram before she set out. She had no free hand to check. If it was poisoned, Oapah would need it now, or the poison would spread, searing him as it moved and incapacitated him with pain.

"No," he growled. "Just an arrow."

His voice was too calm. No man struck with poison, even a man of an iron will, could speak with such calmness. The poison burned as badly as an open flame on naked flesh.

"Row!" screamed Selena. "To the swamp!"

The Serpents were already rowing. The canoe shot forward across the water, headed swamp-ward, due west.

"Turn and pursue!" roared the Galley officer, his voice carrying over the water from the high deck.

Selena looked back.

The rowers on the starboard side pulled mightily on their mutilated oars. The broken shafts plunged into the water, but the Galley did not launch westward. The port rowers, with fully functioning oars, sent the boat headed northwest, at a forty-five-degree angle past the fleeing canoes. With the next plunge, the galley lunged forward even farther to the north, turning away from the canoe and the

Semissari, in the direction of Alwaz Deem. With another pull, the Qhaliffa's River Galley faced due north, aimed at the bloodred rooftops of Sundar Dun.

"Oapah, look!" said Selena, lowering her arrow-ridden shield and pointing at the floundering Galley.

Oapah turned.

Even in his pain, he smiled, squeezing the handle of his scimitarus.

Few had ever broken a ship with a sword.

CHAPTER 27

Through the Mountain Gate

Spatanian Imperial Border
January 21, 1879

As the dawn broke over the eastern mountains, Harold Milton Stanwich did not need any further encouragement to hurry. *The Gressians will not steal the Beserite out from under me, not while I still stand and draw breath. Nor will I inform Lord Harmon, Colonel Caldwell, or Samuel X. Huntington that I have lost Jack Caldwell. No, I will get to the Beserite first, and I will find Jack Caldwell.* Those thoughts swirled in Harold Milton Stanwich's head as the caravan approached the Mountain Gate, the high mountain passage that rose and descended into the Sand Sea.

Three flags snapped in the cold breeze. First was the familiar banner of the Spatanian Emperor, the flag to which Altadige owed its allegiance. It was red-dish-brown, the color of the earth of central Spatan, far to the west in the middle peninsula, the soil that the Spatanians claimed was the most fertile in all of the world. Against the red-brown, a silver lion reared up, roaring with bared claws. The rearing lion was the sigil of the House of Adomingo, the ruling dynasty that had presided over the fractured, many-nationed lands of the empire for two hundred and fifty years.

Second flew the Anglian flag, neither familiar nor unknown to the people of Altadige, with its four white squares, one for each of the home islands, divided vertically and horizontally by a red cross, for the shared blood that held the islands together. On the edge of the flag, enclosing all of the rest was a border of dark blue, blue as the north Titanic Ocean that surrounded the islands and defended them from their enemies. Set against the four white squares, over the red cross, three golden rings interlocked, one for each of the Three Gods of the Faith.

Third flew a new flag that was entirely unknown to the Mountain Gate and the people of Altadige. It was a flag of a nation that had existed scarcely more than a century. On this flag, two boxes were stacked, one on top of the other, one of light blue set above one of dark green, with a rising sun set against the blue, its rays streaking out in diagonals across the blue. It was the banner of the New Anglian Republic, the nation not only of the Caldwells and the Huntingtons, but of Harold Milton Stanwich also, an Anglian by birth, but a New Anglian by choice. The meaning of the New Anglian flag was clear, and its citizens boldly proclaimed it. The dawn belongs to the Republic, not the empires, and the sun rises over new land, against a limitless sky.

The caravan walked uphill at a steady march as it had done for five hours without ceasing. The dawn was cold, and Stanwich was tempted to at least trot the camels. Count Nepopolous was en route, and Demassi surely would not move at a leisurely pace with Jack Caldwell, wherever they were.

The whorehouse woman told Barnes and Hersen that Demassi took Caldwell with the help of others—Beserians—and that they had made for the Mountain Gate in the middle of the night. Barnes and Hersen could not find any others who had seen him, at least not in the half of a day that Stanwich had given them.

The words of a whorehouse Bulbanian—that is a thin reed upon which to hang our fortunes, thought Stanwich, looking up at the towering granite walls on either side of the mountain pass. Long icicles stretched down the granite faces, some extending twenty-five feet or more. Above the icicles on the vertical faces, a vast, steep, snow-covered slope rose past the cloudline.

Stanwich shook his head in disappointment at his choices. *Perhaps I could have sent out more inquiries? No, I could not. Spatanians talk, Spatanians talk to Macmenians, and Macmenians talk to merchants that talk with Lord George Harmon and Colonel Mason Caldwell and Samuel X. Huntington. No, that would not do, not at all. All it would take would be for one of those men to send a telegraph of Jack Caldwell's disappearance, and there is a telegraph office in Altadige.*

What are my choices? Caldwell disappeared from the whorehouse—what was he doing there in the first place, the night before we were to depart? What a damned fool, Jack Caldwell, more boy than man. The whore in the whorehouse said he disappeared through the Mountain Gate. Why would she lie? Well, she would lie because she is a whore. She is paid to lie. Either way, I have no choice. I cannot sit in Altadige. If the crazed guide took him into the desert, then every hour I wait, I give him more of a chance to disappear into the sands.

Stanwich stared ahead, shivering under his thick coat with angry thoughts swirling through his mind as violently as the wind-driven snow up above him on the mountains.

The Gressians are moving south under the count. Under Usor Nepopolous. I know him not, but I know what a Gressian Count is. If this Nepopolous is like any other Gressian Count, he will kill animals, and he will kill men, and he will discard them like they are nothing. He will do whatever is necessary to move into the Valley of Kordon before me. He will steal the Beserite. No, there is no other choice. We move with utmost haste.

"Major Expey, I want to trot the camels," said Stanwich, turning to his left.

As was their custom on their expeditions, as they had ridden into the far interior of Omakhosi, to the Feathermen Highlands where no Westerners had ever ridden before, Hersen Expey always rode to Stanwich's left, slightly behind him, still within ear reach of Stanwich's voice.

"I advise against it, sir," said the LaFrentian Legionnaire.

"Yes, you said that already. I still want to trot them. It is cold. We can move faster."

"Yes, Commander, it is cold, but we are ascending at grade. Our guides will tell you what I am telling you, sir. It will wear out the camels, the footing of the gravel beneath us is unstable, and we have not yet reached even the crest of the Mountain Gate."

"Our guides? I lost faith in our guides when one of them kidnapped Jack Caldwell."

Hersen Expey did not respond to that. They had questioned all of the Beserian guides about Demassi's disappearance. They all swore by their God of the Sands that he acted alone and that they had never trusted him anyway. He scanned the path now where two of the Beserian scouts rode ahead. The steep grade continued, covered in loose gravel, the kind upon which both men and animals found it easy to slip.

"Stanwich," said Peter Harmon, riding up on Stanwich's right.

Stanwich looked back at him and frowned. "What is it?"

"I have been thinking," said Peter.

"About what?"

"About why Demassi took Jack."

"We have that theory only on the word of a Bulbanian whore in an Altadigean whorehouse," said Stanwich, his teeth snapping as his breath made a cloud in front of his lips. His eyes looked ahead at the rising road in front of them. The great granite cliffs on either side narrowed as they approached the Mountain Gate itself.

"Yes," said Peter. "We also have the fact that Demassi is gone, and that he disappeared without explanation."

Stanwich looked at Peter, his eyes impatient.

"I believe we can be more specific than that. I have been talking with the foreman of the porters. His name is Diego. He has information."

"Diego the Vetenan?"

"Yes," said Peter.

"What kind of information?" asked Stanwich after long moments of riding in silence.

"He has information about Demassi—things he saw, and things he observed. They are things you should hear."

"Fine. Bring the Vetenan up," said Stanwich.

Peter nodded, turned his camel, and rode back down the gravel slope toward the main body of the caravan. Between people and crates, more than one hundred camels were making their way up the mountain road, which could hold no more than three camels across, given the narrowness of the pass.

Peter returned following a handsome, long-faced Vetenan, wearing a peaked cap, and a military-style tunic of dark brown. This he wore over black trousers with a gold stripe down the seam.

The Vetenan saluted as if Stanwich were his military commander. The formality came from Hersen Expey, who expected martial discipline to prevail for the totality of Stanwich's expeditions. Hersen had called Stanwich by his name before they embarked, but only "sir" or "Commander" once they were underway. He expected all others to do the same.

"Diego of House Boggarino, yes?" said Stanwich.

Diego nodded.

"Harmon says you have information. What is it?"

"I observed the guide Aurelio Demassi before he departed."

"Before he departed?"

"Yes, Commander." Diego had slowed his camel with a word and a swish of his riding stick, as expertly as a Beserian. He slowed his mount, a tall and lean caramel-colored cow, just as she came in line with Stanwich's cow. The animals eyed each other, their faces mere inches apart. Diego kept his camel a step behind Stanwich's, allowing Stanwich to remain in the lead as a sign of respect. Stanwich did not seem to notice.

Peter did.

"And what was it you observed?" asked Stanwich.

"I saw him packing his bundle," said Diego, his Anglian as clear as a diplomat translator's, and only slightly accented.

"Oh?" Stanwich looked at Peter as if to say, *Of course Demassi was packing his bundle. We were all packing, and you are wasting my time.*

"He packed his bundle earlier than the rest of us," said Diego, "and then he departed."

"What am I to make of that, young Boggarino?" asked Stanwich. His voice was cold as the wind gusting across the Mountain Gate up ahead.

"Perhaps nothing," said Diego, his voice low and calm. "Except for what he said before he packed and left."

Stanwich lifted an impatient eyebrow.

"He said not only that the Year of the Prophecy was at hand, but that the Day of the Prophecy was nigh."

"I am familiar with the prophecy," said Stanwich.

"As are we, Commander. But all of us Vetenans follow the Three Gods, all of us except for Demassi. He follows the God of the Beserians, or what they call the God of the Sands."

"What of it? A man is free to follow whatever God he pleases. In Omakhosi, most of our guides followed shamans and worshipped their ancestors."

Diego blushed under Stanwich's stern gaze, despite the cold wind blowing down the trail.

"He said, 'In the seventh year of the fortieth Qhaliffa, a man shall emerge from the west, and he shall topple the House of the Usurper.'"

"Yes, I too know the words, Boggarino. I even spoke at Peter Harmon's college about it." Stanwich gestured to Peter with his chin. "I'll tell you," he continued, "I've traveled to a lot of places on this Earth, and many a man has a story about gods doing this and gods doing that."

"Yes, Commander, we Vetenans would say the same thing."

"Then, without disrespect, Boggarino, why are you wasting my time with this story?" Stanwich stared.

"Because that is why he captured him, sir. He believes he is the man from the west."

"Three Gods," said Stanwich, softly, shaking his head.

He spit down onto the cold gravel. He continued to shake his head, looking down. They rode on in awkward silence for several minutes. Stanwich did not dismiss Diego, so the foreman remained riding at Stanwich's side. Peter and Hersen rode behind them, keeping their camels' noses just behind Diego and Stanwich's saddles.

Hersen looked at Stanwich, knowing that silence meant Stanwich was weighing choices in his head, turning them over and inspecting them with his keen, mechanical mind.

Whether or not the man is mad, believing his delusions to be real, does not matter. What matters is whether he acted on them, capturing Jack Caldwell because he believes he is fulfilling some prophecy to his desert god. Ridiculous.

"Did Demassi say where this 'man from the west' was supposed to go?" asked Stanwich.

"No, sir," said Diego.

Peter's camel lurched, nearly throwing him onto the sloped path beneath him. The other camels did the same, shuddering as if there were a wolf or a mountain cat crouched on the path in front of them. Peter could see no obvious threat. The camels began to roar.

"Easy," he said, reaching down to rub his cow camel's neck as Diego had taught him. His camel began to turn down the path, continuing to roar. Peter gently struck the camel's neck with his riding stick, commanding the camel to stay facing forward. The camel disobeyed, continuing to turn. He hit the camel's neck harder. The camel continued to turn against Peter's command, now nearly perpendicular to the path.

"A shake is coming!" said Diego, fighting to control his own camel cow. She began roaring in her own voice. Another camel roared, adding to the chorus. Several of the porters started to shout.

"A what?" Peter shouted to be heard over the camels.

And then he heard it, like the sound of an oncoming locomotive.

Peter's eyes widened as the force of the earthquake revealed itself in all of its power. The ground shook, sending bits of gravel up into the air, high as the camels' chests. Porters down the length of the caravan cried out. The camels' cries grew higher pitched as their fear deepened, but they could barely be heard over the shaking of the earth beneath them and of the granite walls that enclosed them on either side.

"Off, get off the camels!" Diego bellowed the order, no longer showing his deference. It was clear to him that the other Westerners did not know what to do.

Stanwich struggled to keep balance, desperately gripping the sides of the dromedary's hump with his legs and grasping the saddle with his fingers as his camel twisted and shook her head. Peter slid off of the back of his beast, holding on to his camel's head rope as he did so. His feet landed on the path as the ground lurched. He stumbled but kept his footing. The trail was narrow, but the ground rose on either side of it, sloping up to the walls of a canyon. The ground shook more fiercely, rumbling as loudly as a raging thunderstorm directly overhead. An icicle three times longer than a man loosened from the granite wall above and fell to the bottom of the canyon, exploding on the path like a chandelier dropped from a roof.

Peter cowered into a crouch, as if under gunfire.

Stanwich drew his pistol as if they were under attack.

Another duo of icicles loosened and crashed. Hersen and Sergeant Barnes had each unholstered their rifles, scanning the path ahead. The ground continued to shake, throwing Peter forward as easily as a child topples a toy soldier. And then as suddenly as it had arrived, the shaking stopped.

Peter held fast to the camel's head rope. His camel cow pulled against the line like a mule. Peter looked down the path past his camel—all nine hundred pounds of her—seeing down the length of the caravan.

The camels faced in every direction—giant animals in a high state of agitation—some stood sideways, some backward, and some still stood facing forward and upslope. Some men were still mounted, but most were not. Many had fallen to the ground. They were rising quickly, afraid that one of the frightened, crate-loaded animals would step on them and grind them into the gravel.

Peter looked with approval down the path at Diego's porters picking up boxes that had fallen off of the camels. Everywhere boxes lay strewn upon the ground. Some had broken open, spilling their contents onto the path as if launched by a catapult. *We will be here for hours trying to piece everything back together.* Peter frowned. *And time is of the essence.* He turned back to the path ahead and looked up the slope toward the Mountain Gate. A pile of stones had fallen onto the canyon path, barring their way.

"Three Gods," he said.

Stanwich was only feet away.

"Stanwich," said Peter.

Stanwich looked at him with wide eyes. To Peter's surprise, Stanwich had remained mounted on his camel throughout the whole ordeal.

"Are you alright?" asked Peter.

"I am fine," said Stanwich, but his eyes remained wide.

Peter's mind raced, playing the other things Diego had told him through his mind.

Demassi said one other thing before he departed. He said that in the Year of the Prophecy, the God of the Sands would repel the unbelievers.

Peter turned and saw Diego as he rode up to him, leaning down from his camel's hump.

Peter looked up. He was still on his feet, holding his camel's woven head rope in his hands.

"Perhaps it is a sign," whispered Diego. "One does not tempt the gods." There was earnest fear in his whisper.

Stanwich holstered his pistol and dusted off the front of his tunic.

Neither Peter nor Diego saw Hersen Expey approach.

"They are not even your gods on the sands," said the LaFrentian, looking at Diego with his harsh grey-blue soldier's eyes. "Compose yourself."

"The ground does not normally shake like that here in these mountains," said Diego, ignoring Hersen Expey and patting the side of his camel to calm her. She had stopped roaring. "Very rare."

"The earth quakes from time to time," said Stanwich.

"It is an ill omen," said Diego.

"Ill omens be damned," said Stanwich, his voice edged with iron. "Expey, get a team to clear those rocks. Boggarino, get the porters picking up those damn crates."

"They already are," said Peter, mounting his camel, finding that he could do it more quickly than before.

"Then tell them to do it faster," said Stanwich.

But Peter was already riding back to the rear of the caravan, toward Barnes, Hannah, and Mrs. Smith.

"He rides to see the women," said Hersen.

Stanwich nodded, frowning, and looking back down the canyon at Peter's camel trotting downhill. "One of the women appears to have fallen from her mount."

Hersen stepped close to Stanwich and whispered, "We should not have brought them, Harold."

Stanwich looked at Hersen, noting the use of his first name, a name Hersen Expey never used on an expedition.

"This is no place for a woman, no matter how rich the woman's father," said Hersen.

Stanwich set his jaw and looked to the crumbled stones blocking the path ahead.

Damn them. Damn them all.

PART III

THE AMAHDI OF THE
WEST SHALL RISE

CHAPTER 28
The Gressian Way

Northwest of the Valley of Kordon
Bulbanian Borderlands, Western Sand Sea
January 21, 1879

Usor Nepopolous looked south to the horizon. A peaked cap rested on his short dark hair. From the back of his cap, a cloth hung down like a set of cotton drapes, covering his neck and ears, guarding them against the fierce sun above. A January chill hung about the desert air, but the sunlight would still sear a northerner's pale flesh if left unprotected. The summer sun merely seared it faster.

Nepopolous wore the stiff green tunic and the red epaulets of an officer of the Holy Orthodox Guard of the Autocrat. He wore the silver eagle of a colonel, not the golden eagle of a general. He did not care, or at least that was what he said. He was a count of one of the Nine Gressian Families, which meant far more than a general's gold eagle. Few generals in the Gressian armies would dare cross a count named Nepopolous even if he were a private soldier, which of course, no Nepopolous could ever be.

For, in truth, all power in Gressia derived from one's proximity to the Autocrat. And over the generations, the Nepopolouses had guarded that proximity like an eagle defending its nest. In most generations, the Nepopolouses had maneuvered to kill or have banished any who threatened their reputation in the Court of the Autocrat, and over the long years, plenty had dared to threaten that reputation.

Count Usor Nepopolous was the third son of the Grand Count. Unlike in Anglia, where only the eldest son inherited the title, all of Grand Count Gungor Nepopolous's sons were called Count. So too was he, Usor, entitled to a share of his father's lands. Tied to Count Usor's estate were four thousand peasants, a paltry share of his father's forty-four thousand, but a position of great power and wealth nonetheless.

Usor's hawk circled high above him, a spot of darkness against the cloudless, bright blue sky. It was a Hon Hawk from the lands of the Hon River, smarter than other hawks, responsive to Usor's commands and trained to do as he wished. Usor thrust out his right arm, whistling loudly.

Without hesitation, the hawk broke into a dive, as if he were dropping down for a kill. As the bird closed, his talons stretched out beneath him.

Usor smiled at the bird's beauty, and then he pointed. The man lay shirtless, stretched out on his back, his arms pinioned by a pair of burly porters. His legs were spread, each tied to a stake that had been driven firmly into the ground.

The giant hawk dove at the man's bared chest and abdomen as if pursuing a fleeing hare, dropping with astonishing speed. Watching with wide eyes, the man screamed.

The hawk landed his talons upon his hairy chest, digging into his flesh. The man howled differently, the sound of pain replacing the sound of fear.

"No, Count, please! Mercy! Mercy!"

Count Usor whistled a new tune—one the hawk knew well. The man tried to turn his face away, thrashing his head from side to side and waving his grey and black hair, long and shaggy in the way of the Gressian peasantry. A thick beard covered the lower half of his broad face. The hawk bobbed its head from side to side, matching his movements as if enjoying a game.

The man thrashed his head more wildly.

"No! No! Get away! By the Holy God, no!"

The bird drew its face closer to the man's, who lurched his head forward, snapping his teeth as if to frighten the bird from his chest. The hawk pulled its head back, looking at the man's face with cold, yellow-black, avian eyes.

The porters holding the man's arms pulled harder on the ropes on his wrists, spreading him far apart. He resisted, but his arms were not strong enough to withstand two men leaning away with all of their body weight.

The predator reached forward, its long, razor-sharp beak only inches from the man's face. Then, as he continued to thrash, the hawk snapped forward and ripped off a piece of the man's face.

A string of flesh dangled beneath his cheek, leaving a deep raw gash beneath. The man screamed in a new pitch, one with which Count Usor was familiar—the tone in which a man's pain gives way to full-fledged terror.

Usor whistled again, and the hawk obeyed, pulling another strip of flesh from the man's face. The full expedition stood arrayed in formation with the riflemen in the rear and the porters in the front. It was important to Usor that the porters have the best view. In his experience, discipline was taught best by showing the consequences of disobedience.

Usor whistled again, again, and again. With each whistle, another line of flesh left the man's face. Eventually, all ferocity left the man, and he stopped thrashing.

With most of the skin torn from his face, and having lost both of his eyes, the man released a queer gurgling sound of pure anguish, barely alive.

Usor then, and only then, after nearly five minutes, drew his long-barreled revolver from the holster strapped to his chest and walked forward. He looked down, satisfied that the raw, bleeding mess beneath him was no longer in any way recognizable as the man that had defied him. His standard met, he pulled the trigger.

The gurgling stopped.

He turned and faced the assembled men.

The eyes that met his own looked at him in great fear. Some men visibly shook.

"Do you see that flag?" asked Count Usor. "Do you see it?" He pointed his finger at the banner, flying taut in the wind. Upon it lay the sigil of the Autocrat of the Gressias—three white eagles upon an emerald-green background, surrounded by a ring of gold, the Holy Ring of Orthodoxy.

"That is the flag of our Autocrat, the flag of our Most Orthodox Ruler. And here on the Sands, I am his emissary. I, Usor Nepopolous!" Usor pointed to the dead, sprawled figure of the faceless, eyeless man. "That man forgot! I hope none of you make the same mistake."

Count Usor snapped his fingers, and his Hon Hawk flew up and landed on the large leather glove on his left hand.

"The Autocrat will not be disobeyed."

Count Usor turned to the nearest sergeant of his riflemen.

"Get my camel. We have already stayed here too long. We will march all night."

"Yes, Your Excellency," said the sergeant, bowing his head in supplication. The sergeant, a man of average height, stood nearly a full head taller than Count Usor. Count Usor stood shorter than most women. At court, for the majority of his childhood, the girls had mocked him as mercilessly as the boys. Some said that was why Usor had become so cruel as an adult. Others said he had always been cruel. But either way, few at court dared mock Count Usor Nepopolous anymore.

The men around him rushed to prepare the camels to march south through the night, moving faster than Usor had ever seen them move before.

CHAPTER 29
Taken

Southwest of the Valley of Kordon
Plain of Gamurian, Western Sand Sea
January 23, 1879

Jack Caldwell opened his eyes to darkness. He jolted awake, thrashing his arms out as if bracing himself for a fall. His mind raced, unsure of its surroundings.

It was not sky above him, nor was he in a room. Not far above his head was a layer of something, like a broad cloth. Jack contracted his stomach to sit up. Immediately a stabbing pain twisted in his abdomen, making him drop back down onto his back. He gasped, waiting for the pain to subside.

Cautiously, he leaned his head forward, straining his neck to look down the length of his body. He could faintly make out that he was wearing clothes and shoes. They were the same clothes and shoes he had last been wearing—his evening dress. He had gone to the whorehouse. Yes, he had gone there, to the last door on the right—the door with the seven on the red sign.

Am I still there now? Did I fall asleep? For how long?

He inhaled deeply through his nose. He could smell animals, sweat, and dust. He sneezed, convulsing his body. The stabbing pain returned to his stomach, forcing his head back down. He groaned.

The cloth peeled back in front of him.

The pale moonlight was radiant compared to the darkness that had just surrounded him. A face filled the open space above him, and the contours of his reality rushed in around him.

I am in a tent. A man pulled the tent flap back and is looking down into my face. I know his face. It was lean and bearded. The eyes were dark and intelligent, sunken deep into a gaunt face.

"You are awake," said the man, speaking in accented Anglian in the manner of a native Spatanian.

"You," said Jack. He named the face in his mind: *Aurelio Demassi. The Vetenan guide.*

"You have slept for nearly three days," said Demassi.

"Where—" Jack attempted again to lean up, but still the pain in his stomach forced him back down onto his back.

"Where—" Jack grimaced, his face racked with pain.

"You are in the Western Sand Sea, upon the Plain of Gamurian, approximately sixty miles west of the Mountain Gate. We are a four-days ride from the Valley of Kordon."

This information swirled inside of Jack's mind. His mind could not assess the information. What had he last seen? Why was he still in his evening clothes? Where did he go after the whorehouse?

"Where are the others?" asked Jack.

"We left them behind," said Demassi.

"Meaning what?" said Jack, jerking his head up and wincing again from the stabbing sensation in his stomach.

"Stay down," said Demassi.

"What did you do to me?" Jack grabbed his abdomen as the pain erupted again inside of him. He lay down, unable to even prop himself up.

Demassi looked at him for long moments without speaking. Jack could see a rich and brilliant carpet of stars in the sky above Demassi's head.

"What was done to you was necessary to bring you here," he said.

"What did you do?" asked Jack again, his voice dropping to an angry growl. He felt a swirling mix of fear and rage. The guide had done something to him. He had hurt him in some way and had taken him out into the desert. Jack was unable to defend himself; he could not even sit up without debilitating pain.

"Tell me, guide, what did you do to me?"

Demassi smiled. "Save your anger, friend, but not for me. You will need it in due time."

Demassi closed the tent flap, and the darkness returned.

Peter. Peter warned me about him. What have I done?

CHAPTER 30
Sanctuary of the Serpents

Semissari Swamp
13th Day, Month of Gandus, 807
Anglian Calendar: January 13, 1879

Selena collapsed on the first patch of solid ground she found beyond the reeds.

They had moved from Saman Keer without stopping for eight days. Whatever strength remained in her after the journey across the Great Mountain, the freezing water and her near misses with the River Galleys had sapped entirely.

She lifted her head, looking around her and marveling that she, Oapah, and Gulana were still alive. She could still hear the drumbeat in her head, and the image of Oapah, roaring as he chopped off the Galley's oars refused to leave her mind's eye.

"Lady Savanar, we cannot stop here," said Gulana. Her eyes were red and weary. Selena had only to look after herself. Gulana was tasked with watching Selena, the one whose escape had marshaled the full might of the Grand Vizer and the Qhaliffa's forces.

Selena moved her eyes but not her body. Despite everything, she felt as if she could fall asleep right there on the cold, moss-covered earth.

"Lady Savanar, we must move. They will not stop. They will press into the swamp. The reserve Galleys already row this way. River Guardsmen will be upon us in minutes. Get up."

As plainly as Gulana spoke the words, Selena heard the Galley drums boom in the distance, and this time not only in her head. Her heart lurched, drawing new adrenaline from some unknown reservoir. She pushed with her palms on the ground, lifting her body as the renewed fear rose inside of her and drove her to her feet.

Oapah and Gulana each reached down to help lift her, one on either shoulder. The Serpents had already removed the arrow from Oapah's shoulder and had given him a vial for the pain. They had many talents, and healing was among them.

"The sanctuary is not far," said Oapah.

Selena turned to look behind her, in the direction of the Great Pool of the Oxus and the booming drums. She could see nothing but the reed wall that had closed in behind them. Selena had heard many tales of the Semissari, a place said to be dark and haunted, populated by dangerous snakes and by other beings worse than the snakes. All children of the flatlands had heard such stories about young ones abducted in the night, taken to the Semissari, and never heard from again.

The place of nightmares was now her refuge.

She looked around her. A half-dozen Sworn Serpents walked past amongst the reeds, moving in the other direction. They stared at her with their strange yellow-green eyes as they glided by, walking in the direction of the Galley drums.

"What will they do?" asked Selena, still leaning on Oapah and Gulana's shoulders as they moved deeper into the swamp.

"They will make any guardsmen foolish enough to land in the reeds pay with their lives," said Oapah.

Gulana's eyes looked forward, staring into the depths of the swamp. The morning sun had risen well above the eastern horizon, baking off the mists of the Great Pool. But the mists still hung about the shallow waters of the Semissari. Selena wondered if they ever departed. Large shaggy trees formed a canopy overhead, their branches connected by a carpet of hanging moss and tangled vines.

Selena looked up and saw one of the vines move. It was a snake, ten feet long and as thick as a human torso. She froze.

"What?" asked Gulana, her eyes intense and warlike.

They all needed rest, and their nerves were frayed. Gulana seemed different to Selena since the scorpion's bolt had struck their rowboat and they had plunged into the water of the Great Pool. Gulana became separated from her at that moment. If Selena had been struck down or captured, Gulana would not have been next to her to intervene.

Selena pointed silently above her, her eyes wide as saucers. The snake's head moved below its body, seeming to stare at Selena. It was no more than ten feet above them. If the snake dropped, it would be upon them.

"Come, Lady Savanar," said Oapah, pulling forcefully on her arm. She felt as powerless as a child's doll in his grip. "In the Semissari, we are in the place of the serpents; some are snakes, and some are Oath Holders. All are our allies. Walk without fear."

Selena looked down and saw a pair of small snakes slither along the side of the path. Her heart fluttered in her chest. They continued for long minutes that felt to Selena like hours, the reed walls on either side of them rarely more than an arm's length away. Yet Gulana and Oapah moved swiftly as if they knew the way.

They were rarely beyond eyesight of at least one snake, and in most sections as soon as Selena took her eyes off of one snake, another came into view. She pondered how many snakes hid in the trees, reeds, and pools of the Semissari. Thousands. Hundreds of thousands. Perhaps millions.

She shivered.

The walls of reeds on either side of them suddenly ended.

They stood in a wide clearing that rose toward its center like an upside-down bowl. Moss and vine-covered trees surrounded the edges, their boughs reaching out far into the center of the clearing. But near the top of the central mound, there was no cover, and there in the sunlight sat a half-dozen Sworn Serpents in their Hahst-sand-colored robes, with their face veils removed. Selena stopped.

All of their eyes were upon her.

Gulana and Oapah stopped and stared. The half-dozen Serpents rose as one, standing shoeless in front of their mats of dried reeds. They bowed in the manner of lords acknowledging royalty, dipping in a way that was at once deep, slow, and deliberate.

Gulana and Oapah returned the bows. Selena did the same.

"Should we approach?" she whispered.

Gulana nodded.

"You must lead the way, Lady Savanar," said Oapah.

Selena walked in as dignified a manner as her exhaustion would allow, stepping upon the moss with her waterlogged cloth shoes.

"Lady Savanar," said the center Serpent, as they approached. "Sit with us."

Selena looked down and saw that three dry woven mats awaited them. They were tan, the color of reeds dried in the sun.

She sat with her legs crossed under her, emulating the manner of the Serpents. She looked into each of their faces, slowly, to remember them. It was immensely difficult to tell one Serpent from another.

She could see they varied slightly in skin tone, eye color, the shapes of their faces and noses and cheekbones and ears and in a dozen other ways that men's and women's faces differ from each other. But in spite of that, there was something staggeringly similar about all of the faces of the Serpents, so much so that it was difficult to tell the men from the women and even the older from the younger. That was, of course, Selena had come to learn, by design.

The center Serpent spoke. "Lady Savanar, I am Asatan."

Any who had heard of the Order had heard the legends of Asatan, Supreme Serpent, one of the Three, along with The Ram and The Lion. There was always one of each to lead the Order, as it had been for generations upon generations, going back to the beginning of the Resistance in the age of the Third Qhaliffa.

None outside of the Order knew the name of The Lion or The Ram, but all knew the name Asatan—even children. However, none could identify her face. Even now, looking into her eyes, Selena struggled to tell her apart from the Sworn Serpents sitting to Asatan's right and left.

Nor was it clear, as Selena looked into Asatan's face, that she was a woman. She could have been a man who had shaved very carefully. Her head was as hairless as her face and her lean neck. Her eyes were yellowish-green and ablaze with intensity. Selena fought the urge to look away.

Something in Asatan's eyes made her deeply uncomfortable, as if she was not worthy of looking into them. They seemed to penetrate as they stared, full of wisdom and lacking any semblance of guilt, fear, or shame. As Asatan's eyes searched her, a strange feeling of familiarity rose as if deep memories were awakening within her.

"You bring us great joy this day," said Asatan.

Selena jolted. It was the voice from the dungeon, the voice behind the veil, the voice that matched the yellow-green eyes that had come to her in the vision.

"Yes, Lady Savanar, I am no stranger to you."

"How?" asked Selena, unable to manage anything else.

"I have watched you across many years."

"You came to me—in a vision. You spoke to me in the dungeon. You told me you would come for me, that the Oath Holders would come, that I should not fear the flames."

"Yes."

"How?"

"I said those words to you long ago, Lady Savanar, when you were still a little girl. I was not in the dungeon, only in your mind."

Selena waited, not knowing what else to say.

"The God of the Mountain and the Sands smiles upon you, Lady Savanar."

Selena felt the gap in her teeth with her tongue, as if to remind her that for all of their mysticism, there was a limit to what these Oath Holders could do.

"Your faith is still growing, Lady Savanar. More will come."

"Will the guardsmen come here, into the Semissari?" asked Selena.

"You need not fear that, Lady Savanar. You are protected here."

"Thank you . . . Supreme Serpent."

Asatan smiled. "You need not call me that, Lady Savanar. Asatan is enough. We are all only Oath Holders here. I am not the first Asatan, nor will I be the last. One will replace me as I replaced the Asatan before me."

Selena nodded. "Then will you also call me Selena?"

"No."

Selena waited in silence, uncertain as to what she was expected to say.

"Before you arrived, Lady Savanar, we waited in great sorrow. But you are the joy to take away our sorrow, the morning to break the darkness."

Selena still did not know what to say to such a thing, so she sat in silence and waited for Asatan to say something else.

But Asatan said nothing. She sat staring with her yellow-green eyes. The other Serpents did the same as their leader. If they were worried about the approaching River Galleys and the men they carried, Selena could not tell. They sat as if ready to fall asleep in the sunshine.

"Why were you in sadness?" asked Selena, at last.

"The Grand Vizer, who serves the darkness, holds the Staff of the Ram. The staff has come alive, and Jemojeen has harnessed its power. We arrived too late. The mission to capture the staff has failed, and all who dared to seize it have been lost."

Selena, understanding little of this, looked at Gulana. She was stone-faced and impassive as a statue, her jaw set in a deep frown. Selena could see that the crease in her forehead—the crease that deepened when she was anxious or angry or afraid—was as deep as she had ever seen it.

Selena turned to look at Oapah, he who had just managed an arrow wound with little more than a growl. A tear now broke free from his eye and rolled down his dark Omakhosian cheek.

CHAPTER THIRTY-ONE
Summoned

Mid-Levels, Alwaz Deem
13th Day, Month of Gandus, 807
Anglian Calendar: January 13, 1879

"You do not have to do this, Ozgar."

"I do."

"There have been plenty of archer officers who did not."

"But I will be one who did, Sergeant."

Ottovan Fanfar shook his head in fear for his young friend. Ottovan was a sergeant, newly risen from the ranks of the ordinary Demissaries. Ozgar was a second-year full Demissary, barely out of training. He, Ozgar Ogatonia, was going to be a Captain of Archers. That was what he always said to Ottovan when no one else was around. He was a quiet young man, serious and determined, but brazen to the point of recklessness.

Ottovan looked at the bridge, barely wide enough for a man to place both of his feet next to each other and still have both of them on the wood. It was, in reality, more of a beam than a bridge. But it was called the Challenge of the Bridge, not the Challenge of the Beam, and many a young Demissary had died in their efforts to meet it.

It is a foolish thing to take on so young, thought Ottovan, even as a young sergeant, when he was not prone to challenge the ways of the Demissaries, even in the smallest of details.

Ozgar's name pulled first. Ottovan knew there was now no turning back. Backing out now would make Ozgar look like a coward, and Ozgar would rather die than look like a coward in front of his fellow Demissaries.

"You have a risk-taker there, Fanfar."

Ottovan knew the voice well.

"For good reason, Jongdar," said Ottovan, looking at the other newly minted sergeant, Jemojeen Jongdar. They were the same year, numbers one and two in their class at the Academy. Ottovan had edged out Jemojeen, defeating him in one-on-one scim-

itarus dueling on the final day of the rankings. Ottovan was never one to let another man win, but when he saw the rage in Jemojeen's eyes, he almost wished that he were such a man.

Six hundred Demissaries stood arrayed, watching. Ottovan could see how nervous Ozgar was in the tension in his shoulders.

Legion Commander Agurleous fired his pistol, the signal to begin. Ozgar leaped onto the beam at a dead run, nocking his first arrow. The scorpion launched out the first target, high and ahead of Ozgar. Ozgar loosed his arrow, barely pausing his pace. His arrow struck the leather ball at its dead center.

Ottovan shouted with the rest of his squadron, shaking his fist in triumph.

"Ottovan. Ottovan!"

Ottovan woke with a start, his torso shooting up and his hand instinctively reaching for a blade.

The voice was Rama's.

He lay in his bed, sweating.

"What, wife?" he asked. His voice was edged as the dagger he kept under his sleeping cushion, his chest pounding.

Rama looked at him with fearful eyes. He felt a wave of shame creep up his face. She was a good wife, as good as any of any man he knew. No, she was better than that. She cared for him and supported the grave risks he took with nearly inexhaustible patience and courage. She was a wise, kind, and sturdy mother for their daughters. She had even kept the beauty of her youth into her middle years. He knew he should be more loving, yet kindness often failed to find its way to his lips.

"Nemakar is here," she said, her voice scarcely above a whisper.

Westerly winds howled outside the clouded panes of the window, its glass intended to conceal. Ottovan Fanfar did not need passersby looking into his house. The fire in the hearth had died down to embers. As well plastered as the house was, the chill had still seeped into his room.

Half of a dozen scenarios raced through his mind to explain why Nemakar would be at his house at this hour. None were good.

The darkness in the window outside meant it was not yet five in the morning. It felt like three.

"Should I send him in?" Rama's hair was disheveled from sleep, but her eyes were alert with alarm. She was no fool. She might not know the details for her own protection, but she knew far more than she pretended.

"Yes," said Ottovan.Better to speak in the bedroom than in the table room. Fewer ears can hear us in here. The girls should neither hear nor see us. They must be kept far away from this.

And yet Ottovan knew that no man who chose the path he had chosen could keep his family out of it forever. There would come a time when normal life would no longer be possible, when the families would have to be hidden.

The children would not understand why they were ripped up from their roots. Ottovan hoped the night of the uprooting was not tonight. He had told Rama there might be a time when they would have to go, and he made sure that she always kept the leather travel sacks ready and stocked with enough hard bread and water for a three-day ride. To her credit, she never asked questions beyond that.

Ottovan threw off his sleeping blankets and pulled his rough tunic over his body. He stepped into a pair of soft linen pants, the kind most men of the Seven Cities wore in their own homes.

The door to his bedroom opened.

Nemakar Hasdruba, Captain of the Fire Demissaries, stood before him. He was tall, a half-head taller than Ottovan. His leanness made him seem even taller than he was. A long drooping mustache framed his mouth on either side, obscuring his upper lip.

Ottovan looked into Nemakar's eyes and knew at once.

Nemakar said nothing for long moments.

Ottovan saw more sadness in his eyes than fear. He was nearly as close to Ozgar as Ottovan was himself. They had all risen together across the long years, building a trust that was almost absolute.

"Tell me," said Ottovan, his voice dropped to a whisper.

"They were ambushed."

Ottovan swallowed a lump in his throat.

"In the Throne Hall itself. Jemojeen holds the survivors in the dungeon."

"May the God of the Mountain and the Sands have mercy upon us all," said Ottovan. "Was he among them? Those that survived and were captured?"

"I do not know."

"Did any escape?"

"I do not believe so," said Nemakar. His hazel eyes were glassy.

Ottovan stared into the cloudiness of the window as if trying to see the wind. He was not a man who cried.

Jemojeen's summons arrived shortly after Nemakar.

Ottovan had steeled himself for it. He knew it would come, but he did not know how quickly it would arrive. Then again, Jemojeen was never a man to waste time.

Jemojeen's Grand Vizerian Guardsmen waited just outside the door. He and Nemakar could not flee, not with his family sleeping inside.

Jemojeen would throw them all in the dungeons as the children of a traitor. He would petition the Qhaliffa to remove Ottovan of his command. He would replace him with a sadistic monster like Ulgur Uggatar, and then he would use Ottovan's men to do his vicious bidding. Those few men who supported the cause would be discovered by the many others who did not.

Rama would be raped, or worse. No, Ottovan could not flee. He was a husband and a father. He had a legion under his command. If he ran away, everything he had ever fought for would be destroyed. Jemojeen knew what mattered to him, and he would burn it all. Indeed, he would try to erase every physical and living memory of Ottovan's existence.

No, there was only one way forward, and it was the way that he, Ozgar, and Nemakar had discussed two dozen times. Each time Ozgar had demanded it, and each time Ottovan had pushed back. *No, I cannot disown you. No, I will not dishonor your memory for this generation and the next*, he said.

But Ozgar had said, *No, Ottovan, my wife is dead, my children too. Perhaps that is why the God of the Mountain and the Sands allowed the sickness to take them. Allow my tragedy to give me strength. They cannot reach me like they can reach you or Nemakar; that is why I must lead them. That is why I must take the Staff of the Ram. I am no worthier of the task than either of you, but the God of the Mountain and the Sands has prepared me for this day—prepared me for this sacrifice, if necessary—by the tragedies He allowed to happen. The fulfillment of the Prophecy will redeem the death of my wife and daughters. You know this to be true, Ottovan.*

Ottovan shook his head that day because he did indeed know Ozgar's words to be true. *But I will not dishonor your memory, Ozgar,* he said.

Ozgar had stood before him, looking him squarely in the eyes—they were nearly the same exact height—and he said, *Fear not for what they might call me, good friend. No man can add or detract from the judgment of the God of the Mountain and the Sands. Let them think of me as a traitor. I shall be clean as the white fleece of the lamb.*

That was weeks ago, weeks that now felt like months, but Ozgar's words still seared Ottovan's heart. He had hoped—as much as he had ever hoped for anything—that the day would not come when he had to choose whether to lie about Ozgar Ogatonia, to publicly call him the vilest of traitors to his legion, his Qhaliffa, and his faith.

"We must not tarry, Ottovan." Nemakar's eyes were strained with alarm.

Ottovan had served with Nemakar under fire a dozen times. He had seen him cross swords with fierce Harafhans and Beserians who knew how to kill with a blade. He did not recall seeing his Captain of Fire's eyes as anxious as they were now.

Ottovan avoided Nemakar's eyes, securing the ties on his leather boots.

"Have you decided?" asked Nemakar.

Ottovan's voice was barely more than a whisper. "He knew the risks."

Jemojeen's guardsmen kept their distance behind Ottovan and Nemakar as they walked in the pale, dawn-lit streets.

If they were traitors, they were not known as traitors yet, and every guardsman knew the reputation of both men. Both carried their wide-bladed scimitari in leather scabbards. Either man's sword had killed too many enemies to count in their long years of service to the Qhaliffa. Both men, Ottovan Fanfar, Commander of the Qhaliffa's Third Demissary Legion, and Nemakar Hasdruba, Captain of Fire of the Third Legion, wore three pairs of pistols on their bodies, as all fire Demissaries did, officers included. With those pistols and the curved swords at their sides, the dozen Grand Vizerian Guardsmen would be lucky to escape with a man alive. The guardsmen could not order Ottovan and Nemakar disarmed. They were Demissary officers of the Qhaliffa and outside of the Grand Vizer's authority—at least for now.

"You need not arm yourselves, Commander," said Sipahi Shaheni, the Sipahi who delivered Jemojeen's summons, just before they left.

Ottovan Fanfar did not acknowledge the statement in any way, continuing to fasten the buckles on his leather holsters.

Nemakar looked at Shaheni with disdaining eyes. He kept his insult in his mind. *You are little more than a propped-up gangman from Sundar Dun, Sipahi.* His pistols were already in his holsters, handles bristling from either side.

They walked south, toward Sundar Dun, on the Upper Ring Road. The Grand Vizerian Fortress of Alwaz Deem, a narrow grey-black tower, loomed before them. It was joked that if the Grand Vizer were a building, he would look very much like his western fortress. There was no joking in Ottovan's eyes now, only a grim gaze facing the road, as dark thoughts swirled through in his mind. Nemakar walked at his side. Sipahi Shaheni's dozen guardsmen walked several paces behind them.

They moved south for the better part of a half-hour, moving at an uphill grade, neither steep nor slight, onto the southern reaches of Alwaz Deem. It was elevated above most of the valley, including the mid-levels where Ottovan and most of the other Demissary officers lived amongst prosperous merchants and the middling aristocrats of the lower Kezelboj.

They passed through the outer wall of the fortress, twenty feet high, with spiked parapets and narrow arrow slots along the upper rim. The portcullis was pulled up above the entrance, its spikes reaching down like pointed teeth, the dense iron mass suspended by its chains as they walked underneath into the mouth of the stone archway.

A pair of guardsmen waited inside the yard, standing next to the door of the tower. The door was opened, revealing a lamplit staircase leading upward.

Ottovan had never been in the tower before. Nor did he wish to enter it now. He failed, however, to see any other choice. It was his duty to come if the Grand Vizer called him. Anything else would be an insult to the Qhaliffa. And only a guilty man would be afraid to heed the summons, especially a man as duty-bound as Ottovan Fanfar. He nonetheless felt better with Nemakar walking next to him. He always felt better with Nemakar at his side, whether facing Beserian tribesmen, Harafhan raiders, or the Grand Vizer himself. Though built like a stork, Nemakar had shown, over the long years, to have the heart of a lion.

Ottovan stepped into the tower, breathing the stuffy air of the stairwell. Nemakar stepped in behind him.

"No," said Sipahi Shaheni. "Only Commander Fanfar."

Ottovan turned and gave Sipahi Shaheni his most withering stare.

"Why is that, Sipahi?" Ottovan could see Shaheni swallow a small lump in his throat before he answered. *He is still frightened of me; that is good.* Ottovan felt a surge of confidence he had not felt since Nemakar had knocked on his door in the darkness.

"The Grand Vizer did not say, Commander. He only asked that you be sent in to him separately."

As quickly as his confidence had arrived, Ottovan felt it receding. He and Nemakar had discussed what they would say to Jemojeen, but he had foolishly expected that they would speak to the Grand Vizer together. They could have coordinated their remarks better.

"Very well, Sipahi," said Ottovan. "Captain, wait here. I shall return." The last sentence was more of a wish than a certainty. Jemojeen had grown bolder of late, and the Order's attacks had made him more so.

CHAPTER 32
A Captured Serpent

Saman Keer
10th Day, Month of Gandus, 807
Anglian Calendar: January 10, 1879
Three Days Earlier

Sendata opened her eyes, and for one glorious moment, she forgot where she was. Then she realized her nightmare was a waking nightmare, one from which sleep was a fleeting and feeble refuge.

The pain reached her first, reminding her like a laughing demon that she was not asleep. Her arms were chained to the cross-plank, as they had been for long hours that might have been days. Gone was any normal feeling, other than a deep ache from which she feared her arms would never recover. The open flesh in her leg burned like fire. They had skinned her, slowly, from her ankle to her knee.

She fought the urge to look down. The feeling—the deep guttural pain that made her stomach empty itself—told her all she needed to know. The skin was gone. The flesh was raw and angry and bloody. If she ever escaped, if she ever left this dark labyrinth to see the sunshine again, they would need to take the leg off. Flesh skinned that deeply did not recover. There was no skin layer from which to regrow.

She heard the footsteps on the stone steps, echoing off of the stone walls, and her heart began to thunder. It was more than one set of footsteps. There were at least two men, likely three.

She waited, her arms tightly chained to the splintery wood. Her legs hung limply with her feet wedged against a small wooden ledge on the up-beam. Her pain was as raw as the flesh on her flayed left leg.

She saw the torturer's face first, round and fleshy in the torchlight. He had a smooth face like that of a boy or a eunuch, except for the small tuft of hair that grew down from his chin, long and bushy like his eyebrows. His eyes were dead, cold, utterly indifferent.

She had looked into his eyes while he flayed her. They reflected back nothing, as sympathetic as a sand-lizard toward a fly. Behind the torturer walked a taller man, a man whose features she knew in an instant, a man whose face she feared more than the torturer's. He, the Grand Vizer, did not do the cutting, but Sendata knew it was his will that moved the knife.

Behind Jemojeen walked another man, one Sendata did not expect to see, one whose face she had only ever seen from afar, like most of his subjects. It was the face of the Sovereign of the Sand Sea and the Great Mountain, the Ruler that held the power of life and death over all, even Jemojeen Jongdar, the mighty Grand Vizer.

Sumetan the Magnificent, Qhaliffa of the Seven Cities, walked with his eyes lowered, watching the stone steps as he descended them, as if resisting the necessity of looking at what had been done to the woman on the crossbeam with the partly flayed left leg, and what was yet to be done.

Sendata watched them as they approached. A shabby cloth covered her small chest and another covered a narrow strip between her hips, but her abdomen, arms, and legs lay naked and exposed. She could swing her head from side to side, but she was as bound to the wood as securely as an insect by a collector's pins.

Jemojeen stood close enough to her that she could smell the garlic coming out of his pores, even over the ever-present stench of the dungeon—the smell of dirt, urine, sweat, blood, and excrement.

Sendata avoided his eyes.

Her leg, the leg they'd begun to flay, began to twitch. She willed it to stop, but the leg did not obey her mind. The cramps in her shoulders had moved from severe discomfort to outright pain, pinching like an iron clamp. Sendata could see that the Qhaliffa stood some feet back as if he might be polluted by her proximity. The torturer stood close to her, ready to act when needed. Sendata's heart raced as fear crept up her spine.

She inhaled, willing herself to fight against her panic.

"Get her attention," said Jemojeen.

The torturer stepped forward and slapped her face with a gloved hand, stinging her cheek with pain and making her ears ring.

The thing about pain, Sendata had learned, was that experiencing the severest pain did not make one numb to the lesser pains. Instead, it made one recognize how much worse it could become, which made the lesser pains more frightening, not less. One's ability to stomach the low pain did not mean that one could stomach the great pains to come. Indeed, once one had undergone the torturer's flaying or the burning irons, one learned that the will was a feeble thing against such weapons. There were pain-bringing techniques that no mind could resist, that the nervous system surrendered to, separate and apart from the conscious will.

Sendata looked up at Jemojeen, still keeping her eyes lowered beneath his chin.

"Look me in the eyes, traitor," he said. His voice was calm, almost pleasant.

The torches along the walls threw shadows across his thin face, making him look excessively gaunt and almost skeletal.

With effort, Sendata raised her eyes, obediently, up into Jemojeen's. In the torchlight, Jemojeen's eyes grew greener, green like an emerald, green as the turban of a Demissary archer. *Yes, green like a Demissary archer. Green like Ozgar's turban. Ozgar. Ozgar's arrow missed Jemojeen in the Throne Room. Ozgar never misses. He could have shot him dead with his eyes closed at that distance. The Staff of the Ram flashed like the sun, and Ozgar's arrow missed. Did he escape? Ozgar is not here.*

Sendata could feel the Qhaliffa's eyes upon her. She moved her eyes away from Jemojeen to look at the Qhaliffa. Her eyes met his own. She could see nothing extraordinary in his face. Beneath his black turban and the giant emerald set inside of it, his eyes were brown and dull.

The torturer's hand struck her face viciously, harder than the first time. She cried out without forethought or intent as her eyes welled with tears.

"Do not look upon that face without permission, traitor," said Jemojeen.

Sendata turned her eyes back to Jemojeen's chest, her twice-struck cheek hot with pain.

"Do you know who that is, traitor? That face you looked upon?"

Sendata did not answer, unsure whether speaking or not speaking was more dangerous.

"Answer me, prisoner," said Jemojeen, his voice low and calm, barely above a whisper, as though utterly certain that his perceptions were correct and his will would prevail. In this place, Jemojeen's whispers could separate a limb from a body or an eye from a face. Surely, the law of the Holy Book required a judgment before such punishments could be meted out. But, as all knew, it was often difficult to remember how a prisoner obtained her injuries. And who would check the will of the Grand Vizer? The priests? Most certainly not. Few were willing to speak out on behalf of justice for traitors.

"This is one of the twelve?" the Qhaliffa's voice was small as if he were farther away from Sendata than where he was actually standing.

"Yes, Your Majesty," said Jemojeen.

The Qhaliffa stepped closer to Sendata, standing adjacent to Jemojeen. He was nearly a full head shorter than his Grand Vizer. Though he was years younger, he looked to be almost the same age.

The torturer tensed as the Qhaliffa neared, almost flinching. He was a man, unlike Jemojeen, unused to proximity to absolute human power. Jemojeen stood still as a statue.

The Qhaliffa looked up into Sendata's eyes.

She met his gaze, her mind confused that such a man wielded the power he did. His eyes were ordinary, brown, and unimpressive. He was neither handsome nor imposing. Though he was called Sumetan the Magnificent, there was nothing magnificent in his face, his form, or his voice.

"Are you a member of the Order? An Oath Holder?" he asked. His voice had a normal, mundane sound to it, less regal than Jemojeen's.

Sendata looked at him, hanging with chains binding her arms to the wooden crossbar, her bare feet caked with her dried blood, resting on a small ledge sticking out from the upright post. Her flayed flesh from her ankle to her knee was red and lumpy, glistening in the torchlight.

"Yes," she said, keeping her eyes looking into the Qhaliffa's.

The Qhaliffa waited long seconds before he spoke. He nodded as if pondering this response.

"Why?" he asked.

His face was frowning but otherwise inscrutable. He seemed more burdened than angry, as if this were among the more distasteful aspects of ruling over other human beings.

Sendata looked at him, despite her pain, feeling something she had not felt in many days, and certainly not in the terror of the dungeon. The feeling was surprise. *The Qhaliffa of the Seven Cities asks me why I am an Oath Holder of the Order. Is this a game to increase my torment, a moment of pleasure for them before I am flayed further or before I am burned before him?*

"Because I believe," she said.

"*Your Majesty*," said Jemojeen, his voice like acid. "When one speaks to the Qhaliffa of the Seven Cities, one uses the phrase, '*Your Majesty*.'"

The Qhaliffa waved his hand in the air impatiently, frowning and silencing Jemojeen. He kept his eyes on Sendata's face.

"You believe what, exactly?" he asked. His frown left his face, and a look of something like curiosity animated his plain features.

Sendata looked at him. The pain in her flayed leg flared. She considered asking the Qhaliffa for a healing balm but then thought better of it. If she trusted the calmness in his voice and the openness in his face, she was a fool. The torturer was calm when he skinned her, like a butcher in a shop, ignoring her cries for mercy as entirely as if she were already a corpse.

"I believe the Prophecy, *Your Majesty*. I believe that by the ending of this year, you will no longer be called *Your Majesty*."

The torturer withdrew his skinning knife and stepped forward. Sendata flinched involuntarily, fear grasping her from her spine and tingling the back of her neck. The Qhaliffa stopped him by lifting his palm. The torturer froze.

"Put your knife away," said the Qhaliffa.

The torturer obeyed.

"Your Majesty, let him take her tongue. We cannot allow this filth to insult you," said Jemojeen.

"I will decide when I have been insulted, Jemojeen."

Jemojeen forced a look of submission onto his face as the rage bubbled inside of him, rising like the contents of an overheated cauldron. *I grow tired of deference to this man.*

"You believe the prophecy. The prophecy says that in the seventh year of the fortieth Qhaliffa, that the line of the Qhaliffas will end, yes?"

"Yes," said Sendata. She felt courage coursing through her, masking her pain, even if only for a moment.

"And what will bring me down? Your Order? The Beserian rebellion? The reunification of the Staff of the Prophet?"

"Yes," said Sendata. "All of these things."

"All of these things?"

"It is written," said Sendata. "Lady Savanar is free. She is of the line of Hom Hommuram, and another shall arise in the west." Her heart beat with something like triumph as she said the words.

"You were captured in my Throne Room."

Sendata looked at Sumetan the Magnificent, not answering.

"You tried to steal from me."

Sendata felt the boldness of conviction, even as her head hung down, her hairless scalp a jumble of bruises and cuts, half of her face swollen from being beaten, her thin bruised arms chained against the rough wood of the crossbeam.

"We sought that which belongs to no man," she said.

"Oh?" said Sumetan. "But you misread your history. You sought the Staff of the Ram, did you not?"

Sendata stared. *I should not speak of the staff. Not to him, not to any of them. All I say can be used against the others, the others who are not here in this dungeon.*

"Answer me," said the Qhaliffa. The torturer looked at the Qhaliffa, waiting for his sign to flay the prisoner.

"We did not succeed that night," she said. "But we will succeed." She kept her eyes away from the torturer, but she could feel his presence, close and terrifying.

Jemojeen stared at her with smoldering eyes. Sendata knew that only the Qhaliffa's presence kept the torturer's knife from flaying her other leg from ankle to knee, or perhaps one of her arms, or perhaps the rest of her left leg, or perhaps her very face. She swallowed, trying to remember the words of the Order, the words that would make her strong and not afraid.

The Qhaliffa continued, "The staff you sought, Oath Holder, was given to me by my father, who received it from his father, who received it from his father, and so on, all the way back to the very beginning." Sumetan stepped forward toward Sendata's hanging face, his eyes locking onto her own. A flash of indignation appeared in his gaze, and his voice rose.

"Our staff has hung in our Throne Room since the erection of the palace of Saman Keer. It has hung there because it has been in the just and true possession of my family since the first Qhaliffa. And do you know who gave the Staff of Ruling to Mamet, the First Qhaliffa?"

"The Prophet of God," said Sendata, the strength of her voice surprising her.

"Yes, indeed," said Sumetan. "The Prophet of God, who received his Staff from the God of the Mountain, upon this Mountain, high above the clouds. And yet you say it does not belong to me?"

Sendata held her tongue.

"Speak, or I shall enlist a knife to help you find your words."

"Mamet betrayed the Prophet," said Sendata. "He is the Usurper, unworthy of the Staff of the Prophet."

"Lies!" shouted Jemojeen. "Your Majesty." Jemojeen lowered his voice. "It pains me to hear such vile heresies spoken in your presence."

"They pain my ears as well, Jemojeen, but if this is my enemy, I should hear her madness."

"As you wish, Your Majesty," said Jemojeen, nodding gravely.

"Tell me your name," said the Qhaliffa.

"My name I gave to the God of the Mountain and the Sands when I joined the Order. I am only a Serpent."

"Tell me your real name, or I shall tell my torturer to cut out one of your eyes."

"Sendata."

"That is a name of Sundar Dun. You once called Sundar Dun home?"

Sendata nodded.

"I see that my punisher removed some of your serpent skin," said Sumetan. "Yet I do not see scales, only human flesh. Have you ever considered that you are perhaps deceived, Sendata the Serpent? Have you considered that perhaps it is you and not I that believes a lie?"

"It is not a lie. Ask your own Grand Vizer," said Sendata.

The Qhaliffa's left eyebrow rose. "My Grand Vizer? Ask him what?"

"Ask him what he did with the Staff of the Ram in your Throne Room."

The Qhaliffa turned to look at Jemojeen. Jemojeen shook his head slowly with the hint of a smile on his face and flames in his eyes. His nostrils flared ever so slightly, like a vent for his rage.

"Very well, I shall play along, Sendata the Serpent. Tell me, Jemojeen, what did you do with the Staff of the Ram in my Throne Room?"

Jemojeen spoke in a slow, low voice. "I protected it from this thief and the fanatics who were with her, with the help of nearly one hundred guardsmen."

"And when an arrow was shot at your face, you called upon the staff's magic, the power that has awakened," said Sendata. "It flared like the sun, and the arrow that would have meant your death fell to the ground."

Jemojeen forced a laugh. "The deranged ravings of a tortured traitor, Your Majesty."

"Ask his soldiers, Your Majesty. Ask the guardsmen. They saw it too. They may be willing to lie to others, but they will not lie to you."

"Ask them if the old wooden staff, the staff that has hung in the Throne Room of my family for eight hundred years, flamed like the sun and protected the Grand Vizer from an arrow?"

"Yes," said Sendata.

"Perhaps the arrow simply missed."

"It did not miss, Your Majesty."

"How do you know?"

"Because—" Sendata paused, considering the ramifications of her words. *Yes, it was I. If I say it was I, perhaps they will kill me before they come to Ozgar. I will not tell them so long as it is in my will, but the Staff of the Ram. If Jemojeen can use it to see my mind . . .*

"Because it was my arrow," she said.

"You tried to kill my Grand Vizer?"

"Only the magic of the staff," Sendata paused. "Only the staff's power saved him."

"Her own words condemn her, Your Majesty," said Jemojeen.

"Kill her," said Sumetan, looking at the torturer. "Kill her quickly. That is my will." He turned and walked toward the steps leading up out of the dungeon.

Jemojeen turned and walked past the torturer. He paused and whispered, just loudly enough for Sendata to hear him, "Cut her tongue out, then her eyes, and then kill her. And yes, do it all quickly. We must obey our Qhaliffa's will."

The torturer nodded.

The Qhaliffa walked up the stairs and into the tunnel. He heard Sendata scream just as Jemojeen closed the door behind him.

"Jemojeen," asked Sumetan. "I thought the Serpents did not use bows and arrows. I thought they used darts from a blowtube?"

"That is correct, Your Majesty."

"Yet she is a Serpent, claiming to have shot an arrow?"

"Perhaps she was lying, Your Majesty."

Sumetan nodded with a swirl of thoughts moving through his mind. Then the thoughts receded, and a far more familiar and comforting array of thoughts advanced. *I need some wine . . . and Maja . . . and to smoke some tar.*

CHAPTER 33
Oapah's Plan

Semissari Swamp—Sand Sea
14th–17th Day, Month of Gandus, 807
Anglian Calendar: January 14–17, 1879

Where the reeds ended, the sands began.

There was no gradual shifting. In one moment, one stood in the tall, dense reeds of the Semissari, and then, as decisively as walking through a curtain to move from backstage onto the stage itself, facing thousands of staring eyes, one was in the sands.

It was precisely those staring eyes that made Oapah afraid, even at night, even on a moonless night such as this.

Jemojeen had dispatched his flame-haired, green-eyed Erassian scouts into the sands to the west of the Semissari. Jemojeen, evil as he was, was an evil strategist, possessing a keen mind that missed little and left little to chance. Of this, Oapah the Hohsa was well aware. As Oapah gazed out onto the open expanse before him, he thought of Jemojeen and of what the Grand Vizer knew.

Jemojeen knew the Order would not have expended the effort and lives to save Selena Savanar merely to cloak her in the Semissari. The swamp was a temporary hiding place, a way station, a launching point. He knew that the Order had revolutionary plans for the daughter of Sah Seg Savanar. Jemojeen was also certain that at some point, those plans must take Selena Savanar west.

The Order did not yet have the people, and so they did not yet have the means of revolution. One may sabotage without the people. One may strike from hiding on occasion, but one may not overthrow a Qhaliffa without an army. There was only one army available, and that army lay to the west. That army, Jemojeen's scouts had told him—the same Erassians that now sealed the caravan routes between Alwaz Deem and Ben Hamur—was forming and growing larger each day.

Abu Akhsa had gathered a host of Beserian tribesmen in the Valley of Kordon, such as had not been seen in ten generations. If the gathering continued, it could become the largest number of Beserians ever assembled since the age of Beseri himself.

Jemojeen, as in most matters of strategic judgment, was correct. They must get Selena Savanar west, but they could not move faster than Erassians across open desert. They could always try to go south, moving far down the Oxus before moving west and then approaching Ben Hamur from the south. It would take more time—far more time—but such might be a safer route. Yet, Jemojeen had eliminated that choice as well.

From the southernmost reeds of the Semissari, Asatan, Supreme Serpent, had dispatched Serpents to search the way. The way was shut, blocked downstream by a half-dozen River Galleys, all loaded with River Guardsmen. No, they could not go south.

"What do you see?" asked Gulana.

Oapah did not answer, lost in his thoughts and mired in frustration.

"Either tell me or make way so I can see for myself."

Oapah turned. "If you wish to look upon the barren sands with your own eyes, do so." He pulled back from the edge of the reeds and made way for Gulana.

Gulana replaced him at the edge of the reeds, scanning the terrain with her large brown eyes. The sands looked grey in the moonless night. She could see nothing but desert. Out there, in the flatness, lay shallow wadis, thornbushes, rocks, and low rises. It was not as severe as the flat, dead whiteness of the Hahst, nor as formidable as the rolling, ever-shifting ridges of the dune lands, stretching out from windblown crest to valley as far as the eye could see.

There were places to hide in this land, but not many and not for long. And none were better at finding a hiding man in the western desert than an Erassian on a long-range sand horse. A man might think himself hidden up until the very moment when the tip of an Erassian javelin pierces his back and sticks out through his stomach.

"I see no one," said Gulana.

"That does not mean no one is there," said Oapah.

"We should return to see her."

"She is sleeping," said Oapah. "Let her rest. We will not rest for long days. Not until Ben Hamur."

"If we ever see Ben Hamur."

"Trust the God of the Mountain and the Sands, and He will redeem you, Gulana of Nor Gandus." The whites of Oapah's eyes stuck out against the darkness of his skin, even on the moonless night.

Gulana looked out into the dark desert, her face hidden by a veil of ten-foot-tall reeds. She felt neither trusting nor redeemed, nor like a Lion.

"When will we go?" asked Gulana.

"Not this night," said Oapah.

"Oapah, I see them."

"Who?" Oapah stepped forward.

"The Erassians. A dozen of them. Far off, but riding south, down from Alwaz."

"Let me see."

Gulana moved aside. Oapah moved his face up to the edge of the reeds yet saw nothing but darkness and sand. He calmed his mind, closed his eyes, and heard their hoofbeats, like a low, distant rumble. The sands were hard in this part of the desert, not soft enough to muffle hooves. Perhaps that was to be their salvation.

"Do you hear them?" he asked.

"Yes," said Gulana.

"Erassians do not move on foot. They think it beneath them."

"Indeed," said Gulana.

"Nor are they moving their mounts at a walk, which would make their steps quieter."

"Arrogant," said Gulana.

"Or in a hurry," said Oapah.

"If we can hear them from a distance, perhaps we can hide, even out upon the sands."

"Perhaps," said Oapah. He opened his eyes, and he saw them, a dozen riders, advancing in a wide *V* formation, covering perhaps a quarter of a mile.

"They do not know if we are still here or if we are yet out in the sands." He turned to Gulana. The hint of a smile hung on his mouth, and his eyes brightened. "Come, let us find Asatan. I have an idea to mask our departure. We may yet see the pools of Ben Hamur alive."

Asatan and her two companions set out boldly, walking into the desert in swift, efficient steps. Oapah stood at the reed line, watching them. The second group of Serpents left next, passing silently through the reed line out into the western desert. The night was nearly moonless beneath the clouds. They had waited three long days for the cloud cover to come in. The clouds had come in at midday on the third day. By nightfall, the clouds blocked out the moonlight and the desert was shrouded in darkness. Until sunrise, they would be cloaked. At least that was Oapah's plan.

The third group set out, headed nearly due south, taking a route that nearly followed the line of the Oxus. They were a group of four. The extra set of tracks would no doubt draw the Erassians' attention.

Perhaps the Order had seen it necessary to give Selena Savanar an extra guard. *Yes, that is what they would think*, thought Oapah, staring almost due west with his large Omakhosian eyes. Every other part of him was massive—from his gigantic feet up to his enormous shaved head. But perhaps most staggering of all were his shoulders, as big and round as flatland cantaloupes at the height of summer.

As he pulled the reeds more widely apart, Selena looked at his shoulders, feeling safer being close to them and knowing what they could do to an enemy when they were wielding his giant curved scimitarus. Others had told her he once cleaved a man in half in a single swing. She did not doubt it, for she had seen what he did to the thick wooden oars of the Qhaliffa's River Galley.

"We will leave shortly," he said, looking up again into the clouds to make sure that the cover still held. It could save them, giving the ruse the time it required. Moonlight would bring the Erassians down upon them, and the Erassians would bring death.

They had all vowed not to be taken alive. They would fight to the death to save the life of Lady Savanar, and if it must be done, Lady Savanar would take her own life.

Oapah watched the fourth and final southbound band of Serpents pass out of sight, dipping into a wadi.

"The time is now," said Oapah, stepping forward out of the reeds. The hardened, sundried earth just underneath the thin layer of sands felt firm under his feet, having trudged through the muddiness and upon the spongy moss of the Semissari for days. Even the firmest parts of the Semissari were damp, and the earth there was always soft, like a soaked cloth that could never quite dry out.

As she stepped out of the reeds, Gulana said the familiar words. Selena watched her walk out. She was an imposing woman, dense with muscle and nearly a head taller than Selena, who was herself a tall woman. Gulana could stand eye to eye with tall men. But behind Oapah, two of her could have hidden with hiding room to spare.

"God of the Mountain and the Sands, guide our feet in Your ways, bring us to water, and deliver us from those who walk in the darkness." And with those words, Gulana walked forward into the darkness of the desert.

Selena walked closely behind her. In front of them, nearly one hundred and fifty miles to the west, lay the deep, clean pools of Ben Hamur. They had until sunrise to put as many miles as possible between themselves and the Semissari, for at dawn, the Erassians would come riding, and the Erassians could track any footsteps made upon the sands.

CHAPTER 34
Found

Southwest of the Valley of Kordon
Plain of Gamurian, Western Sand Sea
26th Day, Month of Gandus, 807
Anglian Calendar: January 26, 1879

Jack shivered under the thin blanket, sitting as close to the fire as he could without burning himself. There was little camel dung for fuel, and the fire barely flickered in the wind. Jack felt well enough to sit up, propped up against a small stone, though he could still hardly stand or walk.

"Eat," said Demassi.

"I have no appetite," said Jack.

The third man watched Jack warily when he finally hobbled from the tent to the edge of the tiny fire. From Demassi, Jack learned that the man had helped him from the beginning, that he carried Jack to the cart and rode with him in the mule wagon they used to bring him up the slope to the Mountain Gate itself.

There, Demassi readily admitted to bribing the Spatanian guards to allow them to pass through. So too had the guards watched over their camels for them while the third man took the wagon down the slope to meet him and Demassi at the edge of the red sign alley, the alley of the whorehouses.

The third man was called Anil.

That much Demassi had shared as well, but Anil had not spoken a single word to Jack. Nor would he so much as look in his direction since Jack emerged from the tent. Every several minutes, Jack would look in his direction, but the man showed no interest in making eye contact.

"Your insides will heal with food but not without," said Demassi, comfortably reclining under a blanket as thin as Jack's. Jack saw that Demassi did not shiver, eating a piece of dried goat meat, cured with salt, hard and chewy.

Jack looked away from the Vetenan, staring into the flames, cold and uncomfortable. The sun had been up for an hour, but the air was still not warm.

The third man spoke.

He spoke in Beserian, a language of which Jack Caldwell did not know a single word. Demassi responded, speaking rapidly and forcefully in the same language, gesturing with his piece of the dried meat as his voice rose and fell with whatever point he was making. Demassi's eyes widened and narrowed as he spoke, his eyebrows rose and fell, and his mouth expanded and contracted underneath his gaunt cheeks.

"What are you saying to him?" asked Jack, rubbing his shoulders for warmth underneath his thin woolen blanket, riddled with holes from years of hard use.

"To Anil? I am only responding. He doubts. I lift his faith."

"What does he doubt?"

Demassi looked at Jack with his dark, intense eyes. "He doubts that you are who I say you are."

"And who is that?"

"A man who has emerged from the west."

"Why does he doubt that?"

"All will become clearer in time."

Jack felt a sudden urge to eat, to feel less weak.

"Give me some of that meat," he said.

"Yes, you must eat," said Demassi as he tore off a long sliver, pulling along the grain of the meat. He handed it over to Jack.

Jack put it in his mouth. The hard, salty texture tasted better to him than the finest beefsteaks he had eaten in Port Calderon or Bay Port City. He chewed a small morsel, slowly working on the tough fibers with his large back molars as the flavor awoke a deep and sudden hunger within him.

"You have eaten nothing in long days," said Demassi.

Jack looked and saw the third man watching him. Like Demassi, his eyes were dark and intense. He too was bearded and gaunt, but he was thicker than Demassi, especially across the arms and shoulders, and his beard was fuller and less ragged. In his eyes, Jack could read distrust and doubt, as clearly as if written in Anglian letters. Jack continued chewing, slowly and with satisfaction.

Within the hour, Jack felt an absence of something, of the burden that had been with him, ever-present since he had awoken after his long, poisoned slumber. His pain had nearly gone.

The third man stood up, facing north. Jack followed his gaze. The man's eyes looked upon the ridgeline, perhaps a half-mile to the north. Between them and the ridgeline lay only scrub brush, thornbushes, gravel, and sand.

A flash of color burst above the ridgeline. It was sky blue, like a bright bird.

Then it disappeared, bobbing back down beneath the ridge. It rose again, now larger, bobbed once more, and then revealed itself in its full size, longer than any bird Jack had ever seen. And then Jack saw, through eyes squinting into the distance, that it was not a bird at all, that it was attached to a staff that rested in the hand of a man, and that the man sat upon a camel. To the man's left and right, other men advanced on camelback, riding toward them at a gallop. They crested the ridge, nine, then ten, then a dozen, then a full twenty riders with their great sky-blue banner dancing above them.

"Who?" said Jack, wishing he had a weapon. "Friend or foe?"

Demassi stood with his hands at his sides, like a soldier at attention.

"Praise be to the God of the Sands," he said, his eyes exultant. "Abu Akhsa has found us."

CHAPTER 35
Ozgar Ogatonia

Upper Mid-Levels, Saman Keer
7th Day, Month of Gandus, 807
Anglian Calendar: January 7, 1879

Ozgar Ogatonia had not tasted water in more than a day since leaving the safe house. He could not go much longer. His loose tunic was ripped. Ugly wounds crisscrossed both of his legs and one of his arms. The deepest gash on his arm stretched across his shoulder and onto his chest. Above the cut, like a round shield atop the shaft of a spear lay an angry, oozing burn. He had done his best to keep his wounds clean, but without water, he could do little.

The pain was his constant passenger, calling out ceaselessly in an unending song of misery that pulsed through Ozgar's body. If he waited much longer to treat the wounds, even the Order's healers would be powerless to help him. He hoped in the deep recesses of his heart that he could avoid the burning treatment. Sometimes that was the only way to keep the wound from festering and killing. When hearing those undergoing the healing fire, however, sometimes death did not seem like the worse alternative.

Slowly, remarkably, he climbed his way from the stone safe house to the upper mid-levels of Saman Keer, traveling by night, taking one alley at a time and hiding from any who came across his way. How he had escaped from the ambush in the Throne Room to the safe house in the first place felt more like a dream than like something he had lived through. The flash pistols fired, blinding the ring of guardsmen. Then came the shrapnel guns, the flame pistols, and then the three-barrelers, all firing in rapid succession in the close quarters . . . Sendata shooting her darts . . . he remembered cutting his way through, but it still should not have been possible for him to have reached the tunnels, and to have found his way out with all of the palace searching for him in the darkness . . .

It is a testament to the God of the Mountain and the Sands, thought Ozgar. *I have been preserved for a reason.* In his pain, Ozgar had sustained himself with those words.

No man should have made it out of that Throne Room alive.Yet, I alone escaped. Did Jemojeen somehow allow it? Of course not. He would never have allowed any of us to escape, especially not me.

How many of the others did he take alive?

Ozgar did not know, but he hoped that the answer was none of them. Ozgar's heart ached with the thought that his companions were dead. They were among the most exceptional Oath Holders in all of the Order, and he had chosen them.

He shuddered at the idea of any of them in Jemojeen's dungeon. He knew what kinds of horrors lurked in that dark place. He knew the pain that encompassed him now was nothing like the pain the torturers could inflict. Few who entered the dungeons ever escaped to see the light of day. And those who did were likely to see daylight only from a stake or the gallows, just before they were executed before the masses.

God of the Mountain and the Sands, please make it so that none were taken alive. Yet doubt lingered in Ozgar's mind.

Ozgar leaned forward, steadying his mind against the pain as he looked and listened. In Saman Keer above all other places, the Grand Vizer had many eyes and ears, and even a look of recognition from the most innocent-looking child could mean a patrol of guardsmen surrounding him in minutes. If they found him, he would not get far.

He would take his own life if it came to that. He would cut his own throat with the Serpent's dagger in his belt. In the melee in the Throne Room, he had lost his scimitarus and his bow. His weapons were unmarked, and Jemojeen and his men could not know of his involvement by studying them. Ozgar had made sure of that. He had escaped with only a dead Serpent's dagger.

Was it Sendata's? Ozgar could not say.

He was prepared to die now. In death, his pain would leave him. And yet, if he could only reach the upper wildlands, he'd find clean streams of running water. Caves and hollows would allow him to rest for a night before he made his way north to Nor Wasura. Between Ozgar and the upper wildlands lay another half-mile of the city—crooked alleys, stone buildings, small gardens, and old trees. But in all of those places, even at night, people could be lurking.

A cracking sound drew all of his senses into high alert.

He looked down the alleyway and out toward the desert. This high up the mountain, the vast majority of Saman Keer lay below him, filling the valley with its green rooftops down to the Ring River, which from this height, looked like a broad silver ribbon.

"This is a waste of time," said a voice.

"We'll see how much of a waste of time it is when we collect the reward."

"I am going to sleep. It is the middle of the night."

"You think someone in the Order is stupid enough to travel by day?"

"No, but he probably died from his wounds."

"If we find his body, we still get the money. Don't you want the money?

"Yes."

"Then keep looking."

Ozgar could not hear the grumbling response.

And then he saw them, two boys, no more than fifteen years old. One carried a small wooden club, and the other had a sling with a sack of stones.

Despite his pain, he nearly laughed at the absurdity. A smile, to Ozgar's astonishment, cracked across his lips. Even if he were tied up, unarmed, and wounded as severely as he was now, those boys would be dead if they came against him. And yet, they were walking around trying to find him with sticks and rocks.

His smile departed nearly as quickly as it arrived. He quietly slid back down into the shadow of the stone wall behind him.

He waited long moments in silence, slowing his breathing. The footsteps vanished.

Painfully, he lifted himself again. He hobbled forward up the alley, against the slope, taking step after painful step. Each time he planted his foot, the pain ran up his leg like a dagger against his bones. And then in planting the other leg, equal pain fired from his nerves. He had been a Demissary long enough to know how to stomach the pain, how to bury it deep within when the body cries out in anguish, for often in the life of a Demissary to cry out in anguish meant death. In his weakened state, it could mean the end now, if crying out meant bringing a patrol of Jemojeen's guardsmen down upon him.

He struggled up the alleyway to a lateral crossroads, staying as near to the dark shadows of walls as he could. There were few lamps this high up the mountain, and few windows were opened in the cold. Most of the windows were dark and shuttered against the night.

"Do not move!"

It was a mix between a whisper and a shriek. Ozgar knew who said it before he turned to see the young adolescent face. It was the boy with the club. He held it raised, comically, above his head, desperately trying to look menacing.

Ozgar, delirious from the pain and dehydration, smiled at the boy.

His partner pulled back a stone in his sling. His forward hand shook in a mixture of fear and excitement.

"Or what?" said Ozgar.

"Or I shall strike you with my club!"

"Are you sure about that?"

"Do not resist, traitor!"

Ozgar's smile vanished.

"Don't raise your voice so loud, boy. You will wake the good sleeping people of Saman Keer."

"I shall wake them all if you do not do as I say!"

"Boy, you should have slept tonight. No reward is worth your life."

"It is your life that you should—"

Ozgar rushed at the boy, swift and deadly, twisting as he ran. The second boy's stone sailed past Ozgar's face as he slashed the blade of his Serpent's dagger across the first boy's throat. The boy's eyes bulged in astonishment as his throat opened. Before the first boy had landed onto the pavement, Ozgar had pulled the curved blade from his neck and had slashed the second boy twice across the chest. The third blow was a stab under his rib cage and into his heart. The second boy was dead before he landed face-first on the alley's cobblestones. Ozgar bent down to pick up the dead boy's sling and his sack of stones.

An oil lamp flickered behind the shutters next to the alley. With his adrenaline depleted, pain surged from his burn, the gash in his arm, and the wounds in both of his legs. He turned and ran farther up the mountain, into the darkness, wishing to cry out in anguish with every step he took.

CHAPTER 36
The Demissary and the Grand Vizer

Grand Vizerian Fortress, Alwaz Deem
13th Day, Month of Gandus, 807
Anglian Calendar: January 13, 1879

"Good morning, Commander. Please sit," said Jemojeen, declining to rise from his gilded stool with the silken cushioning.

Ottovan Fanfar looked down at the hardwood of the backless bench in front of him. He sat. It was low enough for Jemojeen to tower over him from his own seated position. On either side of the Grand Vizer, a fully armed guardsman stood in chain mail, grasping the shaft of a spear in the right hand and the upturned handle of a sword in its scabbard with the left.

Ottovan, as was his prerogative, remained fully armed. He felt the weight of his pistols on his chest. If it came to it, he could take his own life. As quickly as the thought arrived, he dismissed it. He would not abandon his family so he could evade the pain of capture. No, if he were to go, he would do all in his power to make sure the Grand Vizer died first.

"The strangest thing happened, Commander."

Ottovan leaned forward on the bench, taking care to keep his posture confident as his heart thundered. He hoped the fear in his chest did not reach his face. He drew upon all of the powers of discipline and habit he had amassed over the years, arranging his features into a calm mask. He narrowed his eyelids, focused on his breathing, and willed his heart to slow its feverish beat. He met the Grand Vizer's eyes with his own. If Jemojeen could see the fear in his eyes, Ottovan could not find the recognition in Jemojeen's face.

"Several days ago," continued Jemojeen, "there was an attack upon the Qhaliffa's palace."

"How is that possible?" asked Ottovan, his voice low and calm.

Jemojeen looked into Ottovan's face, his green eyes searching deeply into him.

"Leave us," said Jemojeen.

The two Grand Vizerian Guardsmen turned and walked to an arched doorway at the rear of the room. Jemojeen waited for them to pass through the door before continuing.

"Strong as our defenses are, we are not impregnable, Commander. And as you are surely aware, our most dangerous enemies often come at us from within."

"You believe it was rebels?"

"I would not say I believe it was rebels, Commander. I would say I know it was rebels. I caught them."

Ottovan's heart thundered beyond his willpower. His fear rose inside of him like the waters of the Oxus in the spring flood.

"By the God of the Mountain," said Ottovan, feigning astonishment and indignation. "Who was it?"

Jemojeen stared into Ottovan's face without answering.

Does he know? Is he playing with me, like a cat with a mouse? The words raced through Ottovan's mind, swirling and twisting, clouding out other thoughts.

"Some of those we caught were women," said Jemojeen.

Ottovan waited for the words, hearing them in his mind. *And one was your Captain of the Bow, Ozgar Ogatonia.* He would draw his pistols, and he would shoot down as many as he could. He would fight to the end. He would not be led like a sheep to the slaughter like Sah Seg Savanar. No, he would not burn like Sah Seg Savanar, the God of the Mountain and the Sands bless his name.

"One woman, in particular," said Jemojeen, "is a woman with some stature in the Order of the Ram, the Lion, and the Serpent." He spit a large gob of mucous onto the sanded wooden floor beneath him. "May they all bathe in flames."

Ottovan did not say the words, but he nodded in agreement. He would say the words if he had to—his deception demanded it—but not if he did not have to. He sat in silence, listening.

"At first, Commander Fanfar, I was as surprised as you are—stunned into silence." Jemojeen stared into Ottovan's eyes as if Ottovan's eyes were portals to his mind, and Jemojeen was trying to batter down the doors. Ottovan blinked.

"I asked myself," said Jemojeen. "Why would they risk it? Why would they send Oath Holders of the Order into the Qhaliffa's palace? Did they not know they would be captured and tortured? I am told that even upon the way in, they saw that they had been betrayed, finding some of my men waiting for them in the tunnels. And yet they still came into the palace. They went all of the way into the Throne Hall of the Qhaliffa, into the very trap I had so easily laid for them. And why? Why would they do such a thing?"

Ottovan stared in silence.

"Not an easily answered question, I agree," said Jemojeen. "Not easily answered until one finds the key to the door. They were after this." With a flourish, Jemojeen swept the Staff of the Ram out from under a fold in his robe.

Ottovan's eyes widened. *There it is. By the God of the Mountain and of the Sands, it is in his hands. Perhaps I could shoot him and take it. Perhaps, with Nemakar's help, we could fight our way out of the fortress. But then what? There is a full garrison, and the guardsmen would catch us. They would immediately lower the portcullis, and we'd be trapped.*

The thread frayed in his mind, and he could not see farther than blasting Jemojeen and shooting and slashing two dozen Grand Vizerian Guardsmen until their numbers overwhelmed him and Nemakar.

Jemojeen stood up from his chair. He held the Staff of the Ram in his hand.

Ottovan's eyes fixated on the carved ram's head and the horns curving outward from it.

"Some say this is just an old piece of wood, but we know better. Don't we?"

Ottovan looked up at Jemojeen. Standing at his full height, he loomed over Ottovan, his dark robes spread out like a cloud of silk.

"I only know what the legends say, Grand Vizer."

"Yes, yes," said Jemojeen, beginning to pace. Ottovan's eyes followed him as he moved, his fear freezing him in place. He had never feared Jemojeen. He feared the power he held as Grand Vizer, but he had never feared the man. He had bested him in single combat when they were both Demissaries. Jemojeen had always been his inferior. Jemojeen was among the greatest Demissaries of his generation, but Ottovan was always one step greater. Ottovan did not feel greater now.

"They say this wood holds great power, Commander. They say it has the power to protect he who wields it. Some say this piece of carved wood has the power to reveal what lies in the minds of those nearby, even to control their bodies. Have you heard such things?"

"Only in the legends," said Ottovan.

"Yes, in the legends. Tell me, Commander, do you believe the legends?"

"I am just a soldier, Grand Vizer. I do not know about such things."

"Yes, 'just a soldier.' You were always a modest man, Ottovan Fanfar. And it has always served you well. You prefer to show your mettle with your scimitarus and your pistols."

Ottovan said nothing, his eyes trailing Jemojeen.

Jemojeen walked halfway across the wooden plank floor and then pivoted, turning back to Ottovan and facing him with the Staff of the Ram between them.

"What do you know about the Order of the Ram, the Lion, and the Serpent, Commander?"

Ottovan's eyes left Jemojeen's face and stared at the staff. It no longer appeared wooden; it had begun to glow, taking on the color of sunlight. Ottovan averted his eyes from the brilliance of the light.

"Commander, I asked you a question."

"I know very little," said Ottovan.

"Very little?"

Ottovan nodded. Jemojeen took a step toward him. The Staff of the Ram appeared to take on a greater brilliance, with golden light flying off of the curled horns, nearly blinding.

"The staff," said Ottovan.

"What of the staff?" said Jemojeen.

"It is glowing," said Ottovan.

"What am I to do with a legion commander who does not know about the Order?" said Jemojeen, taking a step closer to Ottovan. "Do you not know your enemies?"

"I know that they must be opposed," said Ottovan, squinting at the light of the staff, his eyes beginning to water. "Opposed and defeated. Destroyed."

Jemojeen now stood directly above him. Ottovan turned his face away from the glowing radiance.

The brilliance of the staff disappeared as quickly as it had appeared. Jemojeen returned to his seat. The staff sat in his lap, again a seemingly harmless piece of carved wood.

"They say the staff can search the mind of those who oppose it," said Jemojeen.

"I do not know of such things," said Ottovan.

"Don't you?"

Ottovan stared.

"Do you know what I saw in your mind, Commander?"

Ottovan's heart thundered. The staff had glowed. Perhaps it had opened his thoughts to the Grand Vizer? A feeling of nakedness crept up over his fear, magnifying it. He fought the urge to reach for his pistol.

"Loyalty," said Ottovan, his voice little more than a whisper. "I suppose you saw that."

Jemojeen smiled. "Perhaps you are just a simple soldier, Commander. I saw nothing. Perhaps that is why you still command Demissaries and why I am Grand Vizer."

Ottovan felt the tension in his body release.

"As you are loyal, you will be delighted to know that we caught a Serpent of the Order. Her name is Sendata. She was tortured with knife and fire, partially skinned. They took her eyes and her tongue in the end. Rest assured, Commander. We learned all that she knew."

"When?" asked Ottovan, drawing on every ounce of discipline inside of him to keep his eyes and voice steady.

"Three days ago, just before I departed to meet you, Commander, here in Alwaz Deem. In the meantime, you are to head west with your entire legion. The Qhaliffa has authorized me to command all of the Demissary Legions until the Savanar is captured, and the heretics are defeated."

Ottovan looked at Jemojeen, his eyes for a moment incredulous.

"Do not look so surprised, Commander. You are welcome to read the written edict."

Jemojeen pulled the scroll from underneath his cape and handed it to Ottovan.

Ottovan let the lump in his throat sit there, willing himself not to swallow. Even against the full power of his training and his self-control, his insides still twisted. He had known Sendata since she was a girl. She was among the best Serpents he had ever known. She had volunteered with Ozgar. He had attempted, through Asatan, to dissuade her from the task, telling her to give the mission to a more senior Serpent. But Sendata had insisted. Ottovan's mind returned to Jemojeen's face, which was staring into his own. He had said something that required a response.

"West?"

Jemojeen stood again, nodding, and turning his head. He resumed his pacing.

"You will have two objectives, Commander. On the Orders of the Qhaliffa himself, Sumetan the Magnificent: first, you are to retrieve the traitor Selena of House Savanar. I am told she has escaped south from Sundar Dun into the Semissari Swamp, that den of mud and snakes. She will not stay there long. She will seek refuge in the western desert. Unless I am wrong, and I am rarely wrong, the Savanar will head toward Ben Hamur. She mistakenly believes the Sharef of Ben Hamur will provide her refuge. When you capture her, my preference is that you bring her back alive. If you must kill her, then such is her fate, but I very much prefer that she be returned to me alive.

"Second, once you have captured the heretic-traitor, you are to find the Beserian Hamid Salesi. You, of course, know that name. Do you not?"

Ottovan nodded.

"He now rides, I am told, with the growing forces of Abu Akhsa. Akhsa has amassed a horde of tribesmen near the Valley of Kordon. I trust your own Erassians have told you as much, yes?"

Ottovan nodded.

"Salesi has a staff. It looks like this one. Except, of course, it is a Serpent."

"The Staff of the Serpent was lost, Grand Vizer," said Ottovan, marveling at his own ability to lie with conviction.

"It has been found. Find Salesi. Find the Serpent Staff. Return it to Saman Keer, and do not return until you have done so. This your Qhaliffa commands."

Jemojeen took a new scroll out from his robes.

"Your orders," he said and threw it at Ottovan Fanfar.

Ottovan caught the scroll in his right hand. His reflexes were still as quick as those of a Sworn Ram.

Jemojeen looked at the scroll in Ottovan's hand, and his eyes narrowed.

"You are dismissed, Commander."

"One question, Your Excellency," said Ottovan.

Jemojeen raised his eyebrows.

"Why does the Qhaliffa wish to send an entire Demissary Legion into the desert to retrieve a relic? Should we not be preparing to crush Abu Akhsa with the Third Legion as we have planned?"

"Plans change, Commander. You are a piece to be moved, not the player moving the pieces. Do as you are ordered."

"Yes, Your Excellency," said Ottovan, his true answer staying in his mind. *But I always moved my pieces better than you did, didn't I, Jemojeen?*

Ottovan bowed and turned to go.

By the God of the Mountain and the Sands, he does not know. Ozgar must have escaped.

Hope bubbled inside of him, strong as the Spring of the Prophet.

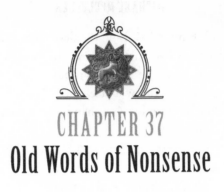

CHAPTER 37
Old Words of Nonsense

Plain of Gamurian
Western Sand Sea
January 28, 1879

Hannah could feel the disapproval of Stanwich's gaze. He did not speak with words, but he spoke with his eyes, as did his LaFrentian shadow, Hersen Expey. It was true; she had fallen from her camel. Even Mrs. Smith, who had ridden camels since she was a girl, had nearly fallen when the giant icicles began to drop, exploding like anarchist's bombs in the narrow canyon.

The camels had lost their minds, calling out in fear and trying to run back down the mountain. Porters fell, boxes dropped, contents spilled. When the shaking finally stopped, it looked as if a battle had occurred and the caravan was on the losing side.

Yet somehow, Stanwich wished to blame her. It was nothing he said. His words were still polite, but he looked at her with distrust, even contempt. His look said, *You have no place here, woman.*

He had excluded her from the first council meeting on the sands, but he had not excluded her from the second, which had yet to begin. After the last meeting, about which she found out only because Peter told her, Hannah reminded Stanwich, with Mrs. Smith scowling at her side, that she was Hannah Huntington, the personal representative of Mr. Samuel X. Huntington, a one-third backer of the expedition, and she would be treated as such.

Stanwich apologized with the correct, polite words—*I am ashamed by my mistake, Miss Huntington*—but his eyes held no shame. And his LaFrentian stared at her as if she were an enemy, his gaze cold and grey as the North Titanic. Under Hersen Expey's gaze, she felt better with Barnes and Mrs. Smith next to her. They would both be coming with her to the next council meeting.

"Miss Huntington."

Hannah opened her eyes. The canvas of the tent was above her. She had slept in her riding pants, with her hair pulled back. The ground was hard. The wool blankets underneath her did little to soften it, and even before she tried to move, Hannah could feel the stiffness in her back and her legs.

Mrs. Smith was already sitting up, her head nearly touching the top of the small canvas A-frame. It was no more than four feet wide from edge to edge and six and a half feet long. If they lay next to each other, it was large enough to accommodate both Hannah's height and Mrs. Smith's girth. Hannah could have had her own tent. But, she had already heard the Spatanian porters calling her, upon Stanwich and Hersen's encouragement, no doubt, "The Princess of Calderon," which she did not so much mind, and "Her Royal Huntington," which she did. Why one bothered her and not the other, she could not say. Nor could she say what she had done to deserve such monikers, aside from being the only woman of a particular class on the expedition.

But having the porters and the camels carry her own tent when all others were sharing A-frames seemed to Hannah to be fuel that she did not need to add to their fire. Moreover, Mrs. Smith's body was warm, and the nights were terribly cold.

Unbathed like the rest of them, Mrs. Smith smelled ripe, but the warmth was worth the aroma. Hannah knew they shared the same kind of tent that the enlisted men used in the LaFrentian War—small, light, and simple as a tent could be. As with everything, they had necessitated a camelback to carry it, and speed was of the essence. Stanwich had insisted that no one use a tent more complicated than a simple A-frame. So, Hannah Huntington woke up next to Matilda Smith, smelling her body odor, feeling stiff as a corpse, and huddling against her for warmth, like a chick nestled up against a hen.

"Miss Huntington, the council is beginning," said Mrs. Smith.

Hannah lurched upward, throwing the blanket off of her. She reached for the tent flap, her eyes red and puffy with not enough sleep. Even when she retired to the tent early, after the exhaustion of a full day's ride, she found that sleep in a tent was not like sleep in a bed. She was always still tired, never quite rested.

The sky was pink, the air cold and clear. Outside of her blanket, the cold enveloped her, and she shuddered.

"Here is your cloak," said Mrs. Smith. It was dirty and stiff from their days of riding, but Hannah took it gratefully. She rubbed the wool as if to clean it. It was no use. On the Plain of Gamurian, the dust found its way inside of everything and settled upon all, ever-present and inescapable.

Hannah looked across the camp and saw a trio of camel-dung fires already burning. The smell of a coffee pot beckoned to her above the odor of the burning dung, an attractive scent amongst the foul ones. She had never been much of a coffee-drinker in Calderon. But she was a coffee-drinker on the sands, as was everyone else. Mrs. Smith alone refused the coffee, being a follower of the New Church of the Three Gods. The New Church said that the Spirit of the Three alone should be sufficient to focus one's mind and alert one's body. *No drink, no matter how strong, can match the power of the Spirit.* That was what their preachers said. Mrs. Smith said it too, but when she did, she smiled in a way that made it unclear whether she really meant it or not.

Hannah walked across the camp, feeling the circulation returning to her legs and the stiffness receding in equal measure. To move felt better than sitting in the cold, and the cold helped rouse her from the miserable night of sleep. The coffee smell grew stronger as she closed in on the steaming pots.

In front of her, Stanwich was already conferring with Hersen Expey, *like the schemers that they are*, she thought, smiling sweetly at them. Hersen glanced at her and then quickly returned his eyes to Stanwich, as if he had not. She could see the desire in the LaFrentian's eyes, plain as day even in a glance, though he masked it with rudeness. She had long ago learned to see a man by watching his eyes and ignoring his words. Most conversations between the two of them—Hersen and Stanwich—seemed to be in secret, as if all the words they said were too important to be shared with any of the other forty-five persons in the expedition.

Stanwich looked at her too, but not like Hersen.

Peter Harmon sat by the fire, drinking coffee and reading a book, as usual, with his long legs stretched out in front of him. He looked up from his book, allowing his eyes to follow her. She met his gaze with her own, seeing the hunger in Peter's. He returned his eyes to his book, self-consciously, and his cheeks blushed pinker than the sunrise.

She shook her head in irritation. *By the Three Gods, I look like a beggar, and he still looks at me like that. And then he looks away like an embarrassed boy. No, he would never do.*

Hannah saw Sergeant Joshua Barnes, from the rear, standing by himself and sipping his own tin cup of coffee. He stared out beyond the tents, looking into the open desert in the direction of the Valley of Kordon. Barnes did not talk much before Jack's disappearance. He spoke even less since. He wore an old army belt, modified, with a revolver on one hip and a large dagger on the other, its brass handguard sticking up above the sheath, as prominently as the revolver's handle on the other hip.

In the same direction, Hannah could see the far-off sentry walking in his arc, several hundred yards out from the camp, carrying a rifle in his arms. He wore a green Spatanian army-style cap with the loose shirt and pants of a Beserian tribesman, the kind that allowed a man to easily mount and dismount a camel, the kind that allowed a man to find warmth in the winter but breathed when the heat began. Most of the porters wore this shabby uniform, whether they served as guards, camel leaders, cooks, or tent men.

Many served in different roles depending upon the day. Hannah liked the porters, more or less. They too ogled her with their eyes, but it seemed to her without intent. They sang, and many of them sang well. Some sang in camp, but they all seemed to sing on the march. Stanwich made no effort to stop them. Singing or not singing, a Beserian patrol would hear, smell and see them from miles away; such was the nature of the Sand Sea, and the Plain of Gamurian in particular. It was flat, and sounds carried far, but smells carried even farther. Barring the errant winter storm, and winds strong enough to kick up heavy clouds of dust, a man could see clearly to the horizon, making even a single rider conspicuous. If a man could gain elevation, on one of the sporadic dome-shaped rises, then he could see for twenty, thirty, or even forty miles upon the plain. On a clear day, a column of men was un-hidable, and it was a clear day.

Hannah continued walking to the fire with Mrs. Smith walking behind her.

"Coffee," said Mrs. Smith, using the Spatanian word, looking at the cook's assistant, standing near the fire, placing clumps of dough into an iron pan to make flat, simple biscuits.

The cook's assistant nodded, taking two tin cups off of his light wooden cook's rack and pouring scalding black coffee into each. The Spatanian handed the cups to Hannah and Mrs. Smith, smiling as he passed them over.

"None for me," said Mrs. Smith, handing her cup back.

"For the princess, only," said the man, smiling more broadly. It was not an ugly smile. The man's breath reached Hannah as he smiled. It was foul in the manner of a man who has eaten salt beef and has not cleaned his teeth in long days, possibly weeks.

Hannah spoke Spatanian well, but she did not correct him in calling her princess. The man's smile was so genuine and friendly.

"Thank you," she said.

"Very well," said Stanwich, placing his hands on his hips, and looking over at Hannah. "It seems we are all here. Follow me, please."

Hannah blew on the steaming surface of her tin coffee cup, holding it close to her face. The steam felt warm on her cheeks against the coldness of the morning air.

Hersen was already walking to the table that lay away from the tents, on its own upon the desert floor. He carried a rolled map underneath his arm, like a Beserian carrying a prayer mat or a Macmenian shepherding a carpet. Hannah stood several steps away from the map table, and Peter Harmon and Joshua Barnes made their way around the dung fires.

Stanwich waited, impatiently tapping his foot, glancing around in all directions to ensure that none could overhear them. The tallest bush in the vicinity reached no higher than his knees, offering nowhere for a sneaking man to hide.

"Very well," repeated Stanwich.

He says that too often, thought Hannah, feeling happiness that she had isolated one of his verbal tics, an imperfection. *Stanwich has many of them.*

"Yes, very well," he said again. "This map is said to be credible. It is of Macmenian make, and caravaners have used it for decades. As you can see, we are here." Stanwich pointed to a location on the Plain of Gamurian.

Hannah looked down, surprised they were still only on the far western edge of the Sand Sea, and the map itself only showed the western most parts, from the Harafhan Mountains in the south to the Bulbanian borderlands in the northwest. Due north lay merely more desert sands, and still more sands stretching to the far north and the Erassian tribe lands of the Gressian steppes. Ben Gamurian, the western most, outer oasis lay on the eastern part of the map. The Valley of Kordon, which, in the scope of the whole Sand Sea, was merely a sliver, dominated the central and northern parts of the map.

"There are two places that Demassi may have taken Jack Caldwell. First, he could have taken him here," said Stanwich, pointing at the southern tip of the Valley of Kordon. "Second, he could have taken him here." Stanwich drew his finger along a line from west to east, moving in the direction of a green oval, marking the oasis of Ben Gamurian.

"He did not go to Ben Gamurian," said Peter.

Hannah looked up.

Peter's voice was abnormally firm. He squinted in the sunlight, looking down at the map with his book stuffed under his armpit.

"Oh? Mr. Harmon? And why is that?" asked Hersen Expey, his LaFrentian accent drawing out the vowels in *Harmon*.

"Because he is taking him to the Beserians."

They all waited in silence, looking at Peter Harmon, who still looked intently down at the map.

"You see," said Peter, putting his finger down onto the map. "The deduction from the prophecy is quite clear. They will be here, in the Valley of Kordon."

Moments of silence ensued as Peter looked up, meeting Stanwich's eyes.

"I am afraid I do not follow," said Stanwich.

"It is simple, Stanwich. Demassi believes Jack is the Promised One of the Beserian Prophecy. It is the clue that pulls it all together."

Hannah let out a small laugh.

Peter turned, his cheeks flushing again, but his eyes sharp. "I am not saying I agree with him. I am merely stating what Demassi clearly believes."

"I have known Jack since he was a boy," said Hannah. "He is like a brother to me. I can assure you he is not a promised one from a prophecy."

"It is implausible, yes," said Peter.

"It is ridiculous," said Hannah, her eyes narrowing in defiance.

Peter looked at Hannah, noting that defiance looked particularly attractive on her face.

"Among other things, a promised one does not get lost by going to whore-houses," said Hannah.

Stanwich, Hersen, Peter, Barnes, and Mrs. Smith all looked at her. It was Hannah's turn to blush. She had barked out the words as if they had been waiting to get out, and she had emotion in her tone.

"Perhaps, perhaps not," said Peter, pulling the book out from under his arm and turning to a marked page. "But the point is not whether it is true, it is whether Demassi thinks it is true and is acting accordingly."

"It isn't true," said Hannah. "Maybe he kidnapped him for some other reason."

Peter began reading aloud. "He shall be broad of shoulder, light of eye, in his twenty-third year. From beyond the sands, from beyond the western mountains, he shall arrive—"

"What are you reading?" Hannah's chin jutted forward, like her father's when he was negotiating.

"It's a lesser-known part of the prophecy, and it is rather astonishing in its specifics. All of those would, of course, apply to Jack," said Peter. "And we could perhaps see how Demassi, in his fanaticism, wished to be the one to find this promised person."

Peter cleared his throat and brought his index finger down the page of the book. The old, tattered cloth cover was a pale, faded green, like a once-bold color that had degraded to pastel with years of usage.

"From weakness, he shall emerge," Peter continued reading aloud, "and he shall depart from the sins of before. Like His people, the God of the Mountain and the Sands shall call him forth to the new time—the time of justice and glory."

The haughtiness in Hannah's face lessened. "Let me see that," she said, reaching for the book.

"You can't read Macmenian," said Peter.

"I can," said Hersen Expey, reaching for the book.

"Very well," said Peter. "See for yourself."

Hersen took the book, more roughly than Peter would have liked.

Hersen held the book close to his face, carefully reading the Macmenian characters. When he reached a particular passage, his face changed. His eyes widened, not much, but enough for Peter to see the difference. He nodded his head.

"Yes, that is what it says," said Hersen Expey.

"Yes, well 'coming from weakness' does not mean 'whorehouse,'" said Hannah. "And Jack is not weak."

Stanwich stood back from the table with his arms crossed, observing the others.

"If he has taken him to the Valley of Kordon," said Stanwich, "he has taken him to the Beserite too. Going to Ben Gamurian would be going the wrong way. In the Valley, we capture both birds with the same net."

"Indeed," said Peter.

"Then we head north?" asked Hannah.

She had promised herself she would be assertive in the meeting.

"There is one more thing," said Peter, reaching for the book in Hersen's hands.

Stanwich looked at him expectantly.

Peter, recovering the book from the LaFrentian, turned several pages.

"If he has taken him to Kordon, there will be tribesmen there—many, many tribesmen," said Peter. "If Aurelio Demassi is not the only one acting upon the prophecy, there will be thousands of warriors gathering from across the Sand Sea."

"Our guides have already told us that," said Stanwich.

"Indeed, but have they told us why?"

Peter drew his finger along the pages of the book. A gust of wind fluttered the pages, causing him to lose his place.

"I doubt your old book has much to say about why men gather in the valley north of here. This is madness," said Hersen Expey, shaking his head.

Peter ignored him, searching back through the old pages of Macmenian texts.

"Here it is," said Peter. He began reading slowly, translating the Macmenian words into Anglian as he read. "And there, in the place of Kordon, the army of the faithful shall gather, and with the aid of the Serpent, they shall march to the liberation of the Mountain."

"These are old words of nonsense," said Hersen Expey.

"These old words caused a guide you hired to abduct my cousin, Major Expey. These old words say precisely what is now happening. Warriors are gathering in large numbers in the north, in the Valley of Kordon. Our guide kidnapped Jack Caldwell because he believes he is this Promised One. Jack is broad of shoulder, light of eyes, and in his twenty-third year. He comes, as do the rest of us, from 'beyond the sands and the western mountains.' Does he not?"

"Jack is not the promised one of the prophecy," said Hannah.

"For the third time, that is not the point," said Peter. "The point is that Aurelio Demassi believed he was and captured him. The point is that these tribesmen believe the prophecy and are gathering by the hundreds and even by the thousands. And they gather for war. Do you think they are going to readily hand Jack back over to us?"

"Yes, when they realize he is not who they think he is," said Hannah.

"And when will that be?" said Peter.

"He can't—" Hannah shook her head with exasperation. "He can't even speak their language. He is just a foolish man from Calderon. A foolish, vain, young man."

Mrs. Smith put a hand on Hannah's shoulder as if to calm her. Hannah shrugged it off, with enough violence to draw glances from the others.

"Harmon has a point," said Stanwich.

"If they are going to war, we should get there as fast as we can," said Hersen Expey. He had a glint in his eye.

"And why is that?" asked Peter.

"Because we have ten crates of Hart-Harold breech-loading .45-caliber rifles, and they have none."

Peter looked at Hersen and then at Stanwich.

"You see," said Hersen Expey, "even if they are foolish enough to believe this boy is the answer to their prophecy, they will also see the rifles we offer them for their war. We can trade. We will trade them the guns for the Beserite, and we will trade them for Jack Caldwell."

Barnes cleared his throat. He looked north with narrowed eyes. He stepped to the side to have a better view of the landscape, unobstructed by the others.

"Riders," he said.

All of the others looked at him. Barnes spoke softly, but when he spoke, others listened.

"What?" said Stanwich.

"Riders," said Barnes, louder, pointing to the north.

The whistle of the northern sentry was shrill—three long blasts, meaning that unknown riders approached. He aimed his rifle into the air and fired the warning shot. The sound carried out, clear and loud across the open desert plain.

Stanwich, Hersen, Peter, Hannah, and Mrs. Smith all looked to the north. At the horizon, a line of figures emerged, mounted and riding swiftly. There were perhaps a hundred of them, possibly more, all riding camels. All moved fast, directly toward the camp, growing larger against the sky as they thundered forward.

"Those are not merchants, Stanwich. That is a raiding party," said Barnes.

Mrs. Smith was already pushing Hannah Huntington back toward the tents and toward the square of crates—a small redoubt—that she and Barnes alone had insisted the porters build before they erected even their tents.

Even in her caution, she did not believe the redoubt would ever be tested so soon.

They ran for their rifles.

CHAPTER 38
Selena Remembers

East of Ben Hamur
Central-Western Sand Sea
26th Day, Month of Gandus, 807
Anglian Calendar: January 26, 1879

"Saliha, Sanda, wake up! Wake up!" Saliha Savanar awoke to see her mother standing at the window. She wore her sleeping dress, a long slip of silk. She was of middle age but still had the figure of a younger woman. Her hair was long, auburn, and woven into a thick braid that reached down nearly to her waist.

Saliha sat up. Her sister Sanda sat up next to her, rubbing her eyes. Sanda was seven, three years older than Saliha.

"Sanda, get up," said Saliha. Their mother stood at the window glancing through the slot in the shutters into the courtyard. Saliha could hear men's voices.

"In the name of the Qhaliffa, Selahim the Second, open this door!" Saliha felt a chill at the sound of that voice. Something was wrong with that voice being shouted in her father's courtyard at that hour of the night.

"Come out, Savanar!" thundered the voice again. Saliha stood next to her mother, glancing out the shutters. In the center of the half-moon of men in the courtyard, a man stood in a purple turban, tall and menacing the torchlight, a dark black beard covering the lower half of his face. Flanking him on either side were giant men in orange turbans, lancers of the Qhaliffa. Every child in Alwaz Deem knew that lancers were the cruelest Demissaries. But the man in the purple turban frightened her the most. He was the one that all of the other Demissaries looked to for their orders. Why was he here, calling for Mother?

"Who is that man, Mother?"

Saliha's mother looked down at her with uncomprehending eyes, paralyzed by worry.

"Why are they here, Mother?"

"Lady Savanar."

"Why are they here?" Selena said the words aloud as she opened her eyes. The low stone ring of the well lay in front of her face. The ground underneath her was hard. A single blanket covered her against the cold of the winter desert night.

"Lady Savanar." The voice was Gulana's.

Selena looked toward the voice and saw Gulana's face above her, with stars in the sky above Gulana. Gulana shook Selena's shoulder with her strong hands.

"You were dreaming," she said.

"How long was I asleep?" asked Selena.

"Four hours," said Oapah. "We have already wasted part of the night. We must move now. We have waited here at the well for too long."

Selena sat up. They were close enough to Ben Hamur that she could smell the fruit trees whose roots reached down into Ben Hamur's pools. In the cool, dry desert night air, scents traveled dozens of miles, often farther.

"How far are we?"

"No more than forty miles," said Gulana.

Oapah nodded his agreement. He had already rolled their blankets. He handed Selena a piece of hard, dried meat.

She sank her teeth into it, savoring its saltiness. A piece of meat slipped into the empty space where her front teeth used to be—teeth that were once considered beautiful, the teeth the torturer placed into his pocket after he slowly ripped them out of her bleeding gums while she screamed. Selena, who had come to know pain, could not remember knowing pain greater than that. Now she looked like a beggar from the alleyways of the flatlands, the beggar Jemojeen made her when he took her family and her home, turning Saliha the Savanar into Selena of the streets. Except even then, she was a girl with the teeth and the face of a young Princess of the High Kezelboj, a Savanar of Alwaz Deem.

"When we reach the Staff of the Serpent, the God of the Mountain and the Sands will heal your mouth," said Oapah, as if reading her thoughts.

Selena looked at him with doubting eyes. "No, Oapah. Even the God of the Mountain and the Sands does not grow new teeth for his faithful."

"The God of the Mountain and the Sands raised the Mountain and scattered the Sands," said Gulana. "The God called forth the seven rivers from the mountain. The God can make you new teeth."

Selena chewed the meat with her molars, keeping it away from the empty space at the front of her gums. *At times I envy them their faith. The God of the Mountain and the Sands may be what they say—Creator of all things—but the Creator of all things will not give me new teeth.*

"Lady Savanar, we must begin walking. The sun has been down for too long." Oapah looked over his shoulder. "We have waited too long at the well."

Clouds still hung low overhead, but not enough to fully block out the moonlight, which turned the sands into the color of silver coins.

They began walking west in their usual formation, with Oapah leading them and Gulana following Selena. The full goatskin of water weighed heavily on Selena's shoulder, the leather strap cutting into her skin even through the wool of her overcloak. Selena's feet had blistered from toe to heel. She had never walked so far. Even traveling across the mountain with the Rams of the Order had not been like this, trudging mile after mile across the sands that grew impossibly hot during the day and freezing cold at night.

The first blisters gave way thirty miles out from the Semissari, but her feet had not immediately hardened. New blisters arose underneath the first blisters, to be replaced by a third set of blisters that now, mercifully, were on the edge of bursting. Gulana said that after the third blisters, Selena's feet would be as hard as hers. As of now, Selena did not feel the hardness in her battered feet, merely pain. With each step, the pain called out to her. Yet she kept stepping, ever westward, following Oapah's massive feet toward the oasis of Ben Hamur, trudging across the hard-packed silver sands.

They had thus far evaded the Erassians for more than one hundred miles. They walked in the night and slept in the daylight under what little shelter they could find, in shallow wadis and in the shadows of small boulders and thornbushes.

None of the three of them knew what happened to the brave Serpents who volunteered to walk into the sands as decoys. Without question, the Erassians had fallen upon some of them, perhaps even all of them. Selena felt a knot twist in her stomach as she thought of the dozen Serpents, and Asatan herself—all of them willing to give their lives so that she might escape to Ben Hamur.

They might all be dead because of me. My life is not worth their thirteen lives, no matter what the old scrolls say. My life was not worth Trendan Rudar and Huralt Donadun. My life is not worth more than the Rams who rowed us across the Great Pool. My life is not worth more than Oapah's or Gulana's.

As the blisters tormented her feet, and as the guilt swirled inside of her, she continued walking west.

"If we can cover twelve miles this night, then we will have water until we see the walls of Ben Hamur," said Gulana, speaking behind her. "The well of Gaz is not far, and its waters are less salty than the last well."

Oapah grunted his assent in front of her.

Selena felt slow and plodding on her tired legs. The pistols the Serpents gave her weighed against her chest, and the waterskin lay awkwardly on her side. The weight of the dagger—a razor-sharp Serpent's fang—rubbed her leather belt against her hip, wearing down the skin as the miles wore along. Even the wool of her cloak felt heavy.

Oapah stopped and dropped to a knee.

"To ground," said Gulana.

Selena was already down, growing faster and more like her guardians with each passing night.

Oapah craned his neck, cupping his ear toward the north. His eyes narrowed as he scanned the darkened desert.

Selena listened.

She heard nothing.

She looked north with wide eyes. She saw nothing but pale silver sand in the moonlight. She cupped her ear, but still she heard nothing.

"They have found us. They ride to an object. Erassians do not gallop in that way when they are ranging," said Oapah.

"Perhaps they ride to the well?" asked Selena, hopefully. They had already put a mile between themselves and the well.

Oapah listened intently as if weighing Selena's theory against the sounds in his ear. For long, silent moments, Selena and Gulana waited, watching Oapah.

"No," he said, shaking his head, "the riders move toward us, not the well, and they will be upon us in minutes."

And then Selena heard them.

It was a soft patter, barely perceptible, sounding like the call of some far-off bird. It was faint, but it was the sound of hoofbeats.

"Do we run?" she asked.

"There is nowhere to run," said Oapah.

"Can we hide?" asked Selena.

"There are no hiding places here to conceal us from Erassians," said Gulana.

"We will fight them then?"

Selena felt the pair of three-barreled pistols in their leather slips. They were heavy on her chest, hanging at a diagonal. They were loaded, but they would not fire until the hammers were cocked back. Asatan gave her both pistols in the Semissari. She asked Selena which Demissary pistol she was most comfortable using.

Before Selena answered, Gulana had said, *Lady Savanar will take the three-barrelers.* And then she had turned to Selena saying, *They are the easiest to use, my lady.*

All of the weapons they had carried south from Sundar Dun, save for Oapah's great two-handed scimitarus, were lost to the waters of the Great Pool. Gulana now carried a borrowed blade she had complained about since they left the Semissari.

"Yes, we will fight, and we will pray to the God of the Mountain and the Sands. Join your hands with my own," said Oapah. They were already kneeling.

The hoofbeats grew louder.

CHAPTER 39
Bring Umahar

Alwaz Deem—Meer Norekah
25th Day, Month of Gandus, 807
Anglian Calendar: January 25, 1879

"Father, why must you leave?"

Ottovan did not respond.

"Why must you go, Father? You will miss my seventh year-ending."

"Ohanna, do not say such things." Rama shook her head at her daughter.

Ottovan turned and looked at his second-oldest daughter.

"Ohanna, when I return, it will be late spring, and I will take you on a ride up to Nor Gandus, and we will fish in the streams. The sun will have warmed the air, and we will go up the Great Mountain, sleeping beneath the stars on the hillside with just you and me."

Ohanna smiled.

She had Ottovan's broad face, and while not conventionally beautiful like her mother, there was intelligence and beauty in her eyes. And there was a fire in her smile, the kind that lies at the intersection of mischief and wisdom.

He would have to watch her. Few would dare risk impropriety with the daughter of Ottovan Fanfar, but still, the young were known for boldness, not forethought. His own youth was robbed of him, but by the grace of the God of the Mountain and the Sands, Ohanna's world would not be the hard world of a training Demissary.

Unless disaster struck, and Ottovan failed in his mission, she would mingle with the sons and daughters of the Kezelboj lords. She already did.

"Where are you riding, out on the sands?" asked Emakah, who was eleven.

Her face was narrower, like her mother's, with the same tiny nose and full lips. She was fair to look at, all agreed, including, perhaps most notably, Emakah herself. Ottovan had caught her lingering at the looking glass, enamored with her own face, more than once.

"You know I cannot tell you that, Emakah." Ottovan sipped his soup, gripping the wooden bowl with both hands. He swallowed a large gulp of broth. "I ride for our Qhaliffa, as always."

"For the Qhaliffa as always," said Emakah, under her breath. Her voice mocked her father's earnest tone.

Ottovan heard the hinges on the gate to the garden open.

He tensed. Evening had descended upon Alwaz Deem, and he did not expect visitors.

The door opened with a crash.

Ottovan lurched to his feet, swiftly placing his full frame between the door and his family. His hip dagger was already drawn and in his hand.

Ottovan nearly slashed the man with his blade before he collapsed onto the sanded wooden planks at his feet.

Beneath a dark, hooded cloak, a turban was wrapped around his head, brown and nondescript, the kind worn by merchants. Blood, grime, and an unkempt beard obscured his face. Yet, still, Ottovan could recognize the man he knew so well.

"God of the Mountain!" shouted Emakah.

"Quiet girl," said Ottovan, kneeling over the fallen man. "Rama, take them away, and come back alone."

Rama was already ushering the girls from the room, a firm hand at their backs, pushing them to hurry.

Ottovan bent down closer to the man's face. His eyes were barely open, and he groaned with weariness and pain.

"Friend, by the God of the Mountain and the Sands, you are alive."

"Water," said Ozgar, his voice a ragged whisper.

Ottovan rose and pulled a cup from the table. He walked to the wall, where the waterskin hung next to a pair of wineskins—one new, one old. He squeezed the waterskin, jetting a stream of water into the wooden cup. He brought it to Ozgar's prone body. He could see the shredding and tears in the fabric of his robes; he could see the dried blood on the wounds beneath.

"Drink, friend," said Ottovan.

Ozgar drank greedily, like a man reaching a well after a long march across the sands.

"Slowly," said Ottovan. "Slowly or your stomach will ache."

Ozgar slowed the pace of his drinking.

"Were you followed?"

Ozgar swallowed heavily and slightly raised his eyelids.

"No."

"Are you certain?"

"By the God of the Mountain and the Sands," Ozgar wheezed. "I was not followed."

Ottovan looked down at him, doubting. Unwounded, he would not doubt Ozgar's word for a moment. But Ozgar was wounded, on the run for twenty days, and, if he was now lying on Ottovan's floor, he had traversed the Great Mountain, from Saman Keer to Alwaz Deem.

"More water," said Ozgar.

"Slowly, friend. I know you thirst, but vomiting will not aid you."

Ozgar placed his hands on the cup and swallowed another mouthful of water.

"You are wounded. Gravely."

Ozgar groaned.

Ottovan leaned back, surveying the damage upon Ozgar's body. "Have you kept the wounds clean?"

Ozgar breathed heavily as if fully exhaling for the first time in long days, at last in a place of refuge. "I have tried."

Ottovan heard Rama's steps behind him.

He rose and walked to her, whispering his words. "I cannot leave him here with you. We must find Nemakar. This is far beyond our powers of healing. Go to Nemakar's house. He is closest. Tell him only one thing, *Bring Umahar and his vials. Make haste, wife, or Ozgar Ogatonia will die.*"

Nemakar sent Rama home as soon as she brought him the news.

By the God of the Mountain and the Sands, Ozgar is alive.

This thought entered Nemakar's mind and would not release it. He rode north from Alwaz Deem to Meer Norekah, keeping up a fierce pace, driving his horse to near exhaustion, his hope spurring him forward.

He rode along the Upper Ring Road, passing through the Grand Vizerian Guardpost without incident. When he reached the main up-valley stretch along the River Meer, he took his horse up along the railing, bypassing the merchant and religious traffic, shouting "Demissary! Demissary!" as he rode.

Seeing the tall, straight-backed officer with the flowing mustache, the people made way for his warhorse, as well they should. Nemakar Hasdruba was not a man to be trifled with.

He rode up and up, past the mid-levels, past the neat courtyards and low-walled houses of the priests and the merchants. And then, he reached the dwellings of those who were paid the highest in the service of the Qhaliffa—the bureaucrats who oversaw the Ring River wharves, the treasuries, and the tending of the roads.

He rode farther up still, where the traffic lessened, up past the upper mid-levels, where the richest merchants lived. He rode onward, past the high levels where the High Kezelboj had built their palaces of limestone and granite. He rode to where there were at last more trees than buildings, where the Meer Norekahn pines grew taller than Galley masts.

At last, he reached a gravel lane, flanked by enormous, ancient trees, straight and narrow as the columns of stone in the Qhaliffa's palace of Saman Keer. At the end of the lane stood a small stone house surrounded by a little stone wall. This high up, it was cool in the summer and cold in the winter, even when the lower valley was sunny and warm, heated directly by the afternoon sun.

Here, in the remote reaches of Upper Meer Norekah, in the mist-cloaked place called the "Cloud Level," Umahar had chosen to make his life when he was not campaigning with the Third Demissary Legion of Ottovan Fanfar.

Nemakar walked down the lane, the gravel crunching beneath his boots. His eyes scanned the lines of trees that flanked the alley to make sure none of Jemojeen's spies placed eyes upon him. Umahar should be unsuspected, but Nemakar had grown to understand that Jemojeen cast a keen eye upon all that served in the Third Legion and upon all of the officers especially.

He wore his cloak over his uniform, his dark brown hood covering the purple of his turban. He did not need word reported that a purple-turbaned Demissary Captain was rushing through a Meer Norekahn cloud lane to find Umahar.

Nemakar opened the low gate, walking through a plot of cabbages, carrots, and peas climbing a trellis. He knocked on the rough wood of Umahar's door. The house lay completely quiet. Umahar's wife had died of the coughing death five years earlier. They never had children, and he had not remarried. He lived alone, like a warrior-monk with his vials, his hanging clumps of herbs, and his small garden in front of his house.

Nemakar waited at the locked door.

Meer Norekah was the correct city for a man seeking peace after the pain of heartache. It was the city of the blue rooftops, not sky blue like Nor Gandus, but dark blue, like the Ring River in the summer, the color of deep waters.

Meer Norekah had always been a prosperous city, competing with Alwaz Deem and Saman Keer itself in its wealth and elegance, but without the grandeur. It had never boasted the population of either of those cities, and for that reason, aging merchants who could afford to live anywhere in the Qhaliffa's realm often chose Meer Norekah for their home. Umahar, the Demissary physician, liked Meer Norekah because it was quiet, and here among the clouds, he was free from the baser ambitions of the valley below.

Nemakar knocked again on the door with a gloved fist.

A pair of hens looked at him warily from a corner of the walled garden. A third hen ignored him, still pecking at the newly overturned earth. Umahar tended to his garden. Nemakar, in a fleeting wave, felt envy for the simplicity of Umahar's life: scrolls, herbs, gardens, and quiet. What more could a man who rode the sands making war wish for when he returned to the Seven Cities?

The door creaked open. Umahar stood in the open doorway, wearing an apron covered in flour.

"Captain," said Umahar, his voice calm and pleasant.

Umahar stood with his hand still on the edge of the door. Nemakar stepped through the door and closed it behind him. He faced the door and locked it, sliding the bolt. Despite the age and roughness of the wood, Nemakar saw that the bolt was oiled and well-tended, and that it fastened securely against the sturdy post of the doorjam. A Grand Vizerian guardsman would have to do far more than deliver a well-placed kick if he wished to break through.

"Have you ridden from Alwaz Deem?" asked Umahar, his hands on his hips.

Nemakar glanced at the open window. The night was mild, especially for the cloud levels, and Umahar liked to keep his garden window opened on all but the most frigid evenings.

"Ozgar is alive," he whispered.

Umahar walked to the window and closed it.

"By the God," said Umahar. "The others?"

"I know not," said Nemakar.

"Where is he now?"

"He burst through the front door into Ottovan Fanfar's house while they ate their dinner. Ottovan sent his wife to me, and I rode immediately."

"What is his condition?"

"Poor. His wounds are deep and many."

"Was he followed?"

"Rama thinks not. Ottovan thinks not. Ozgar says he was not followed."

"He would know," said Umahar, nodding.

"He is gravely wounded, and he was on the run from Saman Keer for nearly three weeks."

"Have sufficient excuses been made regarding his absence from the barracks?"

"Barely. He is said to have a grave illness."

"Who is tending to him in his illness?"

"We have said that you are," said Nemakar. "Have you been seen?"

"I have been here awaiting our orders."

Nemakar nodded, his eyes darting as his mind raced.

"Were you followed here?" asked Umahar.

"No."

"What are his wounds?"

"Flame and blade; he is cut deeply, and he has burns on his legs, chest, and shoulders."

"Have they festered?"

Nemakar shook his head. "I pray they have not."

Umahar walked to the shelves that held his healing vials and the rack from which his herbs hung. He grabbed half of a dozen vials and several bunches of herbs, showing no hesitation in his selections.

"Come," he said. "We ride for Alwaz Deem."

CHAPTER 40
Count Usor Hurries

Northwest of the Valley of Kordon
Bulbanian Borderlands, Western Sand Sea
January 28, 1879

Seven days had passed since Count Usor Nepopolous disciplined the disobedient peasant-porter with his Hon River Hawk. *What was his name, Gabachov? Gabachovsky? Gabovsky? Whatever it was, he died screaming and faceless.*

Since witnessing his demise, the men marched faster during the days, and they had kept quiet around their small campfires at night.

The Beserian scouts and porters had wanted to use dung for his fires.

Nepopolous made clear that unlike dogs from the desert, he did not eat food cooked above a flame of burning shit. His porters would carry his firewood, and any dissent would be dealt with like Gabakovsky's. *What was his name? It was a peasant name. They tend to blend over the years and months, one interchangeable man with another, no better than mules and so often less useful,* thought the count as they headed south.

Usor rode onward in a state of near-sleep as mile after monotonous mile slipped past. They were still far enough north that they could travel by daylight and sleep under the stars. In a hundred miles or so, the sun above would become too hot for day travel for men like Count Usor, and they would march at night, but not yet.

They had reached the vast gravel expanse of the Bulbanian borderlands. It was not flat like much of the Sand Sea but rather undulating like waves upon the ocean. Rarely did a hill of the gravel lands exceed twenty feet in height, and rarely did a depression penetrate the earth any deeper than that in the inverse.

Nonetheless, the undulations were ceaseless, rising and falling, rising and falling, and rising and falling, for as far as the eye could see. On each rise, the camels' feet sank into the gravel, and on each descent, they did the same. Thus, the camels stepped more gingerly than they did across dunes or true flatlands, the going slow and difficult. Yet the men still kept up Usor Nepopolous's demanded pace, resting less and driving ever southward.

The power of discipline, he thought, smiling in self-satisfaction.

Several camels had died from exertion and poor treatment. The remaining camels shouldered heavier loads. The hired Beserian camel-tenders told the count that the camels could not struggle under such pressure indefinitely and that he would lose more if they were not treated better.

Usor repaid the Beserian messenger for his honesty by requiring him to carry a crate on foot for the following three days. He survived, but barely. His hands were bloody beneath the strips of cloth he had wrapped around them. Other Beserians tried to help the man with his load until Count Usor made it clear that any man assisting him would be shot.

So, the others left him to struggle on his own, lagging far behind the rest of the column. Two more camels died.

The Autocrat knew who he was sending, thought Usor Nepopolous, riding in his giant saddle. *Send a man who knows how to discipline his subordinates, and the mission shall be achieved. Send a man who treats his underlings gently, and you shall fail. These men and beasts are pawns to be moved in this Great Game, of which I am a formidable player.*

If I achieve the Autocrat's wishes, I will be added to the Council. Perhaps I shall even take command of the Guards, wearing a general's gold eagle. No Anglian shall move more swiftly than I across this forsaken land. Harold Milton Stanwich? A weakling. The man is from a democracy. An explorer? Let him have Omakhosi. He has never before raced time and space against a Count of the Gressias. He has never before faced me. We shall see what their newspapers think when I secure the Beserite!

For himself, Usor had chosen the most durable and largest camel, even though he was among the smallest of riders, smaller than even the rail-thin Beserians. He had ordered the construction of a special saddle, with added padding and supports, making it appear as if he were riding in a small castle or a woman's litter affixed to the camel's back.

It would be the kind of thing men would readily mock if anyone dared to mock Usor Nepopolous. Sticking out from his saddle, Nepopolous added a shaded perch for his Hon River Hawk. Usor was not the kind of man who wished to have a bird ride along upon his arm for any length of time. Nor was he the kind of man who named a bird. He called the bird "hawk."

"Your Excellency."

Usor heard words interrupting his pleasant walk around the tranquil lake in his mind, like someone shouting from the side of a theater during the middle of a performance.

"Your Excellency, our outriders have spotted tribesmen to our south."

Usor looked up.

He had been nearly asleep in his saddle, dreaming of summer on his estate, when he would order the best-looking peasant women to come and accompany him on his walks around the lakes and upon the forest paths. Many were married. Many were not. He had pictured in exquisite detail one such frolic with a dark-haired beauty in the August just past. She was a virgin before that day . . . Usor opened his eyes with a shudder and a frown as his camel descended yet another tiny gravel hill.

His chief Erassian had spoken and distracted his daydream. Kassan was his name.

Some Erassians served the master to the south, the Qhaliffa, following the religion of the God of the Mountain. Such men believed that yoke to be lighter than the yoke of the Gressian Autocrat, and no small number of Erassians chose to abandon the religion of their birth to serve the Qhaliffa. The others, like Kassan's family, decided to stay and serve the Autocrat. They remained Orthodox in their faith, but that was misleading.

In choosing to serve the Autocrat, they traded the light Orthodoxy of their tribes for the heavy theology of the Gressians. A man who did not make Sunday services could be flogged, at least under the regime of Petros Pavolous Petrovich. The fervent and young Autocrat had been seated for five years now upon the Throne of the Pines and the Olives, the throne of all of the Gressias, north and south, east and west—from the new continent in the west to the shoreline above Hak-Hakkan in the east and from the frozen sea on its interminable northern coast down to the edges of the Sand Sea and the hills of Bulbania in the south. These lands made up the many-nationed empire of the Autocrat, even more diverse than that of the Spatanians and many times its size, an empire so vast as to be said by the Anglian diplomats to be ungovernable.

"How far?" asked Usor, looking at Kassan the Erassian. Usor hated him less than the others. Usor, as a rule, did not care for Erassians, but the man was at least competent. Usor could not deny that.

"Four miles," said Kassan.

"How many tribesmen?"

"Perhaps a dozen."

"All men?"

"Men and boys."

Usor nodded, considering.

"Do they have camels?"

"Yes. Nearly two dozen."

"Excellent."

"What would you have me do, Your Excellency?"

Usor scoffed. *Is that answer not obvious?* "Bring me the camels, all of them."

"All of them?"

"Why would you leave valuable camels to the tribesmen?"

"They may offer resistance," said Kassan. "They are armed, and they will fight for their camels. Camels are a Beserian's most prized possession. They will die for those beasts."

"Of what concern is that of mine, Erassian? Bring enough men to kill them and take the camels. Or threaten them and take the camels without killing them. I care not, but I will have all of the camels." Usor looked at Kassan with his dark grey eyes that made men tremble.

To Kassan's credit, he did not tremble. For this reason, Kassan spoke with Usor Nepopolous more than any other man in the expedition. This was especially true following the hawk's punishment of Gabakovsky. And every man in the column could see the Beserian scout struggling with his crate, which he carried on pain of death, staggering miles behind the last camel in the line. Count Usor ensured that even the most dim-witted man could fully understand his lessons.

Kassan waited, continuing to ride at Count Usor Nepopolous's side.

"You are dismissed," snapped Usor.

"Yes, Your Excellency," said Kassan the Erassian, turning to lead the patrol. He galloped through his men without stopping. They followed him ahead, lurching forward from the column, twenty-five strong, disappearing over the first rise and down into the depression, then rising up again into view, then back down out of sight, until they had finally reached a rise beyond which they were no longer visible.

They came back two hours later.

Count Usor had ordered the column to continue southward in their absence. *They are Erassians. If my scouts cannot find us on the move, what good are they?*

When Kassan and his Erassians arrived, they came from the northwest. Behind them, they trailed a dozen camels. Kassan rode straight to the front of the column, not stopping until he reached Count Usor. None of the other Erassians rode forward with him.

He was alone to face the count.

Usor continued riding, his camel moving at a swift walk.

"How many?" he asked as Kassan approached his side.

"We lost four men, Your Excellency. The tribesmen were well armed."

"I said how many, as in how many camels did you bring me back?"

"We captured twelve camels, Your Excellency."

"I thought you said there was twice that number?" Usor looked askance at Kassan.

"Some escaped, and some were killed in the fighting."

"I see," said Usor, frowning.

Kassan continued to ride awkwardly at his side, unsure whether to return to his place in the column or remain.

"Your men that you lost, did we keep their camels?"

"Three of them, Your Excellency. One was shot out from underneath Kagadan before he himself was shot."

Usor could not much tell one Erassian from another and did not much care to.

"Very well, Erassian," said Usor. "We now have fifteen new camels, not twelve. Allocate the added baggage to the new camels. That should make the ones we have to live a bit longer, no?"

"Yes, Your Excellency," said Kassan, trying to hide the hate from his face.

"And well done, Erassian," said Count Usor. "You are a useful man."

CHAPTER 41
New Orders for the Third Legion

Alwaz Deem
26th Day, Month of Gandus, 807
Anglian Calendar: January 26, 1879

When Umahar—Demissary Fire Lieutenant, physician to the Third Legion, and secret Oath Holder of the Order of the Ram, the Lion, and the Serpent—stepped through the door, Ozgar Ogatonia had reached the height of his fever.

Ottovan Fanfar and his wife Rama both held down Ozgar's arms as he thrashed back and forth in the madness of delusion and semiconsciousness. Their eldest daughter dabbed his forehead with a cloth dampened in cold water from the fountain. They had made clear to her that he was very sick, suffering from a terrible illness. Even in winter, Alwaz Deem rarely saw frost at the mid-levels, but the fountain water, which came from the height of the River Deem, from the spring beneath the glacier, was cold in the manner of newly melted snow, even in summer. In the winter, it felt as cold as snow itself.

"Ahhhh! Begone! Begone!" shouted Ozgar, writhing as if under the torturer's knife.

All of the windows of the house were closed shut. Ozgar and Rama had stuffed cloth underneath the doors and along the windows to stifle the sound. Umahar and Nemakar did not hear the shouting and the moaning until they were against the door, already inside the courtyard.

Nemakar quickly shut the door behind them when they entered, letting only a moment of Ozgar's screaming escape out into the night air.

The mid-levels of Alwaz Deem were prosperous but crowded, with homes near each other, clustered between the banks of the River Deem and the granite mountain slopes that bound the Valley of Alwaz, which at the mid-levels, did not yet widen as it did in the lower levels, as the shoulders of the mountain receded and the wide-open descent to the flatlands began.

Umahar approached Ozgar's body. He looked down to see the fear and worry in both Ottovan's eyes and Rama's.

"Yes," said Rama, looking at her daughter. "Like that. Dip it in the cold water, wring it out twice and then tap the forehead, just like that."

Ozgar shouted as Emakah, the eleven-year-old girl, daubed his flaming forehead. She recoiled, as if Ozgar were a dog, snapping its jaws. Ozgar's eyes opened. They were wild and unseeing.

"You have done well, Ottovan," said Umahar, kneeling next to Ozgar's body.

The powerfully built archer captain had lost considerable weight since the last time Umahar had seen him. His customarily bronzed complexion was pale and sickly, yellowish in the way that the olive-skinned become when suffering from a terrible sickness. Ozgar was, of course, a Bulbanian, like all Demissaries. But he was a south Bulbanian, like Ottovan, nearly dark enough to be mistaken for a native Qhaliffan.

"The fever has done much damage," said Umahar. "The infection has taken hold of him."

Umahar gently urged the girl Emakah to back away. She gratefully stepped back, offering him the damp towel. Umahar shook his head, returning his eyes to Ozgar's face.

"Captain, I am here. I have brought medicines that will cool your mind and your skin." Umahar, like all Demissaries, was first and foremost a warfighter, even if he was a physician and chief healer to the entire Third Legion. He, like the others, had survived the training of the Academy, and he had chosen one of the three: lance, bow, or fire. He had chosen fire, which made Captain Nemakar his commanding officer.

Beneath Umahar's penetrating gaze, Ozgar collapsed into a fitful sleep, neither seeing nor hearing the physician. But he had also stopped thrashing. Ottovan and Rama still held fast to his arms, Ottovan's firm hands holding Ozgar's body down by pressing on his shoulder.

"Commander, you may remove your hands," said Umahar. Ottovan looked back at him with doubt in his eyes.

"He is at rest. His body is exhausted. He is lucky to be alive."

"It is we that are fortunate that he lives," said Ottovan. There was fierce loyalty in his tone.

"Indeed, Commander."

Nemakar stood, observing those crouched around Ozgar's inert form. Ottovan's clean, bald head glistened with sweat. Even Nemakar rarely saw his legion commander without his purple turban.

Rama's hair was drawn back into a pair of long braids. Her headscarf had fallen off of her head, and strands of loose hair fell about her flushed face.

Nemakar observed that she looked like a woman who had just been intimate with her husband. They had exerted themselves to keep Ozgar from thrashing himself against the wooden floorboards or worse.

"We received orders," said Ottovan. "We cannot wait here any longer. I have delayed as long as I am able."

Nemakar nodded, considering Ottovan's words. "Then we must leave him here."

"They will find him," said Ottovan, shaking his head.

"What else would you do?" asked Nemakar, Captain of Fire, stroking his long mustache.

"Bring him," said Ottovan. "Somehow. If they find him, they will find his wounds. Then they will know." Ottovan glanced over his shoulder to make sure that his daughters could not hear him.

"He was injured in training," said Nemakar, keeping his voice low. "This is what we will say. That is what he will say."

"No," said Ottovan, shaking his head. "We cannot leave him here, and we have already said he was suffering from a grave illness."

"Then we hide him," said Nemakar.

Ottovan nodded. *Perhaps we could hide him.*

"We can bring him to the Semissari and hide him there," said Nemakar. "The Serpents can heal him as well as Umahar."

"Who will take him there?" asked Ottovan, shaking his head in dismissal.

Umahar, the physician, continued looking down at Ozgar, carefully running his index finger and his eyes along his body, looking at each point of infection with an expert's eye, assessing the pus in the wounds and the degree of danger each presented.

"Will he live?" asked Ottovan.

Umahar did not immediately answer. "He may live."

Umahar held Ozgar's right arm, looking at it carefully. It was the arm that Ozgar used to pull his bow, the bowstring arm of the finest archer in all of the Seven Cities.

Through the cloth-stuffed opening of the door, Ottovan heard the faint creak of the iron gate to the stone courtyard. It was night, and as usual, he expected no one at this hour.

He jumped to his feet, checking his belt for his dagger. It was there, as always, sharp and ready.

A knock struck the door, loud and imperious.

Ottovan turned with urgency in his eyes. He whispered, "Take him into the back room now. If he wakes up, gag him if you must. Keep him *silent*."

Ottovan walked to the door and cracked it open, peering into the torchlit courtyard.

A pair of thick-chested Grand Vizerian Guardsmen stood staring at him, the torchlight glinting off the chain mail covering their dark grey tunics. Their faces were hard and unfriendly. They were Jemojeen's men, and they did not need to be told how their master felt about the Commander of the Third Demissary Legion.

Ottovan heard the sound of feet dragging on the wooden floor behind him as Nemakar and Umahar pulled Ozgar's body into the far room. There were no doors inside the house. If these men of Jemojeen were sufficiently bold, he would have to draw his dagger to keep them from seeing Ozgar.

Another face moved forward into the torchlight. Turkelan the Erassian stared at Ottovan, green-eyed beneath his red-orange hair, his lips half smiling. His face had always reminded Ottovan of a fox, with a long, narrowed jaw and wide, intelligent eyes. It had long been said that he saw and heard things other men missed, almost in the way Oath Holders of the Order thought of the Sworn Serpents. It was fitting that Turkelan served as Jemojeen's eyes and ears.

"Commander Fanfar," he said, the half-smile growing inside of his orange beard and the corners of his eyes compressing as if he had just heard something amusing.

"Captain Turkelan," said Ottovan.

"I am told that you ride upon the sands on the morrow," said Turkelan. His voice was pleasant in the manner of a cheerful executioner.

Ottovan trusted him even less than he trusted the Grand Vizerian Guardsmen. Indeed, he did not trust any of them, but Turkelan was by far the more dangerous.

Turkelan stepped forward toward Ottovan, who still held the door only cracked open. The Grand Vizerian Guardsmen parted as Turkelan advanced.

"Yes, Captain," said Ottovan, meeting the Erassian's eyes. "I am enjoying an evening with my wife and my daughters before I depart for the sands. May I ask to what I owe this unexpected visit?"

"The Grand Vizer wished for me to inform you of several matters personally."

Ottovan stood at the door, neither opening it farther nor closing it, blocking the gap with his wide body. He kept his face as still as a statue's, in the manner in which Demissaries were trained.

"May I come in?" asked Turkelan. "The information I am to share with you is best shared behind closed doors."

"My wife and daughters are inside," said Ottovan. "I do not wish to disturb them. I assure you my courtyard is quite private, especially at this late hour."

Ottovan did not wait to allow Turkelan to disagree. He stepped out into the courtyard, closing the door behind him. The cold of the winter's night air was sharp against the naked skin on his scalp.

Turkelan looked at Ottovan's bald head, noting the missing, omnipresent purple turban.

"The Grand Vizer is informed that Captain Ogatonia has been absent from the barracks."

"He has been ill," said Ottovan, perhaps too quickly.

"Is he improving?" asked Turkelan.

"My legion's business is my own, Captain."

"No, Commander, it is not. You report to the Grand Vizer, upon the orders of the Qhaliffa. Did you forget?"

"He is improving."

"Will he be able to join your legion on the march?"

Ottovan nodded, his eyes narrowing in contempt.

"Excellent," said Turkelan. "I know the Grand Vizer will be pleased to hear it."

Ottovan waited.

Turkelan stared at him, still smirking.

"Is that why you have come here to disturb my evening, Captain?"

"The traitor and heretic Selena Savanar has escaped from the Semissari Swamp," said Turkelan.

"Oh?" asked Ottovan, hiding the joy in his heart while keeping his eyes level and his gaze hard.

"She has ventured into the western desert with two companions, in the direction of Ben Hamur."

"I see," said Ottovan. "In other words, Jemojeen's guardsmen let her escape from Sundar Dun into the swamp." As he spoke the insult, he looked at the guardsmen squarely in their faces. They glared at him with much malice but little guile. In Ottovan's experience, Jemojeen liked his guardsmen to be obedient, ruthless, and moderately stupid.

"And then," said Ottovan, returning his eyes to Captain Turkelan, "your scouts allowed her and her companions to escape from the swamp. How was that done, Captain? Over open ground? How many patrols did you have? Ten? Twelve?"

Turkelan looked disdainfully into Ottovan's face. The green in the Erassian Captain's eyes locked onto the hazel-brown of the Demissary Commander's. There was flame beneath the green and iron underneath the brown. Neither man blinked. Both were killers many times over.

Turkelan spoke first. "It was most unfortunate that she escaped, Commander. Indeed, my men presently sweep the approaches to Ben Hamur as we speak. They are likely to find her. In my experience, few, if any, escape my men. In fact, I cannot think of one who has."

"It appears she already has," said Ottovan. "A woman."

A wave of hatred passed through the emeralds in Turkelan's eyes. He blinked, forcing a smile back onto his lips.

"As I said, my men are searching. Perhaps they have already found her."

"What is your message for me, Captain?" said Ottovan, his voice growing deeper. His chin jutted forward, and his eyes narrowed.

"You are to go to Ben Hamur at once."

"Were those not already my orders?"

"You are to make the utmost haste."

"To find the Savanar?"

"You may leave that to us, Commander."

"So that she may escape again?"

Ottovan provoked him intentionally, and he could see the anger rising in Turkelan's cheeks and at the edges of his eyes. Ottovan could see the Erassian Captain's visible efforts to control his rage. They were a proud race, the Erassians, and despite their service to foreign overlords, they were unaccustomed to a demeanor of subservience. The Erassian looked as if he wished to stab Ottovan. Ottovan would welcome nothing more. He felt the dagger at his belt, longing to unsheathe it against these men. He would gladly fight them all. If it came to it, Nemakar and Umahar were inside, and no three could defeat the three of them in an even-numbered match with blades. Of that, Ottovan was entirely certain.

"You are to secure Ben Hamur," said Turkelan, with the officiousness of an officer carrying a message from the Grand Vizer himself. "The Grand Vizer no longer trusts the Sharef. Indeed, my men have observed Beserian riders east of Ben Gamurian."

"East of Ben Gamurian?" said Ottovan. There was doubt in his voice.

"That is what I said," replied Turkelan.

Turkelan handed Ottovan a new sealed scroll.

Ottovan looked down, seeing the dark green seal of the Grand Vizer, pressed against the edge, unbroken.

"Will it be just the Third Legion going to Ben Hamur?"

Turkelan laughed. "Of course not, Commander."

At that, Turkelan turned and walked out the gate of the courtyard followed by the heavyset guardsmen. Ottovan did not bid them goodnight.

CHAPTER 42
Caught in the Open

East of Ben Hamur
Central-Western Sand Sea
26th–28th Day, Month of Gandus, 807
Anglian Calendar: January 26–28, 1879

The riders advanced at a near gallop, coming from the northeast, in the direction of Alwaz Deem, moving southwest.

Selena crouched in the shallow ravine with Gulana at her left and Oapah to her right. She gripped the handle of a three-barreled pistol in her right hand, her knuckles whitening as the oncoming hooves shook the hard-packed desert sand.

Gulana and Oapah each held their own pistols, crouching in silence and staring north at the silvery sands. The riders looked massive on their mounts, casting forward shadows as they moved south, backlit by the moonlight.

"How many?" asked Selena.

"Eighteen," said Gulana.

That is too many, thought Selena. *I have six bullets, three in each pistol. I cannot kill six. I will be lucky to hit three, even two. They will throw their javelins. If they mean to capture, they will throw the javelins to wound me, and they can hit a small melon off of a post, every time, at a gallop. I have seen them on the course. I must save a bullet for myself if it comes to that. I will not let them take me to Jemojeen. I will not let them burn me.*

"They will not take me alive," said Selena, her voice vehement.

"They will not take you at all," said Gulana.

Oapah crouched in brooding silence, tapping his pistol with a massive index finger, as long and thick as a gun barrel.

The riders advanced to a quarter-mile away, churning the ground beneath them.

"They are not in a *V* shape," said Oapah.

Gulana stared.

"Look," said Oapah.

Selena looked. She saw only a line of galloping dark shapes, moving swiftly toward them.

"Erassians would charge us in a V, always," said Oapah. "That is a line."

"This is true," said Gulana, squinting at the riders.

Oapah stared at the advancing horsemen, trying to pick out their features in the dark.

"They have helmets," said Oapah, "and their color is wrong. Those are not Erassians."

"Guardsmen of the Grand Vizer?" asked Selena, tilting her head in doubt. *Why would Jemojeen send them? They are not sand riders.*

"No," said Oapah. "Not guardsmen. Not on the sands, not riding that fast."

"By the God of the Mountain and the Sands," said Gulana, her voice rising, "They are riders from Ben Hamur."

"The Ram sent word to the Sharef," said Oapah, his face altering as worry receded and hope advanced.

Gulana nodded.

"Can Ben Hamur be trusted?" asked Selena.

"The Sharef is with us," said Gulana.

"Says who?" asked Selena, glancing nervously at the oncoming riders.

"The Ram, The Lion, and The Serpent."

"All three?"

"Yes," said Gulana.

"Even so, can we trust that these are men loyal to the Sharef?" asked Selena.

Neither Oapah nor Gulana responded, staring at the riders. Men could dress like other men if they were trying to fool others. It was an old trick upon the Sand Sea, used by Beserians and Qhaliffans alike over the centuries. For all they knew, the riders could be Demissaries in disguise.

The riders charged forward in an all-out gallop, like the riders in the Qhaliffa's Race, galloping around the Ring River every spring.

"Let them get closer," said Oapah.

"Ben Hamur is loyal to its Sharef," said Gulana.

"Why are they galloping toward us?" asked Selena. "They ride to a target. They are not roving."

"Perhaps they were sent to find us," said Gulana.

Oapah nodded.

"Perhaps they ride to find us before the Erassians do. They ride like men racing against time," said Gulana.

"Or against other men," said Selena.

They galloped closer.

Even in the darkness, Selena could now see their helmets. They were not conical, like those of Jemojeen's Grand Vizerian Guardsmen. Instead, they were shaped like a large upside-down bowl placed down over a small steel plate, and along the rear edge of the plate, a thin curtain of chain mail hung down, protecting their necks.

"Stay down," said Oapah, using his war voice.

Selena crouched down closer to the earth.

"You too," said Oapah, looking at Gulana.

She stayed where she was.

The galloping horsemen—eighteen of them in a widely dispersed line, were now no more than one hundred yards in front of them. Three saddled horses trailed behind them, horses without riders.

Oapah stood up. "Riders of Ben Hamur!"

His voice carried across the sands.

As if on Oapah's command, the outlying riders drew inward, angling their paths to him.

"If they are not truly Ben Hamurians, we are dead," said Gulana.

"Then we were already dead," said Selena.

Oapah held a pistol openly in his left hand. In his right, he grasped the handle of his two-handed scimitarus, which he alone could wield with a single, massive arm. The triple-hardened steel, forged in the hottest mountain forges of Nor Wasura, reflected the moonlight, its blade shining with beauty.

The riders came closer.

Selena could see the shields on their arms and the spears in their hands. They wore capes that billowed out behind them. She could not see the green of their clothing, for all was muted in the darkness, shaded in grey.

The riders drew closer, no more than twenty yards away.

The center rider raised his right hand.

"Walker on the sands! State your name!"

"Rider of Ben Hamur, I will have your name first."

Even over the hoofbeats of their horses, all of the men could hear Oapah's words, deep and unafraid.

The horsemen came to within several yards of Oapah.

Selena and Gulana remained awkwardly crouched, looking up at the mounted spearmen, a dozen and a half strong. Both women still gripped the handles of their pistols.

Across their chests, the riders wore cuirasses of hardened leather.

"I am Dungar Bin-Guttar, Captain of the Horseguard of Ben Hamur," said the man in the center of the line. "We ride in the name of Ayzah, Patriarch of the family Bin-Ayawad, Sharef of Ben Hamur. Now I will have your name."

Oapah stared at them, slowly scanning each man's face, his finger on the trigger of his three-barreled pistol. He looked carefully into each man's eyes. He could see no Erassian faces, no faces of Grand Vizerian Guardsmen, no faces of Kezelboj he knew. If these were assassins sent to kill them, then they had eluded the Order after years of dedicated study. The Order learned the names and faces of their enemies.

"You may call me Oapah," he said.

"And behind you?" asked Dungar Bin-Guttar.

Selena and Gulana rose.

"You may call me Gulana," said Gulana.

"And you may call the other," said Oapah, "Sendata."

"Sendata?" asked Dungar Bin-Guttar. "We were told we might find another."

"Another?" said Oapah. His hand tightened on his pistol grip. "No, it is only we three."

"A girl, we were told, a young woman of another name—a name of some fame."

"We beg forgiveness, friend. We are merely travelers," said Oapah.

"Travelers on foot, so far from the Seven Cities?"

"We are without mounts," said Oapah.

Dungar Bin-Guttar looked down at Oapah from beneath his wide-brimmed steel helmet. His eyes twinkled in the moonlight. His cheeks were round and friendly beneath eyes that darted back and forth, the kind of eyes that in a merchant and a military man alike missed little that was before them. Dungar Bin-Guttar, who had spent much of his life leading Ben Hamurian caravans, was both merchant and military man.

"You are well-armed for travelers. Are you not?" Dungar Bin-Guttar looked down at Oapah's three-barreled Demissary pistol as he spoke.

"And I know of few Omakhosians," Dungar continued, "that walk across the Sand Sea, especially those of such great size. Yes, you are known, friend, and you have said your name true; you are Oapah the Hohsa, of the Order of the Ram, the Lion, and the Serpent. And behind you, the tall woman of broad shoulders, I should be a fool if I did not recognize Gulana of Nor Gandus, the she-Lion of the same Order."

Oapah's grip remained tense on his pistol.

"Yes," said Dungar Bin-Guttar. "Two mighty Lions of the Order were tasked with bringing a lady to the oasis of Ben Hamur. The Lions and their charge set forth from the reeds of the Semissari Swamp some days ago, following the line of wells upon which you now stand. The Lions were guarding a lady, Lady Saliha of House Savanar, daughter of Sah Seg Savanar, of the ancient line of Alwaz Deem. She is now known by the name Selena."

A moment of silence ensued, as eighteen riders looked down upon the giant moonlit Omakhosian and two women, one abnormally large, one not.

"You speak true," said Selena, stepping forward. "I am the Lady Savanar."

Dungar Bin-Guttar removed his helmet, revealing a bald head beneath it. On the sides of his head, dark-brown hair hung down on both sides of his face, but he was hairless as a fresh-laid egg on top.

He slid off of the side of his saddle, landing in the sand in his leather sandals. The other riders followed the lead of Dungar Bin-Guttar.

Dungar Bin-Guttar fell to his knees and bowed forward, touching his forehead to the sands before returning to an upright position, still on his knees.

"Lady Selena," he said, rising to his feet slowly. "In the name of Ayzah Bin-Ayawad, Sharef of the Oasis, Ben Hamur stands with House Savanar. We request the privilege of escorting you."

The Erassians did not find them until they were two miles from the east gate of Ben Hamur. The horse riders came at a gallop, from the northeast, with the late-afternoon sun shining into their faces and illuminating them from the west. They moved across the sands in a series of V formations, as swift and effortless as birds flying low above the ground.

They crested the ridge like floodwaters flowing over a bank, fluid as a surging stream. Selena had seen plenty of Erassians in her years in the back alleys of Alwaz Deem. They always seemed oddly out of place on the Seven Cities, usually drunk and speaking too loudly. Many wondered why the Qhaliffa kept them around. They were intemperate, impious, and unruly.

Few of the Qhaliffa's subjects liked them. They frequented the prostitutes and the wine sinks, and a drunk Erassian in the flatlands was so common as to be a figure of speech in Alwaz Deem and Sundar Dun. Though they came from the steppes far to the north of the Seven Cities, north of the Sand Sea itself, they generally avoided the northern cities of Meer Norekah, Nor Gandus, and Nor Wasura, cities less tolerant of their preferred behaviors. They seemed to like the afternoon sun in Alwaz Deem and the heat of Sundar Dun and Ganjar en Oxus as much as their wine and their prostitutes.

But in matters of war, the Gressian Autocrat and the Qhaliffa alike relied upon the Erassians as their most trusted scouts upon desert and grassland alike.

As she watched them ride toward her, like predators toward prey, Selena could see now why that was. Were they not coming to capture her, to turn her over to the Grand Vizer so that she could be publicly tortured and burned alive, she would have called them majestic.

Attached to the edges of their round, brimless, burnt-orange caps flowed their cotton neckpieces, the long scarves they wrapped across their faces when the sun burned too hot or when the sand blew too fiercely. The scarves were orange as well, the color of Erassian hair, a color considered both beautiful in their women and terrifying in their men.

Gulana saw them first, pointing over her right shoulder in the direction of Alwaz Deem and Meer Norekah.

"Riders!"

The word struck Selena like a strap of leather against flesh.

Oapah turned in the saddle that was too small for his enormous body, his horse panting with exertion beneath him. He looked at the V formations, his mind racing. The Vs were inverted, so that the wings extended out on the flanks of each formation, like mouths opening to engulf a meal.

Oapah looked to the west. The walls of the oasis and the protection they might afford lay tantalizingly close. Dungar Bin-Guttar and his men had given them each a horse of their own—Selena, Oapah, and Gulana—leading them west and north, to within eyesight of the twelve-foot-high mudbrick walls and the thornbush zareba surrounding Ben Hamur. The zareba rose out of a dry moat, its finger-length thorns a deterrent to tribesmen who would think of scaling the Sharef's earthen ramparts.

Gulana had not seen Ben Hamur since she was a girl, traveling with a merchant caravan from Nor Gandus, but that was the thing she most remembered, the experience that transported her mind back in time: the way the zareba looked from the desert, bushy and almost welcoming, with birds landing upon the upper branches, eating the insects that burrowed into the dead-looking but still living branches of the water-deprived thorns. She looked at it now, forbidding to enemies but a great comfort to those inside of it.

There were deep pools of clean water within the guarded walls of Ben Hamur, some of the deepest of any oasis upon all of the sands, but the Ben Hamurians did not waste such a precious thing on watering their zareba. The rains came two or three times each spring, and that was enough to water the thorns down to their roots, roots that stretched ten, twenty, and even thirty feet deep into the earth. The moat captured all the rain that came down in those rare precious hours, holding it as a resting pool for one or two days a year. Then it turned to mud that sustained the thornbushes that protected the walls of Ben Hamur around the entire perimeter. Their thorns—thorns upon thorns upon thorns—numbered in the tens of millions.

Only four approaches to Ben Hamur were without thorns, one each to the north, the south, the east, and the west. There, at each of those places, a wooden, retractable bridge came down over the thorns, touching down onto the other side of the moat. Travelers and caravans and the soldiers of the Qhaliffa could only enter Ben Hamur from one of these points. But that was not how Dungar Bin-Guttar planned to send Selena Savanar past the walls of Ben Hamur.

"Ride!" said Dungar Bin-Guttar. "Ride for the east gate!"

The armed and armored horsemen of Ben Hamur kicked their heels against their mounts and rode. They could not outride the Erassians across the open desert for any significant length of time. No one could. Perhaps the swiftest Beserian tribesmen across the broken ground in high heat that was too hot for sand horses, but even then, they would struggle to escape the orange-haired riders in only two miles. The east gate was close—less than two miles—and if they galloped now, Dungar Bin-Guttar's men would have a considerable head start. They galloped.

Dungar Bin-Guttar waited until the rest of his men had begun riding before kicking his mount in the sides. He would be the last to ride for the walls and the first to turn and face the Erassians and their javelins, if it came to that.

His horse lurched forward toward Ben Hamur, the others all in front of him moving into a full gallop.

"Lions of the Order!" he shouted. "Lions of the Order, Lady Savanar, to me, to me!"

Oapah continued to gallop but turned his head back to see Dungar Bin-Guttar. Dungar had given Oapah the largest and strongest stallion in all of the Sharef's stables, and still, the horse looked small and strained underneath him, like a pony beneath a bear.

Dungar signaled that Oapah should slow down, waving his hand from side to side across his chest, his palm facing himself. It was a known signal upon the sands, whether one spoke Beserian or Qhaliffan, Macmenian, or Erassian.

"Lady Savanar!" shouted Dungar.

She turned.

He flashed the same signal.

She did not slow her mount, continuing to charge westward.

"Slow your mount!" shouted Dungar, his chain mail rattling against the hardened leather cuirass on his chest. His sword sheath bounced against his thigh.

Selena did as the Sharef's captain of the horse guard ordered her, but not without suspicion. Selena eyed Gulana, and Gulana slowed her mount as well, shadowing Selena's movements, as always. The four of them: Oapah, Selena, Gulana, and Dungar Bin-Guttar were now several horse lengths behind the others, and the gap grew by the moment.

Yes, thought Selena, looking at Dungar Bin-Guttar with worry in her eyes, they retrieved us from the sands, *but these men have not proven their loyalty beyond that.* The thoughts flew through her mind like arrows from a Demissary bow, one after the other. *I do not know this man.*

"You are not riding for the east gate!" said Dungar Bin-Guttar, shouting to be heard.

Selena glanced at Oapah and Gulana, their faces as suspicious as her own. She saw Oapah and Gulana's hands move toward the hilts of their swords. Her hand moved toward the handle of her three-barreled pistol. *If we have to flee, even due south into the sands, we shall.*

Dungar Bin-Guttar's veteran eyes registered their hand movements.

"Listen to me," he said.

They had all slowed to match his speed, which was now a mere trot.

The distance between them and the rest of the Sharef's riders grew by the moment. If it was going to be a race for the east gate, they ceded precious time to the galloping Erassians.

Selena glanced northward.

The orange of their headscarves was now brighter, bright like Erassian hair, and the riders upon the small sand horses had grown markedly larger. They closed with inhuman speed. To hear of Erassian speed was one thing, to see it was another, and to see it when they rode *at you*, was another thing still.

"We are losing time!" shouted Gulana.

"They will not make the gate in time," said Dungar Bin-Guttar.

"Then why did you send them?" shouted Selena. "And why are we slowing down?"

"We are not here to fight the Qhaliffa, and my men cannot be caught with you three in their midst. The Erassians ride to find *you*. That is but one of a dozen patrols, all at least that strong. A Demissary Legion rides this way on the heels of the orange-haired scouts. They ride from Alwaz Deem, and they ride *for* Ben Hamur."

"How do you know?" roared Oapah.

"We have spies in Alwaz Deem," said Dungar Bin-Guttar.

"So, you will leave us here! You abandon us, Captain of Ben Hamur! Is that the allegiance of your Sharef?" Gulana's words struck like whip strokes.

"Of course not! I spoke the truth when we found you! There is another way into Ben Hamur! A secret way."

"Where?" growled Oapah.

"There are tunnels, and that is the only way to keep you safe," said Dungar Bin-Guttar. "I sent my men to divert the Erassians. Now follow me if you want to live!"

Dungar Bin-Guttar did not wait for them to agree. He put his heels into his mount and his horse charged forward, heading not due west, for the east gate, but west and south.

Selena glanced at Oapah and Gulana and saw the same recognition in their eyes that was in her own.

We must follow this captain. We must trust the Sharef, Ayzah Bin-Ayawad. There is no other choice.

CHAPTER 43
For Anglia and the Three Gods

South of the Valley of Kordon
Plain of Gamurian, Western Sand Sea
January 28, 1879

Crouched behind the stacked crates, Hersen Expey aimed his LaFrentian Legonde repeater at the charging tribesmen and pulled the trigger. Black smoke belched from the barrel as the .38-caliber bullet flew toward its target.

It struck, three hundred and fifty yards away, hitting the rider squarely in the chest, knocking him off of his mount like a bird off of a perch.

"One down," said the LaFrentian, ejecting the spent casing with the rifle's underlever, snapping a new brass cartridge into the chamber. His voice and movements were calm and steady, every bit those of a veteran legionnaire. With the exception of Hak-Hakkan, he had seen combat across all of the continents. He had fought in half of a dozen firefights before his twenty-third birthday and dozens more after that.

Peter crouched next to him, gripping his loaded Hart-Henry rifle, looking out at the oncoming Beserians. Several months before his twenty-third birthday, he had never killed anything more than a bird. His father loved to hunt and thought it imperative that Peter loved it too.

"Peter, a man makes his real friends with a gun in his hands, moving across open ground. Those are the bonds that endure, the ones that count." Lord Harmon had given Peter variations of that speech too many times to count over the years.

And so, Peter had gone along, walking through the mud, carrying his loaded shotgun, preparing to kill innocent fowl—birds he would have preferred to leave alone, or better yet, watch living their lives in peace. Birds, in Peter Harmon's mind, were beautiful, intelligent animals.

He had grudgingly killed ducks, pheasant, and doves over the years, but he disliked it. He took no pleasure in watching them fall. He hated the way they looked in the dogs' mouths, bloody and mutilated because of him. In recent years, he had found ways to avoid hunting trips. He contracted the flu and other debilitating ailments more than anyone else in the Harmon family during the hunting season.

Indeed, it was among his favorite times of the year, because that was when he could read in peace. For hours, he could sip his tea until the pot itself grew cold, reading across all subjects and eras with no one to interrupt his numerous trains of thought.

Even most of the servants were gone during those hunting weeks, and those who remained did not reveal Peter's fake illnesses. The servants of Hylebourne House loved Peter Harmon. They always had.

A spattering of bullets struck the wall of crates, splintering the wood and keeping the defenders low and hidden behind it. At Sergeant Joshua Barnes and Mrs. Matilda Smith's insistence, when they first made the camp, the porters added sand to fill in all of the gaps inside the wooden boxes. The porters had complained that this would require emptying the crates and repacking them before reloading them onto the camels. Barnes and Mrs. Smith had insisted nonetheless.

Barnes had looked at Diego and the porters under his command and said, "Even full crates allow bullets to pass through them. Crates filled with sand do not. Fill them."

The porters obeyed, and all were grateful for the precaution now.

The porters now crouched like Spatanian sardines in a freshly opened tin, chest to back behind the redoubt. Every crate in the enclosure was filled to the brim with sand. Before she allowed them to be stacked, Mrs. Smith had personally checked each one. When she was a girl, a daughter of a traveling deacon of the New Church of the Three Gods, her people had survived more than once because they built sturdy redoubts in their desert camps, and Matilda Smith was not one to forget the most firmly ingrained lessons of her youth.

The tribesmen came closer. Bearded, dark-faced men atop tall camels, they fired their long rifles as they rode. Even on the move, they shot well enough to strike the outer wood of the crates. Gripping his rifle, Peter wondered what they would have done if the sand-filled barricade did not lie between them and the Beserian bullets.

Hannah held her own rifle, the Mancaster repeater from Calderon, the same one she had used to shoot the rattlesnake on Mount Agabanzo. She crouched next to Mrs. Smith, her heart thundering. She had killed many animals, loved shooting, and did it well. But she had never before fired a rifle when being fired upon.

"Stay down," said Mrs. Smith, clutching an old model Anglian Army Hart-Harold carbine—one of the very rifles they had intended to trade to the men now attacking them.

"They need me shooting," said Hannah.

"Stay down," commanded Mrs. Smith. Her tone left no room for negotiation.

Sergeant Joshua Barnes crouched on the other side of Mrs. Smith. He looked out at the charging tribesmen, his eyes just above the upper edge of the crates.

Hannah watched him, seeing that he did not duck down even as the bullets slammed into the barricade. He carried a Mancaster, just like Hannah's, but several models older. Hers was a '78. He carried a '75. It had the same mechanisms and effectiveness but without the shiny newness of Hannah's weapon.

Unlike the new Hart-Henrys and older Hart-Harolds of the Anglians, the Mancaster was a repeater of New Anglian make, with one barrel on top of the other. The bottom barrel was not a gun barrel at all, but rather a storage tube with a spring loader, holding fourteen rounds, each of which could be pulled up into the chamber by means of the underlever. When the underlever was jammed forward, the rifle ejected the spent casing. When the shooter pulled the lever back beneath the trigger, it loaded the new cartridge. Barnes had loaded one final round into the chamber, giving him fifteen shots before he had to reload.

The Mancaster did not have the range or the stopping power of the new Hart-Henrys, or even the Hart-Harolds, and loading the undertube took time. Nor were its rounds as long as the Anglian cartridge, reducing both accuracy and power, but at short and medium ranges, no rifle could match the speed of a Mancaster repeater.

Barnes watched the charging riders. His body tensed.

Hannah watched him. *Why is he not shooting?*

She looked at Hersen and Stanwich. Both were loading and firing at the charging riders, still several hundred yards away—Stanwich with a single-shot Hart-Henry, Hersen with his Legonde. The Vetenan porters did the same, quickly shooting their Hart-Harolds before dipping back down behind the crates.

Hannah crept her head up, looking at the riders. Few were falling from their mounts, but they charged closer with each passing ten seconds, growing larger in her view, more vivid in detail and colors. The dark, indistinct objects in the distance began to separate as rider and mount. Faces became visible beneath dark headscarves. The glinting flashes in the morning sunlight revealed themselves as drawn sabers, long and frightening.

"Now!" said Barnes, leaning forward, extending his repeater's barrel out over the crate line. He gave himself room to fire and reload but kept as little of himself exposed as possible.

He fired his first shot followed by his second and then his third in rapid succession.

The underlever of the Mancaster rifle slammed forward and snapped back into place after each shot with Barnes never taking his aim off of the riders.

Mrs. Smith forced Hannah back down below the crates. She could not see what effect Barnes's shots were having, but his rifle smoke wafted down in front of her.

Ignoring her own advice, Mrs. Smith popped up, fired a shot from her Hart-Harold, and dropped back down just as swiftly to reload. The smoke from the Hart-Harold was different from Barnes's Mancaster, stronger, thicker, and more acrid, stinging Hannah's eyes.

Barnes remained in his firing position, leaning forward against the crates. He fired again, shooting and working his repeater's underlever, again, again, and again. With each shot, the underlever moved forward with a click and then backward with a snap. More smoke belched with each barrel flash, deafening Hannah's already ringing ears.

Still hiding behind the crates, Hannah clutched her shiny Mancaster against her chest.

Mrs. Smith looked into Hannah's face as she reloaded her Hart-Harold, pulling the .45-caliber cartridge from her ammunition pouch, jamming it into the breech. She breathed heavily, like she'd just run up a hill.

"Stay *down*," Mrs. Smith shouted again, her eyes bulging.

Mrs. Smith rose with her rifle. In a fluid motion, she lowered her stock onto the crates, her head and shoulders just above the edge. Despite the hail of tribesmen's bullets now crashing into the outer edge of the crates, she did not flinch or jerk her body.

Hannah ducked down further as bullets tore through the air overhead.

Mrs. Smith fired, her rifle smoke wafting back down into the redoubt, into Hannah's face and hair. Hannah coughed. Mrs. Smith dropped back down next to Hannah. Another Beserian volley struck the redoubt, ripping through the flimsy crate wood and lodging into the impenetrable sand within, louder than a hundred ax-heads felling trees.

Barnes fired out another trio of shots from his Mancaster, swiftly, but unhurried with each shot.

"There are many," he said, dropping down again. Even he had begun to breathe harder in the desert heat and in the excitement of the firefight. His voice was loud but calm.

Mrs. Smith raised her head above the crate line to look at the oncoming tribesmen.

Hannah felt the anxiety rising inside of her, like water rumbling to a boil. *I can shoot, by the Three Gods. I am not going to sit here!*

While Mrs. Smith still looked northward, over the crate, Hannah rose from her hidden position, aiming her barrel over the edge. She had fifteen rounds in her

Mancaster too, a repeater she had fired countless times in the year since it arrived via mail coach to the Huntington Property in South Calderon. It had been packed in a long wooden box full of sawdust and covered by sturdy brown paper. When she opened it herself, unscrewing the bolts on the box, the smell of well-oiled metal had greeted her. The only scent filling her nose now was burning black powder.

She looked out into the desert through her rifle sights, her right eye just behind the breech, her rifle's butt securely nestled against her right shoulder. She did not have far to look, seeing and fearing that the closest tribesmen had come far closer than her rifle was sighted. The riders galloped toward her, appearing gigantic on their tall camels like they were made of one flesh, ten feet tall. Some waved sabers, others waved rifles, and all came on fast, fearless, and fearsome, shouting their war cry.

"Akhsa! Akhsa! Akhsa!"

Hannah put a rider in her sights, no differently than if he were a buck in the hills beneath Mount Agabanzo. Through her sights, she saw the rider's face. He was young, barely bearded, beneath a dark headscarf. In his right hand, he held a long thin saber, glittering in the clear morning sunlight. She aimed at his chest.

She fired. He kept charging.

"Three Gods, Hannah!" she barked, cursing herself.

She ripped the underlever forward. The casing ejected skyward. She snapped it back into place beneath the trigger. The new round loaded. She exhaled and placed the man in her gunsights again. *Calm yourself. Shoot the buck.*

She pulled the trigger.

The .44-caliber bullet struck his shoulder, the opposite of the one carrying the saber. The man staggered, his face contorting. His saber in the other hand dropped. He nonetheless kept his mount, still riding forward.

Hannah worked her underlever, reloading. She aimed and fired.

Her bullet found his chest. He fell straight back, tumbling out of his saddle, landing in the sand behind his running camel.

Hannah reloaded and drew another galloping tribesman into her sights. His whole face was covered. She could not see whether he was young or old, bearded or shaven.

She fired, aiming low. He fell.

She ejected the casing, keeping her eyes forward, seeking another target. Forty men rode straight at the redoubt, straight at her. The exhilaration of shooting down her enemies pulled away, and she felt a wave of fear rise within her.

"Hannah!" shouted Mrs. Smith, pulling her down by her shoulder.

"Let her shoot, Matilda!" ordered Barnes. He was crouched low himself, painstakingly reloading brass cartridges into the undertube of his Mancaster, with steady, veteran's hands.

Mrs. Smith looked at Barnes.

"Shoot!" he shouted.

Mrs. Smith obeyed, aiming her single-shot Hart-Harold, working her underlever like a soldier. She pulled a cartridge from her ammunition pouch, slid it into the breech, and fired again.

Peter looked across the redoubt. Hannah fired and reloaded while he still crouched low, hiding behind the crates, wincing as more Beserian bullets struck. A wave of unmanliness washed over him. Despite holding one of the new army-issue Hart-Henrys, he aimed poorly, hurrying his shots so that he could duck down more quickly. He had not, in his reckoning, yet struck a single tribesman, though he had fired nearly ten rushed rounds in their direction. He could feel his barrel growing hot above his hands.

This is no time for wavering. By the Three Gods, be a man!

Watching Hannah, the thoughts steeled Peter's mind as he ejected the spent shell from his Hart-Henry and loaded a new cartridge. He rose and aimed his rifle over the edge of the crates.

The Beserians were close. He could see their eyes above the cloth wrapped around their mouths and covering their noses. He pointed his barrel at a rider in a dark blue tunic, placing the man in his sights. The man's headscarf flowed behind him like a banner as he thundered forward, riding just in front of the camel's hump.

The man shouted a chant along with the others. What first came up like a buzz, the sound of an angry beehive, had now separated into individual words in his ears.

"Akhsa! Akhsa! Akhsa!"

Peter's vision narrowed into the patch of cloth on the man's chest in line with the Hart-Henry's iron sights. He fired.

The bullet crashed into the man's chest, throwing him from his mount.

The tribesmen's bullets had stopped coming. Peter reloaded. He aimed at a man no more than thirty yards away. The man carried a long rifle in one hand and a saber in the other. His camel beneath him galloped forward, headed straight for the redoubt.

Peter fired again. The .45-caliber bullet hit the camel, splashing crimson as it struck the skull. The camel made several more staggering steps, falling forward to its death, spilling its rider onto the sand.

"Why have they stopped shooting?" shouted Peter, half-deaf from rifle fire.

Stanwich crouched next to him. "Single-shot muzzleloaders! They can't charge and reload from camelback!"

Peter nodded, feeling his confidence grow. He slid a new round into the breech and crept up. He had spent much of his life shooting, even if he did not care for it, and even without the shotgun's cone, men on camels did not fly, and they were much larger than birds.

He shot another man dead. His ears rang, and the smell of black powder crowded out all other scents—even the sweat and body odors of the men crouched all around him behind the crates.

The riders began to move away from the redoubt.

"Look!" said Peter. "They are fleeing!"

A wave of exuberance flowed through him—adrenaline mixed with triumph.

"No," said Hersen. "They ride for our camels!"

The redoubt was just large enough for all of the people. It was not large enough for the animals that had been grazing on patches of sand grass when the attack began. At the sound of the shooting, the expedition's camels had spooked, running away, southward and east, in the direction of Altadige, the direction from which they had come.

To make a redoubt large enough to hold the camels would have taken four times the work. With little support from Stanwich or Hersen, Barnes and Mrs. Smith had to argue sternly to get the fortification built large enough for the humans alone.

They all now saw the folly in that decision.

A knot of fifteen camels huddled together, watching the battle, perhaps seventy yards from the redoubt. Fifteen camels could be the difference between life and death, the difference between transporting the rifle-crates and not. Peter saw this clearly as he watched the Beserian tribesmen ride toward the expedition's remaining camels through the gun smoke.

Two dozen Beserians now rode for them, turning to the west, away from the withering gunfire from behind the crates.

"We cannot lose the camels!" shouted Peter, pointing. "Look!"

First Hersen looked and then Stanwich.

"They are going to take them!" shouted Peter again. The thought of being marooned upon the sands without their camels suddenly gripped him with greater fear than his fear of the tribesmen.

Hersen saw that they would not shoot enough of the Beserians to save their animals. They were already fanning out to avoid the gunfire, moving away and laterally at the same time.

The porters' Hart-Harolds still blazed from behind the crates, but the Beserians no longer fell from their saddles.

"We must stop them!" Peter shouted, feeling suddenly bold.

Hersen looked at him, weighing the Anglian's mettle. Hersen thought little of Peter Harmon, but he had learned in his years with the LaFrentian Legion not to doubt the courage of Anglians under fire, however unmartial they might appear before the shooting began. He had seen Anglians he considered even less manly than Peter Harmon fight like Gengali tigers when bullets began to fly.

"He's right," said Stanwich. "Hersen, you come with me." He withdrew the revolver from his chest holster. "Sergeant Barnes! We are running for the camels!" Stanwich carried a rifle in his right hand and pointed with the revolver in his left hand toward the camels.

Before nodding in acknowledgment, Barnes was already rising. Mrs. Smith rose with him.

"No! No! Women stay in the redoubt," shouted Stanwich.

A half-dozen porters still fired their Hart-Harold rifles over the crates at the Beserians.

"Bring them! Those three!" shouted Stanwich, pointing at the porters with his empty rifle. Diego, the Vetenan foreman, was among them.

Barnes ordered them to follow him.

Stanwich leaped over the crate wall first, running toward the camels at an angle to cut off the galloping tribesmen.

Peter ran second, clutching his Hart-Henry. He did not have time to load it, nor did he have a revolver.

Hersen ran after Peter, holding a pair of revolvers. Neither Hersen nor Stanwich fired as they ran.

A pair of tribesmen saw them running outside of the redoubt. Peter watched them confer with a word and a signal.

The riders seamlessly changed direction, breaking off to charge at Stanwich, Peter, and the others running behind them. The Beserian sabers, which seemed to pose little threat when Peter was behind the redoubt, suddenly loomed large in his mind. They were the kind of swords with which a man on a camel could behead a man on foot—curved, thin, and long.

Another camelman turned and followed the first. Then another followed, and another, then another two, then three more.

"Firing line!" thundered Sergeant Barnes. "Firing line, now!"

Stanwich stopped.

Hersen looked at Barnes with respect in his eyes, one hardened veteran at another. Hersen knelt, holding one pistol at his hip. The other he aimed with his right hand, training it upon the nearest rider.

Stanwich dropped his unloaded rifle, gripping his revolver with both hands—his right on the trigger, and his left cupping the bottom of the pistol's handle.

Sergeant Barnes dropped to a knee in the sand, aiming his Mancaster repeater.

Peter dropped to a knee next to him, flanked by Diego on his other side. Peter reached a shaky hand into his ammunition pouch, feeling naked and exposed outside the redoubt.

The galloping tribesmen charged down upon them, their sabers waving in the air.

"Breathe," said Barnes, seeing Peter's nervousness, his voice sharp. He drew in a deep breath himself for Peter to imitate. "Do it now."

Peter obeyed, inhaling and exhaling.

"Now load your rifle and aim low! Shoot the animal, not the man."

"Yes, Sergeant," said Peter, looking at Barnes, drawing strength from his calm, feeling less afraid in proximity to the New Anglian's fearlessness.

"Ready!" shouted Barnes. The others in the line lifted their weapons to match Hersen and Stanwich, readying the volley.

Peter moved the round in his fingers to the breech of his Hart-Henry. His hand still shook, tapping the sides of the breech with the tip of the round. He exhaled, hearing Barnes's words in his mind, *shoot the animal, not the man.* He found the center of the breech and pushed the cartridge inside.

The horsemen closed to twenty-five yards, atop camels running at nearly full speed.

"Aim!" shouted Barnes. Peter's heart pounded.

The tall Beserians camels churned the sand, towering over the kneeling men, now only fifteen yards away. The ground shook.

"Akhsa! Akhsa!"

"Fire!"

The single-file line of kneeling men fired as one, at nearly point-blank range. The sound deafened Peter as the barrels spewed their black smoke in unison.

Peter's rifle recoiled powerfully into his shoulder. The bullet erupted from the barrel, clean and true, straight into the breast of the camel thundering down upon him. The .45-caliber bullet, fired from the long barrel, backed by the power of the Hart-Henry cartridge, dropped the beast and the rider on top of it, stopping them as surely as a wall of Anglian brick.

A puff of wind moved the cloud of gun smoke in front of them. All of the tribesmen that had charged them were down. Some writhed on the ground, crying out in pain.

Stanwich's and Hersen's pistols fired again, silencing them.

Two of the camels still moved, lying on their sides and moaning piteously.

Another three dozen riders still rode away from them, toward the expedition's camels.

A volley of rifle fire cracked in the distance, the sound of neither Hart-Harolds nor Mancasters. A bullet slammed into Peter's pith helmet, ripping it from his head.

"Three Gods!" he shouted, diving down, smacking his face against the sand. His rifle, held with two hands out in front of him, barely broke his fall. He looked to his left and saw two of the porters on the ground. One of them, the porter closest to him, a Vetenan named Gumez, stared back at him with unblinking eyes.

"Gumez, are you hit?" asked Peter, shouting over the ringing in his ears.

Gumez did not respond. The man's eyes were wide open but blank without life behind them. Peter crawled to him.

Another volley sounded in the distance, tearing the air above Peter's head. A bullet struck a foot in front of his face, kicking up sand into his eyes, pelting his cheeks. Peter blinked in time, saving his eyes. Pain called out from his face, as if he had just been stung by a wasp. His eyes watered.

"Stay down!" shouted a voice behind him. Peter looked at Sergeant Barnes. Barnes was prone, with his rifle in front of him, propped up on his elbows. He fired his Mancaster, reloaded, and fired again.

"There are more gunmen on that ridge!"

More bullets struck the ground around them, ricocheting and spraying sand. Barnes fired another pair of rapid shots.

"They are making for the camels!" shouted Hersen Expey, his LaFrentian accent stronger in the intensity of the firefight. He knelt and fired a shot from the pistol in his left hand.

"Come on!" shouted Stanwich, running toward the camels with his revolver and his unloaded Hart-Henry. The camels were close, less than fifty yards away.

Stanwich ran in a crouch as more Beserian bullets ripped past him and peppered the ground around him. Peter lay on his stomach, covering his bare head with his hands, his face still stinging. He looked up and saw Stanwich and Hersen sprinting for the camels, bullets striking the ground in front of them and behind them.

They need my help.

A vision of the duke's face—the face of John Fitzroy Harmon—suddenly flashed across his mind.

Be a Harmon.

Peter pushed himself up from the sand and ran toward the camels. He expected a Beserian bullet to strike him. He did not know what it would be like. He knew the pain would be terrible and that the desert was a bad place to carry a gunshot wound, but he kept running as fast as he could, sprinting with his head ducked, keeping his eyes upon Hersen Expey's back in front of him.

"Three Gods, man!" shouted Barnes behind him.

Peter heard one final Mancaster shot. He did not know whether Barnes was behind him or still shooting from his spot on the ground. Someone still fired a Hart-Harold from the ground, and shots still sounded from the direction of the crate redoubt.

Running on foot, Stanwich reached the camels at the same time as the first galloping tribesman. Stanwich dropped to a knee and fired a revolver shot into the man's chest. He fell. Stanwich did not hesitate, pulling the hammer back again with his thumb as soon as he fired. He stayed low enough that the tribesmen would have to nearly hang off of their camels to strike him with their sabers. Stanwich unloaded another pistol shot. Another tribesman fell.

Hersen fired his pistols, one after the other, until his revolvers clicked empty.

Two more tribesmen galloped at them. One of them tried to swing down at Stanwich from his saddle. His saber sliced the air, grazing the top of Stanwich's helmet and carving a piece out of the light pith. The other launched out of his saddle, landing on the sand next to Stanwich.

Before Stanwich could fully spin around to aim his revolver at the man, the man's sword had already swung. The sharp saber blade struck Stanwich's pistol hand, sending the revolver down into the dirt.

Stanwich gasped in pain.

The man who struck Stanwich backed away, seeing Hersen Expey running at him. Their eyes locked as he retreated from the legionnaire.

A second tribesman ran for Stanwich.

Before he could swing his blade, Hersen Expey had already pulled the dagger from his belt and buried it into the tribesman's belly. He yanked the blade out, turning toward Peter with fierce eyes beneath his LaFrentian Legionnaire's cap. The bloodstained knife was still in his hand.

Hersen stood over Stanwich as the next tribesman charged. The man's saber was at least three times longer than Hersen's knife. The man was lean and spare, like the others, with dark, almost black hair beneath a dark headscarf above a dark tunic over dark brown skin, baked by the sun of the Sand Sea.

The tribesman ran at Hersen, screaming the same war cry as the others, "Akhsa! Akhsa!" His dark eyes showed no fear of the larger LaFrentian in the red-and-blue cap.

Hersen dropped his knife and stepped forward, picking up Stanwich's Hart-Henry rifle in both of his hands, one behind the trigger, one far down the stock.

The tribesman swung his saber in a vicious downward slash.

Hersen's rifle stock caught the blade near its midpoint. Hersen swung his rifle butt at the man's knees, ducking as he did so. The wood struck bone, and the man cried out, missing Hersen with his next slash.

Peter's decision lasted a fraction of a second, but he would later recognize it as a moment that changed his life. He held his Hart-Henry in his hands, the barrel still burning hot. The tribesmen surged toward the camels, a dozen and a half strong, every one of them armed with a rifle, a saber, and a curved killing-dagger in their belt. Another tribesman jumped down and slashed at Hersen and Stanwich.

Stanwich backed up, holding his mutilated hand with no weapon to face his foe.

Peter Harmon raced forward and shouted.

"For Anglia! And the Three Gods!"

He did not mean to say them, but the words came anyway, drawn from some place deep within him. Peter ran to Stanwich and flipped his rifle upside down, gripping the long stock with both of his hands. The barrel burned his palms like a stove-heated pan, but his adrenaline kept both of his hands firmly on the rifle, swinging it like a club. He was taller than all of the Beserians, and in his long arms, the Hart-Henry was like a poleax.

He swung the rifle wildly, making a pair of tribesmen back up. There was no mirth in their eyes, only wariness of the tall, shouting Anglian moving at them, swinging his rifle butt back and forth.

Another pair of tribesmen rushed at him.

Peter swung at them. These two were not as easily cowed. The first man stepped forward and parried Peter's rifle swing, the blade of his saber colliding with the barrel of Peter's Hart-Henry with a tremendous crash.

The other man slashed, and Peter jumped backward to avoid the blow, nearly losing his feet. The first man pressed forward.

Gunfire erupted behind Peter's head, and the man in front of him dropped. Tribesmen were now all around them, jumping off of their camels and running toward them with blades in hand. The expedition's frightened camels were still off to Peter's left. Less than a dozen remained, moaning in fear, huddling together and backing away.

More gunshots rang out behind him. More tribesmen fell.

Peter saw Stanwich down below him, on his hands and knees, reaching for his fallen revolver with his free, unmangled right hand. Stanwich grabbed the pistol and fired a shot at a charging swordsman. The swordsman fell, landing on the ground at Stanwich's knees. Another swordsman charged him. Stanwich pulled the trigger of the revolver at nearly point-blank range. The hammer landed, but nothing fired. The pistol was empty.

Peter leaped forward, striking the man in the side with his rifle butt, and shouting as he did so. "Aaaaaah!"

The man recoiled and grunted, battered by Peter's blow, but still standing and still holding his saber. Peter dropped his rifle and tackled the man, chest to chest, as the man tried to swing his sword.

They landed roughly, slamming against each other on the hard-packed sands beneath them. Peter landed on top of the man with his full weight. In an instant, Peter looked down into his face, which was very brown from the sun. The man was young, likely younger than Peter, with wide, almond-shaped, yellow-brown eyes in a strangely shaped face, as if an Anglian fox had been made into a human. It was the man that had slashed Stanwich's hand.

Other than as a boy, Peter had never before struck the face of another in anger. He made a fist and slammed it down into the man's face. The man twisted, causing Peter to strike his ear.

The man grabbed his left hand before Peter could recoil it and bit down like a wild animal, catching the smallest finger in his teeth. The man bit down with all of his strength, twisting his head as he did so. Peter recoiled in pain and terror, releasing him. Peter fell back onto his haunches, staring at the stump that remained of his finger. All that was above the first knuckle was gone, bitten off by the fox-faced Beserian.

The Beserian rolled and ran.

Peter looked up at the man's back in astonishment and shock, knowing instinctively that the pain he felt now was only the beginning.

The man ran away as fast as his legs would carry him. The others who had dismounted their camels to attack were all now fleeing. Peter heard a barrage of rapid shots from Mancaster repeaters. He looked over his left shoulder.

Sergeant Barnes, Mrs. Smith, and Hannah Huntington advanced, firing as they walked. Hannah's hair had loosened during the firefight, thick and golden, like an avenging angel's.

Peter looked and saw that all of the camels were gone. The Beserians, those that were not lying dead on the ground, were mounted and withdrawing. Peter saw a rider stop and pick up a wounded man in the direction of the redoubt before galloping off to join the others, riding north toward the Valley of Kordon.

Peter looked at Stanwich, the explorer's hand a mangled mess. The saber had removed the better part of three fingers. Their eyes met. Peter could see the distress in Stanwich's face. He looked down at his own half-missing finger.

The pain was incredible.

CHAPTER 44
The Staff of the Serpent

The Valley of Kordon
Beserian Tribal Lands, Sand Sea
30th Day, Month of Gandus, 807
Anglian Calendar: January 30, 1879

No one spoke to Jack as they rode toward the camp.

But to call it a camp was an understatement verging on falsehood. It was an ocean of tents, a sea of livestock, an entire people assembled.

Jack was well enough to ride. They had waited long enough for that. The poison wore off more quickly than he thought it would. When he first awoke, he felt as if he would never walk again. The next day, he could walk, but felt as if he could never ride. Two days after that, he was mounted on the back of a camel, headed east and north, toward the Valley of Kordon beneath a sky-blue banner snapping in a northerly wind.

Two dozen Swordguard riders accompanied him, Demassi, and Anil. Each Swordguard rider represented a different tribe, and each had sworn allegiance to Abu Akhsa personally. They rode swiftly, in the manner of men delivering an urgent message, or in the way of men fleeing danger. To Jack, who could speak with none of them, the speed of their ride felt like both fleeing and pursuing at the same time. Aurelio Demassi, the only man with whom he could speak, rode at his side.

"Behold," said Aurelio Demassi, "the glory of the Year of the Prophecy." Aurelio threw his arm outward as if to embrace all that spread out before them.

Jack stared in awe.

In his lifetime, he had never seen so many people or so many animals in one place. He had seen vast herds in the western grasslands of the New Anglian Republic, and he had seen the great cities, spread out across the land, with their populations in the hundreds of thousands, but he had never seen anything like this. The Beserians covered the earth from east to west, from the north to perhaps a mile or so ahead of them, which was the southern border of the camp. The camp stretched all of the way to the horizon on the northern sky, which was cloudless, clean, clear, and blue, nearly the color of Abu Akhsa's banners.

Aurelio continued, "They are all here assembled. Never in the generations has there been such a gathering of the tribes: Azadeems and Bazadaks, Celadeens and Kateems, Hazims and Hazaks, Sambads and Salesis, and thirty lesser tribes. They come from as far north as the Gressian borderlands, from as far south as the Harafhan Mountains, and from as far east as the banks of the River Oxus. These are the Beserians of the western Sand Sea."

Jack said nothing, shifting his weight on his camel saddle. It did not matter what he did. He could not make himself comfortable. Riding a camel was not like riding a horse, and the tightness in his shoulders and his back would not leave him. Yet, the men around him rode as easily as if they were sitting in carriages on a Sunday morning jaunt through the park.

"They wait for *you*," said Aurelio. "They all wait for you."

Jack shook his head.

He felt the urge to turn his camel and ride away, but he continued forward. He had nowhere to go, and anywhere he rode, any one of the two dozen men around him could ride him down. They rode comfortably, swiftly, without effort, as men who had ridden camels upon the sands since they were small boys. Their camels were like parts of their own bodies.

"You speak madness, Demassi."

"You speak from ignorance, Amahdi," said Aurelio. Aurelio had begun calling him Amahdi since they had started the ride north to the Valley of Kordon. It was the name of the promised one, the man who would arrive from the west in the Year of the Prophecy.

"You speak of ignorance," said Jack, speaking in Spatanian. "I was born in Calderon. I do not believe in your God. I believe in Three Gods, like others of my kind."

"Your hiding from the truth shall make your conversion to the God of the Sands all the greater," said Aurelio.

Anil rode behind them, watching them. Jack glanced back at him and saw that he held the same look that seemed to always be upon his face, a look of stern disapproval. Jack had the feeling that Anil hated him every time their eyes locked. The others looked at him warily, but Anil's gaze was different, more intense, more smoldering.

Anil's brother rode ahead of them.

He was a larger, more handsome version of Anil. He was called Kaleem Salesi, the eldest son of Hamid Salesi, who, according to Aurelio Demassi, was among the richest men in all of the Beserian tribes. Hamid Salesi was Chief

Elder of the council that advised Abu Akhsa on matters of tribal leadership. He had three wives, which was the most allowed by Beserian tribal law. From those wives, he had eight children, two of which were sons. Kaleem Salesi was the eldest child of the first wife. Anil was the only child by his second wife.

Kaleem rode with a straight back, lean as a spear but as sharp and as hard too. Behind him, another black-bearded Beserian rode carrying a long staff, the bottom of which was jammed into a leather sleeve attached to his camel's saddle. From the top of the staff, Abu Akhsa's sky-blue banner blew backward toward the south.

They rode closer to the camp.

Jack could now see the sentries. They were men on foot a full mile south of the camp. They sat on the edge of a low ridgeline with rifles slung across their arms. Their kind of rifle was not broad and powerful like the Hart-Henry or the Hart-Harold; they were long and lean, almost delicate in their proportions.

"Do not be deceived," said Aurelio Demassi, as if reading Jack's mind. "Any one of those men could drop you from your saddle with those rifles. At this range, none of them would miss."

Jack looked ahead, not believing Aurelio. If a man was crazy enough to believe that he, Jack Caldwell of Calderon, was the Amahdi of the Year of the Prophecy, then he was mad enough to believe that a tribesman could shoot him from a quarter-mile away with a rifle that looked like he could break over his knee, barrel and all.

"That is some range," said Jack, with mockery in his tone. He spoke Spatanian well enough to be sarcastic.

"That is nothing for tribesmen. These are Beserian marksmen, Amahdi, and they could kill at twice this distance, even farther."

"I don't know a man who could do that with a modern rifle," said Jack.

"There are many things you do not know," said Aurelio.

They rode on.

In time, Jack could see the faces of the sentries. They were not looking up and down the column. They stared. They stared at him, looking at his face as if trying to solve a riddle.

There was a rumble from the direction of the camp as if a raucous dance had begun at midday. It grew louder, like the sound of thousands of voices at once as Jack had heard at the horse races on the track of Port Calderon. The voices grew louder still. Even the sentries ahead of them broke their stare and were glanced backward toward the camp.

Aurelio seemed to tense.

"What is it?" asked Jack.

"He is coming."

"Who?"

"Abu Akhsa. They chant his name."

And then Jack heard that there was a contour to the roar. "Akh-sa, Akh-sa, Akh-sa!"

The roar rose higher.

From the center of the tents ahead of them, Jack could see a wide aisle jammed with men, women, and children of the tribes, all craning their necks and shifting to see a mounted group of men that was moving toward them through the central aisle of tents.

"Akh-sa! Akh-sa!"

Slowly, the mounted body of thirty or so riders made its way through the crowd. The same sky-blue banner that snapped in the wind above their own small column of twenty was stretched out above the other riders with Abu Akh-sa. Except that above Abu Akhsa's column were three banners, each tugging on the flagstaffs and reaching toward the east, blown by a westerly wind.

"Behold the west wind," said Aurelio, smiling as if beholding something majestic. The winds had just shifted. The winds had been northerly, sending the banner above them backward, toward the south, until this moment, when the flag turned nearly ninety degrees, roughly due east, like a beacon toward the Great Mountain.

"The west wind delivers you. It is written," said Aurelio. His eyes were wide with wonder and belief.

Aurelio, Jack, and their companions continued northward to the camp, slowing their canter to a trot with straight-backed, black-bearded, handsome Kaleem Salesi at the lead.

The riders from the camp continued south, having advanced nearly through the vast assembled mass that had flocked around them.

Jack looked forward, seeing that the riders did not force their way through the crowds with any violence or impatience. The man at the center seemed to pause and look downward, into the faces of all who came in his way. He was mounted upon a horse, not a camel, and his horse seemed to gingerly step forward, making sure not to step upon any of the children massed around the horse's hooves.

Aurelio seemed to grow more nervous, his face and his posture both stiffening.

"This is him, Abu Akhsa?" asked Jack, looking ahead to size him up.

Aurelio nodded.

"Will you translate for me?"

"Yes," said Aurelio, "but, you should not speak unless spoken to."

"Is that written too?" asked Jack, smirking to fight his nervousness, his Spatanian words caked in sarcasm.

Aurelio did not answer. His eyes lay upon Abu Akhsa and the riders around him.

Abu Akhsa and his retinue continued to move south, coming ever closer.

Jack continued moving north with Anil Salesi behind him, the Vetenan Aurelio Demassi at his side, and Kaleem Salesi in front of him.

"Halt!" ordered Kaleem.

The column stopped.

"Dismount!"

The men began to dismount from their camels. Before Jack was out of his saddle, struggling to get his camel to kneel, the others were already standing upon the ground, their camels kneeling at their sides.

"Dismount!" said Aurelio, looking up at Jack.

Jack was still clumsy on a camel. He swung his leg awkwardly over the camel's hump, his foot catching in the saddle. His momentum carried him over the side, and he fell, landing on his chest on the hard-packed earth beneath him.

He rolled onto his back, unable to breathe, gripping his diaphragm.

Aurelio looked down at Jack and then looked up at Abu Akhsa. He, the Chief of Chiefs, had seen Jack fall, as had all of the riders with him—the Council of the Elders and their leading war fighters, the men who rose to take authority, by the vote of the Council, when war came upon the tribes.

Aurelio looked and saw, in the front row of riders next to Abu Akhsa, Handsome Habeen Barcadey, with his diagonal saber scar across the left side of his face and Bazak Bazadak, broad, dark, and bulging with thick muscles from his calves to his shoulders. These were legendary men amongst the tribes, riding out to meet the man Aurelio Demassi, the Vetenan convert, claimed was the Promised One of the west—the Promised One who had just fallen on his face off of a resting camel.

"Get up, Jack," said Aurelio Demassi. Fear and urgency laced his voice. He was painfully aware that he had staked his reputation upon his faith that Jack Caldwell was indeed who he, Aurelio Demassi, believed he was.

Jack was too frantic to pull air back into his lungs above his spasming diaphragm to notice that Demassi had not called him Amahdi.

"Get up," said Demassi, with greater panic. He was speaking Spatanian, a language the Beserians considered the tongue of crass unbelievers, and thus few understood. Few found it worthwhile to learn such a tongue, despite their ancestors living adjacent to the Spatanian frontier for the better part of eight hundred years. Most learned some Macmenian, the language of the men who took the caravans along the sands, not only because it was profitable but because at least they too believed in a single God, the God of the Mountain and the Sands.

But the Westerners—the Spatanians, the LaFrentians, the Gerdic peoples, the Anglians—they all followed some variation of the Three Gods. Beserian riders of the sands and the followers of the Qhaliffa alike held such beliefs to be anathema, false, and barbaric.

"I told you, Demassi, but you did not listen," said a voice from behind him. Aurelio turned.

Anil Salesi said the words, his face pinched with contempt. Jack could not understand Anil's Beserian, but Aurelio understood every syllable.

"Have faith, Anil Salesi," said Aurelio, forcing a calm he did not feel.

"I have eyes," said Anil. "I do not see the Promised One, and neither do they."

Anil Salesi gestured toward Abu Akhsa and his cohort, pointing with his chin. He looked at them intently, seeing his silver-bearded father, Hamid Salesi, riding at Abu Akhsa's right hand, as always. In his hands, he held an old gnarled piece of wood, broken at the top with a carved coil around it. He always held the staff when confronting matters of importance. Inherited from his father, the staff would someday pass down to his sons, and possibly even his younger son. Anil Salesi looked at the staff, hoping one day he might be that son.

The riders came closer.

The spasm ended in Jack's stomach, and he inhaled, pulling the dry desert air into his lungs. He took long, greedy breaths. He looked up at Aurelio and Anil, looking down at him. He turned and looked to the north, in the direction of the camp. The riders were nearly upon them.

The youngest men in the group approached their early middle years, well into their thirties, with dark beards, almost black. The oldest riders were men with white beards, well into their last decades of life. In the center rode a man whose beard was both black and silver, neither long nor short. He seemed neither old nor young, neither large nor small, yet something in his face captivated Jack's eyes. It took several moments before Jack realized the man was staring down into his face.

The riders came closer still, almost on top of Jack, who was still sitting on his rump on the ground, his legs splayed out in front of him. He could see the detailed contours of the feet of the camels and the hooves of the lone horse as they approached at eye level.

"Get up," said Aurelio, under his breath, in Spatanian.

Jack moved to his knees and pushed himself up onto his feet.

The riders edged closer. They were very tall upon their camels save for the one man seated astride his horse—the man with the grey and black beard, the man at the front of all of the others, the man in the middle of the front line.

Jack stood.

The rest of the Beserians around him stood nearby. He was a half-head taller than all of them, including Aurelio Demassi. So too was he considerably broader across his shoulders. Beserians were nomads to a man, and as a rule, they were lean, many verging on looking malnourished. Demassi said the sands did not sustain fat in the land, nor in the animals or men who lived upon them. Men like Handsome Habeen Barcadey and Bazak Bazadak were thickly muscular, but they were the exceptions. Those two were broad and solid, like stone, built like Demissaries of the Qhaliffa.

The man on the horse stopped his mount, giving a slight tug on his reins. He looked down at Jack Caldwell and smiled. His eyes twinkled in the sunlight, and his face was like bronze.

For a moment, the two groups looked at each other. One group, the group of the Elders, remained mounted. The arriving group, the group of Kaleem Salesi, had dismounted in deference.

"Abu Akhsa," Kaleem spoke. "Abu Akhsa, Father, and Elders of the Council, this is the man."

Jack Caldwell could not understand the Beserian words.

Abu Akhsa looked at Jack. His smile stayed upon his face as he dismounted.

Standing, Jack looked down at him. Abu Akhsa stood considerably shorter than he did.

"Vetenan," said Abu Akhsa, "you will translate my words. Yes?"

"Yes, Your Excellency," said Aurelio Demassi.

"I am only a man of faith, a follower of the God of the Sands. We are alike, you and I, Vetenan. You may call me Abu Akhsa."

Aurelio Demassi nodded. He swallowed visibly. "Yes." He paused as if still not comfortable addressing the Chief of Chiefs in that manner. "Yes, Abu Akhsa."

"Tell him this," said Abu Akhsa. "Tell him he is our guest."

Aurelio Demassi nodded again. He spoke in Spatanian, "Abu Akhsa says you are his guest."

Jack nodded, scanning the solemn and warlike faces of the men still mounted on their camels, looking down at him. Even the white-bearded men held a kind of fierceness in their countenance. All of the elders were lean, but none were frail.

"Do you know why you are here?" asked Abu Akhsa.

Aurelio Demassi translated.

"I was brought here earlier than I anticipated," said Jack.

Demassi looked at him, his eyes flashing the need for caution. He translated Jack's words.

The outer edges of Abu Akhsa's eyes slightly wrinkled, as though pondering a pun, as he considered Jack Caldwell's strange response.

"When were you planning to be here?" asked Abu Akhsa.

Demassi translated the question.

"I was traveling to this very place, the Valley of Kordon, with a man named Harold Milton Stanwich. He is an explorer. This man was to be our guide. We came to trade with you," said Jack, pointing at Aurelio Demassi with his thumb.

The men in front of him visibly winced as if Jack had just pulled down his pants and begun urinating in front of them. Jack saw several hands belonging to the younger, black-bearded riders move to the hilts of the swords they carried in sheaths at their sides. Abu Akhsa's face tightened as if Jack had just insulted him.

"Your thumb," said Demassi. "The motion you just made is deeply insulting to the Beserians. It is like making a curse."

Jack flushed with embarrassment. "What does it mean?"

"One who mounts his goats."

Scarlet rose in Jack's cheeks.

"Please tell them that I apologize."

"He is a foreigner," said Demassi, speaking in Beserian, "He does not know what that symbol means. He meant no offense."

Abu Akhsa considered this. He looked at Jack carefully from his feet up to his head. Aurelio Demassi had given him clothes for the sands. After a week of wearing his evening clothes from the Altadige whorehouse, he had begun dressing like Aurelio Demassi, in the raiment of a Beserian. The clothes were too small, and Jack's large feet stuck out from his sandals like a father wearing his boy's shoes. His loose linen trousers left his lower legs and ankles bare and sunburnt, even in the pale winter sunlight.

"His face flushes, and his skin colors even in the winter sun," said Abu Akhsa, slightly shaking his head. His eyes twinkled in mild amusement at the absurdity of the moment. "And yet."

He paused. "And yet," he said again, turning back to look at his assembled people and raising his voice. "We now stand in the Year of the Prophecy. We should not be surprised to find salvation in strangeness, nor should we too soon reject that which we do not expect. Hamid Salesi, ask of this man what you will."

A mounted, silver-bearded man behind him said a quiet word.

His camel lowered itself onto its knees upon the hardened earth beneath. The other men repeated the same word as he, and their camels lowered in unison. The older man stepped out of his camel saddle and began to move forward, carrying his ancient piece of wood in his hands. Jack could see it had been deeply carved and broken off a larger piece, jagged at the top, with protrusions wrapping around it in a spiral, coiled like a serpent around a tree.

The man walked with slow, measured steps. He held the staff forward and began an incantation. Jack did not know the words. The others all stood in silence, staring not at the staff but at Jack.

Jack's mind raced. *What is this? What is this man saying?* He watched in anxious silence, his fear of shaming himself keeping him from speaking aloud.

The white-bearded man stepped up to Jack. He was shorter than Abu Akhsa.

Jack looked down at him, feeling oafish in his presence. He resisted the urge to turn his face away or to back up. The man stepped closer, a mere foot from Jack. He held up the piece of wood, inches from Jack's forehead. Jack looked at the ancient carvings in front of his eyes, into the eyes of the coiled serpent. He could see the minute and intricate details now, the carvings like a scaled serpent's skin. The scales were still visible, still not rubbed away by the years.

Aurelio wished to warn Jack not to move. He wanted to translate but knew that he could not. He dared not speak while Hamid Salesi held the Staff of the Serpent. He prayed softly under his breath that Jack would not make an error, bringing further shame to them both.

The older man's chanting reached a fevered pace. He held the broken staff up above his head with both hands grasping it around the shaft, just above the bottom. He slowly lowered the staff down toward Jack's face.

Jack, held by some force he did not understand, kept his eyes firmly planted on the man's deep, dark brown eyes, and then his gaze moved to the top of the staff, to the jagged edges that had once been part of something larger. A strange light emanated from the wood as if Jack looked into molten silver fused with the green of spring. And then he saw nothing. All around him went blank, as if the bright light had suddenly given birth to total darkness.

Jack blinked but remained blind. Panic rose inside of him . . . and then it slowly receded, leaving him like an exhaled breath.

He felt that he was no longer standing, but floating upon something like warm ocean water, buoyant, and suspended in time and space. A deep, golden light caressed his face, a light that beckoned to him. A penetrating warmth drew him forward, not unlike that of a roaring hearth when one has been out for too long in the cold. The warmth felt like an old memory, perhaps one of home when he was still a child, but nor was he certain he had ever felt it before.

He blinked again. A new light intruded, harsher and thinner than that which had just embraced him.

He lay upon his back, squinting up from the hard desert floor. Abu Akhsa and Hamid Salesi stood above him in the sunlight.

"Do you understand my words?" asked the old man, the man of the dark eyes and the silver-grey beard.

Jack heard the words. *Do you understand my words?* He knew the man was speaking in a language he did not know. Yet the meaning of each word, of each syllable of each word, was perfectly clear as if the man spoke Anglian with a Calderonian accent. The words struck his ears as if they were the language of his heart, his mind, and his soul.

"Yes, I understand your words," said Jack Caldwell. He spoke words he did not know, Beserian words, with the accent of a man born upon the sands. They moved off of his tongue without effort, in the manner of one who has spoken a language since before conscious memories are retained, like the language of early youth, the language of dreams. The words flowed out of him as naturally as the Anglian words of his childhood.

Abu Akhsa stared down at Jack. His face had changed. His wry smile was gone. His eyes were wide and misty, like he'd seen a loved one arriving at the edge of the camp after a long journey upon the sands, from which it was not certain the loved one would return.

"Rise," said Abu Akhsa.

He offered his hand. Jack grasped it. He rose. He looked at the faces of the Beserians around him.

They had all heard him speak. Their faces had changed. He saw Anil Salesi's face. It no longer held contempt, only wonder. Jack looked into the face of Aurelio Demassi. Tears moved down the Vetenan's gaunt cheeks, slipping down into his beard.

"Long have I waited for this day," said Abu Akhsa.

Jack looked at him, standing at his full height.

"Do you know what has happened?" asked Abu Akhsa, his voice barely above a whisper.

"It was light," said Jack, "and then dark, and then I floated in a place like water—like an ocean, but an ocean in which a man might breathe freely as a fish, as freely as we breathe this desert air now."

Abu Akhsa turned to Hamid Salesi. The grey-bearded older man, Hamid Salesi, nodded, closing his eyes in reverence.

"You were in the presence of the God of the Sands and the Mountain, and He has sent you back to us. It is as it is written."

Jack said nothing, standing with Abu Akhsa at his left and Hamid Salesi at his right.

"Your eyes have changed," said Abu Akhsa.

Jack looked at him with his eyes that were indeed different. Jack could not see himself, but he did not doubt what Abu Akhsa said. Indeed, he knew the words the Chief of Chiefs said before he said them.

"They were blue, lighter than ours, we people of the sands. But so too were they darker, like the waters of the Ring River. Blue they are still. But now they are light, light like the sky of the summer. Like the banner beneath which we ride." Abu Akhsa pointed up at the sky-blue banners snapping in the wind, pointing toward the east, blown by the westerly wind.

Jack looked at Abu Akhsa, seeing the awe in his face.

"Tell them your name," said Abu Akhsa.

"I—" he began, using the Beserian word without effort or forethought. He raised his voice. "I am John Joseph Caldwell, son of Colonel Mason Caldwell of Calderon. I come from beyond the western mountains and the sea. My home lies to the west of the lands beyond."

Only the westerly wind replied as the assembled Beserians listened in silence. What was west of the lands beyond?

Jack spoke loudly enough for his twenty companions to hear him. He spoke loudly enough for Abu Akhsa's thirty companions to hear as well, each man standing at the side of a lowered camel.

Behind the thirty lowered camels, and the famous men next to them, keeping a respectful yet anxious distance of perhaps one hundred yards, a great crowd had assembled.

Without speaking and in full view of the assembled crowd above on the slope leading to the camp, Abu Akhsa lowered himself to a knee. Hamid Salesi did the same. The men of the Council of Elders next to their thirty camels followed Abu Akhsa, dropping themselves to their knees upon the hard desert floor. The Swordguard riders who had come to accompany Jack, Aurelio, and Anil, and the riders of Kaleem Salesi, lowered themselves to their knees next. The vast assembled crowd in the distance saw all of this. They followed the example of their leaders, dropping themselves in reverence of the miracle they had just witnessed.

Alone, Jack Caldwell stood, staring over them all. All eyes were upon him, yet he stood, and he felt no shame.

From his knee, Abu Akhsa lifted his right hand and offered it to Jack. Jack Caldwell took it in his own.

"Stand with me, Abu Akhsa," said Jack, feeling an understanding that he had not known before. "You are the leader of these people."

Abu Akhsa listened to Jack's words in amazement, words Jack spoke with a new, formal tone. The accent was the kind Abu Akhsa himself used in the annual festivals, as if Jack were a Beserian of one of the original one hundred families, as if Jack, like himself, like Hamid Salesi, and several others of the oldest and most famous families, had the blood of Beseri flowing through his veins.

Abu Akhsa looked down and saw that he still held Jack's hand in his own. He raised Jack's hand into the air and shouted, with all of the might in his lungs, "Amahdi!"

Hamid Salesi and the Council of Elders followed, shaking their fists in the air as they roared, "Amahdi!"

And then all of the people in the distance were shouting the word, like a mighty thunder upon the sands.

CHAPTER 45
Stranded on the Sand Sea

Plain of Gamurian
Western Sand Sea
January 28, 1879

Peter stared northward into the dusk with despair in his eyes. The camels were gone, all of them. Nine men lay dead. Not counting him or Stanwich, another four were wounded. They had their medicines still, and the rifles, and their crates of food. But they had lost all means of carrying any of it. Behind Peter, tent flaps rustled in the wind. Above their camp, the flags of the Spatanian Emperor, the Anglian Imperium, and the New Anglian Republic extended to the north, blown by the breeze as if taunting them, pointing in the direction of their stolen camels.

Hersen bandaged Stanwich's mangled hand as well as he was able. He had learned a thing or two about treating wounds in his years in the legion. Peter entrusted his half-severed finger to Mrs. Smith, who cleaned it with alcohol.

It burned terribly when she did it. Then she wrapped it in a bandage. So long as he could keep the nub that remained and avoid the actual flames for the burning treatment, Peter would suffer the lesser pain of the alcohol. He did not know if he had the courage to let them burn him.

"You should burn it," said Hersen, looking at Peter across the small fire pit.

"Do not listen to him," said Mrs. Smith. "Your wound is clean."

"Your drink will not clean his wound, woman. The man bit him. Only the flames will ensure the rot does not grow."

"You will not burn me," said Peter. "Nor will you burn Stanwich."

Peter was edgy.

He had slept little. He had hardly eaten. When the adrenaline wore off, the fatigue advanced. The sense that they had all failed weighed heavily upon his shoulders, and he suspected the beginning of their hardship was only just being revealed to them.

"If I save you from the rot, you will thank me," said Hersen.

Hersen held a log into the fire, watching the far end take flame. "Come and be done with it, Anglian. Be a man. Every boy in the legion becomes a man not on his first fight, but on the burning of his first wound." Hersen lifted his shirt to reveal a large, old burn, the size of a small handprint on his abdomen. He was in the early stages of drunkenness, and he slurred his words.

"It will not be better tomorrow, Anglian, or the day after tomorrow," he said, looking at Peter. His smile was taunting. "With each passing day, you will make me burn you deeper and longer if you wish to kill all of the rot. Be a man, and have it done with."

"Stay silent with your madness," said Mrs. Smith, sitting at the midway point between Peter Harmon and Hersen Expey.

"Oh, and how many wounds have you treated, woman?" asked Hersen, his slurred LaFrentian accent making him sound all the more indignant.

Hannah Huntington, sitting next to Mrs. Smith, stood up. "More than you, LaFrentian."

Peter looked up at her. Even in his pain, the look of her face and body was a feast for his eyes. Even covered in desert dust, with her hair falling about her face in disheveled strands, she was a beautiful woman.

Hersen scoffed, dropping his log into the flames and reaching for a whiskey bottle.

"You should not drink," said Peter. "Grave challenges will face us in the morning."

Hersen laughed, pulled the cork from the whiskey, and drew a deep pull of the rich, brown alcohol into his mouth. He looked at Hannah, Mrs. Smith, and Peter each, in turn, swishing the burning liquid around his mouth as if it were water. Then he tilted his head back and gargled the whiskey in the back of his throat. Having sufficiently drawn everyone's surprise and attention, he swallowed.

Hannah shook her head. Peter and Mrs. Smith stared as if observing a disobedient toddler.

Hersen then barked, deep and forcefully like a dog guarding a Laketown steelyard.

Peter winced.

Hersen laughed, swirling the whiskey in the bottle.

Stanwich, lying next to Hersen, groaned.

His face, which had been racked with pain, was now numbed into a stupor. After the battle, he drank half a bottle of North Anglian Whiskey. No one stopped him. He held his mangled but now bandaged left hand with his right, cupping it against his stomach, rocking back and forth. Before Hersen wrapped it, Mrs. Smith demanded that she be able to pour her clear alcohol upon the wound. Stanwich howled when she did it, and Hersen launched into a string of vile profanities in LaFrentian that Peter refused to translate for any of the New Anglians.

Despite the others sitting either demoralized or drunk by the fire, or in some cases both, Sergeant Barnes refused to stay still. He and Diego organized the porters, all armed with Hart-Harold rifles, into patrols around the perimeter of the camp.

Stanwich, in his pain and his drunkenness, had lost all ability to lead. Hersen Expey was second in command, but he was barking and gargling whiskey with the madness of a sailor on shore leave after a voyage across the Empty Ocean. Barnes drank nothing and filled the void, taking functional command as the night approached.

He marched back to the campfire. The sun had fallen beneath the western horizon, in the direction of the mountains they could no longer see, the direction of Altadige.

"Peter," said Barnes. "Hannah, walk with me. Mrs. Smith, you come as well."

They all obeyed, rising groggily from their positions near the fire. When the sun dropped beneath the mountains, the temperature dropped with it, often with shocking quickness. The heat of the day gave way not to coolness but to outright, frigid winter cold, dropping as much as forty degrees from the heat of the noonday sun.

Peter felt himself wishing for a blanket as the cold penetrated beneath his woolen shirt. Hannah walked past him, with a straight back and a calm, rapid gait. She had, weeks ago, exchanged her skirts and dresses for a pair of tight trousers, not unlike those of a cavalryman, and Peter looked yearningly at her legs, long and muscular, and especially so for her height. Barnes waited to speak until they were all standing next to him, some twenty yards or so away from the fire, far enough to be out of earshot.

"In the morning, there will be decisions to make."

The others listened.

Barnes glanced toward the fire. "We have supplies, but we have nothing with which to move the supplies. In the desert, camels are everything. They are as important as ships upon the sea. We are like men floating in the middle of the ocean on rafts. We are too far to make it back to the port from which we came. We must find an island."

Mrs. Smith nodded in agreement.

"We must find an island," said Peter, finding Barnes' mental thread.

Barnes nodded.

"You speak of the oasis, Ben Gamurian," said Peter.

"Yes," said Barnes. "It is the only way."

"Between here and there," said Peter, "the Macmenian maps show there are six wells. The oasis lies along the caravan line. It is well traveled. But it is still more than eighty miles to Ben Gamurian. That is not far on a camel's back. It is an eternity on foot, especially if we will try to carry these crates."

"We cannot leave the rifles," said Hannah Huntington. "They are the only way to trade our way out of this." Sergeant Barnes looked at her, seeing at that moment that she sounded very much like her father.

"That is true," said Barnes.

"We will carry the rifles on foot to Ben Gamurian?" asked Peter.

"Some of us will."

Peter raised an eyebrow. "What will the others do?"

"Some of us must go back to Altadige."

"Why? How?"

Barnes looked down at his boots, scuffing the sand beneath him. His long arms were folded underneath his Mancaster rifle, cradling it with the barrel pointing down at the ground.

"We must send word back to Anglia and Calderon. There is no telegraph in Ben Gamurian."

"Send word of what?" asked Peter.

"We cannot fix this without outside help," said Barnes. "We have failed. This news shall not age like a fine wine. No, this will spread like rot. Our only way of retrieving Jack Caldwell is by sending word to the colonel." Barnes looked Peter square in the face. "And by sending word to your father."

Peter's face betrayed his anxiety. "And what shall we tell him?"

"We will tell him the truth. We were attacked underneath the sovereign flag of the Anglian Imperium. Jack Caldwell was taken, as were our camels."

Peter's mind raced. "And an attack upon our flag is an attack upon Anglia. We shall ask them to send troops?"

"Yes," said Barnes. "And by the enduring grace and mercy of the Three Gods, Jack Caldwell will still be alive when they arrive to teach these tribesmen a lesson in diplomacy."

"I will go," said Mrs. Smith. "I will walk to Altadige."

"No," said Barnes. "It is too far."

"I have traveled more deserts on foot than all of the rest of you combined," said Mrs. Smith.

Peter looked at her, heavyset and fierce, her jaw set stubbornly forward. Peter felt a wave of respect wash over him as he looked into the face of the brave woman. Colonel Caldwell and Samuel Huntington chose well in the companions they sent with their children.

Barnes shook his head, but his voice was gentle and tender. "No, Matilda, you must stay with Hannah, and you must get her safely to Ben Gamurian. There is food and water there, and there is safety behind those walls."

Mrs. Smith said nothing, but her jaw remained stubbornly set.

"Besides," said Barnes, "we have lost a Caldwell. We will not lose a Huntington as well. I will make the journey back. I have failed in my mission, so I must remedy it."

"Then, I shall go with you," said Peter.

Hannah looked at him, and Peter could, perhaps for the first time, feel respect in her eyes.

"No," said Barnes.

"You will need me."

"No," repeated Barnes, shaking his head. "I will bring Diego. We will take the risk. There could still be Beserians roaming the way back."

"There could be Beserians roaming the way to Ben Gamurian," said Peter.

"If that is so, they will have many Hart-Harold and Hart-Henry rifles to contend with. Many of them died here today. Many more are returning to the Valley of Kordon with dreadful wounds that will never heal, wounds that will kill in hours from now, and, in some cases, days or even weeks. Those camels were dearly bought, and they will not soon forget it," said Barnes.

"You need me to plead with my father if you wish to have Anglian troops."

This caught Barnes's attention. He looked at Peter with questioning eyes. "You can give your message to me."

"I will give the message myself to the telegraph agent in Altadige and not otherwise," said Peter.

"Do not be foolish," said Barnes.

"It is a long way, Peter," said Hannah, calling him by his first name for the first time. "You should listen to him."

"And what if the sergeant cannot move my father?" said Peter. "What if the words are not correct? What if my father asks inquiries that require a response? Sergeant, with respect, you know your ways, and I know mine. You are a soldier. I gratefully defer to you in a firefight. Indeed, I just did. But do you know how to persuade a Lord of the Anglian Imperium? Do you know what to say and what not to say? I shall answer for you. Search your heart and know that you do not. If we fail, it must be because we have placed our best foot forward and failed nonetheless, but not otherwise. If we are to convince my father to persuade the Prime Minister of the Anglian Imperium to dispatch an army to rescue my cousin, I will be necessary to convince him."

Barnes stood looking at the dirt for long moments. He looked up, first at Hannah and then at Mrs. Smith. He did not look at Peter.

"In the morning, we shall tell Mr. Stanwich and Major Expey that they are to march with the column and as many rifles as can be carried to Ben Gamurian. Diego the Vetenan, will go with you. He leads the porters well. He also knows Ben Gamurian. Peter Harmon and I will march to Altadige. There we will send word to Lord Harmon in Anglia and Colonel Caldwell in Calderon."

"And my father," said Hannah.

Barnes nodded. "Yes."

A man groaned in the distance. It was the groan of the wounded, piteous and full of pain.

"What of the wounded?" asked Peter.

"We are marching for Altadige. They are out of our hands," said Barnes.

"We are all one expedition, Sergeant. What shall be done with them? Some can barely walk."

"They will walk to Ben Gamurian, or they will die."

CHAPTER 46
The High Kezelboj

Saman Keer
32nd Day, Month of Gandus, 807
Anglian Calendar: February 1, 1879

Palace servants surveyed the circle of stools, examining their work, making sure that they had remembered every detail.

As was customary, they had spent the morning placing the pitchers of water and wine in their correct places, paired with plates of cheese and fruit atop the small tables adjacent to the wide, cushioned stools. They placed water pipes upon the ground, their leather tubes and wooden nozzles all resting on hooks in the same way. In each water pipe, they put finely shredded pinches of Hindean leaf into the smoking bowls, awaiting the sparks that would light them, filling the Hall of the Qhaliffas with sweet, pungent smoke.

The Kezelboj would arrive soon, and Kezelboj lords did not tolerate sitting without their comforts. Most of the servants had overseen Kezelboj meetings and tended to the aristocrats' needs for decades. The Qhaliffas, across the centuries, had seen fit to keep the lords beneath them happy and well-fed during their visits to the palace.

"Properly entertained lords ask fewer questions and cause less trouble," was a well- known phrase in the Qhaliffa's halls.

This luncheon was to be no exception. The stools formed a large circle in the Hall of the Qhaliffas, the same hall through which Ozgar Ogatonia and the Oath Holders of the Order had slipped before Jemojeen had ambushed them in the Throne Hall. Atop the stools, brightly colored cushions rested, each designating the cities from which the High Kezelboj would soon arrive.

Twenty-one stools faced each other, three for the High Kezelboj from each city, except for Alwaz Deem. House Savanar had lost its seat, seventeen years before, and had, in the official records of the Lords of the Seven Cities, ceased to exist.

As a lesson to the remaining Kezelboj, the place of the Savanars remained empty. As continuing punishment for its alleged treason, Alwaz Deem—the great city of the western mountain—the second most populous of the Seven Cities behind Saman Keer itself, would have less representation at the gathering than any of the other Seven Cities.

Three green stools remained, however, for Saman Keer, three orange stools for Ganjar en Oxus, three red stools from Sundar Dun, three yellow stools for Nor Wasura, three sky-blue stools for Nor Gandus, and three dark blue stools for Meer Norekah. But only two purple stools waited for the lords of Alwaz Deem.

At the top of the circle, nearest to the Throne Hall, between the places for Alwaz Deem and Saman Keer, a single black stool rested, awaiting the Grand Vizer, who would preside in the absence of Sumetan himself.

Footsteps approached from the corridor now, for the meeting would begin in minutes. The servants all stood more erect, their nervousness showing on their faces.

Jemojeen emerged into the hall, flanked by the Sipahi Shaheni on one side and Turkelan the Erassian on the other, each man carrying a curved sword on his hip.

With his hands folded together in front of his chest, Jemojeen looked at the circle of stools. His face darkened.

"Who placed food and drink?" he asked.

The servants stood in two crescents, one on either side of the cavernous hall, each man facing inward toward the circle of stools with their eyes directly ahead. None spoke.

Jemojeen's voice rose. "I asked *who* placed the food and drink?"

The Qhaliffa's steward stepped forward. He was a tall and handsome man with short silver hair and an open, earnest face.

"Your Excellency, I arranged for the food and drink to be placed, as is customary. We also placed the water pipes, as is customary. The Lords of the Kezelboj should be most pleased, Your Excellency."

The steward bowed.

He rose, with a look of surprise, as if awaiting compliments for his diligence.

Jemojeen did not look at the steward or, in any way, acknowledge the words he had just spoken. The Grand Vizer walked toward the circle of stools, his frown deepening.

Shaheni looked askance at Turkelan, who met his eyes, knowingly.

Jemojeen looked down at the nearest plate of winter fruits from the uplands of the southern cities, and the carefully cut wedges of fine cheese. All was indeed arranged in a most appropriate, elegant, and customary manner, worthy of the expectations of the Highest Kezelboj.

"Take it away," said Jemojeen. "All of it. Now. Leave only the stools."

The steward looked at the Grand Vizer as if he had misheard him, standing in place with a confused expression on his face.

"Your Excellency?"

"Take it away!" barked Jemojeen, stepping menacingly toward the steward. The steward winced.

Jemojeen reached down, gripped one of the low tables, and flipped it over, toppling it toward the center of the circle. The cheese bounced off the stone floor, and a pair of apples rolled across the hall.

"Remove the tables!" gasped the steward, gesturing at the crescents of silent servants. They rushed forward to erase any trace of their morning's work.

The Kezelboj lords sauntered into the hall over the course of a half of an hour. Those of the northern cities of Nor Gandus, Meer Norekah, and Nor Wasura began to arrive first, five minutes after the noon hour when the meeting was scheduled to start. Jemojeen had departed before their arrival, telling Shaheni not to get him until all of the lords were seated.

A quarter of an hour after the last lord had taken his stool, Jemojeen slowly walked back into the hall.

"My lords," he said, smiling. Again, Turkelan the Erassian and Sipahi Shaheni flanked him on either side.

Few of the lords returned Jemojeen's smile. Each of the High Kezelboj looked as if they wished to know where their food was. They were each told, by the summons, that they would be attending a luncheon. Never before had any of them participated in a luncheon in the palace of the Qhaliffa at which they were not offered even a cup of water.

Jemojeen walked leisurely across the circle to his own stool.

"My lords," said Jemojeen, seated upon his black cushion, atop the stool that was several inches higher than any of those for the Kezelboj. "Today, we meet to discuss the coming war."

As he said this, Jemojeen moved his eyes slowly along the unsmiling faces of the lords. To a man, they thought they were more worthy of being Grand Vizer than the upstart Bulbanian Demissary who now outranked them all. In their view, he had already been Grand Vizer for far too long. Indeed, it had now been more than seventeen years since Selahim the Grim had made his unprecedented and momentous choice, and Jemojeen's powers over his son, Sumetan the Magnificent, seemed to be growing by the month.

Lord Borjis of Ganjar en Oxus spoke first. His eyes were set abnormally close together. When nervous and speaking before a large group, he squinted and knitted his eyebrows, making himself look nearly like a cyclops. He was considered a reasonably brave man, albeit one of, at best, medium intelligence.

"What war, Grand Vizer?" he asked.

"A fair question," said Jemojeen. "What war, indeed? Why would I gather you all here today?"

"Apparently not for a luncheon," said Lord Cerelac of Sundar Dun, wide-faced and pompous beneath his bulbous red turban, in which an enormous ruby rested. Dark bangs hung down over his forehead from beneath the edge of his turban.

Several other Kezelboj lords laughed at Lord Cerelac's quip, mostly those from the southern cities, those that had arrived latest to the meeting.

Jemojeen's mouth opened into a thin smile.

"No, Lord Cerelac, it is not the time for drinking wine, eating cheese, and smoking a pipe."

"Pity," said Lord Cerelac, laughing. Fewer lords laughed this time, their eyes on the face of the Grand Vizer.

"A pity indeed," said Jemojeen. "As you are all surely aware, my lords, the Order of the Ram, the Lion, and the Serpent assisted the prisoner Saliha, daughter of the traitor Sah Seg Savanar, in her escape from these Seven Cities. She escaped recently, I am informed, toward the oasis of Ben Hamur.

"As you should also all know, Beserian tribesmen presently congregate in unprecedented numbers in the western desert beneath the banners of a rebel named Abu Akhsa."

"How does this mean war?" asked Lord Borjis, his eyebrows still raised.

Jemojeen kept his first response to himself: *You, Lord Borjis, are a living example of the stupidity of allowing leadership to be inherited from one generation to the next.*

"Lord Borjis," he instead said aloud, "I am in the process of connecting these items, if you will allow me to do so?"

Lord Borjis nodded.

Lord Cerelac sniggered.

"My Erassians and guardsmen have worked tirelessly to find answers amid these troubling times," said Jemojeen. He glanced over his shoulder toward Sipahi Shaheni and Captain Turkelan.

The Kezelboj lords followed his eyes with their own.

"I trust you are all familiar with the Beserian Heresy?"

The three austere lords of Nor Gandus, tall and gaunt, nodded first. The others followed.

"We have reason to believe the Order is working with Abu Akhsa and the Beserians. We believe the Order seeks to unite the Savanar with the tribesmen."

"What reason do we have to fear that?" asked one of the men of Nor Gandus.

"She is only a girl. What harm can she do us?" asked Lord Cerelac.

"Only a girl. Yes, Lord Cerelac. I am told she escaped through Sundar Dun. Perhaps your fellow southerners had a similarly relaxed view when the Order moved her through your city?"

At this, the Lords of Saman Keer huffed.

Sipahi Shaheni glared at Lord Cerelac with contempt in his dark eyes. Cerelac caravans were amongst those he robbed when he was still a gangman in Sundar Dun.

"Perhaps," said Lord Cerelac, "if she had not escaped from Saman Keer, we would not have had to keep our eyes peeled in Sundar Dun."

Jemojeen's smile tightened, and his nostrils flared. "Saman Keer is not without fault, either, Lord Cerelac. Nor are my guardsmen, and neither am I."

"The risk, Lords of Nor Gandus, is that the Savanar is a symbol of rebellion. She could make the Beserians bolder than they already are. They await the signs of their prophecy, which is, of course, in truth, heresy."

"Why do we fear a false heresy?" asked the same lord from Nor Gandus.

"I do not say we fear anything," said Jemojeen. "What we must be is vigilant. If the Beserians move east—and I have reason to believe they are moving east—we must ride out to meet them."

"Why not remain behind the Ring River, where we are impregnable?" asked a wan, thinly bearded lord from Nor Wasura.

"We could do so," said Jemojeen. "While Abu Akhsa gathers more tribesmen and conquers the oasis of Ben Gamurian and eventually Ben Hamur and others. We could do so, while the Beserians cut off our caravan routes and give hope to those who might be inclined to follow the deluded heresies of the Order."

The circle of Kezelboj sat in silence.

"Or, we could ride out into the sands to crush them," said Jemojeen.

"With your guardsmen and Erassians?" asked Lord Cerelac.

"Or perhaps with Demissaries?" asked Lord Borjis.

"My lords, His Majesty the Qhaliffa has already given me command of the Demissary Legions to meet this threat, and I would not impose upon your valuable time if I wished to deploy Erassians and guardsmen. I need not consult you about that. Rather, I have called you here because your Qhaliffa asks something larger of you."

The High Kezelboj waited in silence.

Jemojeen rose from his stool, towering over the seated men with his black cape framing him from behind.

From his robes, Jemojeen removed a scroll. "The time for half measures is over. The time of sitting in your palaces while rebellion grows will no longer be tolerated. The heretics claim that a promised Amahdi will rise in the west. They claim a child of the line of Hom Hommuram will join that Amahdi to topple the line of your master, the Qhaliffa. I will not sit idly by while the heretics grow stronger beneath the banners of their lies. And nor will you. Your Qhaliffa commands you to muster your levies."

A collective gasp arose from the circle.

"Have we not already mustered our levies to search for the Savanar and the Oath Holders?" asked Lord Cerelac.

"No, Lord Cerelac. I am not referring to your household cavalry. I am referring to mustering for war."

"How many men?" asked Cerelac.

"All of them," said Jemojeen. "A full muster, Lord Cerelac. Your pikemen, your swordsmen, your cavalry, and your cannons."

Several lords grumbled loudly, shaking their heads.

"That will take time," said one of the other lords of Sundar Dun, a fat man renowned for his cruelty toward his household slaves.

"You have two weeks," said Jemojeen.

More lords gasped.

"Does that include the Great Guns? And the pachyrms to move them?"

"Yes," said Jemojeen.

"How many?"

"All of them."

The Lords of Meer Norekah, conservative caravan owners to a man, sat in scowling silence. Such a muster would cost them two years of hard-earned profits, likely more. But they were wise enough to bear their burden in silence.

"That will require a great deal of coin," said Lord Cerelac.

"Of which you have a great deal, Lord Cerelac, do you not? And surely such a sacrifice is the least you can do for your Qhaliffa, is it not?"

Lord Cerelac scowled. "Let me see the scroll."

"Do you doubt that I am telling you your Qhaliffa's orders correctly, Lord Cerelac?"

"No."

Jemojeen stepped closer to him.

"Do you believe the scroll will read differently from what I am telling you, Lord Cerelac?"

Lord Cerelac shook his head, the bangs beneath his turban swishing back and forth across his forehead.

"Then I will not insult you by showing you the scroll."

"House Borjis and Ganjar en Oxus will muster," said Lord Borjis, saluting with his fist across his chest.

"Very good, Lord Borjis," said Jemojeen. "You are an example to us all."

Lord Borjis nodded, his eyebrows scrunched up above his narrow, squinting gaze.

Jemojeen held the scroll up in the air.

"There will be no tolerance for delay," said Jemojeen.

"And what if it takes more time?" asked Lord Cerelac.

Jemojeen stood and faced him, his eyes drilling down into Lord Cerelac's face.

"Do you expect to fail, Lord Cerelac? Are you unable to meet your duties?"

"No," he grumbled.

"What was that?" asked Jemojeen, stepping closer to Lord Cerelac, peering down his long nose.

"No, Your Excellency."

"That is good, Lord Cerelac, otherwise, I will send Sipahi Shaheni and his guardsmen to assist you. Or perhaps the Demissaries of the Second Legion might help remind the people of Sundar Dun of their duties?"

Lord Cerelac blushed. "That will not be necessary, Your Excellency."

"I will be the judge of that, Lord Cerelac. Sipahi Shaheni will observe your efforts and those of your fellow lords of Sundar Dun. He will report to me to ensure you are moving at a pace commensurate with your duties."

Jemojeen moved his eyes along the faces of the others, slowly scanning the entirety of the circle. Some averted their gaze; most observed him beneath hooded eyelids, knowing they were powerless to oppose him.

"Two weeks," repeated Jemojeen, his voice hard as Great Mountain steel. "You will muster beyond the Approach of Alwaz."

"And then, where?" asked the wan Nor Wasuran.

"West," said Jemojeen. He scanned the Kezelboj faces as if daring another to ask a question.

He waited.

"You are dismissed," he said.

The High Kezelboj rose from their chairs, grumbling in hushed tones as they departed the hall.

"Sipahi," said Jemojeen, still standing in the center of the circle.

Sipahi Shaheni approached.

Jemojeen gestured to Turkelan.

The Erassian followed Shaheni to Jemojeen's side.

"You will both keep an eye on Lord Cerelac."

"Yes, Your Excellency."

"Make sure he does all that is expected of him. It is unlikely that he will return from the campaign alive. There are many dangers upon the sands . . . and he has been insolent for the last time."

CHAPTER 47
The Savanar and the Sharef

Oasis of Ben Hamur
34th Day, Month of Gandus, 807
Anglian Calendar: February 3, 1879

The dense, green, thorny thicket formed a protective barrier around the bathing pool, shielding it entirely from view. At least that is what the Sharef's servants had said when they led Selena and Gulana through the wooden arch with the tal, rounded door underneath the canopy of climbing roses.

The roses clung to the trellis like serpents in the Semissari clinging to a mangrove, but instead of snake heads, from each thorny, curving rose stem, a pink or white flower hung down in various stages of blooming.

Selena had not seen anything lovelier since she could remember. Even Gulana, generally oblivious to such things, looked up at the flowers, sniffing the intoxicating scents that wafted down upon them, driven by a light, warm breeze.

The servant led them to the pool's edge, nodded respectfully, turned, and left them, leaving clean clothes folded on a flat, warm stone.

Selena scanned the thicket.

It looked as impenetrable to prying eyes as the servant had said.

The sunlight sparkled on the pool's surface. They were alone.

Selena took off her filthy garments and dropped them onto the gravel shore. She looked down at the flat stone. The garments the servant left were clean, linen, and spotlessly white—the robes of an aristocrat. She smiled at them, suddenly remembering a day she had long forgotten, a flash of an image. A large, bearded man swung her around as she laughed. Other children stood around her, all bigger than she, all laughing as well, all wearing white robes like those folded upon the stone. *Father? My sisters?*

But as quickly as the memory came, the memory of her loss came just as fast. With her tongue, she probed the space where her missing front teeth should be.

She saw something next to the clothes. It was bulky like a stone, but it was pure white, whiter even than the linen next to it. She had not seen anything like it in long months. She picked it up and smiled.

Holding the chunk in her hand, she stepped forward, utterly naked, letting the cool water of the pool cover her feet up to her ankles. Under the water, her feet sank into the ground, with soft moss cushioning her toes. The ground of the pool squished beneath her feet, coming up through her toes, porous, like a sponge. Tiny fish danced around her ankles in the shallows at the water's edge. The water itself was clear as daylight even out into the depths of the pool.

Selena stepped forward, letting the water come up to her knees. The late morning sunlight warmed her olive-colored flesh. Despite the water, few insects circled her. Ben Hamur was as free from flies as any place she had ever been. The only foul thing around her was her own smell, made the more obvious by her nakedness and the pure water beneath her.

She could smell her pungency after the weeks upon the sand, the days in the Semissari, and the escape from Saman Keer before that. Her body was hard and lean, with bits of her ribs showing beneath her small breasts. The muscles in her stomach each stood out, like six rectangles leading down from the bottom of her chest to the top of her groin. She had not felt the clean tingle of soap upon her skin in weeks, not since the Order had allowed her to clean herself in their labyrinth of caverns beneath Saman Keer.

Yet, in her hand, she held a piece of soap that would renew and refresh her mind and body before her meeting with the Sharef. *He was kind to allow me this*, she thought. *Oapah is at the edge of the pool, on the other side of that barrier, if this is a trap.* After the torture of the dungeon, her near execution, and a month on the run, Selena's wariness did not easily leave her. Nor had her life been easy before. She shuddered as the moneylender and the madam entered her mind.

She waded in farther. Her hair was a filthy, tangled knot.

She walked into the pool, waist-deep, slightly shivering in the water. By her feet, the water was colder than near the surface, where even the winter sun warmed the water by several noticeable degrees. She leaned back, dropping the back of her head into the pool and feeling the coolness in her scalp. She leaned back all the way, letting the water cover her face in a cold embrace to wash away the desert, the mountain, and the grime of the Seven Cities.

Selena pulled her head up, smiling and forgetting, for the quickness of a moment, about the front teeth Jemojeen's jailors had taken from her. She felt the strangeness of carefree happiness, fleeting as the flap of a bird's wings. Then she remembered. It was a great burden, Selena's memory. Her muscles tightened, her eyes narrowed, and she scanned the shrub line on instinct, looking for Erassians or other men coming to take her and capture her in her nakedness. But no one was there, only tiny larks skipping from branch to branch twittering, at each other.

Gulana popped her head up above the water. She was already in the deepest part of the pool, up to her neck. She looked different with her hair slicked backward in the water. She swam toward Selena with her arms and legs beneath her like a frog. She swam well, as the watermen did in the summers in the Ring River and on the Grand Canal, in the clean waters of the north, beneath Nor Wasura, Nor Gandus, and Meer Norekah. As Gulana came close to Selena, her face opened into a tremendous smile, twinkling her eyes and flashing all of her teeth. Selena stared at her for a moment, having never seen Gulana, a Lion of the Order, smile like that before. She was, at that moment, not unattractive.

"You are smiling," said Selena, smiling herself.

"That is something I do," said Gulana, smiling even wider.

"Not that I have seen," said Selena.

"We have never before been in the clean pools of Ben Hamur on a warm winter's morning," said Gulana.

"You wear a smile well," said Selena.

Gulana blushed at the compliment. She was not accustomed to people speaking favorably of her face—her strength, courage, and abilities, yes, often, but not her face.

"Thank you, Lady Savanar," said Gulana, continuing her frog swim toward Selena's edge of the pool. Her skin was bright, smooth, and healthy in the sunlight.

Selena rubbed the soap all over her body, using her hands to scrub away all of the caked dirt that had formed upon her over the weeks. She had not felt water upon her since she had fallen into the Great Pool beneath Sundar Dun, but that was not water that cleaned, and that had been weeks ago.

"You should use this," said Selena, holding up the rocklike piece of soap.

"I do not trust that," said Gulana.

"You have never used soap?"

"Once, perhaps."

"God of the Mountain," said Selena. "And the Sands." She shook her head in mock disappointment.

"I smell as the God intended me to smell."

Selena laughed. "That is like refusing to wear clothes, saying, 'I am attired in what God intended me to wear.'"

Gulana did not respond but instead disappeared beneath the water. Selena followed her with her eyes. Gulana kicked swiftly, like a frog in a hurry, heading in Selena's direction. Before Selena could move out of the way, Gulana grabbed her legs and flipped her backward, landing her in the pool on her back.

When Selena brought her head above the water, Gulana stood above her, naked, tall, and powerful, laughing out loud. "Give me your soap, Lady Savanar."

Selena handed it over.

They stood in the courtyard, freshly attired in sparkling white garments. Oapah looked majestic, tall, and broad as a mountain, the white of his clothing made all the whiter by the darkness of his smooth, Omakhosian skin. Gulana had indeed used the soap, and underneath a light cotton head covering, her hair was clean, braided, and scented with oils. Next to her, standing a half-head shorter, Selena Savanar's face glowed like the face of the Kezelboj girl she once was.

In the center of the courtyard, a five-tiered fountain dropped water into a widening series of shallow ceramic bowls. In each of them, a host of bright-feathered birds flitted about, calling out to each other. Bright, aromatic roses covered the low walls of the courtyard, their scent mixing with those of the old lemon trees planted in each of the courtyard's corners. They grew up and over the walls, nearly forming a canopy overhead and pleasantly shading the flat sandstones upon which Oapah, Gulana, and Selena stood. Thick-trunked olive trees surrounded the courtyard, barring any prying eyes. The grove continued down the steep slope to the pools at the bottom.

The Sharef's House stood at the top of the tallest hill in Ben Hamur, which, not counting the building itself, stood a mere seventy-five feet above the rest of the oasis. But in a place as flat as Ben Hamur, the Sharef's Hill commanded considerable views of all around it. The servants, however, had made clear that none of the three of them were to take in any views, as their presence in Ben Hamur was, and very much must remain, a secret.

"Lady Savanar, the Sharef will see you now," said the servant cloaked in tan robes marked with a dark green sash. "And your companions also. You may follow me."

The servant walked through an open iron gate set in a stone wall, the top of which stood several heads higher than Oapah. As they passed through the wall, Oapah observed that it would be a formidable defensive position if one were forced to defend the oasis. It would be the place that a man would wish to make a last stand if the rest of the sanctuary fell to an intruder. The walls were thick and sturdy, made not from mudbricks like the rest of the settlement, but from old stones, well laid and grouted by master stonemasons.

Oapah had laid his share of stones in Ganjar en Oxus. The best stonemasons in the Seven Cities were said to be Omakhosians. Oapah, when he was not serving the Order, was a journeyman stonemason, underneath the master stonemason Oanawayu. He had taken Oapah on as a young apprentice when he was still a large boy from Omakhosi, openly gaping at the massive mountain before him and the high stone buildings in the valley of Ganjar en Oxus, the city of the orange roof tiles. There were few stone buildings in Omakhosi, and especially amongst the Hohsa. Oanawayu was a Hohsa, and he had taught Oapah to look after other Hohsans who came to the Seven Cities seeking a new life—young, frightened pilgrims like he once was himself, fleeing war and famine on the southern continent.

Oapah looked up at the vast stone structure above him now, a place from which archers could loose arrows into an enemy while they struggled up the steep slope. *Those olive trees, however,* thought Oapah, *would allow an enemy to come very close under thick cover before those archers could begin to strike him.*

They passed into an inner courtyard and up a flight of sandstone steps. Fountains flanked either side of the walkway, sourcing small streams in little enclosed troughs, like tiny mountain creeks trickling along the walls. Oapah looked down and saw small colorful fish in the troughs, darting in and out of the shadows beneath tiny lily pads. They turned up another set of stairs, pleasantly covered by vines overhead, shielding the walkway from the sun.

And then they appeared on a large open platform, half-covered with a great slab of sandstone for its roof, supported by ancient columns. The other half was exposed to the north, commanding a view from its edge, of nearly the entire oasis beneath. Beneath, approximately seventy-five feet down, lay the great open sand and sandstone square, where the people assembled to hear from their Sharef on the days of the great festivals and feasts.

Gulana, Oapah, and Selena followed the servant out into the sunlight. They looked underneath the covered portion of the platform, behind the columns.

There they saw him.

Propped up against a low wooden wall, elevated upon a platform, sat perhaps the fattest man Selena Savanar had ever seen. He lay upon voluminous cushions, some purple and others green, the same color as the sashes worn by the servants of his house. Other pillows were pure white, as white as the clothing Selena wore against her smooth olive skin.

Next to the man, a large ceramic carafe sat by a plate with a small mountain of dates, a chunk of goat cheese fit for a giant, and a loaf of bread that was large enough to feed a dozen Beserians and their goats too.

As she stepped forward, Selena openly stared at the man.

From a corner of the room, from behind a potted fig tree, Captain Dungar Bin-Guttar stepped out and stood next to the giant fat man. Selena looked at Dungar and felt relief. He had brought them here to the cleansing pools. Selena felt something like trust for the man, as he had shown himself reliable in every test so far.

He, too, had cleaned himself since they were upon the sands. The dust was removed from his face and the helmet from his head. In the place of the chain mail that hung down from his helmet, oiled hair framed the sides of his face in ringlets, hanging down from the otherwise bald top of his head. He looked, to Selena's astonishment, almost like a Kezelboj lord from the Seven Cities. She felt Dungar's eyes upon her and wondered if the transition in her was as great as his own.

Dungar Bin-Guttar loudly cleared his throat and said, "Most Upright Ayzah, Patriarch of the family Bin-Ayawad, Sharef of Ben Hamur, may I present to you the Lady Selena of House Savanar of the City of Alwaz Deem and her two companions, both Lions of the Order of the Ram, the Lion, and the Serpent, Oapah the Hohsa of Ganjar en Oxus, and Gulana of Nor Gandus."

The tremendously fat man smiled. His mouth was small in his gigantic face, giving him the appearance of a massive rodent, but his eyes were friendly and intelligent. His face was clean-shaven, and he had little hair on his head.

"When I last saw you, Lady Savanar, you were but a girl. Do you remember?"

Selena looked into his eyes. "Honorable Sharef, I do not."

"You were very young, a small child. You came with your father, who was a great man."

"Thank you, Honorable Sharef. Your words are kind."

"You were then called Saliha. You have grown since then," said the Sharef, placing a handful of dates into his mouth.

As have you, I presume, thought Selena. "Honorable Sharef, I am no longer the girl I once was," she said.

The Sharef stared at her, his eyes sharpening. "It was a grave injustice what they did to your father."

Selena nodded.

"You are now a fugitive from the Qhaliffa," said the Sharef.

"Unjustly a fugitive," said Gulana.

The Sharef's eyes hardened further.

"I will ask you not to speak unbidden to the Sharef of Ben Hamur," said Dungar Bin-Guttar, "Gulana of Nor Gandus." He bowed politely, after his stern words.

Gulana did not say another word, but her eyes held the flame of her anger.

The Sharef flared his nostrils in irritation and frowned with his tiny mouth. "Danger follows you here, Lady Selena of House Savanar."

"Your men, led by Captain Bin-Guttar, brought us here," said Selena. "We would not have escaped the Erassians had they not done so."

"That is a debt I have long owed to your father. Do not read into it more than should be read."

"I offer you our thanks, nonetheless, Sharef."

"Your thanks are accepted."

The Sharef ate another handful of dates. While chewing, he ripped a fist-size chunk of bread from his loaf and stuffed it into his mouth. He began speaking before he had finished chewing.

"Your House, Lady Savanar, no longer exists. Sah Seg Savanar no longer commands the Kezelboj of Alwaz Deem, and neither do you."

Selena stood more upright, weighing her words carefully before she spoke, aware that the wrong words could cause them to be expelled from the oasis, this paradise upon the sands.

"We believe, Honorable Sharef, that others will rise."

"Oh, and what others are those?"

"I was rescued from the stake because others were willing to die for House Savanar. They fought through dozens of Grand Vizerian Guardsmen. They guided me out of the Seven Cities. We faced the Qhaliffa's River Galleys and lived. We made it across the sands, from the Semissari to here, with ten patrols of Erassian riders trying to find us, and yet here we are. The God of the Mountain and the Sands is with us, Honorable Sharef, would you not agree?"

"Do not talk to me of the God of Mountains or Sands, Lady Savanar, speak to me of armies. For God will not march upon me from Alwaz Deem and Saman Keer. No, armies will, thousands of men, and if the Qhaliffa sees fit, tens of thousands. So, what armies do you command, Lady Savanar? Tell me that."

Selena again waited before speaking. She inhaled and exhaled. She looked down at the sandstone floor beneath her sandals.

Gulana looked at her, willing herself to not speak for her, fighting the urge to shout out at the Sharef.

Oapah stared forward, his massive Omakhosian jaw set as if it were carved from granite.

Under the Sharef's gaze, Selena raised her head slowly.

"I command no armies as I stand before you, Sharef. These two brave souls were my only human protectors as I walked across the one hundred and fifty miles of sands from the Semissari. But many others have fought with us since I was rescued from the stake, and more shall come. We would not have made it here had not the Serpents of the Semissari walked out to draw away the Erassian patrols. But it is not only the Oath Holders of the Order that push back against the heavy yoke of the Grand Vizer. Jemojeen Jongdar has made enemies in the Seven Cities."

"Oh? What enemies?" asked the Sharef, his eyes small and shrewd. "I see proud Kezelboj lords groveling for his favor, licking the boots of their *Bulbanian* peasant overlord. The man was little better than a slave, a Demissary whose lineage traces back to a filthy village in the hills of the west. No, there are no armies to fight against Jemojeen. The last man with the courage to put that Bulbanian dog in his place was your father, and Jemojeen burned your father alive."

The Sharef reached for the block of goat's cheese, lifted it to his face, and ripped off a piece with his small mouth.

"Abu Akhsa," said Selena.

"Abu Akhsa?" asked the Sharef. "What do you know of Abu Akhsa?"

He was still chewing his mouthful of cheese, muffling the words. But even through the cheese, Selena could hear the contempt in his voice. Or perhaps it was fear hiding behind contempt. Selena looked around at the fine stone lines of the Sharef's grand home. The Sharef had much to lose.

Fear of losing what one has makes cowards of men. The words came to her mind as if from nowhere. The bearded man in the white robe looked down into her face in her mind's eye, brilliant as a living vision. The words came from his face.

"Do you know him, Lady Savanar? Have you met the Beserian rebel?"

"No, Honorable Sharef."

"Then do not tell me what he will or will not do. I know him."

"Abu Akhsa will march west," said Selena. "In accord with the Prophecy."

The Sharef laughed, spitting little chunks of cheese as he did so. "March on the Great Mountain?"

"The tribes unite behind him as they have not united in generations upon generations," said Selena, finding her courage rising inside of her, using the words Asatan the Serpent had given her, speaking them as if they were her own. And with each passing line of his derision, the Sharef's bullying had less and less effect.

"No army has taken the Great Mountain from the Qhaliffas, Lady Savanar, not in eight hundred years."

"It will not only fall from without," said Selena, quoting Asatan the Serpent again. "The people will rise from within."

"The people are afraid, and those who are afraid do not rise up."

"Are you afraid, Sharef?"

Ayzah Bin-Ayawad stared, frowning with his tiny mouth. Selena saw a flash of anger in his eyes.

"I am told, Honorable Sharef, that before my father died, he said that so long as a Bin-Ayawad rules as Sharef, a Savanar can trust Ben Hamur. Is that true?"

The Sharef's face altered. Selena's words had touched some part of him. Something had penetrated his outer armor, but it had not yet struck home.

"You are here," said the Sharef. "You are safe because of my men, are you not?"

"Yes, we are here," said Selena. "And we thank you and Captain Dungar Bin-Guttar." Selena nodded to the captain.

He nodded back.

"And are there not Erassians from Alwaz Deem, sent by Jemojeen to find you, here inside the walls of Ben Hamur right this moment, as we speak?" asked the Sharef, his voice rising. "And yet, you stand here with me, protected by my walls, and they are down below in the oasis. I am hiding you here, Selena Savanar, so do not tell me that House Savanar cannot trust Ayzah Bin-Ayawad. I am as honorable as my father before me."

A man rushed in from the edge of the sandstone platform.

For an instant, Dungar Bin-Guttar tensed, and his sword rose halfway out of its sheath. Then Dungar recognized the man's face beneath the helmet. He was a horse guardsman, one of Dungar's men. The man whispered into Dungar's ear. As he listened, Dungar's face hardened. He nodded and dismissed the man.

"Your Excellency," said Dungar, "a Demissary legion approaches our northern gate."

The Sharef swallowed hard, saliva, and fear moving down his throat in tandem. "Demissaries are here? Now?"

Dungar nodded. "Soon, Your Excellency."

"Which legion?" asked the Sharef. His face had gone as white as the cloth covering Selena's chest.

"The Third, Your Excellency, under the command of Ottovan Fanfar."

CHAPTER 48
We Shall Trust the God of the Sands

Valley of Kordon
52nd Day, Month of Gandus, 807
Anglian Calendar: February 21, 1879

Jack Caldwell had spoken nothing but Beserian for days. It may have been weeks.

He had lost track of time in the ocean of tents, where each day was like the other, surrounded by the vast, ever-present desert. The days on the sands moved at a different pace than days in other places. Individually, each of them felt as if they took a very long time. In the open hugeness of the desert, and even in as comparatively pleasant a place as the Valley of Kordon, everything was paced more slowly than in the outside world.

To get from one place to another took a long time. There were no railroads, no canals, no telegraphs. There were only relatively flat places that tended to connect one watering well to another in a chain of frequently traveled spaces. These were called caravan routes, and these were the roads of the desert. But they were nothing like roads in the New Anglian sense. They were merely foot and animal paths, well-worn with the use of centuries, even millennia. But so too could a sandstorm render one of these passages unrecognizable to an outside pair of eyes between one journey and the next, a mere week, days, or even hours later.

The Beserians, of course, could always see things that others could not. Their world was the sands, and so what they failed to see in the world outside the sands allowed them to see much more deeply in their own place.

The pace of Jack's days changed as the pace of his mind altered. The world appeared to him with less width and more depth. He began to see the world more like a Beserian. A Beserian could tell the tribe of a rider from a single piece of clothing—a headcloth, perhaps, that to a Spatanian eye or even to most Qhaliffans would simply look like a headcloth worn by every Beserian rider upon the sands. A Beserian could tell things about a man based upon his riding posture, the age and health of his camel, his footprints, his camel's footprints, his camel's dung, and his own as well. All of these things a Beserian tribesman could read as effortlessly as an Anglian read a Harmon newspaper.

But as slowly as the days passed in such a place, in succession, they eroded vast amounts of time. Jack had arrived three weeks before, and it seemed that it could as easily have been one week, or four or twenty. Such was the paradox of the sands. Time did not proceed as it did in other places.

To his face, they all called him Amahdi. He had begun answering to that name as naturally as his own. Indeed, the only one who had ever called him Jack Caldwell was Aurelio Demassi, the Vetenan guide, and he saw Demassi less and less. When he first arrived, he was with Demassi at all times. Now he had not seen him in a day. Or perhaps it was two days? Surely not three days?

Now, his days were spent in the company of Abu Akhsa, Hamid Salesi, and others on the Council of Elders and the Council of War. Ever since the miracle of the Staff of the Serpent, none doubted the wisdom of bringing the Western One into all discussions of when and how to march east. The God of the Sands and the Mountain had spoken, and one did not contest such a thing when one had seen it with one's own eyes.

Jack himself had spent the first several weeks only listening in the Council. Beserians, at least older Beserians, are known to be good listeners. But they are also good talkers. Whether the Western One was the fulfillment of the Prophecy or not—and after the miracle of the Staff of Wisdom, virtually everyone believed Jack was indeed the Promised One of the Prophecy—each Beserian leader still had his opinion on what should be done to advance upon the Seven Cities. Few hesitated to make that opinion known. All spoke often, except for the one whose words were most sought—Hamid Salesi.

Abu Akhsa himself led the men not by proclamation but by questioning the others—especially those sitting upon the Council of Elders and the Council of War. He was, by acclaim, Chief of Chiefs, Leader of all of the Beserians. Several leaders in the farthest eastern reaches—those along the Barban Mountains and along the border of Xin itself—might fail to recognize his leadership, but they were very far away. And they had problems of their own dealing with the Barbans of the east and the Gressians of the north.

The others were here, each tribe represented by a leader on the Council.

Few talked more than Cedak Celadeen, Chief of the Celadeens. Like many of the tribesmen he spoke for, Celadeen was short, wiry, handsome, and dark. He could deploy words as swiftly as strikes from his saber, which was among the swiftest of all the tribes. Celadeen was in his early middle years—perhaps thirty-four or thirty-five—but he could ride, slash, and wrestle with the strongest men in their early twenties. The arrogant ones, he called them. He had made many of them less arrogant after they challenged him over the years, and Celadeen was not a man to ever step away from a challenge.

The Celadeens held the lands just to the north of the Salesis. Their grazing properties were as huge as they were barren, stretching from the Bulbanian and Gressian borders in the west to nearly the center of the Sand Sea, the cold, open, windswept desert above the northernmost Qhaliffan city of Nor Gandus. Bounded by the Erassian steppelands and Gressian ambitions to the north and west, and by the Qhaliffans to the east and south, the Celadeens were a warrior tribe, hardened by centuries of fighting.

Cedak Celadeen, leader of the Celadeens, rose to speak now.

Jack Caldwell sat, with his legs folded underneath him. Jack liked Celadeen's voice. It was low and melodic, almost entrancing in its Beserian rhythms. Jack found that when Celadeen spoke, the effect was like the smoke of a water pipe, soothing and somnambulant, even if the words themselves were fierce.

Of course, Celadeen knew the power of his voice as well, for Jack had heard it nearly every day since he had begun sitting on the Councils. Celadeen, young for a Council Member, spoke as much as any man seated around the circle, perhaps more.

Despite it being the middle of the day, it was nearly dark in the Tent of the Councils. To discuss matters of war, Beserian Chiefs did not meet under the sun. When Jack had asked Abu Akhsa why they did not meet under a shade in the ample daylight, which would save the need to waste precious lamp oil, Abu Akhsa had said, with a look of surprise at Jack's ignorance, "Matters of darkness should be discussed in darkness."

And so now, for the tenth day in a row, or perhaps the eleventh—Jack could not readily recall—they met in the lamplight of the tent of the Chief of Chiefs, Abu Akhsa. The air was heavily scented and clouded by the smoke from water pipes.

None but Elders and War Chiefs were permitted to the Council. Elders were men like Salesi, Azadeem, Bazadak, and Celadeen, whose names were synonymous with the tribes they had led for generations upon generations. These names governed large tracts of the Sand Sea, vast areas of grazing where all who approached knew they were entering the lands of a family name.

The War Chiefs were different. They were men that the Elders had elevated from lesser families to lead the tribes against their enemies. These were fewer than the Elders, and they were among the most famous names upon all of the Beserian sands—men like Handsome Habeen Barcadey.

In his thirty-nine years, Habeen was said to have personally killed more than forty enemies of the tribes, some with his rifle, but most with his sword.

The people called him "handsome" after a saber took off his ear and scarred the left side of his face, moving from the place where his ear should have been, to the edge of his mouth, which rarely smiled. Some great fighters amongst the Beserians were said to be "happy warriors." Handsome Habeen was not among them.

Following the miracle of the Staff of Wisdom, Abu Akhsa proclaimed that Jack Caldwell would be added to the High Council as a War Chief. Aurelio Demassi's eyes burned with envy for days after that.

Demassi was too smart to remove his mask of calm and allow the tribesmen to see his rage within, but Jack had seen Aurelio's mask slip. Jack could read his resentment as if it were written across his forehead with a blade.

Abu Akhsa would never have come to possess Jack Caldwell—the Amahdi, my Amahdi—but for my efforts. They did not support me. They laughed at me, and now they claim Jack Caldwell for their own? As if they had been faithful all along? They do not appreciate me. I will not have my glory stolen from underneath me, even by Abu Akhsa, but especially not by Hamid Salesi. It was not Salesi that showed power. It was the Staff. So, while Jack sat inside Abu Akhsa's tent, Aurelio Demassi sat by himself outside of the tent, facing the desert, seething inside of himself.

Abu Akhsa's Swordguard lined the perimeter in a circle, standing, facing outward with their hands folded in front of them. They remained watchful yet unmoving, preparing to meet any who would dare interrupt the meeting of the Councils. Their sabers were sheathed but lay within easy reach of their hands. All men of the Swordguard wore a sky-blue band across their headcloth, the color of Abu Akhsa's banner. It was a color reserved for Abu Akhsa and his men alone, and none mistook it for anything other than what it was—the color of glory.

All of those present, whether Elders or War Chiefs, smoked as they debated. As with the rest—his speech, his meals, his clothing—Jack had adopted this custom as well. Jack pulled a mouthful of water-cooled smoke into his mouth as he inhaled through the wooden nozzle between his lips. Behind the nozzle, a flexible leather hose attached to the pipe, just above the water, drawing the smoke through the liquid and cooling it just before it went into Jack's mouth.

"Members of the Council," said Celadeen, his cadence steady and mellifluous. "My people have fought the Qhaliffa for generations, since the early years of our people's journey, since the expulsion of the great Beseri himself by the first of the Qhaliffan Usurpers, Mamet the Betrayer.

"Beseri—may the God of the Sands bless him and his descendants—did not choose my people to guard the north because we deserved it. He placed us there because we were hardy enough to endure the hot winds of war—the winds that strike our land from east, west, south, and north. He chose us because we Celadeens are like sand grass that may survive the heat of the summer sun for months without rain. We have fought the Qhaliffans to our south and east. We have fought the armies of their Kezelboj lords, we have fought their Erassians with their orange hair, and we have fought the worst they can throw at a man— their Bulbanian killers, the ones they call Demissaries, with their guns, their arrows, their lances, and their cruelty. So too have we fought the pale-skinned northerners, the ones called Gressians, and yet, like sand grass, we are still here. When Abu Akhsa sent word of the gathering, did we hesitate? Of course not. We rallied to the sky-blue banner, as we have before, and as we shall until the Prophecy is fulfilled and beyond."

Celadeen looked at Jack as he said the word "Prophecy." Jack felt an unsettling strength behind Celadeen's smoldering eyes. Unlike Bazadak or Handsome Habeen Barcadey, he was not a large and powerfully built man. But great power lurked inside of him, nonetheless.

A gruff voice spoke from across the tent. "By the God of the Sands."

Jack looked toward the voice and saw Bazak, Chief of the Bazadaks, the tribesmen of the southwest, nodding in agreement. Even sitting down, one could not miss the strength in his body. He had the shoulders and neck of an ox. His eyes were dark brown and intense, nearly black in the lamplight of Abu Akhsa's tent.

"By the God of the Sands," said Azam Azadeem, Chief of the Azadeems, nodding his long beard in agreement. He was tall and thin, as was typical of his people. He was from the central sands of the west, the lands between the oases of Ben Gamurian and Ben Hamur, the grounds upon the sands that had seen more caravans than any others. It was said that the leanness of the Azadeems was contrasted by the fatness of their flocks, fed by far more than the paltry grazing of their lands.

"By the God of the Sands," murmured a half-dozen other lesser Elders— Kateem, Hazim, Hazak, Sambad, and others. All were men in various stages of their middle age, leading tribes of the same name as their own, as had their fathers before them and their grandfathers before that. Each man pulled mouthfuls of smoke from his own water pipe, nodding in agreement.

"None here should doubt the commitment of the Celadeens," said Cedak.

Cedak waited, stopping his pacing and looking at Abu Akhsa, standing so that he faced him squarely. It was a bold way to stand, a challenge without words.

Hamid Salesi, grey-bearded and old, sat at Abu Akhsa's right hand, holding the Staff of the Serpent in his hands, resting the jagged upper edge against his shoulder. To Abu Akhsa's left sat Jack Caldwell, cross-legged upon a small goat-hair cushion like all of the others.

"Stand not as if you are facing an adversary," said Hamid Salesi. His voice was soft and low. Jack found he had to lean in when Salesi spoke. They all had to lean in.

Perhaps it is intentional, thought Jack, looking at the older man, who was not frail. *Other men speak loudly to be heard. Salesi speaks softly so that other men strain to listen to him. Others shout over rival voices. Salesi speaks so quietly that men are afraid they may miss his wisdom.*

"None doubt the commitment of the Celadeens, Cedak Celadeen," said Hamid Salesi. "You are among your people here. We are but parts of the same tribe, as arms and legs are parts of the same body. You are among the followers of Beseri, the upholders of the Prophecy of the God of the Sands. Our decision is not one of commitment but of wisdom. We are all committed. If we were not, we would not be here assembled under the Sky Banner of Abu Akhsa. But if we are all committed, are we all guided by wisdom? That is the question we must answer in this tent. Our enemies are many, wily, and strong."

Cedak leaned backward as if facing a strong wind blowing from where Hamid Salesi sat. All remained silent for long moments. The only sound was that of gurgling water pipes as the Elders sucked on their wooden nozzles, their exhaled smoke filling the air above in a dense, pungent cloud.

Salesi cleared his throat, breaking the silence. All heads turned toward him. "Out there, outside of this tent, our people and our herds await our decision. Our duty is to them. They will follow as we command. We must not fail them."

Celadeen sat down.

Jack turned his head away from Salesi, wondering who would speak next. *Why do they not just speak plainly? Through all of their courtesies, the path that each man desires is far from clear.*

"There are still more tribesmen that are not yet here," said Azadeem. "We would be stronger to march on Ben Hamur when we have them. As Salesi says, the forces of the Qhaliffa are many. Their guns are many, and their cannons are large. No man has advanced that far into the Qhaliffa's realm in force and lived to tell the tale. It is our lands—the lands of the Azadeems—upon which this army must cross. We should not cross until our forces are sufficient."

A light rumble of support rose to meet Azam Azadeem's words. Jack turned to see the Elders Hazak and Sambad nodding in approval.

"By the God of the Sands, Azadeem speaks wisdom," said Cedak, nodding vigorously, and speaking more loudly than the others.

He has courage, thought Jack, *but I know not whether he is wise or foolish.*

Abu Akhsa sat silent and stone-faced. Jack soundlessly sipped smoke from the nozzle of his water pipe.

"And what think the Bazadaks?" asked Hamid Salesi, waiting for the rumbling to die down.

Bazak Bazadak pulled the water pipe nozzle from his lips and exhaled. "When this Council declares it is time to march to the east, the Bazadaks will ride to the east. We are ready to ride now. We will remain ready to ride, by the God of the Sands."

Celadeen stood up again, his voice rising with his body. "I command the Celadeens and no others. I say we wait, like Azadeem. What say you, Abu Akhsa, Chief of Chiefs?"

Abu Akhsa stared straight ahead as if in a trance, unseeing, and unhearing. All eyes were upon him, yet still he waited, staring straight ahead as though asleep with open eyes, except for the stream of smoke slowly exiting his mouth.

Jack Caldwell turned and looked at Abu Akhsa. Abu Akhsa's profile was strong and handsome. His nose was straight, his chin slightly recessed, his brow flat and smooth. His black-and-silver beard jutted outward from his small chin like the ram of a river galley.

"In the days of my youth," said Abu Akhsa, at last, "my father told me that he would die before the Year of the Prophecy. In this, as in many other things, he was correct." Abu Akhsa's voice was strong and fluid. His accent was not easily placed as being from any one tribe. He was from the Valley of Kordon, but his voice blended north, south, east, and west, in an accent that spoke for all of the Beserians.

"In the Year of the Prophecy, he said more tribesmen would gather than had ever gathered before in his lifetime or in his father's or in his father's father's father's. In this, too, he was correct."

He reached down to his water pipe and pulled a mouthful of smoke into his lungs, slowly exhaling it. All waited for him to continue. He rose, with the ease of a man much younger. He was well built, neither tall nor short, but commanding all the same.

"Like many, I doubted whether the Amahdi would come. Like others, I doubted that he was the Amahdi when he did come. I saw him fall off of the camel. Though my lips were closed, my heart mocked him. I saw with the wisdom of a man, but there are other ways to see—" Abu Akhsa stopped speaking and stepped forward. He began pacing, looking down at the ground.

All eyes followed him.

"Others marched on Ben Hamur," Abu Akhsa continued. "We know their stories. They failed against the might of the Qhaliffa and his guns. With respect due to our ancestors, I say this with humility. They saw their enemies as men see. They saw the armies of the Qhaliffa as I saw this man before us." Abu Akhsa stopped and looked at Jack.

"Would the Amahdi come dressed as a beggar in ill-fitting clothes with a Vetenan guide as his companion?" Abu Akhsa continued, bobbing his head as he paced, his hands clasped behind his back. "Would the Amahdi fall off his camel, like a child who does not know how to ride before the eyes of all the Elders and War Chiefs and many of the people?

"I thought not, because I thought like a man. But there"—Abu Akhsa pointed at the broken staff in the hands of Hamid Salesi—"lies the way of seeing like the God of the Sands. There lies the Staff of the Serpent. Wisdom itself inhabits that wood, the wood of the ancient olive tree, the wood given to the Prophet of God.

"The Staff of Wisdom does not see through the eyes of men. The Staff of Wisdom chose that young man of the west, that man from beyond the mountains, from across the ocean, and across the broad lands on the other side. And when the staff touched the man's brow, he spoke in our tongue as he could not speak before. He does not now speak as a man who has struggled to learn our tongue. Do you hear the hint of a Vetenan or a Spatanian? A Macmenian or a Bulbanian? No, you do not. He speaks like a man who has slept in our tents, shared meat across our fires, and tended to our herds his entire life. He speaks our tongue as well as Celadeen or Azadeem, Bazadak or Salesi. Is that not so?"

Abu Akhsa looked at Celadeen.

Celadeen nodded. "It is so."

"And yet, you say we need more men." Abu Akhsa looked at Azadeem.

Abu Akhsa walked to Hamid Salesi and extended his hand. Hamid Salesi handed him the Staff of Wisdom, the Staff of the Serpent, old and gnarled, but still heavy and dense, with the scales of the Serpent carved deeply into its sides.

Abu Akhsa took it in his hands, feeling the weight of the olive wood in front of him, slowly lifting it up and down.

"This staff is broken. It is easy to underestimate. It would be simple to dismiss. Yet, this staff holds the power of the God of the Sands. It holds the power of the miraculous, the power of the Prophet of the One True God."

All of the Elders had stopped smoking their water pipes.

"Amahdi, rise."

Jack rose, his head nearly touching the fabric that formed the roof of the tent.

"Could you speak our tongue, the words of the Beserians, the People of the Sands before this staff touched your brow?"

"No, Abu Akhsa."

Abu Akhsa stepped toward him. Jack towered over the Beserian Chief of Chiefs.

"When you came here, to this desert, did you believe in the God of the Sands?"

"No."

All of the Chiefs stared, their eyes wide.

"Do you believe now?"

"Yes."

"Why do you believe, Amahdi?"

"Because I have beheld the power with my own eyes, my own ears, and my own tongue. My words are my testament. I could not speak, but now I can."

Abu Akhsa turned toward Celadeen and Azadeem.

"Here is my answer," he said. "It is not by our hands that we shall defeat the Qhaliffa. As you have said, my brothers Azadeem and Celadeen, none have toppled the Usurpers of the Great Mountain with the hands of man alone."

Abu Akhsa lifted the staff above his head.

"This staff seeks its companions. Its companions lie to the east. We must find them, and by the Prophecy, we must find another—she of the east, the descendant of Hom Hommuram."

Celadeen's cheeks flushed, knowing it was over and that they would march with the dawn.

"Those who have come, have come," said Abu Akhsa. "Our faith lies not with more men, though some may still rally to our banner, but with the God of the Prophet. Let the Qhaliffa trust his cannons, his Erassians, and his Demissaries. We shall trust the God of the Sands. We ride east with the rising sun."

CHAPTER 49
The Third Arrives

Oasis of Ben Hamur
35th Day, Month of Gandus, 807
Anglian Calendar: February 4, 1879

With a word, Ottovan Fanfar ordered his camel to its knees.

He dismounted, stepping onto the firm ground of Ben Hamur. The sandy dirt beneath his feet was dry and dusty, but he could smell the water of the oasis pools as if they were right in front of his face. At midday, the North Gate Square should have bustled with people. He scanned the merchant stalls on the eastern and western edges of the square. Their doors were still up, and their merchandise was displayed for any who wished to take it. Yet the square, but for Ottovan and his Demissaries, was empty.

Ottovan turned around, facing the north wall. He looked up at the men manning the archer step above the gate, a step from which an archer of Ben Hamur could rain arrows upon any trying to make their way across the wooden drawbridge. Or, if the bridge were up, a single archer could pick off any who were brave or foolish enough to try to wriggle their way through the long thorns of the zareba in the ditch that surrounded the walls of Ben Hamur.

"You there!" shouted Ottovan.

The half-dozen guards on the wall looked at him without speaking.

"Who is the officer in charge of this gate?" asked Ottovan, his voice loud and commanding.

"I am."

Ottovan looked at the man who spoke. He looked like the others, with dark eyes and the dark brown, sundried skin that came from years of patrolling hardened, mudbrick walls under the Sand Sea sun. The only mark that distinguished him was the green sash he wore across his chest. Like the others, he wore the wide-brimmed iron helmet of the men of the Sharef of Ben Hamur with a hard, boiled leather cuirass covering his chest and back, tough as a turtle's shell.

"What is your name?" asked Ottovan.

"Meeraz," mumbled the man, barely audible to Ottovan.

"It is midday, and this is a market square. Where are the people?" asked Ottovan.

"I do not know," said the man.

A massive man with a bright orange turban dismounted his camel next to Ottovan. His face and head were enormous, perhaps one and a half times as large as a regular man's. His jawbone was thick and bovine, as was his brow. In his hand, he held the long lance of a Demissary lancer, thirteen feet from bottom to tip and made of ash. It was long enough for a Demissary riding upon the hump of the tallest bull camel to spear a man lying flat on his belly right through the center, like a fish in a stream. Its point was nearly a foot long and made of dark steel, gleaming in the midday sun. The man himself stood a head and a half taller than his commander, and his scimitarus was a full one and a half times longer than Ottovan's, adjusted for the man's immense size.

"Use respect!" he barked, glaring up at the wall. "You call him Legion Commander Fanfar! You hear me, dog!"

It would have been impossible not to hear him. The tall man's voice was loud, deep, and grating, like gravel being poured into a wheelbarrow from a great height.

Ottovan raised his hand slightly. "Captain Ulgur, that is not necessary," he said, his voice low and calm.

"Apologies, Legion Commander Fanfar," said the leader of the gate guards. "I meant no disrespect."

Ulgur Uggatar, the giant man in the orange turban, said nothing, but he stood next to Ottovan, staring at the guard with malice in his eyes. He drummed the long heavy fingers of his left hand against the pommel of his scimitarus as he stared, his long lance in his right hand, the lance tip held high for all to see. As Ulgur stared, a half-dozen other lancers dismounted their lowered camels and stood next to him. All were tall, broad-shouldered men, but none were as tall as their captain, Ulgur Uggatar.

"There was no disrespect taken," said Ottovan, looking at the Sharef's man on the gate ledge. "Now tell me where the people have gone."

"They are hiding, Legion Commander Fanfar."

"Oh? Why are they hiding? We come here in peace." But in Ottovan's mind, the truth spoke. *No Demissary truly rides in peace.*

"We welcome you in peace, Legion Commander Fanfar. But they hide because they are afraid."

"They have nothing to fear, guardsman, and neither do you," said Ottovan. But again, his mind said what his voice did not. *That is true, so long as I am here. If I unleash Ulgur and his lancers, you will all have a great deal to fear.*

Ottovan preferred to leave Ulgur at the gate, but that posed risks too. Ottovan had learned, in the ten years he had observed Ulgur as his commanding officer, that he was better off keeping his eyes upon him. Ulgur was a sadist. To some men, cruelty must be learned; to Ulgur, it came naturally. He had come from central Bulbania, from a village not far from where Jemojeen had spent his boyhood. Ulgur, like the rest of the Demissaries in the Third Legion, was harvested in the Spring Reaping, taken from his parents and his village at the age of seven.

Some boys died early in the process of Demissary training. They were the ones that should never have been harvested from their villages in the first place. Most of the Bulbanian boys, however, learned to endure because they had the necessary mental and physical hardness to withstand the crucible. Slowly, but inexorably, the barracks of the Demissary Academy would shape them, like rocks carved by a glacier.

They would come to accept the God of the Qhaliffans, the God of the Mountain. They would come to accept the Qhaliffa himself as a kind of lesser God, and his word would become their law. This law was seared into them by the men who had already become Demissaries, men who were once frightened boys like them, fighting to survive the trials of each day, for years upon years.

A few boys, however, a very small few, flourished from the earliest days of their harvesting. Ulgur was such a boy. He was always tall, always broad, and always even heavier than he looked. That was the thing about Ulgur. He was incredibly dense, like the granite of the barracks walls.

Even in the early years, he could beat most of the other boys senseless with his hands and feet. He had killed another boy when he was in his tenth year of life, his third year of training. They were training with wooden scimitari, and Ulgur had hit the boy in the temple. That was the other thing about Ulgur, he was never much with a bow or a gun, but with a sword or a lance, there were none better. He was as quick as a small boy, had the reach of a tall boy, and a power that his age-brethren could not comprehend.

Even at ten, Ulgur could best the twelve-and thirteen-year-olds with a wooden sword or a tipless lance. The boy he killed was near the bottom of their age group, barely making it by. It may as well have been a fully grown Demissary that fought the boy that day. Ottovan, who was in his fifteenth year of life at the time and his eighth year of training, remembered looking at Ulgur and seeing that the ten-year-old showed no remorse over what he had done.

From that day forward, Ottovan knew that he was a dangerous one, one who would be of use to the Qhaliffa if he could be disciplined to use his power only when ordered. The Demissary instructors made Ulgur train with the older boys after that day. They were the only ones that could fight with him and survive the ordeal without serious injury. Even with a wooden sword, he was too dangerous for the others, even those a year or two years ahead of him.

"The Sharef begs your forgiveness for his delay, Legion Commander Fanfar." The Sharef's Head of the Household stood, round-faced and unarmed. He wore the same green sash as the leader of the guards above the north gate. It was nearly the color of a Demissary archer turban, but slightly darker. The skin of the man's face was freshly shaved, except for a long, oiled mustache and a strip of hair beneath his lower lip, extending like an upside-down triangle toward his chin.

As the man stepped closer, Ottovan caught the scent of perfume upon his clothes, drifting toward him in the warm afternoon air. The smell reminded him of Rama, his wife.

The man stepped down the stairs toward them with his hands extended in welcome. Ottovan extended his right hand with his palm facing up. Head of the Household took the hand with both of his own. The man's hands were soft, softer than Rama's.

"Tell the Sharef he is unwise to make the Qhaliffa's messengers wait."

The man flushed slightly, but clearly enough for Ottovan to see. Ulgur Uggatar, Ozgar Ogatonia, and Nemakar Hasdruba stood behind him, the captains each of the lance, the bow, and the fire.

With Umahar's medicines, Ozgar had recovered enough to feign a terrible illness that allowed him to ride upon a litter. He rode with the baggage for the first part of the journey, and none but Umahar were permitted to see him. By the time they arrived at Ben Hamur, Ozgar could mount his horse and carry his bow. He was markedly thinner and weaker, but more or less himself. His men cheered when they saw him, knowing nothing of his true travails.

Each of them carried their full array of weapons, with sharp scimitari swords in their scabbards at their sides. Ulgur gripped his lance in his right hand, Ozgar held his bow with a quiver full of poisoned arrows hanging from his back, and Nemakar carried three braces of pistols with a shotgun slung over his shoulder. Ottovan had left his pistols, carrying only his scimitarus in his scabbard. He did not expect trouble. This was, after all, only Ben Hamur of the Bin-Ayawads, and Ben Hamur had not rebelled in nearly four hundred years.

"Follow me, Legion Commander, Captains." Head of the Household bowed, turned, and led them up the marble staircase.

Ottovan looked at the walls. They were old but opulent, veined with pyrite, shining as if it were pure gold. Ben Hamur had been on the principal trade route with the west for the better part of a millennium. Not every year was a rich year, but there had been enough prosperous years to make the Sharefs of Ben Hamur exceptionally wealthy—enough to rival the richest Kezelboj lords in the Seven Cities.

Indeed, Ottovan remembered Jemojeen saying, long ago, when they were both mere Demissary Lieutenants, that it was the wealth of the great oasis Sharefs that made them weak. They had much to lose, so they were fearful men.

Fear poor men, Ottovan, not the rich. The rich will kneel if they fear for their riches; the poor and the desperate will only kneel if they fear for their lives, and some, if they are desperate enough, and if their despair is sufficiently high, will not kneel even then. Look at us? Are we rich? Of course not. Do men fear us? All men fear us. Jemojeen had always had ideas about such things.

They rounded the gold-veined white wall and emerged into an enclosed courtyard. Large wooden beams made from the trunks of date palms lay over the opening. Vines of aromatic jasmine covered the beams. Their flowers hung down, with thousands of white spots set against the background of green, elegantly shading the courtyard from the desert sun, the scent as pleasant as it was strong.

A massive cushion, wide and deep enough for three men, rested against the far wall, flanked by two others. Set in front of these, four empty smaller cushions were arrayed.

On the vast cushion against the wall sat Ayzah, Patriarch of the family Bin-Ayawad, Sharef of Ben Hamur, fat and enormous, sized more like a horned pachyrm from the banks of the River Oxus than a man.

Ottovan knew him by sight and had last seen him several years before. He was always a fat man, but he had grown considerably larger in the intervening years. His legs, each as thick as a well-fed sheep, stretched out in front of him.

To the Sharef's right, a woman sat. She was of regular size, even thin across her exposed middle section. Her legs were folded underneath her, and jeweled anklets adorned her bare feet, connected to a toe ring with a thin, golden chain. She wore a lavender veil across the bottom half of her face, so sheer as to be almost translucent. A veil of the same color covered her hair. On the other side of the Sharef sat a grim-faced warrior. His hair was long, dark, and hanging from his head beneath his helmet in oiled ringlets. No beard covered his jaw. His eyes focused on the Demissaries that had just emerged in front of him. A sheathed sword sat across his lap.

Ottovan's veteran Demissary eyes took in the entire picture in a moment, seeing from where an attack could come and evaluating where he would escape should an escape become necessary. His eyes considered the half-dozen men standing on either side of the courtyard, each man holding a sheathed sword in his hands, each staring straight ahead as if they were unhearing and unseeing statues. They could fly into action upon a signal from the seated warrior. Ottovan did not doubt that.

He could feel the tension. Something was amiss in Ben Hamur, but he could not yet say, for certain, what that was.

"Legion Commander Fanfar!" The Sharef's voice was loud and welcoming. It was not, however, as large as his body. Indeed, it tended toward being almost high-pitched.

Ottovan looked into the Sharef's face. The Sharef smiled, but the smallness of his mouth in the enormous girth of his face made him look like a massive smiling rodent, like the mud wallowers that lived on the banks of the Semissari Swamp, growing fat on a diet of reeds, of which there was an almost limitless supply.

"Please, sit with us," said the Sharef. "We are not regularly graced by such a compliment as the presence of an entire Demissary legion. To what do we owe this unexpected visit, Commander?"

Ottovan walked forward, smiling his most disarming smile. Remarkably, despite the years of fighting, training, and campaigning, he had kept his front teeth intact, and his smile was still pleasing to look upon.

Ulgur, Ozgar, and Nemakar each walked behind him. In his orange lancer turban, Ulgur walked with slow, measured steps. To his right, coming barely up to Ulgur's shoulder, Ozgar wore the emerald-green turban of an archer. Under normal circumstances, Ozgar would have to walk with effort to keep pace with the stride of the massive lancer. As it was, Ozgar was walking even slower, limping from the "illness" from which he was still recovering.

Ulgur was not an observant man, but nor was he blind. He could see that Ozgar had lost a significant amount of weight since their last campaign, and something was different in the archer's eyes, too, as if he were hiding something. Ulgur did not trust Ozgar at even the best of times, and these were far from that. Ulgur did not like archers, and Ozgar was every bit an archer. Men who did not do their best killing on a lance or a blade were not fully men in Ulgur's eyes.

On Ozgar's other side, Nemakar walked forward, tall and languid, his great mustache drooping down on either side of his mouth, his eyes hawkish above his long, thin nose. Like Ottovan, he wore the purple turban of a fire Demissary.

"We bring greetings from Alwaz Deem," said Ottovan, approaching the Sharef.

None of the swordsmen along the edges of the courtyard moved, but Ottovan could see the tension in the seated warrior's eyes. The eyes of the woman's face, however, were familiar and almost welcoming.

"Not Saman Keer?" asked the Sharef.

"We bring greetings from the Grand Vizer, Jemojeen Jongdar."

"We receive them most warmly, Commander. Please tell the Grand Vizer we are here to serve. Please sit with us," said the Sharef, pointing to the four cushions arrayed in front of him.

Ottovan and the others sat.

Ozgar lowered himself slowly, wincing as he did so. Nemakar offered him a hand as he settled upon his cushion. Ulgur looked at both of them with suspicion in his large dark eyes.

"I am not sure I have met your captains, Commander Fanfar. Indeed, when we last saw each other, were perhaps you still a Captain of the fire Demissaries?"

"You must keep a great deal upon your mind, Sharef," said Ottovan. "For you have met us all. We were here two springs before the last. We are Ulgur Uggatar, Captain of Lancers; Ozgar Ogatonia, Captain of Bow; and Nemakar Hasdruba, Captain of Fire."

Each man nodded when Ottovan said his name, except for Ulgur, who merely stared at the Sharef.

"Then, you must remember the Captain of our humble Horse Guard, Dungar Bin-Guttar," said the Sharef.

The man with the oiled ringlets beneath his helmet nodded. "And to my left," continued the Sharef, "Is my daughter, Alaya Bin-Ayawad. I do not have a son. She is my heir, so she will sit here to learn what Alwaz Deem has to tell the people of Ben Hamur."

The woman in the veil nodded.

Ottovan opened his mouth to speak when a line of servants rounded a wall and streamed into the courtyard. Each servant carried a tray. Upon each tray rested some delicacy or drink. The servants boldly strode into the open space between the Sharef and the Demissaries, bowing before they deployed the contents of their trays. When they left, Ottovan had a cup of cold tea placed in front of him. He still had the taste of goatskin water from the desert on his lips. He looked down at the tea, wanting to drink it down greedily.

"Sharef, you are most kind, but allow me to serve you," said Ottovan, rising from his cushion. He approached the Sharef, bowed, and presented his cup of kiln-hardened clay before the fat face, just under the man's small mouth.

"To another four hundred years of peace and prosperity," said the Sharef, drinking a long gulp from the cup.

Ottovan watched the apple of the man's throat bob up and then retreat to its resting place. Only then did he raise the cup of tea to his lips and drink. *Yes, if the Sharef poisons me, he will condemn his family to death, but I have no wish to trade my life for his.*

"To another four hundred years," said Ottovan, returning to his cushion.

Ottovan looked at the piles of figs, dates, grapes, and oranges piled on trays in front of him. A good poisoner could use any of them against him. Ottovan could feel the saliva in his mouth. After days of dried goat meat and the stink of well water, his stomach growled as he pictured himself sinking his teeth into each of the pieces of fruit.

Instead, he smiled. *The difference of a Demissary is his discipline,* said Ottovan to himself in his mind. *Demissaries are not tricked; Demissaries are not trapped.* Ottovan could see that none of his captains would touch the food either, until he, by eating it, had given them permission to do so.

"We are here in pursuit of a fugitive," said Ottovan.

The Sharef laughed. It was more honk than laugh, like the sound of an agitated Oxus River goose. "All of you for a fugitive? Does the Grand Vizer have so many troops that he assigns such tasks to entire legions?"

Ottovan allowed himself a small smile.

That was a bold thing, for a Sharef of Ben Hamur to mock the Grand Vizer of the Qhaliffa, when a legion of Demissaries was inside his oasis walls. Ottovan locked eyes with Dungar Bin-Guttar, the warrior to the Sharef's right, the man with the freshly oiled ringlets. *His eyes are wary and possibly fearful. The Sharef's bluster is cover.*

"And who is this fugitive?" asked the Sharef.

"A woman," said Ottovan. "She is the daughter of your deceased friend, Sah Seg Savanar of Alwaz Deem. She was last seen fleeing a patrol of Erassians, headed toward your walls."

Ottovan saw the faintest flicker in the Sharef's eyes. *Thank the God of the Mountain and the Sands, she is here.* Ottovan could feel the joy racing in his heart. He fought to master himself, waiting before he spoke, holding onto his frown as tightly as a weak swimmer grasping a raft in a swift river. *I must go through with this charade. Ulgur must report back to Jemojeen in a way that does not make Jemojeen send others before I am ready. The other Legions and the Kezelboj armies must stay away. If Jemojeen suspects otherwise, they will all converge on this place, and it will burn.*

"I know not of whom you speak, Legion Commander Fanfar."

Ottovan nodded, his eyes severe. "If you do see anything, Sharef, I trust we shall be the first to know?"

"Ben Hamur does not support treason, Legion Commander."

"Then I trust you will have no objection to my men patrolling your walls until she can be located?"

The Sharef shifted uncomfortably, adjusting one of his great sheep-sized legs with ponderous effort. "Whatever we may do to assist the Grand Vizer and His Majesty the Qhaliffa, we are honored to do, Legion Commander. Indeed, we would welcome the assistance."

"Very well," said Ottovan, rising from his cushion. Startled, his Captains rose in rapid succession, with the wounded Ozgar moving the slowest.

He is a good liar, thought Ottovan, *a good liar indeed. And that may save us all.*

CHAPTER 50
Anglia Answers

Parliament of the Anglian Imperium
City of Anglia
February 22, 1879

Lord George Harmon rose from the bright red cushion beneath him on the wooden Government bench, brushing his waistcoat with his left hand as he always did when he was nervous. Many in the House believed Lord Harmon was never nervous, but such men were wrong. *All but fools become nervous*, he had once said when asked. *Some, however, through experience, repetition, and position, learn to become less anxious by turning challenges that frighten other men into matters of commonplace occurrence.*

Lord Harmon was indeed such a man, and few men could conceive rising to the challenges of his ordinary days—deciding editorial content that could reach hundreds of thousands on slow days and millions when there was a scandal, shaping government policy, and exerting his will against the leaders of business and governments in Anglia and elsewhere. Nonetheless, speeches to a full House of the Elected—all 479 members filling out every seat in the great Oval of Parliament—were not commonplace. Such a moment still placed a pair of fluttering wings in Lord Harmon's guts and a tension in the walls of his throat.

Lord Harmon cleared his passageway with a fierce cough-like grumble, holding his stack of note cards in his left hand. Each connected with the next in the upper left corner by means of a ribbon running through a punched hole, and each had a number in the bottom right-hand corner. His directions to himself on those cards were precise, and he knew that losing the order of the cards could invite disaster.

It was a trick he had taught himself—to read his note cards while pretending to speak extemporaneously. Over the years, he had acquired a reputation as a formidable Parliamentary debater. Even though he had pulled off his trick for years, he revealed his method to no one, not even after too much wine, and not even to the Prime Minister, beside whom he did not have a better friend in Anglian politics.

He cleared his throat a second time, more softly than the first. He inhaled deeply through his nose, allowing the air to fill his ample lungs.

The House sat silently in anticipation. It was absolutely full, with, from as best as Lord Harmon could tell, all 479 faces of the Elected Members of the House turned toward him: 88 from North Anglia, 94 from West Anglia, 117 from Old Anglia, and 180 from South Anglia, where more than fifty-five percent of Anglians lived, but which had only thirty-seven percent of the Seats of the Elected. This disparity, of course, gave the governing Crown and Country Party much of its commanding majority over the Liberty and Commerce Party, and the Government did not intend to make any electoral alterations that might change that reality. *Tradition is not merely tradition, but also strength.* At least that was what the campaign slogans said.

"Some seated here today," began Lord Harmon, his voice loud and clear, "may attempt to declare the tragedy most recently reported in this nation's newspapers as a private matter affecting only a select few, including, among others, my family. That, of course, is to their grave discredit." Lord Harmon paused—as he had specified in his note cards that he must do—to glare across the dark green carpet of the vast, oval-shaped well at the center of the House and into the eyes of the Opposition. By wearing his monocle and squinting, he could both read his note cards and appear to stare at his rivals at the same time.

"Some say we must not turn a private tragedy into a matter of state concern." Lord Harmon paused again.

He let his gaze sweep across the front row of the Opposition, the row where the leadership of the Liberty and Commerce Party sat in a line, resting upon their dark blue cushions, upon their curved wooden benches, all facing toward the center of the green oval of carpet where three golden rings interlinked. When Lord Harmon's gaze came to Willem Hammerstone, leader of the Opposition, and Orlando Browne, his party Whip, he let his eyes rest for a long, uncomfortable moment.

"And then, of course," continued Lord Harmon, "some have given quotations to certain newspapers saying this tragedy was deserved. Some have even claimed this is not a tragedy at all, but rather the reaping of what has been sown, the harvest of the greed of a certain family. They say what happened in the Sand Sea was merely the justice to which that family was due. That family is—"

Lord Harmon paused.

"—of course—"

Lord Harmon paused again, as was instructed on his notecard, and lowered his voice to its deepest and gravest tone.

"My own."

Lord Harmon paused again and waited.

The Government side of the House, the portion occupied by the majority Crown and Country Party, rose from their crimson cushions as one, erupting into a hurricane of boos. The cacophony came forth as a fully formed tempest and thundered louder and louder until it was impossible for Lord Harmon to speak.

Lord Harmon stood, repressing a smile, as satisfied as an officer who had just unleashed his artillery squarely upon the enemy. The shouting was deafening to the point of hurting his ears, but it was, if anything, a pleasurable pain. His Elected Members, or EMs, as they were called, were enraged on his behalf, and they were enraged as he had perhaps never seen them enraged before. The fights in the newspapers had reached a new low in political decorum, even for the present age, which was not known as an age of political decorum.

Lord Harmon properly feigned, in his official remarks to his own reporters for quotation: fatigue, sadness, and outrage, but most of them—at least the most senior reporters—could see that there was joy in his heart. He could scarcely print newspapers fast enough to keep pace with the scandal.

The *Illustrated Telegraph* had nearly run out of overnight ink, which had never happened before in its forty-four-year history. Lord Harmon, without question, stood at the center of the scandal, but as Lord Harmon liked to say before exhaling the smoke from a victory cigar, *the hurricane does not batter that which stands in its eye.*

At long last, the boos from the Government benches receded. The Crown and Country EMs finally sat down, and as the final boos died off, the only sounds were the pounding of the lone Parliamentarian's gavel and his solitary shouts of, "Order! Order!"

The room quieted enough for Lord Harmon to resume.

"However, I know all of you seated here today are gentlemen. I suspect that none would dishonor themselves with such words, and I hope the debate does not degrade to that which we have seen in the papers."

"Hear, hear! Hear, hear!" thundered the arcs of the Government benches, with fists shaking in the air.

"Shame! Shame!" shouted the Opposition members. "They are your papers! They are *Harmon* papers! Hypocrite!"

Orlando Browne rose from the front row of the Opposition; he was lean, with perfectly tailored pants showcasing his long, mountain-hiker's legs. Many society women in the City commented on the attractiveness of the Opposition Whip's legs. A vain man to begin with, the Honorable Orlando Browne had grown all the vainer in his years in Parliament and in his rapid ascent up the

Liberty and Commerce Party ranks. His hair was jet black, thick, and swept straight backward, not terribly unlike Peter Harmon's—a fact Lord Harmon had not failed to mention with a heavy tone of disapproval to his eldest son more than once. Born of a Spatanian mother, Orlando Browne's skin was olive-brown, without blemish, and glowing with the healthy luster of frequent exercise. Quick, intelligent eyes twinkled with mischief beneath sharp black eyebrows.

"A point of order, if I may?"

His voice was sharp, like a cracking whip, always audible in even the farthest reaches of the great Parliamentary Oval. If Lord Harmon swung his voice like a broadsword, Orlando Browne deployed his own like a rapier.

"You may not," said Lord Harmon, his voice booming.

Orlando Browne shrugged, smiled his most charming smile, and sat down.

"Boo! Boo! Boooo!" thundered the Opposition. "We will not be silenced! Point of order! Boo!"

The Parliamentarian's gavel banged its mark, impotent to silence the Parliamentary horde.

Along the oval of the well, several spots away from Lord Harmon, an older man with silver and black hair sat slumped forward, leaning on a silver-handled black cane. He wore an amused look on his face, smiling the closed-lip smile of a cat, the smile for which he was famous. On his chin, a small silver spike of a beard pointed toward the carpet.

Lord Harmon glanced at him.

The older man nodded, ever so slightly, but unmistakably. Outside of the House of Parliament, the seated man often took guidance from Lord Harmon, especially if it was a matter having to do with how some bill, issue, or message should be presented in the newspapers to reach the public. But in the House itself, there was no master to the older man with the cat's grin. He was the master of masters, against whom few could maneuver, and none could best.

Still vibrant in his seventy-second year, the Prime Minister of the Anglian Imperium, Binyam Aurelian, was the only Macmenian to have ever held a place in the House of the Elected, much less a ministry seat, much less the leadership of the entire government. He had faced down bigotry his entire career. He had prevailed.

Seeing Aurelian's nod, Lord Harmon cleared his throat again and continued.

"Let us cut to the root of the matter! A hostile force has attacked an Anglian diplomatic expedition, traveling beneath the four squares and three rings of Her Majesty's Flag. Shall we allow such an attack to go unanswered by this Government?"

"No! Nooo! Never!" shouted the Government benches. The EMs shouted as if drunk. As the debate was being held after a break for dinner, some likely were.

"And if we allow it this time," asked Lord Harmon, "what shall stop the next band of savage tribesmen from attacking our next diplomatic mission?"

"Stand for honor!" shouted an EM directly behind Lord Harmon. He caught a whiff of wine as the man shouted "honor" a second time, shaking his fist in the air.

The Parliamentarian continued to swing his gavel like a woodpecker attacking a tree. He was also shouting, Lord Harmon could tell from seeing the movement of the man's mouth, but he could not hear him over the furious din behind him.

In the front row, Aurelian continued to lean back with his thin legs crossed, as if ready to fall asleep. He glanced casually at Lord Harmon and nodded again.

"I yield the remainder of my time," said Lord Harmon, "to the Prime Minister!"

Binyam Aurelian rose slowly on his cane.

When he was slumped in his chair, as he usually was, it was easy to forget that he was actually a tall man. Like a coiled snake reaching out, showing at long last its full, formidable length, Aurelian straightened himself into an upward position, standing nearly as tall as Lord George Harmon. Aurelian cocked his head to the left, taking in half of the room and quieting them as he did so. Then he cocked his head to the right, quieting the remaining half.

"When I was a boy," said Aurelian. His voice was not stentorian, nor did he shout. Indeed, in retrospect, it would have been hard to say that he even raised his voice. Rather, he merely spoke in a usual way, as if he were sitting across the parlor on a sofa, expressing his musings about whatever topic was at hand. The effect was that all quieted so they could hear, and all leaned forward—Crown and Country and Liberty and Commerce members alike—so as to hear the old man better. For even as much as the Liberty and Commerce members, or L&Cers, as they called themselves, might detest Lord Harmon and the other Crown and Country members, they could not find it in themselves to hate the Prime Minister. Perhaps it was his age.

Perhaps it was the legend he had become at some point in his fourth stint as Prime Minister, but he had somehow risen above the thrusting and parrying that kept the other EMs entangled in the battles of the day.

Those who had already silenced themselves severely hushed the others, and Aurelian again showed his feline grin.

"Be quiet!" hissed the Crown and Country benches, speaking to their own.

"Listen to the Prime Minister," said the L&Cers, chiding their fellow Opposition members.

"When I was a boy," began Aurelian, again, "I lived near the southern coast of Old Anglia. My father, as many of you will recall, was a cobbler. His shop was on a lane just off the coast road, not far from the town of Destingham. I helped him in the early mornings before he sent me off to school. As he continued working into the morning, I had to walk to school by myself. I had no older brother, no cousin, to escort me.

"For the first year or so, I walked to school without incident. But one day— as I neared the third farm along the road—a boy approached me. He was a big farm boy with flaxen hair. I was not yet tall, and I have never been broad. The boy frightened me. He told me if I did not give him my apple that I carried in my hand, he would throw me into the irrigation ditch, the same ditch he and his family used as a latrine. I gave him the apple.

"Some days later, as I made my way down the road toward my school, I saw him again, barring the way, standing in the middle of the road. I had learned from my first encounter. I had stuffed my apple as well as my small loaf and my wedge of cheese underneath my notebook at the bottom of my pack. He stopped me, he dug through my pack, and he took it all.

"I spent that day hungry. There were many other days like it, after that time. It was the rare day that he did not stop me to take my food. And then one day, another boy was standing with him, blocking my way. His friend was like him, only with a crueler look. That day they took my food and my shoes. I could hide my hunger, but I could not hide my bare feet. My father, the cobbler, did not fail to notice a pair of missing shoes. He asked me what had happened.

"Having carried this secret burden on my own for the better part of a year, I broke down and cried. I told him everything, weighed down by my own shame and cowardice. I expected him to punish me further for wasting all of that food and for losing my shoes. He sat quietly for a long time before asking me, 'Binyam, are you strong enough to beat this boy? If you forget your fears and strike him as hard as you can, could you free yourself?' I said I did not believe I could. He was too large, and I was afraid of him.

"My father considered this for a good long while. Then he called up Benham, his apprentice. Benham was older than I was, tall and strong, well into his fourteenth year. My father told Benham he would be escorting me to school the next day and that if he retrieved my shoes from the flaxen-haired boy, he would reward him handsomely. I still remember his words to this day, 'Benham, your reward will be commensurate with your deed.' My father did not say such things lightly.

"Do you know what happened next?"

The 479 members of the House of the Elected stared in anticipation, like a vast circle of children listening to their grandfather tell them a tale. Except, of course, these children commanded the government of the Anglian Imperium, and by extension, all of the armies and fleets the empire could deploy.

"Benham only needed to strike him once. He struck him hard, and the boy gave me my shoes. He did not take my lunch again."

The House of the Elected waited in silence.

Just as a mob that is whipped into a frenzy continues to rage with a self-perpetuating force, so too does a group that has listened for a long while hesitate to shatter the quiet. Just as a man requires courage to calm a mob, so too does a man require initiative to break the silence, when hundreds are not speaking. Aurelian did not wait for a courageous man to break the peace.

"Flaxen-haired boys and tribesmen are no different," he said. "If we wish to have peace, we must strike down those who break it. The Beserian tribesmen attacked men traveling under our flag. If we wish the Anglian Imperium to remain an Imperium, we will strike them back."

Lord Harmon spoke first. "Hear, hear!"

That broke the dam, and the support flowed out of the Crown and Country EMs like a river in flood.

"Hear, hear! Hear, hear!"

Willem Hammerstone rose ponderously to his feet, all six feet five inches of him. His shoulders were broad as a woodcutter's, and a shaggy mane of silver-brown hair hung from his leonine head. If Orlando Browne was the pretty new foliage of the Liberty and Commerce Party, attracting new voters and new headlines, Willem Hammerstone was its trunk and its roots, without whom, some argued, there would be no Liberty and Commerce Party.

He was born with an orator's voice and a showman's instincts of how to use it.

"A question for the Prime Minister?"

Aurelian was still standing, leaning on his cane for support. He looked at Hammerstone, his rival of nearly three decades, smiled his cat grin, and nodded to the Parliamentarian.

"I yield for a question."

"I thank the Prime Minister," said Hammerstone. "As we can all agree, it is better to deploy Her Majesty's armed forces with the consent of both parties, not just one."

"There are more than two parties!" shouted a voice from the edge of the oval. It was true. There were technically seven political parties, not two. But in most votes, there were only two that counted.

"Order!" shouted the Parliamentarian, slamming his gavel.

Hammerstone looked in the direction of the shout with a Hammerstonian glare, the kind for which he was famous. He stared, stone-faced, with his ice-blue eyes fixed unblinkingly upon his target. Among the many things Willem Hammerstone hated, being interrupted was one of them.

"Might the Prime Minister answer why the Liberty and Commerce Party should vote to deploy Anglian troops into a desert in which we have no Imperial interest? Might the Prime Minister share with the House why Anglian blood should be spilled over a patch of worthless sand?"

"I am told," said Aurelian, "the Beserians were not working alone. I am told they were encouraged to strike us by a foreign power."

"Oh?" said Hammerstone, "and might the Prime Minister tell the House what foreign power that would be? And what proof he holds?"

Aurelian smiled.

While it was often difficult to tell whether Aurelian's smiles arose from genuine mirth or were deployed for deliberate effect, Lord Harmon could see that this smile was genuine. Aurelian had set a trap, and, as he had done for years, Hammerstone had thundered his way into it.

"I offer no proof, except that under a Gressian Count by the name of Usor Nepopolous, an armed expedition traveling under the Gressian flag hurries its way south toward the Valley of Kordon. I offer no proof, except that the Beserians have *not* attacked that Gressian expedition. I offer no proof except that around the same exact time that the Gressian expedition launched south under Usor Nepopolous, the Beserians chose to attack those traveling under our Anglian flag."

Hammerstone stared at the Prime Minister, his boulder of a head leaning forward, his ice-blue eyes seeing the contours of the trap around him.

"I should think," said Aurelian, his words moving forward with the relentless inevitability of a constrictor snake, "that it is rather very much in our Imperial interest to disallow those who attack our flag with impunity to then invite in our adversaries. And I should think the patriotic members of the Liberty and Commerce Party would agree with that."

Hammerstone continued staring, not speaking. Orlando Browne looked up at him. Hammerstone did not like bending to Aurelian on any matter, but Browne could see that on this matter, he must.

Aurelian rose to his full height, no longer leaning on his cane.

He said, "And regarding Anglian blood being spilled on the Sand Sea, as the Honorable Mr. Hammerstone is surely aware, our Imperium possesses a formidable army just south of the Sand Sea. I hereby move this body, immediately, to authorize Governor Freer in Khyderbad to dispatch what regiments he sees necessary and proper to both punish the rogue Beserian tribesmen and to rescue all surviving members of Mr. Stanwich's expedition. And, I ask the honorable members of the Liberty and Commerce Party to vote with us, as loyal subjects of the Imperium."

Hammerstone nodded to Orlando Browne, knowing he had lost. He leaned toward Browne, who offered his ear.

"Release the votes. Hindean troops only."

PART IV

A STRANGER ONCE AND FOREIGN BORN

CHAPTER 51
Colonel Spinner

Camp of the Gengali Lancers, Harafhan Mountains
Southern Border, Sand Sea
March 1, 1879

The blizzard showed no signs of relenting. The wind had declined to join the snow, and the flakes fell nearly straight down, thickly filling the air.

Lieutenant Spears could barely hear his horse's hooves on the path, so muffled were they by the snow blanket beneath them. He looked down into the dark, nearly black abyss to his right. The path was narrow, too narrow for two horsemen to comfortably ride side by side. On his left side, the mountain rose as a nearly sheer face, higher than Spears could see through the falling snow. To the right, the path dropped off several feet away, at the edge of a cliff dropping down into a chasm.

In the summer, it was said that a beautiful, clear stream flowed along the base of the chasm. It was not summer.

Spears could not see any stream now. He could not even see the bottom. His stomach churned. Spears had never liked heights. Nor could Spears envision anything beautiful when the Harafhan Mountains came into his mind. All he could see was the dark abyss to his right and imagine the dark, bearded faces of savage tribesmen waiting to ambush him around the next corner, tribesmen that could climb mountainsides like goats, attack, and disappear before men like Spears had time to unholster their rifles.

"We're close now."

Spears turned around to the voice. Lieutenant Rodes rode just behind him, his face muffled by a dark wool scarf that came up nearly to the edge of his khaki pith helmet, which was lightweight and meant for comfort in the heat of summer. A narrow slit for his eyes remained between his helmet and his scarf.

"We should have waited for the snow to pass," said Spears, his voice tense and edged with fear.

"It will keep snowing," said Sergeant Binda. His red turban was tightly wrapped on his head in the Hindean style, covering both of his ears and leaving an inverted V-shape of skin visible on his forehead. He, too, had stuffed a scarf into the high stiff collar of his tunic, covering most of his lower face against the cold.

"And we have no time to waste," said Rodes. "You heard the Governor."

Spears turned back around, looking at the path with the frustration of knowing that they were right. He was Rodes's senior officer by three months, which meant that he was in command, and if they failed to deliver Governor Freer's message quickly enough, the blame would rest upon him.

"How much farther?" he asked, turning around.

"One mile," said Sergeant Binda.

Binda had campaigned in these hills for several years, and he knew his way as well as many of the Harafhan tribesmen. Neither Spears nor Rodes had yet campaigned at all, much less in a place like the Harafhan Mountains. They had both volunteered, hoping for glory and relishing the chance to meet a hero like Colonel Willem Spinner.

Spears regretted that yearning for glory now, thinking of the warm barracks he had left in Khyderbad with his regiment, replete with fresh, well-cooked food and as much wine as he cared to drink.

"Very well, ride on," said Spears, leaning forward into the snowstorm.

They traveled up and to the left, rounding a sharp corner around the mountain. A gnarled pine tree grew out laterally from the slope, causing him to duck underneath it. The pine needles brushed his back, sending ice-cold snow down his collar.

"Three Gods damn this thrice," Spears grumbled, arching his back as the snow touched the skin along his spine. He rode onward.

Rodes and Binda followed in silence. They completed the journey around the loop and came to the base of a long, straight incline.

Spears looked up. At the top of the rise, at the edge of his vision, he saw colors that did not belong in the mountains. The colors were neither grey nor green nor the ever-present white of snow. He saw red and blue and a flash of gold. He looked more carefully, widening his eyes, and saw an obstruction on the path—the kind a regiment would place as a guard post.

"Three Gods, look!" said Rodes.

"That is the Gengalis," said Binda.

Spears felt a rush of relief. He reined in his optimism and scanned the path. There was nothing he could see, no place for an ambush, only the way in front of him, the sheer face of the mountainside to his left, and the bottomless gorge to his right.

"Ride," he said, kicking his heels against his mare. She quickened into a trot. He kicked his heels again and clicked his tongue against his teeth. His mare moved into a canter, gliding across the snow. Spears looked forward, wanting nothing more than to be on the other side of the barrier that separated the wildness of the tribe lands from the safety of Colonel Spinner's regiment. He cantered forward, the snow falling all around him, the chasm vast and open to his right, the cliff massive and unyielding to his left.

They approached the barrier. The flag was now clear, tall and imposing, standing proudly against the snow. The barricade was a felled pine log, stripped of its needles and barring the approach at the height of a man's chest with a crude lean-to erected just behind it.

A trio of yellow tunics emerged in the path behind the log. Their pants were dark blue, the same color as their angular Gengali turbans, far different from the Hindean style. A stripe of bloodred cut at a diagonal across the blue and a white plume arose from the left center. Spears, like all patriotic Anglians who dreamed of glory, could recognize that uniform at a distance. *By the Three Gods, we are here, with the Gengali Lancers.*

"Halt!"

The order came in Anglian. Spears reined in his mare.

The three men in the yellow tunics spoke with rifles raised, Hart-Henry carbines ready to place .45-caliber bullets in each of their chests.

"I am Lieutenant Spears! I ride with Lieutenant Rodes and Sergeant Binda of Her Majesty's Tthirteenth Hindean Infantry. We bring word from Governor Freer of Khyderbad for Colonel Spinner."

The three bearded men in yellow tunics looked at them warily, not lowering their rifles.

"We were not expecting riders," said the man on the far right with sergeant's stripes on his shoulder.

"We bring orders," said Lieutenant Spears.

The Gengali sergeant looked at him with discerning eyes, searching for any sign of a trap. Just as quickly, his eyes relaxed. He barked an order in Gengali and lowered his rifle. The others did the same. They stepped to the barricade and, with considerable effort, lifted the heavy log off of the X-posts and dropped it into the snow.

"Hurry," said the sergeant. "There are tribesmen near."

Spears rode forward, his heart pounding in his chest.

The camp lay several hundred yards past the barricade, around another curve on the mountain where the path opened into a wide, flat plain, broad enough to host an entire regiment of cavalry. The men at the barricade had made them wait for an escort, which consisted of a tall, grim-faced sergeant and a short, humorless corporal. Both men were lean and bearded beneath their blue turbans with the red stripe and both wore the bright yellow tunics of the First Gengali Lancers, or as it was better known in Anglia, "Spinner's Riders." Neither man wore an overcoat against the falling snow.

Spears looked at them in amazement, grateful for the warmth of his dark navy cloak, the red of his army tunic entirely hidden beneath the thick wool of his outermost winter garment.

"Has it snowed much these past weeks?" he asked.

Neither the sergeant nor the corporal responded as they rode through the camp. The sun had set behind the mountain, and darkness fell fast upon the camp, the temperature dropping with the sun.

Perhaps they did not hear me, thought Spears. He was never quite sure how much a turban might muffle sound. He raised his voice. "Sergeant, has it snowed much these past weeks?"

The sergeant looked at him. His eyes were as dark and cold as the camp. "Yes, Lieutenant," he said.

They rode on in silence, passing neat rows of white A-frame tents on either side of them. Fires burned in front of the threshold of each. Men huddled around them. Few looked up at the new arrivals. Ample trees grew in the Harafhan Mountains, and the Gengalis were burning the wood in copious amounts. If there was any doubt where the camp was, the tribesmen need only follow the overpowering scent of woodsmoke.

"Wait here," said the sergeant, his voice gruff.

He rode ahead, leaving the corporal sitting astride his mount next to Lieutenant Spears with Rodes and Binda mounted on their own horses just behind them. It was cold and getting colder. Rodes shivered underneath his thick woolen cloak. Binda had adjusted his scarf up so it was barely possible to see his eyes. Only a small inverted *V* of forehead skin showed beneath his tightly wrapped Hindean turban.

"Is he getting Colonel Spinner, Corporal?"

"Yes, Lieutenant," said the corporal.

The man who emerged from the tent ahead of them was not Colonel Spinner. He was a large, broad-shouldered Gengali, built more like a Gressian grenadier than a Hindean. The skin on his face was dark brown, nearly the color of a Hohsa tribesman—or at least as dark as Spears had heard Hohsa tribesmen were. He had never been to Omakhosi to see for himself.

Unlike most of the other Gengalis that Spears had seen, the man did not have a beard, but rather, a neatly trimmed mustache, much like Spears's own.

To Spears's surprise, he looked down and saw the man wore the gold markings of a Commissioned Major on his shoulders.

Spears saluted. Seeing him do so, Rodes and Binda followed his example. The Major with the mustache saluted back.

"Sir," said Spears, somewhat tentatively. He had never before met a Gengali Commissioned officer. In the Anglian Hindean Army, all Commissioned Officers were Anglian. He had forgotten that Spinner's Riders were different.

"What is your business here?" asked the major.

"We bear an urgent message for Colonel Spinner," said Spears, using his most forceful voice.

"The colonel is occupied at the moment," said the Major, his voice mild. "You may deliver your message to me."

Spears's cheeks flushed. He was not sure what to do with this Gengali with the golden marks of a major. He resisted the urge to glance at Lieutenant Rodes. Rodes always seemed to know what to do in these moments. Spears often wished Rodes was the senior by three months. The chasm between command and second-in-command was vast.

"If I may, Lieutenant Spears?" asked Rodes.

Spears nodded.

"May I have your name, Major?" asked Rodes with more than a little hint of Anglian superiority in his voice.

The Major smiled. His teeth were starkly white against the dark brown of his skin. "Rasouda."

"Very well," said Rodes, smiling his condescending smile for which a certain high class of Anglian was famous. "We bear word from the Governor of Khyderbad, Sir Bartimus Freer. He has asked us to deliver our message to Colonel Willem Spinner and him only. We would, with the utmost misfortune, have no choice but to relay back to the Governor that Major Rasouda of the First Gengali Lancers refused to allow us to carry out his wishes."

Major Rasouda continued smiling, a bright streak of white stretched widely across his broad, dark face. His eyes, however, had ceased smiling. Indeed, Lieutenant Spears saw the major's eyes and felt like backing his mare up several paces.

"Wait here, Lieutenants," said Major Rasouda, turning and walking slowly away. He rounded the edge of a tent and disappeared behind it.

"An uppity fellow, eh?" asked Rodes.

Spears glanced back at Sergeant Binda, for whom he had great respect.

"He is a major," said Spears.

"A Gengali Major," said Rodes, with the hint of a scoff.

They waited for long minutes in the cold. No one came to meet them.

"Should we ride to find Spinner's tent ourselves?" asked Spears.

"If I may, Lieutenant," said Sergeant Binda, "I recommend that we do not. They know we are here. They will send for us."

"I am not going to sit here to freeze to death under a Three-Gods-damned cloak in a Three-Gods-damned snowstorm to be made a mockery of by a Gengali," said Rodes.

"Then perhaps you prefer a Colonel of Her Majesty's Cavalry?" said a voice, slightly slurring the word "cavalry."

Spears nearly jumped off of his horse, his hand flying to his saber hilt. How the man had approached from behind them, he did not know.

Spears turned his horse around to face the man as Rodes and Binda did the same.

The man stepped forward into the moonlight. Like the Gengalis, he wore no cloak over his bright yellow tunic. Unlike his Gengalis, he was hatless, with closely shaved hair on a nearly balding head, thinned to the point of bareness on top. His face was flushed, pink as a mountain sunrise.

Rodes urged his horse a step forward, preparing to berate the man when he looked down to see the Golden Lion of an Anglian Army Colonel upon the man's shoulder. Rodes snapped his hand up in a salute.

"Colonel, sir, I am Lieutenant James Rodes, Thirteenth Hindean Infantry."

The blush-faced Colonel did not return the salute. He stepped forward another step. Rodes caught the scent of whiskey advancing off the colonel, like a woman's perfume.

"You in charge here, Rodes?"

"No, sir. I am," said Lieutenant Spears, his hand still saluting. His back was parade ground straight. Sergeant Binda followed Spears's lead.

As the slightly overweight man stared up at the pair of lieutenants and the sergeant in the bright moonlight, it dawned upon each of them, in rapid succession, that they were face to face with Colonel Willem Spinner himself, founder of the First Gengali Lancers, veteran of the First and Second Harafhan Wars, Hero of the Xin Concession, and not one, but two-time recipient of the Queen's Rings, the only man in the history of the Imperium to ever receive them twice.

Spears and Rodes in unison flushed in embarrassment and awe. Sergeant Binda stared with wide eyes.

Spinner laughed. "Get off your horses and meet me in my tent."

He did not tell them where that was, but he began walking in the opposite direction from which he had arrived, the same direction Major Rasouda had departed.

———————————————

It took Spears, Rodes, and Binda nearly ten minutes in the falling snow to find a covered shelter to tie up their horses and locate Colonel Spinner's tent, which was supposedly no different than any of the other hundreds of white tents. They inquired of a half-dozen skeptical Gengalis to finally find the correct place.

"No, the colonel, where is *his* tent?"

"That way," said one, pointing vaguely and sauntering off into the darkness.

"Excuse me, where is Colonel Spinner's tent?"

"The colonel?"

"Yes."

"You are authorized to see the colonel?"

"Yes, on orders from the Governor of Khyderbad."

"Khyderbad is far away."

"Yes, but where is the colonel's tent?"

"That way, over that way," said another man, pointing somewhere else.

They entered, at last, through the unguarded and unsecured flaps of a white A-frame tent that indeed looked like all of the others. Once inside, crouching beneath the low ceiling, they stood as upright as possible and saluted again.

Colonel Spinner held a large bottle of North Anglian Whiskey in his hand, half-finished. There was no table, no open map, and no other visible indicia of command. Sitting on the ground, Spinner leaned back against a balled-up cloak and tunic, wearing his dirty undershirt. The smell of body odor hung in the air, pungent as aged Spatanian cheese. A fire blazed outside of the tent, but inside it was cold, despite the other men in close proximity. Two Gengalis reclined in the tent near Colonel Spinner. One was Major Rasouda. The other was a small, wiry man with a sharp black beard and piercing eyes.

"Sit over there," said Spinner.

The lieutenants and Sergeant Binda obeyed, sitting awkwardly across the cramped tent from the colonel and the two Gengalis.

Colonel Spinner and the two Gengalis all puffed on small, strong-smelling cigars, filling the tent with smoke. Colonel Spinner took in a large mouthful and propelled a stream of smoke toward Lieutenant Rodes' face. Rodes coughed.

"What's your message?" asked Spinner.

The two Gengalis looked at the newcomers with alert, unwelcoming eyes.

Spears adjusted himself on the ground, attempting to sit more upright, in a posture of military dignity. "We bring word from Governor Freer of Khyderbad, sir."

"Oh?" said Spinner, blowing more smoke toward Rodes and Spears, partially obscuring their faces.

Spears pulled the encrypted orders from his internal breast pocket. They were still sealed, showing the pressed red wax of the Governor of Khyderbad. He leaned forward and presented the folded orders to Colonel Spinner.

"You're going to make me read it myself?" asked Spinner. The Gengalis on his side of the tent each smiled.

"It is to be read by your eyes only, sir. And it is encrypted. None of us know the cipher."

"Yes, Major Rasouda told me you were fresh Anglian types," said Spinner, breaking the wax with his index finger, still puffing the cigar in his teeth. "You know who Rasouda is, by the way? He's a pretty famous man, our senior major. Of course, that is not his famous name. Most call him Gindal the Reaper."

Rodes looked with his mouth ajar at the dark-skinned Gengali. Spears stared openly at the man they had just dismissed out in the snow.

"It, it is an honor, Major," said Spears, composing himself, trying to stand.

"Sit," said Spinner, scanning the orders from Governor Freer. "No more saluting."

Spears sat, lowering the hand he was raising to salute again.

"Sir, we—"

"Quiet," said Spinner, keeping his eyes focused on the written orders in front of him. His eyes darted back and forth, scanning Freer's words, deciphering the words in his head.

Spears sat, watching Spinner read. Few men could decode an encrypted letter without looking at a written cipher and placing it next to the text. Spinner was reading as if he was doing the symbol translations in his head. Spears wondered whether messages in the Harafhan Mountains needed to be encrypted at all. Few Harafhans could read, much less read Anglian.

"This is Major Rajatnamdar." Spinner gestured toward the other Gengali, keeping his eyes on Freer's message. "You may have heard of him as well. He goes by Rajat Rajatnamdar."

The small Gengali with the sharp beard gave a slight nod.

"We, we are honored, sir," said Spears, looking at Rajatnamdar with wide eyes, again moving to stand before remembering he had just been ordered not to. Spears looked over at Rodes for reassurance.

Any arrogance that had been in Rodes's eyes had vanished entirely, replaced by a look of earnest awe. These were the heroes Spears and Rodes and thousands like them had read about as boys, the heroes they hoped they might have a chance to glance upon by accepting the mission to ride in the snow through the tribe lands and into the Harafhan Mountains to deliver the very message Spinner was now reading.

Legend said that Rajat Rajatnamdar had personally killed more than two dozen enemies of the Imperium, fighting in engagements from Halex to Xin.

For Major Rasouda, or as he was known to all of the Anglian world, "Gindal the Reaper," that number was a time and a half as great. On three continents, three-dozen were said to have fallen beneath his lance, his saber, his carbine, and his dagger. Few men, other than Colonel Spinner himself, carried more medals for valor.

And I insulted him, like a Three-Gods-damned fool, thought Rodes, who, like Spears, had yet to come under his first enemy fire or reach his twenty-third birthday.

Colonel Spinner reached for the whiskey bottle, raised it to his lips, and drank deeply. He at last pulled his eyes off of the page.

"The Sand Sea," said Spinner.

Neither Spears nor Rodes nor Sergeant Binda spoke. Indeed, Sergeant Binda had not said a word since they entered the tent. Anglian boys were not the only ones who had heard of Rajat Rajatnamdar and Gindal the Reaper. If Spinner's Riders were well-known in Anglia, they were even more famous in Hindea. In their presence, Sergeant Binda was speechless.

"What did Freer tell you?" asked Spinner, leaning forward, his cheeks flushed with whiskey and the mountain cold.

No one responded.

"Speak," said Spinner, his voice escalating to an irritated growl.

"He-he-he told us you are to ride into the Sand Sea to re-re-rescue the failed Stanwich expedition," Spears stuttered under stress. He hated himself for it.

"Well, Lieutenant, I suppose that is perfectly acceptable from the view from the veranda in the Governor's palace in Khyderbad, but we have a post to protect here, and I'm not inclined to ride away from it."

Spears looked at Colonel Spinner with confusion, unclear as to what was expected of him. He sat in awkward silence.

"We will be replacing you here, Colonel, to carry out Her Majesty's mission," said Rodes.

"The three of you?" Colonel Spinner smiled. "Very bold." His grin, like his face, was wide, mocking, and reminded Rodes of what he had always expected a pirate's smile to look like.

"The entire Thirteenth Infantry is marching up the mountain, sir," said Rodes.

"Yes, I read the orders. Didn't you? Oh, that's right, I forgot, you're a useless lieutenant who cannot read encryption, who has never seen a firefight, and who insults heroes like Gindal the Reaper, who also happens to be a superior officer."

Rodes recoiled as if struck in the face.

"Let me ask you another question. Who else is on the expedition, other than Stanwich and his damned box carriers?"

Spears looked at Rodes. Rodes nodded as if answering a question, his cheeks aflame with embarrassment.

"Colonel," said Spears. "It is not just Stanwich. The heir to Lord George Harmon is himself there with him, Peter Harmon."

Colonel Spinner's eyes changed. The lieutenants missed it, but Sergeant Binda did not.

"Are you sure of this?" asked Spinner.

"Yes, sir."

Spinner sat up and set down his whiskey bottle.

"Rajat, prepare the men to ride by midmorning, snow, or no snow."

"So, you will deploy, sir?" asked Spears. "Into the Sand Sea?"

"What else would I do, Lieutenant? Disobey the Governor?"

"No, sir. Of course not, sir. But our forces may not be here to relieve you by midmorning."

"No? Then maybe you should ride down and tell them to march faster," said Spinner, crushing the still-smoking end of his cigar.

CHAPTER 52
The Sight of Beseri

Camp of Abu Akhsa, Bazadak Tribal Lands
West-Central Sand Sea
4th Day, Month of Wasura, 807
Anglian Calendar: February 25, 1879

Jabil, the one whose face everyone said looked like a jackal's, rode at Ghani's side. Both were of the tribe Bazadak, under the leadership of Bazak Bazadak. The strangers had launched their invasion into the lands of the Bazadaks—the lands of the south and the west—so Abu Akhsa gave the Bazadaks the privilege of expelling the invaders.

Ghani rode in the lead because Bazak Bazadak gave him the command. Jabil knew in his heart that Bazadak made him second-in-command because Ghani was not a man suited for leadership. Ghani was not the better rider, nor had he ridden farther across the sands, nor had he raided more camels than had Jabil. Nor could Ghani shoot better or fight more fiercely with a saber or dagger. Most insultingly, Ghani was younger than Jabil by three years.

Bazak chose Ghani to lead, with the approval of the Elders, for another reason. Since Ghani was a boy, when his child's teeth fell out, and his adult teeth grew in, a significant gap had formed between the front two teeth. *A lucky man brings luck* was a saying that all Beserians knew. It was not actually in the Holy Book that a gap in the front teeth was lucky, but most believed it was. Many said the Prophet himself had a gap in his teeth and that those with "The Gap" would carry his blessing upon their endeavors for their entire lives. Ghani had indeed been lucky thus far. His flocks had grown, as had those of his father. His sisters grew up beautiful and respectful of all of the tribal ways. What more proof could a man need for the luck of The Gap?

Jabil looked back over his shoulder. A wind of pride swept over him. *Ghani may have had command, but it was I that commanded. And it was I that met the tall, fierce one eye to eye and wrestled him in the dirt.* At the thought, Jabil could again taste the man's blood on his tongue when he had bitten down through the bone of the man's little finger. Jabil smiled.

The string of camels stretched out behind him in a long line, with tails attached to head ropes attached to noses. As they approached the vast camp, the little children ran out first, shouting and cheering. The older boys came second, more reserved and dignified than the little ones, watching with admiration and envy in their eyes. If they survived the manhood testing and showed themselves worthy when the day of trial came, they would one day ride with the raiders too. One day they could be like Ghani of the Gap and Jabil the Jackal. But it was not an easy thing to be deemed worthy of Beserian manhood, and many boys gave their lives in the effort, knowing that death was preferable to cowardice and all that it entailed.

The young women stayed nearer to the tent lines, but they craned their necks to view the returning heroes better. Some searched for ones they hoped their fathers might pick for them to marry. Others searched for brothers. All searched for someone. The returning raiders defeated the invaders, the men traveling beneath the strange flags bearing the symbols of the pale-faced men of the west. If Ghani of the Gap, Jabil the Jackal, and the others had not defeated the invaders, they would not be bringing the long line of camels behind them. Men would die before they let other men take their camels. Even young girls knew that.

Next came the mothers, walking swiftly with a nervous gait and fear in their eyes, looking to make sure their sons rode among the living. As Ghani, Jabil, and the others came closer, some of the mothers began to wail, seeing that their sons were not among those returning. A Beserian mother could know her son by the way he rode his camel, the way he wore his headscarf, and by seeing a half-dozen other details at a distance, long before she could see his face in the morning sunlight.

Ghani of the Gap, Jabil the Jackal, and the others rode onward, deep into the camp, past the mothers rushing forward to embrace their returning sons, the women forgetting their composure and holding their grown sons as if they were still children. The returning raiders walked onward, pulling the captured camels along behind them, walking through the throng toward the tents of the Elders. Only then did the men emerge.

Abu Akhsa, bearded and famous in his sky-blue headscarf; Hamid Salesi, silver and wise, walking with the Staff of the Serpent, more gnarled and older than he was; and Bazak Bazadak, broad, dark, and fierce, led them forward, the three men walking ahead of all of the others.

The strange Westerner stood with them, the one called the Amahdi, the one meant to be the fulfillment of the Year of the Prophecy, the Prophecy that would pull the Qhaliffa from his throne and return God's people, the People of the Sands, to the lands they were promised—the lands of the Seven Rivers of the Great Mountain at the center of the Sand Sea.

Jabil looked at him, the Amahdi, and saw that he looked less strange than he expected, that he looked almost like a man of the Sands. He did not look like the men they had attacked, with their high, rounded helmets, their pants that hugged their legs, and their golden-haired women armed with rifles. The Amahdi's beard was long, full, and rich, even if it was strangely colored with a hint of gold, like the hair of the women with the rifles. Jabil considered this as he approached. *What would one expect from the Amahdi? To look like all others? Perhaps the hint of gold in the beard is a sign that the Prophecy is true.*

"Ghani of the Gap, son of Tamur, you have done well," said Bazak Bazadak, chief of the southwestern lands and ruler of the Plain of Gamurian. "You make all Bazadaks proud." His voice was as deep as his chest was broad. Both seemed best suited to a time of war.

Jabil did not hide the disappointment from his face. *Did I not command as well? Yet Bazak Bazadak cannot find it in him to also thank Jabil, son of Jamachar?*

Jabil, Ghani, and the eighty-five surviving men who rode with them ordered their camels to halt. They lowered them, with a word, to their knees and stepped off of the humps they had ridden behind.

They bowed in supplication to the Elders of the Tribes. They were all there, twenty-three of the leaders of all of the tribes, the Tribe Chiefs and the War Chiefs, a gathering such as the sands had not seen in remembered lifetimes. Rivals that had slaughtered each other and tribes that had stolen each other's herds for generations were assembled, side by side, serving under the sky-blue banner of Abu Akhsa, the flag that all believed would lead God's people to the Great Mountain in this year, the Year of the Prophecy.

"Ghani, son of Tamur, rise and be recognized," said Abu Akhsa.

Ghani of the Gap rose, smiling his fortunate smile. The Elders looked at him approvingly, the expedition's good fortune affirming their good judgment. Ghani was a blessed young man.

Jabil again noted that he still knelt like a common raider. He felt the ache in the ugly dark bruise on his face, where the tall rifle-swinging man had struck him with his hand. The pain mixed with his feeling of rejection. *Ghani steals my glory. What did Ghani do, other than ride along? Did he command in the fight? Did he kill? Did he fight one of the invaders like I did in hand-to-hand combat? No, he did none of these things.*

"Rise also, you men who have ridden with Ghani, son of Tamur. Rise and be recognized."

The others rose. Jabil, though he was in the front, rose last, weighed down by his bitterness.

"There are others who have not returned," said Abu Akhsa, looking over the faces of the young men. His eyes passed over the face of Jabil the Jackal—Jabil, son of Jamachar—as if he were just an ordinary tribesman, a young raider of no particular significance.

Abu Akhsa looked and saw the long bundles wrapped in cloth, each tied to a camel in the long line. In each bundle was a body that was once a man. The women were already moving toward the camels, edging closer to the bodies and wailing as they approached.

"You have done well to return with the fallen," said Hamid Salesi, his voice old and soft, but more carefully listened to than voices that were stronger and younger. "Did you return with them all?"

"Yes, Elder Salesi," said Jabil. The wind pulled at a tent flap nearby, snapping it in the air. A number of the Elders looked at Jabil with surprise, as though wondering why he was answering a question directed to the leader, Ghani of the Gap.

The words then flowed out from Jabil's long, narrow jaw in rapid succession. "We returned in the darkness of night to retrieve most. Others we could only get after waiting behind. The invaders waited in the place where we struck them before they finally walked away."

Hamid Salesi looked at Jabil with penetrating eyes. "To where did they walk, Jabil, son of Jamachar?"

At the mention of his name by such a person as Hamid Salesi, Jabil felt a surge of validation rise up inside of him. In the next moment, in the blink of an eye, he felt shame for his bitterness.

"Elder Salesi"—Jabil bowed his head respectfully—"all except for two of the invaders departed on foot, headed south and east, to the oasis of Ben Gamurian."

Hamid Salesi, nodded, considering these words. "That is a great distance on foot," he said, "but there are wells. They are wise to walk for Ben Gamurian, but you said there were two who did not. Where did they go?"

"Two men walked back toward the Mountain Gate of Altadige," said Jabil.

When he heard the word *Altadige*, Jack Caldwell, who had stood silently, focused his attention on the strange-faced man before him.

"What did he say?" asked Jack, looking to the Elder next to him.

Jabil heard him and spoke louder. "There were two men, one younger, one older. They walked back to the place of the Spatanians. Both men were pale-faced invaders, tall and thin. Both killed many of our men."

"Did you let them escape?" asked Bazadak.

Jabil was silent. He had nearly struck Ghani for refusing to dispatch men to kill them.

"Yes, Elder Bazadak," said Ghani.

Bazadak's eyes proclaimed his incredulity. His words did not need to.

"They fought bravely, Elder Bazadak," said Ghani, speaking with the breezy confidence of one whom life has favored.

"You should have finished the deed, Ghani, son of Tamur," said Bazadak.

Jabil beamed in agreement, looking into Bazadak's face. If Bazadak noticed, he did not show it. He merely glared at the group of them, his eyes disapproving and severe.

The loosened tent flap continued to snap in the wind.

"There is honor in mercy," said Hamid Salesi.

"They were fleeing, walking away from our lands," said Ghani, nodding and flashing his teeth with the lucky gap.

We should have killed them all, thought Jabil. *Bazadak is correct. They are our enemies.* His jackal's eyes were now wide, yellowish-brown, and shaped like sideways almonds. His chin was as narrow as his jaw was long.

Jack Caldwell looked at him, staring at his unusual face.

"Did they have flags, these invaders?"

"Yes," said Ghani.

"What did they look like?"

"I do not remember," said Ghani, omitting Jack's title. He did not say Amahdi, and he had disrespect in his eyes.

Jack looked at Ghani with surprise. Not since the staff touched his forehead had anyone in the camp of Abu Akhsa been rude to his face. Yet this young raider with the gap in his teeth was rude to him in the presence of Abu Akhsa and the Elders.

"How about you? Did you see them?" asked Jack, turning to face Jabil, son of Jamachar.

"Yes, Amahdi, I saw the flags. There were three. One held the silver lion of the Spatanians, the men of the western border."

"And the other two?" asked Jack.

"They are not flags known to me."

"What did they look like?"

"One was white with red and blue and rings of gold."

Jack's eyes widened. "And the other, the third flag?" Jack already knew the answer, but he asked his question anyway.

"The third flag? A sun rose against blue, rising from green."

Jack's heart thundered against his ribs. He turned, facing Abu Akhsa, Hamid Salesi, and Bazak Bazadak.

"Abu Akhsa, these were not invaders. These were my people. We have attacked my people." His face whitened.

Abu Akhsa reached out his hand and placed it upon Jack's elbow. He leaned in toward Jack's ear. "We cannot undo what has been done, Amahdi," he whispered. "Have faith in the Prophecy."

Abu Akhsa swept his gaze along the faces of the assembled throng. "Come, let us slaughter the young goats. We celebrate the return of our raiders and the bounty of the camels they bring us."

The raiders rose, turning to leave. As the Elders turned away back toward their tents, Jack walked toward Ghani and Jabil, placing a hand upon Jabil's arm. "The ones you attacked, did you kill any?"

Jabil turned as if under attack, his hand moving to the dagger at his belt.

Ghani turned and snarled, eyeing Jack with disdain.

Jack looked down at the two Beserians, towering over them both.

"We killed many," said Ghani, boastfully.

"What did they look like?" asked Jack.

"Pale-faced foreigners," said Ghani.

"Were there women? Was there a woman with golden hair?"

Jabil nodded.

"Did she—did she fall?"

"I know not," said Ghani, his eyes flashing in defiance.

"Did you see her? What happened?"

Ghani of the Gap snorted and turned away.

Jabil the Jackal stayed looking at Jack.

"I saw her walking toward Ben Gamurian, Amahdi. The woman with the golden hair lives."

The celebration lasted deep into the night. They roasted the goat meat over open flames, feeding all in the camp, with the first portions going to the returning raiders, the second portions going to the Elders and the Swordguard, the third portions going to the other men, in order of their age, and so on. Jack refused to celebrate or to eat even one morsel of the celebratory slaughter. He sat in his tent, which Abu Akhsa had ordered erected next to his own. An oil lamp provided the only faint illumination in the darkness as his stomach twisted with hunger. *They are alone in the desert. I cannot abandon them. These raiders stole their camels. They cannot be left alone. They will not make it to Ben Gamurian on foot.*

Jack considered sleeping, but as he lay upon his mat, he could not stop the turning of his mind. Yes, something had changed in him when Hamid Salesi touched the staff to his head. He had become part of the Beserians. He could speak their language. He could understand their ways as if they had been his customs all of his life. But such did not erase him. It was as if another man's experiences had been layered into his mind on top of his own. He could be a Beserian, but so too was he still Jack Caldwell of Calderon. He could still feel regret as *that* man.

I should never have gone to the whorehouse. I should never have allowed Aurelio Demassi to bring me here. Had I not gone that night, I would have been with them. I could have defended Hannah and the others. Perhaps we would be in the Valley of Kordon with the Beserite, negotiating with Abu Akhsa from a position of strength . . .

Jack twisted on his floor mat, his mind pulled between two worlds. He heard the goat hair of the tent flap open. He turned, looking for his knife. Outside, when walking amongst the tribes, he had exchanged his long, straight hunting knife with the handguard for the curved dagger of the Beserian tribesmen. Abu Akhsa had presented him with a dagger with a jeweled hilt. Men viewed it with admiration, continually looking at his belt when he wore it.

But inside the tent, next to his mat, he kept the straight-bladed hunting knife he had carried with him from Calderon, the knife Aurelio Demassi had managed to steal along with Jack's Mancaster repeater, which lay against the side of the tent. He reached for it now as the tent flap moved.

"Be at peace, Amahdi," said a familiar voice.

Jack looked up in the faint lamplight to see the silver beard of Hamid Salesi. The shadows of the flickering lamp exaggerated the sun creases on Salesi's face.

"You are of two minds," said Salesi. "This I know."

Jack rolled over onto his side and sat up. He released his grip on the Mancaster.

"When you became the Amahdi, you did not cease being the man that you were. You will still care for those you have left behind, even as you now see what we see."

Jack looked into his eyes, knowing it was true.

"How?"

"I know not all the ways of the Staff of Wisdom, though my ancestors have borne it since the days of Beseri. But I have foreseen this. The Staff of Wisdom adds to a man's mind. It does not detract."

"My cousin. My friends. They are—" Jack's voice trailed off.

"They are alive, Amahdi. I have foreseen it. They are all alive."

"How do you know?"

"The young woman of the golden hair, the one you care for. She currently sits at a well on the route to Ben Gamurian. She has hunger and thirst but not the kind that kills."

"You can see her?"

"Sit up and close your eyes."

Jack did as Salesi asked of him.

Jack felt Salesi's old, gnarled hand upon his hands, and then Jack felt the old olive wood placed into his palms. It felt smooth against his skin, as if polished by time itself. He gripped it in his hands.

"Keep your eyes closed."

Jack sat upright with his eyes firmly shut, with both of his hands gripping the length of the staff. With his fingers, he could feel the curves where the body of the carved serpent coiled around the center shaft of the wood.

"Now, who do you wish to see?"

"Hannah," said Jack.

"Then see her."

Jack opened his eyes.

Hamid Salesi shook his head, looking at Jack as if he were a young boy. "You must close your eyes if you wish to see." His voice was gentle, like that of a kind parent teaching a child a new task.

Jack closed his eyes.

"Now, see her," said Salesi.

The staff in Jack's hands seemed to grow colder as if it had been left out in a snowstorm and had just been brought into the tent. It became colder still.

"Do not remove your hands from the staff," said Salesi.

"It is cold. Very cold."

"If you wish to see, do not remove your hands."

Jack grimaced. Holding the staff was like holding a cylinder of ice.

"Now, draw the one whose name you have said, the one with the golden hair. Draw her into your mind, and you will be drawn to her."

Jack's face tightened in concentration and effort as if he were trying to lift a heavy crate, filled with bricks.

Hannah sat on the ground, underneath a thornbush. The round woman, Matilda Smith, sat with her. Mrs. Smith looked less round now, her dress hanging more loosely about her than it had before. Hannah's face was drawn as if she had aged several years. She was thin, and there was a new darkness in her skin, bronzed by the sun. She was more fragile than Jack had ever seen her, lean in the manner of the dwellers of the desert, thin in the way of those for whom eating a feast is among life's rarest and most treasured moments. Even Mrs. Smith looked thin, far smaller than the woman he had last seen in Altadige. Her face had hardened, and her midsection had narrowed. Her arms and shoulders were still large and powerful. A Mancaster repeater rested in those arms, tilted against her shoulder as she placed her back against the same stone as Hannah, hiding beneath the paltry shade of a thornbush.

"I see her," said Jack, his voice far away.

Hamid Salesi smiled, knowing from the sound of Jack's voice that the staff had opened up his mind to show him what he sought.

"Is she alive? Is this now?" Jack's eyes were squeezed tight.

"Relax your mind, lose the tightness in your eyes. You see not through your effort but by the blessing of the God of the Sands, showing you what the God wishes you to see. You shall see by the light of the Staff of Wisdom, the staff once held by the Prophet, and by it alone. Sometimes the staff shows what is, sometimes what has been, and sometimes even what is yet to come."

Stanwich stood, drinking from a canteen. One of his hands was bandaged. He and Hersen Expey looked out into the desert. Stanwich placed an extendable Gerdic looking glass to his eye. *What is he looking at?*

Jack's view pulled back as if suddenly he was being lifted into the air and could see through the eyes of a bird. He flew higher and higher, yet his gaze remained ever fixed upon the ground as if he could not stop looking at Stanwich.

He flew higher still.

All of the land was a mix of beige, tan, and brown, the colors of the Sand Sea. A color that did not belong moved into his view, the color of Calderon in the winter, when the rains are heavy, when the seeds buried beneath the earth awaken with new life, and the land turns green. The patch of green entered from the southeast. It grew larger, expanding on the edge of his sight. Then a color even more precious than green came before his mind's eye—blue, the color of deep, clear pools of water.

"I see green. I see water. It is green and water surrounded by sand. Stanwich is looking through a telescope now. He can see this place. Stanwich can see it through a looking glass."

"If your people can see it, Amahdi, then you speak of the oasis of Ben Gamurian. They will be in Ben Gamurian. They have survived, Amahdi. I too see through the staff, and I have foreseen your people in Ben Gamurian. Perhaps you will find, Amahdi, that there are indeed things for you to celebrate on this night of celebration."

Jack continued to look through his mind, the Staff of Wisdom taking him where he desired to go—back into the desert with an eye on Hannah Huntington.

"I do not see Peter," said Jack. "I do not see my cousin. Nor do I see Barnes, the man who was tasked to watch over my shoulder, in the way Handsome Habeen Barcadey looks over the shoulder of Abu Akhsa."

"If you do not see them, find them," said Hamid Salesi. He looked at Jack Caldwell's face through the dim lamplight. In the semidarkness of the tent, with his long, full beard and Beserian headscarf, Jack almost looked like a man of the Sands. *He looks more like one of us each day. As his mind embraces the tribal ways, so does his body.*

The skin next to Jack's eyes wrinkled with his concentration.

"I do not see them. I see nothing." Jack's voice was nervous.

"Clear your mind and go to them."

A mountain range emerged in front of Jack, coming up upon him. Again, he soared like a bird, blown westward by a mighty wind. The mountains grew wider, taller, and better defined. Beneath him lay a desert: dunes, gravel wastes, thornbushes rising out of shallow wadis. A herd of wild camels passed beneath him. The skin next to Jack's eyes relaxed, as his mind marveled at the sights flying past him, a mile or more below.

The mountains grew more formidable still, rising and sharpening. As high as Jack was flying, the mountains were still higher. Ahead of him, he saw a place where the sky seemed to penetrate the wall of mountains, as if the stone had been cut away. Jack flew closer, and the gap deepened. Jack felt a wave of recognition. He came closer still. A maroon flag pulled against its tall iron pole, as if trying to escape to the west or flee from whatever might be heading toward it from the sands. On the flag, a silver lion reared up on its hind legs.

Spatania, the flag of the House of Adomingo, thought Jack, recognizing the place.

He came closer to the mountains, lowering in altitude as he flew nearer and nearer to the gap. He saw a grouping of buildings. He saw a wall in front of the buildings with soldiers on duty behind it, looking out into the sands with rifles at the ready.

They were Spatanian soldiers with their black, flat-brimmed visors sticking out from red cylindrical hats, with long sword bayonets affixed to the ends of their rifles. Jack flew closer as if he were about to land on the bayonets. He recoiled, yet the staff drew his mind forward. He braced as if for impact, but there was no impact. He passed through the soldiers and the steel of their bayonets as if they were nothing more than wisps of cloud. Or perhaps he was the cloud?

A low, stone, square building emerged in front of him with a steep shingled roof. The staff drew him toward it, to an arched doorway. The door was closed shut against the mountain air.

Jack passed through it. In the room, a man sat at a telegraph machine, taking instructions from two haggard, thin men. Both were bearded. One's beard was dark and silver, not unlike Abu Akhsa's. Behind the beard, Jack saw the eyes of Joshua Barnes, sunken and intense. The other man's beard was reddish-brown, full and robust, like the beard of some North Anglian warlord in days of old, when men fought in suits of metal and swung heavy maces at each other's shields. Jack's eyes were shut, but in his own mind, he cried out in surprise. *Peter!*

Peter looked different. He dictated instructions to the telegraph man, who was working his keys with intense concentration. Peter gestured in a way that Jack had not seen him gesture before. Peter motioned as if in command.

And then, as if balls of cotton had been pulled from Jack's ears, he heard Peter say, "Send troops. They have attacked our flag. They have dishonored the Imperium."

Jack opened his eyes. Hamid Salesi sat in the tent across from him. Another had entered the tent while Jack's eyes were shut, and his mind was traveling the Sand Sea, from the pools of Ben Gamurian to the Mountain Gate of Altadige, and into the room with the telegraph machine where Peter Harmon sent his message.

"We must move," said Jack. His hands still grasped the Staff of Wisdom. The icelike coldness of the staff had gone, and but for the serpent carved around it, it now felt like an ordinary piece of olive wood.

"Move where?" asked Abu Akhsa, who had slipped into Jack's tent.

"The staff has taken him into its sight, into the divine sight above the sands, the sight of Beseri," said Hamid Salesi.

"Oh?" asked Abu Akhsa, his eyes dropping to look at the staff still in Jack's hands.

Jack looked into Abu Akhsa's face. As usual, his black and silver beard was trimmed tightly around his famous, slightly recessed jaw. His dark eyes searched Jack's own for the wisdom they might contain. Abu Akhsa had long relied upon the journeys of Hamid Salesi's mind and the places the Staff of Wisdom took him. Jack met Abu Akhsa's gaze in the manner of a peer, without fear or self-consciousness, as few men could.

"I sought my companions, those that the raiders attacked."

Abu Akhsa waited in silence.

"I traveled to a place of greenery amongst the sands, a place of deep pools of pure water. It was a place in reach of my companions. They were thin, battered, and on foot. Some were injured, but they were alive."

"Ben Gamurian," said Abu Akhsa.

Hamid Salesi nodded in agreement.

"And then I rose and soared to the west, faster than the fastest falcon in flight. I came all the way to the Mountain Gate of Altadige, the border of the Spatanians. I came to a room. There was a telegraph machine."

Jack said the word "telegraph" in Anglian because there was no Beserian word.

"What is this, you say? What is 'telegraph'?"

"It is a machine that allows a man to send a message far away in an instant."

"Does it draw upon the power of the God of the Sands, like the Staff of Wisdom?"

"No, it is a machine, a small but powerful machine with a very long reach. Using it, a man can send a message across the land and oceans—hundreds, even thousands of miles in an instant."

Abu Akhsa's eyes shifted back and forth, ever so slightly, as if weighing the truth of Jack's words, seeking understanding for how, if this were true, a machine could do such a thing.

"If we had a machine here, we would need to stretch a long metal wire to where we want to send a message." Jack gestured as he spoke, placing his fingers together and showing that the wire was very thin. Then he slowly stretched his hands apart as if unspooling a coil. "We would then place a similar machine on the other end of the wire. We could then send messages from one machine to the other."

"There is such a machine in Altadige?" asked Abu Akhsa. As a boy, he had seen Altadige, the deep gap in the wall of mountains, the gate through which the Western men marched, and from which the Macmenian caravans came.

"Yes," said Jack. "In the west, in my country, or LaFrentia, the Gerdic Empire, Spatania, or anywhere that the Anglian flag flies, most cities have such a machine."

Abu Akhsa's eyes widened at this, marveling at the claim.

"Do the Gressians have such a machine?" The Beserians had a long, mostly unfavorable, and occasionally violent history with the rulers of the vast northern lands, and with the orange-haired Erassians that rode under the green banner of the Three Eagles.

"Most certainly," said Jack.

Abu Akhsa considered this. Hamid Salesi reached for the Staff of Wisdom. Jack handed it back to him, its custodian and bearer by birthright.

"It is a powerful weapon for a ruler to have, thistelegraph," said Abu Akhsa. Jack nodded.

"Do kings and rulers alone have this power, the power to use this machine, to send a message hundreds of miles in an instant?"

"No, any man may send such a message for a price, and the price is not great for anyone of means."

"A man must pay gold or silver to the holder of the machine?"

"Money, generally, yes."

"In your mind's eye, what did the Staff of Wisdom show you in the room in Altadige, the room with the *telegraph*?"

"I saw my cousin, Peter Harmon. He ordered a message to be sent from the machine."

"Peter Harmon, your cousin, who is he?"

"He is the son of a powerful man. His father is famous and rich and part of the government of Anglia. He is like a ruler."

Abu Akhsa nodded. "And your cousin sent a message on this machine?"

"I know only what the staff showed me, Abu Akhsa."

"Tell me."

"Peter asked for troops to punish those who attacked our caravan."

"What troops?"

"I know not, Abu Akhsa."

"Soldiers of Spatania?" The Beserians knew the soldiers of Spatania. Over the centuries, such men had ventured into the edges of the Sand Sea. The Spatanians did not fight well in the desert. This Abu Akhsa knew.

"No," said Jack, shaking his head. "He would not ask for Spatanians. The men he would ask for are more dangerous. He is an Anglian. He would ask for Anglian soldiers, the soldiers of the crimson tunics."

"The person he is asking, this is his father. The ruler?"

"Yes, I believe so."

"Will his father send these soldiers?"

Jack shrugged. "I do not know, Abu Akhsa. But if they come, you are in danger."

"No man is in true danger," said Abu Akhsa, "so long as the God of the Sands protects him. The God of the Sands has given me the tribes of all of the Beserians of the western sands. Look at the army around you. They are not here because a ruler has sent them. They are here because the God of the Sands has called them. They are here by their own free will to serve beneath the sky-blue banner."

"Very well, Abu Akhsa. I, of all people, do not doubt the power of the God of the Sands. But the young raiders should not have attacked my people. They will bring down the wrath of the Anglians, Abu Akhsa, and the Anglians are mighty."

Hamid Salesi's eyes were closed. The Staff of Wisdom was in his hands. Jack saw that its olive wood had shifted in its coloring, moving from its usual yellowish-brown to a colder color, silver with hints of green. Salesi muttered under his breath, his words rhythmic and strange. His eyes snapped open.

"The soldiers will come," said Hamid Salesi, "but they do not come from the Mountain Gate. They are the men of the south, the men of the bright turbans and the brown faces, men in yellow tunics. The soldiers are coming from Hindea."

Jack's mind raced with strange dreams as he slept, as if the Staff of Wisdom was still speaking to him. The face of the arrogant raider, Ghani, the one said to be blessed with good fortune, walked toward him, always smiling, showing the lucky gap between his front teeth. It was not a kind smile.

Ghani walked closer, coming directly at Jack. He smiled, flashing his gap, and said, "You do not belong, Westerner. You are not chosen. You are not the Amahdi. And I am bringing the staff to one who knows how to harness its true power."

"Demassi?" Jack sat up.

He looked over. The Vetenan snored loudly on his back. He had stumbled into the tent, well after the night's fires had burned down to embers, drunk on fermented milk, his belly full of fire-roasted goat.

Jack rose to his feet.

A chill hung in the air.

He opened his tent flap and looked in the direction of the tent of Hamid Salesi, where like every night, the Elder slept with the Staff of Wisdom at his side. All lay quiet in the camp. The lingering smoky odors of the cooking fires still scented the air. But for the few sentries doing their duty, walking out on the perimeter, nothing stirred. Jack exhaled and turned to go back to his tent.

And then he heard the scream.

CHAPTER 53
Bring Me Don Mazarian

Altadige
February 17, 1879
Eight days earlier . . .

Peter Harmon slept, unmoving for a day and a half.

The servants of the Brothers Leboveckian kept an eye on him, making sure he was still breathing. They kept a fire burning in the hearth and a pitcher of water at his side to meet his thirst, should he awake. But they did not rouse him, even after he approached the thirtieth hour of his slumber.

Peter Harmon was not a man with excess meat on his bones when he had first made the passage into the Sand Sea through the Mountain Gate with Stanwich and the others. He was now as thin as a Beserian crossing the barren zones—gaunt, skeletal, and hollow-eyed. Even as he slept, his eyes seemed to have receded into his cheekbones.

Peter Harmon and Joshua Barnes had made the journey back, on foot, in thirteen days. It would have been a remarkable feat for a hardened Beserian raider who had traveled the sands all of his life. For two Westerners, it was almost unbelievable.

When they arrived at the border post, shivering and stumbling, the Spatanians looked at Peter and Barnes and called for a doctor. Peter only said, repeatedly, that they must be taken to the telegraph machine at once. The soldiers relented.

Once the message was sent, Peter and Barnes knocked on the door of the trading outpost of Merchant House Gremanian, stepped inside, and collapsed.

Barnes sat with the Leboveckians' servants now, sipping on a mug of tea made from herbs, watching Peter's chest slowly rise and fall. Barnes himself had drifted off to sleep when Peter finally awoke.

Peter sat up. The room was warm. Outside the window, the sky was dark. The wind blew hard enough outside for Peter to hear its howl through the double panes of the windows—windows meant to keep warm air in and cold air out in the fiercest months of the winter.

"Barnes," he said.

Barnes's eyes opened.

"How long was I down?" asked Peter.

"A day and a half."

"We sent the message," said Peter. "To Anglia, we sent the message."

"Yes," said Barnes.

"Do we have a response?"

"Yes."

"Have you read it?"

"I have."

"Why did you not wake me?" asked Peter, his brow lowering in irritation.

Barnes smiled, like an uncle to a nephew. "There are times when a man should not be woken."

"What does the response say?"

Barnes stood up, walked to the bed, and handed Peter the message.

"From your father," said Barnes.

Peter read it in the firelight.

Troops shall be requested. Stay in Altadige until further notice. LGH

"This is it?" asked Peter, looking up, frowning.

"It has only been a day and a half."

Peter lay back down onto the large down pillows beneath him. A thick red-and-green-checked blanket lay over him. He exhaled, his entire body seeming to collapse into the voluminous mattress.

"Where are the Leboveckians?" asked Peter.

"Not far, I would say," said a voice that did not belong to Barnes. It came from a chair in the far corner of the room.

Peter turned his head, and Yekov Leboveckian, the elder of the two Leboveckian brothers, rose.

"Thirteen days," said Yekov. "I would be inclined to not believe you, except that Sergeant Barnes here swears by it, and the timing makes sense. You would have had to walk that swiftly to be here by now. I daresay you are lucky to have avoided any Beserian raiding parties."

"Time was of the essence," said Peter.

Yekov Leboveckian nodded.

"I asked my father for troops," said Peter.

"I know," said Yekov.

"Will he send them?" asked Peter.

"With his persuasion, Parliament might," said Leboveckian.

Barnes sat watching them both. He was a fighter, not a man who understood the ways of parliaments.

"It will take the Prime Minister, as well," said Peter.

Yekov Leboveckian nodded.

"And the Liberty and Commerce Party must consent," said Peter.

"Indeed," said Yekov.

"That means Hammerstone and Browne," said Peter, frowning.

Yekov Leboveckian nodded again.

"Who will they send?" asked Peter.

"A magic gazing stone, I have not," said Yekov.

"They attacked us," said Peter. "More than a hundred camel riders. They came to kill us. We fought them off only because we had better rifles and because we made a redoubt out of the crates."

Yekov looked at Peter, saying nothing but impressed with the speed and accuracy with which the young man's mind was moving.

"I have a question for you, Mr. Leboveckian," said Peter. "How were we to trade for the Beserite when they seek to kill us?"

"A fair question."

Peter waited with raised eyebrows and a steely look in his eyes.

"We did not suspect that the Beserians would be in such a bellicose frame of mind."

"Are the Gressians behind this?" asked Peter.

"Another fair question."

"How about an answer?"

"You ask questions that do not have answers known to me. You would be asking me to guess."

"Nonsense," said Peter. "You helped formulate our plan. That plan has failed entirely. I believe I am entitled to your answers."

Peter stared into Yekov's face, the firelight flickering in his blue-green eyes. Yekov's own dark eyes looked at Peter appraisingly, showing surprise that there was more of Lord Harmon in the son than he had previously believed.

"Something has changed in the Sand Sea," said Yekov, "and I cannot say what it is. It is not, in our long years of experience, like the Beserians to attack in that way. It is not like Abu Akhsa. He is a pragmatic man. We have traded with him and the tribes under his control for years."

"What tribes?" asked Peter.

"You know the Beserian tribes?"

"Answer my question."

"The tribes of the Valley of Kordon are led by an old man named Hamid Salesi."

"Yes, I know the name," said Peter. "It is famous upon the sands."

"Indeed," said Yekov, his eyes wary.

"What is different about the Sand Sea this year?" asked Peter.

"I do not *know* of any differences in the Sand Sea this year."

"Nonsense," said Peter.

Yekov stared at the young man's insolent tone. *Before they departed through the Mountain Gate, he did not speak this way. Or had I not noticed? No, he has indeed changed. There is an alteration in this one. He has shifted.*

"What do you know of this year?"

"It is the year 1879," said Yekov.

"On our calendar, yes. On the time that matters to the people of the Sand Sea, and to the people of the Great Mountain, what year is it?"

Yekov again stared at Peter Harmon. *What does this boy think he knows?*

Peter Harmon stared back.

Joshua Barnes sat watching both men.

The fire flickered and crackled.

"Eight hundred and seven," said Yekov.

"Which is what?" asked Peter.

Yekov paused for several long moments of silence. "It is the seventh year of the fortieth Qhaliffa."

"It is indeed," said Peter.

Yekov stared. *Let us see what he knows.*

"When Stanwich first recruited me to join him on this journey, he told an elaborate tale, a tale of a prophecy, reaching back to events occurring eight hundred years ago. Did you not think, perhaps, you should have considered such a thing—and the meaning of such a thing—before sending us out to the Valley of Kordon?"

"I am a man of business, Mr. Harmon, not a follower of tall desert tales."

"Tall desert tales?"

Yekov nodded but without confidence.

"Was it a tall desert tale that Abu Akhsa had assembled far more than the Salesis in the Valley of Kordon?"

"We did not know the extent of that, only rumors."

"And is that an excuse not to warn us at all?"

Yekov's cheeks began to flush.

Peter stared at him, waiting.

"Did you tell Stanwich?"

"Stanwich knew of the prophecy."

"That was not what I asked, Mr. Leboveckian. Did you warn him that the Beserians might attack us in force as if we were invaders?"

Yekov did not immediately respond.

"Answer carefully, Mr. Leboveckian, for I intend to see Mr. Stanwich again soon. There will be a reckoning of what was said and what was omitted."

"We could not predict how the Beserians would behave."

"Ha!" Peter laughed aloud. There was no joy in the laugh. "If you were not in a position to warn us, who was?"

"We did not know," said Yekov. His voice was low, almost resigned.

"I think you knew much you did not tell us, Yekov Leboveckian. But if you had told us, perhaps we would not have made the journey, and perhaps you would have been deprived of your profit?"

"That is an unfair accusation, Mr. Harmon."

"Unfair or merely unflattering? I shall make sure my father knows just what exactly you did not tell us, Mr. Leboveckian. I will make sure the Prime Minister knows as well. Oh yes, Binyam Aurelian will receive a detailed recounting of what the Brothers Leboveckian of House Gremanian choose to tell and not tell their Anglian customers."

Yekov stared. He looked ill.

Barnes eyed the Macmenian with suspicion. *Men fearing exposure can become dangerous men.* Barnes did not intend to let anyone become dangerous. There was a pistol at his hip and an iron bar in his sleeve.

Yekov did not move.

"There is, however, perhaps a way that all of that might be avoided," said Peter, still lying in bed.

Yekov stared at Peter in silence.

"There is a man here in Altadige. You know him. Bring him to me before the sun sets tomorrow, and I will refrain from sending these new tidings to South Anglia."

"Who is this man?" asked Yekov.

"Don Mazarian."

Yekov did not move. After long moments of looking at Peter, he said, "Why?"

"Before the sun sets," said Peter. His eyes, unbeknownst to him, looked frighteningly like his father's.

Yekov walked swiftly to the door, opened it, and waded out into the cold mountain night, bending forward against the strong, freezing wind.

As the sun began to set beneath the western rim of the mountains, its descent leaving orange streaks upon the peaks and a purple sky above them, Yekov Leboveckian walked into the small cottage room where Barnes and Peter sat huddled by the fire. Two men followed him in. The younger man was Aaran Leboveckian. The other was an older man, dark and shriveled as a raisin with long white hair and a white wisp of a beard.

"If I am not mistaken, Barnes," said Peter, "the sun has yet to set, which would mean that Yekov Leboveckian has made good on his word. That is assuming, of course, that this is Don Mazarian?"

Peter smiled his most benevolent, winning smile and walked toward the old man with the white hair. In the course of the day, Peter had managed to get out of the bed, eat a solid meal, bathe, and shave. He felt like a new man.

The old Macmenian regarded him cautiously, inclining his head and looking Peter up and down with shrewd brown eyes.

"I am here because I hold these men in high regard," said the Macmenian.

"The Brothers Leboveckian are men worthy of your regard," said Peter.

"And men you have threatened, I am told."

Peter smiled. "And yet you are here by sunset."

"Are you here to threaten me as well?"

Peter did not stop smiling, "I am not here to make threats, only to uncover the truth. You are Don Mazarian. Yes?"

The man nodded.

"Your fame precedes you, Don Mazarian, and I thank you for accepting my invitation."

Don Mazarian's eyes were skeptical.

"I am told, by many, that no Macmenian knows the Sand Sea better than Don Mazarian. I am told no man in all of Imperial Spatania has led more caravans into the Sand Sea. I am told none have traveled deeper into the desert's heart, more extensively into the Seven Cities themselves, or through more desert dangers than Don Mazarian. Did I hear all of that correctly?"

Mazarian's face stayed hard.

Peter waited.

"I am a caravan man, yes," said Don Mazarian, slowly, in a deep, low, quiet voice. "As for the rest, people say what they say."

Peter smiled at Mazarian's modesty. "Very well. I am an Anglian and not a caravan man. I am Peter Harmon, son of Lord George Harmon, publisher of the *Illustrated Telegraph* and Elected Member of the Parliament of the Anglian Imperium. I am here as his emissary. I traveled with the explorer Harold Milton Stanwich into the Sand Sea. I am back here in Altadige because Beserians attacked us. That man"—Peter pointed to Barnes—"is Sergeant Joshua Barnes of the New Anglian Republic. We walked back on foot, without camels, from the Plain of Gamurian to Altadige in thirteen days."

As he said the words "thirteen days," Peter saw Mazarian's eyes shift, only just, but enough for Peter to see. *Unless I am mistaken, that was the first glimmer of respect, thought Peter.*

"A man was to guide our expedition, a man by the name of Aurelio Demassi. Do you know him?"

Don Mazarian stared at Peter.

"You trained him. Did you not?"

Mazarian looked down at his feet. Despite his age, he was not, in any visible way, a frail man. Peter could see that beneath his loose, burnt-orange-and-brown tunic and trousers, his body was lean and hard like a tribesman's. Decades of fierce sunlight had baked the skin of Don Mazarian's face and hands, leaving him nut-brown and wrinkled, but his arms were still wiry like triple-woven ropes.

"I trained him," said Don Mazarian.

"But he did not lead our expedition," said Peter. "He did something else entirely."

Yekov and Aaran Leboveckian shifted nervously in the corner of the firelit room.

"You see," said Peter. "The Brothers Leboveckian here, they hired the Vetenan, Aurelio Demassi, to guide us. They said he is among the finest guides in all of the Sand Sea. They said this because he trained with *you* since he was a little boy and because he journeyed in more caravans with *you* than any other young man living. Yet, Aurelio Demassi did not guide our expedition. Do you know what he did instead?"

Don Mazarian's hands rested on his hips; his eyes rested on Peter's.

"Do you know?"

Mazarian stared.

"Demassi kidnapped my cousin the night before we were to depart. Have you heard this?"

"Altadige is a small place," said Don Mazarian.

"Indeed, a small place," said Peter, looking around the cottage. "So, you do know. Of course, you know. Then tell me, why did he take Jack Caldwell, my cousin, into the Sand Sea instead of guiding our expedition, a mere day before we were to depart?"

Mazarian still kept his mouth tightly shut, frozen into a deep frown.

"Don Mazarian, I am not here seeking a man to blame. I seek neither a head nor even a scalp. I seek my cousin. I am here to find the answers that will bring Jack Caldwell back from the desert alive."

"You may not find them," said Don Mazarian.

"My cousin and his captors?"

"No, you may not find answers."

"I only suspect that I am more likely to find them with you than without you," said Peter.

Don Mazarian's frown loosened. The hardness in his eyes retreated a measure, like the desert's heat at sunset.

"I trained the young Demassi, but I lost him to the Beserian ways some years ago."

Peter waited.

Don Mazarian glanced over again at the Leboveckian brothers. "Six winters ago, I led a trading caravan. We were headed all of the way to the Seven Cities, to Alwaz Deem. In the age of Jemojeen, I am the only Macmenian trader still allowed to journey east of Ben Hamur."

"The age of what?" asked Peter.

"Jemojeen."

"What is Jemojeen?"

"Jemojeen is a man. He is the Grand Vizer of the Qhaliffa of the Seven Cities. In the age of Sumetan, the present Qhaliffa, it is Jemojeen that truly rules."

"Do they not call the Qhaliffa 'Sumetan the Magnificent'?" asked Peter.

Don Mazarian smiled. He had little square-shaped teeth. For an older man's, they were very good teeth—healthy, clean, and almost all still present.

"That name is as mocking as it is true," he said. "His reign is prosperous, but nearly all know he is but a figurehead, a puppet of the Grand Vizer."

Peter looked at the Brothers Leboveckian, his thoughts showing through the indignation that flashed through his eyes. *Did you know all of this and fail to tell me, or did you not know? Either way is unacceptable. Either way, you have failed me, you have failed Stanwich, and you have failed my father.*

"Please continue, Don Mazarian."

Don Mazarian nodded. His voice grew in vigor.

"As I said, Demassi traveled with me on the eastbound caravan. It was the first year of the reign of Sumetan as Qhaliffa. His father Selahim had died in the autumn. We had just learned that Sumetan was keeping Jemojeen, his father's Grand Vizer, as his own. Many had hoped he would not.

"Jemojeen is a Bulbanian who rose from the Demissary soldiers to become the right hand of the Qhaliffa. He is the first to have ever done so. All other Grand Vizers—going back across the centuries—have been Kezelboj lords, aristocrats of the Seven Cities. I say this because one does not make that journey—from Bulbanian Demissary to Grand Vizer—without shrewdness and cruelty, and Jemojeen has ample amounts of both. He is feared across the Sand Sea.

"We took the usual route to the east, from Altadige to the Plain of Gamurian. From there, we went east to the oasis of Ben Gamurian. From Ben Gamurian we traveled far, east and north to the oasis of Ben Hamur. From Ben Hamur, we journeyed north and to the west of the white-sand lands of the Hahst, and then, once around the Hahst, east and south, back down to Alwaz Deem, westernmost of the Seven Cities."

At the word *Hahst*, Peter's eyes flickered.

Don Mazarian saw this, and then he continued, "Before we reached Ben Hamur, well within sight of the oasis walls, a band of Beserians came upon us as dusk neared. They approached us peacefully. There were perhaps twenty of them, and our caravan, with two hundred camels, was well guarded. That night Aurelio Demassi shared a fire with those men.

"In the morning, Demassi told me he was leaving our caravan to travel with those Beserians. He never came to Alwaz Deem. He forfeited his ownership stake in our caravan to go with them instead of staying with us for the end of the journey. His share was four thousand ducats, and that is no mean sum to leave behind, even for the son of an old Vetenan house like House Demassi. But those Beserians put something in his mind that made him leave the money, and he never asked me for it after, not even once. He did not return to Altadige for more than a year. From that day forward, he was different. When he came back to the Veteno after that year, he was a changed man."

"Different how?"

"In many ways," said Demassi. "He became a tribesman in that year, dressing as he does now, no longer wearing the clothes of a man of the Veteno. He talked less and less of things of interest to the people of the Veteno. He ignored friends he had known since he was a boy. He ceased speaking with his family. He spent more and more time brooding. When he talked, he talked of the sands."

Peter turned and looked at the Brothers Leboveckian. His look said all he needed to say. They knew what they had failed to tell him when they had recommended Aurelio Demassi to guide Harold Milton Stanwich and his expedition to the Valley of Kordon. Both Aaran and Yekov looked away to avoid Peter's gaze.

"Don Mazarian, you strike me as a man who prefers plain speaking, so please allow me to cut to the point."

Mazarian looked into Peter's eyes, his chin dipping with just the hint of a nod.

"I am not a caravan man, and I am no great warrior. But I try to observe the world as it is, not as I wish it to be. For that reason, I read, and I remember. I do not believe the Beserian Prophecy is an idle tale. I believe it links all of these events together. I believe Aurelio Demassi became taken with the Beserian Prophecy. Qhaliffans call it the Beserian Heresy. What do you think?"

Mazarian's eyes flickered.

Peter saw the flicker.

He continued, "It states, in part, that in the seventh year of the fortieth Qhaliffa, a promised man shall arrive from the west, and through him, the God of the Sands and the Mountain will return just rule to the Seven Cities of the Great Mountain."

Mazarian continued to look squarely into Peter's eyes.

"I understand that Sumetan, the one they call the Magnificent, is the fortieth Qhaliffa to rule the Seven Cities. Yes?"

Don Mazarian paused before answering.

"Yes."

"And six years ago, you said he was nearing the end of the first year of his reign, yes?"

Mazarian nodded.

"And the Beserians you encountered outside of the oasis of Ben Hamur, they would have known this as well, correct?"

"Of course."

"I also know, Don Mazarian, that though their months are different from our own, the people of the Sand Sea follow a solar calendar, which means their year began when ours did."

Don Mazarian nodded.

"So, in other words," said Peter, "Aurelio Demassi believed he saw a man he thought could be an answer to this prophecy, right when the Year of the Prophecy was beginning. Demassi was positioned here—at the most likely entry point for someone to enter the Sand Sea from the west, was he not?"

Peter waited, allowing his words to hang in the air. No one spoke.

Peter continued, "I was with him, this guide, when the Ship of the Republic *Agobasto* arrived at the Vetenan docks. From the moment he set his eyes upon my cousin Jack as he walked down the gangplank, Demassi stared at him. I found it strange and troubling at the time. He looked at Jack as if he were a beautiful woman who had taken his breath away. I looked at him—Aurelio Demassi—and I saw his face. He was white as a ghost, or perhaps better said, he was pale as a man who has seen a ghost."

All in the room remained silent. Barnes pulled a small cigar from his pocket and struck a match.

"Tell me, Don Mazarian," said Peter. "Is this the kind of thing Aurelio Demassi would do? Capture a foreigner because he believes he is fulfilling a prophecy?"

Don Mazarian stared at Peter for long moments before answering.

"The Demassi I trained, no. The Demassi of today, perhaps."

"And can you think of another reason why he would disappear with him? He had no reason for malice against someone he had never before met. Nor would he kidnap him for some hope of money. There has been no demand. The guide does not care about money. As you yourself said, he forfeited four thousand ducats to ride the sands with Beserians. Indeed, he forfeited a handsome sum he would have earned guiding us, though nowhere near four thousand ducats."

"Your idea is not foolish," said Don Mazarian.

"Then let me ask you another question, Don Mazarian. If my idea is not foolish, and you were to seek Aurelio Demassi in this Year of the Prophecy, where would you go to find him?"

Mazarian's eyes narrowed, and his chin lowered. He clasped his hands behind his back. He closed his eyes tightly, making the crow's feet at the sides of his eyes even more profound, as if the thoughts in his mind were burdensome, like those of a mathematician on the verge of solving a problem, or a father grappling with how to rein in a wayward but beloved child.

"What have you read, Harmon?" Mazarian's eyes were still closed as he spoke.

"I have read *Legends of the Sand Sea: Stories from the Faiths of the Beserians and the Qhaliffans* by the Spatanian Ernesto De Guerre. I read *The Prophet and his Progeny, the Beserians, the Qhaliffans, and their Common Origins* by the Anglian traveler and scholar, John Hoslinger." Peter paused as if deciding whether to add the last part. "And I have read, *The Life of Hom Hommuram* by Agadam Azadeem, the Beserian."

As Peter said the last title, Don Mazarian's eyes opened. "You read those all in your own language?"

"Hoslinger wrote in Anglian. As for the others, I am told the translations are reliable," said Peter.

"You read Azadeem?"

"Yes."

"All of it?"

"Yes, it is a short book," said Peter.

"And an old book," said Don Mazarian. "You may forget the others. Azadeem speaks the only truth that matters."

"Oh?" Peter looked at Don Mazarian, searching the older man's face, uncertain whether he was mocking him or not. Azadeem's work was the least scholarly and the most fantastic in its claims. It was the kind of book one might read to a child before bedtime in Anglia.

Don Mazarian looked over at the Brothers Leboveckian as if trying to communicate something through his eyes alone.

"What do you know of this book?" asked Peter, looking at Yekov Leboveck-ian's face and then Aaran's.

"Nothing," said Aaran.

"Have you read it?"

"Yes."

"And?"

"It is a book of stories," said Yekov.

"Let's have out with it then, Don Mazarian," said Peter, his voice rising. "You say this book of stories tells the truth. I read it. Azadeem tells the same tale Stanwich told at Three God's College to an auditorium of young Anglians. He speaks of a magical staff, a staff that once belonged to the Prophet of the God of the Mountain and the Sands. Azadeem says that on his deathbed, the Proph-et ordered his staff divided into three, giving one part to his younger brother, who became the first Qhaliffa, one part to his greatest general, who disappeared into the sands, and one part to his chief priest, who led the Beserians into their eight hundred years of exile. You say this is true, or that Aurelio Demassi be-lieves it is true?"

Don Mazarian nodded.

"Which?"

"Both."

Barnes exhaled cigar smoke in the corner, watching the old Macmenian caravan leader beneath lowered eyelids.

"If you are not mocking me," began Peter.

"I am not mocking you," said Don Mazarian.

"If you are not mocking me, then tell me how to find my cousin."

"No man can tell you that, at least no man in Altadige. But I can tell you that if Aurelio Demassi took him to Abu Akhsa, and if he is still alive, they will go to the Hahst before the year ends. They must go there."

"The Hahst?"

Don Mazarian nodded.

"The Hahst is the place of the white sands," said Peter, "the driest part of all of the Sand Sea, the land of the swallowing sands, a place of no wells, a place where horses, men, and camels disappear without a trace. This is what Azadeem says."

"Yes," said Don Mazarian.

"And this is where you say they will go?"

"Yes."

"Azadeem also says that in the age of Mamet, the first Qhaliffa, the Gener-al Hom Hommuram journeyed into the Hahst carrying the middle part of the Prophet's staff, the Staff of the Lion, the Staff of Might. Azadeem says that

Hom Hommuram and his companions disappeared into the Hahst, never to be heard from again."

"Yes," said Don Mazarian.

"Azadeem writes that the prophecy proclaims that the place of Hom Hommuram's disappearance shall be found and that the Staff of Might waits for one who is meant to find it."

"Yes."

"And last, Azadeem writes there is a hidden valley, deep in the Hahst, a valley beyond the sinking sands. Azadeem says that once one seeks the valley, he will either find it or perish. This is what you are telling me is true?"

Don Mazarian nodded slowly and gravely.

"If you wish to find your cousin," he said, "you must go there. You may travel across the sands trying to find a single grain, or you may go to the place the wind is blowing. You may seek after him, ever chasing the places he has been, or you may go to the one place he must go."

"The Valley of Hom Hommuram."

"Yes."

"In the Hahst?"

"Yes."

"Then I have only one question, Don Mazarian, for neither Barnes nor I know the way. Will you take us there?"

CHAPTER 54
Welcoming the Weary

Oasis of Ben Gamurian
Southwestern Sand Sea
9th Day, Month of Wasura, 807
Anglian Calendar: March 2, 1879

The dry wind whipped at Hannah's sunburnt face. Her blue eyes were red and weepy, her lips cracked and painful. Mrs. Smith walked behind her, making sure she kept walking east, toward the walls.

"We're almost there, Hannah. Keep walking. That's a girl. Almost there."

Hannah staggered toward the palm fronds that rose above the mudbrick wall. Unlike Ben Hamur, with its deep moat and thorny zareba that rose out of it, Ben Gamurian's walls rose directly from the desert sands, curving in a great oval.

Mrs. Smith carried Hannah's Mancaster repeater slung over one shoulder, and her own Hart-Harold rifle slung over the other. Her canteen hung empty on one hip, and Hannah's rested on the other. They had run out of water half-way through the night. The morning sun had now made half of its journey upward toward the noon hour, and with it rose the heat, drawing sweat down the length of Mrs. Smith's broad back.

The guard on the wall shouted.

Mrs. Smith looked up to see four guards standing above the archway over the wooden gate. Three of them leaned on spear shafts. The fourth aimed a rifle at Harold Milton Stanwich.

"We come in peace," said Stanwich, saying one of the few Beserian phrases he knew. His voice sounded weary and weak.

The guard shouted something again, but Stanwich did not know the words. He looked at Hersen Expey. Hersen shook his head.

"Diego!" shouted Stanwich. The agony of his half-severed hand had frayed his nerves. His face beneath his pith helmet was as red and wind-battered as

Hannah's, but unlike Hannah's, it was pinched with pain. A deep line rose from between his eyebrows to the hairline of his scalp, like a valley dividing his forehead.

"Yes, Commander," said Diego, the Vetenan foreman, already at Stanwich's side.

"Tell these people we come here in peace."

Diego shouted his message up at the wall, speaking Beserian. The guard that had first spoken shouted something again.

Hersen Expey looked up and saw that the man's rifle was still pointed at them. He huffed. Had he possessed the energy, he would have laughed. They were still thirty-two strong, and each man carried at least one modern rifle, either a Hart-Harold or a Hart-Henry; both models were breechloaders and far finer than anything the Sharef of Ben Gamurian could throw at them. He and Stanwich could have dropped all four of them off of the wall, even in their present condition. Hannah Huntington could have shot them dead. *But does it matter? We have the energy barely to load our rifles, much less storm these twelve-foot mud walls. The desert protects this place far better than these weasels on the walls ever could.*

Hersen placed a hand on Stanwich's shoulder. Stanwich looked at him with wild, feverish eyes.

"Save your energy, Commander," said Hersen, his voice gentle, as if speaking to a skittish horse.

"Diego, ask him if he speaks Spatanian," said Hersen, his LaFrentian voice low and commanding. Hersen was not yet confident in his Beserian, but he could speak Spatanian like a native.

"He does not."

"Ask him, you son of a whore, before I stick my knife in your ear."

Diego's eyes widened in fear, and his cheeks flushed. He shouted up Hersen's question in Beserian.

"Are you Spatanians?" asked the same guard, switching to Spatanian. "You look like beggars to me."

Hersen glared at Diego and then looked up at the guard. *So, they do speak Spatanian, you stupid bastard. May all Vetenans roast in the Three Hells.*

Hersen's LaFrentian Legonde five-shot repeater was slung over his shoulder. Every part of him was filthy, but his Legonde repeater was clean and ready for action. Hersen lifted his hands, showing the guard his palms.

"We were attacked by bandits. We have walked for many miles. We seek only to drink from your pools as humble visitors. We will observe all of the laws and customs of the oasis."

The guard stared down at him. The oasis gate remained firmly shut.

"We claim visitors' rights as travelers upon the sands!" shouted Hersen.

The guard stared down at him.

"Open the gates," said the guard. He had no power against the custom of the sands. A thirsty man was entitled to drink from the pools of Ben Gamurian, so long as he followed the laws of the oasis.

The heavy wooden gates began to creak open. The wood was old and weathered, looking to be battered by decades if not centuries of wind, sun, and sands beating against it.

"You will give your rifles to the guard when you enter," shouted the guard as they approached the gate. "No weapons in Ben Gamurian!"

The gates, reaching up fifteen feet to the bottom of the arched, mudbrick parapet above, creaked open farther. Hersen led the procession forward with Stanwich shuffling at his side, softly groaning in pain underneath the paltry shade of his brown pith helmet, a helmet that once sparkled white.

Hannah walked forward with Mrs. Smith at her side. Hannah leaned on Mrs. Smith's shoulder as she passed under the guards on the wooden rampart above. She was too disoriented by the sun to notice the four men staring at her body as she passed underneath them.

The women of Ben Gamurian wore cotton coverings from their heads to their toes, often veiling their faces. Hannah wore riding pants, showing the contours of her long, athletic legs. So too did she wear a military-style tunic, unbuttoned enough for every guard on the rampart to see the curves of her ample chest. One hooted. Another whistled. The others laughed. Mrs. Smith looked up at them, her eyes sharp as Beserian daggers.

"Ignore them," said Mrs. Smith. Hannah was barely responsive, leaning more heavily upon Mrs. Smith's shoulder than she had leaned upon her even moments before. It was as if she had mustered enough endurance to take her through the walls, but no farther.

"We are almost there," said Mrs. Smith. "The pool is just ahead. Come and drink the fresh water."

Hannah groaned.

"Do not stop walking. You need the water," said Mrs. Smith.

Hannah slumped down farther, growing ever heavier on her shoulder. Hannah staggered and fell away from Mrs. Smith, collapsing onto the dusty ground beneath her.

Mrs. Smith caught her just before her face struck the earth. Hannah's wide-brimmed, Calderonian rancher's hat fell into the dust, landing upside down. Her partly loosened braid of golden hair fell over her face.

"Diego, help me!" shouted Mrs. Smith. The Venetan foreman ran, picked up Hannah's hat, placed a shoulder underneath Hannah's arm, and lifted her to help carry her toward the closest pool. Mrs. Smith kept her hands firmly beneath Hannah's other armpit. Hannah's head hung down like a prisoner's, as if her hands were tied to the torturer's beam.

"Almost there, Hannah. Hey! Stay awake! Awake!" Mrs. Smith barked out her words.

Hannah's head jolted up. "I need. To sleep. Just let me lie down."

"You need water," said Mrs. Smith. "Stay awake!" Mrs. Smith had seen what sunstroke could do if someone did not drink enough water soon enough. First came the unconsciousness and then death.

The hard-packed dirt of the square behind the gate ended at the stone steps that descended into the first pool of Gamurian. Several women knelt at the edge of the pool, filling up water jugs, looking at Mrs. Smith with wide, suspicious eyes above veiled noses and cheeks.

Water lilies floated in the pool. Reeds lined the edge, extending out from either side of the stone steps. But in front of Mrs. Smith, Diego, and Hannah, at the bottom of the steps, a pool of clean, clear water glistened in the sunlight. The water came up from springs beneath, springs that had never ceased sending freshwater up into Ben Gamurian for the three thousand years of its recorded history. For as long as men had traveled the sands, they had stopped to drink from the pools of Gamurian.

Mrs. Smith and Diego lowered Hannah to the pool's edge, still holding her up by her underarms. Mrs. Smith cupped a single hand and brought a sip of water to Hannah's chapped, cracked lips. Most of the water fell out of her hand and onto the stone step beneath her, but Hannah's eyes opened at the taste of water on her lips.

"Let me go," she said. "Let me down so I can drink."

Diego and Mrs. Smith released her. To their credit, they watched her plunge her hands into the pool, bring them up to her mouth and lap a mouthful of water before they plunged their own faces into the pool to drink until their stomachs ached. Hannah brought her hands up fiercely, splashing water on her tunic.

It was the custom of Ben Gamurian to allow a parched traveler to drink until he or she was satisfied. No man or camel could drink so much as ever to drain the pools, fed from the springs that released the deep water from the earth, day after day, month after month, year after year, century after century.

Hannah, Diego, and Mrs. Smith drank for long moments.

Stanwich and Hersen, relieved of their numerous weapons, staggered toward the first pool, with Stanwich, the shorter man by far, leaning against Hersen's chest. Hersen wrapped his arms around Stanwich, propping him up from the side.

As they approached the pool, a pair of guards approached them, shouting and shaking their spears. Stanwich and Hersen had left their rifles, their pistols, and their long knives at the gate as they were ordered to do. The guards shouted at Stanwich so forcefully that Hersen almost reached for the small hidden knife he kept strapped above his ankle.

"What?" asked Hersen, using one of the Beserian words he knew, "What?"

The guards shouted, pointing at Stanwich.

"What?" asked Hersen again, this time in Spatanian, hoping the guards might speak to him in that language that he knew infinitely better than Beserian.

The guards continued shouting in Beserian, both at the same time, shaking their spears with the points lowered. Hersen understood most of it but pretended that he did not.

Diego, the foreman, lifted his head from the pool.

"He cannot come to the pool," said Diego.

"What did you say?" said Hersen Expey, his eyebrows lowered, and his eyes narrowed.

"The guards say he cannot approach the pool with his hand," said Diego.

"Why not?"

"No injuries near the water."

"By the Three Gods," said Hersen. "He needs to drink!"

"You must fill up his canteen and bring it to him. They will not let him near the pool."

The guards stepped close to Stanwich with their lowered spears, shouting without ceasing.

"Yes, yes, enough!" said Hersen, placing himself between the guards and Stanwich, raising his palms in submission and backing Stanwich away from the pool.

Hannah finished drinking, rolled onto her back, and lay face up to the sky with her eyes closed. The blazing desert sun beat down upon her sunburnt face, but she lay there, unmoving, with her arms stretched out at her sides. She exhaled, and her mouth shifted up into a smile. *That was the best water I have ever drunk in my entire life.*

Hannah opened her eyes to see five men staring down at her. Four of them wore the same light-colored headscarves as the spearmen who had stood guard above on the gate. Each man, like the men on the gate, grasped a spear that was just taller than he was. But the man in the center looked different. He was not taller or broader, but something about the way he carried himself made him seem larger. A bright yellow border formed the edge of his headscarf, and the fabric he wore seemed both lighter and shinier than the fabric of the guardsmen.

"His Excellency, Tazak Bin-Zaal, Sharef of Ben Gamurian, requests your presence at once," he said, speaking the accented Beserian of the oasis.

Mrs. Smith stood up and looked at the center man, who was clearly the leader.

"We do not speak your tongue," she said, in Spatanian. "Speak Spatanian, and we shall understand you."

The man repeated himself in Spatanian.

"What does the Sharef want with us?" asked Mrs. Smith.

"The desires of the Sharef of Ben Gamurian are not mine to discuss with you, woman."

"Can't you see she needs rest?"

The man looked at Mrs. Smith uncomprehendingly, as if she had just barked like a dog.

"She needs rest," said Mrs. Smith.

"Yes," said the man. His face took on a pinched expression as if there was a foul smell. "His Excellency the Sharef demands your presence at once."

The man turned and began walking away, the four spear-wielding guards trailing at his sides.

They walked past Harold Milton Stanwich, who Hersen Expey had sat down halfway up the path. Cradling his wounded hand in his lap, Stanwich drank from a canteen Hersen held for him, gulping down the water. The leader of the guards with the yellow-fringed headscarf stepped around Stanwich as if he were a carcass, sneering as he passed.

"Animals," he said, in a Beserian accent that he thought neither Stanwich nor Hersen Expey could understand. The spearmen snickered.

Tazak Bin-Zaal, Sharef of Ben Gamurian, wore spotless white cotton robes.

A pair of palms growing out of massive pots shaded his cushion, upon which he sat alone. The containers themselves reached nearly as high as the heads of the guardsmen who stood in front of them, holding their short, head-high spears and glaring like they wanted an excuse to use them. Except for the black hair on his chin and above his upper lip, the Sharef's face was cleanly shaven and oddly pale for a man that lived in a place upon which the sun blazed nearly every day, from season to season, in a clear, cloudless sky.

A lone man, tall and skeletal, stood next to the Sharef. Like the leader of the guardsmen that had escorted them to the Sharef's palace, he wore a head-scarf of a fine, thin fabric, the color of sand except for its bright yellow trim, the yellow of the noonday sun, the sun that in summer baked the sands like coals and felt like a furnace upon a man's uncovered skin.

The Sharef spoke. His voice was low, and his eyes were proud, verging on arrogant.

The tall, skeletal man spoke in Beserian as soon as the Sharef stopped talking.

"The Sharef of Ben Gamurian, exalted be his name, asks if you speak any of the languages of the One True God, the God of the Sands, whom others have rightly called the God of the Mountain. These languages, of course, are Beserian, Qhaliffan, and Macmenian."

"I speak them all," said Diego, in Beserian, kneeling like the others, their legs resting on the hard, hot stone. The Sharef had provided no cushions for his guests to kneel upon, but he had ordered them to kneel nonetheless.

"And the others?" asked the skeletal man.

"They speak Spatanian."

"No Beserian?"

Diego shook his head.

"Qhaliffan?"

"No."

"Macmenian?"

"No, only Spatanian or other languages of the lands beyond the western mountains."

The tall man said something into the ear of the Sharef. The Sharef responded with words that Diego could not hear. The tall man nodded.

"Very well. The Sharef, in his graciousness, will allow you to speak the barbarian language of the Spatanian dogs in his presence," said the tall man, still using Beserian.

Diego looked at the man warily, assessing the danger of the insult. There was no doubt that his face was a Spatanian face, and he was not hiding his Spatanian accent.

"We shall speak to you in the barbarian tongue of the Spatanians, as you do not speak the languages of the people of the One True God," said the tall man, switching to Spatanian.

All of the kneeling Westerners—Stanwich, Hersen, Hannah, and Mrs. Smith—could clearly understand the tall, skeletal man now, and Diego no longer needed to interpret.

"He's a rude skeleton, I see," said Hannah, in Anglian, looking at Mrs. Smith.

Mrs. Smith looked at her, and the tension in her face lessened. *Thank the Three Gods. The waters of the pool have brought her back. Those groaning with sunstroke do not make fun.*

"His Excellency, the Sharef of Ben Gamurian, wishes to know why you have walked across the desert to our ancient oasis," said the tall man.

"We were attacked," said Hersen Expey.

Stanwich groaned.

Hersen looked over at him with concern in his eyes. In all of their journeys, even into the darkest heart of the Feathermen Highlands, when Stanwich had fallen down the ravine and broken his leg, Hersen had never seen Stanwich in so much pain. *The infection is deepening.*

"Attacked by whom?" asked the tall, skeletal man at the Sharef's side.

"Beserian raiders," said Hersen. Stanwich did not speak, grinding his teeth against the pain pulsing up his arm, and starting to lose his balance from the fever gripping his mind.

The Sharef spoke in a low voice that only the tall, skeletal man could hear.

"How do you know they were Beserians?" he asked.

"Because we saw them," said Hersen. "And who else would they be?"

"Where were you attacked?" asked the tall man. His voice reminded Hersen of the long, thin knives assassins had used across the generations in the Veteno, sharp and piercing. A gracious ruler might have allowed them to rise once they had first knelt or to sit differently. The Sharef of Ben Gamurian was not such a ruler.

"South of the Valley of Kordon," said Hersen.

Again, the Sharef spoke in a low tone that was inaudible to the Westerners kneeling before him. The tall skeletal man nodded sharply. He cleared his throat.

"Why do you travel with women?" he asked.

"We travel together," said Hannah.

The tall man looked at her with anger in his eyes.

"Why does this woman speak to me when I have not spoken to her?" He directed his gaze at Hersen.

Hersen glanced over at Hannah, the grey of his eyes meeting the brilliant sky blue of hers. Hersen lifted a hand toward her and widened his eyes.

"We meant no offense, Mr.—what may I call you?"

"My name is inconsequential. I am merely the voice of the Sharef of Ben Gamurian when he wishes to speak to barbarians such as yourself."

Hersen forced a smile onto his face. In his years in the LaFrentian Legion, he had often been outnumbered by the forces of arrogant chiefs in Omakhosi, in Halex, and elsewhere. *One does not allow such men to offend, not until the odds have altered.*

"Hersen," said Stanwich, speaking loudly in Anglian, "you tell that talking skeleton that if he calls me a barbarian one more time, I'm going to take the knife out of your boot and cut his throat."

"Rest yourself, my Commander," said Hersen, nodding and placing a gentle hand on Stanwich's shoulder. Stanwich irritably shrugged off Hersen's hand. Sweat beaded on his forehead as the fever raged hotter and hotter.

"Tell your Sharef this," said Hersen. "My name is Major Hersen Expey. I am an officer of the Legion of the Republic of LaFrentia. I travel with Harold Milton Stanwich, the greatest explorer in all of the world. The woman you speak of, she of the golden hair, is the daughter of the richest man in all of the New Anglian Republic. Any kindness the Sharef shows to us will be remembered and repaid."

The tall skeletal man blocked his mouth with his hand and offered the Sharef a barrage of hushed, rapid words.

"Listen to him, Diego," whispered Hersen, turning to Diego's ear. "You make sure he says what he is supposed to say."

Diego leaned forward to listen better, stretching his neck like a turtle reaching for a leaf.

The skeletal man stopped speaking.

"Did he say it true?" whispered Hersen.

Diego nodded.

The Sharef snapped his fingers. From behind a stone wall at the side of the receiving room, a servant rushed forward, bearing a large silver cup. The Sharef took it in his hands, sipped modestly, and returned the cup to the servant's tray, neither looking at nor acknowledging the servant. The servant rushed off to the place from which he came. The Sharef wiped his lips.

"You look like beggars to me," said the Sharef, speaking Spatanian himself. "The daughter of a man of great wealth, you say? Then why is her face streaked with dirt? And why does she dress like a man, wearing the pants of a soldier?"

"We are not always as we appear," said Hersen.

Hannah looked at the pompous man in the immaculate white robes, feeling the urge to strike his proud face. Mrs. Smith placed a hand upon Hannah's thigh and left it there.

The Sharef's closed mouth tilted upward at the edges into a condescending smile.

Hersen continued, "We request the right to stay here until others come to relieve us. In the alternative, if you have camels, we will pay you."

"Pay me? How many camels do you desire?"

"Fifty," said Hersen, without hesitation.

"Fifty?" The Sharef laughed aloud. He looked at the tall skeletal man who began laughing as well. The Sharef stopped laughing, and his eyes hardened. A fraction of a moment later, the tall skeletal man stopped laughing as well, as quickly as if he were a puppet on a string, obeying the hand of its master.

"And what will you pay me for my fifty camels, you who walk across the desert?"

"We can pay you in gold," said Hersen, pulling a Spatanian ducat from his belt pocket and lifting it up in the air. Sunlight flooded the room from the large square windows in the plastered mudbrick walls, glinting off of the gold in Hersen's hand.

The Sharef laughed again. "I am afraid my camels will cost you more than that, Westerner."

Hersen unfastened the detachable pocket from which he had pulled the gold. He lifted it up in his fist, like a sack full of pebbles.

"This is gold enough for one hundred camels in the Veteno," said Hersen, shaking the sack.

The Sharef smiled. It was not a kind smile.

"We are not in the Veteno, Westerner. How much gold do you have in that sack?"

"Eight hundred and fifty gold ducats," said Hersen.

"A fine sum," said the Sharef. "But I have a different idea."

Hersen looked at him suspiciously.

"You carried rifles when you walked through my gate. They are currently in my gatehouse."

Hersen looked at the Sharef.

"Tell that sand snake he is not taking my rifles, not one," said Stanwich in Anglian.

Hersen nodded at him, noting the feverish wildness in Stanwich's eyes.

"I desire your rifles more than I desire your gold," said the Sharef.

"The answer is no," said Stanwich, still speaking only to Hersen, in Anglian.

"You are not your own commander, are you ,Westerner?" asked the Sharef.

Hersen glared.

"The one who holds his hand, whose face winces in pain beneath his sand-colored helmet, the one who sweats with the fever of infection, he is your commander, is he not?" continued the Sharef.

Hersen looked at Stanwich to his left. Diego knelt next to him. He then turned and looked at Mrs. Smith and Hannah, still kneeling to his right. All were shifting their bodies on their knees, the discomfort beginning to turn into pain.

"Yes, he is our commander," said Hersen.

"He is wounded," said the Sharef.

"He is," said Hersen.

The Sharef looked at Stanwich's pale and sickly face underneath his pith helmet. Sweat gathered on his jawline, dripping from his beard.

"Your commander has a fever, the kind that kills."

"He needs rest," said Hersen.

"He needs strong medicine," said the Sharef.

"Medicine," said Stanwich, grunting in Spatanian.

"We seek medicine as well," said Hersen.

"Yes, Westerner, but medicine also costs, like camels."

Hersen again resisted the urge to reach for the knife at his ankle. There were ten guards, each armed with a spear. Even in his legionnaire's hands, his knife would not be enough, even if the guards were incompetent fighters. They would all be dead—Stanwich, Hannah, all of them—from spear punctures before Hersen could gut the Sharef on his cushion.

"We will pay you gold for your medicine," said Hersen.

"Save your gold, Westerner. You will need it for Ben Hamur."

"Ben Hamur?"

"If your commander wishes to survive, he must go to Ben Hamur."

"What medicines do they have in Ben Hamur?"

"None that we do not have here."

"Then why would we go to Ben Hamur? It is hundreds of miles from here across open sands."

The Sharef rose from his cushion. The Westerners all remained kneeling on the hard stone, their legs stiff, their discomfort growing more acute.

"Rise! Rise! You rise when the Sharef stands!" shouted the tall skeletal man, bellowing like a man trying to douse a spreading fire.

Mrs. Smith stood first, helping Hannah up onto her feet. The men rose with her. Hersen lifted Stanwich by his healthy arm, and Stanwich gritted his teeth against the pain.

"You must go to Ben Hamur," said the Sharef, walking toward Hersen Expey, "because your commander is beyond the powers of our medicine."

Hersen stared into the Sharef's eyes. They were dark and intelligent, eyes that saw much and revealed little.

"With respect, Sharef, we do not have time for riddles."

"No, indeed, you do not, Hersen Expey of the LaFrentian Legion, but I am told that the Staff of Wisdom travels across the sands to Ben Hamur as we speak."

Hersen glanced at Stanwich and Diego, as if unsure whether he had heard the Sharef's Spatanian words correctly.

"You look confused, Westerner. Do you not know of the Staff of Wisdom? Others call it the Staff of the Serpent, the Staff of Beseri, and they are not wrong, for it is a staff of many names, which it has earned through the centuries because of its origin . . . and its power. It was not long ago in the Valley of Kordon, but it has moved west, and it has found a new owner. No longer does the staff rest in the hands of Hamid Salesi, advisor to Abu Akhsa, leader of the Beserians."

Hersen looked at the Sharef, not knowing what to say. *The Staff of Wisdom? Abu Akhsa?*

"Is Abu Akhsa going to Ben Hamur?" asked Hersen, not knowing what else to ask.

The Sharef continued forward. He was neither fat nor thin, and on the shorter side of average. He smiled beneath his black mustache, the ends of his lips curling up to reveal crooked teeth.

Crooked teeth for a crooked man, thought Hersen. Hersen wore his own smile like a mask.

"Abu Akhsa will go wherever Abu Akhsa goes, Westerner, but the Staff of the Serpent makes its way to Ben Hamur whether the Beserians follow it there or not."

"How do you know this?" asked Hersen.

"It is the duty of a Sharef to know what happens upon the sands. Do you know how long my family has governed this oasis? For far longer than your people have had a nation. Yes, I know of your nation, Hersen Expey of the La-Frentian Legion."

Hersen looked at the man, speechless.

"If your commander does not find the Staff of the Serpent, he will surely die. The staff alone has the power to heal such a wound. I have seen it with my own eyes."

The Sharef's Spatanian came out rapidly and accented in a way that made his words difficult for even Hersen and Diego to understand. But Stanwich caught enough of them.

He adjusted his pith helmet, leaning it back on his head, revealing his sweat-slicked blond hair.

"I need medicine, Sharef, not some magic staff. I'll make you a deal. You give me medicine to make the burning in my hand go away, and you give us fifty camels to get us back to Altadige, and I'll give you the gold and half of my guns."

The Sharef paused. From the look in his eyes, it was clear he had understood the poorly accented Spatanian of Harold Milton Stanwich.

"And I'll tell you, Sharef," Stanwich continued, "these are not old rifles that someone is trying to dump off to tribesmen and the like. We carry only modern rifles, some of which were made this very year: Hart-Henry single-shot breech-loading rifles, the rifle of the Anglian Army."

The Sharef's smile faded from his face.

"Your rifles are already in my possession. My guards took your rifles when you entered my gate."

Stanwich smiled through his pain. It was not a triumphant smile; it was a smile of endurance, the smile of a man who has already endured much pain and hardship and knows that he must likely endure still more.

"Your guardsmen are only holding my rifles. I am offering you half of them to keep."

"And what makes you think I will not simply keep what I already have?" asked the Sharef.

"Look, Sharef, I am not in the business of making threats. I've got a bad cut on my hand, and I need some help. Some tribesmen attacked us out there. Those men will be severely punished. We traveled with diplomatic protection, under the flags of the Spatanian Empire, the Anglian Imperium, and the New Anglian Republic. The armies will come, and when they come, they will learn who helped my expedition, and they will learn who helped my enemies. Which one will you be, Sharef, when the armies come? The one who made the Oasis of Ben Gamurian my enemy, or the one who helped me and my fellow travelers in our time of need?"

Hersen looked at Harold Milton Stanwich with a look he did not typically give a man with whom he had spent more time than any other across the past ten years—surprise. He had never heard Harold Milton Stanwich speak Spatanian so well in their entire lives together. His eyes were still wild and altered from his fever, his skin was piqued, and his face was gaunt.

Stanwich nonetheless met the Sharef's gaze. For several seconds they stood almost exactly eye to eye, albeit several feet apart, staring at each other, like cocks in a pit.

"I will accept your offer, Harold Milton Stanwich. Fifty camels and whatever medicine my healers can provide you, you shall have. But I warn you. Your fever is the killing kind. Ride for Ben Hamur or death will find you."

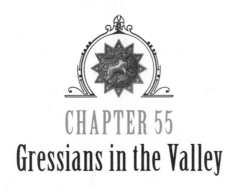

CHAPTER 55
Gressians in the Valley

The Valley of Kordon
Western Sand Sea
March 20, 1879

The wind whipped at Peter Harmon's face, blowing from the northeast. His red-brown beard had grown thicker than he had ever worn it before. His hair grew down, well past his collar, and the sun had altered the color of his face, changing it from pale to red, and then from red to bronze. His own mother would likely have to look twice before recognizing him; had there been a mirror for him to look into, it is doubtful he would have recognized himself.

The strong wind carried a frozen edge, even as the hot sun beat down upon Peter's shoulders. His back ached from his camel's saddle. He had better endurance than he possessed on the route with Stanwich from Altadige to the Plain of Gamurian, but his ability to sit in a saddle was nowhere near that of any of the Macmenians who rode with Don Mazarian. They rode a camel as easily as other men walked a city street.

Peter glanced over at Barnes. He knew Barnes had ridden a camel as few times as he, save one uncomfortable expedition he had executed with Colonel Caldwell's regiment across the southern deserts of the New Anglian Republic in the LaFrentian War. Yet, inexperienced with the humped beasts as he was, Barnes's face betrayed no pain, if pain was indeed what he felt. Barnes sat, straight-backed and firmly in his saddle, looking ahead toward the eastern horizon.

"We should approach the Valley of Kordon shortly," said Peter, glancing down at his compass. He had never much paid attention to things like compasses before. Now every third of an hour, he glanced down at the glass face of his small Gerdic piece—a fine compass manufactured by the Grutt family works of Gruuten.

"We would be better to avoid it," said Barnes, still looking east.

"The Valley of Kordon?"

Barnes grunted and nodded, keeping his eyes on the eastern horizon.

Don Mazarian rode at the fore of their twelve-camel caravan. He had insisted upon personally checking everyone's saddlebags in advance, including those of his men, making sure all of the needed provisions were present and that only those provisions were present. Regarding the expulsion of any extraneous items, he was a fanatic.

"Bring Azadeem only," he said to Peter on the day of their departure. "Leave the other books here."

Peter had protested, to which Don Mazarian said, "You do not understand the Hahst, young Anglian. A man who values his life does not enter the Hahst at all, but if he must enter, he most certainly does not enter with more than he needs."

Peter obeyed the old Macmenian, leaving the excess books in Altadige, in a back room of House Gremanian's trading outpost, under the care of Aaran Leboveckian.

But Don Mazarian did not stop there. He was a detailed autocrat regarding all items allowed in his caravan, even bullets. Each man was allowed forty rounds of ammunition, no more.

Peter and Barnes had both argued for more, with Barnes, as a warfighter, carrying far more credibility. Don Mazarian remained unyielding.

"No man needs more than forty bullets," he said. "If each of us needs to kill forty men, we will most certainly die, and no man should be firing one of his bullets unless it knocks down a hare for us to roast or an enemy that means us harm. Your countrymen might waste bullets as if they are pebbles on a seashore, but upon the sands, a man does not waste a bullet. Bullets must be carried, and more often than not, it is speed that saves a man's life on the sands, not the bullets in his pouch."

In the end, Don Mazarian relented on Barnes's addition of a fifteen round ammunition belt, slung at a diagonal over his chest. Unbeknownst to Don Mazarian, Barnes smuggled another fourteen in the undertube of his Mancaster.

That was in Altadige, long days ago.

They were far from Altadige now. Don Mazarian slowed the caravan, raising his right hand into the air.

Peter looked down at his compass again. They rode nearly due east with a slightly northern bearing, heading nearly face-first into the wind. Peter clicked his tongue the way the Macmenians had taught him and tapped his riding stick on his camel's neck. She lurched forward out of a walk, trotting with Peter awkwardly clinging to her back. The trot was the most challenging movement for Peter to adapt to on camelback. The rare canter and the even-rarer gallop were almost smooth, and easy enough for a horseman to adjust to, but the trot rattled a man like a loaded cart crossing a lane cobbled with river rocks.

"How far to the Valley of Kordon?" asked Peter, slowing his camel alongside Don Mazarian's. Don Mazarian rode with a casual, relaxed stance, as if half-asleep, his eyes narrowed to slits, and his face scarf lifted up like a Beserian's veil.

"Three miles," he said, turning to look at Peter. "That green line there. That is the valley," said Don Mazarian, pointing ahead.

Peter looked and saw it near the horizon, a thin line of forest green separating the bright blue, almost teal sky above, from the monotonous tan canvas beneath it.

"I had no idea the valley was so lush," said Peter.

"Lush?" Don Mazarian smiled beneath his silver-white beard and laughed. "Nonsense, that is the green of thornbushes. Nasty things. But even the thorns will give us a kinder reception than any raiders or encampment guards Abu Akhsa has left behind."

"Should we avoid it?" asked Peter.

"No," said Don Mazarian.

"Barnes says we should," said Peter.

"That is because we should," said Barnes, riding his camel up beside them. Barnes looked more like an aging rancher than a war hero. Like Peter, he was long-haired and scruffy. Unlike Peter, he eschewed the Anglian pith helmet in exchange for the floppy, wide-brimmed hat of a Calderonian ranchman, and his beard was a tangle of brown, with little bits of grey.

"There is water in the Valley of Kordon," said Don Mazarian.

"There are likely enemies in the Valley of Kordon," said Barnes.

Don Mazarian continued riding, saying nothing.

Peter broke the silence. "If not Kordon, then where?"

"We would ride around," said Don Mazarian. "It is not a short ride. Good, seasoned caravan men have run out of water making the ride."

Peter instinctively put his hand to his waterskin, feeling it for its weight. It was, at best, half full, and Peter inclined toward optimism.

"We should avoid the valley. Indeed, we are too close now," said Barnes.

"New Anglian," said Don Mazarian, "remind an old man. How many caravans have you led across the sands?"

Barnes did not answer.

"Enemies with rifles and swords frighten me more than empty waterskins," said Barnes.

"Do they?" asked Don Mazarian, his voice rising, "And how many times have you persuaded or bribed thirst to refrain from killing you? How many times have you seen a camel die, knowing the next well is farther away than you can walk?"

Barnes's jaw jutted forward in a small gesture of defiance, his mouth curving down into a frown. He continued to look forward.

"We walked back to Altadige from south of Kordon in thirteen days."

Peter looked at Barnes, nodding in support.

"An impressive feat, no doubt, but this is not retreating to Altadige, and do not think that because you have seen a little patch of desert you have seen the Sand Sea. You have seen very little.

"There are ways to deal with men," said Mazarian. "In seventy-four caravan rides upon this desert, and I am not counting this ride, a man learns things. This is one of them. Thirst kills without mercy. Thirst is deaf to pleading, impervious to bullets, disinterested in gold. On the other side of the camel, New Anglian, men are susceptible to all three. If I am picking adversaries, I choose a man over the desert every time, and as you may see, New Anglian, after all of these years, I am still alive.

"So, to answer your question, young Harmon, yes, I say we shall ride for Kordon. Perhaps Barnes, while we are there, you will find justification to use those extra bullets you insisted on carrying across your chest. But you will not die of thirst, and neither will I."

Don Mazarian smiled, looking to the east. The thornbushes marking the edge of the valley loomed, greener and larger than before.

Several hundred yards from the valley's rim, Don Mazarian ordered Peter and Barnes to wait back with him, one on either side.

"There is a fine line between courage and foolishness," he said. "Wait, and let my men do what they have learned to do in their years upon the sands."

Two of Don Mazarian's Macmenians waited behind them, holding the camel ropes of the other riders. The camels, to the credit of their Macmenian training, neither grunted nor roared. They stood in silence, waiting for their masters to return.

The other Macmenians, seven of them, ran forward, in three groups of two with one man bringing up the rear. The front three groups spread out across fifty yards, scanning the ridgeline in front of them, their eyes searching for any irregularities in the constant and unbroken line of thorn bushes. They held their rifles in their hands as they advanced, aimed down at the dirt but prepared to fire.

To a man, they carried Legonde repeaters, the same LaFrentian weapon that Hersen Expey so proudly carried alongside Harold Milton Stanwich, Model 1 of the year 1876. It boasted most of the stopping power of the Anglian Hart-Henry, and most of the speed of the New Anglian Mancaster. That the weapon was in the hands of Don Mazarian's Macmenians now was a testament both to the underestimated prowess of LaFrentian industry, and to the fact that the LaFrentians would, more readily than other nations, sell their finest rifles to foreigners that could, depending upon the diplomatic winds, one day use their own guns against them.

"Fine men carrying fine weapons," said Barnes, watching them advance.

Don Mazarian nodded with pride.

Peter looked at Barnes, arching an eyebrow, wondering if serving along-side Hersen Expey had somehow softened Barnes's disdain for all things LaFrentian.

"Too bad you do not let them carry enough ammunition," said Barnes.

Don Mazarian's eyes lurched toward him, flashing annoyance.

"My men carry what they need, no more, no less."

"I'd say less," said Barnes.

Don Mazarian huffed, flaring the nostrils on his long, slightly downward-curving nose.

The men had closed to within twenty yards of the ridgeline. All was quiet.

Peter looked up. A hawk circled overhead, flying directly over them.

"Do you see that?"

Barnes nodded.

"Do you see that, Don Mazarian?"

"What?"

"That hawk. Look at its coloring and its golden beak. Isn't that a Hon River Hawk?"

Don Mazarian looked up at the hawk just as the thornbushes exploded with rifle fire. One of Mazarian's Macmenians fell, crying out.

The rapid-fire of Legonde repeaters filled the air, a shocking departure from the silence of only a moment before. *Crack-crack. Crack-crack-crack. Crack.*

Peter's camel jolted, nearly throwing him from his saddle. He regained his balance.

"Down! Down!" he shouted in Macmenian, correctly wielding his riding stick. The rifle fire notwithstanding, the Macmenian-trained camel lowered onto her knees. As soon as she hit the ground, Peter had already swung himself over her hump, his Macmenian sandals landing in the dirt. His Hart-Henry rifle was out of his saddle's side holster and in his hands.

He was slower than Barnes, who was slower than Don Mazarian. Despite his more than sixty years, Mazarian already advanced ahead of Barnes, moving at a crouch, the butt of his Legonde rifle nestled tightly against his shoulder and his eyes looking down the sights toward the line of thorns.

More shots burst from the thornbushes. Bullets flew past Peter's head, ripping the air as they went, making him duck lower.

"Those are not Beserian rifles!" said Don Mazarian, aiming his Legonde into the thorns. Just ahead of Peter, Don Mazarian's rifle cracked out a shot, deafeningly loud.

"Stay low!" shouted Barnes, firing his Mancaster. The New Anglian rifle made even more noise than the LaFrentian one.

His ears ringing, Peter shouldered his Hart-Henry single-shot breech loader and scanned the thorns for a target. Wisps of grey-black smoke lingered in front of the thorns, but Peter could not see any bodies behind it.

"I can't see them!" he shouted.

"Shoot below the smoke!" said Barnes.

Don Mazarian continued to advance in a crouch, firing his repeater as he glided forward in swift, soundless steps across the sand.

"To ground!" shouted Barnes.

Even through his adrenaline, Peter's mind remembered the phrase they had discussed day after day. Peter threw himself down onto the ground, still gripping his Hart-Henry with both hands. His chest absorbed the fall, like a punch to the sternum.

Peter gasped at the thudding impact as a new volley tore through the air, and puffs of smoke spewed from the thornbushes. On reflex, Peter drew his chin into his chest, like a tortoise to a shell, wincing as the bullets flew past his pith helmet. He looked up to see that Don Mazarian was already on his stomach, firing his Legonde into the thorns. A man cried out in the direction of the thorns.

Don Mazarian shouted in rapid Macmenian, gesturing with his arm from his prone position. His Macmenians jumped up from where they had been crouching, along a shallow wadi and behind a stack of rocks in front of the thorns.

"Support them!" shouted Don Mazarian, using Spatanian words that Peter and Barnes both understood.

Barnes fired, cocked his Mancaster underlever forward, expelled the casing, and fired again. Peter put his Hart-Henry to his shoulder and pulled the trigger, shooting into the thorns just behind the thickest cloud of gun smoke. The rifle kicked back hard against his shoulder, barking out a smoke cloud of its own. Peter ejected the spent shell with the underlever while his rifle shot still rang in his ears. The stink of gunpowder filled his nose. He plunged his hand underneath him into his ammunition pouch, gripped a cartridge, pulled it up, and slid the tip into the breech.

The Macmenians rose on either flank of the smoke clouds accumulating in front of the thorns. Peter fired into the gap between them. Barnes and Mazarian's shots followed just behind his own.

Peter reached for another round. The Macmenians rushed forward, carrying their Legonde repeaters in their hands. A man jumped out of the thorns, gripping a rifle with a fixed bayonet. He was uniformed like a western soldier, but his hat was strange and tall. His tunic was green above black trousers. He charged at the Macmenians. Three of them raised their rifles and fired at once. The man staggered sideways into the sand, dropping his rifle as he fell.

The Macmenians ran into the smoke, disappearing. Peter followed them with his eyes, searching for a target, waiting for the sounds of more gunshots. They did not come.

"Forward," said Don Mazarian, rising from his stomach. Barnes nodded at Peter, rising to follow the old Macmenian. Peter lifted himself, rose to his knees, and stood up. Don Mazarian and Barnes ran forward. Peter followed them into the dissipating smoke.

When they reached the thorns, they saw three dead soldiers hanging by their clothing, the thorns having caught their tunics and trousers as they fell toward the earth.

"Stay low," said Don Mazarian. "Stay beneath the thorns."

Peter looked and saw that near the ground, the branches grew farther apart, rising in separated, perpendicular trunks that did not have long thorns. Peter dropped down and crawled, using his knees and his elbows, his hands still gripping his Hart-Henry. Barnes crawled directly in front of him, following Don Mazarian, creeping as swiftly as the other Macmenians, some of whom were young enough to be Don Mazarian's grandchildren.

Peter crawled farther. His head reached the edge of the branches, and his stomach lurched, his legs jutting out laterally. Below him, the Valley of Kordon opened up, broad and majestic. The drop of the cliff in front of him was severe, falling off perhaps two hundred feet before striking the valley floor below.

Don Mazarian lay with his elbows at the edge of the precipice, flat on his stomach, scanning the valley with an extendable Gerdic looking glass, not terribly different from Peter's own. Peter looked down with his naked eyes and could see dozens of men working in the gravel near the tiny stream that flowed at the bottom of the valley.

Peter pulled his own looking glass from his belt, drawing the edge up to his eye and extending the brass tube to its full length. It stretched out nearly as far as one of his arms.

The workingmen were dressed like tribesmen, in loose Beserian tunics and baggy trousers. They dug, plunging their spades into the dirt and filling wheelbarrows behind them. Peter continued scanning. Another group of men appeared in his lens, standing perhaps fifty feet behind the workers. They dressed like the dead soldiers they had just crawled past under the thorns, wearing green tunics, black trousers, and the same tall, strangely shaped black hats, like a smokestack that grew wider as it neared the top. They appeared to watch the workers.

Peter saw one of them walk forward toward a worker. The soldier began gesturing, but the worker did not appear to respond, keeping his head looking down at the gravel he dug into with his shovel. The soldier in the tall smokestack hat reached the digging tribesman. The tribesman gestured, and then the soldier struck him across the face with the butt of his rifle. The man remained on the ground as if knocked unconscious. Peter lowered his looking glass and looked at Don Mazarian and Barnes.

"They are Gressians," said Don Mazarian. "Those soldiers wear the uniform of a guards regiment of the Autocrat."

"What are the workers doing?" asked Peter, already knowing the answer before the question left his lips.

"They are digging for Beserite," said Don Mazarian.

CHAPTER 56
Night in Ben Gamurian

Oasis of Ben Gamurian
10th Day, Month of Wasura, 807
Anglian Calendar: March 3, 1879

The Sharef agreed to give Hannah Huntington and Mrs. Smith a small, one-room building with a flimsy, rotting wooden door near the northeastern arc of the oasis walls. Like the outer oasis walls and nearly every other structure in Ben Gamurian, the walls of the building were made of old, sun-bleached mudbricks.

Two narrow beds lay just inside the door, each low to the floor. Most who bore Beserian and Qhaliffan blood slept on cushions on the floor, even oasis dwellers and those who lived in the stone houses of the Seven Cities. "Bed dweller" was an insult reserved for pale-faced Westerners.

"We have places for Westerners," the Sharef said. And this was one of those places. Mrs. Smith did not like the Sharef's tone when he said it, nor did she like the look in his eyes.

Mrs. Smith took the bed nearest the door, placing Hannah in the bed near the back of the room. It was little more than a mudbrick hut and smelled of dust and old cloth. Rough and uneven stone pavers covered the dirt below, making the beds sit unevenly on the floor.

"If Ben Gamurians built the Sharef's house, they clearly know how to build and level a floor," said Mrs. Smith. "This place is an insult."

Mrs. Smith looked up at a large spider in one upper corner of the room and a small lizard in the other.

"It is better than sleeping tentless under the sands," said Hannah, pulling off her boots and lying on her back. "And at least we have water in our bellies."

Hannah stretched her feet, exhaling in the manner of those who have been unable to set down their anxieties in long days. At last, she and Mrs. Smith were alone, able to rest away from prying men's eyes. They had made the march to Ben Gamurian, and they had survived. Now, it was a matter of getting word back to Anglia and Calderon. They had done their part. She and Mrs. Smith, Stanwich, Hersen Expey, and Diego the foreman had led the survivors through the sands to the oasis. Now Peter and Barnes must do their part. Would they? Of Peter, Hannah was unsure, but Barnes would do his duty. Even if more Beserians attacked them, Barnes would find a way.

Hannah ran her eyes along the walls of the room. The rotting door and its little wooden slide bolt notwithstanding, the walls seemed sturdy enough, at least to keep out unwanted visitors.

As their Mancaster and Hart-Harold rifles lay in the guardhouse next to the western gate, Mrs. Smith had picked up a stone from the edge of one of the oasis pools. It was no bigger than a fist, but she felt better with it at her side as she pulled an old dirty blanket up over her chest against the cold. She slept in her dress and her stockings, ready to leap out of bed at a moment's notice. Her boots she kept at the foot of her bed. The rock was not much, but if it came to it, swinging a stone was better than trying to fight a man with a fist alone.

"There is a barracks not far from here," said Mrs. Smith, lying on her back.

"The oasis guardsmen are here to protect us. Are they not?" asked Hannah, looking up at the ceiling.

The lizard in the corner had moved to a space above her, hunting for insects in the moonlight. A fly walked unsuspectingly, not far from the lizard. The lizard crept forward, slowly and silently, its sticky feet clinging to the mudbrick surface above it. In the blink of an eye, the lizard's head snapped forward. Hannah thought the fly might have escaped, but then she saw a wing and a leg sticking out of the lizard's mouth. The lizard adjusted its jaws and swallowed.

"I do not like the way they looked at you," said Mrs. Smith.

"Who?"

"The guards."

"I had not noticed," said Hannah, lying to allay Mrs. Smith's fears. In her delirium, she had not noticed at first. Once she drank from the pools, however, she too had noticed. "Where are the others sleeping?"

"Along the western wall," said Mrs. Smith, "across the oasis."

Hannah stared up again at the ceiling. The fly-hunting lizard had retreated to its corner, and moonlight poked through the narrow square window above her, illuminating the far wall. Hannah lifted her hand, making a shape on the wall.

She placed her thumbs together with one hand crossed over the other. Against the wall, her thumbs looked like the bill of a duck, and her hands and fingers made the wings. She moved her hands, and the duck's wings flapped.

"Mrs. Smith, look."

Mrs. Smith looked up.

"A duck," said Hannah.

"I see it," said Mrs. Smith.

"What can you make?"

With one hand, Mrs. Smith made what looked like a large set of jaws.

"What is that?" asked Hannah.

"An alligator," said Mrs. Smith.

Hannah flew her duck over to Mrs. Smith's alligator.

There was a noise in the alley, the sound of footsteps. Both Hannah and Mrs. Smith dropped their shadow animals from the wall.

"Did you hear that," whispered Hannah.

"Yes," whispered Mrs. Smith.

"We should not have let them place us away from the others," said Hannah, still keeping her voice low.

"Shh," said Mrs. Smith.

There were more footsteps and hushed voices out in the alley. They sounded nearly next to the door. Mrs. Smith looked at the door, her eyes moving to the flimsy wooden bolt. She swallowed hard, seeing that the lock was worthless. Any soldier worth his salted goat meat could kick it open on the first try.

The voices grew louder. Men whispered.

"What are they saying?" asked Hannah.

Mrs. Smith put her finger to her lips. She slid out of bed and positioned herself next to the door, grasping her rock in her right hand.

The door moved inward, straining against the wooden bolt, pushed as if someone hoped it was unlocked, and they could slip inside undetected.

Hannah tensed, pulling the blanket up to her chin in fear. She had no weapon, not even a knife. She could shoot like a man, but she had never learned to fight with her fists. Hannah glanced at the windows overhead. They were small open squares in the mudbricks, unobstructed by wooden blinds, shutters, or even cloth coverings. But they were high up the wall and too narrow for any-one larger than a child to squeeze through.

A face appeared in the window opposite her, the open cutout at which she was staring. It was a man's face, dark and bearded.

Their eyes met. Hannah's eyes widened in fear, and her heart pounded in her chest. The man's eyes lingered on her. Hannah stared back, like a cornered mouse unable to break its gaze from the serpent's.

The man in the window spoke, but Hannah could not understand the rough Beserian words. The door shoved inward again, rattling the rotting wood on its old rusted hinges, but the wood and the hinges held.

Hannah's eyes found Mrs. Smith's. Mrs. Smith put her finger to her lips again, crouching down in the shadow near the door in her stockings, hiding from the man's eyes at the window.

The door exploded backward, ripping the wooden bolt from the wall.

Two dark shapes darted into the room. As the door flew open, Mrs. Smith launched up, lifting her stone above her head. She swung the stone down, striking one of the helmetless guardsmen just as he was rising. The rock struck his skull right above the temple. As soon as she swung, she knew she had struck the "kill spot," the place her father had taught her a woman or even a girl could drop a grown man if she hit him correctly.

The man fell, but the other man ran past, headed for Hannah. He dove upon her, covering her on the bed.

Hannah screamed, kicking her legs up at him.

Mrs. Smith ran after him, lifting her stone to smash against his skull. She did not see the third man rush into the room behind her. As she swung her stone down at the man atop Hannah, the third man stepped forward and threw his arm around Mrs. Smith's throat like a noose from behind.

She grabbed his arm at her throat with her free hand, her eyes aflame with adrenaline and fear.

With his free hand behind her, the third man pulled his dagger and thrust it into her back. The blade was thin, slightly curved, and long enough to emerge from her belly, sticking out through the front of her dress.

Mrs. Smith's eyes widened, and the stone dropped from her hand.

Hannah kneed the man above her in his testicles, pulling him to the side as he winced in pain, pushing her hips out to the other side, sliding out from underneath him.

She looked up to see Mrs. Smith, her guardian and protector. The tip of the blade protruded from Mrs. Smith's stomach, just below her breastbone. The man behind her emerged with a sickly smile, still grasping Mrs. Smith's throat with his right arm.

Hannah howled like an animal, her eyes primal.

"Noooooooooooooo!"

At that moment, fear could have pinned her to the bed, or rage could have sprung her from it. Rage prevailed.

She freed herself from the man's clutches on the bed and rushed at Mrs. Smith's killer. Screaming as loud as she could, she swung her right hand at his face.

The man threw Mrs. Smith down to the ground, his knife still in her back. He blocked Hannah's punches with his left arm and struck her straight in the face with his gloved, right fist. Blood burst from her lip. He was not a small man, and the blow sent Hannah staggering back toward the bed. The man stepped forward and struck her again in the side of the face; she stumbled back further into the bed.

The man behind her reached up and clawed her back down, like a spider grasping its prey. He held her from behind, choking her nearly to unconsciousness. But she was not unconscious.

She kicked wildly as the man above her ripped her pants off of her body, forcing himself between her legs.

CHAPTER 57
The Anglian and the Gressian

Gressian Beserite Mining Camp, Valley of Kordon
Western Sand Sea
March 20, 1879

"Count Usor," said Kassan the Erassian, the lone man in the camp with the courage to speak to Count Usor unannounced.

"Yes, Erassian?" said Usor.

He was reading a book with a red cover, seated in a small folding chair with one leg crossed over the other. He rested under the shade affixed to the front of his tent. In the distance, Usor could hear thuds and cries of his soldiers beating a Beserian. Such was the fate of those who did not work swiftly enough to extract Beserite from the gravel of the old, mostly dry riverbed.

The sun shining almost directly overhead meant it was almost noonday, and the sand of the Valley of Kordon was nearly hot enough to burn bare skin, but beneath Usor Nepopolous's tent shade, the temperature was not unpleasant. In the distance, Usor could just barely hear the trickle of what remained of the stream at the bottom of the riverbed. Birds fluttered and chirped as they called to each other from the branches of the tall, old thornbushes, far better shaded than the men sweating with picks and shovels upon the gravel.

"A small band of Macmenians has attacked our pickets on the western boundary," said Kassan the Erassian.

"Oh?"

"Yes."

"How many are in 'a small band,' as you say?"

"Twelve."

"Twelve," repeated Count Usor, still looking down at the page of his book. "And our pickets failed to deal with these men?"

"They have killed our pickets. Only several survived to tell me of the attack."

"I also heard gunshots with my own ears. Did not you, Erassian?"

"I heard the gunshots, Count Usor, yes."

"That is the thing about this valley. It is almost like an amphitheater, no?"

Kassan, the Erassian, stood staring back at Count Usor.

"Do you know what that is, Erassian, an amphitheater?"

"No, Count Usor."

"That is because your people build nothing of significance, Erassian. That is why men like you serve men like me."

Kassan the Erassian looked straight ahead.

"Bring me the men who fled the dozen Macmenians. I will speak with them at once."

"Yes, Count Usor."

The five men marched to stand before Count Usor Nepopolous with fear in their wide, darting eyes. None of them needed a reminder of what dire consequence a poor conversation might bring. Each of their eyes drifted in the direction of the Hon River Hawk resting on its perch underneath Count Usor's shade. Each man had seen what the long golden beak could do. Each man stood, feeling the fear at the base of his spine and the tightness of his throat. None dared to step close enough to share Count Usor's shade, preferring to sweat in the sweltering direct sunlight several feet farther away from the count and his hawk.

"You are the pickets who were fired upon?"

The men stood in silence, each too frightened to speak, each fearing that he who spoke first might be the first to be punished.

"Are these men deaf, Erassian?"

"No, Count Usor."

"Then why do they look at me like mute peasants caught stealing grain?"

"Yes, Your Excellency, we were fired upon," said the corporal, at last. He was the leader, the only man in the group with a pair of stripes on his shoulder, and it was correct for him to speak on their behalf.

Count Usor's eyes moved to the man's sleeve and rested there for a moment. Under his gaze, the man swallowed hard.

"A picket's job is to do what, *Corporal?*" asked Count Usor.

The four men other than the corporal, all tall and broad men, nearly big enough to be Gressian grenadier guards, stared down into the dirt. These were not grenadiers but rather guardsmen of the light infantry, chosen for their proven resourcefulness, endurance, and ability to withstand hardships in the field. The Gressian light infantry regiments were chosen for skirmishing, whether upon the frigid mountains, upon the scorching desert, upon the wind-blown steppes, or under the dark canopy of the vast northern forests.

The corporal opened his mouth to speak, but no words came out.

"Since you are all silent, I shall answer for you," said Usor. "A picket's job is to alert the commander of an approaching threat, so the commander may deal with that threat appropriately. I am your commander. Did you alert me?"

The large veterans continued to stare down into the ground. The corporal's cheeks had flushed red with embarrassment.

"Or rather, Corporal, it would appear to me that you allowed yourself to be surprised, and now I have dead light infantrymen. What good are dead light infantrymen?"

"Count Usor." It was Kassan the Erassian that spoke, his orange hair blowing in the soft breeze, bright as burning grass upon the steppelands.

Count Usor turned at Kassan, his eyes irate. Usor tolerated being interrupted as little as he tolerated most other things.

"Count Usor, they are coming. The Macmenians." Kassan pointed at the western wall of the valley.

The ancient horse path was cut into the wall, cutting back and forth in switchback after switchback, slowly descending the steep grade. As Usor looked, his eyes moved to the dozen camel riders, halfway down the cliff's face, both riders and men visible as darker shades of brown against the tan face of the sandstone cliff.

"By the Orthodox God," said Count Usor, smirking and shaking his head. For a moment, he stared at the western wall, still failing to believe that a dozen men could be so stupid or so bold as to ride directly at his camp. *They ride at my camp. My camp! And after having shot and killed a half-dozen of my men! Clearly, they have never heard of Usor Nepopolous. We shall remedy that.*

"Light infantrymen," said Count Usor, his voice rising. "Consider this the day that the Orthodox God smiled upon you. You especially, Corporal. Get your rifles and prepare to meet those men who shot your brethren. Perhaps you may even chance upon redeeming yourselves. Thank the Orthodox God for the chance; it is more of a chance than I would have granted you."

Count Usor gathered thirty-five riflemen of the Autocrat's own light infantry regiment of guardsmen, or as they were more commonly called, the Guards Light Infantry. Usor and his light infantry made their way to the base of the western wall, the sheer, sandstone cliff that rose one hundred and seventy-five feet from the valley floor. The Macmenians still descended, snaking back and forth on the camel tracks, and they would soon reach the base of the cliff.

Nepopolous left a good many of his riflemen to oversee the Beserians still digging for the Beserite. *The work will not stop; it will never stop until the Beserite is all in the hands of the Autocrat. And then the general's golden eagle shall be mine.* He looked down at the colonel's silver eagle insignia on his shoulder, envisioning the Autocrat removing it and replacing it with the gold.

Count Usor's long-barreled pistol rested securely in his holster, diagonally against his chest, fully loaded and heavy with its eight long bullets.

The Macmenians continued to descend in a single-file line of camel riders, seemingly unafraid.

We shall change that. Count Usor smiled.

Usor enjoyed few feelings better than breaking those who dared to disrespect him, and as he acquired power, he craved his revenge in larger quantities, with ever crueler and more unusual punishments.

It was a dangerous addiction, even for a Count who considered himself above the law, which he often was. Before he ventured to the Sand Sea, Usor's father, Grand Count Gungor, had threatened to strip him of his titles and land, and even to ask the Autocrat, Petros Pavolous Petrovich, to banish him if he did not cease his elaborate tortures. Usor suspected this was not because his father felt compassion for Usor's victims, but rather because rumors of Usor's sadism had begun to tarnish the Nepopolous name at court. Indeed, it was in part to be free from these constraints that Usor volunteered to lead the expedition for the Beserite . . .

Count Usor shifted in his strange saddle now, feeling almost sexual excitement at the prospect of destroying the Macmenians. Like many Gressians, Usor did not like Macmenians to begin with. He distrusted the stateless race of merchants and tradesmen, and carried the prejudice that had, in the past, turned to pogroms against them. Because of this, far fewer Macmenians lived in the lands of the Autocrat than had lived there a century before. Most had fled to the west.

Usor felt a surge of predatory confidence now as he watched them approach—Macmenians that would dare challenge a Count of the Gressias. His father was not within a thousand miles of the Valley of Kordon, and neither was anyone else with the power to stop him from doing whatever he wished . . .

Thoughts of dark anticipation raced across his mind. *These men are arrogant! We'll see how their arrogance holds up when they are tied to stakes and my hawk is peeling the skin from their faces. Or perhaps we'll strip them naked and start at the other end.* Usor smirked more deeply, hearing the screams in his mind.

The line of Macmenian camel riders was almost down to the valley floor. Count Usor's troops assembled their firing lines one hundred and fifty yards from the base of the valley wall. The valley floor between the wall and his firing line was flat, with nowhere for the Macmenians to hide.

Count Usor looked down the line of his troops assembled in front of him, arrayed in a double-spaced, two-deep firing line to his left and his right. Each light infantryman held a Hart-Gorbagos single-shot, breech-loading rifle. It was the Gressian version of the Anglian Hart-Harold. It had most of the stopping power of the Hart-Henry, and most of the range, if not quite the accuracy. It was a fine weapon for killing across all terrain and all circumstances, durable and reliable in heat and cold, dry and damp. Most importantly, the rifle rarely jammed, which to a Gressian commander, was of paramount importance.

"Prepare to fire," said Count Usor.

"Prepare to fire!" ordered the Light Infantry Captain.

Kassan and his Erassians sat upon their sand horses at Count Usor's side, ready to fly out along the flanks, showering their javelins into the dozen Macmenians, aiming to kill or wound, whatever Count Usor's preference happened to be.

"Don Mazarian, they are aiming their rifles," said Peter Harmon, second in line behind the grizzled Macmenian.

Don Mazarian said nothing.

Peter turned back to look at Sergeant Joshua Barnes. Barnes met his eyes but said nothing. His Mancaster repeater rested in his hands, fully loaded with fourteen rounds in the undertube and an extra round already in the chamber.

They reached the bottom of the valley wall, on a level plain with the four dozen green-coated riflemen facing them and the two dozen horsemen behind that. The horsemen wore the orange hats of Erassians, the same color as their long hair that hung down beneath the hats. One small man in a legionnaire's-type hat with a neck guard sat in a large, strange saddle, like a miniature wooden castle atop a large bull camel.

Don Mazarian raised his right palm over his head and urged his camel forward. The other riders moved in beside him, with Peter to his left. Barnes rode at Peter's left, his eyes narrowed and his right hand just off the trigger of his Mancaster repeater.

They advanced to eighty yards from the Gressians. The Gressian light infantrymen aimed their rifles forward, trained upon Don Mazarian, Peter, Barnes, and the others.

"If they fire, we are dead men," said Peter.

Barnes kept his eyes forward.

"Allow me to speak for all of us, Anglian," said Don Mazarian, his voice tenser than Peter had ever heard it before.

Peter held his loaded Hart-Henry carbine, frowning with skepticism. *I am neither a great rider nor a great shot. But I am getting better at both.* He felt balanced on his camel's back, and felt, perhaps for the first time in his life, that he really knew how to knock a man down with his Hart-Henry.

They advanced farther. Only fifty yards separated the green shirts of the Gressian riflemen and the advancing Macmenians.

"Why aren't they firing?" asked Peter.

"I don't know," said Barnes, looking at the hedge of Gressian barrels aimed at him, Peter, and the others.

"Not a word," said Don Mazarian, keeping his open palm above his head. "I tell you, do not say a word."

Peter remembered that his Anglian face was covered. Only his pith helmet and his light eyes could reveal him as a stranger to the sands, and some Macmenians and Erassians had eyes the same color as his own.

The Erassian javelin men streamed out onto either flank from behind the double line of green riflemen. A dozen riders moved onto either side, arching outward to encircle the advancing camel riders, the cloth of their orange hats and their long orange hair trailing out behind them.

"They are cutting off our escape," said Peter.

"Quiet," growled Don Mazarian, his teeth snapping.

Thirty yards separated the front row of the firing line from Don Mazarian's line of camelmen.

The small man with the legionnaire's neck guard moved forward in his strange saddle.

The guardsmen parted like water before a boat's prow, forming up again as soon as the camel had passed through them. Peter looked and saw that a large bird was perched on a small pole protruding out from the saddle.

"It is the Hon River Hawk we saw flying overhead," he whispered.

Barnes nodded. Cloth covered his face and, save for his New Anglian rancher's hat, his clothes were those of a Macmenian caravan man. A loose cloak hung about him in varying shades of brown and tan, the kind of cover that served almost like camouflage upon the shifting hues of the Sand Sea.

"Halt or be shot!" shouted one of the men in the green shirts. His words were Gressian. Don Mazarian knew his Gressian well enough.

"Halt," he said, keeping his right hand raised with his palm facing forward, the caravan sign for *we come in peace.*

Count Usor's Erassians on the wings continued moving outward. They had now enveloped Don Mazarian's riders, placing themselves, their mounts, and their javelins on the sides and rear of them. All wore round, almost tubular hats, nearly as orange as their hair beneath. Attached to the back of the orange hats were long strips of cloth that most of the men had wrapped around their faces. The fabric protected them from both the cold of winter and the heat of summer. Some wrapped the cloth tighter than others, with more or less of their face showing. Those who had bound their faces the tightest revealed only a pair of bright, green eyes, staring forward in the disconcerting way that few who have not met an Erassian on a field of battle can properly understand; it was the gaze of a mountain cat, a pair of glowing emeralds in each Erassian face.

The little man in the camelback castle moved his mount forward. His face was uncovered and clean-shaven. Peter stared at him. The man's eyes were dark grey, almost black, and he smiled to reveal small white teeth.

"You shot my men," said Count Usor Nepopolous, speaking the rolling syllables of the Gressian language, his voice pitched higher than most men's.

"We acted in self-defense," said Don Mazarian, speaking in the same tongue.

"Speak again without being spoken to, and I will feed your tongue to my hawk while you watch," said the count.

Don Mazarian looked at Usor Nepopolous, the light brown of Mazarian's eyes locked upon the darkness of Nepopolous's. Don Mazarian swallowed hard.

"You shot my men," repeated Count Usor.

Don Mazarian did not respond.

Peter glanced at Don Mazarian. Alone amongst the others, Peter spoke Gressian. He could always learn languages faster than others. When studying the Third Gressian War at university, the war in which Lord Harmon had seen combat on the continent, Peter had traveled often to Gressia Town in the City of Anglia, picking up the language in the cafes while drinking plum brandy with old men who had stories to tell.

"Now, Macmenian dog," said Count Usor. "I might shoot you even if you had not attacked my men. Tell me why I shouldn't have my men shoot you now?"

"May I have the privilege of your name, sir?" asked Don Mazarian, his voice low, polite, and deferential.

"My name? I thought Macmenians knew everything. Don't your kind talk to your kind in all nations, telling each other what is happening so you can all steal money from the real people, people with real countries?"

Peter felt a tingle of anger in the back of his neck as he looked at Don Mazarian. If the old Macmenian was outraged by Count Usor's insults, Peter could not see it in his face.

"Answer me, dog," said Count Usor, spitting down into the dirt. The globule landed at the feet of Don Mazarian's camel.

Don Mazarian waited before responding, inhaling slowly through his nose and exhaling through his mouth.

"I meant no disrespect—" he began.

"Silence!" shouted Count Usor.

He smiled with his little white teeth, and Peter could see the danger in his dark eyes. Count Usor had moved his camel forward several steps farther so that he was now staring down into Peter, Barnes, and Don Mazarian's eyes. The Gressian leader was now close enough that Peter could smell the pungent urine on the coat of the Gressian's bull camel.

Peter, at last, saw the value of the man's strange saddle. It was like armor, with wooden walls protecting him almost entirely from three sides—back, left, and right—and significantly safeguarding him from the front. *The man seeks to make the job more difficult for the assassin when he comes.* Peter's eyes moved to the Gressian's long-barreled pistol strapped to his chest.

"I know your name," said Peter.

Count Usor looked at him with indignant eyes. His sadist's smile collapsed.

"Your name is Usor Nepopolous, and you are a Count of the Gressias." Peter pulled his face wrap down, revealing his sunburnt cheeks and his freckled nose, long and straight, in the manner of the New Anglian Caldwells, his mother's principal contribution to his face. The Caldwell parts also made Peter's eyes shine bright blue-green in the blazing desert sunlight as they stared into Count Usor's face.

"You have come to take the Beserite from this valley to take it back to the Autocrat. You believe that if you do," said Peter, looking at the markings on Usor's shoulders and collar, "you might become a General of the Guards, instead of just a Colonel. You hope one day to replace that silver eagle on your collar with the golden eagle of a general. Do you not?"

Count Usor looked at Peter. Surprise overtook the rage in his eyes. The man speaking was not a Macmenian. There was no olive in his skin. There was no Macmenian tilt to his Gressian words. His accent was wrong, and it was wrong in the wrong way.

"It is customary and polite to ask another's name, not to ask them if they know yours. Since you are neither customary nor polite, I shall introduce myself. My name is Peter Harmon. I am a Harmon of Hylebourne House of South Anglia. I am the son of Lord George Harmon of the Parliament of the Anglian Imperium, and Lady Glencora Caldwell Harmon, formerly of Laketown of the New Anglian Republic. Beserians captured my cousin, who traveled with us. We seek to capture him back. We seek to bring those Beserians to justice. That is why we ride through your valley."

Usor looked down at Peter Harmon. Though he was by far the smaller man, his high saddle on the back of his massive bull camel made him taller.

"You are a long way from your home, Anglian," said Usor Nepopolous.

"As are you, Gressian," said Peter.

Their eyes locked, Gressian and Anglian, sons of men who ruled over others, men who themselves might one day rule over tens of thousands.

"You have more guns than I do today, Count Usor Nepopolous, but an Anglian army is on its way here. They ride at my request to seek out those who dared to take my cousin from beneath an Anglian flag. If they would ride to find my cousin, what do you think they would do to punish those who attacked me?"

Usor looked at Peter, his eyes widening and then narrowing in the manner of a man trying to sense a trap and ferret out a lie.

"Men disappear in the Sand Sea," said Count Usor. "It is hard to tell what might have happened to them. There are sandstorms and sinking sands and dangerous tribesmen. Perhaps you should have ridden with more men, Anglian."

"If you fire upon us, perhaps you could hide your deed, Count Usor, or perhaps you won't. Perhaps your vanity will cause you to fire upon us now to show that you are the"—Peter almost said larger—"stronger man. But if you are caught, you will not become a General of the Guards. You will not be a man who succeeds your father. You will embarrass your family amongst the other Nine Families at Court. You will be the Nepopolous son that started the Fourth Gressian War. Does the Autocrat, Petros Pavolous Petrovich, he who sits upon the Throne of the Olives and the Pines, desire a Fourth Gressian War?"

Count Usor looked at Peter again, his eyes flashing. It was only an order away. His Erassians would rush in with their javelins. And then it would be only one more order to begin the torture of the freckle-faced Anglian and the old Macmenian, but there was a hesitation. *How does he know I am a Colonel of the Guards and that I seek to become a general? How does he know my family is one of the Nine Families at the Court of the Autocrat?*

"I know a great deal about you," said Peter, as if reading Count Usor's mind. "I know you are aggressive and cruel. I know you are here because spies in my country sent you information about the Beserite. How do I know these things? Because my father told them to me in Altadige. That is how I know. Did you think you were alone here? Did you think you slipped south along the Bulbanian borderlands in secret? No, Gressian, we see you, and we know where you are. Did you think you had stolen a march on the Stanwich expedition, and no one would be the wiser? No, Count Usor, you are better known than you believed, and as we speak, Anglians know I am here. So, you may weigh that in your mind as you decide whether to order your light infantrymen of the Guards to fire. Yes, I recognize their green tunics, the same hue as your own."

"You talk much, Anglian," said Count Usor. "And you are outnumbered."

"You came for the Beserite, Count. Take it and be rich; take it and be famous. We pass through to find a lost man, not to challenge your rights to these minerals. Kill us, and you may lose all that you care to achieve. Kill us and start a war between Anglia and Gressia. Let us pass, however, and the Beserite is yours."

Count Usor considered the words.

"You fired upon my men. I cannot allow that to pass unpunished."

Peter edged his camel forward, sitting more upright to be nearly eye to eye with the count.

Count Usor's riflemen stared nervously over their aimed barrels as the camel rider in front of them advanced nearly face-to-face with Count Usor. Still, Count Usor had ordered none to fire until his signal. Count Usor was not a man to be disobeyed, even if obedience meant placing him in danger.

Peter spoke in a low voice that only he and Count Usor could hear. "Count, your men fired upon us, so we were justified in shooting back. But more importantly, they are just men. They are not *men* like you and I are; they are not players in the great game. They are only pawns, so move your pawns like the player of the game that you are."

"If it is as you say," said Count Usor, "give me four of your men, blood for blood."

"They are not my men to give, Count Usor, but what I have to give I shall. If you want my gold, it is yours. There are four hundred gold ducats here at my hip. Say the words, and they are yours; that is one hundred for each soldier you have lost. That is far more than what you would take in compensation from another count who killed four of your peasants. Indeed, it is ten times more. No?"

"I will take your gold," said Count Usor. "But, I will take something else as well."

"What is that?" asked Peter, his heart fluttering. He could see that Count Usor was almost done, that he had nearly agreed. *But the last item.*

"I want your rifle."

Peter almost said, *it is yours.* "This rifle was a gift from my father, Lord Harmon. It is of great value to me."

"I will have the rifle, or I will start shooting your men," said Count Usor.

Peter looked down at the Hart-Henry in his hands, a Hart-Henry that meant nothing to him. He had taken it out of a crate of twelve at House Gremanian.

"Very well, Count Usor, you may tell any who ask that you took Peter Harmon's rifle from his own hands in the Valley of Kordon." Peter extended the rifle to Count Usor, leaning forward to hand it to him with both hands.

Count Usor took it.

Then Peter leaned forward again, handing Count Usor the heavy sack of gold.

Count Usor took that as well, smiling with pride in his eyes.

"Now, if we may, Count Usor, we must ride east to find my cousin."

Count Usor stared at Peter, holding both his rifle and his gold. Peter met his gaze without flinching.

"Let them pass!" shouted Count Usor, moving his camel to the side.

"I bid you good fortune with the Beserite," said Peter, bowing respectfully from his saddle.

To the astonishment of all except for Peter Harmon, Count Usor bowed back.

The green-shirted men of the Guards Light Infantry raised their rifles to the ready position, and Peter Harmon ordered his camel forward. Don Mazarian, Sergeant Joshua Barnes, and the others followed.

As they passed, the Gressian guardsmen stared, their mouths open in disbelief.

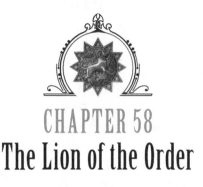

CHAPTER 58
The Lion of the Order

Oasis of Ben Hamur
31st Day, Month of Wasura, 807
Anglian Calendar: March 24, 1879

As she had for the last week, Selena Savanar woke with the sunrise. The nights were not as cold as they had been and neither were the mornings. The orange sky in the east advanced against the still-purple sky in the west. The surface of the pool looked smooth as glass, and steam rose off of it in the cool of the morning air. Winter had almost given way to spring, but the Demissaries would still not leave Ben Hamur. Until they left, Selena could not leave her quarters, even with a disguise. The Sharef feared that, of all things, it was her missing teeth that would give her away.

"Are there not many women with missing teeth in Ben Hamur?" she asked.

"There are no women with the beauty of Selena Savanar whose teeth—but for the missing front two—are otherwise perfect," said the Sharef.

The Sharef's smile reminded Selena of a vastly overgrown rat, with only his front-most teeth visible inside of his massive round cheeks. She opened her mouth to argue for her freedom to roam the oasis.

The Sharef silenced her with a wave of his fat hand. "There is too much risk. You shall stay here."

Yet, he did not neglect her. He seemed to derive joy from her presence. Each day, just before the noonday hour, the Sharef of Ben Hamur traveled down to his private pools, waddling his girth down seven flights of sandstone steps, huffing and puffing like a porter under a load.

The rear of the palace itself and a pair of tall, tree lined interior walls enclosed the pools to the north, east, and west. The southernmost enclosure was the southern outer wall of the oasis, the tallest and thickest in all of Ben Hamur, made higher and wider to better protect the Sharef's palace that was just inside of it. So too, given the proximity of the palace, only the Sharef's most trusted guardsmen patrolled the parapets that overlooked the pools on one side and the southern zareba on the other, the spikes of the dry thornbushes that separated the Sharef's walls from the desert beyond.

Selena was not alone in her opulent, well-guarded prison. Oapah and Gulana trained with their blades daily, and they did so in near silence. Expertly, they stopped just before contact, halting their thrusts and their parries, their slashes and their swings, their feet moving ceaselessly in a silent, beautiful dance with their drawn, deadly, curved scimitari. Selena watched them, amazed at how swiftly they moved and how precisely they could stop their blades only a hair's breadth away from each other.

More than once, they had persuaded Selena to pick up a blade and learn the way of the scimitarus under their instruction, but Selena had long known that her skill with a blade would not be her salvation. She could train every day from the present day until the end of her days and never stand a chance against Gulana of Nor Gandus, much less Oapah the Hohsa.

To Selena Savanar, other preparation mattered more. She did have a skill that neither Gulana nor Oapah could match. Each day, for most of the day, she read the scrolls the Sharef brought down to her, devouring new material each day, from sunrise to sunset. She read scrolls that told of the olden days of Ben Hamur and Alwaz Deem. She was surprised how many times the word Savanar showed up in the annals of Ben Hamur, from century to century, going back almost to the age of the Prophet.

The Sharef's library was extensive, and Selena asked for all that had been written about the Staff of the Prophet and its fracturing into the Staff of the Ram, the Staff of the Lion, and the Staff of the Serpent. She sought all there was to know about the disappearance of Hom Hommuram the Great, and with him, the Staff of the Lion, which was the centerpiece of the Staff of the Prophet. That portion was made from the oak tree raised atop the Great Mountain, the oak tree that kept company with the God of Gods, the One God, the God who created all that was, all that is, and all that will ever be. Others called it the Staff of Might and told of its great power: the power to bend the skies and the sands to the command of the bearer. Others said that such powers would only attend to the bearer if the God of the Mountain and the Sands willed the bearer to hold it.

All writers confirmed that Hom Hommuram and his dozen companions took the Staff of Might into the Hahst and that they were never heard from again. Some said Hom Hommuram was living still, eight hundred years later, in a hidden valley, a land of greenery, fruit trees, and flowing water.

The Sharef's men walked along the top of the wall, patrolling without ceasing, in daylight and in moonlight, making sure the Sharef's guests were still beneath them in the enclosed gardens of the pools, and that none approached the zareba from the south. So too did the Sharef, through the command of Dungar Bin-Guttar, ensure that riders patrolled the southern approaches, making certain that none burrowed tunnels at the bottom of the wadis and ditches, making sure that unwanted men did not hide behind the larger stones sunken into the sands.

Atop the walls, only two men at a time patrolled, hand-picked by Dungar Bin-Guttar for their loyalty and their secrecy. So too did Dungar himself visit every day, bringing news of Beserians marching eastward from the Valley of Kordon. Each day he grew more excited as he told of the Beserians' progress.

Other than the patch of the wall behind the Sharef's palace, however, the Demissaries had largely taken over the oasis. It was known that the Qhaliffa could send his Demissaries whenever he, in his wisdom, so chose, but it was not customary for the Demissaries to stay so long.

A Sharef knew he might have to feed and water a legion of Demissaries for a few days while they prepared to march out into the Sand Sea. In most years, a Sharef had to shoulder that burden. Sometimes the Demissaries stayed for a full week, eating tremendous amounts of food and consuming vast stores of camel fodder. But it had been long years since a Demissary Legion had stayed in Ben Hamur for more than a month.

Their presence made the people nervous. The Third Legion was disciplined, far more so than the infamous Second Legion, but the people of Ben Hamur did not differentiate much between Demissaries. A lancer in an orange turban was still a lancer, and every daughter in Ben Hamur had heard of the mass rapes carried out by the lancers after the rebellion of Ben Rusa, the oasis that was destroyed.

It was said that no woman of Ben Rusa escaped the raping lancers. Those deemed too old or too young were killed outright, impaled on lance points, or slashed apart with scimitari. Lancer after lancer took their turns with the others, and then they killed most of them. A handful, perhaps one in fifty, were determined sufficiently beautiful to take back to the Seven Cities as prizes, to live their lives out as slaves, forfeiting all rights to the particular Demissary who had decided to spare her. When they were finished, the Demissaries burnt the oasis down to the sands, but not before they had castrated the male prisoners.

The Rebellion of Ben Rusa was more than one hundred years ago, but upon the sands, memories do not readily recede. There was not a boy or girl in Ben Hamur who would not hear about the lesson of Ben Rusa before they celebrated their seventh year-ending.

With such knowledge in their minds, the children of Ben Hamur hid from the Demissaries, and the adults looked down toward the earth when one of them passed. Yet, the Demissaries stayed and stayed, almost as if they knew the object they sought lay hidden somewhere in the oasis. Day by day, the pressure upon the Sharef grew. Yet, Selena Savanar remained hidden in his walled garden, and Ayzah Bin-Ayawad remained true to his word.

The Demissaries took over the patrols of the rest of the walls, making the Sharef's men, like the people they were sworn to protect, restless and nervous. Strangely, Dungar Bin-Guttar told Selena, just the previous day, that the Demissary Legion Commander, Ottovan Fanfar, had never demanded that his troops patrol the section of the wall just to the south of the Sharef's palace, the only part of the outer wall that would allow someone standing upon it to see into the rear courtyard where Selena Savanar, Oapah, and Gulana had been forced to call home for the past long weeks.

"We are occupying his oasis. The least we can do is give the man the privacy of his own home," said Ottovan Fanfar to Dungar Bin-Guttar, when the Lancer Captain Ulgur Uggatar had demanded that the southern wall section be made available to his men.

The lancers prowled around the Sharef's palace, loitering about the entrances and asking pointed questions of those who passed in and out. If a Demissary asked a question, a man was obligated to answer him. Fewer and fewer men were walking about, so as to avoid questioning. The business of Ben Hamur ground to a halt. Yet, as the days slipped into weeks, the Demissaries failed to explain to anyone why they still remained in Ben Hamur.

"Sharef," said Head of the Household.

The Sharef remained sleeping, snoring like a hippopotamus, sleeping on his back.

"Sharef," repeated the Head of the Household.

The Sharef jerked up and opened his eyes, like a man coming up from water and gasping for breath. The Sharef looked around him, into the darkness. A ray of moonlight shone through his open window that faced his vast sandstone veranda, the veranda that faced north, looking over the entire oasis.

"Sharef, the Demissary Commander is here."

"Ottovan Fanfar?"

The Head of the Household nodded.

"Why?"

"He would not say."

"Is he alone?"

"He is alone."

"Where is he now?"

"He waits in your receiving room."

The Sharef paused to think, dropping his chin onto his wide chest above his massive belly, making the fat on his neck look like a series of rolling hills.

"Offer him wine. I will meet him in my *private* receiving room."

"Yes, Your Excellency," said the head of the household.

The Sharef entered, wearing a double-layered silk robe, the kind one could only purchase at high cost from the trading men of Xin. It was worth more than a good scimitarus, a good camel, and a new rifle combined.

Ottovan Fanfar, waiting by himself in the center of the room, stood with his wine untouched. He wore a simple tunic over plain pants, greyish-brown in color. His long, collarless coat was deep blue, the color of the Ring River in high summer. Open at his waist, it continued to cover halfway down his legs, the bottom hem reaching his knees. His left hand rested on the pommel of his scimitarus, sticking out from his belted waist.

"Commander," said the Sharef, shuffling into the room. His fat feet were stuck into a pair of soft Xinish slippers.

Ottovan nodded.

"To what do I owe the honor of seeing you in the middle of the night and alone no less?"

The Sharef instinctively looked to the corners of his receiving room. It was well-appointed but far smaller and more private than the vast hall with the columns and the potted trees that he used when needing to impress visitors with the wealth and power of Ben Hamur. Something told him that Ottovan Fanfar neither needed instruction on, nor was impressed by, the capacities of Ben Hamur. Other than the low tables and the cushions around them, the room was empty.

"I need to see Selena Savanar tonight."

"Commander, I—"

"There is no more time to waste," said Ottovan, cutting off the Sharef.

"I have not seen the Savanar traitor."

"Sharef, I am alone. I know where she is, and I know with whom she is hiding. Take me to her."

The Sharef looked around, like an animal in a trap. "Where may I ask, do you believe this traitor is hiding? Surely nowhere inside my walls."

Ottovan stepped forward, his hazel-brown eyes bright and intense.

"Sharef, I *know*."

"I—"

"She is in your garden, beside your private pools. She rests there, reading scrolls from your private collection that you bring down to her. Guarding her are Oapah the Hohsa and Gulana of Nor Gandus, both Lions of the Order of the Ram, the Lion, and the Serpent. They practice with their scimitari, stopping before their blades clash to avoid the clamor and to keep the secret of their presence."

The Sharef stared at Ottovan, dumbfounded. The look of astonishment lasted only a moment before his mask returned.

"Commander," the Sharef smiled his rodent smile. "I am surprised that a commander of Demissaries would think such fanciful things."

"Take me to her, Sharef." Ottovan stepped forward again, his eyes boring deep into the Sharef's.

The Sharef stared, his smile fading from his face like the light at sunset.

"If this were a trap, Ayzah Bin-Ayawad, would I come here alone? No, I would have brought fifty Demissaries with me. We would arrest you. Your pools would already be surrounded, and my men would stand upon your southern ramparts. No, I am here to see Lady Savanar. I have known she was here since the day we arrived. Now take me to her before my men realize I have disappeared."

As the Sharef descended the sandstone steps, with only the moonlight to guide him, his heart thundered in his chest. He was not a man accustomed to physical exertion, and even in his sleeping room, he let his wives and mistresses do most of the work. Such was the demanding price of his appetite, the cost of obesity.

Ottovan walked behind the Sharef, with silent steps, sensing the fear coming off the man in front of him as if it were an odor. Ottovan's purple turban snugly covered his bald head against the night's chill. His gloved left hand rested comfortably on the weighted pommel of his scimitarus. Across his chest, the three pairs of loaded pistols rested with familiar and comforting weight in their leather holsters. It was a burden he had long accustomed his mind and body to carrying, and in time, satisfaction with the power of the pistols supplanted the burden of carrying them. Without them, some combination of spear and sword wielders might defeat him with his scimitarus alone, but with his pistols, those wishing to kill him would need to group themselves by the dozen. And even that many would have to be willing to forfeit their own lives to give others, equally as determined, the chance to take his. *Are there such men in Ben Hamur? Does the Sharef employ such men? I doubt it. Guardsmen are cowards.*

The Sharef loudly cleared his throat, covering his mouth with his fist.

Ottovan glanced around suspiciously.

"Too loud," he said.

"Forgive me, Commander."

"I should not need to warn you, Sharef, but it would be very foolish to call others to observe this meeting."

The Sharef's face flushed with fear and embarrassment. "Yes, Commander."

They reached the bottom of the sandstone stairs. A wooden gate, fortified by iron rods, barred their path. The Sharef pushed on it. It was locked. He plunged his hand into a pocket in his robes, fishing for a key on a ring. The fat of his belly compressed the pockets of his spacious robes, making it harder for him to slip his hand inside.

"Open it," said Ottovan.

The Sharef pulled the ring from his pocket and grasped one of the keys in his plump fingers. It was dark in the archway of the gate, shaded from the moonlight. He missed the keyhole with the key tip and heard the sound of iron tapping against iron.

"Hurry," said Ottovan.

The Sharef's heart raced faster, pattering against his ribs. He found the keyhole in the darkness, plunged the shaft of the key into it, and twisted the lock.

He stepped forward through the gate and under a dark arch, the rose stems above looking black and ominous.

"Who goes there?" said a voice.

The Sharef jumped, gasping with a high pitch.

"It is I, Ayzah Bin-Ayawad."

"Step forward." The voice was a woman's.

The Sharef stepped forward.

"Lift your arms overhead and show me your palms."

The Sharef did as he was told.

The speaker jumped forward out of the shadows, brandishing a drawn scimitarus in the moonlight.

"Demissary!" her words were something between a whisper and a shout.

"Gulana," said Ottovan.

The woman paused, stopping her blade inches from the fat rolls of the Sharef's throat.

"It is I," said Ottovan, stepping forward.

Gulana knew the voice before she saw the familiar curves of Ottovan Fanfar's face. The tension in her face dropped, she exhaled, and a baffled smile rose on her lips.

She bowed her head.

"Greetings, Lion of Nor Gandus," said Ottovan.

The Sharef flinched as Oapah the Hohsa stepped forward out of the shadows on the opposite side of the gateway arch, massive, broad, and gripping the handle of his great curved sword with both hands—the sword that could cleave a man in two, the sword that chopped the oars off of the Qhaliffa's River Galley as if they were kindling.

"Commander," he said, his voice deep as a bass battle drum.

The Sharef turned around with an uncomprehending face, his heart still pounding against his rib cage, his breathing short and rapid.

"Is it?" asked Gulana, gesturing with her chin toward the Sharef.

"Is it safe?" asked Ottovan.

Gulana nodded.

Ottovan let out a small laugh. "By the God of the Mountain and the Sands, no."

The Sharef turned to Ottovan, still unsure whether one of the three warriors was about to slash him with a scimitarus.

"Sharef," said Ottovan, "you have done well to harbor these heroes. You have placed yourself in great danger, and we will not forget."

Comprehension slowly crept onto the Sharef's face. More than anything, the Sharef realized he was not about to be cleaved by Oapah's blade. Color returned to his ample cheeks.

"I—"

"You are safe amongst us," said Ottovan. "We seek to protect the same woman." He turned to Gulana. "Where is she?"

"I am here," said Selena Savanar, stepping out from behind a palm into the moonlight.

"You are correct to hide, Lady Savanar," said Ottovan.

Selena looked at him, her hazel eyes brilliant and feline in the moonlight.

The Sharef looked at her, seeing her eyes. *They are Savanar eyes, her father's eyes in a woman's face.* Of the four of them looking at Selena, the Sharef had known Sah Seg Savanar better than any of the others, as a friend and nearly as a peer.

The others, even Ottovan, mostly knew the great Kezelboj Lord from afar, for his justice and his courage, by his reputation and renown. So too, however, was the Sharef the only one who did not see him burn. It was his burning that brought the others—Ottovan, Gulana, and Oapah—all into the Order. If Selahim the Grim wished to terrify the people into servile submission by making them all hear Sah Seg Savanar's screams, he had failed.

The nobleman lasted longer into the burning than anyone else Selahim burned, but in the end, he screamed. He was human, and humans cannot withstand the flames, not even the greatest, not even the most courageous. But what Ottovan, Gulana, and Oapah saw that day, all from different walks of life, all from different cities amongst the Seven Cities, was the evil of burning a good man. It was that day that made them answer the call when the Order of the Ram, the Lion, and the Serpent came knocking upon their doors in the middle of the night, the Order that sought men and women not only for the strength of their bodies and their swiftness with a blade, but for the power and swiftness of their minds, and perhaps most importantly, the resolve in their hearts.

"You are in grave danger," said Ottovan.

"Is that any different from any other time?" asked Selena.

Ottovan half smiled, lifting the right side of his mouth in a smirk. "My lancers are a problem."

"Then why did you bring them?"

Ottovan half smiled again and shook his head. "A Demissary Legion does not ride out into the Sands without its lancers. If, as Jemojeen wished, the Second Legion were here instead, you would already be in their hands, and many in Ben Hamur would be dead."

The Sharef nodded and swallowed hard, knowing that it was true, knowing what cruelties the Second Legion could inflict.

"Ulgur Uggatar. That is the name of my lancer captain. He is close to Jemojeen. And he is nearly as large as Oapah." Ottovan looked at the massive Omakhosian as if to confirm it was true. "He is every bit a lancer, as sadistic as a lancer of the Second Legion—worse really. He is the kind that finds joy in killing."

"Why did you choose him?" asked Selena. Like most in the Seven Cities, she had heard of Ulgur, the giant Demissary lancer.

"A man is wise to keep those he trusts the least in his line of sight, Lady Savanar." As he spoke, he glanced at the Sharef.

Sharef Ayzah Bin-Ayawad looked at Ottovan, disliking the look in the Demissary Commander's eyes. Under Ottovan's gaze, he felt his confidence shrink, like a chunk of mountain ice melting in the desert sun.

"Nonetheless, Ulgur reports back to Jemojeen directly. He sends his messages through the Erassians. Ulgur thinks he is shrewder than he is. He does not know that I know."

"Do you know *what* he reports back?" asked the Sharef, finding the courage to speak. He felt as secure as a rat amid three cats. Selena Savanar did not frighten him, but the other three were terrifying, even in his own oasis, even if he were behind a line of his finest guardsmen, which he was not. Ben Hamur did not raise warriors to contend with the likes of Sworn Lions of the Order.

"He reports a belief that you are hiding things from him," said Ottovan, looking at the Sharef. "He reports that there are parts of Ben Hamur in which Demissaries are not permitted. He complains about me that I do not deal with you harshly enough. He states that a real legion commander would deal with traitors in Ben Hamur like the Second once dealt with the rebels of Ben Rusa, the oasis that is no more."

The Sharef said nothing, too afraid to speak. *I should never have made my promise to Sah Seg Savanar. This is too much. All of this could have been avoided had I simply turned a blind eye, had I only ignored the news of Selena Savanar's escape.*

"Have courage, Sharef," said Ottovan, the brown in his eyes burning with intensity. "Your choices will define your friends and your enemies, but not just yet. Abu Akhsa marches as we speak. He is within one hundred miles of your walls."

The Sharef stared at Ottovan. He did not know whether Abu Akhsa would treat him as a friend, as an enemy, or as something in between. Over the years of his stewardship and those of his father and grandfather, the Sharefs of Ben Hamur had not been enemies to the Beserians, but nor had they been great friends. Those who paid attention knew that the Sharefs of Ben Hamur had always done what was in their own interest, first and foremost, so long as that did not run directly afoul of the Qhaliffa of the Seven Cities.

"When he arrives with his Beserians in their tens of thousands, who will you have rather served, Sah Seg Savanar's heir or her enemies?" asked Ottovan, a crease forming down his broad forehead.

"I have hidden her thus far. Have I not?"

"You have, Sharef," said Ottovan Fanfar, "but your duty is not yet done. Until she is united with the Staff of Wisdom, we are at risk."

"Why are you at risk? Are you not the *commander* of the very Demissary Legion we are hiding her from?"

"Yes, Sharef. I am. But as a commander of the Qhaliffa's Demissaries, I am obligated to take Selena Savanar back to Alwaz Deem so she can be tried and burned. There are less than ten people in Ben Hamur that know who I am— that know"—Ottovan turned and looked back over his shoulder—"I am The Lion of the Order. And five of them are the five of us."

The Sharef's eyes widened. He had heard, in passing and in legend, that only one Sworn Lion at any given time was called *The* Lion. He never had in his wildest imaginings believed that The Lion of the Order of the Ram, the Lion, and the Serpent could also be a legion commander of Demissaries. *And who is The Serpent? Jemojeen?*

"To help Lady Savanar, I must not see her. I must not see any of you." Ottovan looked up at the wall where one of Dungar Bin-Guttar's men walked along the parapet. His face was still covered in shadow from the rose thicket clinging to the arch overhead. "Those are trusted men. Yes?"

The Sharef nodded. "My Captain, Dungar Bin-Guttar, selected them himself."

"How many of your men patrol that section? How many, other than Dungar Bin-Guttar know that Selena Savanar and her guardians are here?"

The Sharef paused. The number was larger than the amount he wished to say. Dungar Bin-Guttar had ridden with more than a dozen men when he retrieved Selena Savanar from the Sands, rescuing her from the Erassians. There were at least a half-dozen more in the Sharef's household who knew of their guest hiding in the enclosed southern garden.

"Twenty, at least."

"And you trust them all?"

"Yes," said the Sharef quickly. He nodded as if to emphasize his words.

"Twenty is too many," said Ottovan, shaking his head. "Ulgur will soon find out."

The Sharef stared.

"We cannot keep you here, Lady Savanar," said Ottovan, turning to Selena.

"Where shall I go?"

"We must put you out into the desert so that you might meet Abu Akhsa. If we place you into the western deserts, and you move swiftly, you will meet him in days. They know who you are. They believe in the words that are written."

Selena stared, fearing the desert. She had grown to appreciate the gardens that surrounded the deep pool. It was a prison, and she hid in fear each day, but there were moments when she almost forgot her fear. It was a lovely prison.

"What of the Erassians?" asked Oapah.

Ottovan looked at him. "You will have to avoid them."

"That is easier said than done, Commander Fanfar," said Gulana.

"If you are to be caught, it is far better for you to be caught outside of these walls than inside," said the Sharef.

"I should think it far better to not be caught at all," said Selena.

"Of course," said Ottovan. "But if Ulgur's men catch you here, they will not understand. They will seek punishment of both the Sharef and of the people of Ben Hamur for harboring you."

"I can hide underground," said Selena. "We are but three people and Ben Hamur is not small."

"It is not a question of whether you can hide, Lady Savanar. It is a question of who will betray you and when. If we believe that a score of Ben Hamurians know you are here, the number is likely now twice that. Men speak with their wives, at least. And if forty Ben Hamurians know that Selena Savanar is here, harbored by the Sharef in his gardens, it is only a matter of time."

Selena nodded, knowing that it was true.

"I can help with the Erassians. My Demissary guides will learn that you have escaped to the north. I shall send the scouts in significant numbers after you. In the meantime, you will escape beneath the western wall. Are there tunnels, Sharef?"

"Of course."

"Very well, I have already stayed here too long," said Ottovan, looking up at the guardsman on the parapet of the southern wall, his face still hidden by the shadows of the roses.

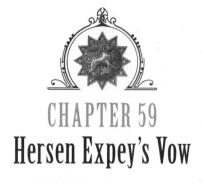

CHAPTER 59
Hersen Expey's Vow

Oasis of Ben Gamurian
12th Day, Month of Wasura, 807
Anglian Calendar: March 5, 1879

"It is not like them not to be here. I feel some evil has befallen them," said Hersen Expey, his face drawn tight from the worry he carried. He looked down at Stanwich's rotting hand. It would have to go. Hersen had seen amputations—removals of limbs by knife and saw—and the thought of Stanwich undergoing one on his left hand made him queasy. Few operations were worse, and chloroform would not be found in a place like Ben Gamurian. Stanwich would have to undergo surgery awake.

Stanwich grunted.

"I am going to find them," said Hersen. "I will not be gone long."

Hersen opened the door of their mudbrick villa and descended the stairs down to the earthen path beneath. The Sharef had given them one of the better guest dwellings in Ben Gamurian, as befitted the leader of an expedition and a man carrying as much gold and as many rifles as Hersen Expey and Harold Milton Stanwich had given to him.

Far finer dwellings have been purchased at far less a price, thought Hersen, already sweating in the hot morning air. The heat descended on Ben Gamurian and clung to it like a woolen blanket, trapping all inside of the oasis in a stifling embrace.

As he walked eastward along the northern avenue, if the wide dirt passage deserved such a name, he passed between dense mudbrick buildings on either side of him. The people of Ben Gamurian opened their doors, going about their morning business, walking to the pools to draw their drinking water, and dragging their wares to the stalls in the bazaar. Young children clung to their mothers, demanding things in a language Hersen Expey found it still hard to understand. The Ben Gamurians accented their Beserian dialect strangely. Though

Hersen's Beserian was improving rapidly, he still only caught spatterings of words as he passed the oasis dwellers.

Hersen continued eastward. The morning sun on his back was hot, making his underarms sweat. Those on the earthen walkway stopped to look at him. The farther he walked, the more self-conscious he became in his LaFrentian clothes, with his legionnaire's navy-blue pants and his red-and-blue peaked cap. He was glad his knife was in his boot, but not pleased to be alone, under the gaze of so many people.

They see me as a foreigner, and their eyes say they do not much like foreigners.

He passed the large pools that he and Stanwich and Hannah and Mrs. Smith had drunk from days before, lapping up the water after their month of trudging across the sands. The water had tasted better in that moment than any water he had ever tasted before.

Hersen passed the gate where the guards had hooted at Hannah in the way that had bothered him and made him move his finger closer to the trigger of his Legonde repeater.

We should not be leaving them alone during the whole of the night, the Sharef's orders be damned. Hersen walked faster. The oasis was larger than he remembered. After long minutes of walking swiftly, he reached the northeastern section, a place of run-down one-, two-, and three-story buildings, with dirty, peeling plaster, poorly mortared bricks, and crumbling rooftops. Most buildings shared a wall with the buildings next to them, making impenetrable barriers between one passageway and the next.

I should never have let them place the women here. I would not have done it had I not been so distracted and worried by Stanwich's hand. Hersen walked faster yet, breaking into a jog. The sweat moved more freely beneath his tunic, rolling down his chest and back. He had not yet felt humid air upon the Sand Sea. He had felt the heat. An oppressive, dry heat hovered amongst them as their constant companion on the march from the crate redoubt beneath the Valley of Kordon to the Oasis of Ben Gamurian. This morning brought a new air, a humid air, as if central Hindea or Omakhosi had gifted their steaming climates to the desert for the morning.

He turned down an alley, then another, and another. The mudbrick houses all looked similar. Some had doors with cracking paint. Some were unpainted. In front of others, hardy herb gardens grew out of narrow window planters, struggling against the heat, and looking like they received less water than they should.

Hersen looked down at the small map he had drawn upon his notepad when Mrs. Smith and Hannah had left with the guardsmen who were ordered to escort them to their overnight dwellings.

"Fear not, friends of the West, my guardsmen shall keep your women safe from any who should wish them harm. You have all traveled far." That was what the trim little Sharef said, smiling beneath his trim little mustache, taking his extorted Anglian guns and his heavy sack of golden Spatanain coins.

Hersen saw his error on his map. He had not gone far enough. The dwelling for Hannah and Mrs. Smith sat two more alleys beyond him to the east and the north. Hersen looked around again at the run-down houses, many of which looked uninhabited. There were fewer people around in this part of the oasis than in the others Hersen had passed.

Hersen turned down the second alley. Near the end of a dark and shadowy passage, he saw the one-room place the Sharef had given to the women. Hersen's eyes moved to the door. Battered off of its hinges, the door lay diagonally, partially blocking the opening. Hersen's heart thundered, and his breathing sped up.

He reached down into his boot, pulled the dagger from its sheath, and ran as if he were charging an enemy. A veiled woman walked down the alley with a little dark-haired boy. Her eyes widened, and she pulled the boy to her chest as she jumped out of the way. Hersen ran through the spot where she had held the boy only a moment before, but he did not slow his gait, running as if he did not even see them.

The woman cursed him in Beserian as he passed.

Hersen reached the broken door.

It was stuck, wedged at a diagonal between the doorjam and the earth beneath. Hersen pushed, but the door did not move.

He reached his hands underneath, first setting his knife on the ground. He pulled up and diagonally with all of his wiry strength. The door gave way, and he threw it behind him with an angry grunt. He swept his knife off of the ground and stepped inside, ready to kill. The smell of blood hit his nostrils in an instant. There was a pool of it beneath him and a trail of it leading out the door, as if someone had dragged a bleeding body out by its feet. Hersen looked up, into the room.

A body crouched in the far dark corner.

Hersen stepped forward. The body was pale and naked, grasping its knees like a baby in the womb. Hersen swallowed hard, hoping he was somehow mistaken. In the dim light, he could still see cuts and bruises on the arms and the legs. The long golden hair was unmistakable, even in its present state, even in the darkness of the room.

"Hannah," he said.

The body moved, slightly rocking forward and then back against the confluence of the two farthest mudbrick walls. Her face was buried in her knees.

"Hannah," repeated Hersen, stepping forward.

Hannah looked up. Her eyes were wild, like the eyes of a cornered animal. Both of her cheeks were battered, massively swollen into her eyes and bruised black. Dried blood crusted around her mouth and nose.

"By the Three Gods!" said Hersen, again setting his knife down on the earthen floor and crouching down toward Hannah. They were alone in the room. There was nowhere for another to hide.

"No," she shrieked, cowering in the corner.

"Hannah, it is me, Hersen Expey. Major Expey of our expedition." His voice was gentle as if he were talking to a small, frightened child.

Through the slits of her swollen eyes, she looked at him. Hersen looked back at her, seeing the fear and confusion on her face.

"Hannah," he stepped closer, nearly within arm's length. He slowly extended a hand out toward her crossed arms, the arms that tightly hugged her knees.

"Get away!" she screamed.

Hersen withdrew his hand as if he had just touched a hot stove.

He backed up a step. He looked around the room, his eyes adjusting better with each passing moment to the dimness. What remained of Hannah's clothes lay strewn across the floor, ripped, tattered, and dirty. He looked back at her. Blood had dried in her hair, matting it wildly. The beautiful blonde hair looked like a rodent's nest, tangled and sticking out at strange angles.

Hersen looked for something he could use to cover her other than her own garments, the clothes that whoever did this had ripped off of her body. He saw a sheet on the side of the bed. He stepped toward it and picked it up. He inspected it with his eyes, looking for blood. He saw none. *She must have kicked it off before they began, or perhaps whoever did this ripped it off.*

Hersen turned back toward Hannah, and she looked at him. Hersen could see the distrust in her eyes, swollen as they were.

"Hannah, please trust me," said Hersen, not knowing what else to say. He walked toward her slowly, carrying the sheet, his mind on fire with rage. *I will kill whoever did this with my own hands. I will get my weapons, and I will make this man pay with his flesh.*

"Put this on," he said aloud. "We will cover you with this, and I will take you to Stanwich, to where we are staying, where you will be safe."

"Safe?" said Hannah.

Hersen looked down at her. She held a new look in her eyes.

"Safe?" she said again.

"Yes," said Hersen, "You will be safe with us."

"You abandoned us," said Hannah, her voice like a low flame. "You left us here in this place. They came at us, Hersen. Mrs. Smith is dead."

"Who did this, Hannah?"

Hannah shook her head from side to side with bitterness in her eyes. "The same men the Sharef sent to protect us. They came in the middle of the night. They kicked down the door, and they—"

Tears streamed down Hannah's face as she sobbed.

Hersen stepped forward again, carrying the sheet from the bed. He placed it over Hannah's nakedness. She drew the cotton cloth over her, shuddering as she did so, sobbing without stopping.

"They killed her. They killed her. She tried to protect me, and they killed her."

Hersen held her, red-faced and silent. He had no words to say, other than the phrase thundering across his mind over and over and over. *I will kill them; they will pay. I will kill them; they will pay. I will kill them; they will pay.*

"I will kill them; they will pay," he said aloud.

CHAPTER 60
Chasing Ghani

West of Ben Hamur
32nd–33rd Day, Month of Wasura, 807
Anglian Calendar: March 25–26, 1879

Jabil and Anil rode side by side. Ghani's camel tracks were fresh in the moonlight.

"Brother Kaleem," said Anil. "Look."

Kaleem Salesi rode up alongside his brother. "What do you think, Jackal?" asked Kaleem, looking past his younger brother as if he were not there. Kaleem's eyes rested upon Jabil's face that all agreed looked like the face of a sand jackal.

"The traitor and his companions no longer ride alone. Others have come to assist him," said Jabil, blinking his large, wide-set yellow-brown eyes and nodding with his long, narrow jaw.

"My eyes also see this," said Kaleem, nodding respectfully at Jabil. He did not look at his younger brother.

"Horsemen have joined him, not camel riders," said Anil, looking at the marks of the other riders in the moonlight.

"Yes, this is obvious," said Kaleem.

Kaleem turned back to look at the others. The two dozen riders looking back at him were young and strong. All volunteered to ride in the flying column; all sought blood from Ghani, the traitor, the ungrateful one who dared strike down Hamid Salesi and take the Staff of Wisdom as his own.

Kaleem Salesi commanded, given the honor to avenge his father. Anil Salesi would command if Kaleem fell. He was his second. But Kaleem did not treat Anil as his second. He looked past his brother to Jabil, the Jackal, as his real second.

Each time Kaleem looked past him, ignoring his words and adding a new layer of disrespect, Anil felt himself hating Kaleem nearly as much as he hated Ghani, perhaps more. Ghani had committed the ultimate disrespect by attacking his father, the greatest man Anil had ever known, greater even than Abu Akhsa. By consensus of the Council of the Elders, they deemed Hamid Salesi—only Hamid Salesi—fit to carry the Staff of Wisdom, and for almost thirty years, no other man did so. For three decades, Hamid Salesi carried the bottom third of the Staff of the Prophet, the holiest relic in all of the tribes, the part carved as a serpent, the part that Beseri himself carried into the desert at the time of the great division, when the faithful fled the corruption of the Usurper, the first Qhaliffa, surrendering the river valleys of the Great Mountain to lesser, evil men, in exchange for the harsh freedom of the sands.

Since that day, more than eight hundred years ago, the faithful sought the guidance of the Staff of Wisdom. For forty generations, the God of the Sands had given the Beserians the sustenance they required from the harsh lands of the Sand Sea. There were famines and years of drought, when even the few great storms, upon which all of the hardy plants in the Sand Sea relied, did not come to drop their fierce, pounding rain. Those were evil years when fathers buried sons, mothers buried daughters, and the people grew bitter. But always, even in the worst of times, a remnant survived, and that remnant recommitted themselves to the God of the Sands. The God of the Sands rewarded their faithfulness with many children, vast herds, and rain enough to sustain them.

Throughout all of those forty generations of men, rarely did the God of the Sands speak directly to the people of Beseri other than through the holder of the Staff of the Serpent. For all of Anil's life, and for that matter, Kaleem's as well, the staff holder, their father Hamid Salesi, heard the whispers of the God of the Sands, and more than once saw with the eyes of God: what was, what is, and what is to come. In such times, it was said that Hamid Salesi saw like the Prophet himself, and like the Prophet, opened his ears to the voice of God.

As they rode eastward, Anil thought on this. *Ghani. Ghani struck down my father. He beat an old man and took that which only the wisest may carry. He stole the staff. He now rides to hand it over to our greatest enemy. He rides to give it to the very men that our ancestor Beseri risked his life to keep it from. Ghani rides to give it to the Qhaliffa.*

And yet, Anil knew in his heart that he did not hate Ghani. Perhaps that was what Kaleem saw. Maybe that was why Kaleem did not trust his own brother.

Do I trust myself? asked Anil in his own mind, folding the question back onto himself again and again in the darkness. *The man has done a great wrong to you and your family. Why do you not desire to slit his throat? Because he was kind to you. Because he saw you when others did not. Because when all of the others were worshipping Kaleem, "the next leader of the Salesi clan," Ghani always took the time to see Anil Salesi. He saw me. He always saw me, and he was always kind. Most forget about Anil Salesi, but Ghani never called me "the other brother."*

As his hate for Ghani failed to catch fire, extinguished as if by a stiff northern rain, Anil felt his hatred of Kaleem rising. It took no special kindling to ignite that flame.

It is true that I am friendly with Ghani. But were not all of the others? And yes, it is true that Jabil hates Ghani, but Jabil hates any that receive more attention than he does. Jabil is a jealous, bitter young man, a sand jackal indeed. He is not to be trusted, yet Kaleem treats him as if he were his real brother. Kaleem asks Jabil for his opinions but ignores the words of his own brother!

Anil turned to look at his brother's arrogant face, made silvery by the moonlight. *Curse you.*

"What think you, Vetenan?" asked Kaleem Salesi, breaking the silence.

Aurelio Demassi rode up out of the darkness.

Anil turned to look at the Vetenan he had known since they were boys, when Aurelio first came to the Valley of Kordon with Don Mazarian. They were the same age, and they had become fast friends in those days, each sons of a famous man, and each seeking to forge a path they could call their own. Anil had taught Aurelio all he knew in those days: the ways of the Beserians, the stories of olden days, and the prophecies of the days that had not yet come. Demassi always listened, desiring acceptance above all else, showing even then in his bright, hungry eyes that he preferred the ways of the sands to the ways of the Veteno.

Anil remembered the first time, six years ago, when Demassi proclaimed it. *Anil, you are my real brother. I was not meant to live in a big stone house surrounded by gold and fine things that make a man weak. I was meant to be here, to be a man who can make his way upon the back of a camel, a man who is content with his tent and his herds.*

That felt like many years ago. In the time since, Aurelio Demassi had made himself more Beserian than many Beserians. When the day came and Demassi told him he had found the promised one of the West, Anil was not truly surprised. He could trace Aurelio's path back in time to the first day of his declaration, when the boy from the Veteno chose his destiny and aligned his life with the people of the sands. *And perhaps it was my destiny to help him. Perhaps our lives are now twisted together, as the carved snake twists around the Staff of Wisdom.*

Aurelio Demassi peered down into the earth, examining the tracks.

"Erassians joined Ghani no more than two hours ago. They ride northeastward with great haste."

Aurelio looked at Anil. "Do you agree?"

Anil nodded.

Kaleem was already riding to the northeast, with Jabil at his side. The others of the flying column followed them, streaming past Aurelio and Anil, as if they were stones stuck in the sand.

They rode through the night.

As the sun rose, orange advanced at the horizon line, moving upward from the desert floor toward the sky, forming a vanguard of light blue above it, and a layer of darker blue above that, advancing against the dark purple that still controlled the western half of the sky, where night held onto its last tenuous territory.

Silhouetted against the orange, just above the horizon line, Ben Hamur rose to the east—squat mudbrick buildings dark against the sky. The Sharef's hill and palace towered above them. Like a vast, shallow bowl, the plain of Ben Hamur slowly descended toward the walls of the oasis and its protective zareba of thorns, the thicket that was taller than a man and three times deeper than it was tall.

The two dozen camel riders emerged onto the ridgeline as one, spread out in a skirmish line. In the clear air of the sunrise, each moving thing below them emerged in high definition, distorted by the rising sun to appear far closer than it actually was. To the north, five desert antelope looked up from their paltry grazing, seeing the line of Beserian riders. They galloped off to the northeast. Over the years, many a Beserian bullet had felled an antelope so that the shooter could roast the rich flesh above his campfire. Over the generations, the antelope had learned to run when men on camels emerged on the horizon.

To the south, some miles off, a pair of desert foxes shuffled eastward, retiring after their night's work, moving toward the shaded crevice or cave that would hide them from the heat of the day, where they could rest until dusk when their hunt would resume.

To the east, three camelmen rode with a dozen horsemen. The horsemen were Erassians, their heads each capped with a flash of orange in the distance, just barely visible as tiny dots of color against the greyish-tan of the plain. They rode swiftly as if they knew the danger that stalked them from the west. They looked to be moving faster than the foxes and nearly as quickly as the antelope.

"They are four miles off," said Jabil, blinking his wide, yellow-brown eyes.

Kaleem nodded.

"Ben Hamur is twelve miles from this ridge," said Jabil, staring forward.

"Can we catch them?" asked Kaleem.

"No. Not if they continue to ride in earnest," said Anil.

Aurelio Demassi nodded, seeing that Anil was correct. They could not ride fast enough to catch Ghani and the Erassians before they passed through the gates of Ben Hamur.

Kaleem frowned. The riders continued to move eastward, tiny figures upon the surface of the large bowl below them.

"Can we catch them before they reach Ben Hamur?" asked Kaleem, as if Anil had not just correctly answered that very question.

"No," said Jabil.

Kaleem nodded, his face grim. *If I do not avenge my father, they will not respect me as a man of honor.* Kaleem cared little for the staff but a great deal about what might occur to his reputation as a warrior if he failed to retrieve it. He had personally never put much faith in the old piece of carved wood.

"But if the traitor rides there," said Jabil. "We have little choice."

"Ben Hamur may not admit us," said Anil. "If there are Erassians with Ghani now, then there will surely be more."

"Are you afraid of the Erassians, brother?" asked Kaleem, smiling with mocking eyes.

"No more than I should be," said Anil.

"What say you, Vetenan?" asked Kaleem, raising his black eyebrows. Kaleem never failed to remind Aurelio Demassi that he was an outsider.

Aurelio Demassi looked at the horizon as if trying to peer beyond Ben Hamur, to see farther to the east, in the direction of Alwaz Deem, a city of which they had all heard, but in which none of those present had ever set foot, save for Aurelio Demassi. He alone had been to the Seven Cities with the caravans of Don Mazarian, the Macmenian. He alone had drunk wine to the point of drunkenness with the merchants of the flatlands, stumbling in the early morning darkness alongside the banks of the Ring River in summer. There Demassi had also seen the ancient glory of which the scriptures speak, where the deep green of the Valley of Alwaz ascends past the clouds, where the River Deem flows down through a countless number of stone buildings topped with the purple roof tiles for which the city was famous.

There also, Demassi saw that which kept the Beserians away across the generations—the Demissaries of the Qhaliffa.

"I say that your brother Anil is correct to fear Ben Hamur. There will not only be Erassians there but Demissaries too."

That word caught the attention of all who could hear it. The arrogance departed from Kaleem's face. Anil nodded gravely. Jabil blinked his wide jackal's eyes.

"You know this, Venetan?" asked Kaleem. "That there are Demissaries in Ben Hamur?"

"No, but I believe it," said Aurelio.

"Then keep your beliefs to yourself," said Kaleem. He spat onto the dry earth beneath him.

"If we ride swiftly," said Jabil, "perhaps we shall catch them. Perhaps they shall slow their flight. Perhaps one of their camels shall stumble in a ditch. Perhaps the God of the Sands desires the Staff of Wisdom to fall back into the hands of His people as opposed to His enemies. But if we stay here debating whether or not there are Demissaries, we will never know, for Ghani, the traitor, will then surely escape."

Kaleem nodded.

"We should wait for the vanguard," said Anil. "Handsome Habeen Barcadey rides with the five hundred, and they are only twenty miles behind us. If there are indeed Demissaries in Ben Hamur, we are fools to ride ahead. We are scouts. We are only two dozen strong. We have tracked the traitor. We have done our duty. Now let us wait for a force that the Sharef of Ben Hamur will fear as much as he fears the Demissaries."

"This is wise," said Aurelio Demassi, nodding respectfully. He had long known Anil to be the wiser of the two Salesi brothers, even if others had not.

Kaleem smiled his unkind smile.

"Perhaps if I were my younger brother Anil, or Aurelio Demassi the Vetenan, I too would claim that I had done my duty, merely by watching the traitor flee. I would wait for Handsome Habeen Barcadey and his five hundred volunteers." Kaleem paused and then raised his voice so all of the two dozen riders could hear him. "But I am not Anil. I am Kaleem Salesi, and I will avenge my father. We ride for Ben Hamur!"

Kaleem clicked his tongue and whisked his riding stick against his camel's neck. His bull beneath him surged forward. The others followed over the ridge and down the slope into the great bowl of Ben Hamur.

Anil looked at Aurelio. Aurelio frowned and shook his head, and then they both rode after the others, galloping toward the rising sun.

CHAPTER 61

The Long Guns of the Demissaries

Oasis of Ben Hamur—West of Ben Hamur
32nd–33rd Day, Month of Wasura, 807
Anglian Calendar: March 25–26, 1879

The villager cloaks on Selena Savanar and Gulana looked believable. Gulana, with her loose turban, looked like a well-shaven man. She was taller and broader across her shoulders than any woman in Ben Hamur. Selena wore her villager robes well. The veil that covered her face made her appear as if she were any other woman venturing out to gather and forage. Oapah was the problem. He could no more hide beneath a villager's cloak than a bear could become a sheep by donning a fleece. No sheep was the size of a bear. Oapah was larger than any man in Ben Hamur by far. A watchful pair of eyes seeing Oapah move beneath a cloak could only mistake him for one man, Ulgur Uggatar, Captain of the Third Legion's lancers.

"Do you have an orange turban?" asked Selena.

"For what?" asked the Sharef, blinking his little eyes nervously.

"Do you have one?"

"I have the cloth to make one," said the Sharef, looking at his Head of Household.

"Can you wrap a turban in the Demissary style?" asked Selena, looking at Gulana.

"Yes," said Gulana of Nor Gandus.

"If we are pursued, they will pause if they think Oapah is the giant, cruel Demissary. Perhaps they will think he has taken us out into the desert to have his way with us. It may purchase us the moments we need to escape. Even other Demissaries fear the lancer captain."

The Sharef nodded. *The seed of her father is strong in her. When fear seizes others in the darkness, she thinks with the clarity of the morning.*

Gulana carefully wrapped the orange cloth around Oapah's head. From behind, with the cloak around his shoulders, it was believable, especially in the darkness. They seemed almost the same size—Oapah the Hohsa and Ulgur the Demissary—with the same shoulders that appeared to span twice the width of an ordinary man's.

"You must go now," said the Sharef, looking nervously at his Head of Household. The Sharef kept glancing at the locked door as if the Demissaries were standing on the other side, listening.

"Under cover of darkness," continued the Sharef, pacing on his wide, pachydermic legs. "That is the only way. I am told the Beserians are moving toward us in great numbers. You must reach them before the Erassians reach you. The tunnels will take you one hundred and fifty yards beyond the wall. From there, you may follow the wadi, unseen from the western wall for another two hundred yards. Beyond that, you must move swiftly, and pray to the God of the Sands that these cloaks hide you as you flee."

"They are colored correctly, Your Excellency," said the Head of Household.

"Who?" asked the Sharef.

"The cloaks."

"Yes, yes," said the Sharef.

"Now go, go before you bring death upon us all."

With that, the Sharef turned to go. At the stone archway, he turned and looked at Selena Savanar and her companions. Fear poured out of his eyes. Whether he feared only for his own life or for theirs as well, Selena could not tell.

Selena stood alone with Gulana and Oapah. The trap-door that led to the underground stairwell was propped open in the corner.

"He is afraid," said Selena.

"Fear makes him weak," said Gulana.

"Come," said Oapah. "Weak or not, he is correct about the darkness. We do not want to sleep in the tunnel beneath the sands."

After Gulana and Selena had disappeared down the stairs beneath the floor, Oapah followed them under the ground, pulling the wooden prop as he did so. Once again, they were underground, surrounded by impenetrable darkness.

"Look," said the Demissary lancer in his orange turban, standing on the western wall of Ben Hamur, looking out over the zareba and pointing to the plain.

The oncoming Erassians rode in a *V*, as always, but the *V* was not inverted as it would be during an attack. In an attack, the riders at the edges of the *V* would advance first and the captain at the apex would ride last, directing his flanks with better vision, sending his javelin men to envelop and enfilade the enemy from his sides where he was almost always weaker, and where he was more afraid of being surrounded. The Erassians rode in a true V now, approaching with the captain at the fore. Inside of the V, a trio of camel riders rode with them, wearing the rough tunics of Beserians.

"I see them," said the fire Demissary. His long gun lay propped against the mudbricks of the wall. The second man of the long gun team, also in a purple turban, yawned. His fork-shaped rifle support lay against the wall next to the long gun, not nearly as long as the long-barreled rifle, though the support was as high as a man's shoulder. The early morning sun painted the desert in bright orange light. The Demissaries had held the watch since the third hour after midnight, one third each bowmen, lancers, and firemen, as always.

"It looks like they have captured a few Beserians," said the bowman in his green turban, grasping the center of his double-curved bow with his left hand. A quiver of arrows hung at his side. Half of them were poisoned with the burn, the poison that made Demissary archers' weapons uniquely feared—even more than the guns of the fire Demissaries and the famous cruelty of the lancers. The poison was strong enough to make men kill themselves if they could not find a salve to stop the burning.

"Give me your looking glass," said the fire Demissary, gesturing at the lancer.

"Why?"

"Give it to me. There are other riders."

The lancer handed over his tube-shaped looking glass, letting a man see at ten times the magnification of the naked eye. The purple-turbaned fire Demissary placed the tube to his eye. In his lens, the two dozen Beserian riders emerged, riding forward at a canter, their camels churning the sand beneath them as they advanced.

"Beserians," he said. "Twenty-four of them. Prepare the long gun and signal the others."

The Demissaries on the wall leaped into action. The lancer lifted a small horn to his lips and blew it once. Up and down the wall, the Demissaries looked in his direction. He waved his lance three times. The other fire Demissaries lifted their long guns. The holders raised their rifle stands, jamming the bases down at the bottom of the firing step so the fork-shaped holders stuck up just above the mudbricks of the parapet.

The fire Demissary who first spotted the riders handed the looking glass to the man holding his rifle base. All Demissary long gunmen operated in two-man teams, one holder, one shooter. The holder was also the range spotter.

"Give me range," said the shooter, pulling back the firing hammer with his whole hand.

The holder held the looking glass to his eye. "Eighteen hundred yards."

"Too long to shoot. We will wait for twelve hundred." He looked up from his rifled long gun. "Inform Captain Nemakar that we have sighted Beserians and we will commence firing at twelve hundred yards."

The lancer nodded. On a parapet, lancers were runners, regardless of rank. Bowmen and fire Demissaries were needed to shoot at the enemy. The lancer ran down the parapet and took the mudbrick stairs two at a time, grasping the wooden railing as he descended.

Tall and clean-shaven except for his massive, drooping mustache, Captain Nemakar reached the parapet, breathing audibly in the still morning air.

"Who are they?" he said.

"Beserians, two dozen."

Nemakar looked out over the thorns of the zareba and onto the upward sloping desert plain beyond. The oasis of Ben Hamur sat at the base of a massive geological bowl, dozens of miles across.

"Scouts?"

"It appears so, Captain, though they ride in the open, en masse."

Nemakar nodded, looking out into the western desert.

"Would you like the looking glass, sir?"

"I see them," said Nemakar. He had always had better vision than most men, and it had held up as he approached his middle age.

"They are nearing twelve hundred yards," said Nemakar. "Long guns! Prepare to fire!"

Down the length of the western wall, the two-man teams on the long guns prepared to fire, resting the heavy barrels against the fork-shaped hardwood holders.

"On my command," said Nemakar.

The shooters who had not done so already pulled back the great firing hammers on their rifles and lowered their faces down over the long barrels, placing their eyes in the sights.

"Fire!" ordered Nemakar.

The barrels erupted in a massive explosion, the gunpowder deafening to all within one hundred yards, as thick black smoke belched forward from the barrels, as if the entire western wall had suddenly burst into flame.

The rider next to Aurelio Demassi was thrown from his horse, just as the distant thunder hit his ears. Two more riders over, to Demassi's left, another rider plummeted over a toppling camel, shouting out as he fell. In front of Demassi, the sand exploded as if struck by a cannonball.

Jabil understood what was happening first.

"Long guns!" he shouted. "Angle! Angle right! Angle right!"

His jackal's eyes were wide, showing the white parts as he turned to look into Aurelio Demassi's face. The look only lasted a fraction of a second, but it stuck in Demassi's mind for far longer.

Demassi turned his camel with a strike of his riding stick to the right place on the cow's neck. She turned swiftly, almost throwing Demassi from her back. Demassi looked to his left; Anil was there, riding with wide eyes, striking his camel to move from a canter to a gallop.

More long guns thundered in the distance. Adrenaline pumped through Demassi, making his skin tingle as he rode.

By the God of the Sands, if long guns are firing at us, Demissaries are here indeed, and we are madmen to ride for Ben Hamur. Another long gun sounded; Demassi crouched forward on his camel, drawing his head down toward the camel's neck. He felt the air shudder above him, as if it were being torn apart.

By the God of the Sands.

"Faster!" shouted Kaleem Salesi. "Faster!"

All of the camels broke out into a full-fledged gallop. Demassi knew there was little swiftness left in his cow. She was a good camel, but she was bred for endurance, not speed.

Two more booms sounded in the distance. Demassi's heart boomed in his chest, the skin on the back of his neck buzzing with heightened awareness. He could still feel the vibration of the air that had ripped apart above him.

Was that the bullet? By how much did it miss me? Demassi had been under fire before, but never by long guns, and never by Demissaries. Long guns were not like rifles. They did not sound like rifles, and what they did to a man's body was not like a rifle. It was more like a cannon held by a man.

Demassi was almost in the wadi by the time he saw it, so fast were they galloping. He could think of nothing but the long guns firing their giant bullets past his head.

And how far are they? At least a thousand yards? Farther? What kind of rifle can fire with accuracy at more than a thousand yards?

The wadi's drop was six feet and nearly perpendicular to the plain.

"God of the Sands!" shouted Demassi as his camel took the decline. He launched forward from his saddle, falling over the camel's head, hitting the ground and tumbling. The camel fell after him, her legs buckling and her neck, chest, and face striking the sand at the base of the tiny ravine. She roared in fright.

The other riders poured into the wadi, with even the most experienced Beserian raiders toppling off of their mounts.

Kaleem Salesi alone remained on his bull camel. The bull camel took the ravine at a leap, keeping both its footing and its rider.

"Stay down!" ordered Kaleem. As if on his command, several patches of sand on the ridgeline exploded with the impact of long gun bullets.

"They have our range!" shouted Jabil, fully grasping their peril.

Demassi looked around at the others. Anil was next to him, pushing himself up from the ground, having fallen onto his face. His headscarf had pulled off of his head, exposing a tangle of thick black hair. All of the others looked as frightened as Demassi felt.

He looked down the length of the ravine and physically jumped in fear.

"God of the Sands! Draw swords! There are others!" Demassi reached for his saber, but before he could do so, the strongest hands he had ever encountered—stronger than any he had ever imagined—grasped his shoulders and ripped him forward like a child's doll of cloth.

Demassi looked up into the man's face. It was black, like an Omakhosian's.

"Who are you?" asked the man, shaking him with one arm. The fingers that gripped Demassi's shoulder and collarbone were like an iron vise. The other massive hand drew a dagger the size of a forearm.

Demassi said nothing, looking up in the Omakhosian's face with wide eyes and an open mouth. Before he spoke, he found himself flipped around, facing the others with the cold of bared steel against his throat.

Before him stood Kaleem, Jabil, Anil, and the others who had survived the long guns. Demassi was too scared to count how many had died, or how many had not made it down into the wadi.

"Release him," said Kaleem. His voice did not shake, nor did his hands that held his rifle. "Release him, or I will shoot you."

"Who are you?" said a woman's voice.

The woman stepped out from behind the giant Omakhosian. She was tall, taller than Demassi, Kaleem, or any of the Beserians facing her. She aimed two pistols. One had orange markings upon it and a single barrel. The second pistol was black with three barrels. The hammers of all three were cocked back and ready to fire. She aimed the three-barreled pistol at Kaleem.

Kaleem stared at her. Jabil had freed his rifle from his saddle and was standing next to Kaleem, aiming his weapon at the tall woman with the pistols.

"If I ask again, it will be after I have pulled the trigger," said the woman.

"I am Anil Salesi, son of Hamid Salesi, Member of the Council of the Elders, Second to Abu Akhsa, bearer of the Staff of the Serpent, the Staff of Wisdom, the Staff of Beseri."

Kaleem turned to look at his brother, taking his eyes off of the enemies before him. Anil stepped forward, unarmed.

"Who are you?" asked Anil.

From behind the massive Omakhosian, another woman appeared. She was of a more ordinary size, but still taller than most of the Beserians, with olive skin and the drab cloak of a villager, like the others.

"You are the son of Hamid Salesi?" she asked.

"I have spoken truly," said Anil.

"And who are these others that point their rifles at us?"

Kaleem cleared his throat. "I am Kaleem Salesi, heir to Hamid Salesi!"

The olive-skinned woman smiled, keeping her lips closed together.

"Why are you here, riding toward Ben Hamur?"

"You tell us who you are!" said Kaleem. "Or we will shoot!"

"If the long gunmen fired upon you, then you are no friend of the Qhaliffa," said the woman, stepping closer to Anil Salesi. She stood forward and to the left from the massive Omakhosian, who still held a knife to Aurelio Demassi's throat. "Perhaps, you are even who you say you are."

The woman took another step closer to Anil. She pulled her head covering back off of her forehead, revealing long, auburn-brown hair with streaks of gold.

"I am Selena Savanar, daughter of Sah Seg Savanar."

All of the Beserians stared at her.

"Now lower your weapons, and Oapah the Hohsa and Gulana of Nor Gandus will lower theirs."

"How do we know you are Selena Savanar?" asked Kaleem, pointing his rifle at her instead of Oapah. "How do we know this is not a trap set by the Qhaliffa? How do we know he is not a Demissary in disguise?" His eyes went to Oapah as he finished speaking.

"First, if it were a trap," said Selena, smiling to reveal her missing two front teeth, "It would be set by Jemojeen Jongdar, the Grand Vizer, who is your true enemy and ours, for the Qhaliffa does nothing. Second, you ask how I can prove that I am Selena Savanar? Look at my mouth, look at the teeth Jemojeen ordered ripped out in the dungeon beneath the Qhaliffa's palace. They ripped them out with pincers while I screamed. They tortured me before they brought me to the stake to burn me alive, as they did my father before me.

"As for these two? They are not Demissaries. They are Lions of the Order of the Ram, the Lion, and the Serpent. They risked their lives to save me and the other two who were to be burned, Trendan Rudar and Huralt Donadun, may the God of the Mountain and the Sands embrace their eternal souls. These Lions rescued me from the stake, and they risked their lives to bring me here. We escaped from Saman Keer to the Semissari Swamp, and from there to Ben Hamur.

We fled Ben Hamur this morning before the rising sun. We fled to escape the very Demissaries who fire their long guns at you."

As if on a signal, a pair of long gun blasts thundered from the direction of Ben Hamur and the rim of the wadi exploded, spraying grains of sand onto all of those standing below. The Beserians all ducked in fear, but Selena Savanar and her companions did not.

"If you are truly the sons of Hamid Salesi, take us to him," said Selena. "We seek him and the staff that he carries, the Staff of Beseri."

"Lady Savanar," said Anil, stepping forward past his brother. "The staff was stolen. We ride to retrieve it. That is why we ride for Ben Hamur."

"Stolen by whom?" asked Selena. She turned to Oapah. "Release him," she said.

Oapah lowered his knife from Aurelio Demassi's throat.

"He is called Ghani," said Anil. "He is a Beserian, a Bazadak, and one considered favored because of the lucky gap in his teeth."

"How did he steal it?"

"He struck down our father in his tent and escaped into the night."

"And he rides for Ben Hamur?"

"Yes."

"Did he ride with the Erassians you pursued?"

"Yes."

"Why?" asked Selena, already knowing the answer.

"He rides to take the staff to the Qhaliffa," said Anil.

Selena nodded. "For the first time in eight hundred years. Where is your father now?"

"With Abu Akhsa," said Anil. "And the main force."

"How many warriors?" asked Selena.

"More than ten thousand," said Anil.

Selena's eyes widened. She nodded. "Come, we must ride to them now. We have little time."

The Beserians stared at her.

"And by the God of the Mountain and the Sands, lower your rifles! We are on the same side, and the war is beginning."

CHAPTER 62
On the Edge

Western Rim of the Hahst
51st Day, Month of Wasura, 807
Anglian Calendar: April 13, 1879

The Hahst appeared as a vast white line at the horizon, like a sea within a sea.

They had advanced without ceasing for nearly thirty hours, sometimes riding when they became too tired to walk, and then walking when the camels became too tired to carry them. They had not seen a well in seventy miles. Their waterskins hung ominously light on their hips. The closer they came to the Hahst, the more Don Mazarian insisted they hurry, as if enemies pursued them. Peter had wanted to drink his remaining water for three hours, but he had steeled his mind against it, willing himself to think of something else.

At last, with the Hahst in sight, Don Mazarian allowed the small caravan to stop. They were still a dozen strong, including Sergeant Joshua Barnes and Peter Harmon, the only ones who had not spent their lives traversing the Sand Sea in Macmenian caravans. Don Mazarian treated the young Macmenian with the Gressian gunshot wound, using the medicines and bandages he carried in his saddle's bag. The man bore his wound admirably, which Don Mazarian had called no more than a scratch. The man kept the pace and did not complain.

After their weeks on the sands, both Barnes and Harmon looked like Macmenians: thin as spears, with sun-browned faces, lined with the wind and the never-ending brightness of the desert light. Peter caught his reflection in a knife blade and laughed. The pink-faced boy of twenty-two who had departed Hylebourne House was not readily seen beneath the brown skin in his reflection. His reddish-brown beard grew longer and thicker by the day. His need for food had lessened, even as he thought about eating more and more.

As he rode and as he walked, Peter marveled at the meals those dining at Hylebourne House took for granted: eggs, bacon, hams, chickens, roasted pork and beef, whole fish and filleted fish, shellfish prepared in four different styles, bread baked six different ways, potatoes and turnips and carrots, and sauces of every variety to please the palate. He thought of these things as the miles slipped by, with days of monotonous terrain slowly, ever so slowly, passing by.

Sometimes as he rode, creeping ever eastward toward the place that was likely to kill them all—the Hahst of the white sands, where men and camels were said to disappear without a trace—he thought of wine. Sometimes, half-asleep, slumped in his saddle, he thought of the white wines of Hylebourne House; some that smelled of flowers and citrus, others that smelled of butter, and still others that tasted like stone. He thought of the sharp, light-bodied whites Mr. Breckenridge, the Butler of Hylebourne House, selected for afternoon picnics in the spring, the kind that paired well with crisp cheeses and LaFrentian rabbit terrine, spread on toast. Somehow, over and over, his mind sought to sit upon Anglian grass, on a blanket with a basket, with the air pleasant but not hot, with birds chirping in the trees, as swans and ducks paddled their way silently across the pond, ducking their heads to forage under the water.

Then Peter awoke from his daydream, seeing nothing but rolling dunes of sand in all directions, like waves upon the Titanic Ocean, for as far as the eye could see from horizon to horizon, without obstruction, without ascertainable landmarks. But then, after days that seemed like weeks, and weeks that seemed like months, they came to the Hahst, the place where the tans and the yellows and the browns gave way to the whiteness of the site that desert men feared more than any other place on the Sand Sea.

When he was not thinking about wine or picnics on the grass in those long weeks, Peter wondered what made the Hahst so frightening. *What makes a man like Don Mazarian, a man who is unmoved by the things that frighten other men, tremble before such a place?*

"This is a good place," said Don Mazarian, looking down at the ground. He did not look ahead toward the Hahst. In the sunlight, the Hahst looked stark white in comparison to the rest of the Sand Sea, as if it were a great cotton sheet pulled tight across the desert.

Peter looked down at the ordinary sand beneath his feet. It looked like all of the other places his feet had trudged across over the past fifteen hours of walking: sandy, vaguely brownish-tan, and hot.

"There is water near," said Don Mazarian.

Peter looked around. *I see nothing but sand.*

"That is the place of the water," said Don Mazarian, pointing at a place a few yards away. "We will place our tents here. We will dig our well there."

Peter looked to where Don Mazarian pointed. He saw only a small indentation of discolored sand.

The Macmenians began unloading their light, hollowed-wood tent poles. They fit together into parts, easily carried in a saddlebag while adding little weight to the camel tasked with carrying them. Peter marveled at their lightness to the point of flimsiness, and yet how firmly they could stand up against the wind when it began to blow. *I suppose centuries of desert crossings teach lasting lessons.*

Don Mazarian walked forward to the place he said they would dig the well.

"This will be good water," he said, looking down intently into the indented, slightly discolored sand.

"I see sand," said Peter, walking up behind him.

Since he had spoken up in the Valley of Kordon, facing down Usor Nepopolous, Peter had grown more assertive, and Don Mazarian had grown more respectful. Upon the sands, Don Mazarian was a man of few words, yet the few words he chose to utter, he uttered with great care.

Over time, Peter could read what Don Mazarian did not say with his mouth, and what he instead said with his posture, his movements, and above all, his eyes. This was how Don Mazarian spoke a great deal, and as the time passed, Peter found himself noticing things in his Macmenian companions that he did not see before.

It was as if before the sands, Peter moved too quickly to see that which occurred before his very eyes. Upon the sands, the time slowed, and Peter began to see with new eyes. Peter saw, for the first time, what Barnes the Sergeant had always seen: details in terrain, slight changes in a man's head tilt, a subtle shift in a voice that might mean the difference between anger and happiness in a man that was not inclined to readily admit or reveal either.

"You see sand because you still see with Anglian eyes, even if you are less blind than you were before. If you could see with the eyes of a Macmenian, then you would see," said Don Mazarian.

Peter looked again. At the edges of the discolored indentation, he saw a wrinkling in the sand, like an old man's hands.

"Where there is wrinkling, there is water," said Don Mazarian.

One of the Macmenians nearby nodded in agreement.

Peter looked at Barnes.

Barnes shrugged.

Don Mazarian's Macmenians dug into the indentation, thrusting their narrow-bladed shovels into the earth. There the sand was heavier but moved easily, as if placed there more recently than all of the rest.

"Who buried this well?" asked Peter.

"Who buries any well?" asked Don Mazarian.

Peter shook his head.

Barnes began digging with the Macmenians.

Peter turned and walked to his Macmenian tent. He pulled his shovel out from under a blanket. It was heavier than the Macmenian shovels. He gripped the handle with his newly hardened hands.

"Let me help," said Peter.

Don Mazarian stepped aside.

Peter thrust his spade down into the hole that the Macmenians and Barnes had begun. The sand on his shovel was heavy and waterlogged. He dug down again, dumping the sand to the side. His arms were thinner than they had been but also stronger, as if all nonproductive weight had departed from his frame, leaving only what was firm and necessary. He thrust his spade into the earth once more, and then he saw it—water. He dug again, pulling out a soggy shovelful. In minutes, an open pool of water lay at his feet.

"Taste it," said Don Mazarian.

Peter dropped down to a knee, placing his rough brown hands into the water. He lifted a mouthful to his lips. The water, shielded from the sun until now, was cool and pure, cleaner tasting, and less salty than the water from the caravan wells he had drunk from to stay alive over the past weeks.

"It is clean," said Peter, looking up at Don Mazarian in surprise.

"Yes."

"Why?"

"Underground rivers."

"I thought the Hahst was dry?"

"It is. They flow beneath the white sands."

"Can you dig for them in the Hahst?"

Don Mazarian shook his head.

"But they are the same rivers that flow into the Valley of Hom Hommuram," he said.

"I thought you did not believe in the Valley of Hom Hommuram?" said Peter.

Don Mazarian stood in silence.

Peter placed his hands into the cool, clear water again. After drinking bad well water from a goatskin—making all water, after enough time, taste more like goatskin than water—the water tasted better than any he could remember.

"They are also the same rivers that swallow men and camels in the sinking sands," said Don Mazarian. "A man may not dig in the sinking sands."

"I see," said Peter, drinking from his hands again, barely listening.

"You see what, Anglian?"

Peter looked up. "What?"

"The sinking sands, I said. Listen. There are many ways to die, and falling into the sinking sands is among the most certain."

Peter looked at him.

"If you wander from the way, you will perish, and the way is hidden."

"Is that why you are all afraid?"

"The only man who does not fear the Hahst is the man who does not know what he does not know," said Don Mazarian. As he spoke, his eyes drifted eastward to the place of whiteness. "Men who do not fear the Hahst die quickest."

"Upon the Prophet's rock I stand, for all other ground is sinking sand." The words were spoken in Anglian.

"What did you say?" asked Don Mazarian, looking at Sergeant Barnes.

Barnes repeated the words.

"Those are words from the Holy Book."

Barnes nodded.

Peter looked at Barnes with surprise in his eyes. He had not thought of Barnes as a book reader.

"What is the way through the Hahst," asked Peter, "the way through the sinking sands?"

"None can say with certainty," said Don Mazarian. "Men claim to walk from one end of the Hahst to the other, crossing straight through it instead of making the long ride around it. But most who say such things are liars."

"Have you known any to claim it?" asked Peter.

"None that I believe," said Don Mazarian.

"Who claimed it?"

"Many have claimed it."

"What does Azadeem say, in *The Life of Hom Hommuram*?" asked Peter, already knowing the answer. When he read a passage, he rarely if ever forgot it, even years later.

Don Mazarian frowned and shook his head.

"You told me to forget the others. You told me Azadeem's was the only book that matters."

Don Mazarian looked out toward the east, out over the white sands of the Hahst.

"Yes," he said.

"Azadeem says that the path curves like a moon sliver, with the same arc as the horn of a ram. Does he not?"

"What does that mean, Anglian, 'with the arc of the horn of the ram'?" asked Don Mazarian. "Such words are a poor map by which to navigate the sinking sands."

"Is there a better map?"

Don Mazarian shook his head.

"Do we know where it begins?" asked Peter.

"Where what begins?"

"The Arc of the Ram, the place a man may enter on firm ground, where he can tread upon the rock of the Prophet instead of falling into the sinking sands."

"Yes, that place is known. There is a place from which a man may advance. But men fall off of the path. The path narrows, and the path curves. Men fall off with their camels. They disappear before men's eyes as if swallowed up by hungry earth. Others say it is not only the sands that swallow. Some say—"

Don Mazarian stopped speaking again, his eyes drifting.

"Some say what?" asked Peter.

"Some say things lurk beneath the sinking sands."

"What things?"

"Serpents."

"What kind of serpents?" asked Peter.

"The kind that are longer than camels and wider than men. They are said to be pale, like the Hahst."

"Have you seen them?"

"No."

Peter stood in silence, looking out upon the plain of whiteness. He turned to Barnes, clearing his throat.

"Sergeant Barnes, what day is it today?"

"Saturday, why?"

"What is the date?"

"April the thirteenth," said Barnes.

"Are you certain?"

"Yes."

Peter nodded. "Then, today is my birthday."

Don Mazarian's eyes widened on his dark wrinkled face. He looked at Peter as if weighing him in his mind. "Perhaps it is auspicious that we enter the place of death on the day of your birth. May the God of the Sands bless you and bring you peace."

"I doubt we shall find peace," said Peter. "But by the Three Gods and yours, Don Mazarian, we will find the path."

CHAPTER 63
"Unclean"

Oasis of Ben Gamurian
19th Day, Month of Wasura, 807
Anglian Calendar: March 12, 1879

Hannah stood barefoot on the cool stone, with a shroud-like garment covering her from her throat to the ground, hiding her feet. Over her head, she wore a veil that covered her face and her hair. She was unrecognizable beneath her coverings. That was as the Sharef of Ben Gamurian demanded.

"Unclean, that is what she is," said Sharef Tazak Bin-Zaal, small, lean, and carrying a smug look upon his face, the face of a man that knows he is in command and that none are present to challenge that command.

"Unclean?" Hersen nearly toppled with rage. His face contorted. He knew his anger was more likely to hurt his cause than to help it, but his honor shouted inside of him, thundering against the injustice, and he could not keep it contained inside of himself.

The Sharef stared at him as if daring Hersen to continue. The guardsmen, standing in a line on either side of the Sharef, stared straight ahead, grim-faced and severe. Hersen knew that each man needed only a word, or even a nod from the Sharef to lower his spear and come for him, or worse yet, Hannah.

Hannah. Control your temper, or they will hurt Hannah worse than they already have.

Hersen and Hannah faced them alone.

Stanwich lay bedridden, back in the house the Sharef had given to them, reeling in pain from the infection. After a brief reprieve, Stanwich's fever had worsened. He had begun hallucinating and would not stop moaning. Hersen had learned long ago that when the delusions and hallucinations began, the fever approached its most dangerous peak. From there, men could pass beyond, into the darkness from which they never returned.

"Pardon my tone, Sharef," said Hersen.

"You are wise to watch your tone, foreigner," said the Head of Household, the Sharef's steward and second in command, the tall man that looked like a talking skeleton.

Hersen blinked slowly and swallowed. Hannah stood next to him, staring down at the ground, her eyes covered by her veil. If there was any fight left in her, it was well hidden, as if she were merely a husk of herself.

"There was another," said Hersen. "Another woman that was with Miss Huntington. Her name is Mrs. Smith. Where has she gone? Miss Huntington says she was stabbed in front of her by men wearing the uniform of your guardsmen. I am told they killed Mrs. Smith because she tried to defend Miss Huntington. They killed her so that they could attack Miss Huntington."

"And where are your witnesses?" asked the Sharef.

"My witness is right here, standing before you," said Hersen, looking at Hannah.

"The unclean may not serve as witnesses. Who are your other witnesses?"

"You call her unclean," said Hersen. "If she is unclean, as you say, it is because your own men attacked her!"

"Do not raise your voice, foreigner," said the Head of Household. "I shall not warn you again."

"Your men attacked me," said Hannah. Her voice was low and distant as if detached from her body.

The Sharef glanced at her as if unsure whether she had spoken or not.

Hannah raised her voice so there could be no mistake as to who spoke. "They killed Mrs. Smith by jamming a knife into her back, like criminals and murderers. And then they raped me."

She pulled the veil from her head and threw it down onto the ground. Her face was discolored to a purplish-black and swollen beneath each of her eyes.

"Cover your face!" shouted the Head of Household. The Sharef turned his eyes as if looking upon Hannah would somehow stain the perfect whiteness of his garments.

"Unclean!" shouted the Head of Household. "Cover your face!"

"So that you can lie while I stand here?" Hannah shouted. "So you can dishonor the memory of an honorable woman? I think not!"

"Guards! Seize her!" shrieked the skeletal man. The guards rushed forward, but not before Hersen could step in front of Hannah, placing himself between her and the line of advancing men.

A dozen guardsmen closed in with their spearpoints lowered.

Hersen stood upright, knowing that a stone ledge above a steep drop lay just behind Hannah. There was nowhere to run. He reached down into his boot and pulled out the hidden dagger, brandishing the blade.

"A blade! Seize him!" shouted the Head of Household.

Hersen backed up, keeping Hannah directly behind him.

Beyeeeu-be-be-euuuuuu.

The trumpet sounded for all to hear, and in a moment, all knew that such was not a sound belonging to Ben Gamurian.

Be-be-be-eeuuuuuuuu.

The vast open view of the southwestern desert lay behind Hersen, the view from the receiving terrace of the Sharef of Ben Gamurian.

"What is it, Hannah? Turn to look," said Hersen, keeping his eyes squarely upon the guardsmen in front of him. "Who is it?"

Hannah looked, squinting in the sunlight.

The broad, open Plain of Gamurian stretched out before her. Along it, long lines of horsemen rode toward her beneath a vast cloud of dust kicked up from hundreds and hundreds of horses.

"They are riders. They are yellow," she said.

The guardsmen advanced ever closer, their spears lowered.

"Yellow? Do they ride beneath a banner?"

"They ride beneath the flag of the Anglian Imperium," she said.

Hersen's heart thundered in his chest. He looked into the eyes of the advancing guardsmen. To his astonishment and theirs, his mouth opened into a smile.

CHAPTER 64
Hannah Huntington's Justice

Oasis of Ben Gamurian
19th Day, Month of Wasura, 807
Anglian Calendar: March 12, 1879

"Tell them to open the gate or face the consequences," said Colonel Willem Spinner, staring at the mudbrick walls from beneath his pith helmet.

The small, black-bearded Major, Rajat Rajatnamdar, nodded sharply, his eyes aflame.

He kicked his heels against his charger's flanks, lurching forward into action. Like all of the others except Colonel Spinner, he wore a blue turban with a red stripe across the front.

Rajatnamdar cleared his throat and shouted, "In the name of Her Royal Highness, Violet Caterina Stephania, Queen of Anglia, Empress of Hindea, Sovereign of the Anglian Imperium, open your gates!"

Only the wind responded.

The guards above the wooden gates looked down at the regiment of yellow-shirted horse riders, each man carrying a lance with a red-and-white pennant affixed beneath the steel tip. The wind blew from the south, as if the riders had brought the chilled air from the Harafhan Mountains with them across the sands. The pennants snapped in the wind—each a solid bar of red above a stripe of white—extending northward, like seven hundred little flags.

Vastly larger than the pennants, the flag of the Anglian Imperium strained against its flagstaff, driven by the same wind, unfurled in all of its glory, with the red cross beneath the three golden interlocking rings, set against four white squares, bounded by a border of blue.

"My patience departed somewhere between the Harafhan Mountains and that gate," said Colonel Spinner. "Show them the crank-gun."

Gindal the Reaper nodded, his eyes dark brown and cold. Unlike most of the men, he still wore only a mustache instead of a beard.

"Bring up a crank-gun," he growled.

A unit of three Gengali troopers rode up upon a team of six horses with three sets of two. Each man rode the right horse in each group of two. Behind them, the horses towed a twelve-barreled gun attached to a small ammunition limber, wide enough for two men to sit upon, riding on top. Like a cannon, the crank-gun sat between two massive wooden wheels, each taller than a man, with flat steel tires on the wheels' edges, wide enough to be hauled across the sands.

The gun team rode up in front of Colonel Spinner. The man riding the front horse carried a whip in his hand and remained mounted. The other two mounted men swung out of their saddles and dropped down onto the sand.

They walked to the limber, unlatched the crank-gun, and wheeled it forward. One of the men adjusted the barrels while the other walked back to the limber, retrieving two heavy cylinders. He set one down at his feet and attached the other to the back of the twelve-barreled apparatus, snapping two steel latches forward and locking them into place. Into the side, the other man then inserted the crank, as long as the man's forearm.

"Where are we aiming, sir?" asked the gunner, standing at the ready.

Gindal the Reaper looked at Colonel Spinner.

Spinner nodded.

"Send a volley into the gate," said Gindal. "Two cranks."

"Yes, sir."

The first man shifted the wheels into place and lowered the barrel. The second man gripped the handle of the crank from behind the ammunition cylinder.

"Ready, sir," he said.

"Fire," said Gindal.

The man pushed the crank forward and pulled it down into an arc. The barrels spun clockwise. The first barrel swept past the twelve o'clock position and erupted with a fierce boom, shaking the air and making the gun shudder. Smoke belched from the six-foot-long, .55-caliber barrel.

The second barrel followed, and then the third, and then the fourth until all twelve barrels had fired. Then the gun continued firing as the man worked the crank.

After he cranked each barrel twice, all fell silent.

A pungent cloud of black smoke obscured the view just in front of the gun. Every man's and every horse's ears rang. The horses, trained around the crank-gun and rifle fire since they were young, did not panic. The horses closest to the gun merely flinched. Colonel Spinner's stallion did not even flinch.

The smoke drifted upward.

The men on top of the gate slowly peeked above the ramparts. Spinner looked at the gate itself. The gun had done its work. In the center of the two wooden gates, the planks had splintered, and daylight shone through where the clustered bullets ripped through the wood.

"Major Rajatnamdar, give them one more chance," said Colonel Spinner.

Rajat Rajatnamdar rode forward and in rough, accented Beserian, he shouted, "Open the gates or die!"

His words hung in the air. No one from Ben Gamurian responded.

"Take down the gates," said Colonel Spinner.

"Prepare to fire until the gates are no more," ordered Gindal the Reaper.

"Ready!" said the man at the crank.

A shout came from the rampart above the gate.

"Halt!" ordered Spinner.

The man with the crank froze.

"Major Rajatnamdar, what do they say?" asked Spinner.

Another shout approached from the ramparts. Spinner could see the man cupping his hands to better yell out into the desert.

"He says they are opening the gates. He says do not shoot."

"Very well, Major. They have one minute," said Spinner, pulling a gold watch from the pocket of his yellow tunic.

Spinner could hear a commotion behind the gates, and then he heard the squeal as the old hinges moved. The wooden gates pulled inward. The wide gate became a window, and lush palms appeared above green reeds.

"Center column, prepare to advance!" ordered Colonel Spinner, pulling his saber from its scabbard.

The lancers behind him lowered their lances from ninety degrees to forty-five, aimed in the direction of Ben Gamurian.

"Forward!" Colonel Spinner tapped his heels against the flanks of his stallion. The horse moved forward at an eager trot. The lancers followed him as one, a wave of yellow tunics beneath a forest of lances.

Like water released from a dam, the mounted Gengalis flowed around Rajat Rajatnamdar, Gindal the Reaper, and the crank-gun crew, who now adjusted their barrels to aim at the guardsmen still standing above the open gates.

Gindal rode to the right flank where his captains each stood ahead of their squadrons, preparing to advance. Rajat Rajatnamdar rode to the left where his own battalion awaited him.

Spinner's center surged forward. Rajat and Gindal had learned long ago to avoid arguing with Colonel Spinner about leading the men from the front.

If I die on the field, that is how I want to die. That was what he always said.

Eventually, they stopped asking. They wanted to die the same way, as did every man in the Gengali Lancers. They were all Gengalis, after all, and it was said that none had more of a Gengali heart than the Anglian Colonel, Willem

Spinner, who had led them across battlefields from Xin to Halex over the past fifteen years. And always Colonel Spinner led from the front. Across the long years, enemies had shot seven horses out from under him, but they had never shot him.

With the steel of his drawn saber gleaming in the sunlight, Spinner crossed through the opened gates of Ben Gamurian. Unlike Ben Hamur, no great trench surrounded Ben Gamurian's walls. No great zareba protected the mud-bricks with countless finger-length thorns. Only a five-foot thick, twelve-foot high wall of mudbricks separated the oasis from the sands around it.

The yellow-shirted Gengalis rode through the gate, following their leader, eight riders across with lances lowered. The guards cowered as readily as the people of the oasis.

Spinner did not slow down, but rather, once he passed under the gate, he increased his stallion's trot to a canter. He rode past the ancient pools without stopping for a drink. If he or his stallion were thirsty, no man could tell.

He rode straight for the palace of the Sharef, the highest building in all of the oasis. His men followed him with sabers in scabbards on their left hips, and rifles in leather holsters hanging from their saddles at their right. In their right hands, their lances remained pointed forward, light, long, and steel-tipped. It took little imagination to see what one of the lancers might do in the face of resistance. Men instinctively covered their stomachs with their arms and crouched into alleyways, buildings, and foliage near the pools, anywhere where the eyes of the riding lancers would not easily find them as they cantered through the oasis.

Spinner rode up to the inner gate, the low barrier that kept the house of Sharef Tazak Bin-Zaal separate from the remainder of the oasis.

The gate was closed.

"Sharef of Ben Gamurian!" thundered Spinner, "open this gate."

His riders formed up behind him, reining in their horses and filling up the totality of the hardened dirt of the path. A low stone wall surrounded the Sharef's home with an iron fence above it. Vines grew through the iron and covered much of the stone.

"Sharef of Ben Gamurian! Open this gate!"

A man appeared on the stone landing overhead. He was remarkably thin, like a living skeleton.

"Who rides into Ben Gamurian making such demands?" asked the man, his tone acid.

Spinner looked up at him.

"Open the gate."

The man stared down.

Spinner unholstered a pistol with his left hand, aimed at a pot on the landing overhead and fired. The ceramic exploded, sending shards at the man. The man who looked like a skeleton fled out of sight.

"Open the gates," said Spinner.

Three horsemen dismounted. One carried a mallet with a heavy iron head. The other carried a cutter with massive handles, each as long as a man's arm. The third man carried an ax.

They inspected the lock on the iron gate. The first man, the man with the ax, looked down and then stepped back without swinging. The second man with the hammer did the same. The third man approached the gate and saw that the lock secured a chain that bound the gate in place. He placed his cutter against a link of the chain and compressed the two long handles. The cutter sliced through the iron lock as easily as garden shears cut a stem. The chain now cut, the first man with the ax pulled the chain. It gave way. The second man with the hammer kicked the gate open. The walkway was too narrow to ride up on horseback.

"Every third man stay with the horses. The rest, onward!" barked Spinner.

He dismounted and ran forward with his pistol in his left hand and his saber in his right. He raced up the stairs, taking two at a time in his tall riding boots. Three dozen lancers followed him, carrying their Hart-Henry carbines in their hands with the short, .45-caliber barrels at the ready, their sabers slapping their thighs in their scabbards.

At the top of the stairs, two guardsmen barred the way with their spears.

"Halt!" shouted one. His voice was loud, but his eyes were tentative and afraid.

As Spinner came closer, charging like a bull, the guardsmen's eyes grew wider. Spinner aimed his pistol at the guardsman on the left. Their eyes locked. The guardsman dropped his spear and ran.

Alone, the remaining guardsman threw down his spear and lifted his hands. Spinner ran toward him. The man threw his back against the stone wall. Spinner ran past him as if he were a statue.

Reaching the top of the stairs, Spinner paused for a split second to scan the broad stone terrace. It was empty.

Spinner turned to the guard who was still standing, frozen by his fear like an ornament on the wall.

"Where are they?" Spinner roared.

The guardsman blinked uncomprehendingly at Spinner's Anglian words.

"Where?" shouted Spinner again, shifting to Beserian. He knew few Beserian words, but he knew how to say that.

"I—I—I—I do not know."

Spinner slammed the hilt of his sword against the man's face. He cowered with a crimson gash on his cheek.

"Where!"

"Below, below!" the man whimpered.

Spinner ran for the doors of the great house, sprinting across the wide, flat stones of the veranda, moving faster than any who had not seen him in action before would have thought possible. He reached the closed doors before any of his troopers. They were set on light hinges, not meant to withstand armed men. Spinner aimed a kick at the place where the door lock met the doorjam and kicked with all of his weight. The door flew open, banging against the stone wall behind it.

Two rifles fired with deafening sound in the enclosed space. Spinner stepped forward, unharmed. He lowered his pistol and fired into a man's chest. He pulled the hammer back with his thumb and fired into the second man, hitting him in the shoulder. The man cried out. Spinner pulled the hammer back again and shot him dead. He ran past where the dead riflemen lay slumped on the ground, stepping over them and down into a dark, descending stairway. Three of his troopers were already behind him.

He ran down the stairs into the darkness, not slowing his gait. The stairs went straight down into a wide room with a low ceiling. The room smelled of wax candles that had just been snuffed out. Spinner ran forward. Another door was closed on the far side of the room.

"Colonel, they may have set traps," said the sergeant running behind him.

"I doubt it," said Spinner. He reached the door and kicked. It held. He kicked again. It still held.

"Three Gods damn it!" shouted Spinner.

He aimed his pistol just above the door handle and fired, further deafening himself and his men in the enclosed space, just as his hearing had begun to recover. He kicked the door again, and it flew open. He ran through into a winding hallway, descending downward at a slope, like a path winding around the side of a mountain.

Spinner ran, ducking forward to avoid the low ceiling and the even lower crossbeams that held it up.

"Colonel, let us lead!" said a trooper, calling out behind him.

"There could be traps, sir!" said another.

Spinner ran forward as if deaf, charging into the darkness. A flicker of light shone ahead, a glimmer that kept the blackness from being total.

The men's ears still ringing from Spinner's pistol shot, they could not hear their own boots slamming on the ground beneath them. The ceiling grew even lower.

A gunshot erupted down the hallway, which had closed in on them more and more with each passing twenty yards. The bullet struck the wall, ricocheting back and into the arm of one of the troopers running behind Spinner. He cried out in pain and then cursed in Gengali.

"Gods of the Plains!" shouted another, as the Gengalis called their gods.

Spinner unloaded one of his two remaining pistol shots into the darkness ahead of him. Two more shots rang out from the darkness, sending bullets into the beams above Spinner's head. Spinner threw himself down onto his stomach. The ground had stopped sloping downward.

"Stay down, Colonel!" shouted the man behind him. The trooper dropped to a knee and fired his Hart-Henry carbine. The hallway magnified the sound as if the walls were collapsing upon them. Two more troopers knelt and fired.

A cry of pain came from the darkness ahead.

"Stop firing!" shouted Spinner. "Follow me!"

He rose and ran forward as fast as a man fleeing for his life, except that he ran toward his enemy.

The flatness of the ground began to slope upward. Spinner's chest heaved from the exertion and sweat clung to him despite the coolness of the tunnel. The space between the floor and the ceiling grew, and Spinner no longer had to run hunched over to avoid the wooden crossbeams above him.

The light grew brighter, and Spinner could see the contours of the stones on the walls. He could see daylight coming in from beneath a door ahead.

"There is a door!" he shouted.

Whatever gunmen had crouched in the hallway crouched there no longer. Spinner ran to the door, climbing the grade, gasping for air, feeling the many cigars he had smoked on the long ride from the Harafhan Mountains to the gates of Ben Gamurian.

He reached the door, slamming into it with his shoulder and his forearm. The door burst forward, and dazzling daylight blinded him, like a mole suddenly finding himself above ground. He squinted to see fleeing men in front of him, perhaps a dozen of them running down a tree-lined dirt path.

He staggered forward, running after the men despite the harsh light in his face. Spinner's troopers poured out of the door behind him, flooding the path with their yellow tunics.

The runners fleeing ahead stopped in the face of forty mounted lancers advancing toward them, moving down the far end of the path with their lance points lowered. The fleeing men turned to run laterally into the trees, but other men in yellow tunics and red-and-blue turbans were already there, emerging from behind the trees with their carbines at the ready.

A dozen men trying to escape turned back toward the path, away from the gunmen advancing from behind the palms. As they turned, they ran into the others of their party, trying to do the same thing but from the opposite side of the path. As each side turned, their eyes widened in the horror of seeing they were surrounded.

The Gengalis with the aimed rifles walked slowly as they moved out of the trees, advancing with the grim certainty of a python constricting around its still-living prey. The lancers advancing down the path slowed their pace as well, pulling their canter back into a trot. The only one still running was the red-faced, heavyset man in the pith helmet and the yellow tunic with the drawn saber and the unholstered pistol, squinting in the sunlight.

He stopped only when he had come to within a few yards of the men. His troopers were still several yards behind him.

"Which one of you is the Sharef?" he asked, taking in a deep breath after he spoke, his chest still heaving from his run.

The Ben Gamurians stared at him. None answered Spinner's Anglian words.

Spinner's Gengali translator rushed forward, repeating the words in Beserian, in a low, clear voice.

"I am the Sharef of Ben Gamurian," said a tall, skeletal-looking man.

"You are?" Spinner's eyes were skeptical. "Is that a fact?" he asked, walking still closer to the man. His translator followed close behind, repeating his words.

The other men in the group looked around them with increasingly desperate eyes. All were armed, some with spears, others with single-shot rifles. All had swords at their sides.

"It is a fact, and you are an invader," said the skeletal man. "You have no right to be here with your soldiers." He cleared his throat and lowered his voice to sound more commanding. "I order you to depart at once."

"You order me? Look around yourself, fellow. I see many yellow shirts. Those are my men. Where are yours? Just these handful? We are here by the orders of the Queen of the Anglian Imperium. We shall go wherever we like. There was an attack upon the sands upon the colors of the Imperium. We are here to punish that attack."

To his credit, the man kept his eyes level, neither looking down nor away. "I know nothing of such an attack, and you have no right to punish anyone here. This is the sovereign territory of the Qhaliffa of the Seven Cities. He is my Su-zerain, and I, Tazak Bin-Zaal, the Sharef of Ben Gamurian, rule in his place!"

"You lie," said Colonel Spinner, stepping closer, to nearly within thrusting reach of the Sharef's spearmen. "You know of another attack, Sharef. You allowed harm to fall upon your own guests, and when that happened, you refused to enforce justice. A woman was killed and another harmed. Do you deny it?"

Spinner stepped closer, pointing his sword at the man who called himself the Sharef of Ben Gamurian. Spinner shook his sword as he spoke. The sword point danced in front of the man's face.

"Do you deny it?"

The Sharef's spearmen did not lower their spears. Nor did they thrust them toward Colonel Spinner. They stood as if frozen.

"There was no evidence," said the skeletal man.

"No evidence? No evidence of what? Was there not a dead body? A blood-stained hovel? Was there not a survivor, a woman? Did not men in the uniforms of your own guardsmen kill a Mrs. Smith and—" Spinner paused to swallow his rage.

He was a rough man, but so too was he born a gentleman, raised and trained not to discuss such things.

"Did not men bearing uniforms of your own guard attack a Miss Hannah Huntington in the very room you had provided to her as your guest? Did they not assault her womanhood?"

"The only witness was a woman," said the skeletal man. "A woman alone may not testify against men."

"So, you do know it, and what I was told is true," said Spinner. He flared his nostrils and snarled. He stepped forward, placing his sword point at the throat of the tall, skeletal man calling himself Sharef.

"How many of you attest that this is the Sharef of Ben Gamurian?" shouted Spinner.

None spoke or made any movement.

"Raise your hand if this man is the Sharef," said Spinner, "and know that I will kill any man who lies."

The hands of the guardsmen remained lowered, gripping their spears.

"Tell me the real Sharef, or I shall cut your throat," said Spinner, touching the steel of his saber blade to the skeletal man's long, stringy neck. The rest of Spinner's troopers behind him had caught up with their colonel, with the stocks of their carbines against their shoulders, ready to fire their .45-caliber bullets into any that resisted. The Sharef's spearmen remained still as statues, like the bronze and marble men in the Grand Piazza of the Veteno.

"I am Sharef of Ben Gamurian," said a small, lean man with a black mustache and a short black beard. "You may lower your sword. My Head of Household shows loyalty to protect me. Surely your men would do the same to protect you."

Spinner turned his eyes to the man, lowering his sword from the skeletal man's neck. The skeletal man exhaled with relief.

"My Head of Household speaks truly. The only sovereign of Ben Gamurian is Sumetan, Qhaliffa of the Seven Cities, Ruler of the Sand Sea. I rule here in his place. You would be foolish to threaten me."

"Major Rajatnamdar!" shouted Colonel Spinner.

The small, heavily bearded man emerged from the palm trees to Spinner's right. He carried no weapon in his hands, but the pommel of his saber stuck out from his scabbard and the handle of a revolver was visible above his hip holster. A handsome, olive-skinned Spatanian emerged at his side.

"Tell me, Sharef, do you recognize this man?"

The Sharef turned to see the face of Diego the Vetenan foreman, the man who had ridden through two days and two nights to find Colonel Spinner's column, to proclaim what had befallen Hannah Huntington and Mrs. Smith. Diego's porters had caught word in the bazaar that an Anglian army advanced from the south. Hersen had dispatched Diego within hours of finding Hannah. Only then did he demand an audience with the Sharef.

Looking at Diego, the Sharef said nothing, but Spinner saw the flash of recognition in the man's eyes.

"Tell me, Sharef, where are the Western women, the explorer Stanwich, and the LaFrentian they call Hersen Expey?"

The Sharef looked at Colonel Spinner with defiant eyes, but he did not speak.

"They are in this man's dungeon, Colonel," said Major Rajatnamdar, gesturing toward the Sharef. "A dungeon from which Major Rasouda's men are freeing them."

"And for what were they imprisoned, Sharef?"

"They were a threat to the peace of this oasis. I jail whom I please," said the Sharef.

"Here they come now," said Rajat Rajatnamdar.

A commotion stirred down the path, behind where the two score lancers sat astride their mounts, drawing all eyes in its direction.

A group of ragged-looking Westerners advanced on foot, flanked on either side by a half-dozen dismounted lancers walking with them. A taller, more healthy-looking man with a mustache on his face helped a lancer hold up a wounded, smaller man, unshaven with the disheveled beard and excessively pale skin of a man fighting a fierce fever. A lone woman, with a wild tangle of blonde hair walked in front of them unassisted, her posture erect, with a lancer on either side.

In front of her, walked Gindal the Reaper, tall, dark-faced, and lethal, holding a bared saber in his right hand and something else in his left.

The Sharef looked at them and then turned back to Spinner.

"You have no right to free those I have imprisoned," he said.

"Have I not? You will learn what rights I have and do not have, Sharef. And then you will learn something else."

As Gindal led the others forward, Spinner could see that the feverish man in the middle was barely conscious, moaning, and looking down at the path with his eyes half-closed.

"Three Gods, that is Stanwich," said Spinner, seeing the stark difference in the face he had seen less than three months before at the Queen's Three God's Day Ball. He shook his head in disgust, looking at the Sharef. Then his head stopped shaking, and the flame rose in his steely, battle-hardened eyes.

"Guardsmen of the Sharef, drop your spears if you wish to live. Or hold your spears and be shot."

Half of the men dropped their spears immediately. The others still held theirs, their eyes darting around tentatively. Three more let their spears fall into the dust below.

"Major Rajatnamdar," said Spinner.

Rajat Rajatnamdar barked an order in Gengali. Two of his troopers fired their .45-caliber bullets into the chests of the spearmen who had refused to drop their spears. The force of the rifles knocked the men backward, flat onto their backs, killing them before they hit the dust and concussing everyone's eardrums.

Spinner shouted to hear himself over the ringing in his ears. "There is courage, and there is stupidity. You will find, Sharef, that I am not a man who likes to repeat himself. Now raise your hands above your heads, all of you."

The men obeyed. The skeletal man was the last to raise his hands, only doing so when the Sharef himself did.

"In Hindea," said Spinner, "I am bound to follow Anglian law. In Gengal, we will follow the law of the Gengali Councils. Here, Sharef, at this moment, you shall find that I am the law."

Stanwich, Hersen Expey, and Hannah Huntington now walked close enough for Spinner to see the sweat beaded on Stanwich's pale face. Spinner looked at him with disbelief. *He has aged ten years since I saw him in the Queen's palace.* In Spinner's recollection, few men were more energetic than Harold Milton Stanwich, and few men seemed younger for their years. The man before Colonel Spinner, however, looked like an old, dying man.

"Miss Huntington, do you see before you the man who attacked you?" asked Spinner.

Hannah stepped forward. Slowly, she swept her eyes across the faces of the men surrounding the Sharef of Ben Gamurian. She stopped her eyes on the face of a handsome young man with dark eyebrows and thick dark hair underneath a white headdress that draped down to the center of his back. Spinner could see the man flinch under her gaze. Then she looked at two other men. One of them looked straight down into the dirt to avoid her eyes. The other met her eyes and then quickly looked away.

"Yes, I see all three of them," said Hannah Huntington. "I see the men who murdered Matilda Smith." Hannah's voice shook, but when she said the words "Matilda Smith," the words came out firm and clear.

"Point to them," said Colonel Spinner.

"Him, him, and him," said Hannah, pointing her right index finger at each man as she identified them.

"She is a liar!" said the first man. "I do not know this woman! I have never touched her! And she is a woman! She cannot accuse me! This is not evidence!"

"What is your name?" asked Spinner.

"Usuf," said the man, spitting down into the dirt.

"Major Rajatnamdar, tell this man, Usuf, that he is to undress."

The man looked at Spinner in horrified disbelief.

Rajat Rajatnamdar stepped forward. "Take your clothes off."

"I will not!" said the man.

"This man is my son, Usuf Bin-Zaal," said the Sharef. "He is the heir to Ben Gamurian! You will not tell him to disrobe before you foreigners!"

"Get on with it," said Colonel Spinner, nodding to Major Rajatnamdar.

"Undress," he said.

"The Qhaliffa shall hear of this," shouted the Sharef, "and his wrath shall be great!"

"My wrath shall be great if this man does not undress!" shouted Colonel Spinner.

"Undress," said Rajat Rajatnamdar.

Rajatnamdar did not shout, but something in his eyes changed the look in the young man's face. He took his white headdress off of his head, letting it fall into the dirt. Beneath his headdress, a tangle of thick black hair grew wildly from a well-shaped head. He pulled the robe up over his head. All that remained on him was a small loincloth. As he bared his chest, the troops in yellow began to murmur. As clearly as if a cat had attacked him with a set of claws, the man had deep scratch marks upon his chest and back.

"From where did those scratches come?" asked Colonel Spinner.

"My wife," said the man, Usuf Bin-Zaal, son of the Sharef. "My wife scratched me."

"Those are deep scratches," said Colonel Spinner. Dark scabs covered the lines from which blood had flown.

"Miss Huntington, what are those scratches?" asked Spinner.

Hannah stepped forward, moving closer to the man, looking into the same eyes that had looked down into hers when he was on top of her, beating her and raping her. She stood nearly as tall as he did.

"I scratched this man with my hands."

"Why?"

"I scratched him because he was on top of me, forcing himself upon me. I clawed at him because he killed Mrs. Smith. I ripped my nails across his skin because he beat me with his fists, here and here." As she spoke, Hannah pointed to two large, dark purple bruises that still adorned her face.

"She lies!" shouted the man.

"Miss Huntington, confirm the others once more," said Spinner.

"Those two," said Hannah, pointing again at the other two men she had already identified.

"Undress them!" shouted Spinner.

Several of Rajat Rajatnamdar's troopers stepped forward, roughly grabbing the men. Others pulled their headdresses from their heads and their robes from their shoulders. In moments, both men stood, like Usuf, in only their loincloths. Their bared legs looked pale and thin in the bright sunlight. One of the men had a gash at the hairline above his ear.

Colonel Spinner's eyes moved up and down their bodies looking for the telltale scratches. On one man, scratches descended at a diagonal down one arm; on another, two half-moons formed what looked like a bite on his forearm.

Hannah Huntington did not hesitate, her blue eyes simmering, her right index finger pecking the air in the direction of her assailants. "I scratched that man, and I bit the other. They held me down while the other one forced himself upon me."

"She lies!" shouted the other men, imitating Usuf's accusation. The fear in their eyes belied the loudness of their voices.

"She is a woman! She cannot testify!" shouted the skeletal man.

"This is not justice, and you may not do this," said the Sharef, Tazak Bin-Zaal.

"I find that these men are guilty of raping this lady," said Spinner, his chin set forward like a plow. "They shall be punished."

The men looked at Spinner with tense, expectant eyes.

"Major Rasouda, show them what will become of them."

Gindal the Reaper stepped forward with black, predator's eyes, indifferent to the fate of his prey. In his hand, he uncoiled a long leather whip with barbs near the end.

"No!" shouted the Sharef.

"You cannot!" shouted one of the men.

"Father, stop them!" shrieked Usuf, naked except for his loincloth.

Gindal lifted the whip and pulled it back so the long strand of black leather uncoiled, hanging for a moment, suspended in the air. Then he whipped it forward with the fearsome force that only an experienced whip-swinger can generate.

The leather launched downward, slicing through the air, fast as a striking snake. The barbs struck Usuf's skin first, snapping against his bared flesh as it wrapped around him. He shrieked in pain. Before he could cover himself, retreat, or cry out further, Gindal had already ripped the whip back and was bringing it forward again, this time against one of the other men. The other man cried out just as piteously as Usuf.

"God of the Sands!" he screamed as tears formed in his eyes.

The third man's eyes were wide with frantic anticipation when the leather struck him. He winced in pain when the leather hit his bared chest, cutting deeply into his flesh and leaving a hot-red mark nearly breaking the skin.

"You may not lash them!" screamed the Sharef. "You will stop now!" The Sharef ran to his son, placing himself between Gindal the Reaper's whip and Usuf.

"There will be no pity for these rapists!" shouted Spinner, his voice like thunder.

Gindal did not stop. He thrust his whip forward, striking the Sharef across the chest.

"Ayyyeeee," shouted the Sharef as the leather cut into his skin, his white robes doing little to blunt the whip's force.

"How dare you!" screamed the skeletal man.

He pulled a curved knife from his belt and ran at Gindal. Gindal drew the saber that he had returned to the scabbard at his belt. As quickly as the blade was freed from its leather sleeve, it was already moving down in a sweeping motion toward the skeletal man's chest. The saber's steel caught the sunlight as it sailed forward, striking the skeletal man across the chest at a diagonal.

The man stopped, frozen by the force of Gindal's blow, his skin opening like a crimson valley across his sternum and stomach. Gindal pulled his sword back and thrust it into the man's abdomen, point first. The point emerged out the man's back, near his spine. The skeletal man dropped his knife, fell to his knees with an open mouth, and collapsed forward onto his face in the dust.

"Murderers!" screamed the Sharef.

Hannah Huntington placed a pale hand on the canary-yellow tunic of Gindal's shoulder. He looked at her, black eyes in a dark brown face. Her blue eyes met his without fear. Gindal nodded.

Hannah revealed a shiny snub-nosed revolver from beneath her body-length robe, the robe they forced her to wear before they threw her into the Sharef's prison, the robe of a raped woman that dared accuse her rapists.

Hannah stepped forward past Gindal, raising the barrel.

She pulled the pistol's hammer back and pulled the trigger. The gun cracked, and Usuf, son of the Sharef of Ben Gamurian, raper of Hannah Huntington, jerked upright. A crimson stain formed in front of his heart.

He fell dead to the ground.

Hannah cocked the pistol-hammer and shot the second man, the man whose arm she had scratched, the man with the gash on the side of his head where Mrs. Smith had struck him with her rock. Her bullet struck his stomach, and he doubled over. She placed a second bullet into the top of his head as he bent down.

She cocked the hammer again and aimed the pistol at the man she had bitten, the man that yanked her hair and pulled one of her legs open so that Usuf could rape her, the man that had smiled when he stabbed Mrs. Smith in her back.

"Mercy!" he screamed.

Hannah shot him in the loincloth. He screamed again, more ragged and astonished, bringing his hands down to cover his wound. Hannah cocked and fired into his chest. The screaming stopped.

For a moment, all ears rang from the pistol shots.

None moved. The wind whipped the tops of the palm trees, moving the long trunks beneath as if in a rhythmic dance.

"To those who show mercy, mercy shall be given. I shall miss you, Mrs. Smith," said Hannah, speaking her words softly.

If she felt like crying, there were no tears in her eyes.

Colonel Spinner bent over Harold Milton Stanwich with the three best medical men in the Gengali Lancers. Spinner had placed Stanwich in the Sharef's sleeping cushions, relegating the Sharef to the dungeon that had held Hannah Huntington and Hersen Expey not hours before. Hersen Expey stood over Stanwich from the other side, wearing the peaked hat of a LaFrentian Legionnaire. Hannah stood next to him, well-bathed, with hair pleated into a flaxen-yellow braid behind her, her face still battered. She wore clean riding pants and a fitted riding jacket. Colonel Spinner looked at her, seeing the sharp, severe lines of her ancestors, like a raiding queen of the ancient Gerdic sailing fleets, her eyes as icy as the northern seas. *She is as beautiful as she is fierce.*

Stanwich lay with his eyes closed. He had ceased groaning. Troubling as the ceaseless groaning had been, his silence was more disturbing.

"He has little time left," said the lead medical man, the bearded, regimental physician, looking up at Spinner from beneath his red-and-blue turban. "We have applied what medicines we have. We have searched throughout this house for what medicines the Sharef may have kept. Most are primitive. Some will be useful. While we have little to work with here, we have more to work with than this man has time."

Spinner looked at the medical man, nodding with respect. They had long campaigned together, from the Xin expedition of fifteen years ago to the Halex Wars of ten years ago to the latest excursions against the Harafhan tribesmen on the Hindean frontier.

"What does that mean?" asked Hersen Expey.

"From what I can see, the sickness of the wound has penetrated his bloodstream. If that is the case, then his body is polluted with toxins. Soon his organs could fail. If we cannot get him better medicine than what is here, he will likely die. But I have been wrong before."

Spinner shook his head, knowing that his regimental physician was rarely wrong.

"What medicine does he need?" asked Hersen Expey, raising his eyebrows so high that his forehead became a series of ripples, like waves lining up against the seashore.

The medical man shook his head. "He needs a master healer. I do not know that even our best Anglian medicines could help him, Colonel. If we were in Gengal, I would call a Shaman. It is that time. There are rare herb combinations that can reverse the process, but we have few of them here. What is needed, perhaps, is a power beyond."

"What about amputating the hand, or even the arm?" asked Spinner. He hated asking it, but if the alternative was death, such things must be discussed.

Hersen looked at Spinner, thinking the same thing, but not wanting to say it out loud.

"No," said the medical man. "We are well past such things. If we cut the hand off now, we only further weaken his body, and his body will tolerate no more weakening. If you were going to amputate, you needed to do it many days ago, perhaps even weeks ago."

"The burning treatment?" asked Spinner, his voice low.

The medical man shook his head. "No. That would be before amputation."

Hersen frowned, looking down at the medical man, feeling both guilt and defensiveness. *I should have administered the burning treatment upon the sands. I should have forced him. I knew better. Perhaps it is I that have brought him to death's door.*

"What do you suggest we do?" asked Spinner, looking at the medical man.

"There is perhaps something upon the sands that could heal him," said the lead medical man, glancing at the other two healers.

Spinner stared, waiting.

"None of us have seen it, Colonel. We have only heard. There is an object said to reside amongst the Beserians. A staff."

"The Staff of the Serpent," said Hannah Huntington, speaking softly. Her voice was raspy but feminine. Spinner looked at her, and for a fleeting moment, forgot Stanwich and his plight. His eyes found Hannah's, wanting her to look back at his own eyes in the same way.

The medical man looked at Hannah and nodded. "Yes, that is the name."

"The staff of what?" asked Spinner, looking at Hannah.

"The Staff of the Serpent," said the medical man.

"What is it?" asked Colonel Spinner.

"An object," said the medical man, "declared by the Beserians to have far greater healing powers than even a Gengali Shaman."

"If it will heal him, we will find it," said Hersen.

"Where is this Staff of the Serpent?" asked Spinner.

"With Abu Akhsa," said Hersen Expey, "the Chief of the Beserians. Give me Diego the Vetenan and a pair of swift camels, and I will find it."

Spinner looked at the LaFrentian, and then he turned to the medicine man. "I do not wish to see an imperial hero die here on my watch. What can be done to save him while Major Expey is out finding this—this Staff of the Serpent?"

"I will do everything in my powers to keep him alive for as long as I can, Colonel."

"How long?"

The medical man shook his head. "Not long. Maybe days, maybe less. Much more would take a miracle. Perhaps he is stronger than he looks." The physician frowned. "Only the Gods of the Plains know for certain, Colonel."

Spinner nodded. He looked down at Stanwich's pale, bearded face. His eyes were closed, hiding his famously bright blue-grey eyes. Even when his eyes were open, the fever had taken the brightness away.

"How long to reach Abu Akhsa?" asked Spinner, looking back at Hersen Expey.

"The Sharef told us, before his treachery, that we must ride for Ben Hamur, that the staff was taken, and that it rests in Ben Hamur," said Hersen.

"Ben Hamur is very far from here," said Spinner.

"Very likely too far," said the physician.

"If it can be done, I will ride for Ben Hamur," said Hersen. "But I will need Diego the Vetenan, for I do not know the way."

"Then ride for Ben Hamur," said Colonel Spinner. He turned to Rajat Rajatnamdar. "Major, see to it that Hersen Expey and Diego the Vetenan are given the two swiftest camels in Ben Gamurian. If we are to save Stanwich, and I do not for a moment know that it can be done, perhaps this is the way."

The physician nodded, keeping his doubts to himself, not wanting to crush the others' hope.

"Is there another way? Without finding this Staff in Ben Hamur?" asked Spinner.

"No, Colonel. He is far gone."

"We will find it," said Hersen Expey, the resolve hardening in his eyes. "We will ride like the wind across the sands."

"I bid you the speed of the Three Gods," said Spinner.

"Colonel, Miss Huntington." Hersen bowed and left.

Spinner looked at Hannah Huntington.

"Miss Huntington, for as long as we are here, this palace is yours. Know that troopers from my regiment will be assigned to protect you at all times. Know that the Sharef and his kind are spending a spell in the Ben Gamurian dungeon. No harm shall befall you again." As he spoke, Colonel Spinner kept his eyes upon hers.

She met his gaze, keeping her eyes upon his, believing his words.

CHAPTER 65
Ghani's Gift

Jemojeen's Camp, East of Ben Hamur
34th Day, Month of Wasura, 807
Anglian Calendar: March 27, 1879

"Listen, my lords," said Jemojeen.

Their gathering had already lasted for three hours, but each Kezelboj aristocrat still sat in the Grand Vizer's palatial tent, which spanned nearly the width of the Qhaliffa's Throne Room back in Saman Keer. Not one Kezelboj lord approved of Jemojeen's plans, but nor did any have the courage to disagree with Jemojeen openly in his tent. Over the past seven years, Jemojeen had broken what remained of the Kezelboj's political willpower. Jemojeen had found that a handful of strategic floggings, imprisonments, and public humiliations went a long way toward keeping the others frightened enough to stay quiet.

"My Erassians tell me that Abu Akhsa advances from the west with all of his force," he said.

Several of the Kezelboj lords nodded.

"Tell me, what do you think of that?" asked Jemojeen, drawing his eyes along the faces of the aristocrats.

As ordered, the Kezelboj had amassed their full forces west of the Approach of Alwaz. As commanded, they had begun the slow march west, toward the oasis of Ben Hamur, trailing their massive baggage trains and the artillery that had not been ordered out beyond the Ring River for a generation—the Great Guns of the Kezelboj. When out of earshot of the Grand Vizer or his men, they complained bitterly about the cost of the campaign that had barely begun, the price that they would come to bear far more than Jemojeen, the man who commanded them without sympathy.

A handful of priests sat in the tent as well. Jemojeen found that the priests scared the aristocrats. The priests could, with a signal, invoke the will of the

God of the Mountain and direct that will in various ingenious ways against the lords with whom Jemojeen was most displeased.

"Must I wait in silence?" he asked. "Have none of you anything to say?"

"I believe we will crush them," said Lord Cerelac, the southern lord. He was one of a handful of men who ruled over Sundar Dun, or at least the parts of Sundar Dun that the gangs did not control. Lord Cerelac's dark hair hung flat against his flat forehead, and his short legs appeared insufficient to support his abnormally long torso.

"That is much confidence from Sundar Dun. So, shall I count on your levies to fight in the vanguard, Lord Cerelac?" asked Jemojeen. "Perhaps first into Ben Hamur?"

Lord Cerelac blushed. No Kezelboj lord wanted his levies in the vanguard. The trick was to make a considerable amount of noise regarding loyalty and mobilization, but to sacrifice as few men as possible in any actual conflict. The levies came from each of their cities, and they would owe a stipend to the family of any man killed fighting the enemy.

"Grand Vizer, I have fewer men than some of the others."

"What concern is that of mine? I asked if you and your men wish to have the honor of the vanguard against the Beserian dogs. Should I say that Lord Cerelac and the men of Sundar Dun are afraid to fight the Beserians?"

"No, Grand Vizer, it is just that—"

"Just that what? You wish to appear helpful to the Qhaliffa but to not actually be helpful?"

"Of course not, Grand Vizer," said Lord Cerelac, his face flushing more deeply than before.

"I have little time for cowards and even less time for liars," said Jemojeen, sweeping his eyes across the frightened faces of the other Kezelboj lords arrayed before him. Each man looked down at the ground or otherwise avoided any prolonged eye contact with Jemojeen. If in accord with the ancient ways, Jemojeen had to show some semblance of deference and respect back in the gathering in Saman Keer, he had dropped any pretense of it now, out upon the sands with the might of the Qhaliffa's army at his command.

"Even if you wished to lead," said Jemojeen, "I would not let your men in the vanguard, especially if you would be leading them."

Lord Cerelac resisted the urge to say that he would not be leading his men. *That will only invite further allegations of cowardice. Perhaps, I should say I will lead them myself? But then I will have committed myself to battle, and I do not care to die. I do not fight well, and I never have.*

"Your Excellency, my men would be honored to fight in the vanguard," said Lord Cerelac, instead of speaking the truth.

"Honored? What do you know of honor?"

Lord Cerelac said nothing.

"Ganjar en Oxus will fight in the vanguard," said Lord Borjis, squinting out from his close-set eyes.

"Very well, Lord Borjis," said Jemojeen, nodding and finding Lord Borjis to be, as usual, a useful idiot. "Your men can bolster the cowards of Sundar Dun."

Several lords winced at the open insult. It was bold to speak in such a way in front of the assembled Kezelboj, even for Jemojeen.

"I cannot allow you to call me or my men cowards," said Lord Cerelac, his voice slightly quavering. *The other lords will mock me if I do not stand up for my house. They will say I have no honor. But what can I do against Jemojeen Jongdar?*

"Be silent, Lord Cerelac."

Jemojeen then looked into every Kezelboj lord's face, except for Lord Cerelac's. "Soon, we will have a weapon that will shatter the Beserians, and you will all be fighting with each other to seize the glory."

"What is this weapon?" asked Lord Borjis. The other lords leaned forward in anticipation. Lord Cerelac fumed.

"Shaheni!" shouted Jemojeen. Sipahi Shaheni entered the tent as if he had been waiting just outside the entrance.

"Yes, Your Excellency?"

"Bring them in."

"The Beserians, Your Excellency?"

"Yes," said Jemojeen, gesturing impatiently for Shaheni to hurry up.

The Sipahi Shaheni bowed and withdrew from the room. He returned, short minutes later, leading three young Beserians. They were short and lean, as was typical of their people. The Beserian walking in the lead had a handsome, sun-browned face and a prominent gap between the front two teeth of his upper rack. In his arms, he carried an object underneath a dark woolen blanket.

The Kezelboj lords rustled and shifted in their seats to obtain a better view of the approaching men. Most frowned as they saw the long, roughly woven head-scarves and loose tunics of the men. Few had seen such tribesmen up close with their own eyes. These men were clearly Beserians, sand people, the traditional enemy of the Qhaliffa, and of they themselves, the Kezelboj of the Great Mountain.

"My lords," said Jemojeen, stepping toward the approaching Beserians, but speaking to the Kezelboj. "There are times when great gifts come from unexpected places."

The Kezelboj shifted in their seats, unsure what the Beserian with the gap in his teeth might be carrying under the blanket.

"Eight hundred years ago," said Jemojeen, "the Staff of the Prophet was broken into three. One part, the Staff of the Ram, the Staff of our Qhaliffas, has hung above the throne in Saman Keer since the age of Mamet the First. Some have considered this to be merely a piece of carved cedarwood. Perhaps some of you have believed this, as I once did." Jemojeen paused again, sweeping his eyes along the nervous faces of the Kezelboj lords. "I tell you today that the Ram has awoken."

Jemojeen reached underneath his robe, withdrew a long wooden object, and lifted it above his head for all to see.

As one, the Kezelboj gazed up at the Staff of the Ram. The staff was as long as Jemojeen's arm, jagged on the bottom as if it had been snapped off of another piece of wood. On top of the staff, all of the Kezelboj could see the bulbous head carved into the shape of a mighty ram with the points of its curled horns protruding outward.

"Some of you may dismiss the power of this weapon." As he said the word "weapon," he stepped toward Lord Cerelac.

"Lord Cerelac, what do you know of this staff?"

Lord Cerelac did not answer but looked at Jemojeen with suspicious eyes beneath his black hair, cut straight across his forehead.

"Perhaps you think it an old relic?" Jemojeen stepped closer.

The wood of the staff in Jemojeen's right hand began to glow, starting near the nose of the ram and extending out into the horns. The light moved outward around the curl and toward the points like a sunrise advancing across the desert floor. It began as a slight yellowing of the wood and continued to deepen, spreading down the staff and growing both darker and brighter at once, like the color of molten gold.

The other Kezelboj lords shifted in their seats, watching with surprise and concern.

Lord Cerelac looked up. "What is this magic, Jemojeen?" His voice was something between a gasp and a croak.

The Grand Vizer smiled. "Tell me your plans for the battle ahead of us, Lord Cerelac."

Lord Cerelac began to tremble as if a man were grasping his shoulders and shaking him.

"I-I-I plan to tell you that I will lead my men into battle, but in truth, I intend to stay safely behind our forces."

"Honesty at last," said Jemojeen, smiling widely, revealing his teeth stained by years of strong tea and sweetened coffee. Lord Cerelac began to shake more violently, his stringy black hair flopping up and down, beneath his loosened red turban.

"And what will you instruct your men to do? What will you tell the commanders of your levies?"

Lord Cerelac gritted his teeth and strained the muscles in his neck as if lifting an immensely heavy weight. "I—"

"Share with us, Lord Cerelac. Do not hold back your words now."

The turban flew off of Lord Cerelac's head, his black hair flopping wildly.

The Ram's head blazed like pure gold, throwing off light like a sun. The Kezelboj lords and the young Beserians all turned their heads away from the brilliant light flowing out of the staff that had looked like old cedarwood only a minute before.

"I will tell them to slow their march so that the men of other lords reach the enemy first so that my men will see less fighting. *Ayeeeee.*" Lord Cerelac began to shudder. His face contorted, racked with pain.

"Thank you for your honesty, Lord Cerelac, and for confirming your treachery in front of your peers," said Jemojeen.

Lord Cerelac shook more violently.

Jemojeen stepped closer to him and brought the Ram's head down nearer to Lord Cerelac's body. Lord Cerelac shook with even more force, his body bending deeply in unnatural ways. The Kezelboj lords coughed as a vile smell entered their noses, the smell of Lord Cerelac's bowels emptying into his robes.

Two loud snaps struck the tent like rifle shots, and Lord Cerelac fell to the floor.

His legs had each broken, snapping like chicken bones. He lay on the ground, his upper body writhing, shaking so hard that his back was bouncing off of the tent floor.

"Goodbye, Lord Cerelac," said Jemojeen. "Behold the Staff of the Ram!" he shouted. The staff glowed even more brightly, and all of the Kezelboj lords hid their eyes behind their arms.

Lord Cerelac's back bent in two, breaking his spine like a chopped sapling. The shaking stopped, and Lord Cerelac lay dead at their feet, a grimace of terror frozen upon his face. The brightness of the staff receded, and the Kezelboj lords lowered their arms, revealing open mouths and terrified eyes.

"Now, young man, step forward," said Jemojeen, looking at the young Beserian in the center of the three.

The young Beserian with the handsome face stepped forward.

"You are called Ghani, of the Bazadak tribe, are you not?" asked Jemojeen, still holding the Staff of the Ram, which had given up its glowing brightness as swiftly as a desert sunset, reverting to its appearance of cedarwood.

"Yes," said the young Beserian, in poorly accented Qhaliffan. He glanced at the faces of the twenty or so Kezelboj lords sitting around him, looking at him with unfriendly eyes from the dim recesses of Jemojeen's vast tent.

"On behalf of His Majesty the Qhaliffa and on behalf of the Kezelboj of the Seven Cities, allow me to welcome you, Ghani of the Bazadaks."

"Thank you." Ghani stared at the staff in Jemojeen's hand, the staff that had just broken a man's legs and snapped a man's back without ever touching him. "Thank you, Your Excellency," Ghani added.

"You are well mannered for a Beserian," said Jemojeen. "And you are welcome. You will find that we Qhaliffans are fierce toward our enemies but kind toward our friends. As I am sure you can imagine, sometimes our enemies are living amongst us. Are they not?"

Jemojeen nodded toward Lord Cerelac's crumpled form as he looked at Ghani.

"Yes, Your Excellency," said Ghani.

"For example, I am sure that Hamid Salesi, the bearer of the Staff of Wisdom, did not expect a young tribesman like you to steal it from him."

Ghani's eyes widened. A small prickle of fear began to climb the back of his neck like a crawling insect.

"No, Your Excellency, he did not."

"How did you do it? How did you steal it from him?"

Ghani stared, fearing what response his answer might bring.

"Did you use physical violence? Did you beat the old man to take it from him?" asked Jemojeen.

Ghani did not answer.

"Let me see it," said Jemojeen.

Ghani looked at him with tentative eyes.

Jemojeen towered over him with his hand outstretched.

"Hand it to me," said Jemojeen.

Ghani obeyed, handing Jemojeen the object with the blanket still covering it.

Jemojeen grasped the object with his left hand, still holding the Staff of the Ram in his right hand.

"Behold, my lords," said Jemojeen, lifting the object, tilting it to one side and letting the woolen blanket slip off. In his left hand, the falling blanket revealed another staff, jagged on the top with the scaled coils of a serpent carved around it.

He lifted the staff so it was parallel with the other. The Staff of the Serpent, thinner and slightly longer than the Staff of the Ram, was knotted and colored differently, the color of olive wood.

"For the first time in forty generations, the Staff of Mamet and the Staff of Beseri are united." Jemojeen's voice grew louder and deeper like a building roar. "In my right hand, I hold the Staff of the First Qhaliffa, Mamet the Great, the founder of our people. We call it the Staff of the Ram, the Staff of Ruling. You have seen its power here this very day.

"In my left hand, behold the Staff of Beseri, the traitor that led so many of what were once *our* people out into the desert. This is the Staff of the Serpent, the Staff of Wisdom. This was never meant to be apart from the others. Today, they are reunited!"

As Jemojeen spoke, both of the staffs began to glow, the Staff of the Ram glowing in its golden yellow. The Staff of the Serpent started to turn silvery green, both dark and bright, the color of leaves in the moonlight.

"You have seen the power of the Ram. Now behold the power of the Staff of Wisdom."

The Staff of the Serpent glowed brighter as if seeking to surpass the glory of the Ram. Jemojeen closed his eyes, and Ghani and the other two Beserians gasped, crying out, grasping the temples on their heads and falling to their knees.

"Yes!" shouted Jemojeen. "Yes, yes! Tell me more!"

Ghani and the others shook their heads as if they were trying to free some animal gripping their scalps.

Then as quickly as it had begun, the men stopped shaking their heads, and the Staff of Wisdom stopped glowing. Its bright silvery green light vanished, and Jemojeen stood over the men, holding two wooden staffs, one in each hand.

The three young men gasped as if just released from a fierce grip.

"You see, my lords, I could have asked these men what their people are doing, or I could just pull their thoughts from their minds. Abu Akhsa plans to ride east with his host, the might of the assembled tribes. A young man travels with them, a man Abu Akhsa and Hamid Salesi believe is the young man of the prophecy, the promised one of the west, the one they foolishly call *Amahdi*."

Jemojeen lowered the Staffs of the Ram and the Serpent.

"From now onward, my lords, I shall see more than the thoughts of these mere boys. I shall see the thoughts of others too. My mind shall move across the sands like a bird in flight. Yes, this is what this piece of living wood shall bring us—wisdom surpassing all other understanding."

The Kezelboj lords looked at Jemojeen with awe and confusion. They had known the power of his informers, but this was something new and terrible. This was some kind of old and powerful magic that no man of the Great Mountain had seen since the days of the Prophet.

"Sipahi Shaheni, pay these Beserian traitors the price we agreed. Pay them their gold and remove them from my sight."

"But I did as you asked," said Ghani.

"Yes," said Jemojeen, "and you beat an old man and stole from your own people, all for some gold coins. Be gone before I become less kind."

Ghani backed away toward the tent's opening, his two frightened companions following him out into the night.

"My lords," said Jemojeen, "we now ride for Ben Hamur."

CHAPTER 66
An Absence Felt

Column of Abu Akhsa, West of Ben Hamur
34th Day, Month of Wasura, 807
Anglian Calendar: March 27, 1879

Jack Caldwell rode at Abu Akhsa's left. The intense heat beat down on a nearly windless day. Sweat dripped down the center of his back.

To Abu Akhsa's right, where Hamid Salesi would typically ride, there was an open space, a gap that all could see, a gap that showed that no man amongst the tribes could replace Hamid Salesi at Abu Akhsa's right hand. Since the night of the beating and the theft of the Staff of the Serpent, Hamid Salesi required a litter, carried by two long poles attached to four camels. It was covered by tent cloth that shaded the great older man from the blazing sun overhead.

On Abu Akhsa's order, ten swordsmen from his own Swordguard protected Hamid Salesi from sunrise to sunset and from dusk until dawn. They were taken from amongst all of the tribes, and no finer swordsmen existed in all of Beseria. The Swordguardsmen changed every eight hours, but a rotating group of ten swordsmen never left Hamid Salesi's side. Kaleem and Anil, Salesi's warrior-aged sons, rode far ahead, scouting Ben Hamur.

Behind Salesi's sons, Handsome Habeen Barcadey ranged ten to forty miles ahead of the main column, clearing the path of all threats. No women rode with Handsome Habeen, only five hundred warriors armed for war. Habeen commanded the vanguard, a vanguard of volunteers, chosen from amongst the tribes, meant to smash any mounted force they might encounter as they moved west to Ben Hamur. They were prepared for Erassians, for Demissaries, or any other swift riding force that the Qhaliffa might place in their way. Abu Akhsa did not doubt that the Qhaliffa stood behind the theft of the Staff of Wisdom.

Abu Akhsa did not hesitate to move rapidly and decisively east when news of the theft of the Staff of Wisdom reached his ears. He understood the power of the staff. Hamid Salesi had shown him the power too many times with the olive wood in his old wrinkled hands.

"It is one thing for a man to doubt who has never seen the power of the God of the Sands with his own eyes. It is another for one who has seen the power," he said.

Abu Akhsa did not doubt.

Since the staff was stolen, Jack could feel that the Beserian he had spoken without effort now became a challenge. He had to now think consciously about each word he used, and some words simply would not come, as if the filing cabinet in his mind that held the word was locked and refused to open. He had not conceded this to Abu Akhsa, but he had grown quieter with each passing day, hiding his disability. Abu Akhsa still included him on his War Council meetings each night with Azadeem, Bazadak, Celadeen, and the others.

"Amahdi," said Abu Akhsa, turning to look at Jack. "You have grown quiet as of late."

Jack looked at Abu Akhsa, concentrating to catch each of the leader's Beserian words.

"Yes, Abu Akhsa," said Jack.

"Why are you quiet, Amahdi?"

"As you see"—Jack meant to say saw—"when I ride here with Aurelio Demassi, the Vetenan, I not speak words of Beserians. Then the Staff of Wisdom and I speak, and I hear, and words come to my mind with easy."

Abu Akhsa looked at Jack with his eyebrows raised and concern in his eyes.

"Are the words leaving you now?"

Jack's cheeks flushed. He nodded.

"But you still can speak some words, words you could not speak before," said Abu Akhsa.

"Yes, but each day is harder. Harder to remember words, harder to say things in the right way."

"Come," said Abu Akhsa, "we must discuss this with Hamid Salesi." He turned his head to the south, where Azam Azadeem led a long column of his people. Abu Akhsa placed his fingers in his mouth and whistled to him.

"Azadeem!"

Azam Azadeem turned to Abu Akhsa. Abu Akhsa signaled to Azadeem. *Take the lead of the full column.* Azadeem nodded and cantered his camel toward Abu Akhsa. His tall, lean Azadeem warriors streamed out behind him.

"Azadeem, keep the column riding forward," said Abu Akhsa. "The Amahdi and I must be with Hamid Salesi for a time."

"Yes, Abu Akhsa," said Azadeem, looking at Jack with questioning eyes.

The Swordguardsmen of the sky-blue bands made way as Abu Akhsa and Jack Caldwell approached.

"Salesi," said Abu Akhsa, speaking softly.

The old man pulled back the curtain of his litter. The light cotton curtains shaded him from the sun, but on the hot windless day, there was no hiding from the heat, even in the shade.

"Salesi, something has happened."

Salesi looked into Abu Akhsa's face with tired, weary eyes. Since Ghani had struck him down and stolen the Staff of Wisdom, Hamid Salesi had appeared to age well beyond his wounds.

"Tell me," he said.

"The Amahdi," said Abu Akhsa. "He is losing our words, the words he spoke with perfection when you placed the Staff of the Serpent to his forehead."

"It is as we can expect," said Hamid Salesi. "The staff's power is leaving him." He nodded slowly, like a man of eighty, not seventy.

"What does that mean?" asked Abu Akhsa. His true question remained unspoken: *Does that mean he is not the Amahdi if his power comes from the Staff of Wisdom and not from within?*

Hamid Salesi heard the question within Abu Akhsa's question.

"The God of the Sands reveals Himself to us, but only as He chooses to reveal Himself, Abu Akhsa. We may have faith that He has placed a great deal of His power in the Staff of Wisdom. It is power meant to guide our people, but that does not stop an evil man from taking it to use the power for other purposes. The power is still there whether a righteous man holds the staff or an evil one. Beseri understood this. That was why Beseri fled into the desert in the beginning, so that Mamet could not take the staff for himself, so that Mamet could not consolidate the power into his own hands. He was dangerous enough with the Staff of Ruling, the Staff of the Ram."

Abu Akhsa nodded, sweating beneath his white headscarf. The sky-blue banner above Hamid Salesi's litter hung limp in the windless sky.

"Was that why Hom Hommuram rode away into the Hahst?"

"Perhaps," said Hamid Salesi.

Jack looked at them both, straining to understand each of the Beserian words the men spoke.

"Do you believe Ghani took the Staff of Wisdom to the Qhaliffa?" asked Abu Akhsa.

"Before Ghani stole the staff, I saw a man more dangerous than the Qhaliffa."

"Who is more dangerous than the Qhaliffa?"

"His minister—the one they call the Grand Vizer—his name is Jemojeen Jongdar. He holds the Staff of the Ram. The Ram has awakened in his hands."

"I thought the Qhaliffas had forgotten about the Staff of the Ram, that they lost the secrets of unlocking its power? Does it not hang upon a chain in the Throne Room in Saman Keer, old and without use?"

"It did. But it hangs there no longer. This Jemojeen has taken it from the Valley of Saman. He carries it into the desert now, preparing for battle. I believe the Year of the Prophecy has awakened all of the staffs, Abu Akhsa. Even the Serpent had grown stronger than I had ever remembered it before Ghani's betrayal."

"What will happen if Ghani takes him the Staff of Wisdom?"

Hamid Salesi shook his head.

"The power that is leaving us will be added unto him. The power that allowed the Amahdi to speak our words in an instant, as if he spoke them his entire life, now moves to the east. It is transferrable power that can accumulate in another. The power that had kept me younger than my years despite the hardness of my life, it can depart too. Look upon my face, Abu Akhsa, as you have done for much of your life. I have seen seventy-two years upon the sands. The staff kept me looking as if I had barely seen sixty-two years. Now my body moves in the other direction. With each passing day without the staff, I become an increasingly old man."

The concern in Abu Akhsa's face radiated out from his dark eyes, as his eyebrows arched, and he frowned deeply.

"What will happen if we do not retrieve the staff?"

Hamid Salesi nodded slowly. "The Amahdi will continue to return to his state when he met us, becoming more of a Westerner and less one of us. I will likely die. But there are far worse things than that. An evil man will hold all of the power you have seen in me over the long years, perhaps greater. And he will use that power far more than I ever have. He will combine it with the Staff of the Ram, and he will see things other men cannot. He will know and do things that make him like the God of the Sands."

"We will stop him," said Abu Akhsa.

"We must," said Hamid Salesi.

Jack Caldwell nodded, understanding only pieces, hearing only sounds where he used to hear words.

CHAPTER 67
Handsome Habeen Barcadey

The Wadi, West of Ben Hamur
34th Day, Month of Wasura, 807
Anglian Calendar: March 27, 1879

Selena Savanar gripped her three-barreled pistol, watching the Demissaries advance in a wide arc.

The center of the Demissary line was a wall of orange: orange turbans above orange capes, with orange pennants streaming off of thirteen-foot lances. Huge horses carried huge men, tall, long-limbed, broad-shouldered, and thickly muscular.

"They are coming for us, straight at us," said Selena, her words rapid and afraid.

"Yes," said Oapah, gripping two pistols of his own. Oapah inhaled through his nose and exhaled through his mouth, his massive chest rising and falling.

The fire Demissaries with their long guns still stood upon the wall of Ben Hamur. They had fired shots into the edges of the wadi throughout the night, keeping Selena, Oapah, Gulana, and the Beserians pinned down and awake. Little water remained in any of the waterskins.

"Ben Hamur is not rising against them," said Gulana. "Look, the Demissaries ride out against us, but Ben Hamur is silent, and men with long guns still stand upon the walls!"

Selena nodded. "The people can still rise, Gulana. The Demissaries have only just left through the gates. There is time."

"There is little time!" said Gulana, raising her voice. She had not slept. None of them had. Gulana was thirsty. They were all thirsty.

The archers of the Demissary left flank advanced—men in green turbans and green tunics with green fletching on their arrows.

Gulana looked at them and swallowed hard. She reached down and felt the small vial of anti-poison at her belt, the vial that would be the difference between burning from the inside, suffering unbearable pain, and merely having an arrow wound.

"Can you see him in the looking glass?" asked Selena.

"I am looking for him," said Gulana, the tube of her looking glass against her right eye.

"Find him," said Selena, looking at the enemy's left flank with naked eyes.

The Erassians rode in front of the Demissary archers in their usual inverted V formations, their orange-red hair blowing toward Selena, driven by an easterly wind. The wind came on strong ahead of the Demissaries, and the scent of sweating men and sweating horses filled Selena's nose, blown across the flat desert plain toward the tiny wadi that held the Beserians, Selena, Oapah, and Gulana. They were at the base of the vast bowl of Ben Hamur.

"I see him!" said Gulana.

Ozgar Ogatonia rode, unmarked by any distinguishing piece of clothing save for a large golden badge on his left breast, the emblem of a Demissary Captain. Ozgar was grim-faced, gripping his bow. If Gulana did not know better, she would think he rode to kill her.

"What will he do?" asked Gulana.

"I do not know," said Oapah.

"Trust in Ottovan. Trust in the Order. Trust that there is a plan," said Selena Savanar, who was not an Oath Holder of the Order, speaking to the Oath Holders of the Order lying against the wadi's edge on either side of her.

A long gun barrel boomed in the distance, belching black smoke.

"God of the Mountain and the Sands!" said Selena, tucking her chin into her chest, just below the wadi's edge. She felt the massive projectile tear through the air above her and smash into the far side of the wadi wall behind them, launching clods of earth into all of their backs.

Selena rose again, her eyes above the wadi's edge. "They must be running out of ammunition," she said.

"They never run out of ammunition," said Gulana.

Two more long guns thundered in the distance. The bullets kicked up more sand at the wadi's edge.

"Stay down!" said Oapah, pulling Selena down as he spoke, the force of his single hand irresistible on Selena's back.

More long guns fired in the distance.

The Beserians clung to their own long, thin rifles at the wadi's edge beneath the lip, offering no target to the Demissary long guns on the wall of Ben Hamur, but also unable to fire at the lancers advancing toward them.

"Get up and shoot!" shouted Oapah, his deep voice audible to all, despite the sand and soil exploding above all of their heads. "Shoot the lancers now!

They are trying to keep you down. If the lancers close the gap, we are all dead men!"

Kaleem looked at Oapah and then glanced above him at the lip of the wadi, a mere two feet above his head. His brother Anil was next to him. The Vetenan Aurelio Demassi crouched next to Anil. Kaleem hesitated.

Anil stood upon a small ledge, aimed his rifle over the wadi's edge, and fired. Oapah looked over the side through a looking glass.

"Well fired!" shouted Oapah as a lancer tumbled down off of his wounded horse, a splash of crimson on its chest. "Another!"

Anil slid back down onto the wadi floor, already beginning the slow and laborious process of muzzle-loading his Beserian rifle. For accurate, long-range fire, few weapons were better; for speed, few weapons were worse.

"You there! Fire! Fire now!" Oapah shouted again, staring his dark Omak-hosian eyes into Kaleem's face.

"You do not command me, dark man!" said Kaleem.

Oapah could see the fear in his eyes. Two more long gun bullets struck the back wall of the wadi. Kaleem flinched. Oapah did not.

"Get up!"

Aurelio Demassi climbed up, aimed, and fired over the edge before sliding back down.

Kaleem looked at the Vetenan, feeling the eyes of his men upon him. Surely, he could not hide from the long gun bullets while a foreigner stood and fired at the enemy. Fear and duty wrestled in his mind. He willed himself to stand. He placed his rifle stock on the edge of the wadi and raised his head above the berm. The charging Demissaries arrayed in front of him were beautiful and terrible at once, with lances at the ready, points gleaming and pennants flying. Their orange capes billowed out behind them, making each man look twice his actual size.

Kaleem Salesi, heir to Hamid Salesi, leader of the ancient Salesi tribe, ex-haled, training his rifle barrel on a massive Demissary with a huge square jaw, riding at the center of the formation. His finger touched the trigger, and then—

The long gun's boom reached the wadi as Kaleem's body dropped.

"Kaleem!" shouted Anil. "Brother!"

Kaleem's body fell limp, down onto his brother, spurting blood out of the jagged wound where there was once a head. Anil looked at the body that was his older brother and screamed.

"Fire! Avenge him!" shouted Aurelio Demassi, looking at the other Beseri-ans clutching their rifles as they crouched against the wadi wall.

They looked at Anil, holding his headless brother.

Aurelio saw the fear in their eyes. "Shoot them now," he said. "Or they will lance us all! Fire at them!"

The man closest to Aurelio Demassi did not move. He gripped his rifle with both hands, curling over it as if trying to wish the charging lancers away.

"Then give me your rifle!" shouted Demassi. He ripped it from the man's hands, rose, and fired a shot over the edge of the wadi. A Demissary lancer toppled onto the hard-packed sand, somersaulting behind the charging line.

Anil Salesi still clutched his brother's torso, blood from Kaleem's neck arteries still pumping crimson onto his tunic. Anil looked at Aurelio Demassi with wide, uncomprehending eyes.

Aurelio slipped back down as a series of long gun bullets struck the lip of the wadi.

"Anil, he is gone! Now get up and fight! Get up and show these Qhaliffans how Salesis fight! You are the heir now, *you!*"

Still, Anil did not move, clutching his brother as the other frightened Beserians clutched their rifles. These were young tribesmen who called themselves warriors, but they were not forged in twelve years of Demissary training. They were men who had raided since they were boys, fighting occasionally. They were good riders, good shooters, and brave young men at that, but they were not hardened to the point of disdaining death. They were not Demissaries.

Aurelio reached down and grabbed Anil by the fabric of his cotton tunic, lifting him. "Stand and kill them!"

Anil blinked as if clearing his eyes of a dream. He blinked again as Aurelio shook him harder. He looked Aurelio square in the eyes and shoved him in his chest, releasing Demassi's grip on his tunic. He reached down, grabbed his rifle, stood up at the wadi wall, and fired. He dropped down just as quickly and ran along the line of the men he now commanded.

Kaleem is gone. I am the Salesi here.

"Get up! Fire at them!" He slapped the face of the closest man. The man rose and fired his rifle. The next man rose and fired before Anil could strike him. The rest of the line rose, firing more bullets into the now charging cavalry.

The hooves of the charging Demissaries shook the ground as if the earth itself quaked.

"Prepare for the charge!" roared Oapah. "Blades, blades! They will fall into the wadi; cut them before they can gain their footing!"

Selena raised her face above the wadi's edge. The horsemen were now too close. The men with the long guns on the wall of Ben Hamur could no longer shoot at the wadi without hitting the backs of their own attacking Demissary riders.

Selena exhaled slowly, controlling her breathing. There was no surer way to miss a charging horseman than to let fear jostle her shooting hand. In thirty yards, they would be in range of her three-barreled pistols. The ground shook more violently. Her heart pounded in her chest like a drum.

Make each bullet count.

A scream rang out from the opposite direction, away from Ben Hamur, deafening and shrill. Selena jumped.

The scream roared as if the sands themselves were shouting. Selena turned and looked behind her, over the back edge of the wadi.

High above her, from one edge of the ridgeline to the other, a flood of horsemen galloped over the crest, charging down the slope, waving bared sabers.

"By the God of the Mountain and the Sands!" she shouted. "Oapah, Gulana, look!"

The two Oath Holders had already turned to see.

Aurelio Demassi saw them first among the Beserians. Tears welled in his eyes. He had never before seen a sight so beautiful. The morning sun struck the sabers as if each rider bore a blade of blazing light.

"Ayyyyyyyyyyyyyyyyyyyyyyyyy! Akhsa! Akhsa! Akhsa!"

And then Anil Salesi looked up to see the five hundred riders of Habeen Barcadey, charging forward to save his life.

Ozgar Ogatonia nocked an arrow in his double-arched bow. It would take more than a scream to scare him and his men.

These men charge me as if they are my enemy. I am not their enemy, and they are not mine. Nonetheless, any who come near me will meet their God.

Ozgar looked down at the fletching on the arrow. It was green, not black. *No poison, good. If I have to kill these warriors, it will be the clean way.* Ozgar's horse, like those of all of the Demissaries in his wing, was still moving forward at a smooth canter across the flat desert floor of the great bowl of Ben Hamur.

"Regular arrows," he called out. "Nock!"

The three dozen horse archers to his left all drew arrows from their quivers, sliding the thin wooden shafts from their leather cylinders and onto their bowstrings as easily at a canter as if the horses were standing still. The wadi lay close ahead.

Selena Savanar is in that valley. Ottovan was clear. I must dismount into there, and by the will of the God of the Mountain and the Sands, Oapah the Hohsa and Gulana of Nor Gandus will be there too. I will need them to defend Lady Savanar from this melee.

The Beserian saber men ahead did not canter; they charged downhill chanting their war cry, a war cry meant to make other men shudder.

I have no choice. Such are the vagaries of war and the twists of fate. There will be fewer of them to chant now.

"Pull!"

Ozgar's men pulled their double-arched bows as one, guiding their mounts with their knees as they had done ten thousand times before, since they had first chosen "archer" when they were young Demissaries in training, wide-eyed Bulbanian boys, still hoping to live through the next year of trials.

Ozgar eyed a Beserian chest for his arrow.

"Loose!"

A storm of arrows launched forward from the left flank of the attacking Demissary arc, the edge moving out to encircle the wadi that was their initial target, and that would meet head-on the charging half-thousand Beserian saber-men now. The arrows sailed up, arching like a shallow rainbow. Ozgar had ranged his own shaft as well as his men had. Even before the arrow struck, he knew what the result would be.

Ozgar was already shouting, "Nock!" again, when his arrow struck the chest of the Beserian tribesman one hundred and seventy yards ahead of him. The man stiffened and fell from his mount. Horses and men tumbled as the arrows found their marks.

"Pull!"

The Beserians were much closer now, less than one hundred yards.

"Loose!"

The angle on the arrows was shallower, and the arrows hit with greater impact as the Beserian tribesmen galloped into them.

Four dozen yards disappeared in a second as the horsemen galloped toward each other with hooves tearing into the sand.

"Scimitari!" shouted Ozgar. In a movement that most had mastered decades ago, each horse archer returned his bow to the leather sheath at his side and in the same action pulled the long, wide-bladed scimitarus from its scabbard, drawing their blades in unison in a terrible, beautiful, flashing sweep of Great Mountain steel.

The faces of the Beserian tribesmen grew large in the last seconds before impact, and their battle scream washed over Ozgar like a howling wind.

"Ayyyyyyyyyyyy!"

The Demissaries charged in silence in the final exhale before the crash. Ozgar leaned and slashed at the man on his right, knowing the man on his left would have to swing across his body to hit him. Bodies and horses blurred as they flew past each other, the horses instinctively looking for the way through to avoid a collision. Ozgar's blade struck a Beserian saber, and the sword handle shuddered in his hand. Then he was through the Beserian line. He allowed his horse to gallop another two dozen yards before reining her in. He turned and looked.

Both men and horses were down on the ground. Demissaries and Beserians alike writhed on the sand, lying next to splashes of crimson. One man, a Beserian, jumped up, gripping a rifle. He lowered it at Ozgar. There was no time to pull his bow from its sheath.

"Down that man!" he shouted.

Before he finished shouting, three arrows already sailed through the air. They struck the man in the knee, the chest, and the throat. He pulled the trigger as he fell.

The Beserians formed a line, preparing to charge back at them. The high ground was still ahead of the Demissaries, a mere three hundred yards away.

"To the high ground!" shouted Ozgar.

"Prepare to charge," shouted the leader of the Demissary Lancers, still facing downhill, toward the Beserians.

Ozgar looked, expecting to see Captain Ulgur Uggatar, the giant with the lantern jaw and the shoulders broader than two men. But he was not there.

Ottovan ordered him to stay in Ben Hamur, by the God of the Mountain and the Sands!

Lieutenant-Captain Bombar, Ulgur's second-in-command, stood at the center of the Lancer line. Ozgar outranked him.

Ottovan, you are brilliant.

"No! Do not charge! Do not charge!" shouted Ozgar, riding in front of the lancer line so they could not claim they had not heard him, and so they would have to ride through him if they wished to obey Lieutenant-Captain Bombar.

"Do not charge!" Ozgar shouted, clanking his saber against the lance points held at the ready above him. "To the high ground! To the high ground!" He stopped in front of Lieutenant-Captain Bombar.

"To the high ground, Lieutenant-Captain!"

"The enemy is before us!" shouted Bombar. The voice that came from his square jaw was deep and loud.

The man is a lancer, through and through, all aggression and stupidity.

"To the high ground. That is a command!" Captain Ozgar stared into the larger man's face.

Bombar blinked.

"To the high ground!" ordered Bombar in obedience, turning his horse toward the ridgeline behind him. The other lancers turned and followed him up the slope.

Ozgar turned back toward the Beserians. They were lined up, preparing to charge.

In that moment, Nemakar's long guns fired a volley from the wall of Ben Hamur into the backs of the Beserian line. Several Beserians flew off of their horses, dead before they hit the ground. Ozgar could see Beserians turning to glance behind them, toward the sound of the thundering long guns. Their shocking loudness shook the air, even at eight hundred yards.

The Beserian line shuddered, taking long gun fire behind them and seeing the Demissary archer line in front of them.

Ozgar returned his scimitarus to its scabbard and drew his bow, nocking an arrow from his quiver.

"Here they come!" he shouted, riding toward his men. "Bows! Bows! Bows!"

The archers returned their scimitari to their sheaths, pulling their bows back out of their leather holders.

"Nock!" shouted Ozgar, riding back down the line. "Prepare for rear shots! Rear shots!"

With arrows on bowstrings, his men turned their horses back toward the ridge, away from the Beserian's line.

"Ride!" shouted Ozgar.

His own Lieutenant-Captain, Adarak, and the archer lieutenants echoed his command. The line broke into a trot, then a canter, moving smoothly and in good order toward the rise and the ridgeline beyond.

Ozgar lingered, waiting for the Beserian line to launch forward. *Flee to the sides if you know what is good for you. Save yourselves for later. Save yourselves for the real fight. Jemojeen is coming, my friends. You can charge me, but I am not your enemy. If you charge me, I will have no choice but to strike you down.*

The Beserian line hesitated as the arrows began to strike.

Ozgar's men rode toward the ridge, away from the Beserians, shooting arrows back over their shoulders behind them.

"Flee," said Ozgar to himself, aloud and sitting astride his mount, a lone rider on the flat land beneath the slope to the ridge. "Flee to the flanks and live. You swordsmen could make the difference."

Ozgar looked to see a rider moving up and down the Beserian ranks, galloping north and then south, flinging his sword arm upward as if punctuating shouted orders.

The Demissary long guns sounded again in the distance, making the plain shudder with their distant boom. More Beserians were flung from their saddles, struck from behind by bullets one-third the size of a fist, as the arrows still struck them from the front.

"Riders of the van!" shouted Handsome Habeen Barcadey. "We will break into three! Left, center, and right, now!"

His group leaders echoed his command.

For another leader, possibly even Abu Akhsa, the men would have already begun breaking, riding frantically to escape the range of the long guns behind them and the archers in front of them. But for Habeen Barcadey, no man of the vanguard would be said to have been the one that broke first. The men volunteered for the van, but only those allowed by Habeen Barcadey had made the ride.

If Abu Akhsa alone could keep the tribal rivalries of the chiefs in line, none could hold their fiercest men together better than Habeen Barcadey. No man chosen wanted it said of him that he was selected in vain. If that meant death, such was the superior alternative to dishonor; such were the men of Barcadey's five hundred, hand-picked from amongst the tribes for this task. The line shuddered as the long guns did their fearsome work, but it did not break.

"Now!" Habeen charged southward to his left.

The center of the Beserian line surged after him, thundering toward the wadi where the Salesi scouts still crouched, taking shelter from the long guns.

The left wing galloped due south, taking a wide arc, riding parallel to the Demissary lines, charging for the open ground beyond. More long guns boomed from the wall of Ben Hamur. No Beserians fell as they galloped, moving laterally away from the shooters.

The right wing galloped due north.

Habeen looked for the wadi. In the plain, it was nearly hidden, but it was not far.

"They are coming at us!" shouted Selena Savanar, peeking her head up above the wadi's edge. "The Beserians are riding for us!"

Anil Salesi stuck his head up above the wadi. He waved his arms, watching Habeen Barcadey as he approached, little more than one hundred yards in front of him.

"Barcadey! Barcadey!"

The Beserians galloped straight for them, one hundred and fifty riders at least. They did not slow, charging directly at the wadi. A mere twenty yards before the wadi's edge, the outer edges of the line moved north and south, galloping parallel to the open ditch before them, then curving westward around it, like the double arcs of a Demissary bow.

Those in the center of the line, including Habeen Barcadey himself, reined in their horses on the ditch's edge. Barcadey looked down at the line of Beserians and the three others, Oapah, the Hohsa, Gulana of Nor Gandus, and Selena Savanar. His eyes widened as if they were a threat. Oapah aimed his flare pistol into Barcadey's face.

"They are on our side!" shouted Anil. "This is Selena Savanar, of House Savanar, daughter of the one who was burned! She seeks the Staff of Wisdom. She seeks my father!"

Two long guns thundered in the distance. One of the enormous bullets ripped past Habeen Barcadey's headscarf, tearing it from his head.

"Get down, or they will kill you," said Oapah.

Habeen Barcadey did not move. "Get up, and you will ride away with us. Stay crouched in this hole, and you will die." Before he finished speaking, Habeen Barcadey was already looking into the distance. "The Demissaries ride for us now. They are coming down from the ridge. Get up. Those of you without mounts, get on ours. You, Lady Savanar, you ride with me."

"No," said Oapah, "I do not know this man."

"He is Habeen Barcadey!" said Anil.

"I do not know him either," said Gulana.

"I ride with this man," said Selena, grasping the edge of the wadi with her hands and pushing herself up. Habeen Barcadey grasped her arm with his right hand and pulled her up onto his saddle in front of him, as easily as if she were a child.

"Ride at our sides," said Barcadey.

Two of Barcadey's men brought horses forward that had lost their riders. Oapah and Gulana leaped up and mounted them. Anil, Demassi, and other Beserians had already mounted the camels in the wadi and now rode out the sides. Others leaped up to join Barcadey's Beserians that had formed on the far side of the wadi, the side where the grade was such that a man could ride up out of the ditch.

Habeen kicked his horse's flanks, and the stallion launched southward. Selena looked to the west as the wind whipped her face. She could not remember when she had last felt the back of a horse between her legs, and never could she remember riding a horse such as this. It felt as if she and Habeen were flying across the sands, so fast were they galloping. Selena smiled in exhilaration as the swift, powerful horse carried them away from the wadi, the solid chest of Habeen Barcadey firmly against her back.

The Demissary line surged forward toward them, with the Erassians on the far edges, the bowmen on the left flank, the lancers in the center, and on the right flank, closest to them, the men in the purple turbans, the turbans of the fire Demissaries charging forward.

Habeen saw the fire Demissaries and kicked the flanks of his stallion harder.

"Hold on, Lady Savanar," he said.

The stallion drew from an even deeper reservoir of speed, racing toward the open desert to the south, away from the Demissary guns.

CHAPTER 68
The Arc of the Ram

The Hahst
1st Day, Month of Saman, 807
Anglian Calendar: April 15, 1879

Peter Harmon stood, with his hand above his eyes, looking for the curve he had already traced for the five miles in from the edge of the Hahst, moving eastward.

Sinking sands lay to the left, to the right, and in front of him. The arc upon which he now stood was no more than five or six feet across. Upon that arc, it was as if they walked upon solid rock. Off of the arc, they would sink as surely as stones swallowed by the sea.

Peter's camel tugged on the head rope.

"Easy, easy girl," he said, continuing to look forward, seeking the curve of the arc in his mind. Don Mazarian walked his camel behind him, with Sergeant Barnes behind him. The nine other Macmenians walked their camels in a line behind Sergeant Barnes.

Peter's camel tugged harder and then roared.

"What is it?" asked Peter, looking up from the arc to his camel. The other camels began to emulate Peter's own, roaring their disapproval and straining to retreat the way that they had come, back to the west.

"What is it?" asked Peter again, meeting eyes with Don Mazarian.

"They can sense it," said Don Mazarian.

"Sense what?" asked Barnes.

"The storm," said Don Mazarian.

"What storm?" asked Peter.

"It is not merely sinking sands that claim men in the Hahst. Behold," said Don Mazarian, pointing to the east.

Peter looked east, into the wind. On the horizon, clouds rose from the desert floor to high up in the sky, miles from bottom to top. Peter kept his gaze upon the clouds. They rumbled upward, growing larger, like giant skyborne mushrooms giving birth to more mushrooms, each expanding higher toward the heavens, and then collapsing back into each other.

"What is it?" asked Peter.

"Sandstorm, a sandstorm of the Hahst, stronger than all others."

The camels roared louder.

"What do we do?" asked Peter.

"We are five miles in, standing upon the path. There is nothing we can do. We cannot retrace our steps all of the way. The storm will be upon us."

Peter looked behind them to the west. Ahead of the storm, the winds drove the sands so that the path of their footprints and those of their camels behind them were already disappearing.

"Can we seek cover?" asked Peter.

"There is no cover in the Hahst," said Don Mazarian, shaking his head.

"How about ahead?" asked Peter.

"Yes, if we find the Valley of Hom Hommuram, if it indeed exists, we will find cover there."

"It exists," said Peter.

The winds around them began to howl, picking up sand and pelting it against the exposed skin of Peter's face and hands. Peter pulled his veil up over his eyes. His cow camel pulled harder against her head rope.

"You tell me, Don Mazarian. You are the veteran of these sands. Do we hunker down here?"

"There is no other way," said Don Mazarian, nearly shouting through his veil, hurling his words against the rising wind that whisked them away.

"Down," ordered Peter, shouting the Macmenian command into his camel's ear. He pulled down on the head rope as he shouted.

The wind roared more fiercely, taking away all other sounds. Peter looked to the east. There was now nothing but the storm in front of him. He could not see over it, around it, or through it. He saw only the swirling sands surging inward and then outward, up and down, tumbling violently like angry, airborne ocean waves that stretched a mile up into the sky.

"Stay low," shouted Don Mazarian, mere inches from Peter's face.

"What?" shouted Peter.

"Stay low!"

"I cannot hear you!"

"Get down!" screamed Don Mazarian, jamming his finger down to the ground. "And stay against your camel!" Don Mazarian pointed at Peter's camel.

Peter crouched down.

Don Mazarian nuzzled up against his own camel, using the camel's body to shield him from the east, a small living wall against the fury of the swirling sands. Peter saw that Barnes was doing the same thing, only feet away from him.

The true front of the storm now raged a mere half-mile away, moving eighty or ninety miles per hour, perhaps faster. Peter looked eastward in awe. The winds grew stronger and louder than he ever believed wind could become. The winds pulled at Peter's body and at every piece of clothing he wore, pushing him toward the west, as if to expel him from the Hahst, yanking him upward, as if to throw him into the sky. Peter looked up, and the storm itself was nearly directly overhead, a towering, swirling madness of sand.

Peter looked up to see Don Mazarian's veiled face. Don Mazarian shouted something over the back of his crouching, terrified camel.

Peter could hear nothing. Don Mazarian rose, crawling over his camel. He pulled a rope from behind him, a line that was attached to both him and his camel. He tied it to Peter's leg and slung it through Peter's belt, working silently in the raging fury all around them. Then he tied the same rope to Peter's camel saddle.

And then all vision vanished, leaving only a stinging, howling swirl of sand, taking away all sight, all sound, all sense of anything save for the raging, roaring, deafening wind, and its desire to lift them up, up, up.

— PART V —
THE USURPER'S WAR

CHAPTER 69
An Ugly Smell

South of Ben Hamur
49th Day, Month of Wasura, 807
Anglian Calendar: April 11, 1879

Hersen Expey could smell the fire before he could see the smoke, and long before he could see the mudbrick walls of Ben Hamur or the Sharef's House on its lone hill inside of the inner stone walls. He could smell something else as well, a smell he had come to know as a LaFrentian Legionnaire, but a smell to which he had never become accustomed—the smell of burning flesh.

"Those are not cooking fires," said Diego.

"No, they are not," said Hersen, pulling his riding cloak over his mouth and nose to mask the smell. The burning humans did not smell like burning meat. They smelled like burning hair, blood, clothes, organs, and leather—a mix of sulfur, sickly sweetness, and coppery metal as the mixture burned.

"Bodies," said Diego.

Hersen nodded.

They were alone on the vast plain, nearly over the rim that would bring them down into the great bowl-like descent down to Ben Hamur. Their camels noticed the smell as well, grunting, wrinkling their noses, and raising their heads into the air.

They crested the rise, and neither man was prepared for what lay before their eyes. Still miles away at the base of the plain, Ben Hamur was aflame.

Four dozen fires—maybe more—spewed smoke into the air, partially obscuring the view of the House of the Sharef on the top of the oasis's lone hill.

The fire, however, had at least given them a warning.

To the west of Ben Hamur, an ocean of men advanced like a tide, more than ten thousand, many of whom were mounted. All advanced toward the east, toward Ben Hamur, like dark water advancing across the sands of a beach.

To the east of Ben Hamur, an even larger force advanced. Hersen's eyes moved to a dozen points of light on the northeastern horizon, bright as fires but the wrong color. They were bronze, reflecting the sunlight overhead. They were the artillery barrels of massive cannons, demonstrably huge even from miles away.

"What is that?" asked Hersen, already knowing the answer in his mind.

As he asked, the earth shook as fiercely as if a quaking fault had just lurched under the sands. The barrels of the artillery flashed, belching smoke. A great thunder rumbled in the distance, rising to Hersen and Diego, mounted upon their camels. The men operating the massive bronze guns looked tiny as ants.

"Great guns," said Diego. "Those are the Great Guns of the Kezelboj, the most frightening weapons of the lords of the Seven Cities."

"How do they move them across the desert? Those barrels alone must weigh thousands of pounds, tens of thousands!"

"Look behind them," said Diego. "The pachyrms."

Hersen looked past the guns, seeing the enormous pachyrms, single-horned animals with rough, grey-leathery hides, and capable of weighing twenty thousand pounds. Hersen thought they were massive stones, but they were living stones, a time and a half at the shoulder as tall as a standing man. Each of their four legs weighed as much as a dozen men, and their thick torsos stretched back for fifteen feet or more.

Hersen raised his looking glass for a better look. Each pachyrm carried a man riding behind its neck, carrying a goad. For each of the great bronze cannons, there were four pachyrms to pull both the massive cannon itself and its colossal ammunition wagon, wide and deep enough to hold the hundred-pound solid shot and array of explosive cannonballs that the Great Guns fired.

Another bronze gun fired in the distance, shaking first the air and then the ground.

Hersen's eyes shifted to Ben Hamur. A portion of the oasis exploded, sending mudbricks and roof tiles hundreds of yards up into the air.

"That is what it looks like when they strike," said Diego.

"By the Three Gods," said Hersen, marveling at the guns' power. He had seen plenty of artillery fire in the LaFrentian Legion, but never from cannons like these.

Another of the Great Guns fired from the eastern position. Another section of Ben Hamur shattered, blowing apart like pottery struck by a hurled boulder.

"That is not an expeditionary force," said Diego. "That is the assembled might of the Qhaliffa. I have never seen such an army."

Hersen's looking glass followed the line of the Qhaliffan force, advancing in a vast crescent and moving toward Ben Hamur like a scythe. On the edges, Hersen could pick out the Erassian cavalry—lean, orange-haired horsemen riding swiftly and carrying javelins.

"Who are those on the flanks?"

"Erassian scouts," said Diego.

Hersen nodded. "And closer in?"

"Demissaries." Diego's voice changed when he said the word.

Hersen took the Demissaries into the lens of his eyeglass. They rode erect, in bright uniforms upon large, strong-looking horses. A third of the line wore purple turbans, a third wore orange, and the final third wore green.

"Which are the archers, the men with the poison arrows?"

"Green," said Diego.

"That means gunmen are purple," said Hersen, looking through his hand-held telescope.

"Yes," said Diego.

"The lancers wear orange," said Hersen, watching the men advance with their thirteen-foot lances, orange pennants snapping in the wind. "Those are large horses for desert fighters," he said.

"They ride camels for the long journeys," said Diego, "They ride those big warhorses when they intend only to fight, not roam."

Hersen saw in his looking glass how much larger the Demissary chargers were than the Erassian sand horses. The Erassian mounts looked like ponies next to the others.

Dozens of bright flags rose above the advancing men. "What are all of those banners?"

"One for each of the Kezelboj houses, some from each of the Seven Cities."

Hersen fixed his eye on a single black banner, taut in the wind with markings of gold. It was ten times larger than any of the other flags, stretching what looked like dozens of feet outward, affixed to an enormous flagstaff.

"The black one, that is the Qhaliffa's, yes?" asked Hersen.

"Yes."

Hersen turned his telescope again to the west, to the advancing Beserians. Above them, sky-blue banners blew eastward, as if pointing to the Seven Cities. The banner lacked any ornamentation beyond its color, the color of the desert sky on a bright, sun-drenched day.

"That is Abu Akhsa," said Diego.

"Those bastards," said Hersen, thinking of Stanwich's hand and how feverish he had been when he last saw him in his bed in Ben Gamurian. Perhaps the very warrior who had struck Stanwich was riding amid the horde up ahead.

"I hope one of those cannons hits them, but not the one who cut Stanwich. I remember his face, the face like a jackal. I am going to find that man, and I am going to kill him myself."

Hersen and Diego rode forward, two men riding toward two groups of thousands and a burning oasis between them.

"Remember, Major. We seek the Staff of Wisdom, not vengeance. Only the staff will heal Stanwich."

Hersen nodded. Diego was correct. But his mind still thought of vengeance against the one who looked like a jackal.

CHAPTER 70
A Sharef's Courage

Oasis of Ben Hamur
48th Day, Month of Wasura, 807
Anglian Calendar: April 10, 1879
One Day Earlier

Ulgur Uggatar pounded on the Sharef's bedroom door.

"Get up!"

No response came from the room.

Ulgur nodded to the lancers in orange turbans at his side.

They nodded back: six tall, thick-boned men with neck muscles that bulged above the rim of their tunics. They swung the heavy battering ram back and hurled it forward against the heavy wooden door. The iron tip of the ram punched through the door as easily as if it were made of palm fronds, ripping the wood apart as it moved through. The ram shattered the crossbar that bolstered the door. The front two lancers kicked in the splintered remains.

Ulgur stepped past them with his scimitarus drawn.

Two of the Sharef's guardsmen stood at the foot of the bed, grasping the shafts of short spears.

"Halt," shouted the guard on the left.

Ulgur stepped forward, rising to his full height. He towered over the guardsmen, neither of whom were large men.

"Step aside," he said, his voice a deep growl.

"You have no right to enter the Sharef's room!" said the same guardsman, lowering his spear. He stepped sideways, coming closer to the other guard and blocking Ulgur's path to the Sharef's bed. Closed curtains shielded the bed from Ulgur's view.

The other lancers followed Ulgur into the room and fanned out behind him, making a human wall of beige tunics, orange turbans, and grim, killers' faces. All of the lancers carried long, curved, wide-bladed scimitari in their hands.

Ulgur lurched forward, swift as an Erassian despite his height and size. The guardsmen stepped forward, raising their spears, but not quickly enough. Ulgur's scimitarus caught the first man cleanly at the throat, taking his head off like a melon from a post.

The second man overcompensated, lifting his spearpoint high as Ulgur swung his blade low from the other side, taking out the man's left knee and cutting off the lower half of the man's leg. As the guardsman dropped, the second blow, swung from top to bottom, nearly cleaved him in two.

Ulgur grunted as his heart pounded with satisfaction. He stepped forward and threw open the curtain. The considerable girth of the Sharef of Ben Hamur lay on the bed before him. The Sharef looked up at him with fearful eyes, the sheet pulled up to his chin.

"By the Orders of the Grand Vizer, get up."

The Sharef did not move, speechless. His eyes moved past Ulgur to his butchered guards on the floor.

"Assist him with his task," said Ulgur. The six lancers walked forward, ripping back the Sharef's sheets and revealing his grotesque fatness. He squealed like an oversized rodent.

The men grabbed him and, with some effort, lifted him, carrying him like the battering ram they had just left outside his bedroom door.

"I can walk," he said, nearly breathless with fear.

Ulgur nodded.

The lancers dropped him, and half of his body landed on his soft mattress. The other half landed on the stone floor below. The Sharef winced with pain.

"Then walk," said Ulgur.

The Sharef of Ben Hamur, Ayzah Bin-Ayawad, looked up at the six massive men and their even larger leader. *Yes, Ottovan told me these men would come. I can be brave. This is what it will take for my people to rise. But I can play my role, and by the blessings of the God of the Sands, both I and my house might live.*

"Get up, fat man," said Ulgur, his voice as compassionate as a bear's growl.

Ayzah Bin-Ayawad turned his fat body sideways, like a porpoise on a beach as he gained enough momentum to sit up.

The six lancers and their leader looked down at him as if they were about to carve him up.

The Sharef, with effort, planted an arm and a knee and rose, exposing his private parts beneath his sleeping robe to the men looking down at him. He flushed with embarrassment. From a knee, he rose to his full height. Standing up, he was only as tall as the lowest shoulder of the standing lancers and was barely up to the mid-chest of Ulgur Uggatar, their captain.

You have no right to be here, said the Sharef in his mind, repeating the words he had prepared. But the words would not come. He looked down at the severed head of his guardsman, and fear grabbed his tongue as securely as a pair of iron tongs.

"Let's go," said Ulgur.

They walked forward, stepping over the dead bodies of the two guardsmen the Sharef had known for their entire adult lives. He knew their wives and their children, and these men had cut them down as if they were wild dogs.

Be brave. Your people depend upon you. They will not rise without your guidance. If you want to avenge those men, be brave.

They walked out onto the open ledge of the north-facing stone veranda, the place from which the Sharef could view all of his oasis below him. From here he could address the assembled people as he did several times a year, on the days of rest each season, when all ceased working to worship and give thanks to the God of the Mountain and the Sands.

As they walked out into the open in the early dawn air, Ayzah Bin-Ayawad felt a chill, the coldness biting into his skin that was covered by no more than a silk sleeping robe. The thinness of the gown made his body look even fatter than his regular day robes.

Ayzah looked down and froze.

Beneath him, hundreds of his people had assembled in the predawn cold. Tied to posts in the center were a dozen or so of his men, including guardsmen and Dungar Bin-Guttar, his captain of the guards.

"People of Ben Hamur," shouted Ulgur, addressing the crowd, "you do not serve this man." Ulgur pointed to the fat man, Ayzah Bin-Ayawad, Sharef of Ben Hamur. "No. You serve the Qhaliffa of the Seven Cities and his Grand Vizer, Jemojeen Jongdar."

"What is this?" asked the Sharef, pursing his lips, making him look more ratlike than usual.

"These men helped a heretic and enemy of the Qhaliffa escape from this oasis!" thundered Ulgur, his eyes still on the crowd, "Now, they will pay the price."

Despite there being hundreds of men, women, and even children, the crowd below waited in utter silence in the cold dawn air.

"Execute them!" roared Ulgur.

As one, men in orange turbans with drawn swords stepped out from the line of lancers separating the crowd of Ben Hamurians from the guardsmen lashed to the posts.

A woman screamed, and then another. "No! That is my husband! That is my son! Stop!"

The lancers advanced regardless, grim-faced men baring the cold, curved steel of their scimitari swords.

"What are you doing?" asked the Sharef. "I demand to see Ottovan Fanfar! I demand to see your commander! You have no right to do this!"

"Silence that fat rat," said Ulgur.

A lancer struck Ayzah Bin-Ayawad, Sharef of Ben Hamur, in his left side, knocking the breath out of him. The Sharef collapsed in a heap onto the cold stone beneath him. Another lancer kicked him in the stomach, harder than the Sharef thought a human could kick.

Ayzah Bin-Ayawad could not see what was happening when the crowd began to wail. He forced himself up, gasping for air. His tears blurred his eyes, involuntary from the pain. He opened his mouth, but no air came into his lungs. He opened and closed his mouth with panic in his eyes.

As the air came into his lungs, at last, the sounds of his people's agony washed over him, entering his ears and searing them.

Far below him, in the open square beneath the veranda, his guardsmen were slumped on the ground, dead. But the orange-turbaned Demissaries stood above them, still swinging their large swords, hacking them to pieces. The Demissaries chopped like crazed butchers, cutting hands from limp arms, severing forearms from elbows, removing legs at the knee, and still chopping, chopping, chopping. The blood sprayed over the execution posts, the bodies of the dead, and the dirt beneath, covering the Demissaries as they continued to hack.

Ayzah Bin-Ayawad watched with wide, horrified eyes as a large Demissary took Dungar Bin-Guttar's head and kicked it across the dirt, sending it toward the crowd, laughing as he did so.

The first stone hit the laughing Demissary squarely in his big, bearded jaw.

He staggered backward, no longer laughing. The second and third stones struck him in the chest and the head. Through his pain and his horror, Ayzah Bin-Ayawad saw the rocks begin to fly, knowing that stone-slinging was not a lost art amongst his people.

The slingers ran along the rooftops, a handful at first, flinging their stones like missiles at the men in the orange turbans.

"Get them off of there!" Shouted Ulgur to the men with him on the Sharef's veranda. "Get those slingers, now!" Ulgur looked around, realizing that he was utterly without support from any bowmen or fire Demissaries. All of the archers and fire Demissaries were out beyond the walls hunting down the Beserians and Selena Savanar.

Ulgur's lancers ran across the stone veranda and down the long stairs. Seventy-five feet below them, the crowd of screaming women, shouting men and wailing children had not yet dispersed, despite the lancers beginning to slash at them with their scimitari. The slingers on the rooftops continued flinging their stones down at the lancers. Ulgur saw two of his lancers down, and they were not moving.

"Get up!" he barked at Ayzah Bin-Ayawad, pulling him up to his feet. The Sharef cringed from the pain in his side.

The Sharef stood, slumping heavily toward the flat, cold stones of the veranda beneath him. Despite his enormous girth, Ulgur held him up easily.

"Order those men to cease. Order them to put down their stones."

"I will not," said the Sharef, looking up at the giant Demissary.

"What did you say, fat man?"

"I said." The Sharef swallowed hard. "I said that I will not."

"Do it," said Ulgur, shaking Ayzah Bin-Ayawad, Sharef of Ben Hamur.

"No."

"Do it!" said Ulgur.

"I will not!" shouted the Sharef, finding greater courage with each denial of the Demissary's demands.

"Then you will die," said Ulgur.

The Sharef stared into Ulgur's face. It was said before this day that Ayzah Bin-Ayawad had led a cowardly life. But all remembered he was not a coward at this moment, the moment that in the history of Ben Hamur and the history of the Ayawads of the Sand Sea was to matter more than any other.

Ulgur lifted Ayzah Bin-Ayawad over his head, all three hundred and ninety pounds of him, and threw him like a giant sack of yams over the edge of the veranda and down onto the open space beneath. The great man fell to his death in front of all of the assembled masses on the square below. Cowardly and self-indulgent in life, he may have been, but his family had ruled the people of Ben Hamur for five hundred years, and he was the last male of his line.

As he flew through the air, many in the crowd stopped what they were doing. They stopped shouting and stopped fighting against the Demissary Lancers that slashed back at them with their scimitari swords.

For a momentous several seconds, the slingers on the rooftops stopped loading the smooth, egg-sized stones into their slings and watched as their leader fell to his death. Ayzah Bin-Ayawad did not shriek or scream as he fell. He flew through the air in silence, as if at peace with his decision to resist in the last moment by which he could be judged in this life under the heavens.

He landed heavily, falling seventy-five feet in the air, in the position from which he would never arise. He landed on his stomach and his face, like a great sea-mammal dropped against a rock. He landed hard, with a sickening crunch.

His bones smashed, his body nonetheless shuddered, still alive for several agonizing seconds as the blood from his crushed organs flooded his torso from the inside, as the pain embraced him like an all-encompassing blanket. Yet he did not make a sound from his throat.

The people of Ben Hamur stared up at the giant Demissary that had just thrown their Sharef from the veranda he used to address them, the terrace from which he would announce the Holy Holidays, and from which he would declare how much bread and dates he would give to the people from his personal reserve. The people stared, and then as one, they rose, shouting as they charged.

The first to strike the Demissary line were cut down like sheep, as were the second and even the third lines of people. But the fourth line managed to grab hold of legs and arms. The fifth line managed to strike a fist or a foot into the faces and the heads and the ears and the groins of the Demissaries whose arms and legs were held by others. The sixth row of men and women engulfed the Demissary line like ants upon a group of giant wounded beetles, biting, kicking, punching, and stabbing with small cooking and eating utensils.

The uprising of the people of Ben Hamur began in this way.

CHAPTER 71
Barcadey Returns

The Assembled Tribes of Beseria, West of Ben Hamur
48th Day, Month of Wasura, 807
Anglian Calendar: April 10, 1879

"There they are," said Jack.

His Beserian accent had fallen off, deprived of the magic of the Staff of the Serpent. But in the past weeks, he had relearned some of what he had lost, as if remembering the details of a place he had once known in early childhood but had not known since. If he relaxed his mind and stopped straining, he could grasp pieces, as if fumbling around in a dark coat closet and knowing the right fabric by its feel alone.

"Where?" said Abu Akhsa. The leader had watched Jack with some caution as he regressed.

"There," said Jack, pointing out into the moonlit desert.

The heat had risen in the recent days, and they had begun moving at dusk, continuing on an hour after the dawn. It was several hours past midnight when Jack heard the low, distant rumble. That had changed too since the staff had departed. He could hear things he had not heard before; he could see things before other men, including Beserians, who themselves could see things on the desert that others, who were not Beserians, could not.

Abu Akhsa stared. He had observed the changes in Jack. He had seen him learn the language, almost like an ordinary man, but not quite. He had seen the changes in his hearing and his sight. So too had Jack begun to smell things, pulling scents off of the desert sky more like a camel than like a man.

"There," repeated Jack.

And then Abu Akhsa heard the faint thundering of mounted camels galloping. Abu Akhsa, at the front of the column, was only fifteen miles from Ben Hamur, deeper into the lands of the Qhaliffa than he had ridden in long years.

"Riders!" shouted a sentry.

"Riders!" shouted another.

Abu Akhsa strained his eyes, staring eastward.

The line emerged as a shimmer of metal, flashing in the moonlight, and then the dark line appeared, riding fast toward them.

"They are ours," said Jack. "Habeen Barcadey returns."

"How do you know?" asked Abu Akhsa, thinking of his largely indefensible column of women, children, old men, and herds of goats and sheep that extended for miles out behind them.

"I can see them," said Jack.

For long moments, Abu Akhsa stared out into the silvery sands as his grey horse edged him ever closer to Ben Hamur. He now rode at the front of the largest column of Beserians since Beseri himself led his followers out from the Ring River and the Great Mountain. Abu Akhsa's hand twitched on his saber's handle.

"They are ours!" shouted the sentry.

"Habeen Barcadey returns! He returns with the five hundred!"

A cheer rose from the warriors leading the column. Abu Akhsa looked at Jack, wondering how he saw things before the sentries, young men picked from amongst the warriors and amongst the tribes for their superior vision.

"Many have died," said Jack. "The five hundred are more like three hundred."

Abu Akhsa stared eastward, hoping that Jack was wrong, but sensing in his stomach that he was not. The riders came closer, a line of darkness advancing toward them across the hard-packed desert sands. They were only a few miles from the ridge that led down the great bowl into Ben Hamur.

"Do you see Handsome Habeen?"

"Yes," said Jack. "Barcadey leads them from the center."

Abu Akhsa nodded, unable to distinguish any of the riders from any of the others.

"There are others with him, others who were not with him when he departed with his five hundred."

"What others?"

"I do not know them. I have not seen them before."

"Describe them."

"There is a giant Omakhosian, nearly black of face, and broad of shoulder. He is a huge man, broader than Bazak Bazadak, broad enough to make Habeen Barcadey look small."

Abu Akhsa continued to stare eastward, seeing nothing but a line of horse and camel riders rushing forward across the sand plain.

"There is another. A woman. She is large, like a man. She has the face of a warrior."

Abu Akhsa continued to stare into the desert, failing to see these things that Jack Caldwell could see as if he were viewing it with a looking glass in the light of the morning sun. Abu Akhsa did not reach for his looking glass, knowing it would not work correctly in the weak light of the moon.

"Aurelio Demassi and Anil Salesi are alive," said Jack.

"But Kaleem is not," said a voice.

Abu Akhsa and Jack Caldwell both turned toward the voice.

"Salesi," said Abu Akhsa, his eyes widening. There was as much surprise in his voice as in his eyes. Hamid Salesi had not ridden with them at the front of the column since Ghani had attacked him in his tent, weeks before.

Salesi's eyes glistened in the moonlight. "My son has died," he said.

"He may be with the riders," said Abu Akhsa.

"He has fallen," said Hamid Salesi. "I know it to be so. The staff may be gone, but its power lingers in me after holding it for so long. I have seen it in my mind."

Abu Akhsa had known Hamid Salesi long enough to know that when he said such a thing, he had indeed seen it, and that it was no idle dream crossing his mind. Salesi had held the farsight when he had held the staff, and Abu Akhsa did not doubt it if Hamid Salesi claimed to contain the farsight within his mind still.

"Do you see him?" asked Abu Akhsa, looking at Jack.

"No, Abu Akhsa."

"Anil is my son now. The God of the Sands has spared him," said Hamid Salesi.

Abu Akhsa nodded, his heart breaking for his friend who had loved his eldest son far more than his words revealed. Abu Akhsa felt the heat in his cheeks, tightness in his throat, and wetness coming to his eyes. He swallowed.

"I am sorry. He was a brave man, Hamid. You may rest assured in that."

"Yes," said Hamid Salesi.

The line thundered closer in the moonlight.

CHAPTER 72
Ottovan's Escape

Oasis of Ben Hamur
48th Day, Month of Wasura, 807
Anglian Calendar: April 10, 1879

"Commander Fanfar, it has begun."

Ottovan looked up at Nemakar, standing with Umahar at his side. "Did you watch?"

"Ulgur acted in excess," said Nemakar, his face grim behind his long, flowing mustache.

"As we knew he might," said Umahar.

"What did he do?" asked Ottovan.

Nemakar's forehead creased severely as he prepared to deliver heavy news. He cleared his throat. "Ulgur burst into the Sharef's palace, dragging him down to the veranda with six lancers. Then with the Sharef next to him, he stood above the square where the Sharef's guardsmen were tied to posts. These men, according to Ulgur's charges, were those who helped Selena Savanar escape. Then, without warning, he ordered his men to cut the Sharef's guardsmen down before the Sharef's very eyes, and before the people of Ben Hamur."

Ottovan stared at them, wrestling with his choice. "How many guardsmen did he kill?"

"Nine of them, including the Captain of the Guard, Dungar Bin-Guttar."

Ottovan winced. "They are all dead?"

"Quite dead," said Nemakar, "chopped to pieces."

"God of the Mountain and the Sands," said Ottovan, shaking his head and leaning forward with his elbows on the table. He reached up and rubbed his temples beneath his purple turban. "Did that start the uprising?"

"Yes," said Nemakar, "but it went beyond that."

Ottovan raised his dark eyebrows. "What did he do?"

"Some Ben Hamurians began slinging stones from the rooftops. Mostly boys. They hit some of the lancers in the open square. Ulgur grew enraged, and he threw the Sharef off of the veranda down onto the stones below. The Sharef is dead."

"May the God of the Mountain and the Sands damn Ulgur," said Ottovan. "He should not have done that. I ordered him to let me deal with the Sharef."

Umahar nodded in agreement.

"We knew the risks," said Nemakar.

"He is like a wild animal, still uncontrolled after all of these years," said Ottovan. His eyes darted around as if looking for a path in darkness.

"Yes, he is," said Lieutenant Umahar, the physician of the Demissary Legion. "But the people of Ben Hamur are now truly in revolt. We have achieved our purpose."

"At great cost," said Ottovan, shaking his head.

A roar rose outside the door.

"There will be greater costs still," said Umahar.

"There was no alternative," said Nemakar. "Ben Hamur must rise. We knew to unleash Ulgur and his men could achieve that."

The dead, hacked-apart body of Dungar Bin-Guttar flashed through Ottovan's mind. *He was a good, honorable man, and I have killed him by unleashing my monster. Ulgur. Ulgur will have his day of reckoning, and so will Jemojeen, who has made all of this sacrifice necessary.*

"How many of our men are still inside these walls?" asked Ottovan, his body tensing.

"We have a half-dozen of ours in the courtyard," said Nemakar. "The others are out with Ozgar and his archers."

"And Ulgur's lancers?"

"They are cutting their way to the gate. Many are falling. Many more Ben Hamurians have fallen."

"And Ulgur himself?"

"Alive, when we left our observation place. He is leading his men, cutting his way to the gate."

"How far is Jemojeen?"

The roar outside of the villa grew louder. A mob grew closer, its rumble rising like an angry ocean.

"Twenty miles at most, pulling with him the Great Guns of the Kezelboj."

"It is time," said Ottovan, rising from the table.

Umahar and Nemakar stood back as their leader affixed his scimitarus to his belt, a sword that had spilled much blood in its long years of service to Sumetan the Magnificent and to Selahim the Grim before that.

Ottovan picked up his heavy leather holsters, already loaded with his six fire Demissary's pistols: two flashguns, two three-barreled pistols, a shrapnel gun, and a fire pistol. He slung his blunderbuss shotgun over his shoulder at a diagonal. Nemakar and Umahar were already armed in this way, three officers loaded up like ordinary troopers, preparing to fight alongside their men, as was expected of a Demissary officer.

Ottovan nodded.

Nemakar strode forward and opened the door to the courtyard. The shouts of the crowd immediately trebled in their intensity. To their credit, the six Demissaries in the courtyard waited silently in their purple turbans, like cats ready to pounce on any who came through the barred iron-and-wood gate. Ottovan could hear the sounds of people rushing by, just outside the gate. Individual voices rose, like floating pieces of wood on a rushing stream, only to disappear again into the general roar.

"Find them!"

"Find the orange turban men!"

"Kill them! They killed the Sharef!"

"Arm yourselves!"

"Revolt! Revolt! Revolt!"

"For freedom! For House Ayawad!"

Ottovan's veteran eyes scanned the wall that separated the merchant villa from the alley. He had chosen well. They were high, sturdy walls, and none in the mob knew that he and his men were there on the inside of them.

Ottovan tensed just as the stone whizzed past him, striking the plaster on the mudbrick wall behind him. Before any of his men, veteran Demissaries all, Ottovan unholstered a three-barrel pistol and fired at the slinger on the rooftop. The man fell.

There was a lull in the roar of the crowd.

"Gunfire! In there! Yes, in there! Behind that wall! Demissaries? I think so . . . there! Yes, in there!"

Fists began to pound against the wood and iron of the gate.

"Find a battering pole! Yes, over here! Climb over! You there, help me up!"

"Let's go," said Nemakar.

A small, low door barred the entrance to the tunnel to the outside, the passage low enough that all of them would have to crouch. One of Ottovan's men already held the door open.

"There they are! Demissaries! Ten of them! In here!" The shouting voice came from the edge of the wall. A man had climbed the corner and was looking down at them.

Ottovan turned. Three more men had climbed the wall, looking down at them in the courtyard and shouting.

"Flash them," said Ottovan.

Umahar turned, pulling the red-handled pistol from his chest holster. He aimed up at an angle, just above the rim of the wall, and pulled the trigger. The flame-colored powder shot out across the air of the courtyard, slithering like the ghost of a fiery serpent, hovering over the ground before the flash.

Then it burst, bright as the sun.

CHAPTER 73

The Glory Shall Be Mine

Jemojeen's Army, East of Ben Hamur
48th Day, Month of Wasura, 807
Anglian Calendar: April 10, 1879

The Erassian scouts galloped eastward on sweat-glistened horses, their bodies illuminated by the rising sun in front of them.

Through his looking glass, Jemojeen saw the familiar contours of the face of the Captain Turkelan riding toward him at the apex of the V formation.

Seeing the riders on the horizon, Sipahi Shaheni sent his hand to the hilt of his curved sword.

"They are Erassians. Captain Turkelan brings us tidings from Ben Hamur," said Jemojeen.

Minutes later, Turkelan stood before them, bowing in salute, with an extended arm and a fist across his chest.

"Grand Vizer, Ben Hamur rises in rebellion."

"Rebellion? Meaning what?"

"The Sharef is dead, killed by the Demissary Ulgur."

"Why did he kill him?"

"His guardsmen helped the traitor Selena Savanar escape. While Ulgur executed those that assisted the traitor, some Ben Hamurians began slinging stones in rebellion. The Sharef would not order them to stop. Ulgur threw him to his death from the Sharef's own veranda in front of all of the assembled people."

Jemojeen nodded. "Traitors should be dealt with severely."

"There is more, Your Excellency."

"Out with it then."

"The Beserians attacked. Commander Fanfar's Third Demissary Legion has repulsed them."

"How many Beserians attacked?"

"At least five hundred, perhaps more."

"That is a mere fraction of Abu Akhsa's force."

"Yes, Your Excellency. The remainder closes in upon Ben Hamur, ten thousand warriors, maybe more. Seemingly, all of Western Beseria rides behind them, under Abu Akhsa's blue banner. Beyond the warriors are herds, carried tents, and women and children in their tens of thousands."

Jemojeen continued riding forward toward Ben Hamur. Turkelan and his Erassians turned their horses back around and rode at his flanks.

The Kezelboj forces stretched out behind Jemojeen, in a column that reached miles backward toward Alwaz Deem and the other cities of the Great Mountain. In the center of the column, massive horned pachyrms tugged the Great Guns of the Kezelboj, the bronze-barreled behemoths that could throw boulder-sized cannonballs several miles out across the desert.

In front of the cannons, thousands of Kezelboj levies marched, the militia of four of the seven cities, ethnic Qhaliffans all, wearing chain mail and leather cuirasses, carrying round shields, axes, maces, spears, and swords. Their leaders, Kezelboj aristocrats, rode in the colors of their cities: the Lords of Sundar Dun in red, the Lords of Saman Keer in green, Ganjar en Oxus in orange, Nor Wasura in yellow. The men themselves all wore the cloth of their city's color underneath the brown, hardened-leather cuirasses that protected their chests and iron chain mail that hung down from their leather cuirasses, like a skirt protecting their groins and upper legs.

On the sides of the cannons marched the Grand Vizerian Guardsmen, all grey and black, carrying curved swords, spears, and round shields. No weaponry in all of the Seven Cities meant more to Jemojeen than the Great Guns, and other than the expert gunners themselves, who were mostly unarmed, save for the occasional single-shot pistol and belt knife, Jemojeen made sure to keep his own men closest to the guns.

Behind the guns rode the remaining militiamen, led by their Kezelboj lords: Nor Gandus in light blue, Meer Norekah in dark blue, and Alwaz Deem, always last, in purple.

This was the might of the Kezelboj and of Jemojeen's forces, eighteen thousand strong. But the army did not end there. Two other columns rode behind the center column, one slightly to the north and one slightly to the south.

To the north, rode the First Legion of Demissaries and to the south rode the Second Legion, each expected to be capable of defeating three times their number in battle. Each legion was nine hundred strong. As with all Demissary legions, their lancers wore orange, their bowmen donned green, and their firemen rode in purple.

For his war council on the march, however, Jemojeen desired the company of neither the Kezelboj lords nor the Demissary commanders, consigning each to ride with their units. Jemojeen was always a man who best preferred his own counsel. If he were to seek an opinion, it was generally that of a competent subordinate and never that of a man who might consider himself to be Jemojeen's equal.

After riding in silence, Jemojeen turned to Captain Turkelan. "What do you propose?"

Turkelan turned his bright green eyes on Jemojeen. "An army that rides with women and children and herds of animals brings its vulnerabilities with it. I would fan out and attack the enemy's flanks. Force them to spread out and break through with a strong force. If they fear losing their families in the rear, the Beserians will break."

Jemojeen nodded. "And how about you, Sipahi Shaheni, what do you recommend?"

"We have the Great Guns of the Kezelboj, Your Excellency. We could set them up within range of Ben Hamur, firing upon the oasis and killing the traitors that have risen in rebellion. If Abu Akhsa ever wishes to attack the Seven Cities, he will need Ben Hamur's water and food stores. He will have to rush to save the oasis, attacking our guns. We can slaughter his men as they ride against our cannons across open ground."

"Or perhaps we can do both of those things," said Jemojeen. "Yes, we can do both of those things. If we slaughter Abu Akhsa's army, we will have made a mockery of the idea that this is the Year of the Prophecy, when the 'promised ones' of the east and west will bring the line of the Qhaliffas low. But we must also show the other oases what happens when a Sharef and his people revolt against the Qhaliffa. They have apparently, after a mere hundred years, forgotten the lessons of Ben Rusa. And yes, Captain Turkelan, we can do better than just killing Abu Akhsa's army. If we can kill his people—his women and his children—we will have destroyed our enemies for generations. There will have been no greater victory on the Sand Sea."

Jemojeen closed his mouth and finished his thought in his mind only.

And they shall remember the name Jemojeen Jongdar as the man who won that victory, the greatest Grand Vizer in the history of the Seven Cities, and the power and the glory shall be mine.

CHAPTER 74
Abu Akhsa's Plan

Camp of Abu Akhsa, West of Ben Hamur
48th Day, Month of Wasura, 807
Anglian Calendar: April 10, 1879

"We should attack here," said Handsome Habeen Barcadey, his diagonal face scar glistening in the firelight. He held a stick and drew in the dust adjacent to the fire. All of the greatest warriors and tribal chieftains of the Beserian tribes gathered around the large blazing fire to make their final preparations. The advance would begin just before the sunrise.

Jack Caldwell could not take his eyes off of Selena Savanar. Her hazel eyes shone with a power he had not felt before when looking at a woman. Her olive skin was without blemish, and even the Beserian great chiefs, men who led full tribes like Azadeem, Celadeen, and Bazadak, seemed to care about her opinion. But for the two front teeth missing from her mouth, she would have been the most beautiful woman Jack had ever seen. Her large woman warrior and her giant Omakhosian flanked her on either side.

"They will bring the Great Guns of the Kezelboj," said Selena, reciting what she had spent weeks studying in the Sharef's scrolls in Ben Hamur. "Of this, I have no doubt."

"My scouts have seen them," said Azam Azadeem.

"How many?" asked Selena.

"Thirty, maybe more," said Azadeem.

"Thirty Great Guns will travel with no fewer than ten thousand men, maybe more," said Selena. "Do you agree?" She turned and asked Oapah the Hohsa.

Oapah nodded. "Yes," he said, in a voice as deep as the war drums that would sound with the dawn.

Habeen Barcadey had already introduced Gulana of Nor Gandus and Oapah as Oath Holders, Sworn Lions of the Order of the Ram, the Lion, and the Serpent. The leaders of the Beserians looked at them with immediate respect.

None had ever met an Oath Holder of the Order—at least none that they knew of—but all had heard of such men and women, and Gulana and Oapah did not disappoint in their appearance.

So too had all of the leaders of the Beserians heard of House Savanar, of the cruel burning of the great Sah Seg Savanar and of his daughter who had escaped once as a girl, and who had survived a second time when Jemojeen Jongdar tried to burn her as a grown woman. All standing there knew that the line of the Savanars descended from Hom Hommuram himself. All believed in the power of the Prophecy and of the words that said:

> *From the east shall come another, a child of Hom Hommuram.*
> *To restore the Staff that was broken, the Serpent, the Lion, and the Ram.*

If this was not the child of Hom Hommuram, then who was?

Jack stared into Selena's firelit face as she looked down at Habeen Barcadey's drawing in the dirt, each line he made showing where thousands would fight, bleed, and die.

Jack's thoughts swirled like a sandstorm. *Could it be so? Am I really the one of the Prophecy, the Amahdi of the West? The one who is to ride with the daughter of Hom Hommuram? Is she my age? Only three and twenty? Her face is young, but her eyes are old . . . and beautiful.*

Selena looked up at Jack. Her eyes rested upon his as if she were drilling into his soul, laying bare his thoughts, naked and exposed.

Could it be? she thought. *Could this strange Westerner be the one of the Prophecy? He is broad of shoulder and light of eyes. Is he a great warrior? He looks as much boy as man, too uncertain in his eyes.* Her eyes judged him harshly, placing him alongside mighty Oapah and Ottovan Fanfar in her mind.

Jack kept his eyes steady upon Selena's, not wanting to look elsewhere despite the intensity of her gaze.

"Far more than ten thousand men are marching with the Great Guns of the Kezelboj," said Azam Azadeem. "There are closer to twenty thousand. My scouts have reported this, and Azadeem scouts do not report falsely."

A general grumble rose from the assembled tribal leaders.

"Twenty thousand?"

"And Great Guns?"

"How can we defeat such a foe?"

"Do not forget the Erassians . . . or the Demissaries!"

"I have fought Demissaries. They are not to be underestimated!"

"Enough!" said Abu Akhsa, his voice slashing like a saber. "We have not traveled all this way to fear our enemy. The God of the Sands rides with us. He guides our sabers and our bullets. We stand in the midst of the Year of the Prophecy." He paused to look at Jack and Selena, his eyes lingering upon each of their faces. "The Amahdi of the West shall rise," he said, looking at Jack. "And from the East shall come another, a child of Hom Hommuram," he said, looking at Selena. "We have nothing to fear. Now listen to your elder, Hamid Salesi."

All sat, waiting in silent anticipation.

Hamid Salesi cleared his throat, leaning forward and holding a walking stick, deprived of the Staff of Wisdom he had carried since he was a young man. He looked older, as if he had aged two decades in several weeks.

"The scouts of the Azadeem have sharp eyes, and they perceive things as they are," said Hamid Salesi, "And I do not doubt that the armies of the Qhalif-fa ride forth with as many as twenty thousand. But nor do I fear that army, and neither should you. We ride as free men, free men in service of the One True God, the God of the Sands and of the Mountain. They ride to battle as slaves of their lords, as slaves of their Qhaliffa, and as slaves of a cruel master to whom that monarch wrongly gives his power. We are not slaves. Jemojeen and his Kezelboj will learn tomorrow of what free men are capable."

A deep boom sounded in the distance and then another and another. A series of crashes rattled the sky.

All of the assembled chiefs and warriors turned and looked to the east. Fear crept up spines. More booms and crashes approached as they turned. They could not see anything in the eastern darkness. But all could hear the man-made thunder, as distant flashes dotted the horizon.

"They have begun firing the Great Guns," said Oapah. His voice itself sounded like a distant great gun.

"What are they firing upon?" asked Cedak of the Celadeens.

"They bombard Ben Hamur itself," said Gulana, speaking for the first time from her grim warrior's face. In the firelight, her brown hair looked dark enough to be black. Her face was long and narrow, contrasting with Bazak Bazadak, who stood next to her, his face as wide as hers was narrow, scowling above his thick black beard.

"Why bombard the oasis?" asked Bazadak.

Hamid Salesi's eyes were closed as if he were using the farsight of the Staff of the Serpent, the Staff of Wisdom, the staff that Ghani the traitor had taken from him.

Abu Akhsa turned to Salesi, waiting for him to open his eyes. Others continued talking about the bombardment, about Ben Hamur, and about what the attack should look like, but Abu Akhsa remained silent, waiting and looking at Hamid Salesi's closed eyes.

Behind Salesi's eyelids, Abu Akhsa watched his eyes dart back and forth as if watching two armies approaching. How many times had Abu Akhsa waited for Hamid Salesi to open his eyes before? Watching his eyes behind closed lids? Waiting to hear what he had seen in the darkness with the aid of the farsight? Five hundred times? A thousand?

Jack Caldwell stopped listening to the chatter of the others around him, turning to watch Abu Akhsa and Hamid Salesi. He had seen Salesi use the farsight. He had used it himself with the old man's guidance, and he understood its power. *But can he use the farsight if the staff is gone? Does the power linger in him after all of these years? Does it still linger in me after only months?*

"Yes, it lingers," said Hamid Salesi, opening his eyes.

Jack's eyes met Salesi's, as did Abu Akhsa's.

"Yes, I still can feel your thoughts," said Hamid Salesi, looking at Jack.

The other chieftains and warriors were still arguing with each other, but Selena Savanar had focused her gaze upon Hamid Salesi, Abu Akhsa, and Jack Caldwell, the bombast of the arguing chiefs receding around her.

Selena stepped forward.

The others ignored her, arguing more loudly with each other about how the forces should attack. Short, wiry Cedak Celadeen and lean, lanky Azam Azadeem gestured wildly, shouting at each other while Bazak Bazadak shook his bearded head with increasing vigor.

"What did you see?" asked Selena.

Gulana rose and followed her. Oapah followed her only with his eyes.

Hamid Salesi locked eyes with Selena.

Jack swallowed uncomfortably. Something about Selena Savanar prevented him from being at ease. Her proximity made him self-conscious about the way he looked, smelled, spoke, and stood.

Selena glanced at him and returned her eyes to Hamid Salesi.

Salesi nodded, clearing his throat again like an old man. His voice was gravelly.

"Jemojeen now holds two of the three staffs, that of Mamet and that of Beseri, the Ram and the Serpent, the Staff of Ruling and the Staff of Wisdom. He will use them both, and so long as he holds those staffs, we will not overpower his army."

The dire words hung in the air, focusing the attention of the few who heard them. The chiefs continued to argue with each other in the background.

"What would you have us do, old friend?" said Abu Akhsa.

Selena, Jack, and Gulana turned their eyes to his black-and-silver bearded face. Oapah watched, seated in the distance.

"The farsight is leaving me, Abu Akhsa, but some remains," said Hamid Salesi. He paused, swallowed, and nodded. "If riders could strike at him directly during the battle, it is possible they could pry the staffs from his grasp."

"Do you see it clearly, old friend? Do you see him losing the staffs in the farsight?" asked Abu Akhsa. He heard a hesitation in Salesi's voice that was not there when he spoke with the farsight.

"No, Abu Akhsa, I do not see it clearly. I see it only as a shadow on a wall, cast by the firelight, but I see it nonetheless. In that way, shaded and in darkness, I see a staff pried from his hands. I believe it can be done."

Abu Akhsa frowned deeply, creasing his forehead and furrowing his brow. He looked east toward the sounds of the booming cannons, the Great Guns of the Kezelboj.

"He will be guarded heavily," said Oapah, rising and walking toward them. Hamid Salesi looked up at the giant, dark-skinned Omakhosian.

"Yes, he cares much for his own skin," said Gulana, echoing Oapah.

Both she and Oapah stood taller than any of the Beserians, who were not a tall race. Both she and Oapah had fought against Jemojeen and his men for long years. The Order had tried to assassinate Jemojeen Jongdar in nearly half of the years he had served as Grand Vizer. All attempts had failed. She had fought with two of the failed attempts; Oapah had fought with three. Jemojeen had grown increasingly on guard with each effort, increasing his guards, growing warier of routes he took, ever afraid of an ambush.

"We must distract him," said Selena.

Jack's heart raced as he heard her voice.

Selena continued, speaking the fluent if guttural Beserian one picked up in the bazaars of the flatlands. "Divide our forces, draw his attention out toward the far flanks. Then we will slip through the gap in his lines. We will strike him once he spreads his forces wide."

"Yes," said Hamid Salesi. "This is sound. Perhaps lead him to believe that he is winning. A man who believes he is on the hunt is often less wary of being hunted himself."

"How?" asked Abu Akhsa. "What do you envision?"

Hamid Salesi did not immediately speak, weighing his words carefully as if each was heavy and difficult to lift.

"Habeen Barcadey?" asked Abu Akhsa, looking to Hamid Salesi for his answer. "Should he lead our force to strike Jemojeen?"

Habeen stood off to the side, still holding the stick with which he was drawing out the enemy positions and those of the Beserians. He was covered in dust and sweat with caked, dried blood covering half of his face. He watched with tired, warrior's eyes. But he stood with a posture of pride, the posture of knowing he was still the most famous swordsman in all of the tribes of Beseria.

"No, I do not see him in the farsight," said Hamid Salesi. "I see another."

"I will take back the staff from him," said Selena.

Oapah and Gulana each turned to look at Selena with disbelief.

"Yes," said Salesi. "It is you."

"Do you see it?" asked Abu Akhsa. "You see her doing this? In the farsight?" Abu Akhsa had long ago learned not to question Salesi's farsight, but that was when he had carried the Staff of Wisdom, when there was no hesitation in his voice, only the certitude of seeing clearly, that which was yet to come, but which always happened.

Hamid Salesi nodded. "I see it as well as I can see without the Staff of Wisdom, Abu Akhsa. It is also what the Prophecy tells us. We may rely upon that."

"I will ride with her," said Jack, stepping forward.

Hamid Salesi's eyes shot at Jack, more alert than they were a moment before. His mind raced. *Yes, perhaps that is it. The promised ones of the east and the west, one for each staff, Hom Hommuram's line to rule, the Amahdi of the west, to be wise, to take over from Beseri—"to the west he fled, and from the west, his heir shall return." Yes, this must be so. Even if I see only dimly, this must be so.*

"Very well," said Hamid Salesi.

Oapah and Gulana looked at Jack doubtfully, eyeing him up and down.

"And I will ride with them," said Aurelio Demassi, stepping out from among the group behind Habeen Barcadey, those of the vanguard who had returned alive, the survivors of the long guns and the Demissary charge.

"How many should we send with them?" asked Abu Akhsa.

"Nine shall ride in all," said Hamid Salesi. "Nine should ride at Jemojeen at the appointed time."

"Then I will ride with them as well," said Anil Salesi, Hamid Salesi's remaining son.

Salesi looked at his son with sadness in his eyes, knowing that he could not shame him in front of his fellow warriors by denying his request.

Anil looked at his father, seeing the sadness, feeling guilty, and knowing that he was the cause. Anil had never loved Kaleem, but his father had loved him greatly. Anil could see the pain in his father's heart in the depth of the creases on his face.

"As will I," said Jabil the Jackal.

Hamid Salesi nodded with approval. *Jabil the Jackal rides well and fights ably.*

The Great Guns of the Kezelboj boomed in the distance, louder than rolling thunder, one after the other, each boom corresponding to a massive cannonball being shot into the crowded oasis of Ben Hamur.

Flashes illuminated the eastern horizon, piercing the darkness.

"Not you, Anil Salesi. I need you here with me," said Abu Akhsa.

Anil opened his mouth to protest.

"I have spoken, Anil Salesi," said Abu Akhsa. "You will be here at my side."

Anil stared.

"Who else?" asked Abu Akhsa.

"The God of the Sands will show us," said Hamid Salesi, slowly nodding his silver beard, looking at Abu Akhsa with gratitude. "Wait for the rising sun."

CHAPTER 75
Ottovan Crosses Over

Third Demissary Legion, West of Ben Hamur
49th Day, Month of Wasura, 807
Anglian Calendar: April 11, 1879

The bombardment obliterated all other noise.

Pieces of mudbrick and shards of roof tiles careened out over the western wall of Ben Hamur, striking into the desert sands like meteors from the heavens.

Ottovan shouted for Umahar and Nemakar to hear him, though they were only feet away. They had united with their division of fire Demissaries, three hundred riders, each man armed with three sets of pistols, a blunderbuss shotgun, and a scimitarus. The men with the long guns had moved off of the mudbrick walls of Ben Hamur to join their division just in time for the bombardment to begin.

Via a swift rider, Ottovan sent a note to Jemojeen to tell him that they would intercept any Ben Hamurians trying to escape the death trap of the oasis. Ottovan proclaimed they would seal off the western retreat route, putting any who came outside of the walls to the sword.

Ottovan found that the lies were coming more easily to him. He had, however, felt a new nervousness in his gut since he had heard that the Staff of Wisdom had fallen into Jemojeen's hands. *Does it give the farsight immediately? Can he see whatever he desires? If so, our time is short . . .*

"What, Commander?" shouted Nemakar as a brick sailed far over their heads.

Ottovan read Nemakar's lips moving underneath his long mustache.

"I said ride to that wadi for cover!" Ottovan pointed westward, toward the broad recess in the ground, wide enough to accommodate hundreds of men. It would not provide much cover, but it was far better than staying out in the open on the plain, under the deadly rain of roof tiles and bricks.

"Yes, sir!" Nemakar signaled to his lieutenants, who signaled to their sergeants, and within seconds three hundred Demissary firemen rode westward on their large warhorses, the sunrise shining upon their purple turbans and the polished barrels of their weapons.

As they descended into the broad, shallow wadi, the entire western horizon darkened with bodies—men, horses, and camels.

"Commander Fanfar!" shouted Umahar.

Ottovan looked up. "God of the Mountain and the Sands, it has begun."

Umahar already held his looking glass in his hand. "The banners are sky blue, fifty of them. Does it mean?"

"Abu Akhsa himself," said Ottovan.

The Great Guns of the Kezelboj continued to roar in the distance, their cannonballs still careening into Ben Hamur with terrible, building-crushing explosions.

A great cry arose from the ridgeline. Horns sounded. Bass drums boomed, the kinds carried by two camels, suspended in the air, struck by a man with a giant drumstick, the size of a battle club.

Boom. Boom. Boom.

Ottovan pulled his own looking glass from his belt. He scanned the Beserian line. Underneath the densest cluster of the banners, he found him.

There he is, Abu Akhsa, bearded in black and silver. Has it been that long? His beard was black. I suppose the last years have aged us all. And, yes, there she is. Selena Savanar.

Ottovan felt his heart rise as he saw Savanar and Abu Akhsa riding together.

Abu Akhsa rides a silvery-white horse, the horse of a just conqueror. And there, Selena Savanar rides a horse of the same color, only smaller, as if she rides the sister of Abu Akhsa's stallion. There. There is the other, the other one of the Prophecy, riding at Abu Akhsa's left hand. He of the light eyes and the broad shoulders. The Amahdi.

"Shall we fire the long guns, Commander?" asked Nemakar.

Ottovan saw that his sergeants were already ordering the long gun pairs to dismount as was their regular combat procedure against mounted men massed together at such a distance.

"No," said Ottovan.

Nemakar glanced behind him, seeing his lieutenants looking at him, awaiting the order to commence firing upon the enemy.

Nemakar did not say his thoughts aloud. *They will think it suspicious, Commander. There is no reason not to fire. We must risk hitting even important ones among them. Our men cannot know where our true loyalties lie—not now, not yet.* His forehead creased.

Nemakar and Ottovan both looked at the western ridgeline.

More mounted men continued to amass, turning the soft tan of the desert sand into a dark brown, the color of mounted Beserians atop camels and horses. Little bursts of light twinkled along the line as the morning sunlight struck looking glasses and rifle barrels. The line continued to grow, thickening and widening, as thousands and thousands of men continued to form a vast crescent.

"There are too many," said Ottovan.

Nemakar looked at him, awaiting an order. *Doctrine says we should fan out into skirmish formation and begin weakening them with our long guns. You know this, and so do our men.*

"I know what doctrine says," began Ottovan, speaking loudly enough for the lieutenants behind Nemakar to hear him. "But that is all of the might of the Beserian force. Lieutenant-Captain Hanrak, Lieutenant Nabak, to me."

"Yes, Commander?" said the men riding up.

Besides Umahar, the physician, they were the most senior officers beneath Captain Nemakar, men who had risen from common Demissaries up through the ranks to become officers based on their tremendous skill. They had risen as all Demissaries must rise, from the bottom, based upon demonstrated ability and leadership, not birth or wealth.

Both Hanrak and Nabak looked at Ottovan with questioning eyes as the Beserian force continued to grow on the ridgeline. Neither of the veteran officers had ever seen such a power on the Sand Sea, or anywhere else they had deployed for the Qhaliffa over the years, from the Harafhan Mountains in the south to the Gressian border in the north.

"This is no time for long guns," said Ottovan. "That is all of the might of Abu Akhsa and the Beserians. What matters is that we screen the flanks so they cannot get around the Grand Vizer's force on the other side of Ben Hamur. Do you understand?"

"Yes, Commander."

"Nabak, you will take A and C squadrons to the north. Hanrak, you take B and D squadrons to the south. You will observe the Beserians, retreating until you reach the Erassians on the flanks of the Grand Vizer's Kezelboj Army."

"Yes, Commander."

"Captain Nemakar, Lieutenant Umahar, and I will ride to face Abu Akhsa himself, to bring him a message from the Grand Vizer. Perhaps there is time yet to show them the futility of this attack."

"Commander, you should not ride yourself," said Lieutenant-Captain Hanrak.

"No, Commander, you should not," said Lieutenant Nabak.

Both lieutenants idolized their commander, as did most Demissaries who had chosen to become firemen, whether they served in the Third Legion or not. No fighting Demissary had achieved more renown in a half-century at least.

"None can carry the message but me," said Ottovan. "The words I carry are for me to deliver to Abu Akhsa himself. Umahar and Nemakar will provide me all of the support I need. Now go!"

Hanrak and Nabak saluted and then rode off, one to the north and the other to the south. The junior lieutenants followed the orders, and the squadrons began to move, the sergeants barking orders as the lines shifted, moving outward, parallel against the vast Beserian crescent.

As his men galloped away, Ottovan Fanfar inhaled deeply.

It is time. At long last, it is time.

Ottovan sat astride his warhorse in the wadi on the vast plain, flanked to the north by Captain Nemakar Hasdruba, and to the south by Umahar of Meer Norekah: three Demissaries, three members of the Order of the Ram, the Lion, and the Serpent, three men standing between the might of the tribes and the might of the Qhaliffa—the army of the sands against the army of the mountain.

"That was brilliant, Commander," said Nemakar.

"Brilliant or very foolish," said Ottovan.

The three men stared at the thousands of riders ahead of them, the sound of the Beserian horns washing over them, punctuated by the artillery explosions behind them and the deep boom of the camel-drawn war drums ahead of them.

"Shall we meet Abu Akhsa?" asked Ottovan.

He had already started riding forward.

CHAPTER 76
The Demissary and the Beserian

Beserian Army, West of Ben Hamur
49th Day, Month of Wasura, 807
Anglian Calendar: April 11, 1879

The three men rode westward—Ottovan Fanfar, Nemakar Hasdruba, and Umahar of Meer Norekah—with Ben Hamur and its exploding buildings behind them, the vast Beserian Army in front of them.

From Abu Akhsa's saddle, they looked no bigger than the tiny figurines used in the Game of the Squares of War, moving across a vast khaki-colored blanket, the sun softening the color of the sands of the Ben Hamurian plain. Their shadows extended out far before them as they cantered toward the Beserian line, three men riding against thirteen thousand.

On the eve of the battle, three thousand Beserians from the far northeastern lands, men from the Gressian border as it neared the Barban Mountains and the Xin frontier, rode into the camp from the north, not wanting to miss the battle of the age, the battle of the Year of the Prophecy. They were strange-looking to the western Beserians, similar in build and facial hair, but clothed differently, wearing thick wool and lining their tunics with fur. The sands beneath the Barban Mountains were frigid in winter, and the winter there stretched for many more months than winter in a place like the Valley of Kordon.

They had come to see the downfall of the Qhaliffa and the fulfillment of the Prophecy. They had come, eastern men across thousands of miles of desert, to lay their eyes upon the Amahdi of the west and the daughter of the line of Hom Hommuram—the two that their Prophecy assured them would arrive.

They stared openly at Jack, at his blue eyes, his square jaw, and his broad shoulders. They nodded respectfully at Selena Savanar, the sharp, straight nose of her profile showing her to be clearly a daughter of a noble line of the Kezelboj.

They now looked eastward, toward Ben Hamur, as the Great Guns of the Kezelboj still sent their deadly cannonballs crashing into the oasis, as three lone Demissary horsemen rode toward the Beserian battle line.

"Are they mad?" asked Cedak Celadeen.

"They do not carry a flag of parley. We should shoot them dead," said Azam Azadeem.

"You will shoot no one," said Abu Akhsa. "Do not fire upon the riders!" he shouted. Do *not* fire . . . give the order to *not* fire."

Hamid Salesi glanced at Abu Akhsa. The Chief of Chiefs was not a man to repeat himself.

"Do not fire! Do not fire!" The orders ran down the line as the Tribal Chiefs and War Chiefs barked them out, and their under-chiefs and elders repeated the words. No Beserian fired as the three men rode toward the line.

"Is that who I think it is?" asked Abu Akhsa, viewing Ottovan, Nemakar, and Umahar through his brass Gerdic looking glass, a treasured gift from a Macmenian trader.

"Yes," said Hamid Salesi and Selena Savanar, speaking at the same time.

"Who is it? Who rides?" asked Jack Caldwell.

"Ottovan Fanfar, Oath Holder and *Lion* of the Order of the Ram, the Lion, and the Serpent," said Selena.

"Like you," said Jack, looking at Oapah and Gulana. "The Order that protects *you*," he said, looking at Selena Savanar.

"Yes, but he is *The* Lion. There is always one Ram, one Lion, and one Serpent to lead the Order. He is The Lion. We are only Lions," said Gulana.

Jack looked at Gulana, just able to understand her accented Beserian and having never heard her speak so much.

"I will ride to meet him," said Abu Akhsa.

"It is not safe!" said Habeen Barcadey.

Abu Akhsa was already riding forward.

Hamid Salesi kicked his heels against the flanks of his horse and rode after him, a half-stride behind Abu Akhsa.

"Then I am also riding," said Jack, urging his mount into a gallop to catch up with the older men.

"We wait," said Selena, watching the three men ride forward, aimed direct-ly at the three Demissaries riding toward the Beserian horde.

The sky blue of Abu Akhsa's headscarf trailed behind him as he charged for-ward. His saber remained in its scabbard, his ancient rifle with the rune-carved stock slung behind his back. Jack alone carried his rifle in his hand, a Mancaster repeater, loaded and ready for action. Hamid Salesi rode forward with no more than an ancestral dagger in his belt.

The three Demissaries kicked up the sand beneath them as their warhorses carried them westward in full view of the assembled tribesmen, thirteen thousand warriors watching the three men gallop toward Abu Akhsa, Hamid Salesi, and Jack Caldwell.

Thousands shifted nervously in their saddles, waiting for the two sets of three to reach each other.

The Demissaries slowed first, on a signal from the center rider, the shortest and most broad-shouldered of the three. All wore matching purple turbans, the turbans that marked them as fire Demissaries, even if one could not see the three sets of pistols in holsters hanging from their chests, or the shotguns in holsters at their sides.

The Demissary fire squadrons that had stood with them to face the advancing Beserians had vanished into two clouds of receding dust, disappearing in the distance along the flanks, fleeing to the north and south of the oasis. The three Demissaries sat upon their mounts, utterly alone to face the tribes.

Abu Akhsa reined in his steed, stopping only a few body lengths from the Demissaries and squaring off against the center man.

"Ottovan Fanfar," he said.

Hamid Salesi and Jack Caldwell came up on either side of Abu Akhsa, their horses panting from the gallop.

"You did not always travel with such a great host," said Ottovan, looking into Abu Akhsa's bearded face.

"Nor you such a small one," said Abu Akhsa, his eyes twinkling in the morning sunlight.

Ottovan swung himself out of his saddle, his boots landing firmly in the dirt. He approached middle age, but through ceaseless physical training, he still held the agility of a far younger man.

Abu Akhsa dismounted more slowly, showing his years more than Ottovan, though they were nearly the same age. Ottovan stepped forward, his arms open and extended. Abu Akhsa stepped forward, his arms out. They embraced for all of the warriors of Beseria to see. They stepped back, looking into each other's faces and smiling.

"The day has come," said Ottovan.

"At long last," said Abu Akhsa.

Ottovan waited to speak, looking into Abu Akhsa's eyes, holding the weight of glory and the light of destiny on his face.

"Will you ride with us, old friend?" asked Abu Akhsa.

"We will, but we will require new clothes."

"New clothes?"

"Jemojeen holds the Staff of Wisdom, the Staff of the Serpent. He will soon gain the farsight, if he does not have it already." Ottovan's eyes drifted up to Hamid Salesi.

"If the farsight still lingers in me," said Hamid Salesi, "Then Jemojeen does not yet see clearly. But he will soon. I can feel him trying to use it; I can feel the power moving out of me and into him. We can disguise you and your companions, but there is little time before the staff relinquishes all of Beseri's power to Jemojeen. And when that happens, even disguises will not keep you or your mind from his gaze."

Ottovan nodded, turning to mount his horse. Nemakar and Umahar nodded to Jack and Hamid Salesi, who nodded back.

Abu Akhsa looked them both in the eyes.

Nemakar and Umahar bowed forward from their horses to the leader of all of the tribes.

Abu Akhsa bowed back, keeping his eyes upon them.

"We welcome you to the rebellion, my friends. May the God of the Mountain and the Sands guide us to victory."

"To victory," said Nemakar and Umahar in unison, saluting with their fists across their chests in the Demissary way.

Abu Akhsa returned the salute, the salute practiced by his most sworn enemies, the Demissaries of the Qhaliffa of the Seven Cities of the Great Mountain, the descendant of Mamet the First.

Jack saw this, and a shiver ran up his spine, a chill of destiny. He glanced at Hamid Salesi and saw that his eyes were moist, as if he had waited a lifetime for this very moment, when the war of the centuries would commence. Salesi looked behind him, seeing the gathered descendants of Beseri—the might of the holy army of the Prophecy—arisen to right the wrongs of forty generations.

And this time, the Qhaliffa shall fall! Hamid Salesi swallowed a lump of emotion in his throat.

Ottovan planted his foot in the stirrup and swung himself back up onto his warhorse. He, Nemakar, and Umahar rode forward.

Jack and Hamid Salesi made room so they could ride interspersed, Beserian and Demissary, next to each other, with Ottovan Fanfar and Abu Akhsa riding together in the center. Abu Akhsa kicked his heels against the sides of his stallion, sending him thundering forward across the plain toward his waiting army. Ottovan and the others followed him, riding up alongside him, six men in line.

Selena Savanar watched them ride toward her.

Her heart pounded against her chest. She had waited for this day, whether she knew it or not, since the day she heard Jemojeen's voice in the courtyard, the day her world ended and her nightmare began, the day she lost her home and her family.

She had waited since the day the Qhaliffa's men raped her mother and her older sisters, the day they took her father away to burn him, based upon the lies of evil men. Since that day, others had plotted Selena's revenge for her, an act of revenge that only an army such as this could deliver, an army that the most celebrated living Demissary, Ottovan Fanfar, Commander of the Third Legion, Lion of the Order of the Ram, the Lion, and the Serpent was now riding to join. And though others had plotted it, though she had lived in ignorance of her destiny, she saw the six men riding toward her and knew, for perhaps the first time, that this would be her revenge nonetheless.

"Abu Akhsa!" she shouted.

The men around her looked at her.

"Abu Akhsa!" she shouted again, louder.

"Abu Akhsa!" shouted Gulana, the only other woman among the thirteen thousand men, adding her voice to Selena's.

"Abu Akhsa!" shouted Oapah, deep as a battle drum.

Handsome Habeen Barcadey looked over at Selena with his deeply scarred face. He pulled his saber from its sheath, the saber that was said to be deadlier upon the Sand Sea than any other.

"Abu Akhsa!" he shouted.

Fifty men followed him, drawing their sabers, and adding their voices. "Abu Akhsa!"

Five hundred more men followed them, their sabers sliding out of their sheaths. "Abu Akhsa!"

Then five thousand joined, the line thundering as loudly as the Great Guns of the Kezelboj.

As Abu Akhsa, Ottovan, and the others rode closer, the shouting only grew louder. The remaining thousands drew their sabers and shouted the name of their leader.

"Abu Akhsa!"

Abu Akhsa reined in his horse one hundred yards from the line of shouting warriors. He pulled his saber from its sheath, the saber that had belonged to his father, and to his father's father before that, forged from the iron of the east, steel from the Barban Mountains, its blade nearly black.

He raised his free hand over his head, lowering it to tell his men to quiet their battle cry. He waited long moments for the shouting to stop.

"Warriors of Beseri!" he boomed.

Ottovan stopped just behind him, as did the others. Abu Akhsa began to ride up and down the line, looking at the faces of his men.

"Warriors of Beseri! For eight hundred years, our people have awaited this day, when the God of the Sands shall bring his righteous justice to the Usurper and his line. Today is the day the House of Mamet falls! By tomorrow, we shall ride east to knock upon the gates of Alwaz Deem!"

Abu Akhsa shouted as loudly as possible. There were too many men to hear him, but those in the front ranks could hear him, as could those near the center of the line. He waited.

The line erupted into a roar. The men shouted, shaking their sabers above their heads. Others waved their rifles in the air, thrusting the barrels up into the sky.

Abu Akhsa waited until the shouting receded, then he waved his hands for the men to listen to him again.

"Today, many of you may fall, but if there were ever a day to fall, today is that day! When your grandchildren and your great-nephews and nieces talk of your deeds, it will be today that is most remembered! Where were you in the Battle of Ben Hamur? Did you fight with Bazak Bazadak? With Celadeen and Azadeem?" As Abu Akhsa said the names of the tribes, each group of warriors sat slightly higher in their saddles, with their chests held slightly more puffed out, with a greater spark of courage in their eyes.

Abu Akhsa continued, "Did you ride with Habeen Barcadey and Hamid Salesi? Did you help break the line of the Kezelboj? Did you kill a Demissary?"

Abu Akhsa waited. He scanned the line and saw that he held all of the warriors' eyes upon him. They were now in his hands.

"And if you live today," he shouted, "yes, you can tell them what you did, but you are humble men, men who would prefer for their deeds to speak for themselves. If you live, yes, some will remember well what you did here today.

"But if you fall? If you fall, others will proclaim your deeds. They will shout your name from the backs of their camels, and they will speak of you around their fires at night. They will tell of you to their children and their children's children, and you will live on. For no man who falls today shall truly die.

"Today shall be the day of the immortals, the day that, many years from now, young men will look back upon and say, 'I wish I had been there to fight and die.' So ride, my brothers, ride to victory, for today is the day of destiny!"

The line roared even louder than before. The men shouted until their voices shook from strain. Abu Akhsa rode forward into the line, headlong into the ocean of roaring men.

Selena Savanar waited next to Habeen Barcadey, adding her voice to the others, shouting and shaking a saber above her head. Her heart thundered in her chest, and for the first time since she could remember, she felt more hope than fear, as if the tide could truly turn, as if Jemojeen Jongdar and the House of the Qhaliffas might actually fall.

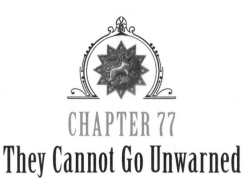

CHAPTER 77
They Cannot Go Unwarned

South of Ben Hamur—Southwest of Ben Hamur
49th Day, Month of Wasura, 807
Anglian Calendar: April 11, 1879

The hooves struck the hard-packed desert sand south of Ben Hamur, shaking the ground like a stampeding herd. They looked to be more than half a thousand strong, orange-turbaned men and green-turbaned men on warhorses, moving in two separate columns, separated by only a few horse lengths.

Hersen and Diego looked at each other and then looked for somewhere to hide. There was nothing: no wadi, no donga, no cluster of boulders, nothing but a sprinkling of low shrubs that came up no higher than a man's knee. The men galloped toward them, coming on fast from the east.

"Demissaries?" asked Hersen, his heart pounding against his ribs and his throat tightening in fear.

"Yes," said Diego, nodding with wide, anxious eyes. "Archers in green and lancers in orange."

"There is nowhere to hide," said Hersen.

"We have only one chance, and that is to ride."

"The way we came?"

"No, look at their angle. We must ride toward Ben Hamur."

As Hersen looked to the oasis, a massive cannonball struck near the Sharef's palace on the lone hill, sending bricks high up into the air. They cascaded in arcs down onto the oasis below, trailing debris behind them and streaking the sky.

"There? Toward the bombardment?" asked Hersen, his voice tight and doubtful.

"There is no other choice! We are only two riders. Only there might they ignore us."

Hersen looked at the column of heavily armed men charging toward them, all riding fast and hard. In his experience, Hersen had learned to see when men rode toward combat, and these men rode to fight and kill.

"What if—" said Hersen, changing his mind before offering an alternative.

"There is no time!" shouted Diego, with more fear in his eyes than Hersen had ever seen before.

Diego whipped the end of his head rope against his camel.

Hersen launched after him, clicking his tongue to urge his camel cow forward. She galloped forward, the swift beast that she was, lean and muscular, taken from the Sharef of Ben Gamurian's finest stock on the orders of Colonel Willem Spinner.

Diego was already galloping toward the oasis ahead.

"That is a flanking force," shouted Hersen, leaning forward to make Diego hear him, despite the sound of the wind rushing past their ears. "They are moving in too much force to be reconnaissance. What lies to the west along that line?"

Diego considered as they galloped north toward Ben Hamur, weighing Hersen's shouted question in his mind.

Then the idea struck Diego like a bolt of lightning into his brain. "They ride for the Beserian herds! For the women and the children!" he shouted backward, over his shoulder, at Hersen.

Hersen rode onward toward the oasis and the bombardment.

Beserian women and children are not my problem. Beserians caused my problem. They attacked us and wounded Stanwich. They have caused me to be here in this Three-Gods-forsaken desert searching for some Three-Gods-forsaken magic stick.

"Major, we must warn them," shouted Diego, still riding toward Ben Hamur but slowing down his camel. The smell of burning grew stronger in his nostrils.

"Not our fight!" shouted Hersen. "Not our problem! We search for the Staff of Wisdom as you said yourself!"

"They cannot go unwarned!" shouted Diego, pointing to the west.

"Let the Beserians warn themselves!" said Hersen, glancing over his shoulder at the advancing Demissary columns. They were closer than before, closer and gaining ground.

"We must ride faster!"

"We must warn them," said Diego, slowing down more.

Hersen slowed apace with him. He needed Diego for his languages. Hersen could not speak the language of Ben Hamurians. He could still not speak well the language of the Beserians, much less the Qhaliffans.

"By the Three Gods, Diego, what is wrong with you, man? They are coming closer!"

The arrow struck the top of Hersen's legionnaire hat, taking it down into the dirt.

"Three Gods!" he shouted.

Diego looked.

Two more arrows sailed by his face.

The archers were far enough away that the arrows came down at an angle, as if launched over a high wall. Hersen looked toward the horsemen, a look of disbelief on his face that mounted men could shoot arrows so far or so accurately.

"Hold this!" He dove off of his camel into the sand below, tossing the head rope to Diego.

"Do you wish to die?" Diego's face was incredulous as he caught the rope Hersen had thrown to him.

Hersen grabbed his hat and leaped back up, slowly pulling himself back onto his saddle with both arms.

A trio of arrows sailed over his body while he lay facedown over the saddle.

"Come on!" shouted Diego, pulling the rope back away from Hersen and smacking the side of his camel with his palm.

The cow needed little encouragement. The camels grew increasingly fearful as the mass of warhorses galloped toward them. Hersen turned the camel to the west, with Diego at his side, and the southern wall of Ben Hamur at their right, to the north. Hersen glanced back over his shoulder to look at the Demissaries. A detachment of lancers and archers, perhaps each twenty strong, had broken off from the main columns to ride toward them.

"Can we outrun them?" shouted Hersen.

"On the sands, perhaps!" said Diego, whipping the sides of his camel and shouting "run" in Beserian.

His camel galloped faster, gliding across the hard-packed desert.

Hersen felt another arrow pierce the air to the left of his face. He galloped forward, wondering at his willingness to dive down to get his hat.

Hersen rode, keeping pace with Diego, the far more experienced camel rider, his stomach in a knot. *Perhaps I dove for it because there is not another Legionnaire's hat on the Sand Sea. And I need my Three-Gods-damned hat. And I will not let those bastards say they took a LaFrentian legionnaire's hat as a trophy! At least not Hersen Expey's!*

"We are riding behind the Beserian lines!" shouted Diego. Hersen looked to the north. The Beserian force advanced toward Ben Hamur, a vast crescent, the southern tip of which was perhaps two miles ahead of them.

"North?" barked Hersen into the wind.

"No, west!"

More arrows fell around them, loosed from bows in the hands of fast-riding men, hundreds of yards behind them, missing Hersen and Diego by mere feet.

Hersen and Diego galloped away from Ben Hamur and away from where the Staff of Wisdom was supposed to be, with Demissaries pursuing them for long miles. When they finally reached the Beserian rear, the young men who shouted to them were little more than boys, no older than thirteen, likely younger, gangly and high voiced.

"Who goes there? Ride any closer, and we shall shoot!"

Diego and Hersen slowed their camels, exhausted.

Their camels heaved for air, their sides surging in and out as they labored for breath. The Demissaries were at long last out of sight, having disappeared behind the ridgeline behind them.

"I am called Diego. I am a Vetenan. This man who rides with me is of the west."

The boys appeared to talk amongst themselves. More arose, seeming to appear out of the earth, jumping up from behind boulders and chattering with each other in rapid Beserian.

"What are they saying?" asked Hersen.

"They say that you look like the Amahdi, like the one that rides with Abu Akhsa, broad of shoulder and light of eyes."

Hersen looked at Diego, the question in his eyes. *Could they mean Jack? Does that mean he is still alive?*

"Behind us ride Demissaries!" shouted Diego. "An entire Legion! They are coming here, and they are coming now!"

The boys' chattering ceased. They lowered their rifles at Hersen and Diego.

"How do we know that you are not lying?" asked one, slightly taller than the others, presumably their leader.

"Listen!" said Diego. The hoofbeats rumbled like a Spatanian locomotive, a distant train coming closer on iron tracks.

Hersen could see in the boys' eyes that they could hear it too.

"They are coming," said Diego. "They are coming for you, for your brothers and sisters, your mothers, and your herds! Now warn the others!"

CHAPTER 78
The Battle Begins

Army of Jemojeen Jongdar, East of Ben Hamur
49th Day, Month of Wasura, 807
Anglian Calendar: April 11, 1879

"Infantry, advance!" The order sounded down the line.

The men already held their swords in their right hands and their conical shields in their left hands. All of the men wore black turbans, a sign that they fought for the Qhaliffa first, and for their lords second. Their tunics varied by city, red for Sundar Dun, green for Saman Keer, and so on. Above each city's levies, the banners of their lords snapped in the wind, the same colors as the men's tunics. At intervals, massive black banners bearing the golden symbol of the Qhaliffa punctuated the sky like vast floating birds, soaring above the ranks.

The long lines of infantry marched forward, edging toward Ben Hamur. The ground descended slightly toward the oasis, enough for the men to see the Beserian horde advancing toward them on the other side, moving down the opposite side of the great bowl-like depression, at the bottom of which sat Ben Hamur and the old and famous pools of the oasis, pools now clouded with blood, shards of tile, and pieces of crushed mudbricks.

The officers carried maces with heads shaped like large fists, bristling with five ridges of steel. In their belts, they carried long-barreled pistols, single-shot muzzle-loaders. They marched in the front line of the infantry, with the shield-and-sword men in the front three ranks. The back three ranks held the pikemen, each soldier carrying a sturdy-shafted, eighteen-foot long pole topped with a deadly spike.

Jemojeen sat astride his great black warhorse, watching the infantry advance.

"Keep your guardsmen ready," he said, looking at Sipahi Shaheni. "When the Beserians charge—and they will most certainly charge—you will secure the position behind the wall. You will deploy your men exactly as I have instructed."

"Yes, Grand Vizer," said the Sipahi.

"Turkelan," said Jemojeen.

"Yes, Grand Vizer," said the Erassian, overseeing the scouting for the entire army.

"Where is the First Legion?"

"South of Ben Hamur, riding to the rear, as planned."

"You will tell me when they have reached the tents and the herds."

"Yes, Your Excellency."

"And the Third Legion?" asked Jemojeen, directing his attention forward, looking through a small telescope at the devastation his artillery was still wreaking upon Ben Hamur.

"They are flanking the oasis, enveloping it on either side."

"Why?" asked Jemojeen, already adjusting his view to look for the Demissaries moving toward him from the north of Ben Hamur.

The vast dust cloud rising up from the oasis, the result of hours of pounding from the Great Guns of the Kezelboj, obscured his view, covering Ben Hamur and its near surroundings like a veil.

"I do not see them," said Jemojeen.

"They are there, Your Excellency," said Turkelan. He had learned over the years that he could speak more frankly with the Grand Vizer than others could. He was useful enough for Jemojeen to permit him his blunt speech.

Jemojeen kept his looking glass trained on the northern wall of the oasis. A flash of purple punctuated the cloud of debris and then another, another, and another. Then a full line of riders emerged from the cloud, their faces veiled against the choking dust.

A battery of Kezelboj cannon fired to Jemojeen's right, three guns at once, with the blasts from their long, bronze barrels shaking the ground. Their heavy metal balls struck Ben Hamur at once, twelve hundred yards in the distance, launching more debris into the air as they hit their targets.

"I see them," said Jemojeen, his words barely audible. The artillery had nearly deafened them all.

Turkelan read the Grand Vizer's lips and smiled in his usual, self-satisfied way.

The infantry had now advanced a third of the distance between Jemojeen's command position and the eastern wall of Ben Hamur. On the far side of the oasis, the crescent of the Beserian attack surged forward, two miles out, closing rapidly across the plain.

"Now!" shouted Jemojeen, gesturing with his long hands. "Adjust the artillery. Tell them now! Prepare to fire over Ben Hamur. Use the markers that were placed in the night. Abu Akhsa will soon be in range."

"Yes, Your Excellency," Sipahi Shaheni shouted back. "Fragment balls?"

"Of course," said Jemojeen, frowning.

A Sipahi should know better than to ask superfluous questions.

CHAPTER 79
The Left Flank—
The Advance of the Azadeem

Northwest of Ben Hamur
49th Day, Month of Wasura, 807
Anglian Calendar: April 11, 1879

Azam Azadeem rode ahead of his men, lean as a spear and, like most of his tribe, tall for a Beserian. He held his long-barreled rifle in his hands with his saber resting in its soft leather sheath at his hip. He had ordered his men to do the same. The Hazim tribe rode under his command, as did many of the Beserians from the Barban borderlands, with their strange dialect and their fur-lined tunics. He had instructed them carefully.

Azadeem had long believed that desert wars were won with accurate rifle fire, not saber charges, no matter how much glory his young men might seek by running their blades through the blood of the enemy.

Let them cheer for Abu Akhsa, waving their sabers in the air, but it is marksmanship that will win this day.

Mounted upon their warhorses, the Demissaries advanced in front of him at five hundred yards and closing. A large banner flowed over them, black with green lettering, showing only two diagonal marks: *II*. The two lines marked the Second Demissary Legion, renowned for its cruelty.

Azadeem could see in an instant that the legion advanced in its classic battle formation. The lancers arrayed as shock troops in dense ranks in the center, the archers spread out along the flanks in looser, curving positions like a series of crescent moons, and broad lines of fire Demissaries formed the reserve: orange turbans in the dense front, green turbans on the loose sides, and purple turbans in the broad back.

Azadeem had fought Demissaries before. Most Beserian warriors had not, and few of those who had fought them had ever lived to tell the tale. Azadeem had learned long ago that just because many orange turban men fall does not mean that the battle is won. He knew that the purple turban men—the gunmen in the reserve—can smash an army after they have been weakened and terrorized by the men in the green, the archers with their vicious poisoned arrows that made flesh feel as if it burned from within.

No, Azadeem vowed, *I will not fall prey to their usual tactics, and I will not fall victim to the men in the purple turbans, not this time, not my wing. The left wing will smash the Demissaries, and glory will hang from the shoulders of the Tribe of Azadeem.*

Azadeem's heart pounded with pride as he looked down the line of his men, all riding camels. *They are good men, good shots, men who will shoot down these Demissaries.*

Azadeem signaled for his men to halt, lifting his left fist into the air. The line leaders mimicked his signal and the line stopped.

He signaled to prepare a rifle volley as he returned to the front line. He looked toward the enemy as his men shouldered their rifles, perched atop their camels, aiming as they had all aimed their family weapons a thousand times before.

The Demissaries continued to advance.

Without a word, Azadeem thrust his hand forward.

The line leaders, watching him, barked the command, "Fire!"

The line to Azadeem's left and right erupted in rifle fire, belching black smoke as all Beserian rifles did. He kept his gaze forward as the thick cloud wafted across his line of sight. A sprinkling of the lancers, the large men on the most massive horses at the center of the line, fell onto the sands. He had discussed this with his line leaders in detail. The first volley must strike the lancers to slow them down.

We Beserians cannot face an unweakened line of Demissary lancers in a hand-to-hand clash; no one can. We must weaken them. They must fall first. Slow the lancers down, and we shall slow them all down. This he had said in his tent not six hours before.

Azadeem signaled another volley.

The second rank moved forward through the gaps in the first line as the mounted riflemen of the first rank slowly but expertly loaded their rifles in their saddles.

Azadeem glanced sideways to make sure the second rank had fully cleared the first line. The second rank men moved ahead and shouldered their rifles.

Azadeem thrust his arm forward again, slashing downward.

"Fire!" Nearly three hundred rifles fired as one, fiercely shaking Azadeem's eardrums, making a new cloud of black smoke.

The lancers' line advanced closer. More men fell.

That was a good volley, thought Azadeem. *My plan is sound. If the Celadeens can hold the right flank, this day shall be ours.*

Azadeem signaled for the third rank to move forward. The men rode ahead. Azadeem looked at them. The third rank held the youngest warriors, those most newly arrived into the ranks of manhood, those that had just screamed the loudest for Abu Akhsa and his speech. Their faces held an anxious pride, those of boys seeking to prove that they were indeed men by killing the enemy in front of them, to show that they could shoot the Demissaries as well as their fathers, uncles, and brothers.

In the distance to the east and south, Azadeem heard the deep boom of the Great Guns of the Kezelboj, the boom of the cannons so different from the crack of rifles, even the roar of hundreds of rifles firing as one. Even with the dullness in his ears—battle deafness, he called it—he could hear the sound that was different from all of the others. He looked up.

"God of the Sands," he said aloud.

The first cannonball struck to his left. Men and camels launched into the air, tossed like the grains of sand that had just erupted beneath them. The earth beneath Azadeem shuddered, and his camel roared in fear, jerking to the side and throwing Azadeem into the man next to him, their shoulders slamming into each other from atop their camels.

Azadeem still kept his balance. He turned to see the next three cannonballs strike the ranks of his tightly packed troops.

Before his eyes, a cannonball smashed a camel, sending its neck and head and hind legs in opposite directions. Of the man that had sat atop the camel, Azadeem could see nothing. In a fraction of an instant, the ball lodged in the ground and then burst into fragments, flattening forty men and their mounts.

Azadeem's eyes widened, and his throat tightened. His stomach twisted, and fear raced up his spine, swift as a rodent fleeing a flame.

His ranks shuddered as camels and men panicked. Three more massive cannonballs struck, fired from the bronze guns that Azadeem could barely see with his looking glass through the smoke and dust on the far side of Ben Hamur. More men and camels scattered about him, thrown to the earth with evil force. Arms, legs, entrails, and other parts littered the desert where Azadeem's formidable ranks had stood only moments before.

Men screamed.

Camels roared, barely audible amongst the explosions.

Azadeem looked forward, marveling in horror that the cannons had found their range so quickly. The Demissaries advanced faster, moving directly at him.

"We cannot stay here, Azadeem!" one of his line leaders shouted at him over the din of the wailing.

Three more cannonballs landed and burst.

More men fell. More men and camels added to the chorus of agony in Azadeem's ears.

Azadeem looked ahead.

The Demissaries had moved into a charge. The lancers in the orange turbans looked larger than he could ever remember them looking before. The terrible archers with their poisoned arrows and their green turbans rode forward at full gallops, like desert wolves moving to encircle a herd. The men in purple turbans followed from the rear, almost lazily, as if utterly confident in the victory coming to them.

A scream rose from the direction of Ben Hamur. It was not a scream of pain, but a war cry, bloodcurdling, and loud enough for Azadeem to hear it over the wailing of his wounded men and camels.

He looked.

By the God of the Sands. Where did they come from? On his flank, two hundred more archers charged, men in green turbans, almost in bow range. The banner above them showed three hash marks—*III*—the marks of the Third Demissary Legion.

I have no choice. We will all die. I will expose our flank, but there is no choice. I will not allow the destruction of tribe Azadeem, not while I still draw breath.

"Retreat! Retreat!" shouted Azadeem as loudly as he could, swirling his arm in a circle. His few remaining line leaders, those who had avoided the fragmenting cannonballs and had retained their composure, saw Azadeem and echoed his order.

"Retreat! Retreat! Retreat!"

The men who could still do so turned their camels and fled to the rear, galloping their camels to the west.

Thus collapsed the left flank of Azam Azadeem.

CHAPTER 80
The Right Flank—
The Charge of the Celadeen

Southwest, South, and Southeast of Ben Hamur
49th Day, Month of Wasura, 807
Anglian Calendar: April 11, 1879

Cedak Celadeen sat high on his camel.

He was a small, wiry man atop one of the largest bull camels in all of the herds of Beseria. He had bred the bull for warfare, and it was said that the size of the Celadeen camels matched the size of their fighting spirit in a way that their own human size did not.

The men of the Celadeens of the northern sands, they that had raided against the Erassians of the Gressian borderlands for as long as any could remember, were among the fiercest tribes of men who rode upon the earth. A Celadeen man was as unlikely to walk into battle as were the Erassian horsemen of the steppes. They and their camels were said to share a special bond, closer than the relationships they held with other men of their tribes and even closer than their bonds with their women.

Cedak advanced at a swift trot, his saber in his hand, the saber his father had handed down to him, the saber that the leader of the Celadeens had carried since the time of Beseri. Yet the sword gleamed in the sunlight, its light blade polished as if newly forged. It was forged of Great Mountain steel, of the kind that went into the blades of the Demissaries, the swords made high above the northern cities of Meer Norekah, Nor Wasura, and Nor Gandus. It was said, in Celadeen legend, that the sword Cedak carried had broken other blades in combat without so much as denting its own steel.

Cedak Celadeen looked ahead of him. Nothing but sand stood between him and the zareba at the intersection of the western and southern walls of the oasis of Ben Hamur.

The oasis itself was smoldering, coughing up smoke and dust. Celadeen did not much care what befell the Ben Hamurians. He did not much trust sedentary men, the kind who dwelled in oases. Unlike other Beserian chiefs, he did not ride in the center of his line. He requested to be on the right flank of the battle line, the place of honor, and he usually was given it.

Pompous he might be, but he was pompous for a reason. Save Habeen Barcadey, and perhaps Bazak Bazadak, few if any had ever shown more courage than Cedak Celadeen. The Celadeens rode on the right flank, and he rode at the extreme right end of the line on the right flank. The fearsome tribesmen of the Hazaks and the remainder of the Eastern Beserians rode with them, but to their left, giving the Celadeens the true flank.

As they advanced, a silent mantra moved across his mind, the words he told himself to remind him of his duty: *I am the flank. I am the right. There is no man beyond me. I am the end.*

Celadeen looked down his line of wiry warriors, browned and bronzed by years in the saddle, bearded and fierce atop majestic camels, men like himself. All rode with their sabers drawn, the backs of the curved blades resting against their shoulders as they glided eastward along the sands.

We do not sit and shoot like cautious Azadeems. We ride with the speed and strength of our ancestors, blessed by the God of the Sands. I will cut down this Grand Vizer, and all upon the sands will forever remember Cedak Celadeen. I will deliver the Staffs of Beseri and Mamet to Abu Akhsa from my own hands!

"Ride for the southern wall!" he shouted, his eyes smoldering, using the booming battle voice that was as loud as any in all of the tribes. "Speed shall carry us this day! Celadeeeeeeeen!" he shouted and goaded his bull camel into a full-fledged gallop.

His men followed his lead, positioned just behind him and arrayed for hundreds of yards to his left, a dense wall of men and camels, all charging at a diagonal to the southwestern corner of Ben Hamur.

The ground rumbled as they moved, kicking up sand as high as the camels' chests. The air was clear but for the billowing cloud of smoke and dust rising above Ben Hamur and then wafting to the south. The northerly wind drove the thick fog south, and then pushed it down toward the desert, all the way to the sand, making a massive tunnel into which the riders of the Celadeen now charged.

Ahead, no enemies marred their path to the confluence of the southern and western walls. To the right, which was south, lay the dense cloud of smoke and Ben Hamurian debris. What lay beyond that, none could say.

If men are there, we shall be through the gap before they can respond to us. Nor shall they catch us before we slay the Kezelboj.

Already, in his mind, Celadeen could see the looks of adoration from the women of the tribes. Already, he could feel the joy of hearing Abu Akhsa proclaim him the savior of the day, more significant than the Amahdi of the West in whom so many hopes had been placed, greater than Azadeem or Bazadak, greater than old Hamid Salesi, Handsome Habeen Barcadey, and even Abu Akhsa himself. *Celadeen! Celadeen!* That is what the people would shout.

Celadeen galloped onward, edging closer to the tunnel of smoke and dust before him, hearing the booming of the Great Guns of the Kezelboj in the distance. The Great Guns had stopped shelling Ben Hamur. *Where are they firing? Not at the Celadeens! The God of the Sands blesses us this day!*

They galloped onward. The burning smells of Ben Hamur increased—flesh and wood and cloth and other things. The smoke began to burn Celadeen's eyes, forcing tears down his cheeks and pinching at the back of his throat. He coughed as he rode. He lifted his sand veil over his face, the fabric of the mesh thin enough to keep out even the smallest grains in a sandstorm.

From the far side of the oasis walls, sounds of agony mixed with the smells of burning—animals, men, and women all wailed in a chorus of pain, loss, and despair. One sound, unmistakable, spoke more clearly than any words. Children cried for parents.

The words rose over the wall, the sound of a young girl. "Mother!"

The wall came closer, as did the still intact thorn zareba that protected all of the twelve-foot-high mudbrick walls, growing up from the mud at the base of the moat to fill the entirety of the deep ditch, rising above the level of the plain to a height taller than a man.

Celadeen eyed the zareba to his left, grateful it was not his task to attempt to breach it or the wall behind it.

Celadeen looked at the wall behind the zareba. No guardsmen looked down upon him or his riders from the parapets as they rode closer and closer, nor did any Qhaliffans stand upon the wall. The southernmost part of the western wall was as empty as if the oasis was already abandoned.

The cloud of debris was now overhead, blocking off the sunlight and eliminating all visibility to the south. Celadeen rode into the artificial twilight. Ash trickled down as if it were snowing, but there was no mistaking the smell of death and burning that now flanked them on both sides and covered them from above.

Celadeen made no effort to be quiet. Raiders were quiet, seeking to sneak up upon an enemy. *This is not a raid. We charge for glory in the Battle of the Prophecy.* The booming of the Kezelboj cannons grew louder, yet wherever they were firing, Celadeen could not see. He could not hear where the cannonballs landed, save for a faint sound of crashing in the far distance somewhere to the north.

"Charge!" shouted Cedak Celadeen as he and his tribesmen galloped through the tunnel beneath the cloud, shaking the ground beneath them. The southern wall and its zareba now bound them from the north, cloaked in smoke. The debris cloud itself now bound them from the south, as impermeable to the eye as a solid wall. Yet far ahead, through the smoke tunnel, the sun shone down from a warm blue sky, a sky of spring, and Cedak Celadeen did not see a single Qhaliffan in his way.

"Do you hear them, you stupid son of a whore?"

"Yes, sir," said the Captain of the Grand Vizerian Guardsmen, bristling under the Sipahi Shaheni's rebuke, but not daring to show it.

"Then put your men tighter together! You want those Celadeen bastards getting in these gaps to slash at you with their sabers?"

"No, sir," said the Captain, turning to his men. "Close the ranks. Close them tighter!"

His men responded immediately, moving closer together so their shoulders touched and their small, round shields overlapped. With two gloved hands, each man gripped a nine-foot spear, a half-spear, as the pikemen of the Kezelboj called them, with mocking in their voice. Dark-grey chain mail armor hung from the torso of each of the guardsmen, covering their bodies down past the tops of their knee-high boots. The same chain mail draped down from their steel helmets, which sat upon their heads in the shape of half chicken eggs beneath tightly wrapped black turbans.

Sipahi Shaheni stood behind the line, pointing with his mace. He shouted at his captains, personally berating sergeants and even regular guardsmen.

"Closer!"

His men were not of the same quality as Demissaries, not even close. They were little better than the levies of the Kezelboj, more accustomed to bullying merchants and criminals in the flatlands of Alwaz Deem than facing a determined force of tribesmen riders.

I have seen the Celadeen. I wish we had been assigned another tribe to face. His heart thumped. His men were not desert fighters. Nor were they men who had met a charge from galloping camelmen, much less *Celadeen* camelmen.

I am the anvil; the Erassians and the Demissaries are the hammer. The anvil cannot break. If we are to fail, it must be Turkelan and the Legion Commanders that fails. Jemojeen will flay me if these men break. He could even burn me. Yes, he is capable of that. Shaheni swallowed the bile in his throat. The ground shook from the charging Beserians and grew stronger. *They are halfway along the southern wall. They will be here soon. The Celadeen are almost here.*

"Tighten the line!" he shouted for the fortieth time.

The line could tighten no more. The men seemed calm enough.

Yes, well, we shall see how calm they are when the fury of the Celadeens emerges from behind that wall.

Shaheni looked to his right, at the corner of the southern and eastern walls of Ben Hamur. He placed the right end of his line right up against the eastern zareba, set back twenty-five yards from the south wall but parallel to it. His infantry line stood shoulder to shoulder, shield to shield, and stacked five ranks deep. They stretched three hundred yards to the east of Ben Hamur, facing due south.

They were a dense block of spearmen, so dense that even if the front men wished to retreat, they would be unable to do so. A man in the front ranks could only do one thing—thrust his spear forward and kill the Beserian in front of him. He could do that, or he could die. Shaheni had long ago understood the value of picking men who did not wish to die, men who saw cruelty as their only path forward. Yes, Sipahi Shaheni had long found such men useful in his service to Jemojeen.

Shouts rose from behind the southern wall. Shaheni gripped his mace handle more tightly in his right hand.

"Prepare!" he shouted.

The captains echoed his order. The men lowered their spearpoints.

Celadeen and his men had nearly passed the southern wall. The sunlight shone brightly at the end of the smoke tunnel just ahead of them. Their line had condensed to a column to avoid riding their camels through the choking smoke of the dense cloud to their right or into the thorns of the southern wall's zareba to their left. Celadeen rode in the front rank, his saber in his right hand.

"We ride to the guns of the Kezelboj!" he shouted.

Celadeen emerged first into the bright sunshine, launching out of the eastern end of the smoke tunnel at a full gallop, like a bullet from a barrel. The path ahead lay open. He looked left. His heart jumped, and his limbs tensed with adrenaline.

The grey-black line of infantry stood like a solid block of Great Mountain granite, stretching for hundreds of yards, like an extension of Ben Hamur's walls, only darker and bristling with spears.

The other Celadeens charging out of the smoke tunnel saw the infantry at the same time as their leader.

"Wheel! Wheel! Turn to charge them!"

The next ranks of horsemen charged out of the smoke tunnel, turning on Celadeen's command and instinct. They veered left in a great crescent, camels and men emerging from the smoke, flowing like a stream around the southeastern corner of Ben Hamur's mudbrick walls.

"Pierce the line! *Pierce the line!*"

Celadeen put his eyes on a man. Thousands stood before him, far many more thousands than he had believed the Qhaliffa could deploy against him at this place, hidden behind the walls. *There, I shall break you there! I will break your line and then cut you down from the rear.*

Celadeen goaded his camel to charge against the solid body of men and the bristling hedge of spearpoints.

His heart thundered, and his eyes narrowed as he closed for impact.

"Celadeen!" he screamed. His men echoed his war cry, shrieking with raised sabers atop their tall galloping camels.

The ground underneath them shook. The camels charged across a narrow but deep front, the riders following those in front of them out from the smoke tunnel behind the southern wall.

Sipahi Shaheni stood behind the line, five rows deep. His front row had knelt, holding their spearpoints at a forty-five-degree angle, in such a way as to impale the chest of any camel willing to charge headlong against them. The standing men behind them stood with lowered spearpoints, and the third row, the second line of standing men, lowered their spearpoints as well.

Shaheni saw him—a wiry man who seemed to draw all attention as he charged. He rode slightly ahead of the others. He would strike the line first. The man shouted with a saber raised above his head. His camel was gigantic and as ferocious as its rider, charging without fear against the hedge of spears.

Shaheni set his jaw for the impact, holding his mace and his breath.

The first man struck the line, his huge bull camel bursting through the first three rows of spearmen. He reared up with a pair of spears jammed into him, kicking and biting as the man on its back swung his saber as fast as Shaheni had ever seen a man swing a sword. Fifty more camels struck the line, knocking through the front ranks, the unarmored swordsmen slashing downward at his mailed spearmen.

The lead rider was still atop his wounded camel, pushing forward against the fifth and final rank. He slashed his saber, somehow avoiding the spearpoints jammed up at him.

Sipahi Shaheni himself ran to reinforce the line. His captains were already there, roaring out orders that no man could hear above the chaos of swords, spears, camel flesh, and chain mail colliding. The final rank of men thrust their spears at the horsemen, shouting as they fought.

Cedak Celadeen looked down and saw the spears jammed into his camel, the finest bull he had ever owned. They were pushed in past the metal tip. It was only a matter of time before the beast fell. A spear tip flashed past Celadeen's face. Another grazed his arm, pain registering as the spear opened flesh. It was not his sword arm. Celadeen saw an exposed arm below him, gripping a spear shaft. He swung and separated the hand at the wrist. Before the man's scream registered in his ears, he was already swinging at a trio of spearpoints, knocking them backward.

Celadeen looked up as his wounded camel carried him further still. He could feel other riders pressing in next to him, burrowing deep into the last ranks of the spearmen, slashing and killing as they pressed the attack home. There was only open space now between him and the Great Guns of the Kezelboj, booming a half-mile in the distance, bellowing great clouds of grey-black smoke.

By the God of the Sands, we are through them.

A Sipahi emerged in front of him. He recognized him as the leader by the badge on his chest and by the cape draped from his shoulders. He carried no spear, only a mace in his hands and a sword in a sheath. Celadeen saw the man drop his mace and draw his sword.

"Ayaah!" shouted Celadeen, slashing down at the final spearman in front of him.

His camel pushed him through and then collapsed, falling onto its chest and neck.

Celadeen leaped from the falling camel's back, landing on the balls of his feet, directly in front of the Sipahi.

The man slashed at him.

Celadeen parried the blow with his saber, the ancient blade of his forefathers. The swords clashed with a metallic screech.

Celadeen rolled and swung low at the man's ankles. The Sipahi, stout and broad across the shoulders, leaped in the air, locking eyes with Celadeen, looking out from a wide, thuggish face.

The Sipahi brought his sword down, fiercely and with great force. Celadeen rolled to the side. The Sipahi's blade struck the earth. Celadeen gained his feet, slashing down with his sword as he rose.

The Sipahi blocked the blow.

Celadeen could feel other tribesmen around him, advancing on foot as he was.

The Sipahi backed up, outnumbered.

Celadeen pursued him, slashing as he advanced.

The Sipahi backed up still, retreating but keeping his eyes on the other Beserian tribesmen advancing toward him on foot, their camels slain on the ground behind them.

Celadeen looked up, past the Sipahi, seeing a flash of orange in front of him. Then he saw a man mounted upon a massive warhorse.

The man in the orange turban emerged as if he had just sprung up from the ground itself. The Sipahi continued to retreat backward, but Celadeen did not pursue him. Other men in orange turbans emerged out of the sands.

God of the Sands, there is a wadi there. How many? How many horsemen could be in there? The thoughts flooded Celadeen's mind as his heart pounded.

More riders flooded the space before him, like demons rising from the abyss, massive men atop huge warhorses. The front rider was among the most towering warriors Celadeen had ever seen. The man locked his eyes upon Celadeen and kicked his warhorse into a gallop.

The man charged, lowering his long lance.

Celadeen looked behind him. There was no place to retreat. Behind him, a melee of men killed each other in a dense mass, camels and unarmored tribesmen falling amongst armored spearmen, the chain mail draped down from their helmets to protect their necks.

He saw a tribesman slash, striking chain mail. Then the spearman thrust his spear into the tribesman's chest, bringing him down from his camel.

Celadeen spun back around. The lancers had grown more numerous, and the lead chargers were much closer. He looked around him. Only a handful of his tribesmen stood near him. There was nowhere to run.

The Sipahi stepped toward him, shouting in rough, accented Beserian, "Today you die, tribesman!"

The lancers thundered nearer, the largest among them riding directly at Celadeen himself.

"Prepare for cavalry!" Celadeen shouted.

Those around him spread out and crouched down, low to the ground, their swords cocked behind their heads.

The horsemen charged closer. The lead lancer, the massive man, lowered his long lance.

God of the Sands guide me. Celadeen exhaled and narrowed his eyes.

The lance head slipped by him, grazing his back, as he leaped across the horse. In the same movement, he swung his saber at the horse's hind legs. The charger flashed past him in a blur, but Celadeen felt the ancient steel bite into the horseflesh. The horse screamed and stumbled, dropping the rider.

Celadeen turned just in time to meet the running Sipahi's blade. The Sipahi attacked in earnest this time, slashing high, low, and then high again, swinging powerful blows that knocked Celadeen backward.

As Celadeen parried the Sipahi's blows, he did not see the massive Demissary Captain rise up from his wounded horse behind him, unsheathing his huge scimitarus. He did not see the tremendous curved blade as it rose in the air like an executioner's ax. The blow struck Celadeen at the collarbone on his sword-swinging arm, passing halfway down into his torso. His eyes opened in astonishment as his family sword fell into the dust.

As he collapsed, nearly cleaved in two, the ranks of Demissary lancers galloped by, riding to kill whatever tribesmen remained in the melee.

The Sipahi Shaheni nodded at Captain Ulgur. Ulgur smiled at the blood splashed across the blade of his scimitarus. Shaheni could not remember the last time he had seen Ulgur smile. He had never liked the man, and he did not like him now.

Ulgur looked down at Celadeen's body and spat.

"Get me a new horse."

CHAPTER 81
The Center's Advance

Oasis of Ben Hamur
49th Day, Month of Wasura, 807
Anglian Calendar: April 11, 1879

The nine of them advanced behind a solid wall of camel cavalry.

They were:

Selena, of House Savanar, daughter of Sah Seg Savanar

Jack Caldwell, of Calderon, called Amahdi of the West

*Ottovan Fanfar, Commander, Third Demissary Legion,
The Lion of the Order*

*Nemakar Hasdruba, Fire Captain, Third Demissary
Legion, a Lion of the Order*

Oapah the Hohsa, a Lion of the Order

Gulana, of Nor Gandus, a Lion of the Order

*Handsome Habeen Barcadey, Leader of the
Swordguard of Abu Akhsa*

Aurelio, of House Demassi, of the Veteno

Jabil, of tribe Bazadak, called the Jackal

When the God of the Sands ordained it, they would ride for Jemojeen Jongdar himself, and they would take the Staffs of Wisdom and Ruling from his
hands, the Serpent Staff of Beseri and the Ram Staff of Mamet. That was the
plan they had agreed upon with Abu Akhsa and Hamid Salesi. Hamid Salesi

saw the nine riding for Jemojeen—seven men and two women—and he saw victory.

But without the staff, Salesi's farsight was not what it once was, and soon, if the Staff of the Serpent remained in Jemojeen's hands, what had once been Salesi's power to see would soon be Jemojeen's. In time, Jemojeen would see what he wanted to see, far and near, future and past. The nine rode for Jemojeen with the understanding that the fate of the Sand Sea rode with them.

Habeen Barcadey rode in the center, flanked by Jack Caldwell to his left and by Selena Savanar to his right.

One hundred men of Abu Akhsa's Swordguard rode with them. To mark them from other warriors, as always, the Swordguard wore a sky-blue band wrapped around their headscarves. There was no more coveted marking a man could seek in all of Beseria. No man could become a Swordguardsman without being chosen by Abu Akhsa himself. The sons of the powerful were no more likely to earn the sky-blue band than were the sons of the poor and unknown. A man could only earn his way by fighting against the enemies of the tribes, and even then, only by showing the most exceptional valor, the kind that places honor above all else. Those were the words they said upon receiving the sky-blue band: *honor above life, indifference to death.*

Even a proud chief like Azadeem or Celadeen would nod respectfully to a man of the Swordguard, even if he were born the bastard son of a goatless mother. Even those who took great pride in being a man of one of the mightiest tribes—be it Azadeem, Bazadak, Celadeen, or Salesi—would look upon a man with the sky-blue headband and feel something approaching envy.

The assembled might of the Bazadaks rode in front of the nine and their Swordguard escort. Three rows of camelmen, with horse riders of the Kateems and the Sambads along the flanks, moved forward at a walk across a half-mile front. Ben Hamur lay broken in front of them, smashed and smoking from Jemojeen's bombardment, but the western wall still stood, twelve feet high and intact behind its thorn zareba.

At the center of the camelmen, in the center of the front line, rode Bazak Bazadak. He did not make decisions quickly or easily, but when he made a decision, he was nearly unmovable. He had decided to advance. He rode lightly in his saddle for being a heavy man, dense with muscle and explosive when he moved. No Beserian had ever defeated Handsome Habeen Barcadey with a blade, but Bazak Bazadak had come the closest.

"What do you see?" asked Hamid Salesi, watching them advance from the rear.

His plain eyesight was not what it once was; it too seemed to have receded since Ghani, the traitor, had stolen the Staff of Wisdom from his hands. There was little high ground to the immediate west of Ben Hamur, once one descended from the far western ridgeline, but Abu Akhsa and Hamid Salesi stood upon the sole hillock, which was little more than a mound. From that mound, they could see most of what lay to the west of the oasis, the vast bowl-shaped plain spread out before them, with Bazak Bazadak's force advancing directly ahead.

"The smoke obscures all that lies beyond the oasis," said Abu Akhsa, lowering his looking glass and shaking his head.

"And to the south?"

"Smoke," said Abu Akhsa. "Celadeen leads his men into that tunnel."

"Into it?" asked Hamid Salesi.

"Yes."

"Not around it? Not to the south?"

"No," said Abu Akhsa, seeing Hamid Salesi's meaning. His right flank was unguarded and exposed. Whatever lay beyond the smoke wall, growing denser by the minute, would be unchecked and unchallenged.

Hamid Salesi looked back behind him. The remaining four hundred of the Swordguard waited, the sole reserve of the army. "Celadeen may have erred, Abu Akhsa, by being too aggressive."

Abu Akhsa nodded, knowing it was true.

"What do you see?" asked Abu Akhsa.

"There is little of the farsight left in me," said Salesi. He slumped in his saddle, looking older than he had ever looked before.

"Can you see beyond the oasis and beyond that tower of smoke?"

"Darkly," said Salesi. "Jemojeen is there. The Great Guns of the Kezelboj are there. The Kezelboj army waits there as well."

"Waits or advances?" asked Abu Akhsa.

Hamid Salesi faced forward with his eyes tightly closed, his forehead wrinkling with concentration.

"They advanced. Now they wait. The army lies in wait: Kezelboj levies, Erassian cavalry, Grand Vizerian Guardsmen, and much of a Demissary legion."

"Behind Ben Hamur? Behind the zareba?" asked Abu Akhsa. He could feel the nervousness in his stomach.

"No," said Hamid Salesi, wrinkling his forehead even more. "They hide behind the wall, thousands of infantry. Demissary lancers hide in a long fold in the ground."

"Then Celadeen rides into a trap," said Abu Akhsa.

A loud boom sounded from the far side of Ben Hamur. A chorus of booms followed just behind, each as loud as the other.

"The Great Guns fire again," said Abu Akhsa, training his looking glass on Ben Hamur, waiting to see the impact of the giant cannonballs. He saw nothing strike.

"North," said Hamid Salesi, his eyes still closed and his forehead still creased in concentration.

Abu Akhsa turned to his left, to the north to where Azadeem's forces advanced on the flank. He could not see Azadeem's force itself due to the undulating ground, but he could mark them by the smoke rising from their ranks. They were engaged, firing rifle volleys against Jemojeen's right flank. The sounds of the Azadeem rifles crackled in the distance, and barrel smoke wafted southward toward Ben Hamur.

The ground looked as if it coughed, sending sand and debris up into the air. A handful of other eruptions followed just after.

"They are firing on Azadeem!" said Hamid Salesi, his eyes still closed.

"I see it," said Abu Akhsa. He turned backward, again looking at his reserve, the mere four hundred of his Swordguard remaining.

"Do not release them," said Hamid Salesi.

Another salvo of Kezelboj cannon fire landed amongst the Azadeems on the left flank.

"I fear they will be overwhelmed," said Abu Akhsa. "If Azadeem retreats, our left flank will collapse."

"Do not release them," said Hamid Salesi, opening his eyes, and shaking his head. "There are greater dangers ahead."

Umahar, the Demissary, and Anil Salesi stood behind them in silence, training their looking glasses forward, at the zareba of Ben Hamur.

Bazak Bazadak held his saber in his hand. He alternated his men, saber, and rifle, prepared for whatever might lie ahead. The desert was a treacherous place, with many flatlands hiding folds in the earth that could hold hundreds and even thousands. Long barreled, single-shot, muzzleloading rifles were excellent when an enemy could be seen and shot at a distance; a Beserian rifle was accurate and deadly, sighted for range. But the same weapons could be a disaster if an enemy was close enough to charge, rising from the earth below, slashing and stabbing at camels and riders with swords and spears. Then a Beserian wished only for his saber. Bazak knew not what Jemojeen would throw at him, but he would be ready either way.

The zareba along the western wall grew more significant by the moment, no more than one hundred yards in front of them, wide and twisting like a tangle of spiny snakes, rising from a pit. Still, no man stood upon the walls of Ben Hamur. No long guns boomed from the ramparts; no Demissary archers flung their poisoned arrows down upon them. The Great Guns of the Kezelboj had turned their fury to the north.

Before they turned their cannon barrels to the north to smash the ranks of Aza-deem, the Great Guns of the Kezelboj had reduced the eastern wall of Ben Hamur to an extensive line of rubble. The buildings adjacent to the wall were no more, crumbled into piles of mudbricks and roof tiles, crushing furniture and bodies beneath, obliterating lives that had until that day been stable and secure for generations. Amidst the rage following the Sharef's murder, the Ben Hamurians who had counseled against revolution were drowned out by louder voices, voices seeking revenge and glory, seeking to grasp the moment of history, seeking the sky-blue banner of Abu Akhsa.

Yet, Abu Akhsa was last said to be descending upon the oasis from the western horizon. His banners had yet to enter Ben Hamur. The Great Guns of the Kezelboj had struck first, deadly, indiscriminate, and relentless. The can-nonballs lodged in the earth of Ben Hamur were now as commonplace as the stones in the Valley of Boulders. What was once a place of greenery, order, and respite from the desert was now a hellscape—a tribute to the destruction of Qhaliffan cannon fire. The dust of the crushed buildings still hung above the air like thick smoke. Mixing with the debris, actual smoke rose upward, choking the air from a hundred fires started by the incendiary balls bursting with fire upon landing, fire so hot that it could ignite a tree trunk upon contact.

Into this place, Jemojeen Jongdar rode at the head of the Kezelboj forces, with the levies of Sundar Dun in the fore. Many were gangmen from the flat-lands, men of the streets, men of crime, only willing to fight for their southern lords upon the promise of great plunder. To meet the Grand Vizer's quota, the southern lords had to resort to bribing such men, men of little discipline and even less honor. The gangmen likely regretted their arrangement now, seeing they were headed into the burning oasis, for dead men could not spend coins.

The men of Sundar Dun laid long boards down across the thornbushes of the zareba, making a passable bridge across the ditch that would hold a lesser force at bay. Jemojeen rode across on his black stallion, haughty and lean, the horse matching the demeanor of its master.

The remaining lords of Sundar Dun rode just behind him, short, wide men, wearing red bejeweled turbans. They were olive-skinned men, like all Qhalif-fans, but being southerners, their olive tint was darker than that of their north-ern brethren. They were far darker than Jemojeen Jongdar, a Bulbanian by birth, like all Demissaries, with the paler complexion to match.

In his right hand, Jemojeen carried the Staff of Ruling, made of cedar, with its top shaped like a ram's head. In his left hand, he carried the Staff of Wisdom, the carved serpent coiling downward around the olive-wood shaft in a spiral.

The lords of Sundar Dun eyed the Grand Vizer and the staffs he carried warily, Lord Cerelac's fate fresh in their minds.

At last, for the first time in eight hundred years, he, Jemojeen Jongdar, had united Beseri and Mamet, Wisdom and Ruling, Serpent and Ram. Pride rose like a flood tide inside of him, making his skin tingle with the feeling of unmatched power.

Though the battle was not yet won, the words of his achievement would not depart his mind. *I did this, not Sumetan, that common fool. Not even Mamet ever achieved this. Ben Hamur burns, and I ride with more of the Staff of the Prophet than any man has held since the Prophet himself. I, and I alone, Jemojeen Jongdar!*

Sipahi Shaheni and his Grand Vizerian Guardsmen still fought to the south, destroying what remained of the forces of the Celadeen. Ahead of Jemojeen rode Turkelan and his Erassians that had first crossed over the makeshift bridges, thrusting their javelins into any Ben Hamurians who crossed their path. The levies of Sundar Dun followed the Erassians, making a pathway through the rubble just ahead of Jemojeen, working furiously and fearing the eyes of the Grand Vizer just behind them.

Jemojeen did not slow the steady walking pace of his horse.

"Faster!" shouted one of the Sundar Dun lords, a short, fat man who had never done an hour of physical labor in his life. The pommel of his sword gleamed at his side, bejeweled and rarely handled. A long whip sat in his right hand, as well used as his sword was ignored. He snapped it at the back of a man who had stopped lifting rubble from the street.

Above Jemojeen, atop a flagstaff held by an armored Grand Vizerian guardsman, the tremendous black banner of the Qhaliffa crackled in the wind, its gold circle, centerline, and outer rim shimmering in the sunlight.

The burnings of rebels had begun, and the acrid smell assaulted Jemojeen's nostrils. He did not flinch as he rode onward. He heard screams as flames engulfed the half-crushed buildings. Mudbricks and roof tiles did not easily burn, but the palm fronds that formed the mats of every home burned readily.

Jemojeen looked ahead as a woman with a young child ran from a thick cloud of black smoke. She emerged from her front door into the avenue, coughing violently and looking around her with darting, frightened eyes. A mounted Erassian launched a javelin into her, spearing her through the toddler in her arms. They both fell dead to the ground.

Jemojeen looked away as if he had seen nothing more than the slaughter of a chicken for his dinner.

"Bring me Turkelan," said Jemojeen.

The Sipahi at Jemojeen's side nodded and rode ahead, spurring his horse into a canter. Jemojeen preferred Shaheni as his Sipahi, but Shaheni had craved battle glory, requesting to command the guardsmen of the left flank.

Very well, thought Jemojeen. *I suppose every sword-swinger must find his glory at some time if he wishes to feel fully a man. Perhaps he would have chosen otherwise if I told him the left flank would face the Celadeens. It would be best if Shaheni returned to me alive . . .*

The Sipahi that Jemojeen had dispatched returned with Captain Turkelan.

Jemojeen kept his gaze forward. "Turkelan, clear out every building along the western wall. And do it now. I intend to fill them with our foot soldiers."

"Yes, Your Excellency," said Turkelan, saluting with a bow and his right arm outstretched. Then he turned to ride ahead.

Jemojeen continued down the main east-west avenue of Ben Hamur, which, before this day, was paved with flat stones, well mortared, and flat as a pool of still water. It was flat no longer.

Ahead of Jemojeen, an array of cannonballs lay lodged in the stones, turning pavers up at perpendicular angles to the earth and tossing others out of place. Broken, jagged shards now lay sprinkled across Jemojeen's path. The Great Guns had done their work well.

"Sundar Dun!" barked Jemojeen without turning around.

A pair of Kezelboj lords rode forward, each dark-skinned, bejeweled, and stout in the manner of men who dine richly every evening.

"Yes, Your Excellency?" said the fattest and eldest of the Kezelboj lords. The people of Sundar Dun were said to greatly fear this man with a reputation for cruelty and ruthlessness. Jemojeen found him servile and could see the fear in his face as he stared into his eyes. None of the Kezelboj lords would soon forget the timely lesson of Lord Cerelac, and not just those of Sundar Dun.

"The time has come," said Jemojeen. "Deploy your levies. If there is a house left unoccupied, I will hear of it, and you shall hear of it from me. I want men in every single house. I want them behind every wall. When the tribesmen come over the wall, your men will draw them in. Am I understood?"

"Yes, Your Excellency," said the Kezelboj.

"What are you waiting for?" asked Jemojeen.

The Kezelboj flushed. They turned and rode back toward the officers of their levies, shouting profanities and turning their fear of Jemojeen into a rage at their underlings.

Jemojeen listened with satisfaction as the Great Guns boomed behind him. He smiled as the impacts of the cannonballs sounded to his right, north of the north wall of Ben Hamur. He had planned the sighting of the guns himself, and he had ordered the markers set up north of the wall. The Azadeem tribesmen rode squarely between the markers, just as Jemojeen had foreseen the night before, looking into the farsight with the Staff of the Serpent.

"Now find me the only two that matter," said Jemojeen, speaking aloud to himself.

The Sipahi riding just behind him glanced at Jemojeen's face and then quickly looked away. The Sipahi did not like magic. It frightened him even more than the man who was wielding it.

Jemojeen's eyes closed again. What the Sipahi could not see was the bright ocean of images flashing behind Jemojeen's closed eyelids.

"Show them to me," he said, gripping the Staff of Wisdom more tightly and feeling its power move up his arm, through his shoulder, up his neck, and into his mind, cooling his face as it flowed, caressing him like a piece of silk.

The Sipahi eased the pace of his horse's stride, creating a few more feet between himself and Jemojeen as the serpent on the staff changed to its unnatural color of silver-green.

Selena Savanar came into Jemojeen's view, riding a caramel-colored camel with a man's Beserian-style headdress covering her hair.

To her left rides the black-faced Hohsa, a massive man. He is the one they call Oapah, yes, the one Shaheni suspected years ago. I should have listened to him then. Oapah, the stonemason. I will kill him and all of the other Omakhosian stonemasons in Ganjar en Oxus. Does he ride with Selena Savanar? Then he is without question an Oath Holder of the Order. He must have been the tall one the guardsmen saw in the back of the alley, the one as large as Ulgur Uggatar who saved her on the day she was to be burned. His face covering does not conceal him from me now!

To Selena's right rode a broad man with a long diagonal scar on the side of his face. Jemojeen knew the face and the reputation that came with the face.

I was there when you were scarred, Habeen Barcadey. That slash should have killed you. You will not escape this battlefield alive.

Another face came across Jemojeen's eyes, behind his eyelids. The man was young, tall, and handsome, no older than a young Demissary sergeant and more youthful than any lieutenant. His jaw was strong and squarish, his eyes bright blue. His beard covering his jawline was as blond as it was brown, in the way of the Gerdic men of the north and some of the Gressians.

Who are you, riding with Selena Savanar and Habeen Barcadey? Are you my enemy of the west? The one they call the Amahdi? Are you the one they claim will bring down the house of the Qhaliffas? I think you are that one. Are you here to defeat me? I think not. You are a fraud. I asked to see you, and here you are. You will fall, Amahdi. You will fall this day, and I will burn you next to Selena Savanar. You will burn for all of the Seven Cities to see. I will burn you both in the Square of the Savanars, and all will know the prophecy is a lie.

Even with the Staff of Wisdom in his hand, and even with the growing farsight, Jemojeen did not let his mind linger on the man who rode to the

Amahdi's right, the broad, shorter man whose face was covered by a veil. Something was deeply familiar in the man's posture and in the way he rode. So too did he carry a broadsword in a broad scabbard, wide enough to be a Demissary's scimitarus. But Jemojeen Jongdar had other things to worry about.

"Where are the reserve archers of the Third?" shouted Jemojeen, opening his eyes, and looking around him, as the olive wood of the Staff of the Serpent resumed its natural color. *I will leave nothing to chance today. Today the rebellion dies.*

"We are here," said Ozgar Ogatonia, Captain of the Bow, advancing at a trot. One hundred of his riders rode behind him, carrying a black banner with the three green slashes of the Third Legion.

Jemojeen looked at the calm face of the archer. Jemojeen had known him since he trained at the Academy. He had won the archer competition across the chasm, the Challenge of the Bridge. That day Jemojeen learned the name Ozgar Ogatonia, and he had never forgotten it.

Something twisted in Jemojeen's mind. It was doubt, a lingering sense that something was amiss, but the thought vanished as quickly as it arrived. He had a battle to win and a revolution to smash.

"We await your order to deploy, Your Excellency," said Ozgar, saluting with his fist across his chest. His gaze rested steadily upon Jemojeen's face, fearless and firm. The mounted archers trailed behind him in two columns, saluting as Ozgar had saluted.

"Very well," said Jemojeen. "Wait until they have tired themselves against the levies of Sundar Dun." Jemojeen flared his nostrils as the smell of burning human flesh wafted by. "I do not waste my Demissary archers on the front line," said Jemojeen, flashing a smile that held more malice than mirth.

Ozgar met his eyes again, saluted, and turned his horse toward the western wall. His men followed as he galloped down the avenue, flanked on either side by smashed buildings, wrecked by the Great Guns of the Kezelboj.

For a moment, a thought entered Jemojeen's mind again. *I know those eyes; I know them from another face.* A knot of discomfort and dread twisted in Jemojeen's stomach, the kind he rarely felt in recent years, the kind that comes before a battle against a dangerous foe. A Beserian horn sounded from just beyond the wall.

Whatever was wrong with Ozgar, the archer's gaze would have to wait for later.

CHAPTER 82
Bazadak Breaks Through

Oasis of Ben Hamur
49th Day, Month of Wasura, 807
Anglian Calendar: April 11, 1879

"Abu Akhsa," said Umahar, from behind his veil. Against his strong objections, Ottovan had ordered Umahar to stay at Abu Akhsa's side to inform him of the ways of the Demissaries, of things he might not know, things that might make the difference between victory and disaster once the battle came underway. Also, at Ottovan's command, Umahar kept his face veiled.

Jemojeen can see with the farsight now. He will see us where no looking glass can see. Neither buildings nor distance can shield us from his gaze. Anywhere on the Sand Sea or in the Seven Cities, he can find us. Let not your face be left unveiled. If he knows to look for you, his gaze will find you. Stay covered!

Those were the last words Ottovan Fanfar shouted before he rode forward with Nemakar, and the others, nine riders in all, nine riders to take back the Staffs of Beseri and Mamet from Jemojeen upon the battlefield.

Abu Akhsa turned to the Demissary Lieutenant, physician for all of the Third Legion, a man of medicine and vast knowledge.

"Be wary of your flanks," said Umahar.

"Azadeem is to our left; Celadeen is to our right."

"Azadeem will soon retreat, and Celadeen has advanced too far," said Umahar.

Abu Akhsa looked into the Demissary's eyes, knowing his words were true.

Ottovan Fanfar swears by this man. He is an Oath Holder of the Order. I can trust him, and I must.

"What would you have me do?" asked Abu Akhsa after a long pause.

Hamid Salesi looked at Umahar with weary eyes, awaiting the Demissary's answer. Anil Salesi waited next to him, in silence, wishing he were with the others riding for Jemojeen.

"Do not commit your reserve," said Umahar, gesturing back at the four hundred men of the Swordguard. He frowned as he looked at them, doubting, despite their fierce reputation, that they would be enough to stop a rout if the flanks collapsed.

Abu Akhsa acknowledged Umahar's words with a nod and turned back toward the front, scanning with his looking glass. Bazadak's men had dismounted all along the zareba. The men with the triple-layered tents were running forward, carrying the thick fabric to the dense thicket of thorns growing out of the wide trench along the western wall.

Umahar raised his own looking glass, skeptical that the Beserian method was capable of crossing the zareba.

The first line of Beserians heaved weighted, clawed javelins at the mudbrick wall. The shafts sailed over the zareba and across the moat. Some of the javelins struck the wall and ricocheted off. Others landed true, gripping the wall's rim, trailing double strands of ropes from the shafts. Umahar scanned the western wall. He could still see no enemies manning the parapets, no Demissaries, no levies of the Kezelboj.

The men who had just thrown the javelins bent down, attaching the tent fabric to the ropes, sticking hooks through grooves. They pulled one end of the line, and the fabric began to advance, like a shadow across the zareba. The men heaved on the ropes, and other men joined them, pulling like rivermen hoisting a sail above a galley. The tent fabric moved closer to the walls of Ben Hamur, covering the zareba.

"God of the Sands and the Mountain," said Umahar, watching intently in his looking glass.

The tent covering masked the entire zareba across a two-hundred-yard front. Bazadak's Beserians leaped out onto the tent fabric, sinking several feet but still running across the zareba. The material held, keeping the men above and the thorns beneath. The men made it across to the base of the wall.

Dozens followed and then scores. Men hoisted others up, gripping the top of the wall. They were over. Beserians ran across the wall in the direction of the gate. They continued running, still alive. No one shot them down. None fell from arrows or gunfire. They flocked to the gate that was also a drawbridge, held upward against the wall by its chains.

Bazadak's mounted men began to ride toward the gate en masse, like a giant herd congregating upon a well.

Umahar lowered his looking glass and looked up at Abu Akhsa. "If they flood into the oasis, they will be massed together for the Great Guns of the Kezelboj. It will be as easy as spearing fish in a shallow pond."

"No," said Hamid Salesi. "The Great Guns will not fire."

Anil looked at his father.

"With respect, Elder Salesi," said Umahar. "I believe they will. Even if it means killing many of his own men, Jemojeen will not hesitate."

"You may be correct about that, Demissary Umahar, but Jemojeen will not order his Great Guns to shoot himself."

Umahar's eyes shifted as he understood Hamid Salesi's meaning.

"Yes, Lieutenant," said Hamid Salesi. "Jemojeen is inside the walls, with much of his army. He waits for us there. I see him. He seeks this battle, and we will give it to him."

"Forward," shouted Bazadak. "Forward!"

He did not wait for the drawbridge to drop. When it fell, his camel cavalry would be ready to flood into Ben Hamur beneath the archway. They amassed along the edge of the zareba, shoulder to shoulder, leg to leg, camel flank to camel flank.

The chains of the drawbridge began to creak, and the bridge lowered several inches. Then the chain creaked again in a prolonged wail. The bridge lowered several feet at once, exposing daylight behind it, clouded with smoke from the fires beyond the wall. Then the drawbridge gave way, falling down to the earth below, its chains flying out of their holes like vast iron snakes, pulled downward by the heavy wooden planks of the bridge. The iron-studded wood landed on the far side of the zareba trench with a tremendous crash that shook the bridge with its violence. The path was open, with nothing separating Bazak Bazadak from the interior of the oasis.

"For Beseri! For Abu Akhsa!" he shouted with all of his might, charging his camel across the drawbridge with his saber drawn, lifted above his head. Two men charged, one on either side of him, the bridge wide enough to accommodate three galloping horsemen. His men followed, and within moments, two dozen were inside the wall, then four dozen, then six.

"Abu Akhsa!" shouted the men, riding into the smoke of Ben Hamur.

Ozgar peered out over the ledge of the third-floor window, his bow in his left hand, an arrow nocked in the bowstring in his right hand. The fletching of the arrow was black, meaning the tip held the poison, the liquid that made flesh feel like it was aflame from within.

He looked across the room at the other archers poised behind broad windows in the thick mudbrick wall. Slanted wooden shutters covered the openings, shielding Ozgar and his men from view but giving them full visibility of the Beserians charging through the gate.

Ozgar gently released the tension on his bowstring, raising his finger to his lips. His fellow Demissary archers nodded to him. All of them believed they knew him well. He had led most of them since they had first left the Demissary Academy. They trusted him entirely as a child trusts a father. They would obey him without question and follow him, even unto death.

From their vantage point behind the closed wooden shutters, they could see the tightly packed groups of Kezelboj levies waiting in the alleys on either side of the main thoroughfare, the only place through which the Beserians could move into central Ben Hamur. The side routes were wrecked by the cannonade of the Great Guns of the Kezelboj. Jemojeen had ordered the Kezelboj levies to block off any side approaches that might still remain. The levies carried out their job as ordered, and only the main central corridor remained for the charging Beserians to advance down.

Ozgar and his Demissary archers waited in anticipation, seeing the trap. The Bazadaks rushed forward, like insects toward an unseen web while Jemojeen's spiders waited.

The Beserian horsemen charged, shouting and brandishing their sabers. A handful rode with their rifles instead of blades, ready to fire upon any who emerged from the rubble. They came closer, closer, and closer still.

Ozgar looked for the signal. It did not come. The Beserian camel cavalry charged onward, deeper into the oasis. They had now run by the first three dense groupings of Kezelboj levies on either side of the central road, screened off from the Beserians' sight by buildings fronting the road.

Deeper still, the horsemen rode, extended in a long column stretching back to the open western gate, with more riders plunging into Ben Hamur across the wooden planks of the lowered drawbridge. Beserian riflemen now manned the western wall, looking down into the oasis for targets, but finding none and holding their fire.

At last, Ozgar heard the drums. They sounded in three deep thumps, as if the oasis had a beating heart, newly come to life. In a furious dash of steel and brightly colored tunics, the Kezelboj levies ran out from behind the buildings that hid them, suddenly flowing out of the side alleys and into the main avenue, gushing forward like blood from a dozen arteries.

The ranks of the levies smashed into the camel riders on the edge of the cavalry column, striking as a mass of infantry from behind their round shields, slashing with their swords at camels and riders alike. Their officers bellowed their war cries, urging them onward and firing their long, single-shot pistols into the Bazadaks.

The men on the edge of the camel column slashed back, awkwardly, trying to turn their camels to face the new enemies on their flanks, but there was little room. Those that could turned and swung down with their sabers, striking the wall of shields. The camel riders on the edges of the column, both left and right, fell before the waves of infantrymen.

The few Beserians with their rifles drawn fired them into the advancing lines at nearly point-blank range, dropping individual men, but the levies were too many. The dense columns of swordsmen pressed forward from both sides of the avenue, striking the column of horsemen perpendicularly. The flow of the horsemen into the oasis slowed as men and camels turned into each other, trying to join the fighting on their left and their right, but unable to move freely.

"Wait," ordered Ozgar, speaking loudly enough to be heard over the screams and shouts of men fighting and dying below them, but not loud enough to draw attention to their position. He signaled with his hands for no archer to rise. They remained crouched and hidden.

Ozgar ran to the far end of the building, facing east, looking out over the center of the oasis and toward the deepest place that the Beserian column had advanced into the oasis.

"Here they come."

As Ozgar said the words, the Kezelboj pikemen appeared at the central square of the oasis, blocking off the Beserian advance at one hundred yards and running out in a column at the double-quick march, pivoting in a manner Ozgar would have thought Kezelboj soldiers incapable. *They have been drilling after all.*

The men formed a solid block of infantry, six rows deep, with each man holding an eighteen-foot long pike, topped with a foot-long iron spike.

The deep battle drums sounded again, beginning a rhythm that did not stop. *Boom. Boom. Boom. Boom.*

With each strike upon the drum, the wall of pikemen advanced. The front horsemen of the Beserians unleashed a desultory volley of rifle fire. A handful of pikemen fell to the ground.

The others marched directly over them, stepping forward with each drum-beat.

Bazadak tugged on his camel rope. His bull stopped charging.

"Fire!" he shouted, waving his sword.

Of the dozen men riding alongside him, only three had their rifles drawn. They discharged their weapons into the advancing wall of pikemen. At the range they shot from, they could not miss. Pikemen tumbled to the ground. The other men sheathed their sabers and drew their rifles, shooting more pikemen down onto the dusty paving stones of the avenue.

As the men fell, others from the rear ranks stepped forward, replacing them immediately as the human wall advanced with the steel tips of their pikes advancing far ahead of them.

By the God of the Sands, their spears are as tall as the trees of the oasis.

Bazak turned to retreat, but there was nowhere to go. The noses of the camels behind him were up to his saddle. The camels in the row behind them were up to his camel's rump, and those behind them were still shoving forward with the momentum of the attack. Bazadak glanced back over his shoulder, pulling his camel's head rope, pulling against the tide behind him, the tide that pushed him toward the advancing forest of steel-tipped pikes. With his head turned back, Bazadak saw the Kezelboj infantry on either side of the avenue, pressing inward.

"Dismount!" he ordered.

There was no way to lower his camel amid such chaos. Sword in hand, he slid off of his camel, landing down on the stone. With his left hand, he drew the curved dagger from his belt. The others, some of the most experienced warriors in the tribe of Bazadak, dropped down from their camels, pulling their swords from their scabbards. There was no time to reload a rifle.

The pikemen advanced faster, closing in as a solid mass. The front row of spearmen lowered their pikes to nearly parallel with the ground, gripping the long shafts of their weapons with both hands. The second rank held their pikes at a slightly higher angle, and the row behind them held their pikes at a steeper angle still. The steel tips marched closer to Bazadak and his men, like the quills of a porcupine backing into a cornered predator.

Bazadak looked around frantically. There was nowhere to run. The pikes continued advancing down the avenue, stretching from the north row of buildings to those on the southern edge of the street.

"Take the sides!" shouted Bazadak, abandoning the head rope of his prized war camel, leaving him to the advancing pikemen.

He moved laterally, weaving through the thicket of men and camels. His men followed him. A camel backed up, nearly knocking him over. He regained his footing and continued moving toward the sounds of sabers striking shields.

The closer Bazadak came to the flank, the denser packed the camels and men became. He could not pass through them to reach the enemy. He turned around to see that his men had followed him so effectively that there was nowhere for them to retreat. They were stuck behind the camels in front of them. The still-mounted camelmen on his left flank, now directly in front of him, battled a mass of infantry so thick that they could not punch through. Indeed, the camels seemed to be backing up as the wall of infantry pressed forward against them, slashing with their swords against the long legs and exposed chests of the frantic, unarmored animals.

To Bazadak's right, the pikemen of the Kezelboj closed in, shouting taunts, close enough for him to see the whites of their eyes and the snarls through their beards.

"Wait for my signal," said Ozgar, peering down from the window.

"They are massed, sir," said one of his sergeants.

"Do not loose arrows yet. We will hit our own," said Ozgar.

"I have a clear angle, sir," said the sergeant, looking down at the dense mass of camels and riders just beneath his window. The other young Demissaries near the sergeant looked up at their captain, the man they idolized.

"Not yet!" roared Ozgar. "I am going down to help the infantry! You will wait for my signal before you loose a single arrow!"

Ozgar moved across the room and dashed down the mudbrick stairs, taking two at a time. The air was thick with smoke and dust. The sun was still bright overhead, piercing through holes in the dense mass of smoke. Ozgar blinked beneath his green turban.

He leaped off of the stairs and turned into an alcove. He ripped his Demissary turban off of his head and tore his tunic from his chest. He found the small bundle of cloth hidden beneath the urn and pulled the sand-colored material onto himself, quickly wrapping it around his arms and legs, saving his head and face for last. In seconds, he was covered by the cloth from head to toe, with only a small slot for his eyes. He placed the arrows in his quiver into the urn and pulled the fresh bundle of arrows out from it.

He glanced up, knowing his men would wait as ordered for his signal to loose their arrows, the arrows that could not miss the dense mass of camelmen stuck between the pikemen advancing toward them and the rows of buildings and massed swordsmen at their sides. The camelmen of the Bazadaks would, by now, be jammed back to the western gate, an entire tribe of warriors stuck on the avenue, unable to turn and unable to retreat, waiting to be slaughtered.

A tinge of guilt struck at Ozgar's heart as he thought of his earnest Demissary archers waiting in the building above him. They trusted him with their lives. He had trained them since they were boys.

Yes, you are betraying them. But you have made your choice. You are an Oath Holder of the Order. Ozgar swallowed heavily, hardening his eyes and his heart.

You will not carry this day, Jemojeen. We will stop you.

CHAPTER 83
The Nine and the Grand Vizer

Oasis of Ben Hamur
49th Day, Month of Wasura, 807
Anglian Calendar: April 11, 1879

The nine of them waited, crouched against the outside of the wall, on the inner side of the zareba, near the corner of the northern and western walls. Habeen Barcadey looked around nervously.

"We are exposed," he growled.

"He will open the door," said Ottovan Fanfar, his face covered with a tight veil that covered all but his hazel-brown eyes.

"He was already to have opened it," said Habeen, his dark eyes glaring with intensity alongside his dark, angry-looking scar. "The Swordguard already moves to the northern gate. They will be there in minutes." His fingers impatiently drummed the pommel of his famous sword. "We must go in *now*."

"Patience," said Nemakar Hasdruba, his great mustache covered by a veil nearly as tight as Ottovan's. His long nose pressed uncomfortably against the cloth.

"I will go over if I must," said Habeen.

"Do not," said Oapah the Hohsa, his voice deeper than any of the other men. "They will see you."

The small wooden door, no higher than a standing man's waist, creaked from the inside. The door lurched forward an inch, catching on the top of the opening as if it had not been opened in years. A force from the inside struck the door again. It swung open, wailing on its old iron hinges.

A man wrapped in sand-colored cloth looked out at the nine, crouched down in the low door.

"You are late," said Ottovan Fanfar.

"My apologies, Commander," said Ozgar, from long habit calling him by his Demissary title. "Follow me."

Handsome Habeen Barcadey stepped through the door first. Ottovan followed with Jack Caldwell behind him and Selena Savanar behind him. The others followed them with Nemakar Hasdruba going in last, closing the door behind him.

Ozgar guided them down an alley, up another at a perpendicular, and then down another alley. They continued in this way, making their way into the oasis, moving ever closer to the sound of the battle raging in the central east-west avenue where Jemojeen's forces had trapped the Bazadaks.

Ottovan moved forward, running parallel to Ozgar. The Demissaries and Beserians ran almost silently along the dirt alleyways. Jack Caldwell self-consciously heard his Beserian sandals slap against the ground.

"He is using the staffs to ambush our forces," said Ozgar.

"How do you know?" asked Ottovan.

"I saw it with my own eyes. He is slaughtering the Bazadaks."

"There are still the Azadeem and the Celadeen columns," said Ottovan.

"I would not be assured of that."

"Where is he? Where is Jemojeen?"

"He was last in the palace of the Sharef, the high point of the oasis."

"Then that is where we must go."

Jemojeen stood on the Sharef's veranda with a panoramic view of the oasis below him. With his naked eyes, looking across the rising columns of smoke of Ben Hamur to the north, he could see the retreating waves of the Azadeem camel and horse cavalry of Abu Akhsa's left flank, as well as the hundreds of dead men and animals, strewn like rags across the desert floor. The Demissaries of the Second Legion pursued them, with the archers riding out along the flanks, raining arrows down upon the fleeing tribesmen. The lancers pursued from the center, spearing men from behind like fish in the shallows. The firemen rode at a leisurely pace in the rear, not yet even using their ammunition.

Jemojeen turned all the way around to see the final remains of the Beserian right flank—the broken remnants of the Celadeens—scrambling to the west and south, with some riding into the dense smoke cloud south of the oasis. Turkelan's Erassians pursued the fleeing Celadeens with their javelins, hurling them into any man who did not ride away fast enough.

"It is almost finished," Jemojeen said aloud.

Sipahi Shaheni stood behind him, still breathing heavily from ascending the stairs to the veranda. His tunic was torn and covered with blood from his battle on the east wall. Jemojeen had ordered him to join him, depriving him of the glory of chasing the retreating Celadeens his men had defeated.

"Soon Ulgur's lancers will join those of the First Legion," said Jemojeen, his heart thundering with pride, his feeling of ecstasy growing by the moment. "They will be behind Abu Akhsa, and the Beserian threat will be gone forever. We will slaughter their herds, their women, and their young."

Shaheni stood stone-faced.

"And I would say we have shown Ben Hamur the price of rebellion. Have we not?" Jemojeen turned to Shaheni, the twist of a smile upon his lips. As he said the words, the screams of a newly set aflame rebel rose from the oasis.

"Yes, Your Excellency," said Shaheni.

The screams rose as the flames rose on the man.

"The Bazadaks are doomed," said Jemojeen, looking down into the oasis. He could not see his infantry beneath the buildings, pressing inward against the flanks of the tribesmen on the central avenue. But he could see his pikemen forcing the tribesmen back farther and farther into a tighter and more compact space back against the western gate.

"The fire Demissaries of the First Legion will seal off the western gate," said Jemojeen. "Look."

As he spoke, a line of purple, the fire Demissaries of the First Legion, wheeled and turned to the north, moving along the line of the zareba and the western wall.

"Your plan has exceeded even my expectations, Your Excellency," said Shaheni.

"Then perhaps you should have set your expectations higher," said Jemojeen.

Shaheni stood, facing out over the oasis as if he had not heard the Grand Vizer.

"Where is the Beserian traitor?"

"He is down with my men at the base of the stairs."

"Bring him to me."

"Yes, Your Excellency." Shaheni saluted, turned, and walked swiftly toward the stairs.

"Sipahi," said Jemojeen.

"Yes, Your Excellency," said Shaheni, stopping mid-step and turning to face his master.

"Send for Turkelan as well."

"Yes, Your Excellency."

Short minutes later, Shaheni returned, pushing Ghani the Beserian ahead of him. Ghani smiled nervously, showing the gap in his teeth that his people considered a mark of great luck. Shaheni's chest heaved up and down, having just ascended the stairs again in his heavy helmet, hardened leather breastplate, and chain mail armor.

"Good morning Ghani of the Gap," said Jemojeen. He did not open his eyes, nor did he turn to face the Beserian. He stood facing the oasis with the Staff of the Ram in his right hand and the Staff of the Serpent in his left hand.

Ghani stood, smiling with flushed cheeks, unsure what to say. The Grand Vizer made him more nervous than any man he had ever met before, and the more time he spent in his proximity, the more worried he found himself becoming.

"That is what they call you, is it not, your fellow tribesmen, Ghani of the Gap?"

"Yes, Your Excellency."

"Clever name."

"It is because of the gap in my teeth."

"Yes," said Jemojeen, turning to face the young Beserian. Jemojeen towered over him as if he were a young boy. "You have given me a great object, Ghani of the Gap."

"Yes," said Ghani, nodding.

"And I am told you feel the gold I gave you for it was insufficient. Is that true?"

"No, not insufficient, just—"

"Just what?" asked Jemojeen, half smiling and edging closer to Ghani.

"I just thought it would be more."

"More?"

Ghani nodded.

"Let me show you something," said Jemojeen. "Here, hold this," he said, handing the Staff of the Serpent to Ghani. Ghani took the staff nervously, his hands gripping the serpent carving around the olive wood.

"Close your eyes," said Jemojeen.

Ghani obeyed.

"Now let your mind move to your people. Put all other things out of your mind. Find an anchor. Find your mother. Do you see her?"

Ghani waited with his eyes closed. The staff grew cooler in his hands as if it had been resting outside on a night that was cold enough to bring frost. His eyes tightened in concentration, bringing wrinkles to his temples.

"I see her," said Ghani, his heart suddenly tugging at him. The guilt nearly overpowered him.

"Is she with her herds?"

"Yes," said Ghani.

"Are there men with her?"

"No, only my sisters."

"Correct," said Jemojeen. "They will soon be gone."

"Who will soon be gone?" asked Ghani, opening his eyes.

"They will all be gone. Your people will cease to exist. Now, look with your opened eyes. You no longer need the farsight." Jemojeen extended his hand, and Ghani handed the Staff of the Serpent back to him. Jemojeen snatched it away greedily, as if Ghani had offended him by holding it too long. It had returned to a normal temperature, losing the cool that had gripped Ghani's hands while his eyes were closed, and the vision of his mother and sisters was in his mind.

"Now look to the north. Do you see that? Do you see those spots?"

Ghani nodded.

"Those are the bodies of the Azadeem. They fled, and Abu Akhsa's left flank is no more. Now turn behind you."

Ghani did as he was told.

"Do you see those horsemen riding for their lives? And the camelmen racing them to flee?"

Ghani nodded, swallowing.

"That is the right flank, the Celadeens. They are crushed."

Ghani's eyes glistened in faint recognition of what he had wrought.

"Now turn and look below you, look into the oasis. Look at that main avenue. Do you see those riders, the jumble of men and camels? Those are your people, the Bazadaks. They will soon all be dead. My pikemen will sweep them from that avenue."

Ghani's face fell. His lips closed over his teeth. Even his nervous smile was gone.

"You see, Ghani, none of this would have been possible if you had not brought me this Staff of Wisdom. If you had not struck down an old man in his tent and fled with this in the middle of the night, I would not have been able to see each movement Abu Akhsa made. I would not have been able to ambush each of his columns perfectly, the way that ensures that his rebellion will fail."

Ghani looked up at Jemojeen, his heart beating violently.

"But it is more than that, Ghani of the Gap. You see, I showed you your mother for a reason. I have another group of Demissaries moving around from the south. They will soon be upon the herds and the women and the children. Your people will all die. And it is because of you."

Ghani looked up at the pale, bearded, rail-thin Bulbanian, smiling beneath his black Grand Vizer's turban. He glanced at the edge of the veranda, only several feet behind him.

"You have killed your own mother. Do you understand that?"

"No," said Ghani.

"What did you say to me?" Jemojeen's lip curled up, and his nostrils flared in anger.

"I said no!" shouted Ghani, pulling a hidden dagger from his waist and running at Jemojeen.

Jemojeen moved the Staff of the Ram in front of Ghani. Ghani froze in mid-step, as if unable to move, as if his limbs had frozen solid.

"You think you can kill me, you little fool? No man can kill me."

The ram's head at the top of the staff began to change color, turning from cedar to gold. The color started in the eyes and nose of the ram and spread out, moving out along the curling horns and down the shaft of the staff.

Ghani stood in a mid-stride, a living statue of a man running with a dagger.

Jemojeen stepped closer toward him.

"You believe you are going to cut me with this, do you? Then do it!"

Ghani's eyes widened in panic, darting from side to side, as no other part of him moved.

"You see, young fool, I now control your body. Take your knife, for instance, and watch it cut your own arm."

Ghani's eyes watched in horror as his own hand moved his dagger to his other arm and carved a deep gash. Blood began to seep into his tunic sleeve, drenching it.

"Oh yes, you can still feel pain," said Jemojeen. "Now, let's try your legs. Left, right, left-right-left, oh, there is no more room, I suppose."

Ghani stepped the final step past Jemojeen, still holding his dagger in his right hand, his left arm dripping with blood from the wound he had just cut into himself.

He fell.

"Let's release him for the scream," said Jemojeen, smiling.

"Ahhhhhhhhhhhhhhhhh—" The scream cut off abruptly with the sound of flesh striking earth from a height of seventy-five feet.

Jemojeen peered over the edge at the smashed body that was Ghani of the Gap, flung from the same veranda as the Sharef of Ben Hamur.

"I could not allow Ulgur to be the only one to fling someone from this veranda. Don't you agree?" asked Jemojeen, smiling at Shaheni. "And I daresay my version had more style. That boy is a traitor to his own people and a fool. Find where he put the gold I gave him. I want it all back."

Shaheni stared, fearing the ease with which Jemojeen had begun using his new powers.

"Where is Turkelan?" asked Jemojeen, no longer smiling.

"Here, Your Excellency," said the Erassian, walking toward him from the direction of the eastern stairwell.

Jemojeen turned and looked at Turkelan. "You missed the Beserian traitor's last moments."

"I heard him," said Turkelan.

"Not nearly as fulfilling," said Jemojeen.

Like Sipahi Shaheni, Turkelan had blood spattered across his tunic. He had wiped the blood from most of his face, but some still clung to his orange hair in caked dark spots.

"My men pursue the remaining Celadeens as we speak," said Turkelan. "Few will survive. Your ambushes appear to have succeeded."

"Yes, they have," said Jemojeen. "They have indeed. As it stands, I have something more important for you to do. An assignment."

More important than slaughtering a wing of Abu Akhsa's army? I doubt that. Turkelan did not voice his thoughts out loud. His face, as always, was a mask of calm.

"There is a group of rebels. They will try to attack me. The traitor Selena Savanar is with them, as is this boy of the west, the one they claim fulfills the prophecy, the one that, in their delusions, they call 'Amahdi.' If they are not already here inside the oasis, they will be here shortly. I have foreseen it."

Turkelan waited for his instructions, his face nearly expressionless.

"Seal the stairways to this palace. Man the walls. They could be here sooner than we expect."

"Yes, Your Excellency," said Turkelan, saluting and bowing.

"How many in your personal guard?" asked Jemojeen.

"Forty. The rest of my men are pursuing our enemies out upon the sands."

Jemojeen frowned. "How many guardsmen have you here, Shaheni?"

"Two hundred inside the oasis," said the Sipahi.

"Bring them all," said Jemojeen. "I will take no chances, and I will not risk my victory by giving these deranged heroes an opening. They will come nowhere near these staffs. Turkelan, bring your men here to the veranda. Shaheni, seal the entrances and patrol the low points of the Sharef's inner walls. I will call you if I need you and your men."

The two men departed to do as Jemojeen commanded.

"Now to find these snakes that believe they can slither their way to me. They forget there is no longer any hiding from me, not here, not anywhere. I will find you now, yes, I will find you." Jemojeen closed his eyes, wrapping his long fingers around the carved serpent winding around the Staff of Wisdom. The staff went cold in his hand, and his mind began to move out from the veranda.

He swallowed with satisfaction, anticipating his gaze soaring out over the oasis and finding the traitors huddled in an alley or against an outer wall. But his mind did not move far. His vision ventured just off the edge of the veranda, and then it stopped.

They were there, directly beneath him, launching up over an unguarded spot on the inner wall separating the Sharef's palace from the rest of Ben Hamur.

Then Jemojeen saw her face, Selena Savanar, flanked by the Sworn Lions of the Order, Oapah the Hohsa and Gulana of Nor Gandus. And there too was the one of the west, red-faced behind his thick, light-haired beard, carrying a foreign rifle. They were all armed and in the company of five more, three masked men and two others, Beserian-looking men whose faces Jemojeen did not know.

Jemojeen paused for a moment, blinking, battling his own vision to assess whether he saw accurately. He opened his eyes wide and shouted, "Shaheni! Sipahi Shaheni! They breach the wall now, just below us!"

Jemojeen walked forward, peering down over the edge of the veranda. The dense foliage of olive trees, palms, fig trees, and vines shielded the lower wall from his line of sight.

Sipahi Shaheni was halfway down the steps when he heard the Grand Vizer's voice. He looked down the steps. The sentries were out of sight. *I am too far to summon the guards.* He exhaled, rallying his weary body. He turned, and for the third time, began running up the steep stone steps in his chain mail, as fast as his tired legs and lungs would allow.

"Sipahi!" shouted Jemojeen, his voice cracking, ragged from the commanding he had done all day.

Sipahi Shaheni ran faster, his chest burning, his legs churning up the great stone steps.

"Hurry!" croaked Jemojeen, peering with intensity down into the thick foliage immediately beneath him. His heart began to thunder with an emotion he had not experienced this viscerally in long years. His throat grabbed, a tingling moved up his spine, and the hairs rose on his arms.

"I hear him. He knows we are here," said Jabil the Jackal.

"He is using the staff," said Aurelio Demassi.

"Then we should hurry," said Jack Caldwell, gripping his underlever Mancaster repeater, the one Demassi had smuggled into the sands with Jack Caldwell himself. He looked down. There were fourteen shots in the undertube and one in the chamber. Jack looked over at Aurelio Demassi, the man who had poisoned him and taken him to Abu Akhsa, the man who had believed, before any others, that he, Jack Caldwell, would lead the revolution and fulfill the Prophecy.

And yet here I am, here to do what Demassi predicted.

Jack felt a warmness in his heart toward the strange Vetenan, the man who wanted more than any Beserian to be a Beserian.

"Demassi," said Jack.

Aurelio turned.

"Thank you for remembering this." Jack held up his rifle and nodded.

Aurelio Demassi nodded back, feeling closer to Jack than he had upon the sands.

Jack held his rifle as if clinging to an old trusted friend, the only piece of Calderon still with him.

"You will not be able to shoot him," whispered Ozgar, in broken Beserian, looking intently into Jack's face from behind his mask.

Jack looked into the archer captain's eyes, uncomprehendingly.

"He holds the Staff of Ruling, Amahdi. I have seen what it can do."

"Follow me," said Ottovan Fanfar, cutting off their discussion with a wave of his hand. The veil and the cloth that wrapped around his skin covered all but his bright hazel-brown eyes. Ozgar and Nemakar were dressed the same way to hide from Jemojeen's farsight.

"Now!" Ottovan leaped out from the tree he crouched behind. He began running up the steep hill, his powerful leg muscles propelling him upward, while the long, broad palm fronds and olive branches overhead covered him from prying eyes on the veranda above. Nemakar and Ozgar leaped up and ran with him, with Nemakar on his left side and Ozgar on his right.

Oapah nodded at Selena Savanar. They rose and ran behind the three Demissaries, with Selena in the center, Oapah on her right, and Gulana on her left.

Jack Caldwell scrambled after them, with Aurelio and Jabil flanking him on either side, Aurelio on the left and Jabil on the right.

Ottovan dodged the varied tree trunks, avoiding hanging vines and leaping over stones with an expert's speed, seeming to gain momentum even as he ran up the steep hill. The three Demissaries reached the base of the wall first, the vertical face of stone that led up to the Sharef's veranda, the veranda atop which a man could survey all of Ben Hamur and much of the plain that surrounded it.

Ottovan looked up. There, staring down at him, stood the Grand Vizer. Ottovan's eyes locked on Jemojeen's—the eyes he had known and loathed since they were boys in the Academy, both frightened children taken by the Spring Reaping from their homes in Bulbania. His heart rushed with adrenaline.

"Jemojeen," he growled, barely audible.

Nemakar pulled his red-handled pistol first and fired it directly upward. The fine dustlike powder launched up into the air and burst into a brilliant flash directly in front of Jemojeen's face.

"Climb before the flash fades!" ordered Ottovan. "You wait," he said, placing his hand on Ozgar's arm.

Ozgar nodded in understanding and nocked an arrow as the others began scaling the stones up to the veranda.

Ozgar waited with his bowstring tensed.

Jabil and Demassi climbed fastest, both rail-thin men, jamming their fingers into the gaps in the stones with their sabers sheathed and their loaded rifles hanging from slings across their backs.

Sipahi Shaheni had nearly reached the top of the steep stone steps when he heard footsteps behind him. He turned to see Turkelan the Erassian running with a dozen of his men, all orange-haired and carrying javelins. Shaheni kept moving, reaching the top of the steps just as the swiftest Erassian ran by him, a javelin hoisted above his head, cocked and ready to release.

A pair of rifle shots cracked and the Erassian fell, tumbling back down the steps.

Shaheni reached the top to see two Beserian tribesmen and a tall bearded man aiming a rifle at him. To Shaheni's surprise, even though the man had just fired his weapon, he flung a lever down beneath his rifle and fired again.

That is no Beserian rifle . . .

The bullet struck Shaheni's helmet.

Shaheni staggered as if struck by a mace. Another Erassian jumped ahead of him with a javelin, only to take a bullet in his chest as he attempted to throw it.

Jemojeen had been a Demissary for far too long, and he had blinded far too many with his own flash pistols to allow Oath Holders to do the same to him. He had crouched down, covering his face with his sleeve as the powder ignited, retreating deeper into the stone veranda.

He rose from his crouch now.

Jemojeen lifted the Staff of Ruling up in his right hand. The ram's head glowed, as it had in the Throne Room, as if Jemojeen held the sun. Jemojeen thrust the staff in the direction of the tall bearded rifleman and the Beserian tribesmen. The rifleman, who was far too tall and fair to be a Beserian, attempted to keep his rifle aimed forward, but he could not face the blazing light in front of him. He covered his eyes beneath his arms, lowering his rifle. The Beserians, having fired their single rifle shots at the running Erassians, pulled their sabers from their sheaths to charge Jemojeen. But they too cowered before the blazing ram's head on Jemojeen's staff, backing away toward the edge of the veranda.

Shaheni looked and saw that others leaped up from the edge of the veranda, only to face Jemojeen's blazing staff. They all cowered beneath the light.

"Take them now! While they are blinded!" shouted Shaheni to the unarmored Erassians running past him. He rushed forward himself with his curved sword drawn.

The light removed all other senses. Jack could neither move nor run. All that surrounded him was the light from the staff in the hand of the tall, thin, black-bearded man in front of him, a man he could no longer see through the blazing glare. He could not see the others. Both Jabil and Demassi had disappeared. He could not sense them in any way. All that surrounded him was the light: total, numbing, and all-encompassing. Jack willed himself to move his feet, yet they would not move. His sandals rested upon the flat stones beneath him, as immobile as if he were made of stone himself. The link between his mind and his body was utterly severed.

He looked down, and, to his astonishment, he saw his hands move, operating the underlever of his Mancaster repeater, the rifle that had made it from the Caldwell Ranch to the Oasis of Ben Hamur. Jack's hands pulled the lever back into place, flush with the rifle stock, sliding the next round into the chamber. Outside and apart from his own will, Jack's arms lifted the rifle to his shoulder and aimed it at Selena Savanar.

Gulana of Nor Gandus looked at Jack with surprise in her eyes, surprise that in the span of a blink shifted into horror. She dove at Selena, pulling her down onto the flat stones of the veranda, just as Jack pulled the trigger. The bullet passed over her head into the place where Selena had stood a half-second before.

Jack began walking as if in a dream, reloading the Mancaster, cranking the underlever, conscious to observe his body, but unable to control it or stop what his own arms and legs were doing.

Selena looked up at Gulana above her, in anger that Gulana had knocked her down onto the stones, the Sworn Lion's far larger body covering Selena almost entirely. Then Selena looked at Jack, at once understanding.

"The Staff of Ruling! Jemojeen is controlling him! Oapah, stop him!" she screamed.

The massive Omakhosian ran at Jemojeen, his huge sword drawn. Oapah ran with his eyes closed, his face unable to face the brilliance of the staff in Jemojeen's hand. He did not see the weighted Erassian javelin that struck him in the chest. He staggered, his arms jutting outward, exposing his chest further. A lightweight javelin struck him in the shoulder.

"Fall down, Oapah!" screamed Selena.

Oapah dropped onto his side with two spears stuck in his body, as three more sailed past where he had stood.

Jack walked closer to Selena and Gulana, who still covered Selena with her entire body. Both Selena and Gulana squinted to see past the blazing glory in Jemojeen's hand. They could not see him or the two dozen newly arrived Erassians running with their javelins, pouring out onto the veranda from the stairs at the far side.

Nemakar Hasdruba pulled himself up onto the veranda from the wall beneath, moving like a spider with his long limbs, withdrawing two pistols from his chest holsters. He pulled the triggers, firing blind. The first shot landed to the side of the running Erassians, igniting a ring of fire that blazed furiously but harmed no one. The second shot exploded nearer to the Erassians, sending shrapnel into those running along the edge of the veranda. The blast knocked two of them off the ledge to their death below, screaming and waving their arms like backstroking swimmers as they fell.

Nemakar reached for the second set of pistols as Jack Caldwell, firmly under the control of Jemojeen's mind, turned and fired his rifle. The shot struck Nemakar in the left leg above the knee, staining his sand-colored cloth in crimson. Nemakar cried out in pain and toppled, falling onto the edge of the veranda. Jack ejected the casing, slamming the lever forward and then pulling it back.

"Perhaps the chosen one of the West is my chosen one!" shouted Jemojeen. *Of all of the victories of this day, surely, this one shall be the finest.*

Jemojeen willed Jack to wheel and aim at Selena. Gulana placed her arms around Selena's face and shielded her head with her chest, offering her broad back to Jack Caldwell.

"You are not answers to prophecies!" thundered Jemojeen. "I can control you with my mind! Where is the God of the Sands, you fools? He is nowhere because he does not exist!"

Ottovan Fanfar, his scimitarus still in its sheath, pulled himself up over the edge. He ran forward, bent over with his face toward the ground, and threw himself at Jack Caldwell's torso. His weight knocked Jack sideways, just as Jack's finger pulled the Mancaster's trigger, sending the shot into the stone, inches from Gulana's exposed back.

Ottovan landed on top of Jack, throwing the rifle from his hands and onto the stone. A pair of javelins sailed past him, thrown by the Erassians who had now nearly reached Jemojeen.

Aurelio Demassi and Jabil the Jackal had dropped down below the ledge, gripping the stones of the veranda, the only place where the Erassian javelins could not strike them and the blazing light of the Staff of the Ram could not blind them. Aurelio Demassi now lifted himself up, peering above the ledge, and wincing from the light from Jemojeen's staff. Jabil the Jackal clung to the wall next to him. Demassi looked into Jabil's wide yellow-brown eyes, his heart pounding.

"Now," said Aurelio. Jabil nodded.

They rose together, pulling their sabers and running at Jemojeen, the source of the light.

"Abu Akhsa!" they screamed. They screamed the words a second time for courage. The javelins sailed past them. They kept running directly into the light, choosing to die facing their enemy.

Jemojeen looked at the two young men running toward him, each thin, wiry, and a whole head shorter than he was. Their eyes were closed as they ran, as if running into the sun itself. Jemojeen dropped the Staff of the Serpent in his left hand down onto the stone beneath him, still holding the Staff of the Ram in his right hand, glowing like molten gold. With his free left hand, he pulled his scimitarus from his belt, raising it to slaughter the two Beserians running at him. He saw the javelins miss them.

Fools. He smiled, preparing to bring his great curved blade down upon them.

Pain erupted in Jemojeen's right hand—blazing, awful pain.

The pain drew his eyes to his hand without any conscious decision. The arrow had penetrated through his palm, and immediately he knew it was poisoned. The Staff of the Ram, still blazing with light, fell to the ground, as the burning feeling consumed his hand like a flame. He wheeled his head, seeing the archer to his right, crouching at the edge of the veranda, wrapped from head to toe in the sand-colored cloth of the Order.

He brought his blade down from his left hand just in time to parry the wild slashes of the two young Beserians. The staff on the ground below still glowed, but its flash of light was gone, like a dying ember of a once-blazing log. Jemojeen swung his scimitarus, and the two smaller men backed up. Jemojeen fought the urge to scream as his right hand burned, involuntary tears filling his eyes.

"God of the Mountain!" shouted Jemojeen, swinging his hand, as if he could throw the poison from out of his wound. "Shaheni, bring me the balm!" he screamed as he swung his blade.

The two smaller men backed up from Jemojeen's great curved blade, for the first time being able to open their eyes, seeing the arrow impaling his hand.

"The staff has dropped!" shouted Demassi. "Attack! Attack!"

Jack Caldwell lifted his head, coming face-to-face with Ottovan Fanfar, who was still lying on top of him. He looked into Ottovan's brown-green eyes, the only part of him not covered by the sand-colored cloth.

"I am free," said Jack, in Beserian.

Ottovan rolled off of him.

Jack ran for his Mancaster rifle, no longer paralyzed by Jemojeen's staff.

Ottovan stood up and turned toward Jemojeen, pulling two three-barreled Demissary pistols from his holsters. He could see.

Aurelio Demassi and Jabil the Jackal both blocked Jemojeen, backing away from his furious slashes. Ottovan aimed at the Erassians running to Jemojeen's side, firing his barrels in rapid succession, dropping a man with each barrel he fired. He dropped his pistols, drew his scimitarus, and charged at the Grand Vizer.

Aiming from one knee, Ozgar's double-arched bow flexed as he pulled back the bowstring with his right hand, trying to find a shot at Jemojeen through Aurelio Demassi and Jabil the Jackal. He could not find it. He twisted to his left. Another dozen Erassians ran onto the veranda, followed by twice that many Grand Vizerian Guardsmen, armored in chain mail and running with lowered spears.

Ozgar placed his arrow into the face of an Erassian. He pulled his bowstring and let another arrow fly, striking another man. He heard the screams as the poison took root.

Sipahi Shaheni reached Jemojeen's side with his curved sword drawn. Sweat poured down his face, and his chest heaved. Barrel-chested and far stronger than the pair of thin tribesmen, he towered over Aurelio Demassi and Jabil the Jackal, slashing at them with mighty blows, forcing them backward. Jemojeen continued to slash as his right hand burned with the poison.

"The balm! Give me the balm!" he shrieked, still swinging his scimitarus.

"I have none, Your Excellency!"

Jemojeen backed up, dropping his scimitarus, unable to withstand the pain any longer.

"Get the staffs!" he shouted at Sipahi Shaheni, backing away toward the Sharef's palace.

The Sipahi stepped forward, swinging his blade in vicious strokes at Jabil and Demassi, driving them away from Jemojeen. The Beserians backed up farther. Through the corner of his eye, Shaheni saw a broad man—one of the veiled Oath Holders—charging at him with his drawn scimitarus.

"Retreat, Your Excellency! Retreat!" shouted Shaheni. He saw something familiar in the man running at him in the sand cloth, and he felt his stomach twist in fear.

"Get the staffs!" screamed Jemojeen.

Sipahi Shaheni bent down as Turkelan the Erassian arrived at his side, throwing his javelin into the tribesman directly in front of him. The point struck

Aurelio Demassi in his throat, punching through like a skewer through meat. Aurelio staggered as his saber fell, his eyes widening in horror.

Sipahi Shaheni picked up the Staff of the Ram beneath him. As Shaheni went for the Staff of the Ram, Jabil the Jackal dove down for the Staff of the Serpent, picking it up, clutching it against his chest, and rolling.

Ottovan Fanfar charged into Shaheni, kicking him to the ground, and slashing him across his chain mail. Shaheni held the Staff of the Ram as he fell.

Turkelan the Erassian slashed at Ottovan, who blocked his blade, slashing back with his wide scimitarus.

"Ayah!" shouted Ottovan, knocking Turkelan backward with the force of his blows.

Jabil vaulted up off of the ground and ran to Selena Savanar, Gulana, and Oapah, who was still lying on his side with two javelins sticking out of him.

"Lady Savanar!" he shouted.

Gulana of Nor Gandus rose, at last uncovering Selena.

She pulled her scimitarus from its scabbard and ran to Ottovan's side in time to meet a half-dozen of Turkelan's onrushing Erassians. She ducked beneath a javelin, lurched up, and nearly cleaved an orange-haired man in half, taking him at his midsection.

Jack Caldwell aimed his rifle. He pointed it at Turkelan and fired as the Erassian captain dove into a roll. Caldwell's shot missed, careening off the stones.

"Give me the staff!" screamed Jemojeen.

Shaheni threw him the Staff of the Ram as Ottovan Fanfar stepped backward to Aurelio Demassi, fighting off sword blows from the mass of Erassians. Aurelio had collapsed onto his knees with the javelin in his throat. Blood poured from his neck like a faucet.

"Demassi!" shouted Jack, running toward him.

The Staff of Ruling fell short of Jemojeen as Shaheni threw it, landing like an ordinary piece of wood, rattling upon the stones. Ottovan stepped forward to retrieve it, slashing at Sipahi Shaheni and the Erassians in front of him, hitting them high, then low, and then high again. He cut a man down, and then another, his blade flashing through flesh as men collapsed before him.

The Sipahi and the Erassians did their best to deflect the deadly slashes of the masked man—the group of gifted swordsmen fighting furiously to fend off the single superior one. An Erassian moved too slowly, and Ottovan cleaved his arm off at the elbow. As that man screamed, another Erassian fell, a crimson valley opening across his chest.

Jemojeen, nearly crazed with the pain of the burning, turned and ran for the steps. The running Erassians caught him as he collapsed in pain, shrieking for a balm holder.

"The balm! The balm! It is the burning poison. By the God of the Mountain, bring me the balm!"

Selena rose, seeing Jemojeen screaming from the burning in his hand.

"Lady Savanar!" Jabil the Jackal emerged in front of her face, handing her the Staff of the Serpent.

Selena placed her hands around it.

"Three Gods damn you!" shouted Jack Caldwell, in Anglian, firing his rifle into the oncoming Erassians. The Erassians now advanced in a dense mass, intermingled with Grand Vizerian Guardsmen.

They ran as a wave. Ozgar shot his arrows as fast as he could, emptying his entire quiver into the oncoming men, who shrieked from the poison as the arrows hit their flesh. At this range, Ozgar's arrows pierced the guardsmen's armor as if they wore none at all.

Ottovan continued swinging his scimitarus at the growing mass of men in front of him, refusing to back up, moving laterally as men tried to flank him, holding them at bay with the whirlwind of his steel.

"Retreat, Amahdi! Retreat!" screamed Jabil, seeing the growing numbers of guardsmen and Erassians getting closer to Jack, despite his rapid firing. "Amahdi, retreat! We have the Staff of Wisdom!"

Jack neither heard him nor heeded him. He stayed in place, loading his final round into his Mancaster repeater. Ottovan moved sideways to cover him, Erassian blades slashing all around him. Shaheni charged after him, emboldened by the massed men coming to his aid. The Sipahi Shaheni's blade met Ottovan's. Ottovan parried the blow and counterattacked, forcing Shaheni backward, yet Jack Caldwell still did not retreat.

"Amahdi, retreat!" shouted Ottovan.

Jack stood where he was, tall and unafraid, full of battle rage. He thrust his underlever forward, ejecting his final shell. He snapped the lever back and pulled the trigger, his barrel aimed into the face of a guardsman, but the rifle clicked empty.

"Amahdi!" shouted Ottovan, but the Grand Vizerian Guardsmen were already upon him.

"Take him alive!" roared Shaheni. "Alive! Alive!" The guardsmen overwhelmed Jack as a wave, knocking him down, and rolling over him as they continued their charge, rushing past Ottovan to Selena Savanar and the others.

Gulana of Nor Gandus fought at Ottovan's side, the two of them quickly becoming an island amid the enemy, fiercely slashing at the horde of guardsmen and Erassians as they surged around them like a river.

Ozgar, out of arrows, pulled his scimitarus and ran to Nemakar, who was still down, shot through his leg.

"Nemakar!" screamed Ottovan. "Flash them! Flash them now!"

Nemakar, wounded as he was, found his final red-handled pistol in his lowest holster, slid it out of the leather sleeve, aimed, and fired. The powder flew toward the mass of Jemojeen's men and ignited, blinding all in front of the blast in a searing flash.

The wave of men stopped, but Jack Caldwell was behind them.

"Shotgun!" shouted Ottovan.

Still lying on his side, Nemakar pulled the blunderbuss from around his back, aimed, and pulled the trigger. The blunderbuss shotgun, at no more than fifteen yards, flattened a span of ten men, spraying them with tiny lead balls from their feet to their faces.

Ozgar bent down, threw Nemakar over his shoulder, and ran to Oapah the Hohsa.

The massive Omakhosian was still down with two javelins in him, but he was still alive, still breathing despite the steel that had impaled his lung.

"Leave me," said Oapah.

Selena Savanar had retreated to his side. "No!"

"Leave me!" he boomed, coughing blood. "I die here. I have done my duty."

"The far stairwell!" shouted Jabil. "That is our only hope! Hurry!"

"The Amahdi!" roared Ottovan, cutting his way back to the others, through the Erassians and Grand Vizerian Guardsmen that had slipped past him and Gulana. "They have the Amahdi!"

The blinded men in the front were staggering back, but new men, those with unimpaired vision, were moving up the far stairwell, making their way through the mob of men who could no longer see. There were now nearly one hundred enemies on the veranda.

"We cannot save him," said Ozgar, carrying Nemakar over his shoulder, looking down at Oapah.

Ozgar's eyes met Oapah's, and said in a glance what all knew, but none needed to say aloud. *You are far too big for any of us to carry.*

"Leave me," said Oapah again, resigning himself to his fate.

"Give me the staff!" said Ottovan, reaching the others, panting through his veil from exertion. He knew of the staff's healing power, though he did not know how to harness it.

"No," said Selena, refusing to relinquish it. She bent down over the dark-skinned face of the giant Omakhosian. She closed her eyes and held the Staff of the Serpent over Oapah.

Under her breath, she chanted old Qhaliffan words, words Ottovan had not heard in long years. They were words of the House of Savanar.

"Pull the javelins from him," she said. The mob of Erassians and Grand Vizerian Guardsmen edged closer.

"They are barbed," said Ottovan.

"Pull them out!" ordered Selena.

Ottovan, against his better judgment, placed his hands down low onto the unweighted javelin and pulled. It ripped out of Oapah, as Ottovan expected, viciously tearing flesh as it came free.

Oapah gasped, his face contorting. But as soon as the javelin left his skin, the wound covered up, as if tended for long months under the care of a healer as gifted as Umahar or Serpents of the Order.

Selena touched the Staff of the Serpent to the other javelin, the weighted one that had first lodged into Oapah's chest, and that was now fatally filling his lungs with blood.

"Run," said Oapah the Hohsa, his voice ragged. "They are coming closer. Save yourselves."

"Pull it out!" said Selena, her voice fierce and wild.

Ottovan pulled. The javelin came free. The wound, rather than spurting blood, covered itself as quickly as the first. Oapah's face altered from a grimacing expression of pain to one of astonished relief.

"In the name of Beseri, rise and walk, Oapah the Hohsa!" shouted Selena.

Oapah rose to his feet, his eyes flashing, wide with wonder. Despite the oncoming men, the others stared at Oapah and Selena.

"His leg!" shouted Ozgar.

Selena spun around, seeing Nemakar still slung over Ozgar's back. She touched the Staff of the Serpent to Nemakar's wound.

"They are coming! We must flee!" shouted Gulana, backing up toward Selena and the others with her sword drawn, still facing the approaching wave of enemies and seeing that the fighters with sight had nearly passed through those who were blinded.

"Put him down," said Selena.

Ozgar did as she commanded, lowering Nemakar, who hesitated to place his weight on the leg that had just taken a bullet.

Ottovan pulled his remaining fire pistol and aimed it at the charging mass, moving toward them across the veranda. He fired. A ring of flame burst amongst the front row, setting the Erassians ablaze.

Selena looked past the burning men, toward where Jack Caldwell had fallen, and where the Staff of the Ram had dropped upon the stone. She could see neither Jack nor the staff now, only the surging horde of Grand Vizerian Guardsmen and Erassians.

"By the God of the Sands! Come on!" shouted Jabil the Jackal, standing by the far set of stairs. They ran with javelins landing at their heels.

CHAPTER 84
The Sword of the Sands

Oasis of Ben Hamur
49th Day, Month of Wasura, 807
Anglian Calendar: April 11, 1879

When Ozgar Ogatonia, Demissary Archer Captain and Sworn Ram of the Order of the Ram, the Lion, and the Serpent opened the gate in the western wall, Handsome Habeen Barcadey left the nine, letting Ozgar replace him. He ran, as Hamid Salesi had foreseen with the last remains of his farsight, up to the unguarded gate on the northern wall, which he opened, allowing one hundred of his Swordguardsmen to rush into the oasis of Ben Hamur. From there, they raced across the small square and slipped through narrow alleys toward the center of the oasis. Handsome Habeen Barcadey led them forward, one hundred and one swordsmen, each with a sky-blue band across his head, toward the sounds of the battle.

As they approached the avenue, they came to a narrow alleyway, running silently across the stones.

As Hamid Salesi foresaw, there was a building to their left, a structure overlooking the avenue where Bazadak's men were trapped. Habeen Barcadey himself led the silent patrol up the mudbrick steps. He kicked in the door and ran, swift as a leopard across the floor, slashing and killing the young Demissary archers in their green turbans before they had time to turn their bows upon him.

The archers were still waiting for their Captain Ozgar Ogatonia's signal when Habeen Barcadey and his Swordguardsmen cut them down. From the window overlooking the avenue, Habeen Barcadey saw in an instant what needed to be done.

The Bazadak camel cavalry fought in an ever-tightening melee, stuck in the central avenue of the oasis and pinned in by Kezelboj swordsmen and mudbrick buildings on either flank. They faced six ranks of pikemen moving from east to west down the avenue, spearing every man and camel that could not flee fast enough.

Habeen Barcadey saw the Demissary firemen as they sealed off the western gate, killing the Beserians on the wall and pouring their shotgun fire and pistol fire into the rear ranks of the Bazadaks. In minutes, the Bazadaks would be destroyed, and with their death, the army of Abu Akhsa would be no more.

"Follow me," said Handsome Habeen Barcadey, running down the stairs.

He ran past his waiting men and found his three most trusted line leaders. He spoke in rapid Beserian. His line leaders nodded back, confirming their understanding. They ran out to their men, barking curt orders, barely audible above the din of the killing upon the avenue.

Three groups of Swordguardsmen began to run, one group to the west, two others to the east, moving parallel to the main avenue.

Habeen gathered the remaining twenty-five men.

"Listen now, and listen well, friends. The survival of our army rests in our hands. The Azadeems have fallen back; the Celadeens have collapsed. We must now rescue the Bazadaks. Cut the way open, and we shall lead them to the gate of the northern wall. It is the only way. Do you see?"

"Yes, Leader," said a man in the front. The others nodded.

Habeen rounded the corner of the alley and charged. The levies of the Kezelboj had their backs to them, never imagining that they as the ambushers could be ambushed themselves. Habeen and his Swordguardsmen hit them, deadly and silent, taking limbs and heads from the rear, slashing backs, necks, and hamstrings. They cut through the ranks of levies like a hot knife.

Habeen reached the final lines. He looked up into the astonished face of a Bazadak tribesman who nearly slashed him with his saber.

"Men of Bazadak! Bazadaks! Flee this way! This way!"

The tribesman shouted, "It is Handsome Habeen! Barcadey! Barcadey! The Swordguard!"

"Hurry!" ordered Habeen, standing to the side of the now-open alleyway.

The tribesman who first recognized Habeen turned his camel down the alleyway and charged into open space. His camel leaped over the dead and dying bodies of the Kezelboj levies. Habeen had left a Swordguardsman at each turn to direct the camel cavalry down the next alley, and the next after that, through the dense two- and three-story mudbrick buildings, all of the way to the northern gate.

"Hurry!" shouted Habeen, with all of the force in his lungs. "Hurry!"

As the Bazadak camel cavalry sensed the open space, they flowed to it and through it, like water pouring from a cracked dam.

Habeen glanced to his left, down the avenue to the east. The Kezelboj pikemen continued to march from east to west, sweeping all before them in the avenue, impaling men and camels, marching over the dead to the ever-present sound of their drums.

"Retreat!" roared Habeen. "This way!"

And then he saw him.

Bazak Bazadak rode toward him, lacerated in five places, dripping blood.

"Ayah!" shouted Bazadak, who had mounted a second camel that was not his own. Two Kezelboj levies on foot pursued him, slashing at his camel's legs. He turned and decapitated one. The second struck his camel in the hamstring. The beast toppled, sending Bazadak tumbling forward.

The camelmen around him did not stop, so exhilarated were beast and man alike to see, at long last, an open place to run, where they stood a chance of not being trampled, slashed, suffocated, or stabbed.

Bazadak hit the ground hard, showing his exhaustion. The Kezelboj levy who struck his camel ran at him, swinging his saber down to kill the chief of the Bazadaks.

Bazak Bazadak rolled and slashed the man across the knees with the sword in his right hand, bringing him down to the ground. He lurched forward and stabbed him through the armpit with the dagger in his left hand, where the man's armor did not protect him.

Habeen saw the dozen Kezelboj levies running toward Bazadak before he did.

As the camels continued to gallop out of the avenue and into the northern alleyway, Habeen Barcadey ran the other direction, onto the avenue and into the melee.

The dozen levies rushed headlong at Bazadak, their swords raised, nearly upon him.

Habeen charged forward, holding his bloody sword with both hands, the steel still glinting in the bright noon sun. The Kezelboj levies did not slow their attack, confident in their numbers against the lone unarmored man running against them.

They could see that the lone man was broad across the shoulders and wore an ugly scar at a diagonal on the side of his face, but he was one, and they were twelve.

Habeen Barcadey glided like a panther, whispering as he ran, "I am the sword of Abu Akhsa, the sword of Beseri, the sword of the sands."

He leaped over Bazak Bazadak and struck the first man from above, cleaving him at his collarbone, cutting down into his chest. He dropped beneath the next man, cutting his legs out from under him. He then rose, spinning and slashing a man on either side of him. He struck forward against a man's shield and then swung to his left, taking a man's sword arm off at the wrist.

Bazak Bazadak rose and, with brute force, chopped through a man's parry, his blade ricocheting off the man's blade and into his face. He joined Habeen Barcadey at his side, the two warriors standing back-to-back, facing the half-dozen levies that remained.

A group of Nor Wasuran levies in yellow tunics ran to assist their brethren but had slowed their pace, seeing what the two Beserian warriors had done. The Nor Wasurans circled them cautiously, lacking the courage to charge.

"Leader Barcadey! Chief Bazadak! It is time! We must flee!" the line leader of the Swordguard shouted from across the avenue. He ran forward. "The pikemen!"

Habeen glanced to the east. The line of pikemen was no more than twenty feet away.

"Come, Bazadak!" he shouted. Habeen ran for the two men who barred his way to the northern alley, the alley his men had cleared for the camel cavalry of the Bazadaks to escape.

Bazadak ran at his side. Habeen saw a flash of purple from the corner of his eye to the left. On instinct, he closed with the man in front of him, dropping down under the man's saber swing.

The gunshots rang out to his left, to the west, where he had seen the flash of purple. The man whose slash he had ducked fell, taking the bullets meant for him.

"Demissaries! Run!" he shouted.

Bazadak was already running. Habeen looked left as he ran with all of the energy that remained inside of him. The Demissary firemen ran unimpeded, aiming their pistols at Habeen and Bazadak.

"Do not look at them!" shouted Bazadak. As he said the words, the flashes exploded to the west, a wall of white light, a light that could blind.

Habeen's head was turned. He could still see. More shots rang out to the west. Habeen felt tremendous heat to his right as the ring of fire exploded near him, but he kept running. Pain struck his legs as a shrapnel shot exploded behind him. He ran onward, and his legs did not fail him.

Bazak Bazadak ran just in front of him. The alley entrance stood only feet ahead. A hail of shotgun pellets slammed against the mudbrick walls of the buildings at the alley's edge. Habeen Barcadey could feel that he was still not gravely hit. He was still running, still alive.

The camel cavalry formed up in front of him, aiming a volley of rifle shots over his head. Habeen ducked as he ran, and the rifles blasted their shots in unison. The black smoke filled the air above him.

"Barcadey!" barked a Bazadak tribesman, holding the head rope of a riderless camel.

Habeen grasped the saddle and pulled himself up onto the tall, standing bull. Bazadak was already mounted. More Demissary shrapnel rounds struck the edge of the alley.

"Ride! Ride!" shouted Bazadak as they sprinted their camels down the stone and dirt alleys, making violent turns around mudbrick buildings and nearly slamming into the walls. The camels leaped over debris and ran over dead bodies.

Habeen clung to the saddle with his left hand, gripping his sword with his right. He knew that to fall off would mean death or capture, which would be far worse.

Habeen's Swordguardsmen still stayed in their posted positions showing the way to the northern gate and mounting their camels only after Habeen and Bazadak, the last fleeing riders, had ridden past them. They turned down alley after alley, until at last the northern gate was before them. Bazadak riflemen manned the ledge above the gate, firing their rifles at enemies Habeen could not see.

He heard the Demissary long guns in the distance, the boom of the guns so different from those of an ordinary rifle.

As Habeen rode to the gate, a shot from a long gun struck one of the Bazadaks above, throwing him off the wall. His chest burst like a wineskin as he flew backward into the thorns of the zareba.

The gate was still open.

Handsome Habeen Barcadey rode out across the drawbridge with Bazak Bazadak at his side, passing through the zareba in a galloping blur.

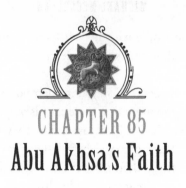

CHAPTER 85
Abu Akhsa's Faith

West of Ben Hamur
49th Day, Month of Wasura, 807
Anglian Calendar: April 11, 1879

"Riders!" shouted Anil Salesi with his looking glass at his eye. He sat mounted on a horse next to his father.

Umahar aimed his own looking glass where the young Beserian pointed his.

"Who are they?" asked Abu Akhsa, squinting in the afternoon sunlight.

"They are not Qhaliffans," said Umahar.

"Nor are they Beserians," said Anil Salesi.

"They are foreigners," said Hamid Salesi, looking older than he had looked even hours before. He did not look through a looking glass as he spoke. He did not even look at the riders. "They ride to warn us."

"Warn us of what?" said Abu Akhsa.

"An enemy approaches," said Hamid Salesi.

Abu Akhsa placed his hand above his eyes to shade them and survey the battlefield. He looked north. The Azadeems, collapsed on the left flank, streamed westward in ones and twos, running from the Qhaliffa's Demissaries that had slaughtered their fellow tribesmen. The fleeing riders stayed to the north as they fled westward, coming nowhere near the hill upon which Abu Akhsa sat astride his mount and behind which the Swordguard waited. *They are too ashamed to face us.*

Abu Akhsa looked south. The Celadeens fled far to the right flank, with seemingly fewer survivors than the Azadeems. The men of the Celadeens stayed far to the south, avoiding Abu Akhsa and the Swordguard as well, flying westward as fast as their camels could take them. *They too are broken and ashamed.*

Anil had begged to ride to rally the Azadeems. His father Hamid said nothing when Abu Akhsa refused Anil's request.

"I need you here," said Abu Akhsa. "Those men are beyond rallying. You will stay here by my side and by that of your father."

The two foreign riders rode closer, galloping across the plain, sending up a trail of dust behind them.

"He wears a hat of red and blue," said Anil, "of the style of the Western soldiers."

"And the other looks to be a Vetenan," said Umahar.

Abu Akhsa shaded his eyes with his right hand, looking at the ruins of Ben Hamur.

"What has befallen the Bazadaks?" he asked to no one in particular.

No one answered him as the foreign riders continued their wild ride across the plains, headed directly at Abu Akhsa.

"Should I stop them?" asked Anil.

"No," said his father. "They ride in peace."

"Umahar," said Abu Akhsa, "take ten of the Swordguard and ride to them. Escort them here."

Umahar, the Demissary, nodded in acknowledgment, stopping his salute midway into the gesture. Abu Akhsa was not his commander, and Beserians did not salute. Umahar turned to the rear of the hill where the four hundred of the Swordguard still waited, lined up upon their horses and camels, itching to join the fight but always obedient to Abu Akhsa's commands. Nearly all could see the remnants of the Azadeems fleeing along the northern stretches of the plain and the Celadeens fleeing to the south. Still, Abu Akhsa held them back.

"We are missing the battle," grumbled some.

"Our swords could make the difference," said others.

Yet their line commanders held them in place, reminding them that they were sworn to Abu Akhsa and breaking his orders would cost them the sky-blue band across their headscarves, the band that was worth more to any one of them than their own lives.

Umahar rode out past Abu Akhsa's small hill with nine Swordguardsmen and a line leader streaming out behind him in a galloping arc. Umahar rode in the center, wrapped from head to toe in the sand-colored cloth of the Order, the only man without a sky-blue band across his forehead.

"Halt, foreigners!" shouted Umahar, in Qhaliffan, as they approached.

The riders did not slow their pace.

Umahar repeated himself, this time in Beserian.

The riders slowed their gallop.

"They are coming! They are coming from the south!" shouted the darker one, the one that did not wear the soldier's hat and looked like he came from the Veteno.

"Who is coming from the south? The Celadeens?"

"No!" shouted the man, breathless with agitation. "The Demissaries!"

"What Demissaries?" asked Umahar.

"Hundreds of them! In orange turbans! They have ridden far to the south and are riding for whatever is behind you! Your camp! Your herds, your women!"

Hersen Expey looked at Umahar and the Swordguardsmen with suspicious, narrowed eyes as Diego spoke.

Umahar did not hesitate. He turned and galloped to Abu Akhsa, the Swordguardsmen riding behind him. Hersen and Diego followed.

"These men say Demissaries are riding far to the south, riding to attack the herds and the women," shouted Umahar before his horse had come to a stop.

Abu Akhsa's eyes widened, grasping in an instant the full magnitude of the danger.

"Yes," said Hamid Salesi, clinging to the final fading remnants of his farsight. "The God of the Sands has brought these men to us to bring us this warning."

"Part! So I can see these men!" ordered Abu Akhsa to Umahar and the Swordguardsmen who blocked his view of Hersen Expey and Diego the Vetenan.

"What did you see?" asked Abu Akhsa, looking down the small slope at Hersen Expey and Diego. Abu Akhsa's eye took them in from their shoes to the hats on their heads.

"You attacked us!" said Hersen Expey, his Beserian heavily accented but understandable.

"I attacked who?"

"We came to the Sand Sea on a peaceful expedition, and you attacked us!" barked Hersen, jamming his finger into the air toward Abu Akhsa.

Several of the Swordguardsmen slid their hands toward their saber handles.

"I know not who you are, foreigner," said Abu Akhsa.

"I am Major Hersen Expey of the LaFrentian Legion! I am the executive officer and second-in-command of the Stanwich Expedition, traveling underneath the flags of the Anglian Imperium, the New Anglian Republic, and the Spatanian Emperor. This is Diego of the Veteno, a Spatanian. Your riders attacked our encampment south of the Valley of Kordon! In that attack, you wounded Harold Milton Stanwich, who now lies dying in the oasis of Ben Gamurian. I come seeking the Staff of the Serpent to heal him."

"The staff is no longer with us," said Hamid Salesi. "It was stolen. The staff lies there." Salesi pointed to Ben Hamur, the smoke rising above it.

"There is no time for this," said Abu Akhsa.

"If you wish to know what I know, you will make time for this!" shouted Hersen, again jamming his finger in the air at the Chief of Chiefs of the Beserian people. Again, the Swordguardsmen reached for their swords, this time leaving their hands on the sword handles.

"Then say it quickly, man," said Abu Akhsa. "Major Expey of the Stanwich Expedition, what do you want?"

"I will lead you to the Demissaries riding to your rear. After the battle, you will bring me to the Staff of the Serpent."

"If it can be done, you have my word," said Abu Akhsa.

Hersen nodded. "Then, you shall have mine! The riders rode out in a vast arc, perhaps gaining four miles, enough to be south of that ridgeline." Hersen turned and pointed to the south. "They could be in striking distance of your herds within minutes."

Abu Akhsa turned to Hamid Salesi.

"Release the Swordguard," said Hamid Salesi.

"Can you see it, or is it gone?"

"I can see it. The man speaks true," said Salesi. "Release the Swordguard. It is the only way, and we must ride with them."

Abu Akhsa looked at Hamid Salesi, aware that the fate of his people was upon his shoulders, and he was about to retreat from the field of battle with his left and right flanks collapsed and the future of his center uncertain.

"If I retreat, we will have abandoned Bazadak and Barcadey," said Abu Akhsa.

"If you stay, you will have ensured the destruction of our people," said Hamid Salesi.

Abu Akhsa drew his sword and faced the four hundred of the Swordguard.

"Men of the Swordguard! The Demissaries ride to our south. They ride for our women, our children, and our herds."

Abu Akhsa paused for his words to sink in.

"Will we stop them?"

"Yes!" shouted the four hundred, deep voices shaking the sky with their roar.

"Will we slaughter them?"

"Yes!"

"Follow me!"

Abu Akhsa charged forward on his horse, with Hamid and Anil Salesi, Umahar the Demissary, Hersen Expey, and Diego the Vetenan, all riding behind him. They rode through a gap in the Swordguard, and as they passed, the Swordguardsmen followed, the afternoon sun shining down upon the sky-blue bands upon their heads and the blades in their hands.

Ulgur Uggatar galloped for four miles to catch up with his men. Having faced the Celadeens, and having cut down Cedak Celadeen himself, Ulgur rode with renewed energy, the energy that only killing gave him. Killing did not satiate his appetite for slaughter; it enlarged it. He reached his men on the far side of the southern ridge, slowing his gallop to a canter, his borrowed stallion panting.

"How far to the turn?" he asked Lieutenant-Captain Bombar, who was nearly as large as he was, and who had led the men in his absence. Ulgur glanced up at the black banner over their head, bearing the *III* in orange, for his lancers. They will remember that flag today. *They will remember it as the flag that flew over the death of the Beserian race, and I, Ulgur Uggatar, will be remembered as the commander of that slaughter.* A warm tingling feeling spread out across Ulgur's back as he envisioned the glory in his mind.

"Less than a mile, Captain," said Bombar.

Ulgur looked at Bombar's face, seeing a hint of disappointment that Ulgur had arrived. "You did not think I was going to let you lead this attack. Did you?" Ulgur laughed.

"No, Captain," said Bombar.

Ulgur looked ahead. The sun was still high in the sky and would give plenty of light for them to carry out the slaughter.

Perhaps this day I will stake my claim to replace Ottovan Fanfar as Legion Commander.

Ulgur looked back upon his men: all tall and strong, all hardened Demissaries trained by him for the last several years, all proven killers. Their orange pennants streamed back from their lance tips as they rode.

Ulgur looked ahead at the scouts. In the near distance rode groups of three lancers. In the farther distance, patrols of Erassians led the way. The Erassians stopped.

The groups of three rode to their assigned positions and stopped, just behind the ridgeline.

Ulgur looked at the closest group, waiting for the hand signal.

The signal came.

"They are there," he said, kicking his horse into a swifter canter. The others followed him, increasing their pace.

Ulgur came to the ridge and looked down. Before him, as far as he could see, stretched the Beserian camp: women, children, old, and infirm. And far more expansive than the people stretched the herds: goats, sheep, horses, and camels, all spread out, searching out the meager forage afforded by the mid-desert plain.

As planned, the lancers of the Third Legion lined up just beneath the ridgeline in three long lines. The lancers of the First Legion lined up to their left.

Ulgur turned and rode down the line. "No mercy! We slaughter everything! Every woman! Every goat! Every baby! Today the Beserians end! Your rewards will be great! Know that! Jemojeen remembers those who do as he asks! No mercy! No mercy! No mercy!"

Ulgur's words were unnecessary. Demissary lancers were not men disposed toward mercy. They were chosen for their ruthlessness, and Ulgur had taken great pains over the years to make them more ruthless than any others. A thousand acts of hardening devoured their hearts. For the Lancers of the Third, killing had largely ceased to surprise or to evoke feelings within them. It was merely physical work. Ottovan had tried to rein in Ulgur's ruthlessness, but there was little he could do when the Qhaliffa, on the advice of the Grand Vizer, heaped rewards upon those who were the most ruthless.

"Today the Beserians die!" shouted Ulgur one last time. He charged over the ridgeline first. The light blue southern sky turned black and orange with Demissary tunics and turbans atop huge warhorses.

A small boy, no more than eight years old, tending to a flock of sheep, saw them first. He reached for his sling. He slung a stone at the wall of lancers charging down upon him. The lancers did not even bother spearing him. They simply crushed him under their hooves. His terrified sheep tried to run before the galloping warhorses, but they were not nearly swift enough. The lancers speared the sheep as they galloped down the slope toward the main camp, turning the white fleece scarlet as they extracted their lances without slowing their pace.

At their tents, the women saw them. They screamed, grabbing their children and running to the north, in the opposite direction of the horsemen.

"Run! Demissaries!"

"Where?"

"Here! From the south! Run, run!"

The little children screamed as their mothers ripped them up from the ground, leaving their simple toys and stick figures lying in the dust.

The panic swept through the camp like wildfire, striking humans and animals at once.

Ulgur struck the tent line first. His charger trampled a small tent, crushing the small poles that held it up and pounding the wool beneath his stallion's hooves. He rode onward, not around the tents, but over them and through them.

A woman's back appeared in front of him. He speared her with his lance, cutting off her scream. She arched her back as the lance struck through her. He ripped the lance out and kept riding as she fell into the sandy soil, never again to arise.

An older man and a young boy leaped up and ran at him with knives. Ulgur speared the boy through the chest. Before he could spear the old man, another lancer did it for him.

Abu Akhsa could see in an instant that he was too late. The screams reached him before he could see their cause. Now he saw.

The Demissary lancers had cut through, over and across the tents, crushing and spearing all in their path. They had already destroyed much of the camp, and the swift orange tide had begun to cut into the flood of running humanity and animals trying to flee to the north across the open plain. The humans ran on foot with no chance of outrunning the lancers.

The animals, swifter than the people, formed a wave ahead of the women and the children. Most of the elderly stood and accepted their fate, trampled by heavy hooves or speared by long, steel-tipped lances. The women did not give up themselves or their young so easily. Thousands were slaughtered nonetheless.

Abu Akhsa paused for no more than a moment in his grief and outrage, his eyes watering and his throat grabbing.

"Charge!" he shouted, swinging his sword forward. His Swordguardsmen did not need prompting to ride to the defense of their mothers and sisters, or their wives and daughters. They charged forward, whipping their mounts to ride as fast as they would carry them.

The Swordguardsmen thundered down the slope in a wave of beige and sky blue, kicking up a cloud of sand and dust above them.

"Kill them! Kill them all!" shouted Abu Akhsa.

Anil Salesi screamed at his side, a bloodcurdling war cry of the ancient Salesis, "Ayoyoyoyoyoyoyoooo!"

His father Hamid kept pace at his side, carrying his own ancient saber and screaming the same words. He rode to the defense of his wives, children, and grandchildren.

Hersen rode with his LaFrentian Legion service revolver in his right hand, ready to gun down any in his path.

Diego rode with his Hart-Henry carbine at the ready.

Umahar held a three-barreled Demissary pistol in his left hand and his scimitarus in his right, riding to stop the lancers of his own Legion. The physician charged into battle as the fire Demissary he had first trained to be, preparing to carry out the killing he had learned long before he had learned to heal.

Many of the Swordguardsmen carried rifles slung across their backs, but none of them sought to shoot the enemy now. All four hundred charged with their swords drawn, seeking to avenge the defeats they had witnessed of the Azadeems and the Celadeens, desperate to avenge the killing in their camp, seeking only Demissary blood to splash across their blades.

Ulgur finally broke his lance on the nineteenth or twentieth body, snapping the shaft as he pulled to free it of yet another torso. No matter. He pulled his huge scimitarus and killed with it. He cut down a fleeing woman with his sword and looked up, seeing the wave of men in beige and sky blue charging down the slope. His men were wild with the slaughter, as he was himself. Most of those he speared from behind had been women. Many were children.

"Horn!" he shouted. "Horn!" he cried even louder, bordering on a scream. "Horn!"

The Legion hornman galloped to his side, riding next to the bannerman with whom the hornman was always to ride for circumstances precisely such as this. The black banner showing the orange *III* snapped in the wind above them.

"Sound the withdrawal! To the west!" barked Ulgur into the man's face. His sword was dark with Beserian blood, the same blood that covered much of his legs and his horse.

The hornman swallowed the fear that always arose when he found himself too near Ulgur Uggatar. He nodded and did as Ulgur commanded, inhaling and placing the long, curved horn to his lips.

He blew three long blasts and then four short ones. He repeated the three long blasts, meaning "withdraw," and the four short bursts, meaning "to the west."

The men in the orange turbans stopped as they were, reining in their war-horses and looking to the bannerman. The black banner was already fleeing to the west.

They stopped slashing and ceased thrusting their lances. As one, they began moving to the west, following the banner. First, they trotted, and then they broke into a canter. Then they galloped as they cleared the bodies and tents of the camp.

As the great wave of charging Swordguardsmen approached, the mass of Demissaries began to ride away, fleeing to the west as the Beserian warriors galloped toward the camp from the east.

As the Demissaries withdrew, the full scope of their destruction opened before Abu Akhsa and the Swordguardsmen's eyes. Thousands of dead women, children, elderly, and sick Beserians lay crumbled and broken upon the ground, growing more vivid the closer they galloped. With the dead, thousands more sheep, goats, and camels lay slaughtered.

The wave of black tunics and orange turbans consolidated as they withdrew, executing a movement they had trained a thousand times. Their open, chaotic pursuit of the camp dwellers gave way to an orderly withdrawal, all before the eyes of the enraged, charging Swordguardsmen. The charging warriors were still a quarter of a mile away when the last Demissary lancer cleared the westernmost tents, joining the main body of cavalry retreating to the west.

The Swordguardsmen reached the camp with no one to strike, only thousands to mourn.

"Cowards!" shouted Anil Salesi, charging forward ahead of his father and Abu Akhsa, shaking his saber at the backs of the retreating Demissaries, a half-mile to the west and riding as fast as their stalwart warhorses could carry them.

Abu Akhsa looked across the camp at the dead and the dying. His Swordguard riders slowed their pace, looking around them. They stopped, no longer able to continue, seeing the faces of Beserian women and children looking up at them with dead, haunting stares.

Hamid Salesi rode next to Abu Akhsa, his eyes darting back and forth and leaping from dead body to dead body. Tears formed in the corners of his eyes.

"Abu Akhsa," he said, "It was not—" Salesi's voice caught in his throat.

Abu Akhsa turned and looked at him.

"It was not supposed to end this way," said Salesi. "The Prophecy. The Prophecy said otherwise . . ." His voice trailed off.

Abu Akhsa looked at him, staring into his face but saying nothing. A baby's piercing wail rose, wafting across the plain and into their ears, carried on the westerly wind.

"The staff is gone," continued Hamid Salesi, slowly shaking his head from side to side. "Perhaps I have failed you, Abu Akhsa. Perhaps I have failed the God of the Sands. If I had not lost it—if Ghani of the Gap had not stolen it."

Abu Akhsa sat astride his silver-white horse for long moments, saying nothing. The baby continued to wail.

"No, Hamid, it is not on you," he said.

"The Azadeems. The Celadeens. They were smashed," said Hamid Salesi, shaking his head from side to side. "The Bazadaks, I fear their fate is no better." Salesi looked out over the devastation of the Beserian camp as if trapped in a nightmare that refused to end, waiting for a morning sun that would not come. "I should have foreseen this. I have failed you. I have failed us all."

"We do not know the end of the Bazadaks, Hamid," said Abu Akhsa.

"I cannot see them," said Salesi. "My farsight is gone. There is only darkness."

"Yet we remain, old friend," Abu Akhsa's voice was soft. "They did not kill all of our people. Look to the north. Thousands live. We came in time to save them. The Year of Prophecy is still at hand."

Salesi looked to the north. Indeed, thousands of Beserians, mostly women, had slowed their running. Some had stopped, beginning to look back to the camp as they saw that the sky-blue bands of the Swordguard had replaced the terrible orange turbans. They saw they had been rescued and that death no longer pursued them on warhorses.

Hamid allowed his eyes to drift back to the camp, darting back and forth amongst the smashed tents and bodies.

"So much death," he said.

"We never believed our cause would be an easy one. The power of the evil ones is great. But all is not lost. No, all is not lost," said Abu Akhsa.

The afternoon sun shone upon his dark, bronzed face as he looked west, making the grey streaks in his beard look white. The brightness of the sunlight seemed to mock him in his grief.

"Where are your wives, Abu Akhsa? Where are mine?" asked Salesi.

"I do not know, old friend. We will find them. If the God of the Sands and the Mountain has preserved them, we will praise him for his mercy. If they are lost." Abu Akhsa paused as if seeking the strength to muster the next words.

"If they are lost," he said, "we shall fight onward in their memory. Our lives are no longer our own, Hamid. Our lives have never been our own. The God of the Sands and the Mountain has built our lives for this moment, old friend. All of the strength we have acquired in our lives, we have acquired for this moment. Men do not require strength to ride triumphantly into the Qhaliffa's palace in Saman Keer. No, men require strength to continue fighting now, at this moment, when lesser men would flee and when lesser men would surrender to despair. Our lives are passing things, old friend, but the ages endure. We must rise now. For this reason we are here. I am willing to sacrifice all, as are you."

"I fear—" Hamid Salesi paused, watching his son Anil—his only remaining son—shake his sword into the air, impotently shouting his rage at the line of Demissaries disappearing on the horizon, riding into the west. "I fear the cost is too great."

"So do all men who stand against the darkness. You are not wrong to fear it, Hamid of the Salesis, but you must never believe it. I need you now more than ever."

The horn sounded in the east. Both men turned, straining their eyes to see.

"That is ours. That is the horn of the Bazadaks," said Abu Akhsa, seeing the riders emerge on the ridgeline from the direction of Ben Hamur.

Habeen Barcadey crested the ridgeline first, with Bazak Bazadak galloping at his side. The others emerged, hundreds of riders, and then hundreds more.

The Swordguardsmen looked up as the western sun shone into the faces of the Bazadaks, the Kateems, the Sambads, and the contingent of their Swordguard brothers who had survived the Battle of Ben Hamur.

"By the God of the Sands," said Abu Akhsa.

Hamid Salesi shook his head. "We cannot win battles by celebrating retreats."

"We are not here to win battles. We are here to win the war, the great war, the war of the Prophecy. These men have survived, Hamid of the Salesis. Wars are won by surviving. Celebrate, old friend, celebrate the small victory we have. These men live."

Abu Akhsa raised his sword, riding forward and shouting, "Bazadak! Barcadey!"

In their devotion, the handful of Swordguardsmen around the Chief of Chiefs still imitated their leader, "Bazadak! Barcadey!"

Their small cheer was a pitiful echo of the battle cry of the morning, the roar of the thirteen thousand who had risen with the dawn, thundering from the ridgeline overlooking Ben Hamur.

Habeen Barcadey galloped down into the destruction beneath him, into the crushed tents and massacred bodies. Bazadak rode at his side. Both men bled from a half-dozen wounds or more. But both men sat upright in their saddles, as if their posture defied the direction in which they rode—away from the battlefield in retreat.

Hersen Expey looked up with Diego at his side.

"Who are they?" he asked.

"Survivors," said Diego. "Survivors of the battle."

Hersen and Diego stared as the men rode closer. They were formidable men. All appeared to be bloodstained with tattered tunics, riding upon wounded horses and camels.

"The large one, his name is Bazak Bazadak, chief of the Bazadaks," said Diego, his voice little more than a whisper.

Hersen could hear Diego's respect for Bazadak in his voice.

Diego's voice rose as he recognized a second rider. "The other, the one who rides next to Bazadak, the one with the scar on his face and the blue band on his head, he is Habeen Barcadey, Leader of Abu Akhsa's Swordguard, the greatest swordsman upon the sands."

The surviving Bazadaks and Swordguardsmen rode closer, reining in their mounts ahead of Abu Akhsa, camelmen riding intermixed with horse riders.

Abu Akhsa sat upon his mount with Hamid Salesi at his side. They waited in silence as Habeen Barcadey and Bazak Bazadak approached at a walk. Abu Akhsa waited for them to speak.

"We were ambushed," said Bazadak, his voice deep and growling. "They knew where we would attack. They waited. Thousands waited in silence. They caught us along the main avenue, coming at us from both sides before we could spread out into the city. Their infantry clogged the alleyways. Pikemen barred the avenue. Then Demissaries sealed us off from behind."

As he spoke, Hamid Salesi's stomach churned. *It is the staff. Only the Staff of Wisdom would have allowed Jemojeen to set such a trap. If I had not lost it, far more would be alive.*

"How did you escape the oasis?" asked Abu Akhsa.

"We would not have survived but for Barcadey and his Swordguardsmen."

Bazak Bazadak looked over at Habeen Barcadey, lowering his head in gratitude. A handful of men nodded, affirming Bazadak's words.

"Barcadey's men cut a way through the alleys to the north. They cut down the levies of the Kezelboj from behind. We rode through the alleys to the northern gate, and from there out into the desert—north, then northwest, then west, and then south to this place." Bazadak looked around him in horror, as if for the first time realizing how much of the camp was destroyed.

"Who did this?" he asked, his voice rising.

"Demissaries," said Abu Akhsa. "Lancers of the Third and First Legions."

"What of the Staff of the Serpent? What of the Amahdi and Selena Savanar?" asked Hamid Salesi. As he asked his question, Hersen Expey, Umahar, and Diego approached.

Bazadak eyed the foreigners with suspicion. Of the three, Bazadak had only ever seen Umahar before.

"Who are they?" he asked, pointing past Abu Akhsa and Hamid Salesi.

Abu Akhsa turned to follow Bazadak's finger.

"They are friends, fellow travelers of the Amahdi. They seek the staff and the Amahdi both."

"You trust these men?" asked Bazadak, looking at Hersen in particular with hard eyes.

"Yes," said Abu Akhsa. "Tell us what you know, Bazak Bazadak. Time is scarce."

"Selena Savanar lives. She holds the Staff of the Serpent, and she rides north with companions."

"Praise the God of the Sands and the Mountain," said Abu Akhsa.

"How do you know that she rides north?" asked Hamid Salesi.

"We rode with them north of Ben Hamur. They ride for the Hahst," said Habeen Barcadey, speaking for the first time.

"The Hahst?" asked Hamid Salesi, with fear and confusion in his voice.

Habeen Barcadey nodded.

"Who are her companions?" asked Abu Akhsa.

"Five of those who rode with us into Ben Hamur ride with Selena Savanar still."

"Which five?" asked Umahar.

"Ottovan Fanfar, Nemakar Hasdruba, Oapah the Hohsa, and Gulana of Nor Gandus. Jabil the Jackal rides with them, as does the Demissary Ozgar Ogatonia. Aurelio Demassi fell facing the enemy."

Diego's face fell as he heard the words. He had known Demassi since they were boys. "How did he fall?"

"Demassi the Vetenan died facing the enemy, fighting Jemojeen Jongdar himself and fighting to defend the Lady Savanar and the Staff of the Serpent."

"What has befallen the Amahdi?" asked Abu Akhsa, dread rising in his voice.

Habeen Barcadey looked at Bazak Bazadak.

Bazadak nodded, his face grim.

"We do not know, Abu Akhsa," said Habeen Barcadey. "He fell facing the enemy. He is either dead or in the hands of Jemojeen."

Abu Akhsa and Hamid Salesi looked at Habeen and Bazadak in stunned silence. Hersen looked at them and then turned to Diego, making sure he had understood the Beserian words properly.

"Yes, they say that Jack Caldwell has been captured or killed," said Diego.

"Jemojeen lives?" asked Umahar.

"Yes," said Habeen.

"And he still holds the Staff of the Ram?"

Habeen nodded gravely.

"How did they recover the Staff of the Serpent?" asked Umahar.

"The nine found him upon the veranda of the Sharef of Ben Hamur. They fought him. Ozgar, the Demissary, shot Jemojeen through the hand with a poisoned arrow, causing him to drop the staff. Jabil the Jackal recovered it. All of the nine fought like heroes. The Amahdi killed many until he was overwhelmed, when hundreds of Erassians and Grand Vizerian Guardsmen flooded onto the veranda to rescue Jemojeen. He fought like the man who was prophesied. That is what the survivors told us as they rode to the north."

All within hearing distance let these words sink into them. No one spoke for long moments.

"Why do they ride for the Hahst?" asked Abu Akhsa.

Hamid Salesi answered. "They ride for the Hidden Valley, for the Valley of Hom Hommuram. They seek to recover Hom Hommuram's staff—the Staff of the Lion, the Staff of Might."

"Yes, this is so," said Habeen Barcadey.

"Tell us where they have gone, and we shall ride to meet them," said Hersen, interrupting loudly in Beserian.

Diego glanced at him, noting that Hersen's fluency in the language of the sands seemed to increase by the hour.

Habeen Barcadey and Bazak Bazadak looked at the LaFrentian with indignation, distrusting him and the loudness of his voice.

"Tell them," said Abu Akhsa.

"They ride north and east, into the Hahst," said Habeen Barcadey.

"Tell me how to get there," said Hersen Expey.

"I will take you there," said Umahar. "I will take you to the Hahst."

"Go, with my blessing," said Abu Akhsa.

"And I will go," said a new voice.

Hamid Salesi turned to see his only living son, Anil.

"No," he said faintly.

"Do we need the staff for our vengeance?" asked Anil, looking into his father's face with flames in his eyes.

"Yes," said Hamid, speaking in barely more than a whisper.

"Do not tell me it is dangerous, Father. Look around you. Where are your wives? Where are my sisters? We know not. We are left with only vengeance. Let me go."

Abu Akhsa looked at Hamid Salesi, unwilling to force his hand.

"Go," said Hamid Salesi, bowing his head to his son. He looked up at Abu Akhsa.

"Go and find your families," said Abu Akhsa in a voice that carried over the Bazadaks and the Swordguardsmen. "Go and tend to them. Go and find your flocks. I ask no more fighting of you this day."

The Bazadaks, led by Habeen Barcadey and Bazak Bazadak, rode past Hamid Salesi and Abu Akhsa, moving into the camp and to the north to find their families.

Hamid Salesi and Abu Akhsa stood motionless as Anil Salesi, Umahar, Hersen Expey, and Diego the Vetenan rode to the northeast.

They sat upon their horses, watching in silence.

When they crossed over the ridge and out of view, Abu Akhsa looked at Hamid Salesi. His old advisor looked into his eyes with great sadness in his own.

Then Abu Akhsa's eyes narrowed in resolve.

"Yes, Hamid Salesi," he said. "They ride for the Valley of Hom Hommuram into the treachery of the Hahst. They may not return, but this war is no longer in our hands. It was never in our hands. Our beginning has ended."

"And our end is beginning," said Hamid Salesi.

"Yes, old friend. Have faith. It is all we have, and it is all we have ever had."

Then Abu Akhsa turned, at last, back to the west, to the ruined camp, to learn if his wives and children still lived.

PART VI
A CHILD OF HOM HOMMURAM

CHAPTER 86
The Daughter of Sah Seg Savanar

Southern Rim of the Hahst
52nd Day, Month of Wasura, 807
Anglian Calendar: April 14, 1879

"Stop here," said Ottovan. "We cannot enter in darkness."

"Why not?" asked Selena. "They may find us by the morning."

"Better to risk that than the sinking sands. We cannot find the path by night. The moonlight is too faint. We will all die."

"The Lion is correct," said Oapah the Hohsa. Like the rest of them, Oapah had ridden more than eighty miles, showing no signs of the two javelins that had stuck into his body less than three days before.

"Our camels are exhausted, and we have little water left," said Jabil the Jackal.

"Fine, we rest here," said Selena, grasping the Staff of the Serpent to her chest. Already she could feel its power entering her, changing her perception, allowing her to see, hear, and feel things she could not perceive before.

Gulana was already preparing the tiny, makeshift tent they would share.

The sands of the Hahst stretched out in front of them like the surface of a vast lake, extending farther than the eye could see to the north, east, and west, white as bleached bones in the moonlight.

"Rest assured, Lady Savanar," said Ottovan, "that the reality of the Hahst is as bad as its reputation."

"Have you ventured into it?"

"Only once," said Ottovan, looking at Nemakar and Ozgar. "Only once."

Nemakar and Ozgar nodded.

Selena stared out over the smooth whiteness of the Hahst. "It looks almost peaceful."

"Yes, it does, until one is swallowed by the sinking sands."

Selena walked to Gulana to help her with their saddlebags.

"We will rest for a few hours. I will take the first watch," said Ottovan.

"And I the second," said Jabil, the lone Beserian with them.

"Riders!"

Selena lurched up, swinging her arms out and striking Gulana, who was still asleep. She looked and saw Jabil the Jackal pointing out into the desert to the south. It was still dark.

The staff! Selena frantically felt beneath her and found it, rigid against her body.

"How many?" asked Ottovan, leaping up from a dead sleep.

"Four riders," said Jabil, swinging his rifle around from the sling across his back and pulling the butt up to his shoulder.

Ottovan lifted his extendable looking glass to his eye.

"God of the Mountain and the Sands," he said, still looking through his glass. "Unless the moonlight deceives me, it is one of ours."

Ozgar and Nemakar stood at Ottovan's side, looking through their small telescopes.

"Westerners," said Nemakar.

"And a Beserian," said Ozgar.

The riders continued to gallop toward them.

"Those are Bazadak camels," said Jabil, knowing his own tribe's camels as well as he knew his own siblings.

The riders came closer. Ottovan walked forward, waving both of his hands over his head.

"Is it true?" shouted Umahar, still far off. He pulled his face covering down. If it was true, he no longer needed to hide his face upon the open sands because Jemojeen could no longer see him.

"It is Umahar!" said Nemakar. "Umahar lives!"

"Is it true?" shouted Umahar again.

He and the others slowed their gallop.

"Is it true?" asked Umahar a third time. His camel breathed heavily, looking to be near exhaustion, as did the other three.

"Is what true?" asked Ottovan.

"Did you recover the Staff of the Serpent? Did you take it from Jemojeen himself?"

"Yes."

"Is it here?"

Selena Savanar walked forward, flanked on either side by Oapah and Gulana, each of the Oath Holders towering over her. Umahar's eyes only saw what was in her hands—the ancient, gnarled piece of olive wood, with the carved serpent coiled around it.

"By the God of the Mountain and the Sands," said Umahar, his voice reverent.

He ordered his camel down to its knees, and he slid out of the saddle, never taking his eyes off of Selena. He walked toward her.

Selena waited, wary of the man's naked desire.

"As you know, Lady Savanar, I am of the Order," he said. "And I am a healer. May I hold it?"

Selena looked to Ottovan. He nodded.

The other riders approached, Anil Salesi, Diego the Vetenan, and Hersen Expey. Hersen stared intently at Jabil the Jackal in the moonlight.

Selena handed the staff to Umahar.

Umahar took the staff into his hands, holding it gingerly as if it were far more precious than gold, more valuable than all of the gems in the Qhaliffa's treasury.

"All of my life, I have wondered at this," he said, slowly turning the staff in his hands. "Have you healed with it?"

Selena nodded.

"Have you healed yourself?"

"Myself?"

"Where the men of the dungeon hurt you, have you restored yourself?"

Selena shook her head. *Is it possible?*

Umahar looked into Selena's face.

"Open your mouth."

Selena did as Umahar asked.

Umahar looked down into her mouth, into the dark space where her two front teeth once were.

Umahar tilted his head, looking at Selena like the trained physician he was.

Umahar hummed, closing his eyes. His lips curled up into a smile as the healing power of the staff flowed into him, the feeling better than he had ever imagined in his many years of imagining.

With his eyes still closed, he lowered the staff down to Selena's lips, seeing with perfect precision in his mind, seeing more clearly than he had ever seen with his eyes. He saw the roots forming in Selena's gums as the teeth began to lower, filling the dark open space, remaking that which could not be remade, restoring beauty that Jemojeen and his torturers, in their cruelty, had intended to destroy forever.

Selena reached up toward her mouth in fear and astonishment.

"Wait," said Umahar, his eyes still closed. The teeth continued to form, straight, white, and beautiful.

"Now," he said, opening his eyes.

He looked down into Selena's face, his eyes radiant.

Selena smiled, feeling the back of her teeth with her tongue, thrusting it into the same place she had every hour since they had ripped the teeth from her gums, the place that had served as a reminder of her pain, her torture, and her loss.

Selena turned, looking at Oapah, Gulana, and the others, smiling with an open mouth as she never had since her torture in the dungeon.

"Lady Savanar," gasped Gulana, falling to a knee.

Oapah beamed and lowered himself to a knee as well.

Ottovan, Ozgar, and Nemakar bowed deeply.

Jabil and Anil looked upon her face with pride, seeing the power of the Staff of Beseri, the staff that had been with their people since the days of the Prophet.

Hersen Expey watched with wide eyes, marveling at what had just taken place before his eyes. *By the Three Gods, it is magic. It is a miracle. There is nothing else to call it. A woman cannot grow teeth that are gone.*

"Lady Savanar," said Umahar. "You are beautiful."

Selena said nothing, her eyes glassy with tears.

"You look like your Lady Mother, the Princess of Alwaz Deem. What evil takes, the God of the Mountain and the Sands restores," said Umahar.

Selena stood in dumbstruck awe, The Ram's words in the labyrinth of the Order returning to her. *What has been taken from you shall be returned . . .*

"May I make a request?" asked Hersen Expey, still eyeing Jabil the Jackal warily.

All of the others looked at him, strange and out of place in his legionnaire's tunic and peaked red-and-blue hat.

"You must first tell us who you are," said Ottovan.

"I am Hersen Expey, Major of the LaFrentian Legion, Second Commander of the Stanwich Expedition into the Sand Sea. I entered this place through the Mountain Gate to find Jack Caldwell, the one the Beserians call the Amahdi. He was part of our expedition. Our guide, Aurelio Demassi, kidnapped him."

Hersen's Beserian accent was still a work in progress, but it was good enough for the others to understand all of his words. They stared at him without speaking.

"The Amahdi was captured," said Ottovan.

"Yes, Habeen Barcadey told us this," said Anil, speaking at Hersen Expey's side.

"And Aurelio Demassi, the Vetenan, gave his life at the Amahdi's side. He fought bravely, as did the Amahdi," said Ottovan.

"Jack Caldwell is a brave man from a brave family," said Hersen, finding himself unable to acknowledge any heroism by Aurelio Demassi. Bitter thoughts rumbled across his mind but did not leave his lips.

Had Demassi not taken Jack, none of this would have happened. Stanwich would not lay dying in Ben Gamurian, and Jack Caldwell would not be dead or captured in the hands of the Qhaliffans, with them believing he is someone he is not. Demassi is not a hero. He is a murderer.

"And Aurelio Demassi is an honorable and brave man," said Anil, looking at Hersen with a challenge in his eyes.

Ottovan saw the look.

"What is your request?" he asked. *And what is the LaFrentian Legion?* Ottovan looked at Hersen's hat in silence. *Are you a Demissary of a Western Qhaliffa?*

Hersen Expey looked back at Ottovan, deciding how to speak to these strange people, people so different looking from his own, so different looking from each other. His eyes moved along the faces of the group: three Demissaries with the paler faces of Bulbanians; two olive-skinned Qhaliffan women, one beautiful, and one built like a warrior; a dark-faced Hohsa who was among the largest men Hersen had ever seen; and a Beserian who looked like a jackal. *Is it the same son of a whore who attacked Stanwich? It must be! How many of them can look like a jackal?*

"The Beserians attacked our camp," he said aloud. "And one of them wounded our leader, Harold Milton Stanwich. It was that man! That man did it!" Hersen's finger pointed into Jabil the Jackal's face. He fought the urge to draw his pistol, knowing these men would not allow him to gun down one of their own and live.

"Our leader," continued Hersen, "his wounds became infected. He is dying in Ben Gamurian. I rode here to find the Staff of the Serpent. I am told it is his only chance."

"You are a loyal soldier," said Ottovan, nodding respectfully. "It is a long ride from Ben Gamurian to Ben Hamur. And you have ridden farther still, to join us here."

Jabil eyed Hersen warily, keeping his distance.

"But no man rides alone over such a distance and lives to tell the tale," Ottovan turned his eyes to Diego, whose Vetenan face reminded him of a more handsome version of Aurelio Demassi's. "Who is your companion?"

Diego's cheeks flushed.

"Diego Boggarino, of the Veteno," said Hersen. "I would not be here without him. Time is short, friend. I beg you for permission to use the staff to heal Stanwich."

"Do you believe it can heal at such a distance?" asked Ottovan.

"I do not know what I believe," said Hersen. "Before arriving here, I did not believe an old piece of carved olive wood could grow new teeth in a woman's mouth."

"You did not know yet you rode here anyway?"

"Stanwich is dying, and the best healers in Ben Gamurian told me there was no other way."

"And so you risked your life to save another's?" said Ottovan. "Your faith is great."

"I know nothing other than that he is dying," said Hersen. "Please do what you can."

Ottovan nodded to Umahar.

Umahar stepped forward, raising the Staff of the Serpent into the air. He extended his arms outward, holding the staff in his right hand. His left hand extended out with his fingers spread. He began uttering words Hersen did not understand, whispered phrases in what sounded to him like Qhaliffan, but different, more archaic. Umahar's head started to move in small circles, his eyes still closed.

Umahar continued for long minutes. All in his presence watched in silence in the cold, clear desert air. Umahar looked to be a man under significant strain. Despite the cold, beads of sweat formed on his temples.

At long last, he exhaled, and his shoulders dropped as if he had been carrying a great weight that he had just released.

Hersen looked around as if seeking an answer on the others' faces.

"What happened?" Hersen asked.

No one answered him.

"What happened?" he asked again, louder, stepping closer to Umahar.

"I cannot heal him," said Umahar.

"Why not? Is he alive?"

"Yes, he still lives, but not for long. There is little left of his spirit."

"What does that mean? You saw him? You saw him as he lay dying?"

"I saw him."

"Is he in Ben Gamurian?"

"He is in Ben Gamurian. A woman attends to him. A woman with yellow hair."

"That is Hannah Huntington," said Hersen, his voice rising, "What else did you see?"

"She mops the sweat on his head with a cold cloth, dipped in water."

"Why can't you heal him? Use the magic! Use the magic you used to grow her teeth back!" Hersen pointed at Selena, his tone growing more frantic.

"It is too far. He is too far gone."

"Nonsense. Give me the wood. I will try it."

"No," said Selena.

Hersen looked at her with indignant eyes, as if he were ready to get his way with the pistol in the holster at his side.

"Give me the staff," said Selena.

Hersen looked at her with wild eyes.

"I will try," said Selena.

Umahar handed her the staff.

Selena bowed her head and knelt in the sand, holding the staff in two hands in front of her. Her lips were closed. All watched her in silence. Even the camels watched with quiet curiosity.

The coldness flowed through her.

Her mind began to ascend from their small camp.

She continued up into the air, as high as a desert eagle might fly scanning for prey. Her mind continued upward, higher than the upper levels of Alwaz Deem, and then higher still. The camp below her was but a dot in the vast desert beneath her. She continued higher still until the outer borders of the Hahst came before her, a vast lake of white in a sea of moonlit grey. She soared higher still, seeing the great smoke plume above Ben Hamur, drifting south like a dark smudge across the moonlit sands.

And then she soared south and west, crossing vast tracks of the desert, flying across sands in seconds that would take men days. In half of a minute, she covered distances that would take even the swiftest Beserian camels weeks to conquer. Ben Gamurian appeared before her.

Harold Milton Stanwich, the leader of the Westerners, the one who brought the Amahdi. By your power, bring him to me, Prophet of the Most High, he of the God of the Sands and the Mountain.

Selena descended from the sky.

She lowered down past the tallest palms of the oasis, and into the palace of the Sharef, into a large room. In the center of the room sat a large, low bed, upon which lay a man, white as a ghost. Oil lamps illuminated the room, but even in their yellow light, the man's face was white, behind a yellow-white beard. He was small and frail, his chest barely rising with each weak breath.

A woman sat upon her knees, looking down at him. Her hair was golden in the lamplight, braided and hanging over her shoulder on one side. The features of her face were strong and beautiful, and her energy was as powerful as the dying man was weak. But her eyes were red and weary for lack of sleep, and she bore old bruises upon her face.

As Selena descended to the floor, the woman looked up, scanning the room as if sensing a visitor.

Go to him, said Selena, speaking only in her mind.

Hannah Huntington, looked around, her eyes wide and wary.

Go.

Hannah rose and bent over Stanwich's body.

Pull back the sheet.

Hannah pulled back Stanwich's sheet to his navel, showing the pale, sickly skin, spread thin over his ribs.

Show me his hand.

Hannah carefully moved her hands to Stanwich's infected arm, now nearly black with rot and infection. She placed a hand under his palm, and one at his elbow.

"Ahhhh," cried Stanwich, opening his eyes and feeling the pain but with no energy to do more than cry out. "Nooooo."

Hold it there.

Hannah held it.

Selena spoke aloud, "In the name of the Prophet of the God of the Sands and the Mountain, in the name of Beseri who stayed faithful, in the name of Hom Hommuram who was lost but shall be found, in the name of Sah Seg Savanar, a righteous man who burned in Your name, in the name of Trendan Rudar who would not renounce You to avoid the fire, in the name of the faithful martyr Huralt Donadun, heal this man."

Selena watched as Hannah held Harold Milton Stanwich's black, putrefied hand. Beneath the rot, the skin began to crackle as if burning from within.

"Ahhh!" screamed Stanwich.

"Hold fast and do not release his arm!" shouted Selena aloud, still kneeling with closed eyes at the edge of the Hahst.

"Let me goooooo," screamed Stanwich, pulling his arm with all of the little strength that remained inside of him.

Hannah held his arm, aware that whatever was happening, whether real or in a dream, required her to obey the woman's voice in her mind.

The crackling intensified, giving off a silver-green light from within Stanwich's arm. The black began to fall off, like the skin of a molting serpent. Stanwich collapsed onto his pillow, passing out from the pain.

Hannah held his arm, her eyes widening in astonishment, barely believing what was occurring in her own hands.

The blackness in Stanwich's hand eroded further, and then it began to disintegrate, falling off like a husk of dust.

Selena, standing on the edge of the Hahst, began to shake violently, as if taken by a seizure.

"Stop her!" thundered Oapah, stepping toward her.

"No!" shouted Umahar, stepping between the giant Hohsa and Selena.

The silver-green in Stanwich's arm brightened until the blackness of the rot was no more. The silver-green stretched up into his shoulder and into his chest, the sickly whiteness receding like a cloud driven by a powerful wind. The flesh over his ribs filled out, and his ragged breathing deepened and slowed. The silver-green continued up into his face, giving life, like spring rains to parched land, and turning his beard silver-white and his hair the same color.

Hannah looked at Stanwich, her mouth ajar, but her hands still held his arm.

"Colonel Spinner!" Hannah shouted. "Come fast! Something is happening!"

The door burst open, and Colonel Willem Spinner stood above Hannah, wearing only a white undershirt and a pair of long underwear. He looked down as if in a waking dream, uncertain what to make of the vision before his eyes.

Stanwich inhaled deeply and sat up, looking, but for the silver of his hair and beard much like the man who had first set foot into the Sand Sea, like the man Spinner had met in the City of Anglia at the Three Gods Day Ball.

Stanwich looked up into Spinner's and Hannah's faces with bright blue eyes that lacked any trace of pain or worry.

"Where am I?" he asked, his voice strong and his cheeks ruddy, looking to be in the prime of health.

Hannah and Spinner stared down at him, their jaws open and their eyes wide.

Selena collapsed onto the sand beneath her. Oapah, Gulana, and Umahar rushed to her.

"What happened?" shouted Hersen.

"It is done," said Selena, looking up at him from the ground, speaking in a whisper.

"He is dead?" asked Hersen, his face falling.

"No, he is not dead," said Selena. "He lives new life. By the God of the Mountain and the Sands, he will not die for a long time."

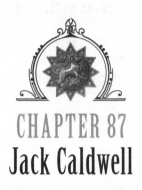

CHAPTER 87
Jack Caldwell

The Way to Alwaz Deem, West of the Great Mountain
52nd Day, Month of Wasura, 807
Anglian Calendar: April 14, 1879

Jack Caldwell opened his eyes and for a brief, kind moment forgot where he was. Then pain struck him first. He was seated on a cart with his hands chained behind him and his legs stretched before him. He tried to shift his position, but his legs sent daggers of pain into him. He gasped. He inhaled and winced at the pain in his ribs. Men with torches walked alongside the cart, in front of him and behind him.

The pike was directly in front of him so he could not miss it. Atop the pike was a head, roughly severed, with shaggy dark hair and stringy strands of flesh hanging down from the butchered neck. Men in turbans, iron helmets, and Erassian hats rode on horses just in front of the pike with the head.

"Your Excellency, he is awake," said a voice behind him.

Jack looked up and saw a pair of men standing behind him. The faces looking down at him bore cruel smiles inside of black beards. They wore mailed shirts and iron helmets like the men who had fought against him on the Sharef's veranda, the men he had shot down.

The veranda! Where are the others?

Three of the riders turned around to approach the cart.

The man in the center held the Staff of the Ram. Jack recognized him in an instant as Jemojeen, the man from the battle of the veranda.

They captured me. No. No. No. I should have died on the veranda.

The horsemen came closer. Jack recognized the others as well. One was the burly man in the chain mail, and the other was the orange-haired Erassian. The captain.

"The sun will soon be rising, Amahdi of the West," said Jemojeen. "But your revolution is dead."

Jack looked at him, feeling hatred and fear.

"You may recall Sipahi Shaheni and Captain Turkelan," said Jemojeen, as if introducing friends.

Neither man smiled, spoke, or nodded. Both just stared at Jack with cold, hard eyes.

"You will also see that your friend the Vetenan is being properly recognized for bringing you to our Sea of Sand," said Jemojeen, smiling.

The Sipahi barked an order. The man carrying the pike turned the spear around so the severed head faced Jack.

Jack looked and saw the face of Aurelio Demassi, its eyes plucked out, and its mouth opened as if screaming.

"Some may say, regarding your fate, that he is the lucky one," said Jemojeen.

Jack felt the fear race up his spine, grabbing his throat.

"You see, he is just a pawn in the grand chess game of this war. Do you play the game of chess? They have that game in your country, yes? In the Seven Cities, we play a similar game. We call it the Game of the Squares of War. I am rather good at it."

Jack said nothing, too scared to speak.

"Very well, speak or do not speak. It makes little difference to me. Your friend, what was his name? Demassi? He was a pawn, a small piece. He was a fool who believed in prophecies. But you, you are something altogether different."

Jack looked into the man's dark-green eyes, the eyes of a snake, almost black in the torchlight.

"You are one in which others placed their hopes. You are like a castle, even a queen, a piece that deserves much consideration. Now, however, I must ask because I do not believe much in prophecies, do you think you are a castle or even a queen?"

Jack said nothing, wanting to take his eyes off of Jemojeen's but feeling himself unable to.

"I will tell you what I think. I think you are a pawn pretending to be a queen. You are just an ordinary man, a little older than a boy. You are not the Amahdi. You are nothing."

Jack stared, paralyzed by his fear.

"I know that, and I suspect that you know that. But you see, others in the Seven Cities and in other places all across this vast Sea of Sand think you matter. They believe you are significant—an answer to a prophecy. They believe you will topple the Qhaliffa. Ha!

"You give them hope. That hope must be extinguished like a candle by the wind. I will now have to show the people that you are nothing and their prophecy is nothing. You will have to die before the eyes of the thousands. I cannot merely place your head on a spear, like your friend. No, you must die before all of the assembled people.

"Do you know how I know you are nothing? Because I was inside of you. I controlled your pathetic body, making you move to shoot your own friends."

My friends. Shooting. The arrow. An arrow struck his hand, and he dropped the staff. Jack looked at Jemojeen's right hand. A thick bandage covered it. He held the Staff of the Ram in his left hand.

"Yes," said Jemojeen, "one of your band of traitors shot my hand. The arrow had the burning poison on its head. That was why I dropped the staff. Burning. Burning brings great pain. But, you see, my burning was quite temporary. I applied the salve, and it went away." Jemojeen held his bandaged hand up for Jack to see.

"Your burning will be different. Have you ever seen a man burn? I have. As have Sipahi Shaheni and Captain Turkelan, here. Oh, yes. It is different from any other death. I learned long ago that men can bravely face the noose, and men will walk to the ax with their head held high and their shoulders back. They face death like heros, full of dignity. That is no good. They die as martyrs. They inspire other heroes, other martyrs. Are you a hero? Are you full of dignity? I think not, but if you are, let me tell you about burning."

Jack swallowed the massive lump in his throat, wanting to fight, to run, to scream, to do anything but sit and listen, which is what he did, his eyes stuck on Jemojeen's face.

"Have you ever held your hand over a candle?"

Jack said nothing.

"Maybe you have, maybe not. It hurts. It hurts worse than any other kind of hurt I have seen inflicted upon a person, and I have seen most kinds. The fire bites your feet first, taking off all of the skin, like a thousand candles underneath you. You will wrestle against the chains, but they will hold you tightly while your feet burn, like roasting steaks of beef. The pain will be unbearable, but rest assured, that is only the beginning. Then the flames will move up your legs. Most men begin screaming as soon as the flames touch their feet, but some last beyond that. As your legs burn, you realize the pain is worse than anything you could imagine and anything you could ever prepare for. It is surprising, actually, how long it takes to kill you this way. Perhaps a minute in, the flames will reach your midsection. That part—the part between your legs—actually burns quickly, and that is when all scream. That final minute, you will scream as loudly as any. Neither strength nor heroism will make you scream any less loud, or any less ragged, any less pitiful, any less full of agony. Your last memory will be of the flames reaching up to your face, taking your hair, your beard, and everything else. That is how you will die, Amahdi of the West, and all of the people will see that you scream just as easily as any other man."

Jack forced himself to speak. "You are missing a staff. The Staff of the Serpent, where is it?"

Jemojeen's face flickered. The flicker only lasted a fraction of a moment, but Jack could see the glimmer of fear. He had asked the correct question.

"My friends took it. Didn't they?"

"Your friends are traitors and thieves. No piece of wood will save them. Nor will they save you. You will never see them again."

"So they did take it," said Jack. "And they escaped. Didn't they?"

"Your last memories will be of pain," said Jemojeen. "You will die screaming, wishing you were never born."

CHAPTER 88
All Other Ground is Sinking Sand

The Hahst
2nd Day, Month of Saman, 807
Anglian Calendar: April 16, 1879

At long last, the wind stopped. Peter lifted his head and opened his eyes. All around him lay white sand. There was no sign of anyone, neither the Macmenians nor Sergeant Barnes, nor their camels.

Peter lifted himself, the sand falling off of him but still covering every crevice. His veil alone had kept the grains from entering his mouth, his eyes, and his nose. The buried camel next to him was stiff and cold.

He untied himself and stood up. All was quiet, even peaceful, with nothing but sunshine above and white sand all around.

"Mazarian! Barnes!" he called out. His voice was loud and strange, carrying out into the nothingness of the sands, unanswered.

"Don Mazarian! Sergeant Barnes!" he called again.

The silence mocked him.

Peter looked all around him, brushing the white sand off of his brown Macmenian robes. He pulled his veil down and felt the sun on his face. His pith helmet was gone.

"Don Mazarian!"

Silence.

Several yards away from Peter, the sand rustled. A hand appeared. Peter ran to the rustle, forgetting the narrowness of the path through the sinking sands. His left leg went down as if he had stepped in water, sinking to his hip. His arms flailed as he tipped to his left.

"Help!" he shouted.

The shifting sand gave way, and Don Mazarian leaped up, the arm rising beneath the sands emerging as a man. He dove at Peter, grabbing for his arms as Peter fell sideways into the sand. He fell short, grabbing only air.

A pair of powerful hands gripped Peter by his wrists. He looked up into the face of Sergeant Joshua Barnes, his face half-veiled and covered with sand.

"Help me!" said Barnes, shouting through his veil into Peter's face.

Don Mazarian reached forward, grabbing Barnes around the waist and holding onto him. Peter was now up to his chest in the sinking sands. Barnes pulled. Don Mazarian pulled on Barnes. Mazarian leaned back and pulled with all of his strength. Slowly, the sands released Peter, making a sucking sound and giving Peter up reluctantly, like an animal unwilling to release a piece of food. Peter collapsed on top of Barnes, with Don Mazarian at their side.

Don Mazarian pulled down his veil and gasped for air.

"I forgot about the sinking sands," said Peter.

"You will not forget again," said Don Mazarian, breathing hard.

Peter looked back at the sinking sands that had nearly swallowed him. The place where he had nearly drowned was now merely a slight indent in the otherwise smooth white surface, as transient as a ripple on a lake.

Peter looked around him. All was flat whiteness.

"The others. Our camels," he said.

Don Mazarian stood up, shaking his head and dusting the layer of white sand off of his robes. "They are lost. If they still live, they will need to break the surface now, or they will suffocate."

"Should we dig?" asked Peter, looking around him, seeking a rustle in the sands or any sign that a man might lurk beneath the smooth white surface.

Don Mazarian scoffed with defeat in his voice. "Dig where?"

Barnes looked around for signs of buried Macmenians.

Peter looked around them. All lay white and flat, like the frozen top of a winter pond back in Anglia. "Dig around us. Dig anywhere."

"We should not have come here," said Don Mazarian. "It was arrogant and foolish to believe."

Peter continued looking across the white sands, scanning to the west, then north, then east, and south. The sand did not move. Everything was white and smooth. He looked west again. Perhaps two hours of daylight remained in the day.

"Perhaps with the sunset," said Peter. "The legend says the setting sun will reveal—"

"I know what the legend says," said Don Mazarian, cutting him off. "Do you have water?" he asked.

"Azadeem says." began Peter again.

"I know what Azadeem says. Do you have water?" asked Don Mazarian.

Peter's hands moved down to his belt. He had nothing, not his extendable telescope, nor his rifle, nor his waterskin.

"Perhaps they are on my camel."

Don Mazarian looked at Peter with arched, skeptical eyebrows. "And where is your camel?"

Don Mazarian looked around at the empty sand that surrounded them.

"Do you have water?" asked Peter.

Don Mazarian lifted his goatskin and shook it, the water sloshing in the bottom. It was less than a quarter full. He drank from it without offering any to Peter and sat down in the sand.

"Sit, Peter. Sit, Barnes, for we will likely die here. We will not be the first fools who believed they could find the Valley of Hom Hommuram, nor likely the last."

"If I can find my camel—he was buried next to me," said Peter. He looked and saw the faint lump of his buried camel, resting on the firm narrow ground of the path, covered in white sand. Carefully, he walked in slow, tentative steps.

Barnes walked toward him and took his elbow in his hands. They walked to the lump and began digging with their hands, plunging them through the thick layer of sand to the dead, stiff animal beneath. Their hands moved up and down along the body. Peter's fingers touched smooth leather. He grasped the satchel and pulled. He heaved and lifted it out of the sand. He found the strap that attached it to the camel and unfastened it. Setting the satchel down, he plunged his hands back into the sand, groping along the camel corpse. His fingers touched another leather object. He grasped it with both hands, pulled, and his goatskin rose out of the sand.

"Have faith, Don Mazarian!" said Peter, his voice triumphant. He lifted the nozzle to his lips and took a long sip of the water. It was cool, having been buried beneath the sand and hidden from the sun. Peter exhaled in satisfaction.

He handed the waterskin to Barnes, who took only a small sip of the water inside of it.

"Very well," said Don Mazarian. "We are still here, stuck without a path."

Peter looked down, seeing another lump near his camel. He walked toward it, plunged his hands down, and pulled his pith helmet up from the sands.

As he lifted the helmet, he saw something in the distance that he had not seen before.

"What is that?" he asked, looking to the east.

"What is what?" said Don Mazarian.

Peter, his helmet back upon his head, was already reaching into his saddle satchel, pulling out his extendable telescope.

"What is that?" he said, now pointing with his left hand, as his right hand held the small telescope up to his eye.

Don Mazarian stood up.

Barnes was already at Peter's side, looking with his naked eyes beneath an extended hand, shading them from the sunlight.

"That, what is that," repeated Peter.

"Give me your telescope," said Don Mazarian, who no longer had his own. Peter handed it over to him.

"That is—" Don Mazarian did not finish his sentence, but his mouth opened. Peter looked at him. "What is it?" Peter's heart began to race.

"That is a rock."

"Yes, a rock in the middle of the Hahst," said Peter, "a rock that signifies, a rock that should not be there unless—"

"Unless it marks that which only exists in legend," said Don Mazarian.

"And with the setting of the sun, the path shall be revealed," said Peter.

"We wait," said Don Mazarian, sitting down on the path, "For the setting of the sun."

Three hours later, the sun hung just above the western horizon.

"Now. It should appear now," said Peter.

Don Mazarian said nothing, looking to the east, toward the rock that was not supposed to be there, toward the rock that stood alone, perhaps twice as tall as a man in a vast lake of white sand.

The sun dipped lower.

"Say the words," said Peter.

"What difference does it make?" asked Don Mazarian.

"Just say them with me."

Don Mazarian shook his head.

"Say them."

Don Mazarian continued looking east with a frown on his face.

"Upon the rock of the Prophet we stand, for all other ground is sinking sand," said Peter.

Don Mazarian made an uncomfortable smirk, as if in proximity with a fool, insistent upon saying foolish things.

"Upon the rock of the Prophet we stand, for all other ground is sinking sand," repeated Peter.

Barnes joined in, echoing the words Peter said, two Westerners, each raised in the faith of the Three Gods, saying the words of the Beserian faithful.

The Macmenian shook his head again.

The sun sank lower.

"Upon the rock of the Prophet we stand, for all other ground is sinking sand," said Barnes and Peter, in unison, louder than before.

Don Mazarian continued staring to the east, toward the rock, while Peter and Barnes repeated the words. The sun dipped lower, halfway beneath the horizon behind them, a half arc still above the desert floor.

A line began to form in the sands, the color of the sun, like molten gold, darker than the yellowing whiteness of the Hahst sands, their color shifting in the setting sun.

"See it!" shouted Peter.

"I see it," said Barnes.

The sun dipped farther, and the dark line grew firmer and brighter against the surrounding sands.

Peter looked down at his own feet and could see the outlines of the path beneath him, seeing that they were standing to the right side of the firm ground, a mere foot from the edge.

"Look down!" said Peter.

Barnes and Don Mazarian looked down.

Then Peter looked forward. Several hundred yards in front of them, the path ended, opening up into a vast area that stretched ahead, all dark gold like the color of the way beneath them.

"Don Mazarian, look! Look ahead! It is all solid! Look!"

Mazarian looked at Peter and understood. The sinking sands ended two hundred yards in front of them—the *Rock of the Prophet*.

"We must run to reach it before the light goes," said Peter.

Don Mazarian nodded. Barnes reached down and grabbed one edge of the saddle satchel. Peter grabbed the other side, holding his waterskin in the other. They ran with the path illuminated before them.

The sun dipped down beneath the horizon behind them. The color of the path began to fade.

"Run faster!" said Peter. They were already sprinting as fast as their legs could carry them.

The path grew fainter still. Peter looked ahead at the vast area of dark ground ahead of them. His legs screamed at him in protest. His arms cried out in pain. His chest heaved with the labor of breathing.

Don Mazarian, far, far older than the other two, began to slow. Barnes reached over to pull him along.

"No, do not slow. The light is going!" shouted Peter. "Come on!"

Don Mazarian shouted out in pain but increased his pace.

The light faded further.

"Come on! We are almost there!" shouted Barnes, half carrying Don Mazarian with his right arm, as he lifted his end of the satchel with his left.

The sunlight vanished. They leaped, three men, flying across the path that disappeared with the light.

They landed on solid ground. The three fell to the ground, gasping for air. They looked up at the emerging blanket of stars in the darkening sky to the east, at the purple sky above them, and the last flickers of blue sky surrendering in the west.

Peter stood up, embracing Barnes in his arms. Barnes reached out and grabbed Peter, stiffly.

"Well done, Harmon."

They turned to look at Don Mazarian.

The wrinkled corners of the old man's eyes began to glisten as he stared in silence.

"Upon—" he began.

He swallowed, beginning again.

"Upon the rock of the Prophet we stand, for all other ground is sinking sand," he said. He swallowed harder as a tear traveled down each of his weathered cheeks.

CHAPTER 89
The Valley of Hom Hommuram

The Hahst
3rd Day, Month of Saman, 807
Anglian Calendar: April 17, 1879

Peter, Barnes, and Don Mazarian slept soundly upon the solid ground beneath them. They woke, drank water from the two waterskins, and began the long march toward the rock before them. As they moved eastward, the rock grew taller, far taller than it had seemed from the path. They also realized they were now walking uphill, that what had looked flat from the path through the sinking sands was not flat at all.

"It is the third day of the Qhaliffan month, the day on which the veil can be lifted," said Peter.

Don Mazarian nodded.

"Do you still doubt?" asked Peter. "After what we have seen?"

"I have doubted all of my life," said Don Mazarian. "It has served me well. It has kept me alive."

Peter kept walking. "I am sorry about your men, Don Mazarian. They were good men."

"They believed," said Don Mazarian. "They believed in me, they believed in the Prophecy, and they believed in the legend of Hom Hommuram. Now their children will be fatherless, and their wives will be widows."

"They were not wrong to believe," said Peter. "We will care for their widows and children."

"You presume that you will survive," said Don Mazarian.

They walked onward to the east.

Holding the Staff of the Serpent, Selena led the others through the Hahst with the rising sun, well aware that the veil could be lowered only on this day, the third day, and that such a day would not come again for another Qhaliffan month, long after their food and water would be gone.

Selena rode forward with her eyes hooded, the Staff of Wisdom showing her where to lead her camel. The others followed behind her in a single line, with Anil Salesi directly behind her and Ottovan Fanfar in the rear. All behind Selena watched the white sands with nervous eyes.

"Lady Savanar," said Anil.

Selena raised her eyes, broken from her near trance, turning to look at Anil.

Anil shifted in his saddle, made uncomfortable by Selena's beauty, and the piercing hazel eyes that seemed to look inside of him.

"In all of the years my father carried the staff," said Anil, "I have never seen anything like that—anything like the healing. Its power seems greater in your hands than in the hands of any other."

Selena looked at Anil with her brown-green eyes, her gaze profound and unblinking. In the sunlight, her eyes seemed to be flecked with gold.

"How did you do it?"

"I did nothing, Anil Salesi. The God of the Mountain and the Sands healed the man in Ben Gamurian."

"The names you said: Beseri, Sah Seg Savanar, Trendan Rudar, Huralt Donadun, why did you say them?"

"They died for truth. Their sacrifice gave more power to the healing."

"How?"

"Not all questions have answers," she said, turning back around toward the white sands in front of her.

Anil's heart beat more quickly, Selena's eyes still looking at him in his mind. Selena had lowered her head covering, and her hair that was once auburn-brown seemed flecked with the same gold as her eyes, shimmering in the sunlight.

"We must ride faster," said Selena, turning around. She urged her camel into a trot. The others followed.

Selena lowered her eyelids again, knowing with a sixth sense—the sense of the staff—that they were approaching a place of great danger, not merely the place of the sinking sands but the place of the serpents—not mere snakes like those of the Semissari, but the true serpents, the pale serpents of the Hahst.

The rustling sound advanced from both sides at once.

The eerie, tranquil white sands of the Hahst lay flat no longer. Beneath the surface, ripples approached like waves upon a pond into which a child had just tossed in a stone—all of the ripples aimed for the column of camel riders, riding in single file behind Selena.

"Then the legends are true," whispered Ottovan, bringing up the end of the line, silently pulling a pair of three-barreled pistols from his holsters.

"What is it? What is happening?" asked Hersen Expey, his LaFrentian service revolver in his hand.

"Serpents," said Diego, his eyes darting to the approaching ripples.

"Silence," said Ottovan. "Do not speak."

Oapah and Gulana slowly drew their scimitari swords from their sheaths, taking short, tense breaths in their saddles while scanning the ground.

Hersen looked around him. For hundreds of yards all around them, the ground wrinkled and rippled, making a sound like slow, heavy breathing. A tingle of dread moved up his spine.

"God of the Sands," whispered Jabil, his jackal's eyes wide and afraid.

"Stay close," whispered Ottovan. "And be silent."

They were quiet enough to hear the steps of their camels. The camels, however, began to strain against their head ropes, looking around them. They eyed the sand like the humans above them, seeing the same movement and hearing the same rustling sound coming beneath the ground.

Only one camel did not begin to glance around in agitation and fear, the one camel beneath the only calm rider. Selena Savanar slowly turned her head from her right to her left, looking at the sands.

She raised a hand for the column to stop.

They obeyed.

Then, with a whisper, she ordered her camel to its knees. The camel lowered, bending its legs and touching its knees down onto the sands that from all sides continued to move.

Hersen Expey saw a long shape moving differently from the other ripples, four, maybe five times longer than a man. It advanced in a swiftly undulating line toward Selena's camel.

Selena stepped down, feeling the ground beneath her sandals.

"Come close behind me," she said, her voice calm and low, but carrying clearly over the growing rustling beneath the earth.

Ottovan, Oapah, and the others all looked at her, still feeling the fear in their camels and fighting the rising terror in themselves. Selena stood erect, with her shoulders back and the hint of a smile upon her face.

"Hurry," she said.

The others drew their camels as close behind her as they could, a tight knot of riders upon the vast whiteness of the now rippling sand plain.

Selena inhaled through her nose as the first serpent breached the surface of the sands, directly in front of her, as if knowing her path and barring it.

The serpent rose steadily and slowly into the glaring sunlight. Its body was massive and pale as the sands from which it emerged, perhaps thirty feet long and as wide as Oapah the Hohsa. Its head looked large enough to swallow a grown man whole.

The camels roared in panic, turning to run and nearly toppling their riders, but they stopped as they saw another serpent, equally large, approaching them from behind the column, rising over Ottovan Fanfar. He frowned in fear as the great snake extended itself above him, his eyes widening.

Through his peripheral vision, Ottovan saw other serpents breaching the surface from either flank. They were smaller than the first two but still larger than any snake Ottovan had ever seen before. The camels turned in to each other, seeing nowhere to run, and their eyes flooded with terror.

Ozgar nocked an arrow onto his bowstring.

"Lower your bow, Ozgar," said Selena, not looking at him.

Ottovan and Nemakar looked at her, holding their pistols, their faith hanging by a thread, despite the miracles they had already witnessed.

"Holster your pistols," said Selena, her eyes upon the serpent in front of her. "Your weapons are of no use here."

More serpents emerged, their pale heads rising higher in the air than the camel riders they had surrounded, their yellow-green eyes looking down into the intruders' faces, unblinking with black, vertical pupils.

The largest serpent continued rising, more than half of its body still flat upon the white sand, the end of its tail still submerged in the depths. It looked down at Selena as if preparing to devour her.

Selena closed her eyes.

She stretched her arms out, holding out the Staff of the Serpent to her side.

Hersen stared in horrified awe, still gripping his pistol. He alone knew nothing of the legends of the Hahst serpents, but his fear was no greater and no less than the alarm in any of the other faces, whether Beserian, Qhaliffan, Sworn Lion of the Order, or Vetenan.

"What is this?" he cried out to no one in particular, his eyes darting to all points of the compass.

"Be silent, Westerner," said Ottovan.

Gulana and Oapah looked at Hersen as if they would swing their swords into him if he spoke again.

Selena stood in silence, her eyes closed with the serpent's head looming above her.

Behind her closed eyelids, vivid images rushed across her mind. So too did the smells, voices, and the feeling upon her skin.

The light was suddenly different, as was the air. Selena felt herself atop a horse, riding not far from where she now stood.

A body rode directly behind her, the arms wrapped around her. She felt the chest of the rider against her back. The horse raced beneath her, thundering between her legs. She and her companion behind her rode faster than she had ever remembered riding before, not cantering but galloping at an all-out pace. A featureless desert passed by—a canvas of tan. She looked down and saw her legs, the legs of a child. Her legs burned in the saddle, rubbed raw by the leather.

She looked to her left and then to the right. On either side, an Oath Holder rode. The riders each glanced toward her, showing her their yellow-green eyes, the eyes of Serpents of the Order.

The scene shifted, and Selena saw them grabbing her in the outer garden, carrying her beneath a woolen blanket and telling her to be silent. She heard men's voices, the smell of burning, the screams of her sisters and her mother.

Then the scene shifted again. They were riding through the streets, the flatlands of Alwaz Deem, toward the bridge, the Approach of Alwaz. The rider behind her slashed down at a guardsman with a knife. He fell.

The sunrise lay behind them, on the far side of the mountain. They crossed the bridge over the Ring River, the guardsmen shouting, the rider behind her slashing down at another man with her knife.

Then they rode across the sands . . .

Her vision shifted again. They were no longer riding. The rider who had been behind her now carried her, as a mother carries a toddler, her child's chest against the rider's, her face looking over the rider's shoulder.

Behind her, over the shoulder, a broad line of galloping men approached on horseback. There were forty, perhaps more. They rode swiftly toward her. The body carrying her was now walking fast, nearly running.

Selena saw a boundary separating her from the oncoming riders, a line where white sand met the tan, dividing the two sharply, like where a lake meets its shore.

The riders continued galloping toward her. She saw the orange hair of Erassians and the turbans and chain mail of Grand Vizerian Guardsmen.

A tall man rode in the center. *Jemojeen.*

Yes, Jemojeen rode directly at her, though his face was far younger than that of the Grand Vizer she knew now. He was nearly handsome and not nearly so gaunt. His beard was black and full.

Selena's vision shifted again. Her little feet—the feet of a child—now stood upon the white sands. She looked up into a veiled face.

"Saliha," said the voice.

Selena stared into the yellow-green eyes without speaking. Selena heard hoofbeats in the distance.

The woman pulled down her veil, revealing the face of Asatan, Serpent of the Order.

"They cannot follow us here," she said. "You are safe here. They protect this place from their kind, not ours."

Selena turned and looked behind her. The ground had opened, and the sand flowed down as if into a waterfall, yet beneath them was no lake, but merely more sand. A shallow wadi opened beneath her feet, just deep enough to conceal an Oath Holder and a child.

At that moment, a great white body moved past them, brushing against Selena's leg. She felt a fleeting moment of fear, but Asatan took her hand in her own.

"Do not be afraid," she said. "They will protect you now, and in the years to come, Saliha."

Selena watched as the great white serpent twisted past her, slithering out onto the white sands above.

The sound of hoofbeats in the distance had vanished.

Asatan turned to the other Oath Holders.

"It is time," she said, holding Selena's hand.

The other two Oath Holders leaped up above the ground.

They withdrew their curved daggers from their robes.

Selena's vision shifted again, looking up over the edge of the white sands, her little head peering up from the wadi.

"Turn away," said Asatan, still holding her. But Selena did not obey. She looked.

Upon the surface, Erassians and guardsmen screamed in terror as Jemojeen watched them from the edge, looking onto the white sands from a rise in the tan sands beyond.

The serpents struck the men from below, pulling them down into the sands. They bit with fangs longer than hands, ripping the men apart and tearing limbs as they pulled them beneath.

More grown men screamed as Asatan squeezed her hand.

Selena opened her eyes, her vision receding, seeing that she was once again a grown woman, facing the great white serpent above her. She could sense her companions now behind her: Anil Salesi, Ottovan, Oapah, Gulana, and the others. She could sense the fear in the camels, though they had now all fallen into a terrified silence.

"You rescued me long ago," said Selena, looking into the eyes of the snake.

The serpent stared back at her. Its face was bent down toward her own.

"You have not forgotten me," said Selena, "though I was but a child then. I remember."

The snake continued to look into Selena's eyes, its head lowering farther as if preparing to swallow her.

Oapah and Gulana gasped involuntarily. The others did the same, too afraid to move.

Selena reached up to the snake's face, extending her hand that did not hold the Staff of the Serpent. The staff now shone brighter than any had ever seen it shine, brighter even than when Selena healed Stanwich from the edge of the Hahst, days before.

The serpent lowered its head to Selena's, close enough to touch her face with its long, forked tongue. Selena touched its nose with her fingertips.

For long moments, Selena's ten companions stared. Her hand rested on the great snake's face, as if she and the leviathan spoke to each other in the silence.

Then the snake lowered itself, turned, and rested on its belly, slithering to the side and making way for Selena to pass. The other snakes followed the lead of the first, turning to the sides and lowering onto the white sands.

Selena and the others looked ahead, seeing that the serpents had made a path through which they could lead their camels.

Selena turned her head back, looking at her companions.

They stared at her as if she were a ghost, as if she were something other than the daughter of Sah Seg Savanar, different from the woman that had led them into the Hahst.

"They are old," she said. "They protect this place from the enemies of Beseri, those who oppose the Prophet of the God of the Sands," said Selena, as if that explained what had just occurred.

Then she mounted her camel, riding to the west. The others followed her, riding in silence toward the sinking sun, through the path between the pale serpents that still watched them from either side.

Approaching from the west, Peter, Barnes, and Don Mazarian stood in front of the rock. To call it a rock was an understatement. What from a distance had looked like a rock, perhaps twice as tall as a man, was a towering column of granite, perhaps five feet across and fifty feet tall, standing alone just past the peak of the rise that Peter and Don Mazarian had ascended all day.

Below the granite tower, a plain of sand extended outward, flat, and featureless.

"We wait here?" asked Peter.

"For the sunset, yes," said Don Mazarian.

"And then the veil will lower?"

"If the legend is true, yes."

"Do you have water?" asked Peter.

"One mouthful left," said Don Mazarian, his voice grave. "You?"

"The same," said Peter, sitting down in the shadow of the granite tower, where the sand was cooler.

As Selena and her companions crested the ridgeline, the plain of the serpents receded behind them, to the east. The tall granite tower stood alone to the west, across a new wide-open plateau of sand. They ascended the rise from the east and now descended into the narrow open plain, white as salt and so empty a single blade of sand grass would have stood out upon it, casting a shadow.

"That is it," said Selena, pointing the Staff of the Serpent at the lone column of granite.

All followed her.

"We must be there by the setting of the sun," said Selena, flicking her camel to send the animal into a canter.

They rode steadily, closing the final mile as the sun sank toward the western ridgeline. They approached in a straight line, eleven riders, shoulder to shoulder, riding across the solid ground beneath them. The tower soared over them, dark and formidable, protruding like the rock sword of a buried giant, alone in the void.

They stopped just before the tower's shadow.

"We wait here," said Selena.

Peter sat on the ground, nearly asleep, his stomach churning from having not eaten food in three days. His lips were chapped and bleeding, and his waterskin was almost empty. He looked down at the goatskin, desperately wanting the final sip of water inside of it but fearing to drink his last sip. *What if the veil does not drop? Then what? Then we are here, marooned inside the sinking sands?*

"Drink it," said Don Mazarian.

Peter looked at Don Mazarian as he lifted his own waterskin to his mouth.

"Drink it," repeated Don Mazarian, "If the veil does not drop, we will surely die. If it does drop, we shall drink from the stream of the valley." Don Mazarian upended his waterskin and squeezed the last drops into his mouth.

Peter looked behind him. The sun fell beneath the ridgeline, and the shadow of the granite tower grew long, stretching at a diagonal toward the east.

"Here, Barnes," said Peter, gesturing with his waterskin.

"No, it is yours," said Barnes.

"We will share it," said Peter, knowing Barnes was just as thirsty as he was.

"There is too little to divide. Drink the water. I am not thirsty."

Peter looked at him, doubtfully.

"Drink it," said Barnes.

Peter lifted his goatskin and drank his last sip of water. As he lowered the skin, now light and empty, a bubbling sound broke the stillness.

Peter looked at Don Mazarian.

Don Mazarian looked back at Peter, his eyes showing he heard the same sound.

The sound grew louder, the sound of water moving over rocks, the gurgle of a waterfall striking a stream.

"Do you hear that too?" whispered Peter.

Don Mazarian nodded.

"And you?" asked Peter, looking at Barnes.

"Yes," said Barnes, nodding.

The three of them looked out past the granite column, into the empty desert.

"We wait here," said a woman's voice, speaking in Qhaliffan.

Peter winced in surprise.

His eyes widened.

He looked at Don Mazarian and Barnes and could see they heard the same voice.

Barnes's hand went to the dagger at his side.

Peter jumped up, looking to the east, into the flat empty plain of bright white sand before him, the direction from which the voice had come.

No one stood before him. Nothing but the shadow of the tower broke the monotony of the glaring sands for as far as his eyes could see.

"Who goes there?" said a man's voice. The words were Qhaliffan, spoken with a foreigner's accent.

All but Selena reached for their weapons.

Oapah and Gulana pulled their swords.

Ozgar Ogatonia drew his bow.

Ottovan, Nemakar, and Umahar pulled Demissary pistols from their chest holsters.

Anil Salesi, Diego the Vetenan, and Jabil the Jackal aimed their rifles to the west, from where the noise had come.

Hersen Expey slowly raised his revolver, with the look of a man who was no longer certain whether he was dreaming or awake.

Selena urged her camel a step forward.

She raised her left palm to calm the others. She looked across the plain, across the shadow of the column.

Nothing but open desert lay in front of them. The voice had come as if on the wind, clear and near. All had heard it.

"Who goes there?" asked the voice again.

"Lady Savanar, back up," said Ottovan, aiming his pistol forward, toward the voice.

"Who is that speaking?" asked the voice again.

All of the riders looked around anxiously, clutching their weapons.

"Lower your weapons," said Selena.

"I am not holding a weapon," said the man's voice.

"I am Selena, once Saliha of House Savanar, daughter of Sah Seg Savanar, Lord and High Kezelboj of Alwaz Deem. Who speaks to me?"

Peter Harmon heard the question.

He turned to look at Don Mazarian and Barnes.

"Is it the veil?" he whispered.

Don Mazarian lifted his hands. "I know not, Peter Harmon."

Barnes shook his head.

"Where are you, Selena of House Savanar?" asked Peter, speaking in the Qhaliffan his father had mocked him for learning with such diligence.

"State your name," said the woman's voice.

The sun dropped down beneath the western ridgeline.

Peter looked in front of him, across the shadow, to the east.

The air moved in front of him, rippling like water. The ripple grew stronger. The desert before him began to alter.

Objects formed in the emptiness, and then the objects became camels with riders on their backs, no more than forty paces in front of them.

Peter backed up, extending his hands outward toward Don Mazarian and Barnes, who flanked him on either side. His eyes looked down at the shifting earth. A chasm opened upon the desert at their feet as the sound of running water grew stronger.

What began as a murky haze, like an object viewed through water, clarified, and the walls of the gorge revealed themselves: solid granite, with lush vines clinging to them. The tops of trees ended at Peter's feet, so close he could have stepped out and touched the leaves.

Beneath the trees lay bright green grass, and through the grass ran a pure, clear stream along a bed of rock. Peter's eyes followed the stream to the north. There, from a hole in the rock, just beneath the tower, a clear, steady spring flowed out of the rock, cascading down into the stream below and watering the narrow valley.

Peter looked across the chasm.

Eleven riders looked back at him.

In the center, with five riders on either side of her, upon a camel's back, sat the most beautiful woman Peter had ever laid eyes upon.

Unlike the others, she held no blade, no gun, only an old piece of gnarled olive wood.

"Lower your weapons," said Selena.

The others obeyed, their eyes wide, marveling at the valley that had just opened at their feet and at the three men who stood before them, on the other side of the chasm, emerging from the nothingness of the sands that had been there only moments before.

"Who are you who stands at the Valley of Hom Hommuram?" Selena asked, her voice carrying easily across the chasm and over the sound of the running water beneath them.

The three men stood with the setting sun dropping behind their backs.

"I am Peter Harmon," said the man standing in the center, wearing a tan pith helmet.

Selena could see he was thin but broad-shouldered, tall, and handsome. A reddish-brown beard covered his jaw.

"This is Don Mazarian, of the Macmenians," said Peter, pointing to his left. "And this is Sergeant Joshua Barnes of the New Anglian Republic."

Hersen Expey stared, his mouth gaping.

Barnes's eyes caught sight of Hersen and widened.

"We must descend," said Selena.

Peter stepped forward, looking down into the gorge. He saw the steep stone steps leading down the rock walls from either side.

Selena dismounted and began leading her camel down the narrow stairs. The others on the eastern side followed her lead.

Peter walked forward and placed a tentative foot onto the first granite step, then another and another. He could smell the water beneath him and the grass and the trees. *How long has it been since I have smelled green grass and trees?*

Don Mazarian and Barnes followed Peter down the steps.

At the bottom of the stairs, Peter stepped forward into the grass, the trees above him forming a canopy overhead. He looked up and saw dense fruit hanging down: pomegranates, apples, oranges, and pears. He knelt at the stream, thrust his hands in, and raised the water to his lips. It was pure and cold. He drank until he could drink no more. He looked up and saw all of the others doing the same.

He sat up, feeling Selena's eyes upon him.

"Come with me," she said, standing across the stream.

Peter stood up, looking at her across the narrow span of water, sensing the full power of her beauty. He saw the perfection of her proportions, the golden shimmer of her hair, the intense radiance of her eyes.

"This way," she said, pointing to the northern end of the valley where the waterfall poured out of the granite wall into the stream.

Peter followed, walking along the western edge of the stream as she walked along the eastern side.

As they approached the wall, Peter saw that they approached a cave.

From the cave came voices, like men singing before a battle. The words were Qhaliffan, or perhaps Beserian, or even Macmenian, the languages blending in his ears.

"They are the words of the Old Language," said Selena, as if reading Peter's mind. "The language from which all of the other languages flow, even yours. They are the words of the Prophet, the language of the God of the Mountain and the Sands, the words that spoke all things into existence."

Peter walked forward, and the voices grew louder. They reached the end of the valley, covered by the shadow of the granite wall. The smell of the waterfall was overpowering. A pathway led beneath the waterfall and into the cave. Behind the waterfall, and before the mouth of the cave, lay a patch of flat, dry rock.

"Walk with me," said Selena, standing upon the rock and extending her hand toward Peter.

Peter grasped her hand, soft and strong on his own. Their fingers interlocked. From Selena's hand, a current flowed into Peter's. It moved up into his body, enhancing all of his senses and making his limbs tingle as if he had been drinking whiskey. But with the tingle came greater clarity in his senses, not less. His heart beat furiously in his chest.

"Take off your shoes," said Selena, "for this is holy ground."

Peter released Selena's hand and did as she asked him, untying his Macmenian sandals.

"Take off your helmet," she said.

Peter obeyed. His reddish hair was slicked back with sweat, the same color as his beard.

She gave him her hand again, and Peter rose.

Selena and Peter walked into the cave, Peter's right hand clasped with Selena's left, their fingers interlocked.

The floor of the cave was cold against their bare feet. The voices grew louder as if Peter had just entered an Anglian church where the chorus of the Three Gods was reaching its crescendo.

Peter looked around him. He could see neither the walls of the cave nor the source of the voices, only a void in all directions.

Selena led him deeper into the darkness. The voices surrounded him.

Peter stepped gingerly with uncertain steps, unsure of what might lie in front of him.

"Walk boldly with me, Peter Harmon. You will not fall, and nothing is in our way," said Selena. "Look ahead."

Lights emerged in the distance, like torches advancing from far down a road on a moonless night.

The lights separated, and Peter saw that there were thirteen, advancing like a *V* with the apex torch moving ahead of all of the others.

"Wait here," said Selena.

In the advancing torchlight, Peter could see that the staff in Selena's right hand had taken on a new color, glowing a deep silver-green and giving off a light of its own, nearly as bright as the torches.

The torches came closer, and Peter could see that beneath the flames rode men—tall men in silver breastplates upon enormous white horses.

The men wore golden helmets, plumed with white, with bright white capes hanging from their shoulders. They were warriors all, carrying drawn swords, except for the man in the lead, who carried only a wooden staff.

As the riders approached closer, the coldness of the cave receded before them, as if the morning sun had entered the darkness of the cave, bringing both warmth and light. Peter stood waiting, holding Selena Savanar's hand. The singing continued, rising louder and louder around them.

Peter could now see the men's faces. They were dark, olive-colored men, like native-born Beserians, Qhaliffans, and Macmenians.

The horsemen dismounted.

Their horses vanished like vapor.

The men, Peter saw, did not carry the torches, but rather, the bronze shafts, topped with flames, floated above them as if suspended in the air.

The lead man approached and stood before Peter and Selena. Two torches advanced with him, floating above each of his shoulders and framing his face in radiant light. He stood eye to eye with Peter, the features of his face handsome, bearded, and strong. He was neither old nor young, but a man in his middle years, powerfully built with a look in his eyes that appeared long familiar with both living and killing.

Peter fought the urge to turn and run. Selena stood perfectly still at his side, firmly gripping Peter's hand.

The man stepped closer, standing close enough to strike Peter with the staff in his hand.

The singing ceased.

All fell silent.

Peter looked above him and saw that the torches made no noise as they flickered in the darkness.

"You are not real," said Peter, his voice extending out into the recesses of the cave. He heard no echo, no ricochet off of any wall. All of the hairs on his arms stood on end.

"Then you have no reason to be afraid," said the man. His voice was calm, powerful, and without accent. Peter heard the man's words as if he had just spoken them in Anglian.

Peter looked at him, afraid.

"How? How is this possible?"

"I was born to carry this in my lifetime," said the man. "Given to me, by the wisdom of the Prophet, in the name of the God of the Mountain and the Sands, the God that carries many names in many places, but who needs no name, who was, who is, and will always be."

Peter looked into the man's hands. The staff the man held bore the carving of a lion.

"Do you know what this is?"

Peter did not answer.

"Peter Harmon of the Islands of Anglia," said the man, "do you know what this is?"

"How do you know my name?"

The man looked at Peter, unhurried and unyielding beneath the bronze torches that flamed above his shoulders.

Peter looked at the staff, and then he looked into the man's face. "It is the Staff of Might, the lost center of the Staff of the Prophet."

"Yes, it is that," said the man.

Peter looked at the man's dozen companions, their faces all clear and shining in the light of the torches that floated above them. All looked directly at him, or perhaps even through him, with firm, expressionless faces, like men that would not hesitate to swing their long, straight swords against his flesh.

"Do you know who I am, Peter Harmon?" asked the man.

Peter looked back at him.

"It is not possible," said Peter, shaking his head.

"And yet here I am, speaking to you in this place, in a language I cannot know, riding to you in a cave that does not end, amongst singing with no singers, on horses that vanish, beneath torches that float in the air, in a valley that opened before your eyes from a desert floor."

"Then you are Hom Hommuram," said Peter.

"Yes, that was my name," said Hom Hommuram, his eyes twinkling in the torchlight, glowing as if they contained torchlight of their own.

"You died eight hundred years ago," said Peter, his voice little more than a whisper.

"Do you think that is the end, death?" Hom Hommuram laughed, the sound washing over Peter and Selena like a warm wind, penetrating inside of them. His teeth were white and straight in his powerful jaw, like Selena Savanar's, like Peter Harmon's own. "When it is your time, you will learn that death is not the end. It is the end of the beginning and the beginning of that which endures."

Peter looked into Hom Hommuram's face. He lowered his eyes, unable to meet his gaze, unable to look into his eyes.

"Look at me, Amahdi," said Hom Hommuram.

"What did you call me?" asked Peter, looking up into his face.

"I called you by your name."

"You called me Amahdi."

"I do not speak names falsely. You do not hold the hand of my descendant of forty generations by chance." Hom Hommuram looked at Selena Savanar and smiled. "Yes, she is faithful like her father before her, he who held the truth, even into the flames. We are a faithful line."

Peter looked down at his and Selena's hands, which were still interlocked, finger for finger.

"I am not the Amahdi. I am only here by—"

"By chance? Mamet the Usurper believed in chance," said Hom Hommuram. "He believed he could shape the world to his desires. He believed that this world exists to serve him. He thought that death was the end, and that he could rise higher by bringing death to others that God had called above him.

"His descendants, the ones that call themselves 'Qhaliffa,' they believe the same. They are wrong. They are a jealous and foolish line. Still more wrong is the schemer who seeks power for its own sake, the self-made tyrant, the one who believes he can surpass the Qhaliffas, he who seeks to harness the power of the Prophet to his own ends, as if the power ever belonged to the Prophet. I speak, of course, of the one who is called Jemojeen. It is fitting that at the end of their line, the Qhaliffas will be displaced by one who is worse than they."

"He will replace them?"

"What you have read in the old books is true, Amahdi. Mamet sent me here, into this desert, into the Hahst, wishing me to die, and for the power of this staff to die with me. With me gone, he believed he could rule over the Seven Cities, over the Sand Sea and beyond, using the Staff of the Ram. But certain things do not die, Amahdi. Mamet believed he could defeat the good priest, Beseri. But Beseri fled, and his people endure. Even in the sands, the God who has many names and no name has sustained them."

"The Qhaliffas have ruled the Seven Cities for eight hundred years, and the Beserians have wandered the deserts," said Peter. "Was Mamet wrong?"

"Was he wrong?" asked Hom Hommuram.

"Yes," said Peter. "You died. Beseri died. Mamet ruled for the rest of his years and died peacefully in his bed. His sons and their sons have ruled the Great Mountain for eight hundred years."

Hom Hommuram looked at Peter without speaking. His eyes warmed as if looking into the face of a young, questioning child.

"Is that a long time," he asked, "Eight hundred years?"

Peter looked at Hom Hommuram, meeting his eyes.

A hint of a smile returned to Hom Hommuram's face. "Does the mountain think so? Do the sands? Does the ocean that surrounds your islands shudder before eight hundred years? For how long have the waves lapped against the Anglian shore?"

"I do not know."

"If your little islands laugh at forty generations of men, then what of the God that raised them up from the seas?"

Peter stood in silence.

"The Usurper Mamet, brother of the Great Prophet, is dead, under the earth, and yet here am I, a living voice, speaking into your listening ears. Except for that which is built of the spirit, Amahdi, all empires fade, crushed into the dust. What the God wishes to preserve does not die, and that which the God wishes to cast aside cannot endure. Know this, Amahdi, though I came before you, I am from nowhere near the beginning, and you are from nowhere near the end.

"Mamet believed he retained the mountain, that he built upon the rock. He believed he succeeded in banishing Beseri and his followers into the sands. But it was Mamet that built upon the sands, Amahdi, and it was Beseri that understood the rock.

"An understanding that does not know what came before and knows not what lies ahead is not true understanding, Amahdi. You are wise to seek that which has come before, for such is the root of wisdom on your side of the great beginning, which is death. From the other side of the door, the side that sees all that was and will ever be, I tell you now what lies ahead. The time has come for your page in the Great Book, and for hers," said Hom Hommuram, looking at Selena.

He looked back into Peter's face. "Jemojeen has captured your cousin, an innocent man, falsely believing he is you. He brings him in chains to Alwaz Deem. There he will burn him alive, slowly and with great cruelty."

"I will stop him," said Peter, his voice rising.

The eyes of Hom Hommuram's warriors flickered behind him as if they were preparing to advance upon him.

"With this, it is possible," said Hom Hommuram, nodding, and extending the Staff of the Lion before him.

Peter looked down at the Lion in the center of the staff, staring up, as if alive, into his eyes. He looked across the staff into the eyes of Hom Hommuram, seeing the same eyes that looked up at him from the staff.

Peter reached out and grasped the staff. As his fingers gripped the wood, Hom Hommuram and his dozen companions disappeared, vanishing beneath the flickering torches, which remained suspended in the air. Peter looked down at Selena. Their hands were still clasped together. Then the flames vanished, leaving darkness. The cold returned to the stone beneath Peter's feet.

The only light came from the Staff of the Serpent in Selena's hand, still steadily glowing, silver and green.

"Come. It is time," she said, turning and leading him back toward the entrance of the cave.

They walked in silence, covering in mere steps walking out what had seemed a vast distance while walking into the cave. They stepped out from behind the waterfall into the warm dusk air. Together, they walked onto the eastern side of the stream, where all of the others stood speaking to each other. As Peter and Selena stepped with bare feet out onto the grass, the others stopped talking and looked at them in hushed silence.

As one, they saw the staff in Peter's hand.

Ottovan Fanfar knelt first. The other Demissaries followed him: Ozgar, Nemakar, and Umahar. Then knelt the Sworn Lions, Oapah the Hohsa, and Gulana of Nor Gandus. Then followed the Beserians, Anil Salesi, and Jabil the Jackal, who had bitten off part of Peter's finger on the Plain of Gamurian. Diego, the Vetenan knelt, and Don Mazarian followed him. The last two standing were Joshua Barnes and Hersen Expey, the New Anglian soldier, and the La-Frentian Legionnaire, men who had fought against each other. The former enemies knelt together.

Peter held the Staff of the Lion, the Staff of Might, his long, strong hands curled around the oaken wood. He walked forward in the dying light. He turned to the east where the darkness had already set in, where the stars sparkled, as numerous as the grains of sand beneath them. Peter held the staff out before him and closed his eyes.

Hom Hommuram charged across a desert plain, mounted upon a warhorse, the Staff of Might in his left hand, a sword in his right. A mighty host galloped behind him. The earth rattled beneath him, and thunder shook the sky overhead. A great mountain lay ahead of him with a city of green roof tiles rising up a valley from the wide river at its base all the way up the mountain to above the clouds. Between Hom Hommuram and the city on the mountain, Peter could see an even vaster army, dark and forbidding. Peter's mind raced forward, and he could see the fear on their faces.

His mind's eye returned to Hom Hommuram in his saddle, galloping across the sands, thousands of riders flanking him on either side.

"This is your army," he said, staring directly into Peter's face.

Peter opened his eyes, looking at the twelve faces staring back at him, kneeling on the valley floor. His hand still held Selena Savanar's at his side.

He walked forward, seeing the intensity of their gazes, but feeling neither self-consciousness nor shame, only a calm, quiet peace, advancing like the dawn.

Selena walked at his side.

She released his hand. He walked toward the twelve, barefoot in the grass. They stared at him, uncertainty and fear upon each of their faces. They had first looked at the staff, but now they looked at him, into his eyes.

Peter looked down into each of their faces, knowing each of them as he had not known them before. As he looked into their eyes, the fear left them, like darkness fleeing the sunrise.

Peter raised the staff into the air, standing in the midst of the twelve. The sky above them thundered and a sudden great wind passed over the valley, blowing from the west.

He looked east, with his eyes wide open, in the direction of the Great Mountain and the city of Alwaz Deem, the city where Sah Seg Savanar had burned for truth.

"Jack, you are not alone," said Peter. "I am coming for you."

"Amahdi," said Selena.

Peter turned to look down into her face.

"We are all coming for him."

And as they heard her words, the twelve rose.

Epilogue
South Anglia

April 17, 1948

She set the manuscript down on the small side table next to the easy chair from which she had been reading for hours, her ninety-two-year-old eyes tired beneath her reading glasses, the cup of tea next to her still half-full and cold.

"That is enough for tonight."

They had missed dinner, and the moon had risen many hours before. A chorus of crickets and frogs called out from the darkness through the open window. A blanket of stars covered the rural Anglian sky on the mild, cloudless night, the constellations all clear. Had they leaned out the window, they could have picked out each of the Ram, the Lion, and the Serpent on the edge of the eastern sky. The embers burned low in the fireplace.

Her daughter Elizabeth leaned forward on the couch.

"Is it true?" she asked. Tear tracks marked her cheeks. The makeup smudged around her eyes.

"Every word," said her mother.

Elizabeth shook her head, her eyes wide. New tears formed as she wiped her face with an already soggy handkerchief. Her head spun as if she were only now meeting her father for the first time, seeing him more clearly than she had in life.

"Were you really raped, Mother, in Ben Gamurian? Did you really kill those three men with a pistol?"

Hannah Harmon nodded, the flame low, but still flickering in the blue of her eyes.

"And you were there when Selena healed Stanwich? You sat next to him?"

"Yes."

"Did it really look like that when the gangrene left, like a crust falling away?" Elizabeth had served as a nurse in the war, as had all of the women in her class. She had seen her share of gangrene.

"It is as your father describes."

"And you heard Selena's voice from across the desert when she healed him?"

"As clearly as I hear yours now. He describes what happened that night as I explained it to him. There are times when he wrote through my eyes, sometimes through her eyes, others through his own."

"Father wrote that? All of it?"

Hannah nodded.

"Why does he write as if he is only one of the characters? Why have I never seen this until now?"

"He wrote this for me, Elizabeth. Sometimes, the great truths must be cloaked. The many books he wrote for the world are well-known, but this one, the real book, is mine. Even in the end, he never thought the world was ready for this story, the story from which all of the others flowed, the story that would force men to believe differently."

"Hom Hommuram, in the cave? The staffs?"

"All real. As real as that helmet sitting on his desk."

"What happened to the staffs? What happened to Jack in Alwaz Deem?"

"We will read more tomorrow, Elizabeth. Now it is time to sleep."

"One last question. Did you and father—do you believe in the God of the Mountain and the Sands?"

Hannah Harmon smiled. "Wouldn't you?"

Elizabeth stood up, walked across the study, and helped her mother to her feet.

As they walked toward the hallway, Elizabeth looked up, seeing a small, faded picture of an eastern woman seated on a camel, wearing desert robes. It was a picture she had passed beneath a hundred times, a picture she had never truly looked at.

She looked carefully now, holding her mother's arm in her own, seeing the woman's beauty, even in the smallness of the picture, even in the faded shades of grey.

"Is that?"

"The Lady Savanar? Of course."

Author Bio

Michael McClellan lives in California with his wife and their two daughters.

He received his history degree from Yale, with an emphasis on the late nineteenth and early twentieth centuries.

Since childhood, he has loved reading large-canvas historical and imaginative fiction the most.

He eventually realized there was a book he wanted to read that had not yet been written.

That story became *The Sand Sea*. It is his first novel.

Acknowledgments

It is often not possible to write a book during normal working hours, and this is perhaps especially true of a first novel. *The Sand Sea* was accordingly written in the dark, either before the sun rose or long after it had set.

That arrangement required a great deal of encouragement from friends and family, and from no one more so than my wife. Churchill once said:

> *Writing a book is an adventure. To begin with, it is a toy and an amusement, then it becomes a mistress, and then it becomes a master, and then a tyrant. The last phase is that just as you are about to be reconciled to your servitude, you kill the monster and fling him out to the public.*

Samantha, you've lived through all of those phases. In the early years, when I was obsessed with researching from an ever-expanding reading list but never seemed to get enough words onto the page, you gave me the best advice: "Just write your book." You were right—as you usually are—and now, at long last, we are flinging the tyrant out. I am grateful for you every day.

This book would not have happened without Steven Pressfield.

The vast majority of us require mentors to show us the way, and it is always difficult to adequately thank one's own. Steve, when I was a wild-eyed young man intent on writing a ridiculously big book, you didn't tell me to "live in the real world" or "start with something smaller." You told me to "tattoo it on my brain" that I would never surrender to Resistance. You told me to keep working until it was done.

You gave me those marching orders in September of 2008. As they say about raising children, "the days are long, but the years are short." Your friendship is among the greatest blessings in my life, and you were there for me in all of the moments on this journey when it mattered the most. That is not a debt that can be paid back. I can only hope to someday pay it forward.

Shawn Coyne, you are an editorial genius, and *The Sand Sea* would never have reached its potential without you. With a veteran's steady hands, you saw beyond the rookie's rough edges in the early manuscript and shaped it into the story it was meant to be. The three years we've worked together have been an education most writers can only wish for, and I look forward to the years to come as we complete the Rubric of Conquest series. Thank you for your vision, your guidance, your wisdom, and your courage.

Mom and Dad, many creators draw from the hardships of youth to make their art. For me it is the opposite; it is the light of those early years to which I often return when I think of warmth and goodness in the world. You always let me follow my own star, play how I wanted to play, and pursue whatever I was interested in, even when your ten-year-old was asking for Civil War battlefield books for Christmas and your eleven-year-old was reading Pakenham's *The Scramble for Africa*. You have always encouraged me. You encourage me still. I am grateful to be your son.

Matt Newman, thank you for your friendship, your artistic talent, and your willingness to be a sounding board. Some of my favorite moments have been working on maps for *The Sand Sea* in front of your computer screens, surrounded by your kids' plastic dinosaurs, seeing places that had previously only existed in my mind suddenly appearing in plain sight, at the tip of your pen. And Timree, thank you for allowing so many late-night visits while your husband and I talked about strange places in a nineteenth-century desert. I owe you for many homemade lattes and ice creams.

Bob Burge, thank you for your friendship, for founding our group, and for your guidance across the long years. Our meals, conversations, and times spent together have been a joyful place of rest and restoration for me from the very beginning.

To the rest of the "Broup"—Jeff B., Bob K., Keith C., Evan M., T.J. F., and the former members too, Ken K., Bill W., Len S., Will S., Pat M., Jeff T., and Sam W.—thank you for reminding me that life is not a dress rehearsal and to think carefully about how I use my "wallet and watch." And thank you for patiently listening to my decade of updates regarding this project. Our Tuesday mornings are the highlight of my month most months, and I am grateful for each and every one of you. Bob K., Ken, Will, and Jeff B., extra thanks for being early readers and for the wind you put in my sails.

Jay, Shari, Steve, and all of the others at Little Church by the Sea who pray over the blue cards each week, thank you for your steadfast perseverance. I am sure you wondered many times across the years when (and maybe if) I was going to finally finish my book. Know that your faithfulness helped push me across the line, and I am grateful for all of you.

Jeff T., thank you for your pastoral wisdom regarding this process and so much else, and for teaching me that it's always about the heart and doing the work for the right reasons. Your words continue to inspire me to be a more authentic man.

Paul, Jason, Greg, John, Jack, Jon, John, Michael, Michael, Richard, Carl, Manoosh, Bahaar, Melanie, Xochitl, and other ND friends that either read early excerpts, encouraged me across the years, or both: thank you.

Paul, you helped give me the courage to move beyond my inner George McFly and share my work. A humble Minnesotan that I know says if one person wasn't standing in the breach at a particular moment, then someone else would have. I've never believed that. There is always the man in the moment, and who that man is makes a difference. Keep growing into your inner George Marshall and thank you for being the patient, wise, and empowering friend and leader that you are.

Jason M., you're one of the toughest, hardest-working, and smartest people I know, and you make it look way too easy. You have less time than anyone else to help me talk through the occasional stuck sentence, yet you've done it anyway. Thank you for your friendship.

Greg and John, there are lots of people that know how to make small problems seem bigger; there are far fewer that know how to do the opposite. Thank you for teaching me that and so many other things about life across the years. You have always had my back and have always encouraged me. I am lucky to have you both as mentors and as friends.

Eric, thank you for being a formidable and diligent lawyer and for making sure I was doing things the right way.

Jacob L., Cousin M., George S., Patrick S., and Brett H., thank you for our many discussions in the garden and in front of the fireplace back in CDM. You knew this story in its earliest youth, with all of the gangly awkwardness that comes with that. Thank you for your patience and for the many years of encouragement and friendship. Your words and feedback always made a difference.

Jacob, you have a great heart and a great mind, and you have always pushed me to be better as few can. Our conversations across the years have fed my heart and my mind, and they have improved the work.

Reza, as I've told you many times, you are an artist masquerading as a businessman; though you are so gifted at each, it is often hard to tell which is the truest identity. Thank you for a lifetime of friendship and for always pushing me to be my best self. You are among the most generous and thoughtful men I have ever known. You have encouraged me in this project from the very beginning. You are the ally and friend that every man wants, but few ever get.

Katy, thank you for all of the encouragement along the road and for inspiring me with your own artistic path. You are amazingly talented and I'm grateful for your friendship.

Matt G., your enthusiasm for *The Sand Sea* has lifted me up more than you know. You were the voice I needed to hear, the validation at the right time. You asked all the right questions and encouraged me to finish the race strong. Thank you for your friendship.

Kenneth R., thank you for keeping me alive and moving for so much of this process. Writing a book this long can take a lot out of you, and it would have taken more if I did not have you as an early morning confidant and friend. You have brightened more days than you know.

Cameron F., you are a great friend and one of the most thoughtful readers I have ever known. Talking with you across a Weber BBQ with a good bottle of wine is some of the best that life has to offer. I once heard it said that you should pick a single reader when you are writing. You have often been that reader.

Adam L., you are a great man living out a life of faith and meaning. I am honored to be your friend. I will never forget the sound of your voice when I called to tell you that I had finally finished my manuscript and that things were truly moving forward. It was as if it had happened to you. There are moments through which one can see many other things. That was one of those. I love the courage and fire within you. So will history when all is said and done.

GN Forum mates—John, Glen, Ben, Jordy, Scott, Brian, Kevin, and Michael—thank you for your interest, support, insights, and patience in tracking this journey across the years. And thank you for believing that I could get it done. I am grateful for you all. And an extra thank-you to John and Michael for being thoughtful and encouraging early readers.

To Michael A., Daniel V., Tommy Mc., Michael K., John O., Mike D., Tom L., Chris L., Scott W., Kurt A., Nick T., David S., Nick S., Justin N., Brian S., M. Bailey, Scott C., Scott L., Eddie H., Tom O., Tom G., Matt P., and Tate L.: Thank you for the years of friendship and for joining me on travels and adventures across the world that in part make writing a book like this one possible. You all make this life a joyous journey, and I am honored to know you. Among the things I am most grateful for in this life are my friends, and you are the best that a man could ask for.

K. Caldwell Harmon, you have been there since this was just a far-fetched idea, and long before that. You were there for Gunpowder Empires, the Barcelonan Incident, Chartwell, the Pampas, Easter Sundays, Axis and Allies, the Baron Kay, the NBAC, Belgravia, the Bolivar, Salisbury Plain, St. Peter's in the rain, uSuthu into Big Corona, the Broken Spoke, Sonoma Mountain, and so much of the rest. Indeed, you were often driving the train. I am grateful that fate brought us together so many years ago. You will see so much in these pages that others cannot. And if you read this book aloud, I am sure you will read "Kezelboj" in Admiral Ackbar's accent. You are a heroic man, and I am grateful to be your friend, always.

Tyler and Gunnar, I am grateful to call you my brothers. You are the kind of men worth writing about, and I am sure there are bigger pieces of each of you in these stories than I have ever consciously realized. You are men to look up to, especially for your older brother. Thank you also for indulging your older brother in the years of war games. They are some of my favorite memories, and that goes for you too Taylor, Matthew, Patrick H., Jeff B., and Michael P.

To all of my cousins, my aunts and uncles, and my in-laws—Nicholses, McClellans, Cessnas, Demases, Nicolsons—thank you for always making the concept of family so much bigger than just the nuclear. I love you all. Know that few things make my heart happier than being with all of you on the nights when there is no reason not to open the best wine and the oldest whiskey. You have all supported me along this path.

Uncle Patrick and Jennifer, thank you for showing your nephew how to blaze an artistic trail. I admire you and your work.

Matthew Nichols, Renee Nichols, Bill Demas, and Elizabeth McClellan: know that I miss you. You left us far too soon. Matthew, I started writing every day, seven days a week, in the days just after you left us. This never would have been finished without that step, and thinking of you helped keep me on the long course when Resistance was fighting hard.

To my grandparents—Bee, Bud, Pat, and Jerry—thank you for your love and for showing us what it means to be a generation worthy of honor and remembrance. Grandpa Jerry, when I hear the words "Great American," I see your face. Thank you for always taking the time for your grandchildren and your great-grandchildren, and for teaching me about our history. Grandpa Bud, I wish you were here to read this too. Your Michener and Catton books stand proudly on my shelves, and so long as I still have a say, they always will. You were a formidable man, and there are strong parts of your spirit in these pages. And thank you both for serving our country in perhaps the most righteous war ever fought.

Kay Cessna, you were always so supportive of this and such a thoughtful reader. We love and miss you. Please know that as this project finishes, Samantha and I are thinking of you.

Jess, thank you for the great pictures and for your artistic vision and talent.

D.G. and M.G., thank you for your friendship and for making our community what it is. Grateful for you.

Lastly, thank you to the whole Story Grid team. Tim, thank you for your vision, mentoring, and guidance in bringing this to its final form. John, Derick, the cover is stunning. Spring, the design is beautiful. KC, thank you for your amazing work getting everything to look right. It is a privilege to work with you. Amanda and Christi, thank you for your amazing patience and diligence with a very long manuscript. You caught much that I would have missed. It is without question a better book because of all of you.

I have unquestionably forgotten a debt of gratitude above, and quite possibly more than one. Please forgive the omissions. They are inadvertent, and any errors that remain in this book are solely my own.

Catherine and Violet, one day you will be old enough to read this book. I treasure every day we spend together. The future belongs to you.

MBMc
April 13, 2020